Ovid's Metamorphoses

Ovid's *Metamorphoses*

A New Translation

———

Translated, Annotated, and Introduced by
C. Luke Soucy

UNIVERSITY OF CALIFORNIA PRESS

University of California Press
Oakland, California

© 2023 by Luke Soucy

Library of Congress Cataloging-in-Publication Data

Names: Ovid, 43 B.C.–17 A.D. or 18 A.D. | Soucy, C. Luke, translator, writer
  of introduction. |Title: Ovid's metamorphoses : a new translation /
  translated, annotated, and introduced by C. Luke Soucy.
Other titles: Metamorphoses. English
Description: Oakland, California : University of California Press, [2023] |
  Includes bibliographical references and glossary.
Identifiers: LCCN 2022058898 (print) | LCCN 2022058899 (ebook) |
  ISBN 9780520394858 (paperback) | ISBN 9780520394865 (ebook)
Subjects: LCSH: Mythology, Classical—Poetry. | Metamorphosis—
  Mythology—Poetry. | LCGFT: Narrative poetry.
Classification: LCC PA6522.M2 S68 2023 (print) | LCC PA6522.M2 (ebook) |
  DDC 873/.01—dc23/eng/20230501
LC record available at https://lccn.loc.gov/2022058898
LC ebook record available at https://lccn.loc.gov/2022058899

Manufactured in the United States of America
32   31   30   29   28   27   26   25   24   23
10   9   8   7   6   5   4   3   2   1

publication supported by a grant from
The Community Foundation for Greater New Haven
as part of the **Urban Haven Project**

To Hannah Semmelhack and Kyle L. Freiler

CONTENTS

ILLUSTRATIONS

MAP

FIGURES

Introduction

Whether they know it or not, when people talk about mythology they are usually talking about Ovid's *Metamorphoses*. Casting the entire mythos of classical legend as a cosmos-spanning series of its titular transformations, Ovid's irreverent Roman epic has done more even than the works of Hesiod and Homer to codify what has become known as "Greek" mythology. From Narcissus and Icarus to Pygmalion and Medusa, many of the world's best-known stories take their familiar form or even their origin from Ovid's telling. Much as the Neo-Confucian Classics did for Chinese writers and the *Mahabharata* for Indian literature, the *Metamorphoses* stands apart as a truly seminal text, at once the foundation of a literary canon and one of its highest peaks, holding all subsequent works in its indelible shadow. In the European tradition, it is rivaled in this respect only by the Bible.

Yet in many ways, the *Metamorphoses* is the opposite of the traditionalist, highfaluting work its stature suggests. With its unique blend of silliness, mockery, and subversion, if Ovid's poem is less famous today than the *Aeneid* or the *Odyssey,* that is largely because educators have found it *too* entertaining. Unlike those grand, reverent narratives that give the epic genre its name, the *Metamorphoses* overthrows all things stately, weighty, and heroic to depict an unstable universe ruled by capricious gods and men, one where virtue, vice, and even excess of feeling are at constant risk of turning mortals and lesser deities alike into the natural features of our known world. The poem is shot through with a rebellious streak, satirizing Roman values of tradition and stoic gravity while taking every opportunity to point up the injustice of the divinities and royals who enforce them. In Ovid's telling, the hero Perseus is a feckless brute reliant on a *deus* to spring out of the *machina,* the Argonauts are at sea for a whole four lines, and all the effusive praise for Rome's gods and rulers is belied by the tell-tale whiff of mock zeal. Best and worst of all, Ovid refuses to take his world seriously. Continually skirting his poetic predecessors, he deploys a constant stream of wit and rhetoric to turn moments of drama into melodrama, while saving true pathos for the victims of powerful oppressors whom other poets would make their protagonists.

Small wonder, then, that the *Metamorphoses* should have proven unpopular with Victorian readers and the orthodox scholars who followed them. In sharp contrast to their treatment of Homer and Virgil, critics largely steered clear of Ovid's work until well into the twentieth century, dismissing it as self-indulgent and amoral even as translators exerted themselves to rob the poem of its most colorful qualities, assigning Ovid their own homophobia and humorlessness while evincing a level of indifference toward sexual assault and misogyny not to be found in the original. This derisive attitude was typified by Edith Hamilton, at one point America's most popular classicist, whose 1942 collection *Mythology* retains a stranglehold on high school curricula despite being dated, bowdlerized, and openly disdainful of its foremost source. In its preface, Hamilton concedes that "no ancient writer can compare" with Ovid as "a compendium of myth," yet continues:

> I have avoided using him as far as possible. Undoubtedly he was a good poet and a good storyteller and able to appreciate the myths enough to realize what excellent material they offered him; but he was really farther away from them in his point of view than we are today. They were sheer nonsense to him. . . . He says in effect to his reader, 'Never mind how silly they are. I will dress them up so prettily for you that you will like them.' And he does, often very prettily indeed, but in his hands the stories which were factual truth and solemn truth to the early Greek poets Hesiod and Pindar, and vehicles of deep religious truth to the Greek tragedians, become idle tales, sometimes witty and diverting, often sentimental and distressingly rhetorical (15–16).

It is a matter of taste whether the reader agrees that Ovid's rhetoric is "distressing," that his being "a good poet and a good storyteller" is insufficient grounds to engage with him, or that his work deserves to be "avoided . . . as far as possible." But where Hamilton must be challenged is her contention that Ovid's myths are "sheer nonsense," blasphemous aberrations from a mind too clever by whole to appreciate the solemn truths revealed to the credulous likes of Hesiod and Pindar. What she takes as dismissive misunderstanding is in fact calculated subversion, and there is no subverting what one does not thoroughly understand. Presumably also no fan of the riddling antics of Socrates, Nasreddin Hodja, or the wise Shakespearean Fool, Hamilton cannot conceive that there may be a point to all Ovid's pretty dressing, a deeper *irreligious* truth to his out-there point of view.

The political and cultural shifts of the last half-century, however, have made it less objectionable to "speak truth to power" or to shed satirical light on old, accepted ideas. In recent years especially, Ovid's blend of irreverence toward authority, skepticism toward tradition, and compassion toward victims has become especially timely. Such shifting of sands is part and parcel of all literary reception but seems particularly suited to the metamorphic nature of this work, which wears the idea of fluctuation as a badge, a shackle, and a spine, not to mention as a title. Though few would be surprised that prudish mid-century authorities failed to understand Ovid's approach, part of what makes his poem so essential and worthy of study is that its contents— the shared cultural basis for a whole artistic tradition—have always been controversial, both among those who failed to understand them and those who did not like what they understood. Indeed, Ovid's biography has long made him a symbol of oppressed writers in every age. After all, was it for telling merely "idle tales" that he was banished by the Emperor?

OVID'S LIFE AND TIMES

When Publius Ovidius Naso was born at Sulmo on March 20, 43 BCE, some forty miles east of Rome, the internecine wars that had marked the last century of Roman Italy were reaching a fever pitch. Julius Caesar had been dead for less than a year and the next month's battle between his heir Octavian and his lieutenant Mark Antony saw the last hopes of a free republic die on the besieged walls of Mutina. But Ovid was only twelve when Octavian polished off his rival at Actium, and not yet sixteen when he proclaimed himself Augustus and founded the Roman Empire. While these enterprises of great pith and moment would have colored the young poet's worldview, the Rome in which Ovid spent his adult life, though still freshly scarred by battle, was one in which power, conflict, and change had moved behind the scenes. On the surface, society would experience a prolonged stability unavailable to his immediate literary forebears.

According to Ovid, his own poetic instinct was innate. Born to a prosperous but not patrician family, he was apparently destined for a life in politics, yet although his father warned him that even Homer had died penniless, Ovid claimed that his attempts at writing always came out in verse. Sent to be educated in the capital, the teenager was wildly successful in the schools of rhetoric, even as he became a celebrated reciter of his own poems. After a few half-hearted stints in minor bureaucratic roles, he resigned to become the youngest fixture of the Roman literary scene, then blossoming into what has since been deemed the Golden Age of Latin literature.

The golden boy of that Golden Age was undoubtedly Virgil. Author of Rome's court-commissioned national epic the *Aeneid,* Virgil is traditionally grouped with Horace and Ovid as the three major "Augustan" poets. Augustus, however, enjoyed a very long reign, and Ovid later wrote that he only ever clapped eyes on the older writer. Instead, Ovid's introduction to cultural circles would come through friendships with the elderly didactic poet Aemilius Macer and Ovid's slightly senior contemporary Propertius, the third (after Gallus and Tibullus) of the great love elegists. Upon publishing the *Amores* (*Loves*) in 16 BCE, Ovid would make his name by establishing himself as the fourth.

The very notion that there existed such a genre as the Latin love elegy, or that there were four primary contributors to it, is itself a sign of Ovid's influence. Developing tropes from the Hellenistic Greeks, early Augustan writers had penned strings of subjective first-person poems that dramatically recounted the joys and especially the miseries of being in love. These were invariably set in the elegiac meter, an uneven form of couplet (one hexameter paired with one pentameter) that would be Ovid's go-to form for his entire life, the *Metamorphoses* excepted. Tibullus and Propertius expanded the variety of topics elegy could address in mounting ever higher heights of melancholy, but the genre achieved its actualization in the hands of the twentysomething Ovid, who returned love elegy to its basics even as he approached them from new angles, practicing the pose of the anagrammatist of desire who narrates much of the *Metamorphoses*. Unlike their self-serious predecessors, the *Amores* are lighthearted and funny to the point of flirting with parody. At a stroke, Ovid seemed to fulfill the genre's promise and kill its future. Later in life, he would look back on his early success and place himself at the end of the Roman elegiac canon; no subsequent critic has revised his list.

The approach Ovid took with love elegy would become a blueprint for his whole literary life: pick a genre, zero in on its idiosyncrasies, and stand them on their heads. Much as he had done for Propertius' elegies, he soon upended Aemilius Macer's genre of didactic poetry, pretending that love and sex could be taught from a literary manual in the same manner as farming (Virgil's *Georgics*) or writing (Horace's *Ars Poetica*). The resulting *Ars Amatoria* (*Guide for Lovers*) made a tongue-in-cheek show of teaching the art of seduction in three books—two for men and one for women—that quasi-systematically explored, explained, and exploded social conventions for relations between the sexes in cheeky defiance of the Emperor's campaigns for public morality, and extolling among other things the importance of mutual orgasm. The *Ars* was succeeded and subverted by the faux-serious *Remedia Amoris* (*Cures for Love*), and the sadly fragmentary *Medicamina Facei Feminae* (*Women's Facial Cosmetics*), whose surviving lines contain five surprisingly plausible makeup recipes put, absurdly, into verse. The strength of these works, all written in elegiac meter, catapulted Ovid to unparalleled fame and notoriety. On the deaths of Propertius and Horace, Ovid was by age thirty-five the leading poet in Rome.

Somewhere along the way, Ovid composed the two works (both of uncertain date) that most obviously prefigure the *Metamorphoses*. These are a tragic drama on the mythical sorceress Medea, one of the most bemoanedly lost works of the period, and the *Heroides* (*Heroines*), a collection of letters written in the voice of female characters from mythology, each addressed to an absent and often traitorous male lover. This innovative narrative choice prefigures several of the most prominent speeches in the *Metamorphoses*, including those of Medea (Book 7), Scylla and Althaea (both Book 8), Byblis and Iphis (both Book 9), and Myrrha (Book 10). These extended monologues take the same tactic of breathing new life into old stories by viewing them from an entirely unexpected angle, granting unprecedented voice and character to women traditionally depicted as somber queens, evil witches, sex-crazed maniacs, or even devoted ciphers. (Medea, for instance, appears in both extant works, occupying a full six hundred lines between them that barely mention the infanticide for which she is otherwise best known.) Though likely deriving from a much earlier time in Ovid's career, the *Heroides* are the clearest antecedent to the *Metamorphoses,* in whose stories Ovid shows the same knack for reinventing familiar myths through the minds of their neglected female characters.

Shortly after the turn of the millennium, Ovid's output underwent a distinct shift in both form and content. Instead of glittering collections of unconventional love poetry, he began laboring concurrently on two monumental works treating Roman religion: the *Fasti* and the *Metamorphoses.* Straddling the didactic and the epic, the *Fasti* was to be a twelve-book encyclopedia of Roman religious practice set against the outline of the Julian Calendar (one book per month), delivered in the form of jocular interviews with the Roman gods. In contrast, the fifteen books of the *Metamorphoses* would capture the whole of the Greco-Roman mythos in both epic voice and epic hexameter—the sole deviation in Ovid's corpus from his elegiac standard. The *Fasti* was halfway done and the *Metamorphoses* all but complete when, in 8 CE, the Emperor Augustus banished Ovid to the Black Sea town of Tomis, in modern Romania, in the furthest reaches of the Roman world.

It does not appear that Ovid committed a crime, and his famously vague explanation for his exile—"a poem and a mistake" (*carmen et error, Tr.* 2.207)—has led to the spillage of vast tides of scholarly ink. In the moralizing context of the Augustan regime, Ovid's most obviously offensive poem was the *Ars Amatoria,* though it was hardly a recent publication and alternatives (including the *Metamorphoses*) have been suggested. The *error* in question is murkier still but seems to have been a scandal; more fanciful scholars have invented an affair with the Emperor's daughter Julia. Whatever happened, the writer and his writings had plainly become dangerous, and his career fell into a disfavor from which it would never recover. Ovid's last two works, the *Tristia* (*Sorrows*) and the *Epistulae ex Ponto* (*Letters from the Black Sea*), consist of elegiac letters to friends, family members, and political operatives, reflecting on his life and pleading for pardon with ever-diminishing hope. If the *Fasti* was ever finished, its second half does not survive, nor do the poems he supposedly composed in the local language of Getic. The death of Augustus in 14 CE did nothing to alter the poet's circumstances, and Ovid died three years later after a decade in exile. He was about sixty.

STRUCTURE AND THEMES

While Ovid's own popularity has waxed and waned in the two millennia since his death, there has never been any question as to which was his most significant work: Ovid's one epic has always defined his legacy. Yet despite its epic scale, epic form, and clear place in the epic tradition, *epic* is a strange word to describe the *Metamorphoses,* whose artistic program seems predicated on defying any easy description. No other work from antiquity is so unsubtle about being so slippery. Far from the epic norm of pursuing a single hero on a singularly heroic pursuit, the poem endlessly shifts its focus, tone, pace, and place in a flouting of convention and expectation that dazzles with its taxonomies of scale, cramming all of time and space into a uniform structure, even as its themes of identity, credibility, and power continue to register on a humble human level.

The structural point is made clear through comparison with Virgil's *Aeneid,* to whose paramount position in Roman literature Ovid is constantly reacting. In true epic fashion, Ovid's poem is divided into a series of books. But where the *Aeneid* set a neat bar of twelve episodic books per epic, later followed by the likes of Statius and Milton, Ovid instead plumps for the three-upmanship of fifteen, only then to ignore the framework he has chosen. Multiple books cut off in the middle of a story, while several more begin on a conjunction, as if lampooning the structural division by showing how easily it can be bridged. Further complications arise when attempting to group the books by theme, as is easily done with the *Aeneid*'s six-book halves. At the most general level, the *Metamorphoses* progresses chronologically from the creation of the universe to the death of Julius Caesar, in the process gradually shifting focus from a divinity-dominated cosmos (Books 1–5) to an age of heroes (Books 6–10) and on into human history (Books 11–15). This pattern only holds, however, so long as one wears pattern-colored glasses. Once the reader is down in the storytelling trenches of the poem, Ovid's narratorial force will carry them here and there, jumping o'er times in a series of kaleidoscopic transitions—some natural, many utterly ridiculous, but all highly stylized—making the poem difficult to classify or segment, in large part because it just keeps rolling along. The difference is evident even in the poems' titles. The *Aeneid* is about Aeneas, a lone hero of heroic qualities embarked on a hero's journey. The *Metamorphoses* is about change.

All this flies full in the face of how a good epic ought to behave. Where the *Iliad* and the *Aeneid* channel the will of fate, making plain in omniscient narration where they are headed from the opening verse, Ovid takes a meandering approach that belies the very notion of a neat, destiny-driven plot. Accordingly, a good third of his poem is occupied by nested sets of stories within stories (often compared to Russian dolls and Chinese boxes) such that the Book 10 tale of Atalanta and Hippomenes—a parable narrated by Venus to Adonis in a song sung by Orpheus to a collection of walking trees—is not even close to the most layered moment of narration in the poem. Despite appearances, however, this device does not make the plots difficult to follow so much as difficult to believe, as droves of secondary narrators pop up to take over for a story or seven, import their own biases, and conflict with one another. Such contradictions were long ascribed to simple sloppiness, the result of a foolhardy attempt to fit so much into a single work, yet the poem's anachronisms and discrepancies are often so ostentatious that it would be silly *not* to view them as an intentional rebellion against the typical epic's pursuit of its inexorable ending. In the *Metamorphoses,* chronology is a haze, credibility an open question, and the finality of fiction rendered undisguisedly fictional. Amid the blur of space, time, and narrative, what remains are the thematic resonances to be found as one story transforms into another.

Transformation is, after all, the name of the game. Boldly jettisoning a traditional unified narrative in favor of variations on a theme, the critical understanding that Ovid uses to construct his epic is the pinpointing of metamorphosis as the one great thread running through Greco-Roman myth, whose stories are made mythical by the presence of supernatural transformative power. Yet despite being the stated theme of the work, the act of metamorphosis remains fundamentally ambiguous, without consistent rationale or moral bearing. Transformations occur as punishments, as rewards, as escape mechanisms, plot devices, memorials, and mysteries, with every body at potential risk of bursting out into something as new and variable as the world of the poem itself—a world, however, that becomes increasingly recognizable as metamorphosis after metamorphosis explains the origin of some familiar real-life feature. The poem's metamorphic playground is the scene of a tug-of-war between permeability and permanence, where forces as different and unpredictable as the whims of gods, the sorcery of witches, or even the strongest mortal emotions are liable to yank the rope in a new direction.

At stake throughout is one of Ovid's main concerns: identity. With each transformation offering an opportunity to compare the before and after, questions naturally arise about what it is to be human or inhuman, and to what degree such distinctions are societal, theological, and/or scientific. Some characters' metamorphoses equate with the freeing of some inner, truer self; for others, their essence is horribly perverted. Yet although describing such a variety of changes may make the poem sound like one great muddle, so many colors swirling into brown, the observance of categorical distinctions in spite of categorical shifts is a precondition to having a metamorphosis: the magic lies in distinguishing what changes from what does not. In Book 1, when the nymph Daphne turns into a laurel tree to escape Apollo's assault, Ovid writes that "just life's glow remained" (1.553), indicating a complete metamorphosis that would seem to fulfill an inevitable fate, since *daphne* means "laurel" in Greek. Yet the trunk's bark continues to shrink before the god's touch, and the passage's final line, "like a head the treetop seemed to nod" (1.567), teases the possibility that some aspect of the vanished woman has survived her transformation, imbuing the wood with her will. There must be a point in each metamorphosis when the human ceases to be one, and the fascination is in the uncertainty of when that is and what is left of them thereafter.

The story of Apollo and Daphne has acquired further renown for its relation to Ovid's other main thematic interest, the abuse of power. In spite (or, inevitably, because) of his status as a poet of empire, Ovid exhibits a refreshing problem with authority, and the reader is constantly treated to tales of deities and rulers subjecting unlucky mortals (or even less mighty gods) to horrifying wrongs on the flimsiest of pretexts, with the poet often changing the details from his mythic sources to accentuate the cruelty of these powers that were. In one stark example from Book 4, Ovid invents for Medusa a human backstory in which the monster's monstrosity results from a double mis-carriage of divine justice: first at the hands of Neptune, who raped her in the temple of Minerva, then from Minerva herself, who punished the sacrilege by turning the girl into her famously snake-haired self. In no tradition prior to the *Metamorphoses* had Medusa ever been any-thing but a monster, and the liberties taken in Ovid's revision are revealing of both the poet's priorities and his influence, since this ver-sion of Medusa's legend underpins most modern retellings. Hearing her origin story narrated dispassionately by Perseus, whom we have witnessed dandling Medusa's severed head for several scenes, instantly flips our view of the feats we have watched Perseus perform. Suddenly invited to pity the monsters slain throughout the poem, we are simul-taneously forced to question the heroism of the myths' accepted pro-tagonists. Considering Ovid's eagerness to destabilize any narrative expectation with an oddly timed pun or mannered exaggeration, the frequency with which he chooses to punch up when faced with a power dynamic reveals an authorial agenda of at times breathtakingly subversive sympathies.

Bearing this in mind will aid in discussing one of the poem's most delicate aspects—namely, rape. In addition to Daphne and Medusa, the pages of the *Metamorphoses* contain seventeen other extended sto-ries of sexual assault (many more are mentioned), nearly all of which are suffered by women, mostly at the hands of gods and kings. Even now it is not uncommon for scholars to meet this fact with a mere grimace or shrug, and there are collegiate horror stories of students whose professors have guided them through passages detailing pro-found acts of abuse with little comment other than on the beauty of the poetry, a callous oversight historically exacerbated by translators disinclined to call a rape a rape. Compared to the Latin original, Eng-lish versions of the *Metamorphoses* reliably have more victim-blaming spread out across fewer assaults, resulting in editions of the epic at odds with Ovid, whose general sympathy for the oppressed against their celestial or lordly oppressors often results in near parables on the effects of power abused. The story of Callisto in Book 2, for example, paints a startlingly intense portrait of psychological trauma as the dis-graced former huntress suffers ostracism, insomnia, personality changes, and misplaced guilt at the hands of three unconscionably malicious and unfeeling gods. As in the *Heroides,* Ovid takes special interest in giving maligned mythical women a degree of feeling and focus almost unheard of in Roman writers, a narrative choice of enormous transformative potential both for how a tale is told and what is made of it in the telling.

This is not, of course, to say that Ovid is some kind of present-day feminist out of time. With few exceptions, these earnest investigations of power are compromisingly conducted through a male gaze quite willing to take aesthetic pleasure in the distress of victims whose plight, however piteous, seems always to increase their paradigmatic beauty. Yet wrong as it is to teach the rape scenes of the *Metamorphoses* while dismissing all but their artistic properties, it is also wrong to dismiss the poem as a hopelessly antiquated work with no insights of value to the contemporary reader. In Book 12, when the maiden Caenis is granted a wish by her divine rapist, the sea-god Neptune, she makes a chilling demand expressly intended to be as mighty as his crime: "make me immune to rape" (12.202). When the god accedes by transforming her into a man, how else are we to interpret his act but as the poet's caustic assessment of his society? For the newly-transitioned Caeneus, there is a newfound security; for women outside the poem, the only solution Neptune proposes was not possible.

The uneasy, fascinating truth is that there exists in the poem a strange balance of sympathies that defies reduction. The natural tendency to focus on individual stories can only lead to unpleasant simplification, since each story has its own circumstances deserving of analysis, some more challenging than others to societal norms and sensitivities, ancient and modern. Yet for the structural reasons described, there is much more to be gained from taking the poem as the continuous whole it is, where the tales of Daphne, Callisto, Medusa, and Caenis do not stand alone but must be read and reread in light of the tales that precede and follow them. While such a reading does not lessen the individual tragedies, it does reveal a greater, critical purpose to all the pain and suffering. Unlike so many Disneyfied and YA retellings of the Greek legends, Ovid's mythos does not overlook the flaws and transgressions of its most powerful characters, pretend it can fix them, or try to make them less awful than they are. Instead, it presents them, plays them up, and calls them into question. For all its fantastic miracles and magical transformations, Ovid's *Metamorphoses* is disarmingly modern in its humanist depiction of a fragile and inequitable universe, where heroes are drained of their heroism, victims deserve to be heard, and the earth is always holier than heaven.

STYLE AND POLITICS

Even so, viewing the *Metamorphoses* from the airy vantage point of themes and structural composition cannot begin to capture the actual experience of reading the poem. This is because the poet, faced everywhere with the horrors of an unjust world, prefigures the absurdists by confronting them with a sardonic smile. From its opening lines, the work is pervaded by the wit and wobble of Ovid's poetic style. The narrator is delightfully intrusive, often addressing characters and readers in the second person (though most translators edit this out), and his repetition of such phrases as "they say," "rumor has," and "if we can believe it" in the midst of narration reminds the reader that, for all their divine characters, the tales being recounted are far from divinely revealed truths.

Yet muddying the waters of narratorial credibility is only one of the many tricks up Ovid's sleeve. In the tales of abuse discussed earlier, he can be deadly serious, but when handling familiar myths of heroism and glory, the poet's tongue is never far from his cheek. Scenes of high passion are hyperbolized into burlesque, while less impressive moments are lavished with flights of rhetoric they have obviously failed to earn. The death of Achilles ("Pelides") is a fine example:

> Now he is ash, and all that yet remains
> Of great Achilles scarcely fills an urn;
> But still his fame lives on and fills the world,
> And in this, the true measure of the man,
> Does Pelides endure and shun the void.
>
> (12.615–19)

At first, this seems an impressive eulogy for a great hero tragically slain. The only problem is that Ovid's Achilles has done nothing to lend his demise real impact: his victory over Hector is barely mentioned, Patroclus—the fallen comrade usually so central to Achilles' character arc—has yet to appear, and the only feat we have watched him perform is his confused killing of the demigod Cygnus, who does not even figure in Homer. The silliness of Ovid's grandiloquent epitaph is made plain by the preceding sentence, which relates the corpse's cremation: "Now, he—Troy's fear, the guard and grace of Greece, / Aeacides, the tireless warlord—burned."

Such anticlimaxes abound. Heroes are particular targets of irony, and the narrator calls characters by that name only when doing so is ridiculous, as in moments of cowardice or repose ("Autonoë's heroic son turned tail," 3.198). But incidental bits of farce lurk in every story, as situations of would-be intensity are undercut by excessive alliteration, dissonant puns, or bizarre displays of metaphoric language that amuse the reader even as they highlight the artificiality of the plot, as when Ovid strings together ten lines of sparkling wordplay for the last gasps of a dying lover. In one extreme example from Book 12, Ovid uses his favorite trick of pairing verbs with their own participles to propel a battle forward with appalling consonance:

> Then, rushing forward, trailing his own guts,
> He trod what trailed, the trodden entrails burst,
> And, tripping, down he tumbled, disemboweled.
>
> (12.390–92)

The gruesomeness of the image is belied by the playfulness of the poetry in a scene whose brutality—the reader will be unsurprised to hear—is too incessant to be taken seriously, landing more like a lampoon of such set-pieces in other epics. The wit and invention involved here are undeniable, yet one should remember that these are the very features historically dismissed as the unrealistic devices of an overactive mind.

Critics unable to imagine any worthwhile meaning in such stylized lapses of verisimilitude have taken special offense to Books 12–14, which dance around the tales of the Trojan War and the voyages of Aeneas, characterizing them as poor efforts in comparison to the *Iliad, Odyssey,* and *Aeneid.* This criticism completely misunderstands how Ovid revels in the very act of running circles around his predecessors, uninterested in retreading the same narrative or tonal ground. The entire story of the abduction of Helen leading into the Trojan War is dispatched in a mere three verses (12.5–7), yet the action grinds to a halt for a three-hundred-line digression on a completely different battle between humans and centaurs. Considering the themes discussed above, however, what some scholars have disparaged as impish iconoclasm is instead seen as carrying profound political intention: Ovid's verbal frolicking "fails" to produce the epic effects of Virgil and Homer not because he cannot but because he does not wish to confer such grandeur on the gods, kings, and heroes whose traditional supremacy, authority, and worthiness he meets with unstinting skepticism. Since the narrator often makes it clear that he is speaking from the perspective of a Roman in the time of Augustus, there is a subversive quality to the poem's attitude that is often at its most brazen where it pretends to be most obsequious. One almost gaspworthy moment comes near the end of the poem, where Ovid explicitly states the Machiavellian motive behind Augustus having the Senate deify his adopted father: "Then, lest the son should spring from mortal seed, / The sire must be made god!" (15.760–61). Only after the deification has been baldly exposed as a political machination do we realize that these are the thoughts of the goddess Venus, who is orchestrating the apotheosis from heaven. In every instance of Ovidian ovation, it is difficult not to come away thinking that the poet doth prostrate too much.

This, then, is the *Metamorphoses*. By turns ironic where one expects sincerity, irreverent in the face of authority, bombastic to the point of teasing, and yet somehow shocking in the sensitivity of its humanism, the *Metamorphoses* is as surprising as it is rewarding, balancing subversion and sympathy on the beam of a rapier wit that deserves much more credit than it has gotten. Besides—the wordplay is fun. While Edith Hamilton and so many other prudish voices have faulted Ovid for his blaspheming repartee, there is another long tradition that has been unabashedly willing to find enjoyment in what is enjoyable. In Book 6, when Latona turns a band of Lycian peasants into frogs, Ovid quietly slips an onomatopoeic "ribbit" into one of the lines describing the metamorphosis (6.377). It's an Easter egg for the reader who happens to notice, little more. How great is that?

RECEPTION

Even if the *Metamorphoses* were a dull slog with nothing to interest the modern reader, the work's preponderant artistic influence would still make it worthy of intense study. Whereas critical appraisals have fluctuated across time, there has been a far steadier current of artistic appreciation for a poem whose myriad multitudes unsurprisingly contain something for everyone. Era after era, not only writers and poets, but painters, sculptors, composers, and artists and storytellers of all stripes and media have drawn inspiration from Ovid's narratives, style, and narrative stylings. Every age gets the Ovid it prefers.

Ovid's influence stayed strong for the remainder of antiquity, as evidenced by the unmistakably Ovidian techniques and motifs cropping up in later poets from Seneca to Statius to Claudian, despite grumblings from Roman teachers of rhetoric that the poet's turns of phrase could be a bit much. The stature of the *Metamorphoses* is further attested by the influence of both its form and content. Both the elegiac couplet and the epic hexameter line, each of which had been adapted from Greek to Latin verse through a centuries-long process of *carmen* and error, attained their final Roman form with Ovid, after whom experimentation effectively ceased. As for content, the many innovations, interpolations, and recombinations Ovid contributed to the mythological canon were thenceforth transmitted as definitive. The once-separate stories of Echo and Narcissus were forever paired. Pygmalion held onto his new job as a sculptor. Pyramus and Thisbe kept on existing. In all the mythos, a few tales apiece from Hesiod, Homer, Sophocles, and Virgil are perhaps the only stories of any cultural currency that have reached us unrefracted through the prism of Ovid.

Throughout the medieval period, the poem known simply as *Ovidius major* ("Ovid's Big One," if you will) was continuously read as a kind of pagan Bible. Even in the first centuries of post-Roman Europe, when rejection of the pre-Christian classical was at its highest, teachers valued the *Metamorphoses* both as a school text from which to learn Latin—the better to read the Vulgate and St. Augustine—and as a source text on the falsehoods of heathen belief. (Some thousand years later, the puritan Milton would still be found using this approach in *Paradise Lost,* where Ovid's gods are enlisted by name in Lucifer's army of demons.) As the High Middle Ages brought a renewed tolerance for antiquity, enthusiasm for the work ballooned to such a degree that scholars commonly refer to the twelfth and thirteenth centuries as the *aetas Ovidiana* ("Age of Ovid"), a period when the poet was routinely consulted as an authority on not only mythology, but cosmogony, natural philosophy, and literary style. The goliard satirists of Germany cribbed his verbiage and the chivalric romancers of France adapted his stories. A full tenth of the lines in the *Romance of the Rose,* perhaps the period's most ubiquitous poem, are para-phrased or translated from Ovid.

But it was the age of the Renaissance that pushed the influence of the *Metamorphoses* to its towering summit. Ovid's combination of eru-dition and bawdiness appealed alike to the naughty humanism of Boc-caccio and the northern ribaldry of Chaucer, and nearly every local literary culture was greatly affected by vernacular versions, from the anonymous fourteenth-century French *Ovide moralisé* to the Italian adaptation by Giovanni Andrea dell'Anguillara (1561), the Dutch ren-dering of Joost van den Vondel (1671), and the never out-of-print Eng-lish heptameter translation by Arthur Golding (1567), whose effect on Shakespeare was so pronounced that excerpts often appear as appen-dixes to editions of *A Midsummer Night's Dream, The Tempest, Titus Andronicus,* and *The Winter's Tale.* Still, even this is not so impressive as the gale-force Ovidian wind that swept through European art and music. The *Metamorphoses* dominated the worlds of ballet and opera for centuries, with individual myths often put to music dozens of times, as with Book 14's lovers Acis and Galatea, who titled operas by Antonio de Literes, Jean-Baptiste Lully, Franz Josef Haydn, and two different works by Handel. In visual art, Michelangelo's sketches, Tit-ian's paintings, Cellini's metalworks, and Bernini's marbles are all crawling with Ovid, not only in the subjects depicted but often in the minutest details. Rubens' *Feast of Achelous* (c. 1615) is an exact visual rendition of the décor Ovid describes at 8.562–64, and the spectators in Bruegel's vastly different *Landscape with the Fall of Icarus* (c. 1560) are clearly drawn from 8.217–19. To walk through the Renaissance and Baroque galleries of an art museum unaware of the presence of Ovid is to stand in the blast of a firehose without recognizing one is wet.

Although the mania for Ovid temporarily dipped in the late Enlight-enment, when philosopher-critics like Winckelmann dismissed Ovid-ian transformations as debasements of the human ideal, Ovid's status as a symbol of suppression of speech and oppression of writers kept him personally popular as a Romantic motif, enrolled alongside Dante and Thomas Chatterton as the underappreciated artists *par excellence.* Indeed, expatriate authors from the ninth-century Carolingian poets to the Romantic Pushkin (*To Ovid,* 1821) and the Communist Bertolt Bre-cht (whom Ovid greets at the door in his "Visit to the Banished Poets," 1939) have all written voluminous self-lamenting works identifying with the woes of the original exile-poet. It is a scholarly commonplace to say that in periods of high patriotism and settled morality, the (at least superficially) dutiful and obeisant *Aeneid* gains in popularity, while in turbulent times of transition and transformation, the disruptive *Metamorphoses* retakes the fore. But even in those reverent Victorian ages, there are still artists and visionaries alienated by their own eras who turn to Ovid, creation or creator, for inspiration and identification. Somewhere, there is always a Johann Gottfried Herder scolding his pupil for enjoying Ovid's "unnatural" urbanity, only for that pupil (whose name was Goethe) to turn around and write Ovid's characters into his *Faust*.

And with its endless vagaries and pendulum swings, the twentieth century was rife with both periods. The modernists who overthrew the orotund Edwardian style and proclaimed themselves the voice of the disaffected Great War generation made Ovid their antique emblem. He is threaded through the pages of Pound and Rilke and the stages of Richard Strauss, in the epigraph to Joyce's *Portrait of the Artist* and the endnotes of Eliot's *Waste Land*. But the rising swell of nationalism swept Virgil back into favor in the lead-up to World War II, and only in the anticipation of Ovid's two thousandth birthday in 1957 did his work begin to receive its present degree of attention, this time with renewed scholarly interest as an international phenomenon encompassing German thriller novels and Japanese anime. His influence on the works of later twentieth century writers from Italo Calvino to Ted Hughes and Salman Rushdie was thoroughly treated in *Ovid and the Moderns* (2005) by Theodore Ziolkowski, who dubbed Ovid the "exemplary 'post'-poet," resonating with postmodernity, postrealism, and the postwar era in his ability to appeal to "feminists, postmodernists, the urban satirists, the multiculturalists, and the aficionados of sex, violence, and the fantastic" (224–25). Since those last three nouns are major components of virtually all stories, the influence described may be imagined.

Still, as Ovid and time both tell, change is only natural. Writing in 2006 at the dawn of the new millennium, the preeminent Ovidian scholar Philip Hardie drew on this understanding to wonder:

> It remains to be seen whether the rapid dwindling of Latin in schools in the last quarter of the twentieth century will finally have the effect of choking off the Ovidian literary reception that produced such riches in the twentieth century (261).

Given the course of history, Hardie was only reasonable in being uncertain. So far, however, the answer has been a clear and resounding no.

THE PRESENT MOMENT

Which draws us down to our times. Not only has Ovidian literary reception not been "choked off," his cultural influence has continued to skyrocket. While I was preparing this translation, the tabletop fantasy game *Dungeons and Dragons* released a classical myth–inspired campaign guide, *Hadestown* won the Tony Award for Best Musical, Methuen published the landmark *Greek Trilogy* of Luis Alfaro, a Tik-Tok trend drove Madeline Miller's novels *Circe* and *Song of Achilles* to the top of the fiction bestseller list, and Disney announced a new television adaptation of Rick Riordan's beloved *Percy Jackson & the Olympians* series, whose first installment I remember being read aloud by my fifth-grade teacher in a school district where no one taught Latin. Artists and writers as wide-ranging as Chris Ofili and Natalie Haynes continue to engage large audiences with their reimagined Ovidian myths, while the YouTube channel *Overly Sarcastic Productions* routinely uploads amusing analyses of Ovid's storytelling in viral videos that have broken the top tier of the platform's trending content. There can be no doubt that Greco-Roman mythology is enjoying renewed popularity on a massive scale, and particularly among the younger generation of which I happen to be a member.

It is not going too far to trace this phenomenon back to the *Metamorphoses,* for of all the source-texts for classical myth, Ovid's epic is the primary wellspring of not only the stories themselves but also the adaptive spirit that is the heartbeat of modern retellings. The classical scholar, mythological anthologist, and popular novelist alike cannot grapple with the mythos anew without taking reams of pages from Ovid's book. Consequently, when readers are drawn to mythology (and the above shows that they very frequently are), whether they come in pursuit of the "original" story or out of interest in its potential for revision and retelling, their paths will run through the *Metamorphoses.*

There they can find much that speaks to current concerns. Of the major ancient poets, Ovid is undoubtedly the most interested in women, the most egalitarian in his conception of human relationships, and the readiest to abandon traditional worldviews in favor of different perspectives—all with an impish smirk at the universe, all with incorrigible style. In giving modern context to the *Metamorphoses,* and especially in introductions like these, the normal thing is to compare Ovid to Vladimir Nabokov, another literary exile whose penchant for teasing, wordplay, and quasi-amoral aestheticism won his sportively inscrutable works admiration and condemnation in ample measure. The point is fairly taken, but I think we would do well to add in at least a dash of another famous writer: Oscar Wilde. Also appreciated in his own time for his genius rather than for his artistry, Wilde too was a moral adventurer who died in exile and disgrace, having good-naturedly gibed and mocked his way through a stringent society where he appeared to thrive, but that ultimately would not let him get away with it. Yet within that scaffolding of wit and subtle derision, his work hides an unexpected proximity to the darkness of the world, along with a profound sympathy for all that is essentially human. The cleverness, critique, and creativity are inextricably bound up in one another, as has been understood by a dedicated readership even in times of relative unpopularity. In a final resemblance, when once acquainted with his fate, it is hard not to see even his pre-downfall writings through the looking-glass of that knowledge.

There is one more reason I am comparing Ovid to a maligned gay playwright out of his time. While classical mythology is in the midst of a revival, the once-preeminent field of classics itself is now under unprecedented scrutiny for its discriminatory past and exclusionary scope, with many understandably wondering what such old and thoroughly gone-over works can still have to tell a modern audience. At the same time as these laudable, good-faith questions are being discussed, however, another segment of the population has proven all too ready to claim the classical heritage for its chauvinist self, cherry-picking the literary record to find justification for patriarchal and white supremacist prejudices in an imperial past they mangle into their own image (a phenomenon that received its first major treatment in 2018's eye-opening *Not All Dead White Men* by Donna Zuckerberg). Through assumption and willful misrepresentation, such misreaders have convinced themselves and others that the legacy of Rome is a monolithic paean to male conquest, an early manifesting of the white West's masculine destiny. But despite their assertions that Ovid, whose seduction advice in the *Ars Amatoria* they take seriously, is one of their number, few relics of classical culture should challenge their views so much as the *Metamorphoses,* read as it actually is. They would be disgusted that this foundational work of "Western civilization" contains a positive depiction of a trans man, confused by its inclusion of admirable Black African characters, and aghast at its panoply of same-sex couples, with whom Wilde himself once identified. Nothing good will come of yielding the floor to those who would pervert, mistake, and (above all) reduce the poem into a simple, evil, and hopelessly dated tract.

And the *Metamorphoses* still has many things to say, much of it unexpected and inimitable. There, in one of the loftiest works of Latin literature, lie investigations of identity, credibility, and power whose emotional immediacy and embrace of the inevitability of change pose a mighty challenge to the exclusive edifices of classical culture as conventionally conceived, the kind on whose justly immutable marble steps we are supposedly meant to worship the dour past without question. But the world of the *Metamorphoses* is not dour, conventional, exclusive, just, unquestioning, or immutable, but surprising, funny, and all-encompassing, rife with injustice yet perennially open to question and change. In translating Ovid's epic, I have been awed by how easily the poem takes me along for the ride, jumbling the gamut from regular to revisionist as it transforms old into new. Translation, too, is itself a kind of transformation, predicated on changes in language and context; and, as much as anything, the welcoming force of the epic's riveting fluidity is what has inspired me—queer, biracial, twentysomething as I am—to compose this new verse translation of a very old poem, the latest transformation in a long line of Ovid's ever-renewable metamorphoses.

Translator's Note

The goal of this work is to provide an accurate, poetic, and open-minded translation of the *Metamorphoses,* the first to use the blank verse of English epic while keeping the same number of lines as the original. Since literary translation is a case-by-case affair in which consistency, though a virtue, comes second to poetry itself, my practices are most closely detailed in the appendix at the back of this volume, which addresses some of my specific choices in vaulting the text's various rhetorical and grammatical hurdles. There are, however, a few broad strokes worth addressing on the topics of meter, wordplay, and the depiction of controversial themes, which together explain why a new translation is needed now.

First and foremost, my intent has been to translate the poetry as poetry: mine is a verse translation. More specifically, it is a blank verse translation equal in length to the Latin, meaning that for each unrhymed line of Ovid's original epic, there appears in my version one line of unrhymed iambic pentameter. Since Ovid wrote in the standard meter of Latin epic poetry, iambic pentameter is the natural choice for analogous translation, being the traditional meter of English epic and therefore evoking much the same tonal register and cultural associations. However, because a line of iambic pentameter is several syllables shorter than the hexameter Ovid used, previous blank verse renderings have invariably swollen the poem's length, often to a drastic degree—Charles Martin's 2004 translation runs nearly five thousand lines longer than Ovid's original twelve; Ian Johnston's is even longer. In addition to making translated editions unwieldy for academic purposes since line numbers will not match, my opinion is that such expansive methods result in a flaccid, dispirited translation, prone to wild recalibrations of pace and emphasis that are particularly ill-suited to capturing Ovid's engaging and unpredictable style. Worse still, it gives a false sense of fidelity, since the expanded translation is formatted with line breaks and spacing that in no way correspond with the verses composed by the poet.

By contrast, my work endeavors to show that equality in length not only preserves the feel of the poetry but need not come at the expense of accuracy in meaning. On the contrary, I have used the tight literary idiom necessitated by my approach as a means of *restraining* license. Where previous translators unmoored from Ovid's line count were free at any time to slacken the beat in order to make a subtext explicit or untangle a knot better left to the endnotes, all while sacrificing momentum and balance, I found that sticking to the literal meaning kept the lines proportionate, lyrical, and relatively neutral for the reader's interpretation. I have accordingly striven above all to tune my ear to Ovid's diction, repeating words when (and only when) his Latin does and avoiding the filler phrases so common in classical translations. Deferring to his word choice gave my lines the desired succinctness, without letting fear of elevated language sacrifice the poetic in pursuit of the colloquial or vice versa.

The difference between approaches is evident even in very short excerpts. Consider, for instance, the description of the goddess Hunger in these three arresting, but fairly straightforward lines, printed here alongside both an academic prose translation and my own verse rendering:

> ossa sub incuruis exstabant arida lumbis,
> <u>uentris erat pro uentre locus</u>; pendere <u>putares</u>
> pectus et a spinae tantummodo crate teneri
> (8.804–6)

her skinny hip-bones bulged out beneath her hollow loins, and her belly was but a belly's place; her breast seemed to be hanging free and just to be held by the framework of the spine

(Miller–Goold, p. 461)

> Dry bones protruding from her crooked crotch,
> <u>Her paunch a paunch-shaped hole, you'd think</u> her chest
> Was dangling, scarce supported by her spine
>
> (Soucy, 8.804–6)

Aside from Ovid's constant sense of consonance, my translation is guided by what strike me as the two main points poetically at play here. First is the grippingly odd turn of phrase *uentris erat pro uentre locus* (literally, "there was a stomach's place instead of a stomach"), which calls for similar pithiness in translation. This is followed by an abrupt second-person address, *putares* ("you would think"), which unexpectedly pulls the reader into the narration. Neither feature, however, is evident in the three most popular translations purported to be in pentameter:

> The hip-bones bulging at the loins, <u>the belly</u>
> <u>Concave, only the place for a belly, really,</u>
> And the breasts <u>seemed</u> to dangle, held up, barely,
> By a spine like a stick-figure's
>
> (Humphries, p. 206)

> [. . .] beneath her hollow loins
> Jutted her withered hips; her sagging breasts
> <u>Seemed</u> hardly fastened to her ribs; <u>her stomach</u>
> <u>Only a void</u>
>
> (Melville, p. 195)

> [. . .] hip bones protruded
> from underneath her withered, sunken loins,
> <u>her belly, nothing more than an indication</u>
> <u>of where a belly might be found</u>; her breasts,
> dependents of her spine
>
> (Martin, 8.1128–32)

Of these editions, now in print through Indiana University Press, Oxford World's Classics, and Norton Critical Editions, respectively, none recreate Ovid's tidy series of three uniform lines, and only Melville keeps to the original length (he averages about an extra twenty verses per hundred). Yet in doing so, he jettisons Ovid's pointed repetition of *uenter* ("stomach") and switches the order of images—

not a cardinal sin, but committed here without clear payoff. For their parts, Martin and Humphries do replicate Ovid's odd phrasing, but they overexplain it, fleshing out with a whole extra line the fleshless stomach that takes only two-thirds of one to describe in the original. And nobody keeps the second-person address, opting instead to flatten the dynamism of the Latin into, at most, a mere *seeming*. Finally, although it is a matter of taste, all three translations evince a far looser handling of the meter than mine.

Admittedly, in any work as long as the *Metamorphoses,* excerption makes easy targets of translations, and it is not my intention to proffer these comparisons as some kind of triumphal display. Each version has its own rationale, and it is not as if my edition captures every poetic device or never spends an extra half-line on a sentence (though I always get it back!) This example, however, is symptomatic of our differing approaches, and I do think it remarkable that the very features I find most interesting in Ovid's language are often those most frequently ignored by translators, who rush to sand away anything unusual in the text the point of which is not immediately obvious. Among the charming devices regularly lost on their chopping blocks are clearly intentional repetitions,

> siue <u>dapes</u> auido conuellere <u>dente parabat,</u>
> lammina fulua <u>dapes</u> admoto <u>dente premebat</u>
> (11.123–24)

> [when he tries]
> The <u>meat</u>, with every <u>bite the fellow takes</u>
> The <u>meat</u> turns into <u>bitten yellow flakes</u>!
> (Soucy, 11.123–24)

> [and when Midas] greedily
> prepared to sink his teeth into his meat,
> the teeth encountered golden dinnerware
> (Martin, 11.172–74)

meaningful ambiguities,

> cum manus impia saeuit
> sanguine Caesareo Romanum exstinguere nomen
> (1.200–1)

A wicked band once raged to sponge away
The name of Rome with [Augustus or Julius?] Caesar's blood
(Soucy, 1.200–1)

when assassins
Struck Julius Caesar down
(Humphries, p. 9)

and sudden authorial intrusions, as when the narrator apostrophizes a character in the story:

Te maestae uolucres, Orpheu, te turba ferarum,
te rigidi silices, te carmina saepe secutae
fleuerunt siluae, positis te frondibus arbor
tonsa comas luxit . . .

(11.44–47)

For you, O Orpheus, sad birds and beasts,
For you the solid stones, for you the woods
Wept tears, while trees who'd thronged to hear your songs
Shed leaves like grief-shorn locks . . .
(Soucy, 11.44–47)

The sorrowing birds, the creatures of the wild,
The woods that often followed as he sang,
The flinty rocks and stones, all wept and mourned
For Orpheus; forest trees cast down their leaves,
Tonsured in grief . . .
(Melville, p. 250)

If their notes are any indication, translators tend to avoid these narratorial choices on the grounds that they are foreign to the English storytelling idiom. To me, however, their unexpectedness reads not as exoticism but as an almost modern flair for formal adventure. Unsurprisingly, paring away the antique and unusual can weaken the force of an unusual antique text; compared with the stylistic banalities typically left in their absence, preserving these expressions can be positively refreshing.

This is especially the case with antonomasia, the practice of calling characters by epithets, nicknames, and patronymics instead of by their proper names. Seen as pompous, confusing, or simply not worth the trouble, antonomasia is invariably edited out in English versions, though Ovid often dramatically employs it to delay a name-drop that can still delight in translation. The god Mercury, for instance, appears in disguise throughout the first two books of the poem, during which he is mentioned exclusively by alias, as "Jove's son," "Atlas' grandson," "bearer of Caduceus," and so on. His real name is not stated until the end of Book 2, where the reveal neatly coincides with the moment he finally shows himself, having just been asked his name (2.741). By this point, however, Melville's translation has printed "Mercury" six times and Martin's seven, while Humphries has named the god on a full ten occasions, only to skip it right when Ovid includes his first. My rendering instead follows Ovid's lead, simply clarifying through footnotes a system of nomenclature whose literary flavor is well worth preserving—and which is anyway still less disorienting than that of many Russian novels.

Just as likely to be left on the translating room floor is Ovid's signature penchant for wordplay, much of which translators either ignore as untranslatable or render stale through overexplanation. Yet because brevity is often the soul of Ovid's wit, which is itself often the soul of Ovid's work, I have made a point of taking extra pains each time such a device has attracted my attention. The most obvious and easiest to replicate is certainly alliteration, which can be either glaring—

> *perspicit et placitas partim radice reuellit*
> (7.226)

> She raked through, ripping roots from plants that pleased

—or subtle: *uirgis ac uimine* (3.29) ("sprouts and sprigs").

Much trickier to tangle with, however, is Ovid's slant-rhyming anaphora, in which a couplet will repeat a phrase pattern while altering its meaning:

> *'Pars ego nympharum quae sunt in Achaide' dixit*
> *'una fui, nec me <u>studiosius altera saltus</u>*
>
> *legit nec posuit <u>studiosius altera casses.</u> . . .'*
> (5.577–79)

Cases like these pose a true test to the translator's patience, and Humphries gives up, skipping line 579 entirely. Martin, who has temporarily abandoned pentameter, makes no attempt to replicate the mirror effect but does a good job of capturing the literal sense, albeit while adding a filler phrase ("for small game"):

> 'Once I was one of the nymphs who dwell in Achaea,'
> she said, 'and none had more zeal than I for traversing
> the mountain pastures or setting out snares for small game. . . .'
>
> (Martin, 5.753–55)

Melville tries harder and does well:

> 'One of the nymphs whose home is in Achaea
> I used to be, and none <u>more keen</u> than I
> To roam the glades, <u>more keen</u> to place the nets.'
>
> (Melville, pp. 116–17)

My concern, however, was on keeping the doubled phrase *studiosius altera* in the same metrical position across both lines while also mimicking the phonetic qualities of the *saltus / casses* pair. Here's what I came up with:

> 'I once was one of those Achaean nymphs,'
> She said, '<u>the keenest one of all to traipse</u>
> The glades; <u>the keenest one of all with traps.</u> . . .'

Ultimately, which version meets with most success is a matter of taste and therefore of a translator's priorities—some may consider these lexical niceties little more than poetic frills. For a final example, therefore, I would like to highlight an instance where the interpretive weight carried by Ovid's verbal gymnastics is undeniably crucial. Many of the myths related in the *Metamorphoses* are etiologies, origin stories accounting for various natural phenomena. In a number of these tales, Ovid drives home the relation between legendary character and real-world result with an etymological pun, as when the daughters of king Minyas are transformed into bats, a fate Ovid states only implicitly:

> *tectaque, non siluas celebrant lucemque perosae*
> *nocte uolant seroque tenent a <u>uespere</u> nomen.*
>
> (4.414–15)

> Houses they haunt, not woods; they loathe the light;
> From <u>dusk</u> they take their name, and flit by night.
>
> (Melville, p. 86)

Melville's rendering is literally accurate, but consequently loses the point in translation: "bat" in Latin is *uespertilio,* from the word *uesper* ("dusk"). Again, wordplay poses a test of a translator's priorities. Martin's interpolative answer is full of filler phrases, but delightfully cheeky:

> Shunning the woods, they congregate in houses,
> nocturnal fliers fearful of the day,
> creatures named for the time they first appear:
> *vespertilians.* [Or, as we say, bats.]
>   (Martin, 4.567–71)

My solution is shorter, stricter, and simpler:

> Now, haunting eaves—not woods—and hating light,
> They're named for how they bat their wings by night.

Each translation has its witty moments, and the main distinction in how we rendered these lines is whether we found the effect worth the try. The opinion guiding my work, however, is that one should try as often as possible. For me, Ovid without his wit is not Ovid, and I have found that sufficient effort can usually recreate, without marked deviation in meaning, the wordplay that makes reading him so fun.

In the end, there are just two primary features of the *Metamorphoses* I consider truly beyond translation. The first is that the extreme flexibility of Latin word order is impossible to mimic in English without mounting a profound assault on syntax. Consider the following word-for-word translation of 13.395:

purpureum	*uiridi*	*genuit*	*de*	*caespite*	*florem*
purple	green	birthed	from	grass	flower

Literally, this line means, "it birthed a purple flower from the green grass," but so long as English is English, no translation will ever capture the balance of the original line, in which the verb keeps the adjectives away from their nouns like animals in nested pens. In these situations, there is little do be done but try to write a good line and move on.

The same holds true with the second untranslatable, which has to do with intertextuality: many of the strands Ovid weaves into his poem are spun from the poetry of his literary predecessors, especially Virgil, from whose work entire lines are borrowed and cleverly repurposed. Such was the Roman readership's knowledge of Virgil that allusions of that kind would have been readily recognized, constituting a major part of the audience experience. For the modern English reader, however, no such knowledge may be presumed, nor could the effect be reproduced in any case since there is no standard translation of Virgil to crib from. Such occasions merit at most a footnote and a shrug. As it is, translators have a difficult enough time grappling with Ovid's moments of *meta*textuality, in which the poem creates echoes between wildly disparate stories by alluding to itself. One fascinating example is the phrase *tanta est fiducia formae* ("so self-assured is beauty!"), versions of which appear in very different circumstances at lines 2.731, 3.271, and 8.434, applying to Mercury (where the tone is jocular), Semele (menacing), and Atalanta (derisive). The effect is not difficult to preserve in translation and, with my focus on Ovid's diction, mine dutifully does. But of all the English versions ever published, the *prose* renditions of Henry T. Riley (1851), Mary Innes (1955), and Michael Simpson (2001) are the only ones I am aware of that do likewise.

Before moving on from formal matters, I would like to reiterate that these comparisons are presented not to prove the superiority of my artistry but to illustrate differences between translations. To varying degrees, Humphries, Melville, and Martin are trying to do different things than I am, which is even truer of the free verse, prose, and hexameter translations largely left out of this discussion (but to which I make frequent reference in the appendix). Naturally, my translation is the only one that embodies the blend of lyricism, archaism, colloquialism, and cynicism that I think best captures Ovid's tonal spectrum; hearing Ovid differently, other translators will concoct other recipes. But the *raison d'être* for my translation is that no prior attempt has been made to create a readable literary translation in English epic meter with such fidelity to the original's meaning and playful verbiage, let alone to its length. Measured by these criteria, I do claim to have done something new.

Where form gives way to content, however, there is a major variance in my translation philosophy that lies outside mere differences of taste in meter, diction, and authorial license. To elaborate on a point made in my Introduction, previous translators of the *Metamorphoses* have made indefensible choices in their renderings of the poem's rape scenes, betraying a readiness to overlook, downplay, and make light of sexual assault that runs quite independent of what Ovid originally wrote. It is both difficult and inadvisable not to read in these choices the same cultural attitudes that have long made it so normal for abuse survivors to be disregarded, their stories distrusted, and their sufferings dismissed. The effect this awareness has had on guiding my translation is evident throughout my endnotes, but the full scope of the phenomenon can be demonstrated only by example. I will furnish two.

The first case has gained some attention from Stephanie McCarter's excellent essay "Rape, Lost in Translation" (which I did not read until after completing my version). This is the story of Leucothoë, who finds herself visited and, in short order, raped at the hands of the splendiferous Sun—not that you'd know it from even the three latest translations in print:

> *at uirgo, quamuis inopino territa uisu,*
> *uicta nitore dei posita uim passa querela est.*
> (4.232–33)

> This sudden apparition
> Terrified the girl, but the god's splendor won out,
> And she endured his advances without any complaint.
> (Lombardo, 4.259–61)

> Shocked as she was by this sudden appearance, the girl was utterly
> dazzled. Protest was vain and the Sun was allowed to possess her.
> (Raeburn, 4.232–33)

> This unexpected apparition frightens
> the virgin, but its radiance overwhelms her,
> and she gives in to him without complaint.
> (Martin, 4.321–23)

In these tellings, the previously frightened Leucothoë has clearly been seduced by the Sun's brilliance, with only Raeburn's hexameter rendering even hinting at continued opposition. Melville and Humphries are similar, and Horace Gregory's 1958 version (still in print through Signet Classics), makes the girl positively pleased by the outcome:

> At which she trembled, yet could not resist it;
> She welcomed the invasion of the Sun.
> (Gregory, p. 118)

What's going on here stems from an undue emphasis on the clause *posita querela* (literally, "having dropped her complaints"), which these translators invariably read as a change of mind. Yet this is a disturbing interpretation because it untangles those words from the verb phrase around which Ovid wraps them, *uim passa est* (literally, "she suffered his violence"), which is the standard Latin construction denoting rape. Worse still, it directly contradicts Leucothoë's later protestation *ille uim tuli inuitae* ("He forced himself upon me!," 4.239), which translators are also not above weakening, as Martin does by describing it as "her own explanation of events" (4.331)—an editorial comment with no counterpart in the Latin. Loath as I am to say it, these translational choices are rape culture in a nutshell, straining past both the victim's story and the author's account to seize on the slightest indication of the most coerced, silent signal of quasi-consent, all while hiding clear indications of rape from the reader. For my part, I see *posita querela* more as a chilling indication of how panic-stricken Leucothoë is in the moment, the shock and awfulness of her situation; accordingly, my translation reads:

> the girl,
> Though scared at such a sight, was vanquished by
> His godly light and raped without a word.

A brief second case study shows that these prejudicial choices can apply even when the rape in question is universally unquestioned. Since Daphne (however tragically) manages to escape Apollo, the first figure in the poem to endure sexual violation is Io, raped by the god Jupiter. This occurs in line 1.600, *tenuitque fugam rapuitque pudorem*, which literally means "and he seized the fleeing girl and robbed her of her honor." Yet Humphries writes only that Jove "stayed her flight, and took her" (p. 21), and Gregory that he "overcame her scruples and her flight" (p. 48). This handwaving daintiness has persisted into the present century, with Martin writing that he "seized her and dishonored her" (1.832), and Lombardo that he simply "stole her chastity" (1.638). As I see it, the emphasis ought to land on the girl's resistance in fleeing and on the violence of the verb, however euphemistic; consequently, I render it "And, grabbing hold, despoiled the struggling girl." As I note in my Introduction, Ovid's poem contains an incisive investigation into the abuse of power; it is a task of the translator not to occlude it.

Unfortunately, such watered-down assault scenes are only the most egregious examples of translators' mishandling of sensitive subjects: slaves are replaced by servants, homosexual references are suppressed, and depictions of women in general become hypersexualized (see the appendix's discussion of 5.393 for a particularly gross example). Between the pentameter, puns, and political considerations, my work is based in the belief that the time has come for a translation that is conservative in its treatment of the poem's text but not in its attitude toward its content.

We are fortunate, therefore, to be on the cusp of a new wave in Ovidian translation. In addition to my own, I am aware at time of writing of two other editions in simultaneous preparation, one by Stephanie McCarter and another jointly composed by Jhumpa Lahiri and my friend Yelena Baraz. In light of the above discussion, this promises to be an exciting development, not least because my three contemporaries will be the first women to publish English translations of the epic since Mary Innes in 1955. To the best of my knowledge, Lahiri and myself are also the first non-white authors to translate the work, while I am likely its first queer translator and surely the first from the generation commonly known as "Z." How much these firsts will factor into our translations remains to be seen; certainly, each of us is more than the sum of our demographics, and our writings are not simple reflections of our identities. Yet speaking only for myself, the pleasure in watching this translation make it to press will go far beyond getting to share these sublime stories and secondhand witticisms with the world. As a classical translator, there is an element of going against the grain in both my process and my person that makes me extremely proud to meet the present moment, especially since doing so was inconceivable to me growing up, when I assumed such pursuits were for other people. Even when I began this project, I could only hope to take part in opening the study of classics to others like me, for whom pursuing this path might become a little more conceivable. The great opportunity granted to me here is thus not only a form of scholarly satisfaction, but a printed-and-bound affirmation that even in classics I can, in fact, do more than only hope—I can write, I can engage, and I can belong.

C. Luke Soucy
Minneapolis
October 2022

The Latin text of the *Metamorphoses* has no paragraph indents, story headings, or divisions other than those between books. These features have been added to the translated text solely for ease of reading and interpretation, with notes in the commentary signaled by a dagger (†). At points where the text is likely corrupted, lines believed to be spurious are marked by [brackets]. A few of the most notable are discussed in the commentary, while the especially interested reader can find more on these and other textual matters in the appendix.

MAP 1. *The World of Ovid's Metamorphoses*, Blue from Overly Sarcastic Productions (2022).

Metamorphoses

Book 1

OF NEW† embodied shapes transformed, my mind
Is moved to speak! O gods (for you have shaped
These matters, too)† inspire what I've begun
And draw the first creation of the world
Down to our times† in one unbroken song.†   5

[THE FIRST CREATION]†

BEFORE THERE were seas, lands, and arching skies,
Throughout the whole world nature bore one face,†
Which was called Chaos, an unordered, rough
And tumble mass of lifeless weight, wherein
Lay packed the jangling elemental seeds.   10
No Titan then brought sunlight to the earth,
No Phoebe yet wrought full her lunar curve;
Nor hung the Earth self-poised in swaddling air,
As Amphitrite's waves embraced her banks.†
For though the land, the sea, and air were there,   15
The land could bear no tread, the waves no stroke,
The mist no light. No being retained its shape
And each opposed with each, for in one self
Heat battled cold, wet strove with dry, soft parts

39

Struck against hard, and weight fought weightless things.   20
   A god and better nature broke this strife.†
He tore the lands from sky and seas from land,
And from the dense air split the crystal heaven.
Then, after he released the separate forms,
Plucked from that sightless mass, he fastened them   25
In place with common peace. Next, weightless fire
Leapt up and claimed its place in vaulting heaven,
With air beneath, the next by lightness placed.
But denser earth sank under its own weight
And drew down heavy masses by its side.   30
The circling water took hold last of all
And wrapped the solid earth within its flow.
   Once he—whichever of the gods he was—
Had so reduced the whole to living parts,
He spun the land into a giant sphere,   35
And to begin, lest all sides be alike,
He ordered straits to stream and swell beneath
The sweeping winds and clasp the circled earth.
And he made springs and lakes and boundless pools
And tilted banks hemmed in by slanting streams,   40
A share of which the earth absorbs; the rest
Runs to the sea where, in a freer flood,
It pounds no banks but breaks on ocean shores.
He ordered fields unrolled and valleys sunk,
The forests wreathed with leaves, the mountains raised;   45
And, as two regions on both left and right
Divide the sky (a fiery fifth between),
So did the might of god segment its load:
The same five bounds are stamped upon the earth.†
The middle zone is home to heat alone,   50
The outer two to snow, but those between
He gave both flame and frost in measured fare,
And over all, the air—as great a weight
Compared to fire as water feels from earth.
   He ordered there the mists and there the clouds,   55
And thunder, soon to frighten mortal minds,
And, mixed with bolts of light, the flashing Winds.

To them, the maker did not grant the air
Outright (for even now, when each one blows
In his own realm, those brothers quarrel so   60
They scarce withhold from shattering the world).
So Eurus sought Arabian lands of dawn
And Persian peaks aglow with morning rays,
While near the western shores by sunset warmed,
Dwells Zephyrus; and wintry Boreas seized   65
The Scythian North, while southern lands drip wet
With constant clouds and rain by Auster's hand.[†]
Above them all, the god let aether flow,
A liquid lacking weight or earthly trace.[†]
    Such boundaries he had scarcely set in place   70
Before the stars, which had so long been crushed
In sightless gloom, began to light the sky.
And, lest some realm be left devoid of life,
The stars and godly forms took hold of heaven;
The waves made way to house bright schools of fish,   75
Beasts gained the earth, and birds the fluid sky.
    But still there lacked one holier than these,[†]
A creature fit for thought to rule them all:
The human race was born. Perhaps it was
That same creator's sacred seed that brought   80
A better world; or maybe the fresh earth,
New-rent from aether, kept some seeds from heaven,
Which, washed by waves, the son of Iapetus[1]
Shaped in the image of almighty gods;
And downward though all other beasts may gaze,   85
He gave to man a face turned toward the sky,
And bade him stand and look upon the stars.
And so the earth, but lately crude and bare,
Was changed and clothed with unknown human forms.

1. Prometheus

[THE AGES OF MAN][†]

A Golden Age came first, when with no laws   90
And no enforcers, good faith freely reigned.
No punishments were feared; no warning words
Were read on plaques of bronze;[2] no frightened crowd
Faced judgment kneeling—peace was unenforced.
Not yet were pine-trees, seeking foreign lands,   95
Hewn down their mountainsides to part the waves,
For mortals knew of no shores save their own.
Not yet did sheer-cut trenches circle towns;
No brazen trumpets straight, no twisting horns,
Nor helms nor swords were there, nor need for arms: 100
The nations lived in safe unwarring ease.
The Earth, untouched by plough and ploughshare wounds,
Herself gave all from self, and men, full pleased
With fare won free, plucked bitter strawberries
On mountainsides, hard cherries, thorny fruits,   105
And acorns dropped from Jove's wide-spreading tree.[†]
Spring saw no end. With gentle warming breath,
The Zephyrs brushed through flowers that bloomed unsown,
And soon, the untilled land brought forth its fruit,
While never-fallow fields grew white with grain.   110
And streams of milk by streams of nectar rolled,
While groves of verdant oaks dripped honeyed gold.
    Once Saturn was dispatched to darkest Hell
And Jove made king,[†] there came a Silver race,
Of lesser worth than gold, but more than bronze.   115
Then Jupiter abridged the span of spring,
So through the summer, winter, fickle fall,
And shortened spring, the year in seasons ran.
For the first time, dry air glowed white with heat
And icicles hung frozen in the wind.   120
Then, for the first time, houses too appeared
(Which up till then were caves or huts of thatch).
And, for the first time, Ceres' seeds were sown

---

2. Laws were announced to the public on bronze tablets

While underneath the yoke young bullocks groaned.
   Next, third in order, came the race of Bronze,   125
With crueler souls more keen on savage war,
Yet upright still. Last came the race of Iron,
An age of baser mettle when all sin
Burst forth, and prudence, truth, and faith took flight,
Replaced by tricks and plots and treacheries   130
And violence and vicious lust for gain.
Soon sailors spread their (then unheard of) sails,
And keels that long stood still on mountain slopes
Now danced and leapt about on stranger tides.
The ground—once shared, like light and air—was marked   135
With lines drawn by surveyors in the dirt.
Men scoured the land's rich soil not just for food,
But, diving through the bowels of the earth,
From out the Stygian gloom where they lay hid
They gouged its treasures—stimulants of sin: 140
Vile iron appeared, and gold, far viler still;
And so came war, which battles with them both
And clangs its clashing arms with bloody hands.
Men lived by theft. No guest slept safe from host,
No in-law safe from son; with brothers, too,   145
Love vanished. Spouses wished each other gone,
Sons sought to see their sires untimely dead,
And evil stepmothers pale poisons brewed.
At last, with virtue killed, the final god,
The maid Astraea,[†] fled the blood-soaked earth.   150

[THE GIGANTOMACHY][†]

   And lest high heaven be more safe than earth,
They say[†] the Giants fought to rule the sky
And built a tower of mountains to the stars.
But the Almighty[3] shot Olympus down
And wrenched Mount Ossa from Mount Pelion.   155

3. Jupiter

The Giants lay pinned by their giant size,
And when their blood seeped through their Mother Earth,[†]
They say that she revived the acrid gore,
And so some vestige of them might survive
Transformed them into men—but this breed too   160
Was hateful of the gods and lived to kill:
Thus you could tell that they were born from blood.

[LYCAÖN][†]

Above them Saturn's son, beholding all,
Bemoaned the thought of foul Lycaön's feasts,
Which, being new, were not yet widely known;   165
And, having roused a wrath befitting Jove,
He called a council,[†] summoned straightaway.
In cloudless skies, one sees an astral road,
Famously bright and called the Milky Way,
On which gods travel toward the Thunderer's house   170
And royal court. Through doors on every side
Patrician halls are thronged, while common gods
Find places all around; and there the powers
Who dwell on high have set their household gods.[†]
Such is the place—if I might be so bold—   175
That I regard the Palatine[4] of heaven.
Once all the gods had taken seats inside
That marbled hall, the ivory-sceptered one,
Aloft his throne, shook out his fearsome locks
Three times and more, and rattled earth and heaven.   180
Then, from his scornful lips, there came these words:
"Never have I been so upset to rule
The world! Not even when the monsters[5] made
To cage the heavens in their hundred hands.
For, savage though they were, that foe waged war   185
With but a single form and single source.

4. The Palatine Hill of Rome, site of the imperial palace
5. The Giants

But now, as Nereus[6] rings the earth, I shall
Lay waste the race of mortals—this I swear,
Upon the streams and Stygian groves† below!
All else has now been tried; the cureless limb   190
Must be cut off to stop infection's spread!
My demigods, my rustic gods and nymphs,
My satyrs, fauns, and mountain-dwelling powers—
Since they are held unfit to live in heaven,
Let us at least allow them their own lands!   195
Or do you think they will be safe, when plots
Are set for *me*, the lord of gods and storms,
By cruel Lycaön, infamous and wild?"
   In uproar, all the gods with burning zeal
Demanded him who dared perform such deeds.   200
A wicked band once raged to sponge away
The name of Rome with Caesar's blood†—then, too,
Such fear of ruin shook the earth and gripped
The human race. Nor does your subjects' love
Mean less to you, Augustus, than to Jove.   205
Once he, with hand and voice, had stilled their shouts,
All held their tongues, and, having stayed their cries
With regal force, he broke the silence thus:
   "He has indeed been punished (have no fear!),
But I will tell his sentence and his sins.   210
The age's sorry state had reached our ears,
And, hoping it were false, I flew from high
Olympus, cloaked in human form, to see.
I cannot count now all the crimes I found,
The rumors were so far outstripped by truth.   215
Round Maenalus, replete with lurking beasts,
Cyllene, and Lycaeus'[7] frozen pines,
As evening twilight turned to night, I reached
The hostile home of that Arcadian king.
On seeing the signal that a god had come,   220
The crowd fell praying, but Lycaön mocked

6. A primordial ocean deity, here representing the sea
7. Three mountains in Arcadia

Their pious vows and said, 'I shall divine
Beyond a doubt if he be god or man.'
   "That night he planned to kill me in my sleep—
Such was the test he chose to seek the truth! 225
But, not content with this, he grabbed a knife,
Took a Molossian hostage, slit his throat,
And tenderized some of the half-dead limbs
Within a stew; the rest he baked with fire.
But as he set the table, my bolt sent 230
The roof down on his worthless household gods.
He fled in terror to the silent fields
Where, howling in his vain attempts to speak,
His mouth grown mad with wonted greed for gore,
He turned to sheep and reveled in their blood. 235
Then clothes changed into fur, and arms to legs!
Though now a wolf, some signs of old remain:†
The same grey hair, the same fierce fiery eyes,
And wildly savage look are all the same.

[THE DELUGE]†

   "One house is felled, but more than one must fall. 240
Where lies the land, the Furies† rule these beasts.
You might (as I do) deem all joined in crime,
So let them swiftly pay a fitting price!"
   Some voiced approval with the roars of Jove,
While some by nodding played their silent parts, 245
But all were sad to lose the human race,
Unsure how an unpeopled earth would work:
Who would bring incense to their altars then?
Would he give all the earth to plundering beasts?
The king of gods forbade such searching fears 250
(For he would see to all) and promised them
A new and different race of wondrous birth.
   But as he was about to rain his bolts
Upon the earth, he feared their flames might spread
And torch the axis of the sacred sky, 255
For he recalled a day was prophesied†

When sea and land and sky would each catch fire,
And all the crafted cosmos be in threat.
So he set down the Cyclops' hand-wrought shafts
For a new plan: to damn the mortal race   260
Beneath the waves, with storms in every sky.
   Straight off, he shut within Aeolus' caves
Aquilo and such winds as scatter clouds;
But Notus† he let fly with dripping winds,
His fearsome face a shroud of black-hot pitch.   265
His beard was filled with clouds, his hair with streams,
His brow with mists, his chest and wings with dew,
And when his wide hands struck the hanging clouds,
There came a crash as each disgorged its rain.
Then Juno's herald Iris, rainbow-robed,   270
Drew moisture from below to feed the clouds
Till all the crops and farmers' hopes lay lost—
A whole year's work transformed to worthless waste.
   But Jove was not appeased by rain alone
And so his sea-blue brother[8] sent his waves   275
And summoned all the rivers to his court.
"This is no time," he said, "to give a speech.†
Now (as your duty calls) pour forth your strength!
Fling wide your doors, away with dams and docks,
And give your streams unbridled leave to flow!"   280
So he decreed. The streams returned, and from
Fresh-flooded mouths, they raced down to the sea.
As Neptune, with his trident, shook the land,
The quaking earth cracked wide new waterways
And wandering rivers rushed through open fields.   285
As one, the crops and orchards, flocks and men,
Their homes and household shrines were borne away.
If any house remained that had withstood
Disaster, vaulting waves now stretched across
Its roof and sank its towers beneath the flood.   290
And now there was no telling sea from land,
For all was sea: a sea without a shore.

8. Neptune

One man takes to the hills; one to his skiff
And plies his oars where yesterday he ploughed.
Above his fields and sunken house, one sails;   295
Another catches fish atop an elm.
Ships now might anchor in a verdant plain
Where underwater vineyards scratch their hulls;
And where once graceful goats had grazed the grass,
Misshapen seals now find a place to rest.   300
Nymphs gape at human groves and towns and homes,
And, in the forests, dolphins roam the oaks,
Which quiver as the creatures ram their boughs.
Wolves swim with sheep, and golden lions float
With tigers on the waves. The boar's swift strength,   305
The drowning stag's fleet foot are no use now.
The wandering bird finds nowhere it can land
But drops with weary wings into the sea.
The hills are crushed beneath the boundless deep,
A strange new tide that beats on mountain peaks.   310
The waves wash most away—those whom it spares
Are met with hunger and soon starve to death.

[DEUCALION AND PYRRHA]†

Between Aonia and Oetaea's fields,
Lies Phocis, once a fertile land, but now
An ocean plain within a sudden sea.   315
There a steep mountain reaches for the stars:
Parnassus,† whose twin peaks surpass the clouds;
And (since the flood engulfed all else) there sailed
The ark that bore Deucalion and his wife.
Once safe, they thanked Corycian's gods and nymphs   320
And Themis, then the god of oracles,
For, of all people who had ever lived,
He was the fairest, she the most devout.
    When Jupiter saw earth a stagnant pool
And, from thousands of men, just one alive,   325

And just one woman out of thousands more,
Both innocent, both faithful to the gods,
He bade Aquilo sweep the clouds aside,
And show the sky the land and land the heavens.
Nor raged the sea once Neptune quelled the tides   330
Beneath his trident and sent Triton forth,
Who, rising from the depths with shellfish strewn
About his sea-green arms, answered the charge
To sound his conch and, by this song, recall
The floods and streams. So Triton raised his horn—   335
A single spreading curve of spiral shell,
Which, sounding in the center of the sea,
Was heard on every shore under the Sun.
Thus touched by dripping beard and godly lips,
It rang the called retreat into the air.   340
Through land and sea, all waters heard the sound,
And every wave that heard held back its flow.
Soon, seas had shores, full streams kept to their beds,
[The rivers ebbed and hills were seen to rise]
As land appeared, and waves gave way to ground.   345
In time, the trees revealed their naked tops,
Their leaves still covered in residual slime.
   The world had been restored. But when he saw
Its lands were bare and cloaked in silence deep,
Deucalion cried to Pyrrha, through his tears: 350
"O wife, O sister, last woman alive,
Who shares with me, as cousins, race and birth,
Whom marriage and misfortune joins to me—
In all the land, from sunrise to sunset,
We two gather alone. All else is sea.   355
I am not fully sure yet of our lives;
Those clouds strike terror in me even now.
If fate saved you without me, my poor dear,
How would you feel? Alone, could you withstand
Your fear? How would your grieving be consoled?   360
Believe me, if the sea now held you, too,
It would hold me, for I would follow you.

Oh, would that I might, with my father's skill,[9]
Breathe life anew into these reformed lands!
Instead, we two live on (as heaven sees fit),   365
The final specimens of humankind."
    This said, they wept and, turning then to prayer,
Begged heaven's help in holy oracles.
At once, they made for the Cephisus' waves,
Which, murky still, now kept inside their banks.   370
Their heads and clothing cleansed within its flows,
They next sought out the goddess' sacred shrine,
Whose gables still hung bleached by putrid moss
Above the altars, now devoid of flame.
Upon the temple's steps, they both fell down,   375
Embraced the icy stone with fearful lips,
And cried, "If righteous prayers can soften gods
And curb their wrath, then tell us, Themis, how
Our vanished race may be restored.† Bring aid,
O font of mercy, to our sunken realm!"   380
    The goddess, moved to oracles, replied:
"Depart with shrouded heads and open robes,
Behind you strewing your great mother's bones!"
They stood awhile amazed; then Pyrrha spoke.
To carry out such orders she refused,   385
But begged with trembling lips for clemency,
Lest, scattering bones, she wound her mother's ghost.
They pondered, all the while, the goddess' words,
So dark with meanings hidden from the mind,
Until Prometheus' son, in gentle tones,   390
Soothed Epimetheus' daughter with these words:
"Unless I cannot think, the oracle,
Which, being holy, never counsels sin,
Means *Mother Earth*—whose bones must be her rocks!—
And bids us cast stones backward while we walk."   395
    This insight moved Titania,[10] but she paused,
So little hope had they in heaven's advice.

9. Prometheus (cf. 83)
10. Pyrrha, granddaughter of the Titan Iapetus

Yet why not try? With veils and unclasped robes,
Back in their tracks they strewed the ordered stones.
Then (who'd believe but on the ancients' word?)†   400
The stones began to lose their hardened form
And soften slowly into softer shape.
Soon, grown in size but mellowed overall,
There could be seen in them some human form,
Not yet distinct or fully clear, but rough   405
Like marble statues only just begun.
Those earthy parts of them that had retained
Some sap or moisture changed to working flesh,
While what was hard and rigid turned to bone.
The veins of rock retained their former name,   410
And before long, through divine will, the stones
Thrown by the hand of man were men in form,
And women sprang from those the woman cast.
And so, we are a hard and toiling race,
For thus we prove the way we first were born.   415

[THE SECOND CREATION: PYTHON]†

All other beasts the land willed into being,
Once sunlight warmed the moisture that remained
And swelled the mire and marshes round with heat,
The fertile seeds of nature, nursed in soil
As in a mother's womb, gained life and grew   420
And gradually took on a different shape.
So, when the seven-channeled Nile† withdraws
From flooded fields to find its former bed
And heavenly light has baked the fresh-laid slime,
The tilling planters unearth much that is   425
Alive: some things complete, awaiting birth,
And some things just begun and lacking limbs.
And often, in one body, parts are live,
While other parts are only shapeless earth.
For, naturally, where liquids mix with heat,   430
There life begins—all things arise from this;

Though flame must fight with water, still their steam
Forms all—a clashing chord that causes life.
So when the Earth, made muddy by the flood,
Grew warm again beneath the lofty sun,   435
She spawned unnumbered species, some with shapes
Familiar, but some monsters newly framed.

    Against her will, she bore you then, as well,
Great Python, serpent hitherto unknown,
Who terrorized the newborn populace,   440
So vast you spread upon the mountainside.
This beast was slaughtered by the archer-god,†
Who'd killed mere does and goats before, but flung
A thousand darts—his quiver nearly out—
Until black venom spouted from its wounds.   445
And, lest time should erase his famous deed,
He founded there the sacred Pythian games,†
So-called in memory of the vanquished snake.
Each youth who won by hand or foot or wheel[11]
Received an oaken garland, for there were   450
No laurels then and Phoebus wreathed his brow
And flowing hair with any kind of tree.

[APOLLO AND DAPHNE]†

    The love of Phoebus fell on Daphne first,
And not through thoughtless chance but Cupid's wrath,
For when the Delian lord[12] had slain the snake,   455
He spied the boy-god[13] bending back his bow
And said, "What are you doing, impish child,
With such fierce weapons, fitter for our frame?†
For we can deal grave wounds to hostile beasts,
And Python, who plagued acres with her girth,   460
Have we laid low now, bulging with our darts.

---

11. That is, in throwing, running, or chariot-racing
12. Apollo, born on the isle of Delos
13. Cupid, generally depicted as a child, often with torch in hand

Content yourself with stirring small desires
And let your torch lay no claim to our praise!"
    Then Venus' son replied, "Your darts pierce all,
But mine pierce you. And, as beasts next to gods,   465
So low will fall your glory next to mine."
This said, he beat his wings and soared on high,
Alighting on Parnassus' shady peak,
And, from his store, took two opposing darts:
One forging love, the other causing flight.   470
(The first was sharp and made of gleaming gold,
The latter blunt, its reed shaft tipped with lead.)
This dart the god sent the Peneian nymph,[14]
Launching the other through Apollo's bones.

    He loved at once; she fled her lover's name,   475
Rejoicing in the woods and spoils of beasts
Like unwed Phoebe[†] [free with flowing hair].
Though many sought her, she refused all suits,
And, free and single, roamed the pathless woods
With no regard for Hymen, love, or mates.   480
Her father cried, "I'm owed a son-in-law!"
Her father cried, "You owe me grandsons, too!"
But nuptial torches were, to her, a sin
And modest pink would flush her pretty face.
Her coaxing arms about his neck, she'd say,   485
"Grant me the joy of staying always chaste,
Sweet sire. Diana's father did the same!"
    He yielded. But your beauty blocked your wish
From coming true—your form opposed your prayer!
At sight of Daphne, Phoebus loved and longed;   490
His visions failed, and longing turned to hope.
Soon, just as straws of harvest grain catch fire
And thickets burn when wayfarers, by chance,
Bring torches close or leave them after dawn,
So was the god aflame. His whole heart burned   495
And on his hopes he fed his fruitless love.
He saw her hair hang down her neck and said,

---

14. Daphne, daughter of the river Peneus

"How would it look arranged?" He saw her eyes
Which shone like stars; he saw her lips,
Whose sight was not enough; he cheered her hands,   500
Her fingers, wrists, and half-bared arms—and thought
What's unbared may be finer! But she fled
Faster than wind and did not pause for these
Recalling words: "Peneus' daughter, nymph—
I beg you, wait! No foe pursues you—wait!   505
Lambs flee from wolves and stags from lions; doves
With trembling wings flee eagles—each their foes!
But love inspires my chase. Poor me, if you
Should fall and thorns should scrape your shins—and I
Have caused you pain! The ground you tread is rough—   510
Slow down, please! Check your flight—I'll slow my chase!
Just learn by whom you're loved: no mountain-man,
No unkempt shepherd guarding herds and flocks—
Rash girl, you don't—you don't know whom you flee!
That's *why* you flee. For Delphi calls me lord—   515
Patara, Tenedos, and Claros, too!¹⁵
Jove is my father. Through me, all that is
Or was or shall be becomes known. Through me,
Do strings and lyrics harmonize in song.
My darts are sure, but one more sure than mine   520
Has made a wound inside my empty heart.
I, who discovered medicine, am known
As Aid-Bearer and wield all herbal powers.
Alas, there is no herbal cure for love:
My craft, which succors all, does naught for me!—"   525
    He might have said more, had the nymph not left
Mid-sentence and fled down her frightened path—
But graceful still! The winds blew bare her frame;
While crossing breezes ruffled through her clothes,
Light air pushed back her flowing hair: her flight   530
Increased her beauty. But it would not last!
The youthful god, now through with wooing words
And spurred by love, stepped back into the chase.

---

15. Sites of Apollo's oracles and cults

FIGURE 1. *Apollo and Daphne*, Gian Lorenzo Bernini (1622–25).
Epitomizing the dynamism of Baroque statuary, Bernini's life-sized
marble may be the most famous artwork based on Ovid. The
sculpture shows Daphne at the moment of metamorphosis, her mouth
agape with horror as leaves shoot from her extremities. Where
Apollo's hand touches her, the nymph's skin has already become bark.

A Gallic hound who spies a hare afield
And seeks his prey while it seeks to be safe   535
Will, when about to grab hold, now—and now!—
Think that he has and chomp upon its tracks.
The hare, too, cannot tell if it's been caught,
But flees the fangs and leaves the crushing jaws:
So ran the god and girl, with hope and fear.   540
    Love's wings proved faster; he denied her rest,
Gained ground, and gasped the hair about her neck.
Her strength used up with toil from such swift flight,   543
She paled and, seeing Peneus' waves, cried out,   544a
"Help, father! if your streams bear godly might,   546
Let change destroy my all too pleasing shape!"
This prayer but said, dull numbness seized her limbs
And thin tree-bark wreathed round her slender waist.
Her hair grew into leaves, her arms to boughs;   550
Her feet, but now so swift, slowed into roots;
Her face, a treetop. Just life's glow remained.
    But Phoebus loved her still and touched the trunk
To feel her heart beneath the new-grown bark.
The branches he embraced as human limbs   555
And kissed the wood, which shrank before his kiss.
"Since you can't be my bride," the god proclaimed,
"At least you'll be my tree! My quiver, harp,
And hair shall bear you, Laurel,[†] evermore.
You'll be there when Triumphal cries resound   560
As Roman generals mount the Capitol,
And at Augustus' doors, a faithful guard,
You'll stand and watch the oak that hangs between.[†]
And, as my brow is young and hair unshorn,
You'll always keep the honor of your leaves."   565
    While Paean[16] spoke, the laurel's branches stirred,
And like a head the treetop seemed to nod. . . .[†]

16. Apollo, in his capacity as a healer

FIGURE 2. *Daphne.* © Kiki Smith, courtesy Pace Gallery (1993). With its rough plaster and shards of glass, feminist artist Kiki Smith's sculpture is a modern response to traditional renditions of the Daphne story. Far from the classical ideal of Bernini, this Daphne's transformation has left a brutalized and broken body, beheaded but still suffering violation.

[IO, PART 1]†

In Thessaly, there is a wooded vale†
Called Tempe, through which the Peneus flows
In foaming waves down from Mount Pindus' foot   570
Which, falling, cast up clouds of finest mist
That rain their spray upon the tops of trees,
While far-off regions weary of its roar.
This is the home and seat and deepest shrine
Of the great stream, who, in a cliffside cave,   575
Makes laws for waves and nymphs beneath the waves.
The local river gods arrived there first,
Unsure whether to toast him or console—
Poplared Spercheus, old Apidanus,
Calm Amphrysus, the wild Enipeus,   580
And Aeas, followed by all streams whose waves
Unwind their well-worn ways down to the sea.
    Poor Inachus alone, deep in his cave,
Stayed home, and swelled his stream with tears to mourn
For his lost daughter Io. If she lived   585
Or now was with the shades, he did not know,
But since he could not find her anywhere,
He thought her nowhere—and feared even worse.
    But Jupiter had seen her heading home
And called, "Girl fit for Jove! You'll someday bless   590
A marriage bed—but now . . . seek shady woods!"
(And here he pointed to some shady woods.)
"Now, while the sun burns at its midday height!
But if you fear to cross the lairs of beasts,
Then know you walk protected by a god—   595
And not some lowly god, but him who wields
Heaven's scepter and who hurls its wandering bolts!
Now flee me not!"
                    (She fled.) And she had left
Lyrcea's wooded plains and Lerna's fields17
Before the god cloaked all the land in mist,   600

17. Regions near the Inachus; the flight is brief

And, grabbing hold, despoiled the struggling girl.
    But meanwhile Juno had gazed down at Greece,
Surprised to find the daylight turned to night
By sudden clouds no stream or land gave vent.
Then, glancing round her, looking for her spouse,   605
Whose secret loves she'd often caught before,
She found him nowhere in the sky and said,
"I'm either wrong or wronged!" and, soaring down,
Alit on earth and bade the clouds depart.
But he had sensed his wife's approach and changed   610
The child of Inachus into a calf—
A gorgeous cow! Saturnia[18] liked its looks,
Despite herself, and asked whose cow it was
And whence it came, as if she did not know.
To stop her search, Jove answered, "From thin air!"   615
But when Saturnia sought it as a gift,
What could he do? How cruel, to give her up!
But not to give, suspicious. Love and shame
Pushed him opposing ways. Shame would have won,
But if he had denied his sister-wife   620
A meager cow—no cow would it have seemed!
Her rival gained, the goddess did not yet
Lose fear of Jove's deceit, but passed the cow
To Argus, one Arestor's son, to keep.
    The head of Argus held a hundred eyes,   625
Which slept in pairs while all the rest kept watch;
They stared at Io any way he stood,
Still watching Io when his back was turned.
By day she grazed, but when the sun had set,
He penned her in, bound fast by unfair chains.   630
She fed on leaves of trees and bitter turf,
And, bedless, slept on seldom grassy ground,
And, luckless, drank the flow of muddy streams.
She wished to reach out supplicating arms,
But had no supplicating arms to reach,   635
And all her tries at groans came out as moos.[†]

---

18. Juno, daughter of Saturn

[Which scared her, for she feared her voice's sound.]
   She even roamed the banks where once she played,
Her father's banks, but, glimpsing in the waves
Her new-grown horns, she fled herself in fright.   640
No Naiads knew her, nor did Inachus
Know who she was, but she pursued them both
And let herself be petted and admired.
And when old Inachus plucked her some herbs,
She licked his hand and kissed her father's palm,   645
While tears gushed forth—if only words had, too,
She would have begged for help and named her fate!
Instead, with hoof-drawn letters in the dust,
She witnessed to her sadly altered state.
"Poor me!"† exclaimed her father, squeezing tight   650
The groaning calf, its horns and snowy neck.
"Poor me!" he groaned, "Are you she whom I sought
In every land—my daughter? You were not
A greater grief unfound than you are now!
You don't reply, but only heave deep sighs   655
And answer the one way you can: in moos!
For you, I'd hoped to ready wedding rites
And gain a son-in-law—grandchildren, too!
But now you'll have a husband from the herd
And in the herd will you bring sons to birth.   660
Nor may my torments end, even in death!
To be a god is pain: death's doors are shut
And all our woes stretch on from age to age!"
   Then eye-bespangled Argus checked his wails
And dragged the girl away to further fields,   665
Where, staking out a lofty mountaintop,
He gazed down from his seat at all below.

[ARGUS: PAN AND SYRINX]†

   The king of heaven could no longer bear
Phoronis'[19] miseries and charged his son,

---

19. Io, sister of Phoroneus

Bright Pleiad's child,[20] with having Argus killed.   670
At once, he donned his wingèd shoes and cap
And took his slumberous staff[21] in mighty hand.
So clad, Jove's son leapt from his father's mount
Down to the earth, and there removed his hat
And dropped his wings. His staff alone he kept   675
As shepherd's crook, to drive a flock of goats
Through backwoods farms while he played on his pipes.[†]
The novel sound enchanted Juno's guard:
"Whoever you are, share this rock with me,"
Said Argus. "For no place has richer grass   680
For herds; and, look, for herders—perfect shade!"
So Atlas' grandson[22] sat and spent the day
In ceaseless talk, while with his pipes he tried
To overcome those watchful eyes through song.
But he fought back against sweet sleep, and though   685
Some of his eyes had slipped into repose
The rest stayed wide awake. And when he asked
How reed-pipes (then quite new) first came to be,
The god said,
              "On Arcadia's windswept peaks,
Among the wood nymphs of Mount Nonacris,   690
There lived a famous nymph called Syrinx, who
Had more than once escaped a Satyr's chase
And outrun gods of woods and fertile fields.
She mirrored the Ortygian[23] in her ways
And chastity, dressed in Diana's style,   695
And as Latonia could have posed or passed,
Except her bow was made of horn, not gold.
    "Still, pass she did. For, on Lycaeus' slopes,
Pan spotted her, his head begirt with pine,
And said these words—"

---

20. Mercury, child of Jupiter and the Pleiad Maia

21. Mercury's sleep-inducing caduceus, depicted as a wand entwined by two serpents

22. Mercury, son of Maia, daughter of Atlas

23. Diana (or Latonia), born to Latona on the isle of Delos, also known as Ortygia

                              The words remained unsaid   700
Along with how the Naiad spurned his prayers,
Fled to the sands by Ladon's peaceful stream
And, stopped from running further by its waves,
Implored her sisters[24] there to change her form;
And how Pan, thinking Syrinx in his grasp,   705
Clutched no nymph's body but the marsh's reeds;
And how his sighs sent air among the stalks
Which issued forth a gentle, plaintive sound.
Enchanted by the sweet and novel tone,
The god cried, "This will stay my bond with you!"[†]   710
And to the reeds—uneven, but conjoined
With bands of wax—he gave the maiden's name.
   When poised to tell all this, Cyllenius[25] saw
That all the eyes had fallen shut in sleep.
He stopped his voice and used his staff to cast   715
The spellbound eyes into a deeper doze.
Then, straightaway, with curving sword, he smote
The nodding head right off and hurled it down
The rockface, smearing blood across the cliff.
Now, Argus, you lie dead with all your light: 720
A hundred eyes, extinguished by one night.

                     [IO, PART 2]

   Saturnia used his eyes to plume her bird,[26]
And so filled up its tail with starry gems.
This done, she took no time, but flamed with rage,
And cast a fearsome Fury in the eyes   725
And mind of her Greek rival, in whose heart
She set a secret spur to make her flee
Around the word, till you, Nile, stopped her toil.
Beside your banks she fell upon her knees;
Then, on her back, with neck reared high, she raised   730

---

24. The water nymphs
25. Mercury, born on Mount Cyllene
26. The peacock, whose feathers show eye-like orbs

All that she could—her face—up toward the stars.[†]
With groans and tears and most pathetic moos,
She seemed to cry for Jove to end her strife.
   So he threw arms around his spouse's neck
And begged her to at last end her revenge: 735
"She'll cause you no more pain,"[†] he cried. "Fear not!"
And bade the Stygian marshes hear his words.
The goddess thus assuaged, the girl regained
Her face and all she'd been: the bristles fled,
The horns withdrew, her eyes decreased in size,   740
Her jaws compressed, her hands and arms returned
And hooves dissolved, transformed into five nails,
Till whiteness was her only bovine trait.
Now pleased to use two feet, the nymph stood straight,
Afraid at first, lest, cow-like, she should moo,   745
As she tried out her long unspoken words. . . .

[PHAËTHON, PART 1][†]

   Now, she is worshiped by a linened throng[†]
And Epaphus, believed her son by Jove,
Shares with his mother in each city's shrines.
Yet Phaëthon, child of the Sun, his peer   750
In years and yearnings, would not yield the floor,
But proudly bragged that Phoebus was his sire.
The heir to Inachus could bear no more:
"You fool!" he cried. "You heed your mother's lies
And swell with pride at a false parentage!"   755
   With shame did Phaëthon suppress his rage,
Bring Epaphus' cruel words to Clymene,[27]
And say, "You'll hurt the more, mother, that I,
So fierce and free of speech, had naught to say.
It shames me that such words had no reply!   760
But if I am indeed a son of heaven,
Then give some sign and prove my claim on high."

---

27. Phaëthon's mother, now wed to King Merops of Aethiopia

He said this and embraced his mother's neck.
By his and Merops' heads—his sisters' too—
He swore and begged for signs of his true birth.   765
Then Clymene, moved either by his prayers
Or by her slandered name, reached toward the sky
And, gazing at the sun, cried out, "I swear
To you, my son, by this far-flashing light,
Who hears and sees us and who warms the earth: 770
You gaze upon the Sun who are his son.
If I speak false, may his light reach our eyes
No more. But you may see his household gods
With ease: the house of dawn is near our land.†
Go! If your mind's so moved, ask him himself."   775
　　His mother's words caused Phaëthon to leap
With joy as, sky-obsessed, he hurried from
His Aethiopian home to star-scorched Ind,
And reached the region of his father's rise.

Book 2

[PHAËTHON, PART 2]†

THE PALACE of the Sun, raised high aloft
Tall columns, gleamed with gold and burned with bronze.
A glint of glistening ivory graced its eaves
And silver shone upon its double doors,
Whose worth was by their workmanship surpassed;   5
For Mulciber himself had there engraved†
The globe, begirt by seas, with heaven above.
Within the waves were shown the sea-green gods:
Melodious Triton, changing Proteus,
Aegaeon with two monstrous whales in hand;†   10
Of Doris and her daughters,¹ some group swims,
Some perch on rocks to comb their verdant hair,
And some ride fish. Nor do they share one face,
Nor do they not, but look as sisters should.
The land holds men and cities, woods and beasts,   15
And streams and nymphs and other country gods.
Above all sits the likeness of the sky
With each door flashing half the Zodiac.
    Now when the son of Clymene had climbed
To reach the house of his supposed sire,   20

---

1. The Nereids, sea-nymphs sired by Nereus

He turned at once to glimpse his father's face,
Yet stood aside: he could not bear such light.
Bedraped in purple vestments, Phoebus† sat,
His throne ashine with brilliant emeralds.
To right and left were Day and Month and Year   25
And Century, spaced out with all the Hours.
Young Spring stood by, wreathed in a floral crown,
And naked Summer, garlanded by grain;
The Autumn, too, befouled from foot-worn grapes,
And icy Winter, rough with hoary hair.   30
Amidst these shapes the Sun, with all-seeing eyes,
Beheld the youth, who quaked to see such sights.
"What brings you here?" he asked. "Why seek this height,
My Phaëthon, son not to be disclaimed?"
He answered, "O shared light of the wide world!   35
O Phoebus, should you let me use that name!
If Clymene has not lied out of shame,
Prove to the world that I am your true son,
And so cast doubt," he said, "out of my mind."
    His sire took off his crown of shining rays,   40
Bade him draw near, then clasped him close and said,
"You've not deserved to be denied as mine!
And, lest you doubt that Clymene speaks true,
Ask any gift and I shall make it yours—
And may the waves by which gods' oaths are sworn,   45
Though unknown to our eyes, bear witness here!"
This scarcely said, he asked the reign and reins
Of his father's swift chariot for a day.
Regretting then his oath, the father shook
His glowing head three times and more, and said: 50
    "You prove me rash: I wish my oath undone!
For this alone, my son, would I deny.
But be dissuaded†—your wish is unsafe.
Dear Phaëthon, you ask a gift too great,
Too unmatched to your strength and boyish years.   55
Though mortal-born, you want immortal things;
Unknowing, you seek more than is allowed
The gods! For though they each do as they please,

Still none have strength to guide the wheel of fire
But me. Even the high Olympian king,   60
Who hurls fierce thunder with his fearful hand,
Can't take my place—and what surpasses Jove?
The morning path's so steep my freshest steeds
Can scarcely crawl. The middle sky's so far
From sea and land that, gazing down, I too   65
Am struck with awful fear that shakes my heart!
The last stretch, hurtling down, wants such firm hands
That Tethys,² who receives me to her waves,
Fears lest I should be thrown in headlong dive.
Then there's the constant motion of the heavens,†   70
Which swirls the vaulted stars with vastest speed.
Fighting this force, which conquers all but me,
I fly against the turning of the spheres.
    "Suppose you take the chariot—what's your plan?
Could you run counter to the spinning poles   75
That snatch all things? Perhaps you think the gods
Have groves and cities there, shrines rich in gifts?
But look—the path lies thick with snares and beasts!
Should you hold course and not be drawn astray,
You still must pass your way through Taurus' horns,   80
By Thessaly's bowman,³ cruel Leo's maw,
And Scorpio, whose savage, swiping arms
Are matched by Cancer, length for curving length.
Nor will the four-hooved creatures, whose souls burn
With inner flames their mouths breathe out as fire,   85
Be lightly ruled by you; they scarce heed me,
But warm their blood in battle with the reins.
    "But now, before I grant your fatal gift,
Take care, my son, while you can change your plea!
You wish to know that you are of my blood   90
And seek sure proof? Sure proof I give through fright:
Fatherly fear affirms my fatherhood—
Behold my face! And if your eyes could pierce

2. A goddess of the sea and wife of Ocean
3. Sagittarius

Inside my heart, they'd see a father's cares.
So look at all the riches of the world—   95
Land, sea, and sky—and from their countless goods
Ask anything. I'll have naught be denied!
Only not this! which, truly, is no prize;
O Phaëthon, the prize you seek's a curse.
    "You fool, why clasp my neck with pleading arms?   100
Doubt not (I've sworn it by the Styx): you shall
Have what you choose—but make a wiser choice!"
    This warning heard, the boy still paid no mind,
But, longing for the chariot, pressed his suit.
To linger while he could, the father led   105
The lad before his Vulcan-gifted coach.
Gold was its axle, gold its pole, and gold
Its towering wheels, ringed round with silver spokes.
The yoke, arrayed with chrysolites and jewels
Reflected Phoebus with a brilliant glow.   110
    While dauntless Phaëthon admires its craft,
Behold the shining east, where watchful Dawn
Throws wide her purple doors and rose-filled halls!
The stars disperse and, last of all, their lord,
The Morning Star, deserts his heavenly post.   115
On seeing him plummet toward the reddening earth,
Just as the moon-horn's tips† slipped out of sight,
The Titan called the Hours to yoke his steeds.
They did as charged and, from high stalls, led forth
The creatures—spewing fire, ambrosia-gorged—   120
And swiftly strapped their halters with a clank.
The father next besmeared his son with balm
To proof his face against the greedy flames.
With rays he crowned him—but, presaging woe,
He heaved his chest with anguished sighs and spoke: 125
    "If you'll at least take fatherly advice,
Then spare the rod, my boy, and seize the reins.
They tend toward speed; your task's to slow their flight.
Nor should you steer through all five heavenly coils—
The road curves wide and splits the sky aslant: 130
Confined within three zones, it skirts round both

The South Pole and the North Wind's nearby Bears.
Make this your path (my wheel ruts mark it out)!
And, so the same warmth reaches earth and sky,
Your airy course must neither sink nor soar: 135
Too high and you will burn the roof of heaven;
Too low, the earth. Fly safest in midair!
Swerve neither rightward toward the coiling Snake,[4]
Nor drive too leftward, where the Altar sits,[5]
But keep between them. All the rest I leave   140
To Fortune. With her guiding aid, may you
Outdo yourself!
                    "Now as we speak, night's dew
Has touched the western shore. We can't delay:
We're summoned. Shadows flee and Dawn glows bright.
Come, grasp the reins—or, if your mind is changed,   145
Then take our counsel, not our chariot,
Now [while you can, still standing on firm ground,]
Not while, unskilled, you press its ill-sought wheels.
Look on in safety—let me light the earth!"
But, mounting the light chariot, the youth   150
Now reared with pride and took the reins in hand
As joyously he thanked his grudging sire.
   Meanwhile, Pyroïs, Aethon, Eoüs,
And Phlegon,[6] flying horses of the Sun,
Neighed flames into the air and kicked their gates.   155
When Tethys, mindless to her grandson's[7] fate,
Unhinged these, laying clear the spreading sky,
They bounded on their way with pounding feet
That cleft the clouds and, borne aloft on wings,
Passed Eurus by, who shares their eastern source.   160
But he weighed less than what the Sun-god's steeds
Could feel—the yoke lacked its accustomed load;
And, just as ships, when poorly laden down,

---

4. The constellation Draco
5. The constellation Ara
6. "Fiery," "Scorch," "Dawn," and "Flame"
7. Phaëthon, son of Clymene, daughter of Tethys

Will, being too light, drift swaying through the sea,
So, void its usual weight, the chariot jerked   165
And wobbled as if nothing were inside.
On sensing this, the four-horse team went wild
And left the beaten path to run amok.
He trembled now, not knowing how to wield
The borrowed reins, nor knowing where to go,   170
Nor, had he known, could he have led them there.
    Then, for the first, the Oxen thawed from heat
And vainly tried to swim forbidden seas.[†]
The Snake, who's closest to the icy pole
And long had been too cold to conjure fear,   175
Now boiled with heat and burned anew with rage.
They say, Boötes,[8] you too fled in fright
As slow and plow-encumbered as you were.
Poor Phaëthon, from paradise's peak,
Peered down upon the distant, distant lands,   180
Then paled and knocked his knees in sudden dread.
His eyes dimming to dark from so much light,
He wished he'd never touched his father's steeds
Nor learned his birth nor seen his wish come true,
But longed now to be known as Merops' son.   185
Now he's a boat tossed in a northern gale
Whose helmsman leaves its broken helm to heaven:
What should he do? Much sky is passed, but more
Now greets his eyes. He charts them in his mind,
Now looking to the west he'll never reach,   190
Now glancing east, uncertain how to act,
Too dazed to hold the reins or let them go.
He does not even know the horses' names!
And there are marvels strewn throughout the sky,
Immense and beastly shapes he quakes to see.   195
In one place curve the double arching arms
Of Scorpio and, opposite, its tail,
With two signs' worth of space about its limbs.
When he beholds it drip black-venomed sweat

8. A northern constellation characterized as a plowman

And poise to wound him with its twisted sting,   200
Cold terror grips his mind—he drops the reins.
   The horses feel them fall upon their backs
And veer unbridled through strange realms of air.
Where impulse leads them they, unruly, rush
And ram set stars, the coach in pathless tow.   205
And now they seek the heights and now they drop,
By plunging pathways, nearer to the earth.
The Moon is shocked to see her brother's steeds
Run underneath her own; scorched clouds belch smoke;
The highest lands are all engulfed in flames—   210
They split in cracks, lose all moisture, and parch.
The hay turns white, trees burn amidst their leaves,
And withered grain lends fuel for its own loss.
But I am quibbling! Mighty cities fell
Beneath their walls, whole nations turned to ash,   215
And woods and mountains blazed! With Athos burned
Cilician Taurus, Tmolus, Oeta's peak,
Mount Ida, thick with springs but now run dry,
Chaste Helicon, and Haemus—not yet known†
For the Oeagrian. Then doubled flames   220
Burned Aetna, Eryx, twin Parnassus' peaks,
And Cynthus, Othrys, Mimas, Rhodope
Soon to lack snow, Mycale, Dindyma,
Sacred Cithaeron, and, through Scythia's cold,
The Caucasus. Then Ossa, Pindus too,   225
And—greater than them both—Olympus burned.
[And airy Alps and cloud-capped Apennines.]
   Now Phaëthon saw all the world ablaze
But could not bear to breathe such sweltering air,
Which boiled as from a forge. Feeling the coach   230
Glow white, he could no longer stand the ash
And upcast sparks, but swirled in seething smoke,
Unsure, in darkness, where he was or went,
Dragged onward at the will of wingèd steeds.
   It's thought that then the blood rose to the skin   235
And turned the Aethiopian peoples black.†
Then Libya dried, its moisture seized by heat.

Then long-haired nymphs bewailed their lakes and springs:
Boeotia longed for Dirce; Argos for
Lake Lerna; Corinth for Pirene's waves.   240
No safer were streams blessed with broader banks:
Steam rose from old Peneus and the Don,
Ismenus swift, Caïcus' Mysian flows,
Arcadian Erymanthus, and the blond
Lycormas, Xanthus, doomed to burn again,[†]   245
Meander, too, which frolics through its curves,
Eurotas' Spartan stream, and Thrace's Til.
Then Babylon's Euphrates burned, as burned
Orontes, Phasis, coursing Thermodon,
The Danube, and the Ganges. Alpheus boiled;   250
Fire scorched Spercheus' banks and melted gold
Into the Tagus, while the singing swans
Of Lydia's shores cooked in Caÿster's streams.
The Nile, in terror, fled to the world's end,
And hid its unfound head,[†] then drained to dust   255
Its seven mouths, now seven streamless beds.
Thus dried the Thracian Hebrus and Strymón,
The western streams of Rhine and Rhône and Po,
And Tiber, pledged to someday rule them all.[†]
    The ground burst everywhere and, through its cracks,   260
Light entered Hell and scared its queen and king.[†]
The ocean shrank as well: where once was sea,
Now dried a plain of sand, and, from the depths,
The mountains rose and joined the Cyclades.
Fish sought the sea-floor; dolphins dared not leap   265
Their usual airborne curves above the waves;
Atop the deep, dead seals swam on their backs,
And rumor has that Nereus himself
And Doris and their daughters hid in caves.
Thrice Neptune stretched his fearsome face above   270
And thrice could not withstand the fiery air.
    But kindly Earth, encircled by the sea,
By ocean waters, and by shrinking springs
That sought for refuge in her dark insides,
Raised up her battered face and shriveled neck,   275

Then, shielding her brow, with mighty quakes
That shook all things, sank slightly in her place
And spoke these broken tones: "If I've deserved
That this should please you, why hold back your bolts?
Should fire destroy me, let the fire be yours,   280
For dying by your hand would ease my death,
O lord of gods! I scarce can breathe these words. . . ."
(The fumes had choked her.) "Look, my hair is singed,
My lids and lips are all, all caked in ash.
Are these my bounty's fruits and this the prize   285
For duty paid? For bearing wounds all year
From crooked ploughs and hoes? For furnishing
Green leaves to flocks, ripe nourishment and grain
To humankind, and incense to yourselves?
Yet, say I've earned my doom—what have the waves,   290
What has your brother done? Why do the seas
Allotted him decrease beneath the air?
    "But if both he and I mean naught to you,
Still spare your skies! Look all around: from pole
To pole they fume. If fire should weaken them,   295
Your homes will fall! See, Atlas toils himself,
Scarce shouldering the glowing vault of heaven.
If seas, if lands, if heavenly halls all die,
Then we are thrown in ancient Chaos! Save
What's left from flames and see to the remains!"   300
This said, the Earth (who could no longer bear
The smoke and spoke no more) withdrew her face[†]
Inside herself, down to the haunts of shades.
    Then the Almighty Father told the gods—
The chariot's source, too—that, without his aid,   305
Cruel fate would end the world. Then up he rose,
Whence he was used to cloud the spreading lands[†]
And, thundering, to fling his flashing bolts.
But having now no clouds to bring the lands
Nor rains to send the sky, he weighed a bolt,   310
Then thundered, raised it to his ear, and dashed
The charioteer from life and perch at once,
And so put out the savage fires with fire.

The horses, in confusion, leapt apart,
Unyoked their necks, and quit the severed reins.   315
There falls the bridle! there, the axle wrenched
From pole! and here, the shattered spokes of wheels:
The chariot's mangled wreck, strewn far and wide.
But Phaëthon, his flame-red hair afire,
Whirled headlong like a comet through the air,   320
As sometimes, in an empty sky, a star,
Although unfallen, still may seem to fall.
A world from home, he's taken in by long
Eridanus,[9] who bathes his burning face.
There, Naiads bury him, still fuming from   325
The flash, and set this verse upon the stone:

> HERE PHAËTHON, WHO DROVE HIS FATHER'S STEEDS,
> LIES DEAD: HE CRASHED. STILL, DARING WERE HIS DEEDS.

[THE HELIADS AND CYGNUS][†]

His father, sick with sorrow, hid his face,
And—if we just believe—they say a day   330
Passed without sun. Still, firelight shone,
So even the disaster had some use.
But Clymene, when she had said what must
Be spoken at such times, was wracked with grief,
And, tearing at her chest, combed all the earth,   335
First for his lifeless limbs, then just his bones—
Bones found already laid in foreign shores.
She lay there on the cherished marble name,
Wet with her tears and warmed by her bare breast.
    Nor did the Heliads[10] mourn less! They gave   340
Their tears in idle tribute, beat their breasts,
Called day and night to Phaëthon, now deaf
To any cries, and fell upon his tomb.

---

9. A western river, possibly the Italian Po
10. The daughters of Clymene and the Sun, and the sisters of Phaëthon

Four times the moon filled out its crescent orb,
And, in their way (for ways are set with time)   345
They still shrieked on. But when the eldest girl,
Named Phaëthusa, would have fallen down,
Her feet were rigid. Fair Lampetia tried
To help her, but was held by sudden roots.
A third, on reaching up to tear her hair,   350
Plucked leaves instead. A trunk enclosed one's legs;
One grieved to find long branches at her arms.
And while they wondered, bark wrapped round their loins,
And, by degrees, round waists, chests, shoulders, hands—
Till only lips that called "mother!" remained.   355
    What could their mother do but rush at will,
Run here and there, and kiss them while she could?
It would not do: she tried to wrest the wood
Away from flesh and tore the tender twigs,
But drops of blood gushed forth as from a gash—   360
"Please, stop, mother!" each cried out at her wound.
"Please, stop! It's us you're mangling in the tree!
And now—goodbye!—" Bark sealed these final words.
    Their tears flowed on and, hardened on the boughs
By sunlight, dripped as amber in the stream,   365
Borne on, someday to tempt the wives of Rome.†
    To see this sight, the son of Sthenelus,
One Cygnus, came. Though joined to you by blood,
He was still closer, Phaëthon, in heart.†
Leaving his realm (Liguria's tribes and towns),   370
He poured laments by the Eridanus'
Lush, verdant banks and sisters-swollen woods.
And, as he went, his manly voice thinned out,
White feathers hid his hair, his neck stretched forth,
Webs joined his reddish toes, wings clothed his sides,   375
And on his mouth, he grew a rounded beak.
So a new bird was born: the swan, which stays
Far from both Jove and sky. Keeping in mind
His bolt unjustly thrown, it seeks still pools
And spacious lakes, and, loathing fire, prefers   380

To dwell in floods, the opposite of flames.
   Meanwhile, the unkempt sire of Phaëthon,
Devoid his splendor, as when he's eclipsed,
In hatred of his daylight and himself,
[Gave all his mind to grief; to grief, his wrath;   385
And] shunned his cosmic charge. "Enough!" he said.
"My lot's been without rest since time began.
I tire of ceaseless tasks and thankless toil!
Let him who pleases drive the wheels of light.
If none will and the gods own that they can't,   390
Let *him* drive! While he tries our reins, at least,
He'll put his father-robbing bolts aside.
Then, once he's felt the fire-steeds' strength, he'll know
Their unskilled driver did not warrant death."
   While thus he spoke, the gods drew round the Sun   395
And begged him not to cloak the world in shades.
Then Jupiter upheld his use of flame
And backed his pleading words with kingly threats,
Till Phoebus called his steeds, still crazed with fear,
And raged his lash against them in his grief.   400
[(Raged: for he charged and blamed them for his son.)]

[CALLISTO]†

   Then the Almighty toured the walls of heaven,
Lest what the fire had weakened should collapse.
Their strength affirmed, he looked to human works
On earth. Arcadia being his foremost care,   405
He gave its pastures grass and leafy trees,
Restored its springs and streams, still scared to flow,
And bade its injured forests sprout anew.
But while he went and came on Nonacris,
A girl† there caught his eye and fired his bones.   410
She had no need to weave in wifely wool†
Nor style her hair, but held her robes with clasps
And bound her tangled locks with bands of white.
With spear in hand, or else with bow, she fought
For Phoebe. No maid on Mount Maenalus   415

FIGURE 3. *Jupiter and Callisto*, Angelica Kauffman (c. 1781). A
founding member of the Royal Academy, Kauffman was the
first woman to achieve major recognition as a history painter.
Like Ovid's retellings, her mythological scenes often redirect
attention to the stories' female characters. Jupiter's disguise as
Diana was popular with artists as a rare excuse to portray
female homoeroticism.

Pleased Trivia[11] more. But no power lasts for long.
 The sun was high, just after noon, when she
Snuck off into a wood untouched by time.
With quiver doffed and pliant bow unstrung,
She lay down on the grass-encovered ground,   420
The painted quiver pillowed at her neck.
To see the guardless girl asleep, Jove mused,
"Here, surely, my deceit won't reach my wife;
And, if it does, still—how, oh, how worthwhile!"
Then, taking on Diana's form and dress,   425
He called, "Dear fellow maiden, on what slopes
Went you to hunt?" Arising then, she cried,
"Hail, goddess! you whom I'd prefer to Jove,

11. Diana, guardian of "three-way" (*trivia*) crossroads

Though he himself should hear!" He laughed to hear
That he'd surpassed himself, next kissed her lips—   430
And with abandon, not as virgins should—
Then stopped her tries to tell him where she'd been,
But gripped her tight and showed himself through crime.
   She fought as fiercely as a woman could.
(Saturnia, you'd have softened, had you seen!)   435
She fought back, but how could a girl prevail?
Who conquers Jove? The victor soared for home.
Regarding now the knowing woods and wilds
With hate, she scarce recalled while heading back
To take her quiver, darts, and dangling bow.   440
   But look! Dictynna,[12] coming with her band
Down Maenalus, disporting slaughtered beasts,
Calls out to her. Though summoned, first she flees
For fear it may be Jupiter disguised;
But having watched the nymphs approach as well,   445
She sees deceit is done and joins their line.
How hard her face worked not to show the crime—
Her eyes scarce left the ground! Now, in her place
Beside the goddess, first in line, no more,
She blushed in silence for her wounded shame.   450
Were she not chaste, Diana would have known
Guilt's thousand signs. (As did, they say, the nymphs.)
   Nine times the moon had filled its crescent orb,
When, tired from hunting in her brother's rays,
The goddess found an icy glade wherein   455
A babbling brook flowed over fine-worn sands.
She praised it, dipped a foot into the waves,
And praised them, too: "All eyes are far from here,
So I say we swim naked in this stream!"
Parrhasis[13] blushed, and she alone delayed   460
While all the girls disrobed. So, she was stripped,
And starkly her bare body shared the crime.

---

12. Greek goddess of hunting, here syncretized with Diana
13. Callisto, from the Parrhasian region of Arcadia

In shock, she waved her hands to hide her womb.
"Go! far from here!" cried Cynthia.[14] "Don't taint
These sacred springs!" and bade her leave their band.   465
 The Thunderer's wife had known this all along
But saved her vengeance for its proper time.
She paused no more now, for her rival had
Birthed Arcas, a young boy (to Juno's grief).
At once, she turned her gaze of cruel intent   470
And cried, "Of course! Adulteress, what was left,
Once pregnant, except publishing my pain?
You've borne a witness to my Jove's disgrace!
But now you'll pay me with that form which so
Delights my husband and your irksome self!"   475
This said, she grabbed her hair and hurled her down.
As from the ground her pleading arms reached out,
The arms began to bristle black with fur,
Her hands to bend and grow with crooked claws
That served as feet, her lips—once praised by Jove—   480
To alter into wide and ugly jaws.
And lest she move by pleas and pleading words,
Her power of speech was taken and replaced
With wrathful, threatening, fearsome, guttural roars.
 Though now a bear, her former mind remained.   485
With ceaseless groans attesting to her grief,
She raised what hands she had toward sky and stars
And felt, though mute, the thanklessness of Jove.
How often, too afraid to sleep alone,
She roamed through fields that once had been her home!   490
How often hounds would drive her on the rocks
As she, a huntress, fled the hunt in fear!
She oft forgot herself and hid from beasts,
A bear who quaked to see the mountain's bears,
And feared wolves, though her father then was one.[†]   495
 Lycaön's grandson, Arcas, unaware
Whose child he was, had now reached thrice-five years.

14. Diana, born on Mount Cynthus

While chasing quarry, choosing where to hunt,
And setting Erymanthus' woods with snares,
He met his mother, who, seeing Arcas, stopped   500
As though she knew him. Running from her still
And ceaseless eyes, he felt an unknown fear,
And when she eagerly approached, he would
Have sent his wounding spearpoint through her breast,
But the Almighty stopped him and removed   505
The stain of sin from them, and them to space,
And placed them side by side and made them stars.†
    But Juno seethed to see her rival shine
And plumbed the depths for white-haired Tethys' home
And the old Ocean's, whom the gods revere.   510
And when they asked her why she'd come, she said,
"Do you seek why the queen of heaven is here?
Another has displaced me in the sky!
Unless I lie, tonight, when darkness falls,
You'll see stars freshly honored—to my grief—   515
Atop the skies where, at the furthest pole,
The last and smallest circle orbits round.
Who would hold back from wounding Juno now?
Who fears to vex one who *helps* those she hurts?
[Oh, I have done such deeds! Vast is my might!]   520
I kept her from being human? She's a god!
Such are my punishments! So great my powers!
Let him restore the beauty to his beast,
Just as he did for Greek Phoronides![15]
Why not, with Juno gone, give her my bed   525
And make Lycaön father to his bride?
    "But if your nursling's† wounds have pained you, too,
Then ban the Oxen from your sea-green swirl!†
Reject these stars, whose fling has won them heaven,
And keep that concubine from your pure waves!"   530

15. Io, sister of Phoroneus (cf. 1.669)

[THE RAVEN AND THE CROW]†

The sea-gods gave assent. Then, taking rein,
Saturnia soared on painted peacocks' wings—
Winged peacocks painted fresh from Argus' death,
As you, too, gabbling Raven, once so white,
Had lately been transformed to sudden black.   535
For that bird once bore plumes of silver snow
To vie with spotless doves; not to the geese
Whose watchful wails would save the Capitol,†
Nor to the river-loving swan he bowed.
His tongue's what did him in: that tattling tongue   540
Made whiteness the antithesis of white.
    In all Thessalia lived none fairer than
Coronis of Larissa. She, while chaste—
Or while uncaught—appeased you, Delphic one;
But spying her adultery, Phoebus' fowl,[16]   545
A hard informer keen to show her guilt,
Rushed off to tell his lord. A nosy Crow,
Her wings aflap, fell in and asked his news,
But, having heard his purpose, cried, "You wend
A worthless way! Heed what my tongue portends: 550
In all I was and am and have deserved,
You'll find good faith undid me.
                              "Pallas once
Locked Erichthonius, whom no mother bore,
Within a chest of Attic reeds she gave
To those three maidens two-formed Cecrops sired,†   555
Along with orders not to look inside.
An elm's dense foliage hid me as I watched
Their doings: Pandrosos and Herse did
As charged without deceit. Aglauros, though,
Jeered at her sisters' fear and loosed the knots: 560
Inside, she saw an infant—and a snake.†
I told the goddess, but for my reward
Minerva drove me from her house and ranked

16. The raven, associated with Phoebus Apollo (the Delphic one)

Me underneath the Owl![17] My punishment
Should warn birds not to run the risks of speech.   565
   "I'm sure you'll think she never liked me much,
But *she* sought *me*—ask Pallas! She's enraged
But even raging, this she won't deny!
For I was born to famed Coroneus
Of Phocis (it's well known).[†] While there I lived   570
My princess' hand (don't laugh!) was richly wooed,
But looks undid me. For, upon those shores
Where I would gently stroll atop the sands,
The sea god saw me pass and fell in heat.
When prayers and praises proved a waste of time,   575
He violently gave chase. I fled in vain:
The beach's softer sands sapped all my strength.
I called on gods and mortals, but I reached
No earthly ears—a virgin goddess[18] saved
This virgin: as toward heaven, my arms reached out,   580
The arms began to bristle black with down!
I would have dropped my robes, but they held fast
As feathers, driven deep into my skin.
I tried to beat my hands against my breast,
But found I now had neither breast nor hands.   585
I ran; my feet, no longer bound by sand,
Rose high above the ground. Soon, through the air
I sailed—and was Minerva's blameless aide.
But what good is it if Nyctimene,[19]
Made fowl for her foul sins, outranks me now?   590
   "Have you not heard? All Lesbos knows of how
Nyctimene debauched her father's bed!
So she's turned bird, but, conscious of her fault,
She flees both sight and light to hide her shame,
A universal outcast from the sky."   595
   The Raven answered, "May this curse be yours

17. Associated with Minerva
18. Minerva
19. The Owl

Who keeps me back! I'll heed no hollow threats!"
And, pressing on, he told his lord he'd seen
Coronis bedding a Thessalian youth.
On hearing this, the lover's laurel slipped,   600
And, in one move, the god's face, heart, and hand
All fell. His spirit swelling hot with rage,
He seized his usual weapons, strung his bow,
And pierced with an unerring arrow's head
That breast he had so often clasped to his.   605
She wailed with wounds and wrenched away the dart,
Then cried, her pale limbs drenched in purple gore,
"O Phoebus, I'd have paid a proper price,
Were I not pregnant—now two die as one!"
With that, her life and life-blood ebbed away.   610
[And deathly cold possessed her soul-less corpse.]
    Repenting his cruel vengeance—late, alas!—
The lover loathed himself for having heard
What caused his anger, loathed the bird who'd told
The hurtful sin, and loathed his bow and hand,   615
And, with his hand, his reckless arrows, too.
He clasped the fallen frame and tried—too late!—
To vanquish fate with his vain healer's arts.
But once he'd given up and seen the pyre
Prepared to burn her with funereal flames,   620
Then truly he (for tears are not allowed
On godly cheeks) gave forth, from in his heart,
A pleading groan, as bullocks do on seeing
A hammer, poised by the right ear, crash through
The hollow temples of a suckling calf.   625
He then poured thankless incense on her breast,
Embraced her, and performed unrighteous rites.
But, lest the seed of Phoebus fall to ash,
From fire and mother's womb, he ripped his son
And brought the child to two-formed Chiron's cave.†   630
The Raven, who had hoped to gain by talk,
Instead was banned from wearing wings of white.

[OCYRHOË][†]

The half-breed, meanwhile, reared the child of heaven,
Delighting in the honor of the task,
When look! with shoulders veiled in flaming hair,   635
The centaur's daughter comes, whom Chariclo,
A nymph, bore by a rushing stream and named
Ocyrhoë.[20] Not satisfied to learn
Her father's arts, she sang fate's secret songs.
And now, prophetic frenzy gripped her mind: 640
Fired by the god[21] that held her heart, she seethed
And, seeing the child, cried, "Healer of the world—
Grow up, dear boy! How oft shall mortals owe
Their lives to you! For you'll have leave to raise
Departed souls and scorn the gods—but once: 645
Your grandsire's flame will stop your second try!
From god to lifeless corpse, from corpse to god
Again—twice you will mold your fate anew![†]
    "You, too, dear father, though immortal now,
Ordained by birth to outlast every age,   650
Will wish you could die,[†] as vile serpent's blood
Torments your wounded limbs! Freed by the gods
From your eternity, you'll suffer death:
The threefold goddesses will cut your thread—"
    More fates remained to tell, but here she sighed   655
And spoke these words as tears ran down her cheeks:
"Fate stays my further speech and stops my voice!
These arts were not worthwhile that bring on me
The wrath of gods—I wish I'd never known
What things will pass. For now, it seems, I'll lose   660
My human form; now grass feels fit for food;
Now comes an urge to run through open fields—
I'm turning into my ancestral mare!
But why in full? My father is two-formed . . ."
The final part of this complaint could scarce   665

20. "Swift-flowing"
21. Apollo, god of prophecy

Be understood, so jumbled were its words,
Which soon seemed neither words nor horse's sounds,
But like a mocking horse. Yet, before long
She neighed for real and trod the grass with arms,
Her fingers joined, their five thin nails combined   670
In hooves of solid horn, her face and neck
Stretched out, her robe's long train was now a tail,
And her stray hairs became a rightward mane.
And so, remade in form and voice alike,
The monstrous marvel was renamed as well.†   675

[BATTUS]†

   Through tears did Philyra's heroic son[22]
Beseech your help in vain, O Delphic one:
You could not cross Jove's will, and if you could,
You were not there, but tending to your herds
In Elis and Messenia, wrapped in skins,   680
Your left hand round a weighty wooden staff,
Your right round seven pipes of unmatched reeds.
But while you thought of love and played your pipes,
They say your cattle strayed to Pylos' fields,
And, spied by Atlas' daughter Maia's son,[23]   685
Were hidden, through his cunning, in a wood.
   No one observed the theft, save one old man
Of country fame (called Battus[24] in those parts),
Who, in rich Neleus' fertile fields and glades,
Stood guardian over packs of purebred mares.   690
This man the god stayed with a touch and said,
"Whoever you are, stranger, if you're asked
If you saw any herds here, just say no—
And take this heifer to reward your pains!"
The stranger took it and replied: "You're safe!   695
That stone will tell your secrets first!" And he

22. Chiron
23. Mercury
24. "Chatterbox"

Marked out a stone. Jove's son appeared to leave
But soon returned in altered form and voice.
"Hey, country clod!" he said, "If any cows
Went by, help out and tell me. They were poached!   700
You'll get a cow and bull as your reward."
For twice the bribe, the elder said, "They're there,
Just past those hills!" (And past those hills they were.)
Then Atlas' grandson laughed, "Would you betray
Me to myself, you traitor?—to myself?"   705
And turned the fraudster's heart to firmest flint.
Still called by the informer's name,[†] the stone
Unjustly bears his ancient infamy.

[THE ENVY OF AGLAUROS][†]

The bearer of Caduceus[25] then took flight
And saw below the land Minerva loves,   710
Munychia's fields, and learnèd Lyceum's groves.[26]
It chanced to be the feast when virgin maids
Bear baskets crowned with blossoms on their heads
With holy gifts for Pallas' hilltop shrine.[†]
Seeing them return, the wingèd god did not   715
Aim straight their way but circled round and round.
As swift-winged kites, at sight of sacral meats,
Will soar away and flee the priestly crowd,
Yet dare not leave but flit round their desire,
So, too, Cyllenius set his course above   720
The Attic mount and reeled back through the air.
And as the Morning-Star outshines all stars,
And Phoebe's golden glow then outshines him,
So far were all the other maids surpassed
By Herse, fairest of her friends' parade.   725
Jove's son, struck by her beauty, hung midair
And burned like lead a Balearic sling

25. Mercury
26. Sites in Athens, sacred city of Minerva (Athena)

Flings forth, which warms by flying through the clouds,
Discovering fire it never had before.[†]
Next, changing course, he left the skies for earth;   730
So self-assured is beauty, which he had,
That he went undisguised, though he took pains
To smooth his hair, to set his cloak just so
Its gold trim would be seen, to keep in hand
His narrow staff which calls or counters sleep,   735
And to adorn his well-wiped feet with wings.
     Deep in their house of tusk and tortoise-shell
Were three rooms: Pandrosos, yours,[†] on the right,
Aglauros' left, and Herse's in between.
And, seeing him first, the left-side sister dared   740
Ask Mercury[†] his name and why he'd come.
"Born unto Atlas' child with Pleione,"
He answered her, "I ferry through the air
The orders of my father, Jupiter!
My plans are plain—just treat your sister true   745
And let the babes she bears me call you aunt:
I've come for Herse. Please smile on my love!"
Instead, Aglauros fixed him with those eyes
That had beheld what blonde Minerva hid,
And, seeking for her help a hefty sum   750
Of gold, she meanwhile forced him from the house.
     The warrior goddess'[27] savage gaze then turned
On her, and, with such deep and tortured sighs
That both her breast and breast-borne aegis rang,
She thought of how those sinful hands had bared   755
Her secret, when she'd glimpsed the Lemnian child[28]
No mother bore and broke her promised pledge.
Soon she'd be blessed by god and sister both—
And rich to boot, with greed-exacted gold!
At once, the goddess sought the rotten house   760
Of Envy,[†] hidden deep within a gorge

27. Minerva
28. Erichthonius, whose father Vulcan resided at Lemnos

Devoid of sun, unknown to wind—a place
Of bitter numbing cold, where firelight's glow
Gleams never round and gloom ever abounds.
    When first the fearsome maid of war arrived,   765
She stayed outside and rapped her pointed spear
(Heaven's laws forbade approach) upon the posts.
At that, the battered doors flung back, and there—
Devouring viper's flesh to feed her sin—
Was Envy! She looked once, and looked away.   770
But, rising slowly from her half-chewed feast
Of snakes, the creature came on sluggish steps;
And, seeing the goddess armed with looks and spears,
She groaned and formed a face to fit her sighs.
A creature pale of cheek and lean of frame,   775
With eyes askew and teeth grown green with mold,
Breasts full of bile and venom in her tongue,
She never smiles, except at others' pain,
Nor can she sleep, perturbed with wakeful cares.
Forced to watch human gain, she rots within,   780
Then strikes out and is struck—forever cursed
To be herself.
                Tritonia[29] loathed the thing,
Yet choked out this short speech: "Infect the child
Of Cecrops with your rot! It must be done.
Aglauros is her name." She said no more   785
But jabbed the earth and spear-vaulted away.
    Askance, the monster watched Minerva's flight,
And grumbled at the goddess' soon success.
Still, taking up a spine-encircled staff,
She set out, wreathed in storm clouds. As she went,   790
She trampled flowery meads, burned fields of grass,
Attacked the treetops, and polluted towns
And homes and nations with her breath. At last,
She spied Tritonia's city, rich in gifts
And flourishing in happy peace; she would   795
Have wept to see so little cause to weep,

29. Minerva, born near Lake Triton

But, having reached the room of Cecrops' child,
She did as told and, with a rust-stained hand,
Caressed her breast and filled her heart with thorns.
Exhaling venomed breath, she laced the bones   800
With toxins that spread black into the lungs.
And, lest the malice wander aimlessly,
She conjured visions of her sister's luck
In joining with a god—and magnified
The beauty of it all.
                Spurred thus, the child   805
Of Cecrops—gnawed within, vexed day and night—
Bemoaned the painful, slow, and wretched rot
Dissolving her like ice in fitful sun.
Consumed by thoughts of Herse's blessèd luck,
She slowly burned like brambles on a fire,   810
Which show no flames yet slowly turn to ash.
She thought she'd rather die than see such things,
And longed to tell her sire, as though it were
A crime. At last, she sat outside the door
To block the god's advance, and met his pleas   815
And praise and kindly words by saying: "Cease!
I shall not leave this spot unless you're stopped!"
"We'll stand," said swift Cyllenius, "by those terms!"
And, with his godly staff, unbarred the doors.
She tried to rise, but found she could not move: 820
Her folded, sitting limbs were numb with weight.
She fought to stand, but met with stiffened knees,
While stony cold spread through her fingertips
And paled her bloodless flesh. As cancer tends
To creep its cureless spread and add what was   825
Unharmed to what's diseased, so by degrees
Did lethal winter enter in her heart
And close the passages of life and breath.
She did not try to speak nor, had she tried,
Would words have come; her neck and lips were rock.   830
A marble statue, stiff and dead, she sat,
But not of white: her mind had stained the stone.

[EUROPA]†

The price of sinful words and mind thus paid,
From Pallas' lands, the heir of Atlas soared
To heaven. Once there, his sire drew him aside   835
And told him, without saying love was why,
"My loyal son, who always heeds my words,
Halt not but speed your downward journey for
The land that spies your mother from the left!†
(The natives call it Sidon.) There, you'll see,   840
Out grazing far away on mountain grass,
The royal flock—go drive it to the shore!"
No sooner said than done; forced from the hills,
The bulls made for the bidden beaches where
The princess[30] and her Tyrian maidens played.   845
    Now, majesty and love do not mix well,
Nor share one home for long: his scepter's weight
Put by, the lord and father of the gods—
Who wields the tri-forked flame, whose nods shake earth!—
Became a cow. Disguised, he joined the bulls   850
To moo and walk in beauty through the grass,
As white as snow unmelted by the rains
Of Auster and untrod by heavy tracks.
Brawn ridged his neck where dewlaps dangled down,
And though his horns were small, you'd swear they were   855
Hand-crafted—clean and clearer than two gems!
His brow supplied no threats; his eyes, no fear.
His whole face promised peace.
                              Agenor's child
Was awestruck at his fair and peaceful air.
Kind though he seemed, she feared his touch at first,   860
But soon brought blossoms for his pearly lips.
Thus cheered, the lover dreamt of thrills to come
And kissed her hands—and scarcely, scarce held back!
And now he frolicked, leaping in the grass,
Now stretched snow-white upon the yellow sands.   865

30. Europa, daughter to king Agenor of Tyre

As time allayed her fears, her virgin hands
Would stroke his proffered chest, or deck his horns
With new-made wreaths. The princess even dared
(Not knowing whom she rode) to mount his back!
And, bit by bit, away from land, from shore,   870
The god drew his false hooves into the waves.
Then—out to sea and through the swells he bore
His spoils! In fear, she watched the shore recede,
One hand around his horn, one on his back,
Her fluttering garments streaming in the wind.   875

Book 3

[CADMUS AND THE DRAGON'S TEETH]†

AND NOW the god cast off his bull disguise,
Revealed himself, and reached the land of Crete.
  Their clueless father then bade Cadmus find
His kidnapped sister, threatening exile should
He fail—an act both dutiful and wrong.   5
So, round the world (for who could thwart Jove's tricks?),
In refuge from his father's realm and rage,
Agenor's son roamed. At the oracle
Of Phoebus, he inquired where he should live.
"A lonely cow shall meet thee," Phoebus said,   10
"One yokes and crooked ploughs have never pressed.
Follow its lead: where it lies on the grass,
Lay walls and call them by Boeotia's name!"
And Cadmus scarce had left Castalia's cave†
When, seeing a guardless calf pass slowly by   15
Without a sign of service on its neck,
He trailed its tracks and, keeping to its pace,
Gave silent praise to Phoebus as his guide.
The cow, once past the plains of Panope
And the Cephisus, stopped and raised to heaven   20
Its high-horned brow, and filled the air with moos.

Next, watching as he followed from behind,
It knelt and dropped its flank into the grass.
Then grateful Cadmus kissed the foreign ground,
Hailed greetings to the unknown slopes and fields,   25
And made to worship Jove, dispatching aides
To seek libations in the running springs.
   Amidst an ancient wood no axe had harmed,[†]
There stood a cavern, thick with sprouts and sprigs,
Its meager stones conjoining in an arch,   30
Whence flowed rich waters, but whose depths concealed
The golden-crested dragon-snake of Mars[†]
With eyes of fire, a body bulging banes,
And three tongues flicking triple rows of teeth.
And when the Tyrian scouts, by luckless steps,   35
Had reached its grove to fill their splashing jars,
This sea-dark serpent, deep inside its cave,
Stretched forth its head and gave a dreadful hiss.
The jars fell from their hands, their blood ran cold,
And trembling seized their horror-stricken limbs.   40
In twisting knots, it spun its scaly coils,
Then leapt up, curving in a giant bow;
Half-lifted in the air, it glowered down
On all the woods—the same in size, if you
Could see it whole, as that which parts the Bears[1]—   45
Then fell on the Phoenicians[†] readying
For fight or flight, or stopped in fear from both.
Some died amidst its fangs, some in its grasp,
And others from its rotting poison breath.
   By now, as shadows shrank in midday sun,   50
Agenor's child, grown worried from the wait,
Was searching for his men. With lion-skin
For armor, armed with iron lance and spear
And courage, which surpasses any arms,
He reached the wood and found them lying slain   55

---

1. The constellation Draco, which separates Ursa Major and Ursa Minor

And, over them, their vast triumphant foe,
Whose bloody tongue now licked their doleful wounds.
"O loyal hearts!" he cried, "I either shall
Avenge your deaths or share it!" Then he heaved
A stone and gave the mass a massive throw.   60
At such a blow, high ramparts would have caved
Beneath their towers: the serpent stood unharmed.
Protected by its scales and hard black hide
As by a breastplate, it rebuffed the stroke.
And yet, that hardness could not brook his spear   65
Which stuck amidst its tough and curving spine,
The iron tip sunk deep into its loins.
Gone wild with pain, it twisted back its head,
Beheld the wound, and bit the sticking shaft,
Then eased around and nearly wrenched it free,   70
But could not coax the iron from the bone.
Then, truly, its old anger gained new drive.
Its throat swelled round with bulging veins; white foam
Poured from its noxious jaws. The clearing rang
With rasping scales as blackened breath escaped   75
Its hellish mouth to spoil and taint the air.
First ringing round itself in giant coils,
It next stood straighter than a running beam,
Then surged forth, like a flowing stream in flood,
And split the hindering forest with its breast.   80
   Agenor's son stepped back, absorbed the blow
Upon his lion's pelt, and used his spear
To check the gaping jaws, which raged in vain
To wound the iron point lodged in its teeth.
The venomed gullet now began to gush   85
With blood, whose spatter stained the verdant grass.
And yet, its hurt was slight, for it fell back,
Its wounded neck drawn out of range of blows,
And, giving ground, staved off a deeper stroke,
Until Agenor's son came near and stabbed   90
The iron through its throat. Backed up against
An oak,† the neck and trunk were pierced as one.
Beneath the serpent's weight, the oak tree bent

And groaned within to feel its lashing tail.
   As victor gazed on victim, there was heard   95
A voice (of unknown source, yet it was heard):
"Agenor's son, why do you stop to see
A serpent slain? A serpent seen you'll be!"
But just as terror seized his face and mind
And icy horror stood his hairs on end,   100
Look! Pallas, patroness of heroes, comes
Down from on high and bids him till and plant
The dragon's teeth to grow a future race.
Obeying her, he ploughs the furrows wide
And sows the ordered mortal seeds: the teeth.   105
The soil (beyond belief) begins to stir
Till, from the furrows, spring the tips of spears,
Then helmets fluttering with painted plumes,
Then shoulders, chests, and weapon-laden arms.
Thus grew a crop of soldiers bearing shields,   110
Like rising curtains at the theater
Which lift their figures upward, faces first,
The rest at measured pace, till all is seen,
Their feet set flush against the bottom edge.†
   These fresh-made foes scared Cadmus into arms.   115
"No, don't take arms!" one of the groundlings cried,
"Nor any part here in our civil wars!"†
At that, he stabbed an earth-born brother close,
Then fell himself beneath a far-flung spear.
His slayer, too, did not outlive the slain,   120
But breathed his last of lately-given air.
As all the horde raged likewise in their strife,
The sudden brothers fell by mutual wounds;
And soon the short-lived striplings lay and thrashed
Their bloodied mother with their cooling breasts.   125
Just five remained, Echion being one.†
Warned by Tritonia, he threw down his arms,
Then sought and forged fraternal pacts of peace.
And so the Tyrian stranger had these men
To found the city Phoebus had foreseen.   130

[ACTAEON]†

At Thebes, though banished, Cadmus, you seem blessed!
Besides your in-laws, Mars and Venus, you
Had family worthy of your wife: boys, girls,
And grandsons—cherished promise of the line—
And these now grown! And yet, one must await   135
A man's last day and call none happy who
Has yet to pass and lacks his funeral rites.†
Of all your blessings, Cadmus, you first grieved
Your grandson, with strange antlers on his brow,
When you, his dogs, gorged on your master's blood!   140
But should you ask, you'll find it's fortune's fault,
Not sin's. For what sin is there in mistake?
    There was a mountain, soiled with slaughtered beasts,
Where, when the shades had shrunken in midday,
The sun being equidistant from its bounds,   145
The kindly young Boeotian² thus addressed
His fellow farers through those pathless wilds:
"Our nets and blades, my friends, drip beastly blood—
We've had our share of fortune for one day!
When Dawn, on saffron wheels, brings back new light,   150
Our work resumes. Now Phoebus cracks the fields
With heat, being equidistant from his bounds,
So cease your work and raise the knotted nets!"
The men obeyed his words and paused their toil.
    There was a dell of spruce and cypress trees—   155
Gargaphië, close-garbed Diana's† spot—
Whose sacred depths contained a wooded cave
No artist carved. But Nature, through her wit,
Had imitated art: from living rock
And travertine, she'd formed a natural arch.   160
Nearby, a fountain crashed its crystal waves,
Which fed the grass that fringed its gaping mouth,
And in whose spray, when weary from the chase,
The woodland goddess dipped her virgin limbs.

2. Actaeon

Arriving then, she gave a squiress-nymph   165
Her spear, her quiver, and her unstrung bow.
Another's arm took her discarded cloak,
And two unlaced her feet. More skilled than these,
A Theban maiden, Crocale, tied up
The hair about her neck, though hers flowed free.   170
Rhanis, Hyale, Psecas, Nephele,
And Phiale[3] then doused her from great urns.
    While in her usual spring Titania[4] bathed,
Look! Cadmus' grandson, his own toil deferred,
Strayed through the unknown woods on furtive feet   175
And happened on the grove; for such was fate.
And as he breached the fountain-misted caves,
Seeing a man the naked nymphs began
To beat their breasts and fill the forest whole
With sudden shrieks, then ringed Diana round   180
To make themselves a screen. The goddess, though,
Was taller and stood head above the rest.
The tint that colors clouds at sunset's touch
Or with the rosy dawn at once suffused
The visage of Diana, viewed unveiled.   185
Though closely crowded by her comrades, she
Still moved aside and turned her face away.
Much though she wished to have her darts, she drew
On what she had—the water—drenched his face,
And, spraying vengeful droplets in his hair,   190
Pronounced these warning words of coming doom:
"Now you may speak of having seen me stripped—
If speak you can!"
                        Without more threats, she then
Gave long-lived deer's horns to his spattered brow,
Gave length unto his neck, points to his ears,   195
Changed hands to feet and arms to lengthened legs,
And, clothing him in spots, filled him with fear.
Autonoë's heroic son turned tail[†]

3. The attendants' Greek names all have watery associations
4. Diana, daughter of Latona, daughter of the Titan Coeus

And wondered at the speed with which he ran.
[Till, seeing his face and antlers in a pond,]   200
"Poor me!" he would have cried, but all his voice
Could voice were groans, as tears rolled down those cheeks
That weren't his. Just his mind remained unchanged.
What should he do? Go home? Hide in the woods?
One course was stopped by shame; the other, fear.   205
    But as he mused, his bloodhounds spotted him!†
First Blackpaw and keen Tracer barked the trail—
Blackpaw was Spartan; Tracer hailed from Crete—
Then others rushed in, faster than the wind:
Now Sharpeye, Bottomless, and Mountaineer,   210
All three Arcadians; strong Deerslayer next;
Fierce Hunter, Hurricane, fleet Flyingfoot;
And sharp-nosed Chaser; Woody, lately gored
By boar-tusks; wolf-sired Vale; and Shepherdess,
A herder, joined by Harpy with two pups;   215
Then, Sicyonian Ladon, flanks reared high;
And Runner, Barker, Tiger, Plucky, Spot,
Pale Snowy, black-haired Ash, quick Whirling-Wind,
And Spartan, of surpassing strength; Lightfoot;
Swift She-Wolf and her brother Cypriot;   220
Black Snapper, marked out by his brow's white spot;
Then Sable, soft-haired Shaggy, and two sons
Born to a Cretan sire and Spartan dam,
Wildtooth and Rager; Yelper, shrill of voice;
And others still it would waste time to name.   225
    Round cliffs and rocks and stones, they ran their prey
Where trails were steep or nowhere to be found.
Now fleeing where he'd often chased (alas!),
He fled his household dogs and longed to cry,
["I am Actaeon! Know me for your lord!"]   230
But words failed—all the heavens rang with howls.
First Blackfur gouged his back, next Beastbreaker,
Then Cragside latched himself upon his arm,
(These three left late, but cut across a ridge
And got there first)† and, with their master pinned,   235
The pack converged on him with all its teeth.

Soon, there was no place left to wound. His groans—
No human sound, but one no deer could make—
Filled the familiar peaks with woeful wails.
Then, kneeling like a suppliant at prayer,   240
He raised his silent face in place of arms.
    But cluelessly his comrades' cries urged on
The raging pack. Wishing Actaeon there,
They vied to call "Actaeon!" back from leave
(His head turned at the name), lamenting that   245
His sloth kept him from seeing their quarry caught!
Well, he may wish to leave, but he is here,
Wishing he could just see, not feel, his dogs.
All round him, savage snouts sunk in his flesh,
They shred their master in his deer disguise.   250
It's said that, till his wounds robbed him of life,
Diana's huntress wrath was unappeased.

[SEMELE]†

    Opinion here was torn. The goddess seemed
More harsh than fair to some, while others praised
Her strict virginity—both sides had cause.   255
Jove's wife alone spoke neither praise nor blame,
But cheered that woe had struck Agenor's house.
Her hatred of the Tyrian⁵ having turned
Upon the dynasty, new grief joined old:
For Semele was heavy with Jove's seed.   260
But just when she'd have loosed her scornful tongue,
She thought, "What have I ever gained through scorn?
She must *feel* my attack! She'll be destroyed,
If 'greatest Juno' I am rightly called,
If heaven's jeweled scepter's mine to hold,   265
And if I'm queen, Jove's sister, and his wife!
Sister, for sure. But I think she's content
With mere affairs: our bed's abuse is brief.
Still, her full womb (that's done it!) shows her crime;

5. Europa, who first drew Juno's anger to the House of Agenor

She wants what I scarce have: a child of Jove,   270
So self-assured is beauty†—set that straight,
I will! Nor call me Saturn's daughter if
Jove does not sink her in the Stygian waves!"
   With that, she rose and, veiled in saffron mist,
Reached Semele's threshold, nor did her clouds   275
Clear off till she'd become a greying hag,
With wrinkle-furrowed skin, stooped shaky steps,
And crone-like voice: the form of Beroë,
Young Semele's own Epidaurian nurse.
They spoke at length, but when talk turned to Jove,   280
She sighed, "I hope he's Jove, but I'm afraid:
Gods' names are often used to gain chaste beds.†
Nor is being Jove enough! Let love be pledged,
If he is real; bid him embrace thee with
The form and face, the size and state he takes   285
High Juno in—full splendor on display!"
   Beguiled by Juno, Cadmus' clueless child
Asked Jove to grant her yet-unstated wish.
The god said, "Choose, I'll have naught be denied!†
To earn thy trust, I'll swear it by the might   290
Of swirling Styx, the god whom all gods fear!"
Pleased by her peril, drunk with power, and doomed
By her obedient lover, Semele
Said, "With that form Saturnia holds you in
For Love's embrace—so give yourself to me."   295
The god wished he had clamped her speaking mouth,
But since her voice sped through the air, he groaned,
For she could not unwish, nor he unswear.
Thus, in despair, he scaled high heaven. His glance
Drew clouds to mingle with the lights and winds,   300
The thunder and the unstoppable bolt.
Yet, where he could, he tried to stay his strength,
Nor took he to Agenor's house the flash
That laid the hundred-handed Typhon† low,
But a far weaker bolt the Cyclops' hands   305
Had forged in lesser flames for lesser wrath,
Known to the gods as "Firearm Number Two."

But even so, her body could not bear
The rush divine—her wedding gift—and burned.
Then, from its mother's womb untimely ripped,   310
Her infant (if it bears belief) was sown
Inside his father's thigh to grow till due.
In secret, his aunt Ino reared him first,
Then gave him to the nymphs of Nysa, who
Concealed him in their caves and suckled him.   315

[TIRESIAS]†

    While this took place on earth by fate's decree,
With twice-born Bacchus[6] safely in his crib,
They say Jove, drunk with nectar, chanced to lay
His cares aside and pass the idle hours
With Juno and in jests. "Your sex," he said,   320
"Achieves more pleasure than befalls us males."
She disagreed, and so they went to ask
The wise Tiresias, who knew both loves.
    For, striking with his staff, he'd once profaned
Two giant serpents mating in the woods,   325
And been made woman (wondrous sight!) from man
For seven autumns. In the eighth, he saw
Them once again and said, "If striking you
Should have such power to change your striker's state,
I'll beat you now as well!" He hit the snakes,   330
And so regained the form he had at birth.
As judge, therefore, he tried this playful case
And ruled for Jove. Saturnia, so it's said,
Was grieved past what the matter warranted
And damned her judge's eyes to endless night.†   335
But the Almighty Sire (since gods may not
Undo the deeds of gods) exchanged lost sight
For prophecy, so honor eased his pain.

---

6. "Born" a second time upon emerging from Jupiter's thigh

[ECHO AND NARCISSUS]†

Renowned and famed throughout Aonia's towns,
He gave his seekers answers past reproach.   340
The first to test his voice and prove it true
Was sea-blue Liriope, whom the stream
Cephisus trapped and raped once in his swirls,
Whereon the beauteous nymph's full womb brought forth
A baby fit for loving even then—   345
By name, Narcissus. Asked whether the boy
Should see a ripe old age, the prescient sage
Said, "If he never knows himself."† For years,
The seer's speech seemed vain, but what occurred—
His death and novel passion—proved it true.   350
  When the Cephisus' son passed thrice five years
And could seem either boy or man, he drew
Desire from droves of youths and droves of maids.
But (such hard pride possessed that soft young frame)
Nor youth nor maiden ever felt his touch.   355
While out once snaring stags, he caught the eye
Of sounding Echo, a loquacious nymph
Who could not hush, nor speak till spoken to.
In those days, Echo had both form and voice,
But no more use for her glib tongue than now,   360
Returning but the last of many words.
This Juno wrought.† For, often, when his wife
Had almost caught the nymphs sprawled under Jove,
She slyly kept the goddess deep in chat
While they escaped. Saturnia soon caught on   365
And said: "Your tongue, which tricked me, hence shall be
Of less avail—and briefer in its speech!"
Events confirmed these threats: all she could do
Was twin last words and double what she heard.
  On seeing Narcissus roam the pathless fields,   370
She burned with love and stole along his tracks;
As she stole closer, warmer grew her fire,
Not unlike sulphur smeared atop a torch,
Which quickly catches when it nears a flame.

How oft she longed to go to him with pleas   375
And fawning words! But nature barred the way;
Nor could she try, but readied how she could,
Awaiting sounds her own words might return.
Split from his friends by chance, the boy had said,
"Is someone here?" "Here!" Echo then replied.   380
Amazed, he cast his eyes to every side
And hollered, "Come!" She called the caller back.
He glanced again, saw no one there, and said,
"Why run from me?"—words which he then received.
Tricked by the mirrored voice, he stood and cried,   385
"I want you to come here!" And Echo made
The gladdest of replies: "I want you, too!
Come? Here!"† To aid these words, she left the woods
And threw her arms around his longed-for neck,
But he took flight and, fleeing, cried, "Hands off!   390
I'd die before I'd give myself to you!"
Her sole response: "I'd give myself to you!"
    Thus spurned, she lurked in woods and veiled her shame
With leaves, to dwell then on in lonesome caves.
But her scorned love survived and grew with grief;   395
As sleepless cares laid waste her wretched frame,
Her skin shrank and its moisture thinned to air,
Till only voice and bones remained, they say,
Then, just her voice: her bones had turned to stone.
[She haunts the woods, on no peaks to be seen,   400
But heard by all, for she lives on in sound.]
    So had he toyed with her; so, too, with nymphs
From seas and slopes; so in the beds of men.
One downcast lad threw up his hands and cried:
"So let him love himself and lose in love!"   405
Far off, Rhamnusia[7] heard his righteous prayers. . . .
    There was a siltless spring of silver waves,
Untouched by shepherds, mountain-grazing goats,
Or other flocks, which neither bird nor beast
Nor fallen tree-branch ever had disturbed.   410

7. Nemesis, goddess of revenge, had a shrine at Rhamnos

Fed by its moisture, grass grew all around
And trees, which let no sunlight warm the ground.
Here did the boy, worn from the hunt and heat,
Lie down, drawn to the fountain's form and place.
[But as he quenched his thirst, a new thirst grew:]   415
While drinking, he is seized by what he sees
[And, loving fleshless hope, takes waves for flesh!]
He wonders at himself, with his face fixed
In place, as though from Parian marble carved.
Stretched out, he gazes on two stars—his eyes,   420
Hair fit for Bacchus' or Apollo's head,
Smooth cheeks, an ivory neck, and such a face,
Its splendid blush mixed in with snowy white,
Admiring all that all admire in him.
Unknowing, he desires himself; when praised,   425
He praises and, pursuing, is pursued;
In perfect parallel, he fires and burns.
How often he tried kissing the false spring!
How often he sank arms into the waves
To catch the neck he saw, but was not caught!   430
Not knowing what he sees, he burns at sight;
The selfsame lie tricks and attracts his eyes.
You fool, why vainly seek a fleeting shape?
You seek nothing—turn, and your love is lost!
You see the shadow of a mirrored shade,   435
It has no form! With you, it comes and stays,
And with you it will go—if go you can!
    No thought of food or rest can drive him off.
Sprawled in the shady grass, he views the lie
With quenchless sight and dies through his own eyes.   440
Rising a bit, he reaches for the trees
And cries: "Ah! trees, was any love more cruel?
You know, for lovers often use your shade.
Well, is there anyone that you recall,
Being centuries old, who wasted so away?   445
I see and want, but what I want and see
I cannot find!" (How fooled the lover is!)
"To pain me more, we're parted by no seas,

Nor roads, nor peaks, nor walls with fastened gates;
Mere water stops us. He longs to be held!   450
For when I reach my lips to those clear waves,
Then, on his back, he lifts his mouth toward mine!
You'd think we'd touch, so little bars our love.
    "Whoever you are, rise! Why flee from me,
O peerless boy? When sought, where do you go?   455
It's not my looks or age you shun: I'm loved
By nymphs! Your friendly faces give me hope,
When my arms reach for your arms, yours reach back.
I smile and you smile, too; I've seen your tears,
When I am tearful; you return my signs;   460
And I suspect that, when your fair lips move,
You're sending words that do not reach my ears. . . .
    "*He's me!* I'm sure—my shade won't leave me fooled!
I burn *for me* with flames I fuel and feel.
What should I do? Woo or be wooed? And why?   465
My wish is with me! Gain has made me lose.†
Would I could leave our body!—a strange prayer
For lovers, to be parted in our love.
And now grief saps my strength. Nor have I long
To live; I am extinguished in my prime.   470
But death is light for me: grief lifts with death.
I would wish longer life for him I love,
But now we two shall die with single breath."
    Then, nearly mad, he turned back to the face
And churned the pool with tears until the waves   475
Obscured its features. Seeing it fade, he wailed,
"Where are you going? Stay, don't leave me here
In love, cruel boy! Let what I cannot touch
Be seen and feed my passion, crazed and sad."
And while he grieved, he tore his tunic's top   480
And, beating his bare breast with stone-white palms,
Drew from his beaten breast a rosy blush,
As apples often have, with some parts white
And some parts red, or else like clustered grapes
Which range, when not yet ripe, in purple hue.   485
And when he saw this in the fresh-stilled waves,

He bore no further, but as golden wax
Melts under gentle flame, or morning frost
Warms in the sun, so did he waste with love,
Consumed by slow and hidden fire until   490
That mix of red and white, that power, that strength
And all that pleased to see were now no more.
    Nor did the form that Echo loved remain.
On seeing him, though remembering and upset,
She grieved; and when the poor boy cried, "Alas!"   495
Her voice repeated every cry: "Alas!"
And when he beat his shoulders with his hands,
Then, too, did she return the sound of blows.
His last words, gazing at the pool, were these:
"Ah—boy, beloved in vain—!" The same came back.   500
"Farewell!" he said, and Echo cried, "Farewell!"
His feeble head drooped on the verdant grass,
The self-admiring eyes now closed in death.
(But in the world below—there, too, he looks
Upon himself within the Stygian waves.)   505
    For him, his shorn-haired Naiad sisters wailed,
The Dryads wailed, and Echo's wails replied.
But when they'd readied pyre and torch and bier,
They found the body nowhere: in its place,
A yellow flower with petals ringed in white.   510

[PENTHEUS AND ACOETES]†

    This story spread the prophet's[8] just renown
Through all of Greece: great was the seer's name!
Just Pentheus, Echion's son, who spurned
Religion, laughed his auguries to scorn,
And mocked his darkness and his stolen sight.   515
The elder shook his silver locks and said:
"How lucky you would be to lose this light
As well and never see the Bacchic rites!
Some day—not long now, I foretell—will come

8. Tiresias

The new god Liber,[9] son of Semele.   520
Unless you honor him with worthy shrines,
Your thousand scattered shreds will soil with blood
Your forests, aunts, and mother! This shall be;
For you'll dishonor his divinity,
And groan that I, in darkness, saw too much—"   525
Echion's son pushed past him as he spoke.
    But he spoke true. His warnings were fulfilled,
For Liber came and cheering shook the fields!
Men, wives, and daughters, high-born folk and low
Rushed thronging to perform his unknown rites.   530
"What madness ails you, Snake-born race of Mars?"
Asked Pentheus. "Are hornpipes, brass on brass,
And magic tricks so powerful that you,
Who fear no swords of war nor trumpets' sounds
Nor lines of weapons drawn, are overcome   535
By women's cries, drunk fits, perverted mobs,
And hollow drums? Should I praise you, the old,
Who sailed so far from Tyre to here lay down
Your exiled household gods, when now you let
Them go without a fight? Or you young men,   540
Whose keen age nears my own, who should bear arms,
Not thyrsi,† and wore helmets once, not leaves?
Recall, I pray, the stock of which you're sprung!
Take up the serpent's spirit,† which alone
Destroyed so many. For his pool and spring   545
He died; may you fight likewise for your fame!
He sent the strong to death; now strike the weak!
Uphold your family name! If fate forbids
That Thebes endure, let catapults and men
Pull down her walls! let flame and sword resound!   550
Though wretched, we'd be blameless and our fate
Lamented—not concealed—with shameless tears!
But now Thebes falls before an unarmed boy,
And not in war with spears and cavalry,
But locks adrip with myrrh and tender wreaths   '   555

9. Bacchus, so-called after liquor's liberating effects

And robes enwrought with violet and gold.
Now (stand aside!) I'll force him to confess
His father's borrowed and his rites are lies!
Acrisius[†] was brave enough to scorn
This god as false and close his Argive gates;   560
Shall Pentheus and Thebes fear his approach?
Begone!" (this to his slaves) "Retrieve their chief
In chains—and halt ye not in my commands!"
    His grandfather[10] and Athamas[11] and all
The crowd rebuked his words and vainly tried   565
To stop him, but reproofs just spurred his rage:
Restrained, it rose and worsened with the wait.
(So I've observed a river flowing free
Which calmly ran its gentle babbling course,
Till, meeting with obstructing stones and trees,   570
It frothed and boiled, made fierce by obstacles.)
But look, the bloodied slaves return! He asks
For Bacchus; they reply he's not been seen.
"But we have seized," they said, "his slave and priest,"
And brought him forth, hands bound behind his back,   575
[This Tyrrhene-born[†] disciple of the god.]
With eyes of dreadful anger, Pentheus
Regarded him, scarce stalling punishment:
"You're doomed," he said. "Your death shall teach the rest!
Now state your name, your parentage and home,   580
And why you practise this new, teeming cult."
Unfazed, he said,
                "Acoetes is my name.
My home is Lydia. My birth was low.
My father left no ox nor field to plough
Nor fleecy flock nor herd; for he was poor,   585
And, baiting hook and line, would ply his rod
On leaping fish. His fortune was his skill.
Handing it down, he said, 'Accept my wealth,
And be heir and successor to my craft!'

10. Cadmus
11. The husband of Pentheus' aunt Ino (cf. 3.313)

In death, he left me nothing but the seas: 590
Them only can I call my heritage.
Soon, lest I cling forever to those crags,
I learned to pilot ships and sail by stars—
By Olenus' Goat-child who brings the rains,
Taÿgete, the Hyads, and the Bear—   595
To mark the winds, too, and what ports are best.
   "While bound for Delos once, I chanced upon
The Chian coast, made land with skillful oars,
And, leaping lightly, gained the sea-soaked sands.
We spent the night there. Then, at dawn's first blush,   600
I called for fresher water to be brought
And pointed out the path down to the spring.
Myself, I climbed a hill to gauge the wind,
Then called my crew and went back to the ship.
Opheltes, the first mate, soon cried, 'We're here!'   605
And brought to shore a prize—as he thought—found
Lost in a field: a boy fair as a girl,
Who seemed weighed down with wine and sleep, and scarce
Kept pace. His air and look and walk I saw,
But naught that could be mortal did I see.   610
I told my men, 'What god is in that form
I do not know, but that form holds a god!
Whoever you are, grant aid to our works
And pardon to these men!'
                            "'Don't pray for us!'
Said Dictys, who was readiest of all   615
To scale high masts or run hands down a rope.
This, Libys, blond Melanthus, who kept watch,
Alcimedon, Epopeus, whose voice set
The rowers' pace and rest and cheer, and all
The crew approved—so blind is plunderous greed.   620
'I won't allow these planks to be defiled
With sacred freight,' I said, 'while I'm in charge!'
And blocked their way, enraging Lycabas,
Their rashest member, whom a Tuscan town
Had banished as a heinous murderer.   625
While there I stood, his young fist clutched my throat

And would have plunged me in the deep, had I
Not blindly grasped a rope that held me back;
The godless mob cheered. Bacchus then, at last
(For Bacchus he had been), as though the noise   630
Had scattered sleep and roused his wine-drunk sense,
Cried out, 'What are you doing? Why this noise?
How—tell me, sailors—did I get here? Where
Do you intend to take me?' 'Have no fear'
Said Proreus, 'Name the port you wish to reach,   635
And we'll stop there.' 'To Naxos,' Liber said,
'Direct your course. My home will welcome you.'
By all the gods and seas, the false ones swore
They would and bade me sail the painted ship.

　　"With Naxos rightward, I sailed to the right.   640
'What's this?' Opheltes said, 'Have you gone mad?'
'Turn left!' they cried. Most nodded pointedly;
Some whispered what they wanted in my ear.
In shock, I said, 'Let others take the helm!'
And freed myself from service to their crime.   645
All roared against me, grumbling as a band;
Then one, Aethalion, jeered, 'Of course, we'll all
Be *hopeless* without you!', assumed my post,
And, leaving Naxos, set a different course.
The teasing god, as if he'd only now   650
Caught on, gazed seaward from the curving stern
And, faking tears, cried out, 'These aren't the shores
You sailors promised me! These aren't the lands!
Have I deserved this fate? What glory's yours,
That many men have fooled a single child?'   655

　　"Since I wept, too, the godless handful mocked
Our tears and smote the sea with speeding oars.
Now, by that god himself (for there's no god
So close as he),[†] I swear that what I say
Is true as it seems false: the ship stood still,   660
As though a dry-dock held it in the waves.
Amazed, they kept on rowing, spread the sails,
And strove by twofold means to work up speed,
But ivy stopped the oars in back-bent knots

And slithered heavy clusters round the sails.   665
With grapes bunched round his brow, the god himself
Brandished a spear enveiled in leafy vines,
While round him tigers, lynxes' phantom shapes,
And spotted panthers' beastly bodies lay.
The men leapt up in madness or in fear,   670
And Medon's body started darkening first,
Spine bending backward in a straining curl.
'What freak,' asked Lycabas, 'have you become?'
Yet as he spoke, his open mouth grew wide,
His nose arched out, his skin turned hard with scales;   675
Then Libys, as he tried the trammeled oars,
Saw that his hands were shriveling in place,
And soon they were not hands—soon they were fins!
Another reached out arms to seize a rope,
But found he had no arms; his arching form   680
Fell limbless in the waves, his tail's far end
Hooked like a crescent moon's round-curving horns.
On every side, they leapt and splashed around,
And rose and sank at sea, time after time;
Like dancers playing, their lithe bodies dashed   685
While their wide blowholes sucked and sprayed the sea.
Of twenty men (the ship had held that sum),
Just I remained, though shivering with fear
And scarce myself. To cheer me then, the god
Said, 'Now, take heart. To Dia!'[12] There, I joined   690
His cult and since have thronged the Bacchic rites."
    "We've lent our ears to this unending tale,"
Said Pentheus, "that time might cool our wrath.
Now seize him, slaves, and plunge his body, wracked
With fearsome torments, into Stygian gloom!"   695
At once, Tyrrhene Acoetes was dragged off
Into a dungeon. While death's instruments,
Cruel iron and fire, were readied as decreed,
All on their own, it's said, the doors flung wide;
And on their own, the chains fell from his arms.   700

12. An archaic name for Naxos

Unmoved, Echion's son now sent no word,
But sought Cithaeron, the cult's chosen site,
Whose slopes rang clear with bacchant voice and song.
As fierce steeds braying at the tuneful call
Of brazen war-horns feel their bloodlust rise,   705
So did the lasting howls that struck the air
Stir listening Pentheus to white-hot rage.
    Near halfway up the peak, ringed round with woods,
A treeless field lay visible to all,
And there, he watched the rites with profane eyes.†   710
The first to spy him, first to rave and run,
And first whose thyrsus flung toward Pentheus
Was his own mother. "Sisters, come!" she cried.
"A giant boar is roaming in our fields—
I'm going to kill that boar!" All rushed as one,   715
A crazed joint charge, and, howling, followed him
As now he feared, now spoke with milder words,
Now cursed himself, and now confessed his sin.
Though wounded, he cried out, "Help, aunt! And may
Actaeon's specter stir Autonoë!"   720
But as he pled Actaeon's name, she tore
Off his right arm!† Mad Ino cleaved the left!
Now, luckless, shorn of mother-reaching arms,
He showed the wounds of his dismembered trunk
And said, "Look, mother!" Seeing, Agave howled,   725
Her head lolled, and her hair whipped through the air.
Then, wrenching off his head with bloody hands,
She screamed, "Here, friends—this feat's our victory!"
Nor are scarce-clinging autumn leaves, once chilled
And swept with wind, more swiftly stripped from trees   730
Than were his limbs plucked off by sinful hands.
    Warned by example, Thebans thronged the rites,
Burned incense, and revered the newfound shrines.

Book 4

[THE DAUGHTERS OF MINYAS, PART 1]†

BUT† MINYAS' child, Alcithoë, still dared
Reject his godly revels and deny
That Bacchus was the son of Jove—a sin
Her sisters shared.
           A priest then called a feast
When ladies and their slave-girls, freed from toil,   5
Would cloak their breasts in skins, let down their hair,
Garland their locks, and wield the thyrsus' leaves,
For he'd foreseen the way the god would rage
If slighted. All the wives and girls obeyed,
Put basket, loom, and half-spun wool aside,   10
Burned incense, and called Bacchus "Bromius,"†
"Lyaeus," "Twice-Born," "Lone Two-Mothered Son,"
"Unshorn Thyoneus," "Nysan," "Child of Fire,"
"Lenaeus," "Planter of the Merry Grape,"
"Nyctelius," "Iacchus," and "Elelean Sire,"   15
And "Euhan," and the many other names
You, Liber, have in Greece. O timeless boy,
Forever young, you fairest form in all
The vaulted heaven! Your head, when lacking horns,
Is like a girl's! To you, the East bows down,   20
Far as the Ganges bathes dark India!

You, most revered, smote godless Pentheus
And two-bit-axed Lycurgus, and submerged
The Tyrrhenes in the deep! Your painted reins
Bind lynxes, yoked in pairs, and in your wake   25
Come bacchants, Satyrs, and the drunk old man
Whose cane-braced limbs scarce ride his crookbacked mule;
And where you go, boys' shouts and women's cries,
Combined with hollow drumbeats, crashing brass,
And long-holed boxwood flutes, ring all around.   30
"Be kind and mild with us," the Thebans pray
And worship as decreed.
                                   Just Minyas' girls
Stayed in and, with ill-timed Minerval tasks,†
Upset the feast: they spun wool, thumbed the threads,
Kept to their looms, and heaped their slaves with work.   35
Said one, as her thumb deftly drew the thread:
"While shiftless women throng these liar's rites,
Let us who hold with Pallas, a real god,
Relieve our useful toil with varied talk:
Let each in turn, lest time pass slowly by,   40
Relate some tale to fill our idle ears!"
Her sisters, in accord, bade her speak first.
    She weighed which tale to tell (for she knew scores),
Unsure, O Dercetis of Babylon,†
To speak of you, whom Palestinians hold   45
Were wrapped in scales to swim within a lake;
Or of your daughter, who gained wings of white
And spent her later years atop a tower;
Or how a naiad's over-mighty herbs
And charms turned youths to silent fish, then did   50
The same to her; or how a tree whose fruit,
Once white, is black now, stained with blood—that's it!
And since that story's not well known, she draws
A thread of wool and so begins to weave:

[PYRAMUS AND THISBE]†

"Once, Pyramus and Thisbe—far the most   55

Attractive boy and girl in all the East—
Lived next each other in that city which
Semiramis, it's said, walled round with brick.
Proximity bred fondness, step by step,
And time brought love. They would have joined and wed   60
But for parental ban, yet bans could not
Restrain their hearts, both rapt with mutual fire.
They had no go-betweens but spoke in nods;
The more they hid their flame, the more it burned.
  "Since it was built, a slender chink had split   65
The common wall that stood between their homes.
For many years, this fault had gone unseen.
(But what can hide from love?) You lovers found
And made from it a pathway for your words,
Where whispered wooing sighs could safely pass.   70
On his side, Pyramus would often stand,
And Thisbe hers, to catch the other's breath.
'O jealous wall,' they'd say, 'why foil our love?
How hard is it to let our bodies meet,
Or part, if that's too much, and let us kiss?   75
But we are grateful: we owe it to you
That words find passage to our loving ears.'
Thus vainly set apart, they talked till dusk
And said 'goodnight' as each one gave the wall
A kiss that could not reach the other side.   80
When dawn had sent away the glow of night
And rays of sunlight dried the frosty grass,
They met in their old place. They first complained
In whispers, then resolved, by hush of night,
To venture past their guards and slip outside,   85
Then, leaving home, to quit the city, too!
And, lest they stray apart in open fields,
To meet at Ninus' tomb and hide beneath
Its tree—a tree of snow-white mulberries
Beside an ice-cold spring: so had they set   90
This pleasing plan.
                    "The sun seemed slow to slip
Into the waves, yet from those waves rose night.

In darkness, Thisbe slyly cracked her door,
And, slipping past her guards with shrouded face,
She reached the tomb and sat beneath the tree.   95
Love made her bold—but look! a lioness,
Its jaws still foaming gore from fresh-killed cows,
Draws toward the nearby spring to quench its thirst.
By moonlight, Babylonian Thisbe sees
It from afar, flees toward a gloomy cave   100
On frightened feet, and, fleeing, drops her cloak.
Its thirst quelled drink by drink, the wildcat turns
Back to the woods, finds it—without the girl—
And shreds the sheer cloak in her bloody maw.
    "In time, when Pyramus arrived and saw   105
The beast's deep-printed tracks, his face turned pale.
But when he found the garment stained with blood,
He cried, 'One night shall strike two lovers down,
But of them she deserved long life the most!
The fault is mine—I killed you, piteous girl: 110
I bade you come by night to this dread spot,
And did not come here first! Now rend my corpse
And feast your savage fangs on sinful flesh,
O lions, you who live about this rock!
Yet only cowards merely wish for death. . . .'   115
Beneath the tree, as planned, with Thisbe's cloak,
He gave the cloth his kisses, gave it tears,
And cried to it, 'Now drink my blood as well!'
Then, drawing out his sword, he stabbed his loins,
And, dying, wrenched it from the seething wound.   120
While on the ground he lay, his blood gushed high,†
Much as a faulty pipe whose lead has burst
Will, through its hissing fissure, shoot long streams
Of water, slicing through the air in spurts.
The spray of gore turned black the tree's young fruit,   125
And, through its blood-soaked roots, a purple hue
Suffused the hanging mulberries.
                              "And look!
Still fearful, but afraid to miss her love,
The girl returns and seeks him, eyes and soul,

Eager to tell what dangers she's escaped.   130
And though she sees the spot and knows the tree,
Its colored fruit confounds her: is this it?
While stopped, there on the gory ground she saw
The body writhe and thrash! Then she leapt back,
Went boxwood-white, and shuddered like a sea   135
Whose plane is ruffled by a gentle breeze.
But soon enough she recognized her love
And beat her guiltless shoulders as she shrieked
And tore her hair. She clasped the cherished corpse,
Filled up the wounds with tears that mixed his blood,   140
Then, kissing his cold features, cried, 'What fate,
O Pyramus, has taken you from me?
O Pyramus, my dear, your Thisbe calls!
Say something, listen—lift your hanging head!'
At Thisbe's name, his death-encumbered eyes   145
Unclosed and, having seen her, shut again.
    "But seeing the cloak and swordless ivory sheath,
She said, 'By your own hand and love, you died,
Unlucky boy! For this, my love and hand
Have strength to wound as well: I'll follow you!   150
And of your death, may I be called the cause
And wretchedmost companion. You, whom death
Alone would part from me, death will not part!
Yet, be entreated by this couple's plea—
O all ye wretched parents, mine and his—   155
That they whom true love and last moments joined
Shall not be grudged the sharing of a tomb!
And you, the tree whose boughs now shade the corpse
Of one poor wretch and shortly shall shade two,
Preserve death's marks and always bear dark fruit   160
In mourning memory of our twin demise.'
This said, she fixed the blade beneath her ribs
And fell upon his sword, still warm with death.
Her prayer, though, reached the gods and parents both;
For when the fruit is ripe, it turns to black,   165
And in one urn lie both their pyres' remains."

[THE LOVES OF THE SUN]†

She ceased. Then, with a pause, Leuconoë
Began to speak; her sisters held their tongues.
"The Sun, whose starlight lights all, also loves.
Now we'll recount the lovers of the Sun.   170
    "It's thought that this god, who sees all things first,
Was first to see Mars' tryst with Venus, too.
Appalled, he showed her husband, Juno's son,[1]
Not just their lie, but on whose bed they lay!
The blacksmith dropped his work with drooping heart,   175
And forged at once a net of brazen links
Too fine for eyes to see (a feat unmatched
By even the most slender woolen threads
Or spider-webs that hang from attic beams),
Designed to spring up at the lightest touch   180
Or smallest stir. He spread this on his sheets,
And when the wife and lover went to bed,
Her husband's craft and cunning scheming chains
Caught both of them, held fast in their embrace.
The Lemnian[2] then flung wide the ivory doors   185
And called the gods to see them bound in shame.
Not unamused, one deity[3] wished he
Might be so shamed! All laughed and, for some time,
This was the best-known tale in all of heaven.
    "But Cytherea[4] knew who had informed,   190
So he who'd bared her love was met in turn
With barren love. What use, Hyperion's son,†
Are all your beauty, beams, and brightness now,
When new flames burn in you, whose flames burn all?
As you, who ought to view all things, now see   195
Leucothoë, and fix upon one girl
Those eyes you owe the world, now in the East

1. Vulcan
2. Vulcan's forge was located on Lemnos
3. Perhaps Mercury (cf. 4.288)
4. Venus, born on the isle of Cythera

You rise too soon, now reach the waves too late,
Or stop to gaze and stretch the winter's hours;
At times, your weakened mind infects your light,   200
Which fades and frightens mortals with the dark—
And not because the moon glows white between
You and the earth! Your color comes from love,
Love just for her, not Clymene nor Rhodes
Nor fair Aeaean Circe's mother now,   205
Nor Clytië, who still lusts after you,[†]
Though spurned and gravely wounded from before.
All were forgotten for Leucothoë,
Born to Eurynome, the fairest maid
In all the lands of spice, until her birth,   210
When her surpassing mother was surpassed.
Her sire was Orchamus, a Persian king,
From ancient Belus[5] seventh in descent.
        "Now under western skies, the Sun-god's steeds,
Who graze ambrosia in the place of grass,   215
Stretched out their limbs, grown strained with daily toil.
While there the four-hooved creatures fed by night,
The god transformed into Eurynome
And entered his love's chamber, where he saw
Leucothoë with twice-six slave-girls near,   220
All spinning slender thread by light of lamps.
Then, kissing her as mothers kiss their dears,
He said, 'This matter's private. Slaves, depart—
Don't bar a mother's right to secrecy!'
They left the room. Then, unobserved, the god   225
Said, 'I am he who marks the running year,
Who sees all things, through whom all things are seen,
The cosmic eye—and (trust me) I like you!'
Afraid, she dropped her wool and rod in fright,
But fear became her and, as he resumed   230
His true form and accustomed light, the girl,
Though scared at such a sight, was vanquished by

5. A mythical Assyrian king, likely derived from the god Baʾal

His godly light and raped without a word.[†]
  "For spite, the jealous Clytië (who loved
The Sun beyond control) made widely known   235
Her rival's tryst and shamed her to her sire.
This cold, cruel man, despite his daughter's pleas,
Her hands stretched toward the Sunlight, and her cries—
'He forced himself upon me!'—buried her
Deep underground beneath a mound of sand.   240
And though the radiance of Hyperion's son
Cleared you a path to lift your buried face,
Beneath that earthen weight you lay, too tired
To raise your head, dear nymph: a bloodless corpse.
  "No sight had brought the lord of wingèd steeds   245
Such anguish since the fires of Phaëthon.
With all his beaming strength he strove to call
Her icy body back to seething life;
But fate withstood his mighty tries, so he
Rained scented nectar round the corpse and cried,   250
'You'll still reach heaven!' and other plaintive things.
At once, the nectar-sodden corpse dissolved,
And soaked the earth in scent. Then, through the soil,
A deeply rooted sprig of frankincense[†]
Rose slowly up and broke the mound apart.   255
  "But Clytië, though love explained her grief,
And grief her slander, met the Font of Light
No more, for she no longer stirred his lust.
And so, deranged with love, she pined away:
Through night and day and cloudy skies, she sat   260
Unkempt and naked on the naked ground.
For nine whole days, devoid of food and drink,
She starved herself on tears and drops of dew,
And never left the ground, but only watched
The passing god and turned her face toward his.   265
They say that part of her stuck in the soil,
While part became a pale and bloodless plant,
But part was red and round her face there grew
A purple blossom which, though held by roots,
Turns with the Sun[†]—transformed, but still in love."   270

[HERMAPHRODITUS AND SALMACIS]†

She'd told and they had heard a miracle.
Some said it could not be; some said true gods
Can do all things, though Bacchus was not one.
Once hushed, the sisters called Alcithoë,
Who ran the shuttle through her loom and said: 275
"I need not tell† of Daphnis' well-known love—
That Idan shepherd, whom a jealous nymph
Changed into stone (so burn the pangs of love!)
Nor shall I tell how nature's laws were changed
For unfixed Sithon—now woman, now man,   280
Poor Celmis, you, who once were Jove's true friend,
Now steel; nor the Curetes, sprung from rain;
Nor Crocus, who, with Smilax, shrank to flowers.
Instead, I'll thrall with something sweetly new:
    "Now learn how Salmacis won infamy,   285
And why limbs weaken in its crippling waves!
Its powers are famous, but few know their cause.
    "Once, Cytherea bore to Mercury
A son the naiads nursed in Ida's caves
Whose sire and mother both were to be seen   290
Within his face, and also in his name.[6]
At thrice-five years, he quit his native peaks
And left his Idan homeland, pleased to roam
Through lands unknown and gaze on unknown streams,
His toil eased by delight. At length, he came   295
To Lycia and, beyond the Lycian towns,
To Caria. There, he saw a crystal pool,
Clear to its bottom, where no marshy reed
Nor barren sedge nor sharp-hooked rushes grew,
But all was clear, though round the pool's far edge   300
Grew thriving plants and grasses, ever green.
    "There dwelt a naiad, but one loath to hunt
Or race or bend a bow—the only nymph

6. Hermaphroditus is a Greek portmanteau of Mercury (Hermes) and Venus (Aphrodite)

Diana never knew. And rumor has
Her sisters often urged her, 'Salmacis,   305
With either spear or painted quiver, come
And mix your leisure with the lively chase!'
Yet neither spear nor painted quiver came,
Nor mixed she leisure with the lively chase,
But in her spring she'd bathe her lovely legs,   310
Brush out her hair with a Cytoran[7] comb,
And ask the mirrored waves what fit her best.
Or, wrapped in a sheer robe, she'd settle down
Among soft grasses or amid soft leaves,
Or pick bouquets, as she was picking when   315
She saw the boy—and longed for what she saw.
But she held off, on though she yearned to rush,
Until she'd calmed herself, arranged her robes,
Composed her face, and earned her loveliness.
    "'O boy, most fit for worship as a god!   320
If you're a god, you're Cupid!' she exclaimed.
'If mortal, bliss is theirs who gave you birth!
Blessed is your brother! Lucky to be yours
Is any sister, any suckling nurse!
But far more blessed than all of these could be   325
Is any bride, any you'd deign to wed!
If she exists, let stolen love be mine;
If not, then marry me and share my bed!'
With this, the nymph fell still. The boy turned red
(For he knew not of love), but handsomely   330
He blushed the shade of fruit on sunlit boughs,
Stained ivory, or a white-on-red eclipse
When cymbals idly crash to aid the moon.[†]
With ceaseless pleas for just a sister's kiss,
She moved to clasp his ivory neck. 'Enough!'   335
He cried, 'Or shall I leave this place, and you?'
'To you I yield,' said Salmacis with dread,
'Dear stranger,' and she seemed to walk away,
But, glancing back, she stole into a bush

7. Boxwood, of which Mount Cytorus had a famed supply

And hid there, crouching on her knees.
                           "The boy,   340
As if unseen amidst the vacant grass,
Walked back and forth and, in the playful waves,
First dipped his toes, then waded ankle-deep.
Charmed by the soothing waters, all at once,
He stripped his body of its slender clothes.   345
This pleased her well. Lust for his naked form
Ignited Salmacis: the nymph's eyes blazed
The way a mirror, shown the cloudless orb
Of brightest Phoebus, will return its light.
Scarce holding back, scarce stalling her own joy,   350
She craved his arms, too crazed to check herself.
With curving palms, he clapped his sides and dove
Into the pool where, stroke by stroke, his arms
Glowed through the waves like ivory figurines
Or shining lilies in a crystal glass.   355
'I've won, he's mine!' the naiad cried and threw
Her clothes aside. Then, leaping in the pool,
She forced her kisses on the struggling boy,
Slid fondling hands up his unwilling chest,
And wrapped—now here, now there—around the youth.   360
At length, she stopped the gleaming boy's escape
As does a snake, caught by the king of birds
And borne aloft (which, hanging, wraps its tail
In coils round head and feet and flapping wings),
Or ivy twining round a tree's tall trunk,   365
Or else an ocean octopus, which grasps
Its prey with tentacles on every side.
Though Atlas' heir[8] strove to deny her joy,
The nymph, who clung as if completely stuck,
Cried, 'Rascal, you can fight but you can't flee!   370
O gods, decree that no day ever shall
Disjoin this boy from me nor me from him!'
Her prayers found gods; for, locked together still,
The two were joined in form and face—as one.

---

8. Through Mercury's mother Maia, Hermaphroditus is Atlas' great-grandson

Just as, when someone grafts a branch in bark,   375
The joint is seen to seal through mutual growth,
So merged their forms in passionate embrace;
Nor were their two shapes twinned, that one might call
Them boy and girl: they seemed neither and both.
    "On seeing how he'd breached the waves a man   380
To surface semi-male and weak of limb,
With upraised hands and voice emasculate,
Hermaphroditus shouted: 'Mother! Sire!
O grant your son, who carries both your names,
That he who comes into these springs a man   385
Will leave unmanned and weakened by their touch!'
His parents, moved to heed their two-shaped son,
Then steeped the fountain with its queering† power."

[THE DAUGHTERS OF MINYAS, PART 2]

    Their tales all told now, Minyas' girls worked on,
And scorned the god, dishonoring his feast,   390
When suddenly the crash of unseen drums
And curving horns and jangling brass rang forth.
As scents of myrrh and saffron filled the air,
Their looms defied belief by turning green,
Thick fronds of ivy draped the hanging cloths,   395
Parts turned to grapevines, what was lately thread
Transformed to twigs, and shoots shot down the warp,
With vibrant grapes to match the violet dyes.
    And now, the day is done; now comes that hour
In which you cannot tell the light from dark,   400
Though light still tints the hazy bounds of night,
When suddenly the oil-lamps seem to flare,
The rafters shake, red flames shine through the house,
And phantom shadows loose their beastly howls.
Throughout the smoke-filled halls, the sisters hide   405
In separate refuge from the lights and fires.
There in the dark, a membrane spreads across
Their limbs and wraps their arms in slender wings
But how they come to lose their former shape

Is hidden in the dark. No feathers raise   410
Them up, yet on translucent wings they rise;
And when they speak, they make a meager sound,
As suits their size, and vent their grief in shrieks.
Now, haunting eaves—not woods—and hating light,
They're named for how they bat their wings by night.[†]   415

[ATHAMAS AND INO][†]

  Then all of Thebes knew Bacchus truly was
Divine; and everywhere, his aunt[9] extolled
The new god's might. Unlike her sisters, she
Had known no grief, save when she grieved for them.
Proud of her sons, her husband Athamas,   420
And her godchild the god, she was a sight
That Juno could not bear: "My rival's son,
Whose power could shape and sink a Lydian ship
And make a mother hack apart her child,
Has now lent Minyas' girls three sets of wings!   425
Can Juno only weep in unearned pain?[†]
Should this appease me? Is this my one power?
He's taught me what to do (foes, too, can teach!):
In slaughtered Pentheus, he's more than proved
The strength of madness. Why can't Ino go,   430
Through her own madness, where her kin have gone?"
  There is a pathway, dark with deadly yews,
Whose silent hush leads to the underworld.
Along that route, where breathes the misty Styx,
Descend fresh shades, the spectral buried dead.   435
A wintry pallor grips this rough expanse
Where new ghosts strain to reach the Stygian seat
Or find the fearsome palace of dark Dis.[†]
A thousand entrances and gaping gates
Lead to the town, and as the sea receives   440
All earthly streams, so this place takes all souls.
No multitude won't fit; it knows no crowds.

_____

9. Ino (cf. 3.313)

Devoid of blood and bone, the formless shades
Roam: some the forum, some the dark lord's house.
While some ply trades and ape their former lives,   445
[Some others languish in their punishment.]†
    Departing heaven (awash in hate and rage),
Saturnian Juno dared to venture here;
At her approach, the threshold groaned beneath
Her holy weight, and Cerberus' three mouths   450
Let loose three cries. She then called forth a power
Ruthless and grim: the sisters born of Night.[10]
Before the adamantine doors of Hell,
They sat and combed their smoky serpent hair;
And, seeing the goddess part the mists, they rose.   455
    That spot is called "the Seat of the Accursed."†
There Tityos lends his innards to bestrew
Nine acres; there you, Tantalus, are fled
By stream and hanging tree; you, Sisyphus,
Now chase, now push a stone that will roll back;   460
Ixion, round himself, there turns and twists;
And there, for daring deal their cousins death,
The Belides must ever seek lost waves.
Saturnia set her savage eyes on each,
And on Ixion most; to Sisyphus   465
She turned then, asking, "Should *this* brother toil
In timeless torments, when proud Athamas,[11]
At his rich palace, scorns me with his wife?"
She told what drove her hate, what drove her there,
And wished her wish: the House of Cadmus felled   470
And Athamas dragged madly into sin.
Her orders, pleas, and pledges joined in one
As Juno urged the goddesses. This heard,
Tisiphone—for she it was—shook out
Her hair and moved the snakes that blocked her mouth: 475
"No need," said she, "for this unending tale.
Your bidding's good as done. Leave this dread place

10. The Furies (Alecto, Megaera, and Tisiphone)
11. Ino's husband Athamas was brother to Sisyphus

And seek again the fairer airs of heaven!"
So Juno left and entered heaven in joy,
Once Iris, Thaumas' child, cleansed her with dew.   480
    That instant, cruel Tisiphone took up
A blood-soaked torch, put on a bleeding robe,
And, with a snake wrapped round her waist, left home.
Along with her went Terror, Grief, and Dread,
And twitching-featured Madness. When they reached   485
Aeolus' house,† it's said the portal quaked,
Its maple doors turned pale, and sunlight fled.
And when these portents drove his frightened wife
And frightened Athamas to leave their house,
The dooming Fury stood and stopped their flight.   490
Then, reaching out, she tossed her tangled knots
Of viperous hair, whose shaken serpents hissed,
As down her arms, or coiling round her breasts,
They rasped and gushed with pus and flicked their tongues.
Then, from her locks, she tore and threw two snakes!   495
Hurled from her fatal hands, all round the forms
Of Ino and of Athamas, they spewed
Their noxious breath, but dealt no fleshly wounds:
It was their minds that felt the fearful stroke.
    And with her, she had brought vile poisons, too.   500
The spit of Cerberus, Echidna's bane,
Confused delusions, blindness of the mind,
And crime and tears and rage and lust for death—
With these she mixed fresh blood and hemlock greens,
And stirred them all within a vat of bronze.   505
This maddening brew she poured on both their chests,
And while they shook, it struck their inmost hearts.
Then several times around she whirled her torch
So fire caught fast from fire. Her task complete,
In victory she sought again the realm   510
Of mighty Dis—and took her snake-belt off.
    At once, Aeolus' son raved through the halls
And cried, "Oh, comrades, set these woods with snares!
I saw a lioness here with twin cubs!"
The witless madman hunted for his wife   515

And snatched Leärchus[12]—laughing, arms outstretched—
From her embrace, then swung him like a sling
Around and wildly round, till on a stone
He smashed the baby's face. The mother, too,
Gone mad from grief or from the poisoned spray,   520
Ran howling with her hair undone and you,
Young Melicertes, in her arms. She cried,
"Hail Bacchus!" Juno laughed at Bacchus' name:
"May this be how your nursling blesses you!"

    A cliff rose by the sea, whose base the tides   525
Had hollowed out to shield the waves from rain
And whose rough heights stretched far across the depths.
This Ino scaled (insanity breeds strength)
And, free from fear, plunged self and cargo both
Into the deep, churning the waves to white.   530
But Venus, pitying her grandchild's plight,
Beguiled her uncle thus: "O Lord of seas!
O Neptune, you whose powers near those of heaven!
Though I ask much, take pity on my kin,
Whom you see sunk in the Ionian swell,   535
And let them join your gods. I should hold sway
With waves, if depths of foam once gave me rise,
As has remained my name among the Greeks."†
So Neptune heard her prayer and, trading all
Their mortal portion for dread majesty,   540
He changed their names and forms and called the queen
"Leucothea," her son "Palaemon"—gods.

    Her Theban friends pursued as best they could,
But saw her footprints end upon the rock.
Sure of her death, they beat their breasts and mourned   545
The House of Cadmus, rent their clothes and hair,
And drew the goddess' malice, saying she
Had cruelly wronged her rival. Juno could
Bear no reproach and said, "I'll make from you
Vast monuments to my malignity!"   550
Deed followed word, for when the staunchest girl

---

12. With Melicertes, one of the two sons of Athamas and Ino

Cried, "Drown me with my queen!" and would have leapt,
She could not move, but stuck upon the cliff.
Another strove once more to beat her breast
And felt her striving arms grow stiff. A third,   555
By chance, was reaching out her hand to sea:
A hand of stone now stretches toward that sea.
One more was ripping out her hair, and you
May see her hardened fingers ripping still.
Each holds the pose in which she then was caught;   560
And some, once Theban maids, were turned to birds,
Whose wings now skim the waters of that flood.

[CADMUS AND HARMONIA]†

   Agenor's son was unaware his child
And small grandson were sea-gods. Crushed by grief,
His string of woes, and omens he had seen,   565
He fled the town he'd founded, as if wracked
By its luck, not his own. He wandered long,
But reached Illyria's borders† with his wife,
Where, fraught with age and woe, they now reviewed
Their family's fate, recounting their old toils.   570
"Was it a sacred snake my spear transfixed,
When first I came from Sidon," Cadmus asked,
"And sowed the soil with serpent seeds—its teeth?
If that has caused the gods' avenging rage,
May I be stretched into a curving snake!"   575
With that, he stretched out, curving like a snake.
He felt his skin was growing hard with scales
That flecked his swarthy body bluish-green,
And fell flat on his chest as, by degrees,
His mingling legs thinned into a smooth tail.   580
His arms were left and, as they left, reached out,
While tears flowed over his still-human face.
"Come here," he cried, "O wretched wife, come here!
While part of me remains, touch—take my hand,
While hand it is—while all is not yet snake!"   585
He would have said more, but just then his tongue

Was cleft in two; so words refused his will,
And every time he tried to vent his griefs,
He hissed. This voice had nature left to him.
    While beating her bared breasts, his wife cried out: 590
"Poor Cadmus, stay! Cast off this monstrous shape!
What—Cadmus! Where's your feet, arms, hands, and face,
Your skin and, as I speak, your—everything?
Why not, O heaven, make me a serpent, too?"
This said, he licked her face and slid between   595
Her cherished breasts as if familiar there,
Then held her fast and sought the neck he knew.
All who were there (some friends were there) stood shocked,
But she caressed the crested dragon's neck,
And suddenly their two coils snaked as one   600
And slithered to a nearby shady grove.
They neither flee nor injure humans now;
Mild dragons, they remember what they were.

[PERSEUS, ATLAS, AND ANDROMEDA]†

    Though changed in form, both cheered their grandson's might,
For India had fallen to his cult,   605
While his new-risen temples thronged with Greeks.
Just Abas' son Acrisius† remained;
Born of their line, he shut the Argive walls,
Took arms against the god, and called the boy
No son of Jove! Nor was Jove's son, he said,   610
One Perseus, begat by raining gold
On Danaë.† But soon Acrisius
(Truth has such power) repented having both
Disclaimed his grandson and defamed a god,
For one reached heaven, and one bore through the air   615
His monstrous, viperous spoils on whistling wings;
And as this victor passed the Libyan sands,
The Gorgon's head let bloody droplets fall,
Which Earth received and gave reptilian life,
And so that land still teems with swarms of snakes.   620
    Next, driven through the sky by warring winds—

Now here, now there—he floated like a cloud
And looked on distant lands from high above
As round the world he flew. Three times he saw
The frigid Bears, and three times Cancer's arms,   625
As often east and often west he whirled.
When sunset came and roused his fear of night
He stopped in Atlas' western realms to rest
Until the Morning-Star should call the fires
Of Dawn, and Dawn the chariot of day.   630
And there, surpassing every man in size,
Was Atlas, son of Iapetus, who ruled
This edge of earth and sea, whose waves received
The Sun-god's gasping steeds and weary wheels.
A thousand flocks and just as many herds   635
Roamed through his pastures, neighborless and free.
And he had trees whose shining leaves of gold
Enfolded golden boughs and golden fruits.
"Dear host," said Perseus, "if noble birth
Can move you, know my sire was Jupiter;   640
Or, if it's feats you prize, you will prize mine—
Please host me!"
                    But his host had long recalled
Forewarnings (which Parnassian Themis warned):
"Know, Atlas, when your tree's despoiled of gold,
A son of Jove shall take its plundered fame."†   645
In fear of this had Atlas walled his groves,
Kept a huge dragon standing guard, and drove
All strangers from his lands—as he did now:
"Get back," he said, "in case your phony feats
Abandon you—and Jupiter with them!"   650
Force backed these threats, but his expelling hands
Were met with stubborn might and friendly words.
In strength, he lost (to whom could Atlas lose
In strength?), but said, "Since you so little prize
Our thanks, accept our gift!" and raised aloft,   655
With his left hand, Medusa's sordid head.
   A peak the size of Atlas stands there now:
His beard and hair are trees; his shoulders, cliffs;

And what was once his head is mountaintop.
His bones turned into stone, each part has grown   660
Immense in size (for so you gods decreed)
That heaven and all its stars might rest on him.
   The son of Hippotes[13] had locked the Winds
In Aetna's caves, and the bright Morning Star,
Who heralds daily toil, had risen high,   665
When he strapped wings to feet and sword to waist,
And, on his flying sandals, split the air.
He passed unnumbered nations, till he spied
The Aethiopian lands of Cepheus,
Where, for her mother's tongue, Andromeda   670
Hung innocent by Ammon's cruel command.[†]
On seeing her arms were tied to stony crags,
King Abas' heir[14] (but for the fluttering hair
And tearful eyes, he would have thought she was
A statue)[†] burned at once with thoughtless love,   675
And, dumbstruck by the gripping, gorgeous sight,
Almost forgot to beat his airy wings.
   Alighting, he cried, "Oh, you've not deserved
These bonds, but those of sweethearts linked in love!
Reveal to me this country's name and yours—   680
And why you bear these chains!" She paused at first,
For maids don't speak to men, and would have veiled
Her modest face had not her hands been bound;
But she could weep and filled her eyes with tears.
He asked again, and lest she seem to hide   685
Some fault, she told the country's name and hers,
And how her mother's boasts of beauty brought
Her there. And while she spoke, the waves let forth
A roar as, from the boundless deep, there rose
A monster whose broad chest engulfed the sea.   690
The maiden screamed. Her sire and mother both
Stood wracked with pain, which she[15] more rightly felt,

13. Aeolus, Keeper of the Winds
14. Perseus, great-grandson of Abas
15. Cassiope

But brought no help save cries and beaten breasts,
As fit the scene, and clasped her shackled frame.
The stranger said: "Long is the time for tears,   695
But short the hour of aid! If I should woo
As Perseus—the son of Jove and she
Whom, in her cell, Jove filled with fertile gold—
The snake-haired Gorgon–slayer Perseus,
Who dares on wings to soar, I would surpass   700
All men as son-in-law! I'll try to prove
My worth in deeds (gods willing); in exchange,
I ask that she my valor saves be mine!"
Her parents took the deal (who would refuse?)
And, pleading, pledged as dowry their whole realm.   705
    But look! where, like a ship whose speeding prow,
Propelled by sweating rowers, ploughs the waves,
The beast tears through the waters on its chest,
No further from the rocks than is the range
At which fly shots from Balearic slings.†   710
Then, suddenly, the youth leapt from the ground
To vanish in the clouds. Next, on the sea,
His shadow fell, the beast fell on the shade,
And, as Jove's bird will spy a spotted snake
Sunbathing on its back in a bare field   715
And seize its scaly neck, grasped from behind
To keep the deadly maw from turning round,
So, headlong through the void, Inachides[16]
Swooped from behind, attacked the roaring beast,
And plunged his blade's whole curve in its right flank.   720
With grievous wounds, it now reared high above,
Now plumbed the depths, now whipped round like a boar
Who hears a fearful pack of baying hounds.
On speeding wings, he fled the hungry teeth;
All he could reach—there on its shell-pocked back,   725
There in between its ribs, there where its tail
Thinned like a fish—his curving sword assailed.
The beast next spat a mix of purple blood

16. Perseus, a tenth-generation descendant of Inachus

FIGURE 4. *The Rescue of Andromeda*, A. van Diepenbeeck (1655). Flemish engraver Abraham van Diepenbeeck was among a small number of early modern artists to recognize Ovid's Andromeda as a Black African. This image was originally published alongside a churchman's disapproving commentary that questioned how a dark-skinned woman could be beautiful. In most renderings, Andromeda is exceptionally pale.

And water, weighing down the wings with spray,
So Perseus dared trust his sea-soaked plumes   730
No more, but spied a rock which, in still tides
Rose high, though covered now in roiling waves.
While there he leaned, the crag gripped in his left,
Three times and more he stabbed the monster's groin!
    Cheers filled the shores up to the halls of heaven.   735
Cassiope and Cepheus rejoiced
And hailed their son-in-law, whom they avowed
The salve and savior of their house. Unchained,
She came who was his labor's cause and prize!
Then he fetched water, washed his victor's hands,   740
And, lest coarse sands should bruise the snaky head,
He smoothed the ground with seaweed and with leaves
To hold Medusa, Phorcys' daughter's, head.
The weeds, still quick and spongy to the pith,
On contact, felt the monster's hardening power,   745
And strange new stiffness seized their stalks and fronds.
The sea-nymphs tested out the miracle
On many seaweeds, cheered the same result,
And scattered them as seedlings in the waves.
It is in coral's nature to this day   750
To harden in the air: a pliant stalk
Beneath the deep, above it turns to stone.
    He then built three grass altars to three gods:
The left was Mercury's; yours, warlike maid,
The right; and Jove's between. In sacrifice,   755
Minerva gained a cow, the fleet-foot one
A calf, and you, the highmost god, a bull.
Then, for his pains, he wed Andromeda
Undowered, while Love and Hymen bore the brands.
Strong incense fed the fires, wreaths decked the eaves,   760
While lyre and flute song—proofs of happy hearts—
Rang round. The golden palace doors swung wide
To show a well-laid banquet, where the court
Of Cepheus joined in the royal feast.

[PERSEUS AND MEDUSA]†

Once fed, their hearts awash in Bacchic wine,   765
He asked the life and lineage of the place
And next the mien and manner of its race.   767†
So Cepheus enlightened Lynceus' heir,[17]   769
Then asked, "Pray tell, O mighty one, what craft,†   770
What courage let you seize the snake-haired head?"
Agenor's heir[18] then spoke of how the foot
Of frigid Atlas† held a rock-ribbed cave,
Whose mouth was home to Phorcys' daughters—twins
Who shared one eye.† While this they passed around,   775
He'd captured it with guile and sleight of hand,
And so, through long and pathless hidden ways
And jagged woods and bristling rocks, he reached
The Gorgons' land. Its fields and trails, he saw,
Were rife with forms of humans and of beasts   780
Who'd seen Medusa's face and turned to stone;
But, gazing in his left hand's shield, he watched
Her fearsome shape reflected in the bronze;
And while she and her snakes were dulled with sleep,
He ripped her head off. From their mother's blood,   785
Winged Pegasus and his swift brother† sprang.
    He spoke, too, of his travels' many trials—
All true—of straits and lands he'd seen on high,
And of the stars he'd touched on beating wings;
But when he finished, they still wanted more,   790
And one lord asked him then why she alone,
Of all the sisters, grew hair mixed with snakes.
"You seek a tale worth telling," said their guest.
"Now hear its cause! Her looks were famous once,
When she was many suitors' jealous hope,   795
And best of all her features was her hair—
A man who said he'd seen it told me so.
The sea lord raped her in Minerva's shrine,

17. Perseus, the great-great-grandson of Lynceus
18. Perseus, a ridiculously distant relative of Agenor

FIGURE 5. *Medusa*, Harriet Hosmer (c. 1854). Hosmer was the first female sculptor of international renown and among the first American artists to gain prominence in Europe. Neoclassical artists were drawn to the challenge of depicting the snake-haired Medusa, but Hosmer's sympathetic bust focuses instead on an earlier moment in Ovid's story, when the still beautiful girl is just beginning her metamorphosis into a monster.

It's said, while Jove's pure daughter hid her face
Behind her aegis. To punish the deed,   800
She made foul serpents of the Gorgon's hair.
And now, to strike her foes with fearsome dread,
Upon her breast, she wears these self-made snakes."†

Book 5

WHILE DANAË'S heroic son regaled
The Cephene crowd, a roaring rabble filled
The palace halls. These were no wedding guests:
Their shouts weren't songs, but cries of savage war!
At once, disruption overtook the feast—   5
Which you could liken to a sea whose calm
The raging wind whips into rolling waves—
Led by the rash warmonger Phineus,
Who shook his bronze-tipped spear of ash and said,
"I'm here—here to avenge my stolen bride!   10
No wings or Jove changed falsely into gold
Can save you from me now!" He poised to strike,
But Cepheus cried, "Brother! What is this?
 What ails you? Is this how you thank such feats?
The dowry you think fit for her saved life?   15
It wasn't Perseus, if truth you seek,
Who stole her, but the Nereids' dread lord,[1]
Horned Ammon, and the beast come to devour
Flesh of my flesh! You lost her *then*, when she
Was bound to die! Unless that's your cruel wish: 20

---

1. Neptune (cf. 4.670–71)

That, with her dead, you'd ease your grief with ours.
Her uncle and betrothed, you saw her chained
And brought no help—but now that someone has
You cry and steal his prize? If you desired
It so, you should have seized it[†] from the rocks!   25
Now let the man who did and saved my age
From childlessness bear off the spoils he gained
Through merit and my pledge—and know that he
Was not preferred to you, but certain death!"
    The foe made no reply, but looked from him   30
To Perseus, not knowing which to strike.
After a pause, with all the strength of wrath,
He hurled his spear—in vain—at Perseus,
And struck his chair. At last, fierce Perseus
Sprang up and sent it back to pierce his heart,   35
But Phineus had hidden himself where
(For shame!) an altar kept the sinner safe.
The spear still found some use in Rhoetus' head;
He slumped and, with its point wrenched from his skull,
Convulsed and sprayed the banquet spread with blood.   40
By now, the crowd burned wild with rage: spears flew,
And some said Cepheus deserved to die—
His son-in-law, too! Cepheus, though, fled
To swear by Law, Faith, and the gods of Guests,
That he was blameless. Warlike Pallas, then,   45
Came with her aegis to her brother's[2] aid
And gave him cheer.
              There was an Indian boy[†]
Named Athis, whom it's held the Ganges' child,
Limnaeë, bore beneath her crystal waves.
His peerless looks, still fresh at twice-eight years,   50
Were helped by fine attire: his Tyrian cloak
Was fringed with gold, gold chains adorned his neck,
And circlets held his hair, which dripped with myrrh.
An expert marksman with a far-flung lance,
He was more expert still in bending bows,   55

2. Minerva and Perseus are half-siblings, being children of Jupiter

As now he pulled the string, when Perseus,
Beside the altar, snatched a fuming stake
And smashed his features into splintered bones.
    On seeing his fabled face awash in blood,
Assyrian Lycabas—his dearest friend,   60
His comrade, and his true admitted love—
Lamented Athis, who breathed out his life
Through bitter wounds, and seized the bow he'd drawn.
"Your fight's with me!" he cried, "Nor shall you long
Gloat over this boy's death, which earns you more   65
Of hate than praise!" With this not even said,
He loosed a piercing arrow from the string,
But missed and struck his target's flowing robes.
The grandson of Acrisius then turned
And drove Medusa's death-blade in his chest.   70
But though his dying eyes swam black with night,
He looked around for Athis, fell his way,
And joined the shades, content to share his death.
    Then Phorbas of Aswan, Metion's son,
And Libyan Amphimedon came, keen   75
To fight; but slipping on the blood-soaked ground,
They fell and, rising, met a sword which cleaved
The latter's ribs and slit through Phorbas' throat.
On Actor's son, two-bit-axed Eurytus,
Did Perseus restrain his curving sword,   80
But, lifting up a huge and heavy bowl,
Embossed in high relief, with both his hands,
He launched it at the man, who gushed red blood
And hit his dying head upon the ground.
Semiramis' heir Polydaemon, too,   85
With long-haired Helix, Scythian Abaris,
Lycetus of Thessalia, Phlegyas,
And Clytus formed a mound of trampled dead.
    But Phineus dared not approach his foe
And flung a shaft at Idas by mistake,   90
Who'd vainly shunned the fray and backed no side.
He fixed cruel Phineus with hateful eyes;
"Since, Phineus, you've forced my choice," he said,

"Know I'm your foe—and suffer wound for wound!"
The spear, drawn from his side, would have flung back,   95
Had not his bloodless limbs then buckled down.
    Hodites, the chief Cephene (save the king)
Next fell to Clymenus, while Hypseus, who
Killed Prothoënor, fell to Lynceus' heir.
There, too, was old and just Emathion,   100
Who feared the gods and, being too old to fight,
Came armed with words and damned their wicked strife,
Then, shaking, gripped the shrine. There, Chromis' sword
Sliced off his head into the altar fires,
Where his half-living tongue still spoke its curse   105
As he expired in flames. A pair of twins,
Named Broteas and Ammon, boxers both,
Would have prevailed, if one could box with swords:
Like Ceres' priest, white-ribboned Ampycus,
They fell before the hand of Phineus.   110
    You too, Lampetides,[†] not meant for this
But for the peacetime task of lyric verse,
Were present, called to sing before the feast.
He stood aside, his peaceful pick in hand,
When Paetalus laughed, "Sing the rest in Hell!"   115
And speared him on the left side of his head;
Yet as he sank, his dying hands still strove
To strum his lyre and struck a wretched chord.
But fierce Lycormas would avenge his death:
He seized an oaken crossbar from the door   120
And crushed the killer's neck as, to the ground,
The man fell like a bullock sacrificed.
Cinyphian Pelates then tried to take
The other oaken bar, but Corythus
Of Carthage fixed his hand there with a spear;   125
Then Abas gouged his side, but he stayed up,
And died there with his hand pinned to the post.
    Next Melaneus died for Perseus,
Like Dorylas, the wealthiest of all
The Nasamones—Dorylas, whose wealth   130
In land and stores of grain was unsurpassed,

And whom a sidelong spear ran through the loins
(A lethal spot). The man who dealt the wound
And watched his dying gasps and rolling eyes
Was Bactrian Halcyoneus, who said,   135
"Of all thy lands, keep this where thou dost lie!"
And left his corpse. But vengeful Perseus
Drove back the spear, torn from the seething wound,
Through nose and neck to jut out on both sides.

   With Fortune's help, Clanis and Clytius,   140
Born from one mother, died of different wounds:
With one fell throw, an ashwood shaft pierced both
Of Clytius' thighs, while Clanis ate a spear.
With Celadon of Mendes, Astreus died
(His mother Syrian, sire unknown); and wise   145
Aethion, once a seer, but whose sight
Now failed; and, with Thoactes, the king's squire,
Agyrtes, infamous for parricide.[†]

   Still more were left than dead, for all were of
A mind against the hero. Joined as one,   150
The hostile host opposed his worth and word.
His bride, her mother, and her useless sire
Took his side, staunchly screaming through the halls,
But arms and groans rang louder as, in blood,
Bellona[†] soaked and soiled their household gods,   155
And kept the battle fresh. With Phineus,
A thousand Phineans surrounded him.
More plentiful than winter hail, their spears
Flew past his sides and round his eyes and ears.
Against a great stone column, he stood braced   160
And, with his back safe, turned to meet the charge.
Chaonian Molpeus charged him from the left,
Arabian Echemmon from the right.
Then, like a starving tigress hearing herds
In separate valleys, who cannot decide   165
On which to rush but longs to rush on both,
So, striking left or right, paused Perseus.
Then, halting Molpeus with a wounded leg,
He would have spared him, but Echemmon left

No time for thought but dashed to strike his neck,   170
And stabbed with willful strength but such poor aim
The sword blade broke against the column's edge
And, leaping back, lodged in its owner's throat.
While this blow was not deadly, as he reached
In vain, his bare hands trembling, Perseus   175
Ran through him with Cyllenius' curving sword.
   But Perseus, seeing that the throngs would crush
His might, cried, "Since you force me, I shall seek
Help from a foe. If any friends be here,
Avert your eyes!" and raised the Gorgon's head.   180
"Find someone else to scare with miracles!"
Said Thescelus, his death-spear poised to throw—
And, as a marble block, he held that pose.
Next, Ampyx sought the full and great-souled heart
Of Lynceus' heir at sword-point, but his hand   185
Grew stiff and could seek neither here nor there.
Then Nileus, the sevenfold Nile's son—
Or so he claimed to be—whose shield displayed
Those seven streams in silver and in gold,
Cried, "Perseus, see of what stock I'm sprung!   190
You'll bear this comfort to the silent shades,
That such a man has slain you—" His speech stopped
Midsentence, so you'd think the open mouth
Was speaking still, but words had lost their way.
"It's your weak hearts," cried Eryx, in reproach,   195
"That hold you, not the Gorgon's power: let's charge
And hurl him and his magic to the ground!"
He started in—earth stopped him in his tracks
Where he remained, a still and armored rock.
   These men deserved their punishments, but one   200
Aconteus, who fought for Perseus,
Glanced at the Gorgon and was shod with stone.
Astyages, though, thought him still alive,
And swung his sword, which rang out loud and sharp.
While dazed, Astyages was likewise struck,   205
A look of wonder on his marble face.
The common ranks would take too long to name:

After the fight, two hundred men survived;
The Gorgon saw two hundred petrified.
　Now Phineus regrets his unjust war,   210
But what to do? He sees the sculpted lot,
He knows them, calls their names, asks them for help,
And, scarce believing, touches those nearby:
All marble! Turned aside, he reaches out
In sideways supplication and defeat: 215
"You win! That petrifying *thing* of yours,
Medusa's face—whoever she is—take,
Take it away! Please, Perseus! We fought
For neither hate nor throne, but for a bride.
Your deeds have proved your claim, though mine came first: 220
I feel no shame to yield. Grant naught to me,
O brave one, but my life—the rest is thine!"
He spoke, but dared not face the man he begged.
"O meek one, what I'll grant," said Perseus,
"I'll grant: a giant gift for one so weak.   225
No sword shall harm you. (Put your fears aside.)
I'll make you last for ages: in the house
Of my father-in-law you shall be seen
And cheer my wife with her intended's face!"
This said, he held out Phorcys' daughter's head   230
Where Phineus had turned his fearful face.
Then, even as he tried to look away,
His neck and streaming tears hardened to stone.
In marble, his meek supplicating face,
Defeated hands, and lowly look live on.   235

[PROETUS AND POLYDECTES]†

　In triumph, Abas' heir marched with his bride
Home to avenge his mother's worthless sire,
Acrisius, whom Proetus had expelled
Through force of arms to seize his citadel.
But neither arms nor ill-gained citadel   240
Outmatched the snake-haired monster's awful eyes.
　Lord Polydectes of small Seriphos,

You, too, for all his strength, his feats and toils,
Were still not softened, but grew hard with hate
And tireless in your endless, groundless wrath.   245
Rejecting, too, his glory, you declared
Medusa's death a lie. "We'll give you proof,"
Said Perseus, "Don't look!"[†] Then, face to face,
Medusa changed the king to bloodless stone.

[PYRENEUS AND THE MUSES][†]

Till now, Tritonia[3] had accompanied   250
Her gold-born brother. Now, from Seriphos,
She rode her clouds past Cythnus, Gyaros' isle,
And by the shortest sea-route made for Thebes
And maiden Helicon, upon whose peak
She gave the learnèd sisterhood this speech: 255
"A tale has reached my ears of some new spring
Medusa's wingèd child sprang from his hoof.[†]
I've come this way to see that wondrous sight;
Himself I saw born from his mother's blood."
Urania[4] answered her: "Whatever cause   260
Brings you here, goddess, our home welcomes you!
It's quite true: Pegasus produced a spring."
And she led Pallas to the sacred font.
    She marveled long before the hoof-struck waves,
Then, gazing round their groves of ancient trees   265
And caves and grasses graced with countless flowers,
She called Mnemone's daughters[5] doubly blessed
In how and where they lived. One answered her,
"O great Tritonia, who might join our band
Were not your virtue bound for better things,   270
In truth you've rightly praised our arts and home;
Our lot is happy—were we only safe!
But our chaste minds fear all (crime being so rife)

3. Minerva, born near Lake Triton
4. Muse of astronomy
5. The Muses, daughters of Mnemo(sy)ne, goddess of memory

And vile Pyreneus sticks in my mind's eye,
For I have yet to recollect myself.   275
    "That fiend seized Daulis and the Phocian wilds
With men from Thrace, then ruled his wrongful realm,
And, seeing us heading for Parnassus' shrine,
Feigned worship for our godliness, and said,
'Mnemone's daughters, stay!' (He'd heard of us.)   280
'Don't wait, come shelter from the sky and rain'—
(It rained)—'with me. The gods have often stayed
In humbler homes!' The weather and his words
Gained our assent and brought us to his house.
The rain soon ceased; with Auster vanquished by   285
Aquilo and dark clouds cleared from the sky,
We made to leave. Pyreneus locked his doors
And threatened force, but we donned wings and fled.
As if in chase, he climbed his ramparts' height
And cried, 'What path you take, I'll take the same!'   290
Then leapt in madness from the rooftop tower.
Face-first he tumbled, shattering his skull,
And, dying, tinged the soil with sinful blood—"

[THE PIERIDES, PART 1][†]

    But while the Muse spoke, flapping filled the air,
And greetings came, voiced in the boughs above.   295
In search of such a clearly talking tongue,
Jove's daughter thought a human speaker spoke
But saw a bird! For there, bewailing fate,
Sat nine true-mimic magpies in the trees.
Said goddess to awed goddess: "In defeat,   300
These creatures lately joined the ranks of birds.
Rich Pierus fathered them in Pellan lands
On Paeonian Euippe, who invoked
Lucina's[6] guidance nine times in nine births.
Their numbers puffed the senseless sisters' pride,   305
And all through Greece and all of Thessaly,

6. Goddess of childbirth

They journeyed to wage war on us through song.
'Spare artless crowds your hollow charms!' they cried.
'If you're so self-assured, come vie with us,
O Thespian powers![7] Though matched in count, we'll win   310
In song and skill. If you should lose, you'll yield
Medusa's font and Aganippe[8] of
Boeotia; or we'll yield Emathia's plains
Up to Paeonia's snows. The nymphs shall judge!'
   "Shame though it was to vie with them, it seemed   315
More shame to yield. Sworn in upon the streams,
The chosen nymphs took seats in living rock.
With lots undrawn,[†] our challenger began
To sing of gods at war, and wrongly praised
The Giants while debasing godly acts: 320
She told how Typhon, sprung from deep in Earth,
Shook heaven with fear and put the gods to flight
Till Egypt and the seven-channeled Nile
Received them, sapped of strength; and how the gods,
When Earth-born Typhon chased them even there,   325
Took lying forms: 'Jove's ram disguise,' she said,[†]
'Is why the Libyans show Ammon horned.
The son of Semele turned goat. A cat
Was Phoebe's mask; the Delian's was a crow;
Saturnia's, a white cow. Cyllenius hid   330
Inside an ibis, Venus in a fish.'
   "Here ceased her singing to the lute, and we
Aonian maids were called—but have you time
And would our song give pleasure to your ears?"
"Of course," said Pallas, "let me hear it all!"   335
And sat down in the forest's gentle shade.
The Muse said: "We chose one to fight for us,
And with her flowing hair in ivy bands,
Calliope[9] rose, thumbed her plaintive strings,
And, with a forceful chord, began this song: 340

---

7. The Muses; pertaining not to acting but to the nearby village of Thespiae
8. Another spring on Mount Helicon, with similar powers
9. Appropriately, the Muse of epic poetry

[THE RAPE OF PROSERPINE]†

"'The first to split the soil was Ceres' plough!
She first gave lands their ripened food and fruit!
She first gave laws! All things are Ceres' gift!
Of her, then, I must sing—if only I
Could sing her worth, who's surely worth a song. . . .   345
    "'Atop the Giant's limbs lay heaped the vast
Three-cornered isle,[10] beneath whose massive weight
Sprawled Typhon—he who'd dared to seek the skies.
And though he strained to rise, Ausonia's capes†
Pelorus and Pachynus held his hands   350
While Lilybaeum bound his legs. His head
Was crushed by Aetna, through which, on his back,
Fierce Typhon spews forth sand and vomits flame.
He often tries to fight his earthen weights
And roll the towns and mountains from his frame.   355
Then earth quakes, and the king of silent shades
Fears lest the ground crack open to reveal
His trembling spirits to the light of day.
    "'The darkling lord† once, dreading this event,
Rode forth his chariot, drawn by sable steeds,   360
And surveyed all of Sicily's supports,
Till, pleased that all was sound, he shed his fear.
But on her mountain, Erycina[11] saw
Him wandering and embraced her wingèd son.
"My arms and hands, my might—my son," she said,   365
"With those swift shafts you use to conquer all,
Now, Cupid, strike the heartstrings of the god
Allotted but the last of three domains.†
You rule the gods, the spirits of the sea,
Jove, and the god of spirits of the sea: 370
So why not Hell? Why not expand our realm,
Mother and son? It's one third of the world!
And yet, in heaven (as we have long endured)

---

10. Sicily
11. Venus, worshiped in Sicily on Mount Eryx

We're scorned: Love's forces dwindle with my own.
You've seen how Pallas and the markswoman   375
Diana shun me! Ceres' daughter, too,
Will stay a virgin, if we let her hope!
But if you care for our shared realm, unite
The goddess and her uncle!" Venus said.
So, from his quiver, as his mother wished,   380
He chose, out of his thousand darts, the one
Most sharp and sure and heedful of the bow,
Bent back the pliant wood across his knee,
And drove its spike into the heart of Dis.
    "'Not far from Henna's walls is a deep lake   385
Called Pergus, which hears more from singing swans
Than even the Caÿster's coursing waves.†
Woods crown the waters, ringing each side round
With screening leaves to ward off Phoebus' rays
And cool the boughs so moisture flowers the earth   390
With endless spring. In this grove, Proserpine
Played, picking lilies, or else violets,
And while, in girlish zeal, she stuffed her clothes
And baskets, vying to out-pick her friends,
Dis saw, adored, and seized her all at once: 395
So quick was love! The goddess, sad and scared,
Called for her friends and mother—mother more—
And since she'd torn her clothes up at the top,
Her sagging dress let fall her gathered flowers.
So innocent was she, and young in years,   400
That still, at such a time, this gave her grief.
Her captor sped his chariot and spurred
The steeds by name, then tugged their necks and manes
With rust-stained reins, to bear her through deep tarns,
And the Palici's sulphurous pools,† which boil   405
Up through the ground, and where the Bacchiads
From Corinth of two seas set city walls
Between twin harbors of unequal size.
    "'With Pisan Arethusa, Cyane
Surrounds a bay there, bound by narrow capes,   410
And there lived Cyane, for whom the pool

Is named, the best-known nymph in Sicily.†
Waist-high amid the flood, she recognized
The goddess and said, "Stop there, both of you!
You can't be Ceres' son-in-law by force: 415
You need rapport, not rape! For, if I may
Mix great with small, Anapis loved me, too;
But pleas—not panic, like hers—made me wed!"
This said, she reached both arms to block his path,
Yet Saturn's son restrained his wrath no more   420
But spurred his awful steeds as his strong arm
Cast down his royal scepter to the depths;
The earth, where stricken, cleared a path to Hell,
And in the crater plunged his chariot!
    "'At seeing the goddess raped and fountain's rights   425
Rejected, Cyane despaired and nursed
Her silent wound till she dissolved in tears.
In waves where she had been a mighty god,
The maiden melted. You'd have seen her limbs
Grow soft, her bones turn pliant, and her nails   430
Lay stiffness by. Her thinnest parts thawed first:
The sea-green hair, the fingers, legs, and feet
(For it's a minor change from meager limbs
To icy waves). Next, shoulders, back, and sides
And chest all vanished in the shallow streams.   435
At last, in place of blood, her breaking veins
Ran clear till naught was left that you could touch.
    "'The frightened mother, meanwhile, vainly sought
Her child through every land and every deep,
Nor rose the dew-haired Dawn or Evening-Star   440
To find her resting. Bearing in each hand
A torch of pinewood lit in Aetna's fires,
She wandered restless through the night's cold shades;
And still, when kindly day snuffed out the stars,
She sought her daughter, sunrise to sunset.   445
Worn down with toil and thirst, her face unwashed
By springs, she chanced to spy a straw-roofed house
And battered its small doors. A hag appeared,
Beheld the goddess and, when asked for drinks,

Brought her sweet draughts with toasted barley flakes.   450
But while she drank, a cheeky coarse-tongued boy
Stood by and mocked the goddess for her "greed."
The goddess, slighted, splashed his speaking face
With her unfinished drink, barley and all!
His face soaked up the flakes, arms changed to legs,   455
And, as a tail joined these mutating limbs,
He shrank till he had no more strength to harm
Into a lizard's form, but smaller still.
And when, with awe and tears, the hag reached out
The creature fled and hid. Its naming fits   460
Its shaming, for the gecko's flecked with specks.[†]
    "'To tell what lands and seas the goddess roamed
Would take too long. She scoured the globe in vain,
Returned to Sicily, and, searching still,
Found Cyane, who, were she not transformed,   465
Would have told all and wished to, but she had
No lips nor tongue nor aught with which to speak.
But still she gave a clear, familiar sign:[†]
Where it had chanced to fall, her holy waves
Displayed the girdle of Persephone.   470
On sight, the goddess tore her hair as though
She'd learned of the abduction only then,
And beat her breast with countless brutal blows.
Still clueless where she'd gone, she cursed all lands
As unfit ingrates for her gifts of grain—   475
And chiefly Sicily, to which she'd traced
Her loss. Enraged, she cruelly smashed the ploughs
That tilled the earth, and dealt to death alike
The farmers and their cattle, bade the fields
Betray their plants, and made their seeds go wrong.   480
The land's fertility—famed round the world—
Lay shattered: crops died young as early shoots,
Destroyed by too much sun or too much rain,
The stars and winds turned toxic, hungry birds
Pecked up the scattered seeds, and grain was lost   485
In cockles, tackweed, and unyielding grass.
    "'Then Alpheus' nymph rose from her Elean waves,[†]

Wiped ears and forehead free of hair, and said,
"O mother of the maiden sought worldwide
And of all grains, leave off your boundless toils   490
And unearned rage against your loyal lands,
Which spread wide for the rape against their will,
Like this land, for whom I, a stranger, plead.
My home is Pisa.[12] Born of Elean stock,
I dwell in foreign Sicily, the land   495
I love the most, where, with my household gods,
I, Arethusa, live upon this spot—
O gentlest one, please save it! Why I moved
Here to Ortygia's[13] bay across such seas
I'll tell some better time, when cares are light   500
And you're of brighter face. The pathless earth
Conveyed me through its hollow depths to here,
Where I looked up and saw the long-lost stars.
But while I drifted past the sunken Styx,
I spotted Proserpine with my own eyes: 505
How sad she looked, and not yet free of fear—
But she's a queen! She reigns in that dark world,
The mighty consort to the king of Hell!"
        "'The mother heard these words in stony awe,
And long stood stunned. But once great shock gave way   510
To great despair, she rode her chariot
To heaven, where she stood wrathful before Jove
With clouded face and streaming hair and said,
"I beg you, Jupiter, to aid my blood
And yours! If motherhood means nothing, may   515
Your daughter move her sire. Nor let your care
For her be less, I pray, since she is mine
When, look—my long-sought daughter's found at last,
If you call 'finding' to more surely lose,
Or 'find' out where she is. Rape I can bear,   520
So long as she's returned, but no thief can
Deserve to wed *your* child, if she's not mine."

---

12. A village in the Greek region of Elis, not the Tuscan town known for its tower
13. An island in the bay of Syracuse

And Jove replied, "She is our charge and care,
My child and yours. Yet if we give affairs
Their proper names, no harm's been done: it's love!   525
Nor will he bring us shame as son-in-law—
With your divine consent. All else may lack:
He is Jove's brother, though he lacks all else,
And yields to me by lot! But if you wish
Them parted, Proserpine shall come to heaven   530
On one condition: no food there may pass
Her lips," he said, "for so the Fates decree!"
    "'But Ceres was resolved to have her child.
Not so the Fates: by then the maiden's fast
Was broken! Through the garden grounds the fool   535
Had roamed and plucked a branch's crimson fruit,
From whose pale rind she'd taken seven seeds
And chewed them down. The only witness was
Ascalaphus, whom Orphne, it is said—
Not the least famous of Avernal nymphs†—   540
Once bore to Acheron in groves of gloom.
Her flight stopped by his cruel report, Hell's queen
Groaned and transformed him to an unclean fowl:
She splashed the Phlegethon into his face,
Which grew a beak and feathers and great eyes.   545
Robbed of himself and cloaked in tawny wings,
He grew into a head with long bent claws,
And scarcely stirred the plumes of his dull arms.
He had become a vile ill-omened bird:
A lowly owl, portending mortal woe.   550
    "'Though his tongue's tattling may have earned his fate,
Why do you, Acheloüs' daughters, bear
Both birdlike feathered feet and girlish looks?
Is it because you went with Proserpine
To pick spring flowers, O Sirens skilled in song?¹   555
As soon as you had scoured the lands in vain,
You wished to bring your efforts to the sea
And prayed to sail the waves with wings for oars;
You found the gods receptive and beheld
Your bodies sheathed in sudden plumes of gold.   560

But lest your songs so soothing to the ears,
Those inborn gifts of lips and voice, be lost,
Your maiden looks and human voice remained.
    "'Between his brother's loss and sister's grief,
Jove, out of fairness, split the rolling year,   565
So now, a goddess shared between two realms,
She spends half with her mother, half her spouse.
At once, her look and outlook were transformed,
For she, who'd late seemed sad to Dis himself,
Beamed brightly as the sun which, cloaked in mist   570
And clouds, breaks through the cloud-cover to shine!

[ARETHUSA]†

    "'Kind Ceres, with her daughter safely home,
Asked Arethusa why she'd fled, and how
She was a sacred spring. From silent depths,
The goddess rose, dried her green locks, and spoke   575
About the Elean river's¹⁴ former love.
"I once was one of those Achaean nymphs,"†
She said, "the keenest one of all to traipse
The glades; the keenest one of all with traps.
But though I sought no fame for being fair,   580
And though I'm fearless, fairness made my name.
Nor did I profit by my too-praised face,
For beauty, which cheers some girls, made me blush
In rustic shame: I thought it wrong to please.
    ""'Returning tired from the Stymphalian woods   585
(As I recall), the swelter twinned by toil,
I found an unwhirled stream whose soundless flows
Shone clear, straight down to where each pebble might
Be tallied up, so still they'd seem to you.
The waves fed poplars and white willow trees,   590
Which freely gave the sloping banks their shade.
Approaching, I first dipped my feet, then sank
Up to my knees. Not satisfied, I stripped,

14. Alpheus

Hung my soft garments on a willow branch,
And plunged in naked. While I splashed and sprayed   595
And dove and threw my arms a thousand ways,
I heard a sound from deep within the pool,
And leapt in terror for the spring's near bank.
'Why hurry, Arethusa?' said the waves;
'Why hurry so?' rasped Alpheus once again.   600
I fled him as I was—disrobed (my robes
Were on the other bank); he raced and burned
The more since, naked, I seemed ripe for him.
So I ran, so did he in hot pursuit—
As doves will flee a hawk on shaking wings;   605
As hawks will give pursuit to shaking doves—
Past Psophis, Elis, and Mount Maenalus,
Cold Erymanthus and Orchomenos,
And Mount Cyllene, nor was I outsped.†
Though I, outstripped in strength, could not run long,   610
While he could bear a longer trial, still on
Through plains, through mountains thick with trees,
And rocks and cliffs and pathless wilds, I ran.
The sun was at my back; ahead, I saw
His shadow gaining—or else my fear did.   615
But certainly I heard his frightful steps,
And felt him panting on my braided hair.
Worn out, I cried, 'Bring aid or I'll be caught!
Diana, help your squiress, whom you gave
Your bow and arrowed quiver countless times!'   620
    """The goddess, moved, cast down a heavy cloud
On me alone. The stream surveyed the gloom
And searched the hollow cloud unknowingly;
He twice passed where she hid me, unawares,
Twice 'Arethusa! Arethusa!' called.   625
How was I then to feel? Not wretched as
A lamb that hears wolves howling round its fold?
Not like a briar-hidden hare, who spies
A dog pack's fatal fangs and dares not move?
Nor did he leave (for he observed my tracks   630
Did not go on), but watched the cloud and place.

Then, as cold sweat possessed my cornered limbs,
My body rained blue drops, my footprints pooled,
My hair rained dew, and faster than I now
Can tell, I turned to water. But the stream   635
Saw his desired's waves, shed his male disguise,
And mixed his flows with mine to mix with me.
At this, the Delian[15] split apart the earth,
Through whose dark depths she bore me to the isle
Ortygia, named for her,[16] and which I love,   640
Since it first brought me back the air above."

[LYNCUS AND TRIPTOLEMUS][†]

"'Thus, Arethusa. The grain-goddess then
Hitched up her chariot, harnessed its two snakes,
And steered between the earth and sky to reach
Tritonia's city[17] and Triptolemus,   645
To whom she gave her coach, seeds, and command
To plant some in uncultivated soil,
And some in fallow fields, now farmed anew.
Past Europe and all Asia soared the youth
To Scythia's royal house where Lyncus reigned.   650
Asked why and how he'd come, his name and home,
He answered, "Far-famed Athens is my home,
My name Triptolemus. My path was not
By ship and sea nor foot and land, but air.
I bear the gifts of Ceres, which, if sown   655
In your broad lands, will bring ripe food and fruit!"[†]
The jealous savage, that he might himself
Give such a gift, received the guest, then stabbed
Him in his sleep; but Ceres, as he tried
To pierce his heart, made him a lynx and bade   660
The Mopsian youth return her sainted team.'[†]

15. Diana, born on Delos
16. Ortygia was an ancient name for Delos, birthplace of Diana
17. Athens, sacred to Minerva

[THE PIERIDES, PART 2]

"Here ceased our foremost sister's skillful song;
As one, the nymphs announced the goddesses
Of Helicon had won. The losers jeered,
So she replied, 'You've earned small punishment   665
In contest and add insult to your crimes,
So since our patience is not limitless,
We'll punish you and follow anger's lead!'
    "Then the Emathians[18] laughed and scorned her threats,
But as they tried to speak and cry aloud   670
And shake their shameless fists, they saw their nails
Sprout plumes while feathers spread across their arms;
Each watched another's face fuse in a beak,
Then joined the forests as a strange new bird.
Beating their breasts, they rose on flapping arms,   675
And hung there—magpies, windbags of the woods.
Now, too, the birds' old prattle still persists
In their hoarse chat and boundless will to speak."†

---

18. The daughters of Pierus, associated with Emathia at 5.313

Book 6

TRITONIA HEARD these words with full support
For the Aonians'¹ songs and righteous rage,
But thought, "To praise is one thing—to be praised
Will save our might from being so lightly spurned!"
    Her mind then hatched the fate of Lydian   5
Arachne, said to match her fame in wool,
And not through birth or birthplace—only skill!
By trade her sire, Idmon of Colophon,
Dyed Phocian purple wool. His wife was dead.
But though his orphaned daughter and her spouse   10
Were low-born, through all Lydia, her craft
Had gained renown, despite her start in life:
A humble home in humble Hypaepa.
At times, to see her wondrous work, the nymphs
Would quit Timolus' dens, while still more nymphs   15
Would quit Pactolus' waves—for it brought joy
To see the clothes she'd made, as well as those
Still in the making: so great was her style!
To see her form fresh balls from unspun yarn,
Or mold them in her hands, or soften out   20

---

1. The Muses

The fleecy cloud-like threads time after time,
Or thumb the spindle round, or simply weave,
You'd know that Pallas must have trained the girl.†
   But she denied such mentorship and said,
"Let her compete with me: I'll stake my all!"   25
So Pallas, in a grey-wigged hag's disguise,
Her feeble body leaning on a cane,
Unspooled this speech: "Old age is not all bad,
Since years bring wisdom! Heed my warnings, then,
For you may seek the utmost mortal fame   30
In woolens—but before a goddess, yield!
And humbly ask her pardon for these words,
So rashly said: she'll pardon you if asked!"
Her threads half-spun, the girl rose, glaring back
With scarce-stayed hands and open looks of rage,   35
And made the hidden Pallas this reply:
"Your mind is senile and decayed with age
From too-long life! If you have any girls
Or daughters-in-law, make them hear you talk—
I can advise myself! And lest you think   40
Your words have swayed me, know we're of a mind:
Why *won't* she come? Why *does* she flee a fight—?"
   "She's come!" the goddess cries, and sheds her guise,
Revealing Pallas, to whom all the nymphs
And Phrygian girls but her kneel down in fear.   45
Still, she turns red; her cheeks blush suddenly
As if by force, then fade, much as the sky,
Although grown rosy with the Dawn's first steps,
Soon pales to white before the rising sun.
Persistent in her fool's quest for the prize,   50
She hurls toward doom. Nor does Jove's daughter more
Decline, dissuade, or else delay their fight.
   At once, both stand their looms on either side
And stretch a slender warp across the frames;
Bound to the beam, the threads are split with rods,   55
While sharpened shuttles weave the weft between,
Pulled by their fingers; once run through the warp,
The weft is tapped down with a reed-comb's teeth.

They work in haste, their clothes hitched round their chests;
Arms soar with skill and zeal relieves their toil.   60
Through purples dyed in Tyrian vats, they weave
An imperceptible array of shades
Which look as sunlight does when struck with rain
And all the sky is painted in a bow,
The length of which shines in a thousand hues   65
To trick discerning eyes: how similar
The tints are, yet how distant the extremes!
There, too, they inlay strings of rigid gold
That weave into the weft an ancient tale.
    First, Pallas shows the Areopagus   70
In Cecrops' city, and the ancient fight
To name that land.† Round Jove, august† and grave,
The twice-six gods are sat in lofty thrones.
She captures each one's face: Jove looks a king;
The sea-god stands with his long trident thrust   75
Against a stone, whose stony crack spurts forth
A salty stream in token of his claim;
She gives herself a shield, sharp-pointed spear,
And helmet, while the aegis guards her chest.
Struck by her spear, the earth is seen to sprout   80
An olive tree replete with pale-green fruit,
Which awes the gods as Victory ends the work.
    Then, as examples to her challenger
Of what prized praise awaits her reckless risks,
She sets four contests in the corners four,†   85
Bright miniatures with palettes of their own:
The first holds Haemus and Queen Rhodope
Of Thrace—now icy peaks, but humans once,
Who called each other by the names of gods.
Next comes a Pygmy mother's wretched fate,   90
As Juno wins their contest and enjoins
Her, as a crane, to war on her own tribe.
Then, she depicts Antigone, who dared
Oppose Jove's consort till queen Juno turned
Her to a bird. Neither Laömedon,   95
Her sire, nor Troy could help; no, winged in white,

The stork clatters its bill in self-applause.
In the last corner, childless Cinyras
Enfolds his daughters' limbs, now temple steps,
And, lying on the stones, is seen to weep.   100
With peaceful olive leaves (to make an end),
She frames the work, concluding with her tree.
　　The Lydian likewise wove† the bull disguise
That tricked Europa. Seeing that sea and bull,
You'd think that they were real; the girl, too, seems   105
To see the land she's left, call to her friends,
And lift her feet for fear of leaping waves.
She shows Asteria in the eagle's grasp;
She shows the swan with Leda in his wings;
How as a satyr, Jove filled Nycteus' child   110
With twins; and, as Amphitryon, caught you,
Tirynthian wife; and Danaë as gold;
Asopus' child as flame; Mnemosyne,
A shepherd; Deo's child, a spotted snake.
　　She drew you, Neptune,† with Aeolus' girl,   115
In bull form; and how, as Enipeus,
You sired the Aloads; and, as a ram,
You tricked Bisaltes' child; how, as a steed,
The crops' kind corn-haired mother knew your force;
The winged steed's snake-haired mother knew your wings;   120
And how Melantho knew your dolphin ways.
To each she gave their proper face and place.
　　Next† Phoebus: here a peasant, now a hawk,
And now in lion's skin. His shepherd guise
Tricks Macar's daughter Isse; Liber's grapes   125
Deceive Erigone; and Saturn sires
Twinned Chiron as a horse. To end the weave,
She spins a braided fringe of vines and flowers.
　　Neither could Pallas nor could Spite itself
Fault her success. Enraged, the warlike blonde   130
Tore up the painted cloths, those heavenly crimes,
And, with her shuttle of Cytoran box,
So beat Arachne's brow three times and more
The wretch broke down and proudly hanged herself.

In pity, Pallas raised her where she hung,   135
And said, "Live! but keep hanging, wicked girl,
And banish hope, for this same punishment
Shall plague thy kind for all posterity!"
Then, as she left, she sprayed an herbal sap
Of Hecate's;† on contact, this dire drug   140
Removed the girl's hair, nose, and ears, and shrank
Her head and all her frame, while to her sides
Her slender fingers stuck in place as legs.
The rest was stomach, from which spun a thread,
And so the spider weaves its former web.   145

[NIOBE]†

All Lydia rumbled as the rumor ran
Through Phrygia's towns and filled the world with talk.
Niobe, when unwed, had met the girl,
While living close on Phrygian Sipylus.†
For all Arachne's fate, her neighbor still   150
Would not yield to the gods with humbled speech.
Much made her proud—her husband's art, their blood,
Their kingdom's power—but (though these pleased her well)
Her children pleased her more. She'd have been called
The happiest of mothers, but for that   155
Niobe had appeared so to herself.
    For Manto, daughter of Tiresias,
Had strode the streets, a seer moved by heaven
To cry out, "Wives of Thebes, in laureled throngs,
Go to Latona and Latona's twins   160
And give them pious prayers and frankincense:
Latona rules my tongue!" Obeying her,
The wives of Thebes, with temples duly wreathed,
Presented prayers and incense for the flames.
And there, ahead a crowd, Niobe came,   165
Distinct in Phrygian robes inlaid with gold,
And fair as wrath allowed. Her flowing hair
Cast down her shoulders with a graceful toss,
She reared up, looked round haughtily, and said,

"What madman would prefer these rumored gods   170
To those you've seen! Why throng Latona's shrines,
When my divinity lacks incense still?
My sire was Tantalus,† the only man
To dine in heaven; my aunts, the Pleiades;
My grandsires, Atlas whose neck holds the sky,   175
And Jove, who is my husband's sire as well!
The Phrygians fear me. As the Cadmeian queen,
Those peoples and the walls my husband's lyre
Once built† are ruled by us as man and wife.
Within our house, wherever my eyes fall,   180
I see great wealth! Besides, my looks befit
A goddess, and what's more, I've seven girls
And seven boys—with in-laws on the way!
First ask what's caused our pride, then dare prefer
That child of Coeus, whoever he was,   185
The Titaness Latona, whom all lands
Refused a scrap of ground to birth a child.
Earth, sea, and sky all forced your goddess out,
A cosmic outcast, till one pitied her
And said, 'You roam strange lands; I roam the sea!'   190
And so, on floating Delos,† she bore twins,
One seventh of the output of my womb!
      "I'm blessed—who would deny it? Blessed I'll stay!
My safety lies in numbers—who'd doubt that?
I am too great for Fortune's powers to harm;   195
Much as she takes from me, she'll leave much more.
My blessings transcend fear, for if some part
Of my brood should be lost, they'd never be
Reduced to only two, Latona's haul.
She's close to childlessness! Now go and leave   200
These rites undone—and lose those laurel wreaths!"
The wives obeyed and left the undone rites,
Yet worshiped how they could: with whispered words.
      On Cynthus' peak, the slighted goddess raged
Before her twins: "Your mother, who was proud   205
To give you birth, and who—spare Juno—yields
To none, has had her godhood questioned! Help,

My children, or my worship shall be banned
For all time! Nor is this my only pain:
The child of Tantalus, to swell her sins   210
With slanders, dares set her babes over mine,
And calls me *childless*—may the curse fall back
On her, who's shown she has her father's tongue!"
Her story told, Latona would have begged:
"Cease!" Phoebus said. "Your litany forestalls   215
Our vengeance!" Phoebe said the same. And so,
They soared in clouds to Cadmus' citadel.
    Before its walls, there lay an open plain
Where horses stamped their stony hooves, and wheels
Crushed through the clods beneath. Astride their mounts   220
Caparisoned in Tyrian red, there rode
Two of Amphion's seven stalwart sons,
Who steered their steeds with heavy golden reins.
Ismenus, the first load his mother bore,
Led his four-leggèd charger round the course,   225
But as he tugged its foaming mouth, he cried,
"Ah, me!"—for then an arrow pierced his heart.
As he slid slowly down, his dying hands
Let fall the reins across the steed's right side.
At that, a quiver's rattle split the air   230
And Sipylus gave rein, like helmsmen who,
Foreseeing a gale, will flee the hanging clouds,
And give full sail, lest any breeze be missed;
So he gave rein, but the unyielding dart
Gave chase, caught up, stuck quivering in his neck,   235
And stood, its point protruding from his throat.
Prone as he was, he tumbled past the mane
And pounding hooves to warm the earth with blood.
Unlucky Phaedimus and Tantalus,
Named for his grandfather, their tasks complete,   240
Switched to the oiled-up exercise of youths.
And now they wrestled, struggling in embrace,
Pressed breast to breast, when from a tight-drawn string
An arrow ran them through, joined as they were.
They groaned as one; as one, they arched in pain   245

Upon the ground; as one, they rolled their eyes
And lay there till, as one, they breathed their last.
Alphenor saw them, clawed his chest and ran
To lift their cooling bodies in his arms.
In this duty he died: the Delian god   250
Sliced through his torso with a fatal blade;
Withdrawn, its spikes drew out a bit of lung,
So life and blood went spurting through the air.
But unshorn Damasichthon suffered more
Than one wound: in the fleshy spot above   255
His shin, he took an arrow to the knee,
And while he tried to free the deadly dart,
Another sank its fletching in his throat.
His blood expelled the arrow, bursting high
In a far-flinging stream that slit the air.   260
Last, Ilioneus came with arms outstretched
In pointless prayer. "O all ye gods!" he cried—
Not knowing he need not have prayed to all—
"Spare me!" Though moved, the archer god could not
Recall his arrow. Still, the fatal wound   265
Was slight: the shaft just barely pierced his heart.
     Dire rumors, general grief, and friendly tears
Informed the mother of their sudden fate.
In shock that it could be, she raged to think
The gods dared go so far and had such rights.   270
Their sire Amphion, too, with breast and blade,
Had killed himself to end both life and pain.
Now this Niobe's not that Niobe
Who lately drove the throngs from Leto's² shrines
And proudly walked her town of jealous friends—   275
Now she wins pity even from her foes!
She fell on their cold corpses uncontrolled
And gave each of her sons a final kiss,
Then raised her bruise-black arms up to the skies.
"Feast, cruel Latona, on my grief!" she said.   280
"Feast on my sorrow till your heart is full!

2. Greek for Latona

[Gorge your wild heart," she said, "while seven times]
I'm mourned. Rejoice, in your vile victory!
And yet . . . why 'victory'? Grief leaves me more
Than joy leaves you: despite these deaths, I win!"   285
   But with that said, a tight-drawn bowstring twanged
And left all but Niobe terrified;
Grief made her bold. Black-robed, with hair unbound,
The sisters stood before their brothers' biers.
One of them, freeing an arrow from his guts,   290
Sank dying on her brother, cheek to cheek.
Another, as she soothed her mother's pain,
Fell silent, buckling with an unseen wound
[And kept her mouth shut till she passed away].
One fell in flight, one died on top of her;   295
One hid herself, one huddled in plain sight.
   Now six had suffered various wounds and died;
The last remained. In all her clothes and arms
Her mother wrapped her, crying, "Leave me one!
Please, leave my youngest, just my youngest one!"   300
But as she begged, the one she begged for died.
Childless, she sat with her dead daughters, sons,
And husband, stiff with pain, her hair unstirred
By wind, her face a bloodless pale, her eyes
Stock-still with grief—an image void of life.   305
Inside, the tongue stuck in her hardened mouth,
Her veins no longer pulsed, nor bent her neck,
Nor moved her arms, nor could her feet now walk:
For all within was stone. And still she wept.
A strong wind whisked her to her native slopes,   310
Where, set upon the mountain, she dripped on,
As, even now, her tears bedew the stone.†

[LATONA AND THE LYCIANS]†

   Then truly did the goddess' open wrath
Affright all men and women to revere
The great twin-bearer's godhood all the more.   315
And since new deeds bring tales of old, one said:

"In Lycia's fertile fields, some peasants, too,
Once scorned the goddess—nor went they unscathed.
Those men's low state has made their tale obscure,
Though wondrous. I myself have seen their pool,   320
That site of miracles. Back then, my sire,
Too old to travel, charged me to procure
Some special cows and picked one of that tribe
To guide me. As we crossed the grassy wilds,
We saw an ancient altar in a lake,   325
Ash-blackened and begirt with shivering reeds.
In fear, my guide paused, whispering 'Favor me!'
And so I whispered 'Favor!' too, then asked
If Faunus, Naiads, or some local god
Were worshiped at that shrine. My host replied,   330
'That altar's for no mountain sprite, my boy.
She calls it hers who once, when heaven's queen
Barred her from solid ground, scarce landed on
Then-wandering Delos, on whose floating isle,
Latona, braced by palm and Pallas' tree,[3]   335
Gave birth to twins, despite their stepmother.
It's said she then fled Juno, with the pair
Of newborn deities clutched to her breast.
   "'And so to Lycia, the Chimaera's land,[†]
Where plains grow parched beneath the heavy sun,   340
The goddess went, worn out from heat and thirst,
Her breasts sucked dry of milk by hungry babes.
Deep in a gorge, she spied a modest lake,
Where country-folk were picking bushy reeds,
Fine shoots, and swampgrass. Kneeling on its bank,   345
Titania[4] tried to reach its frigid flows
And quench her thirst, but peasants blocked her way.
The goddess asked those blocking her: "Why keep
Me from these waters? Water is for all!
For Nature gives no deeds to sun or air,   350
Or crystal waves—I claim a common right!

---

3. An olive tree
4. Latona, daughter of the Titan Coeus

Still, I'll beseech you for it: I did not
Intend to bathe my body's weary limbs,
But quench my thirst! My mouth has gone so dry
My voice scarce passes through my scratchy throat.   355
I know this water—nectar to me now—
Will save my life: give me the waves of life!
These little arms that reach out from my breast
Must move you, too!" (The babes, by chance, reached out.)
To hear the goddess plead, who'd not be moved?   360
But they pressed their denial, adding threats,
Lest she fail to depart, and insults, too.
Not satisfied with this, on hand and foot
They churned the lake and caused the sticky mud
To rise up from the bottom in their spite.   365
Her thirst displaced by wrath, soon Coeus' child
Could no more beg the lowly, no more speak
With words less than divine, but reached toward heaven
And cried, "May you live always in this pool!"
"'Her prayer transpired. They live to swim the waves,   370
And now sink fully in the marshy depths,
Now rear their heads and float atop the flood,
And often rest ashore, and often leap
Back in the icy lake. But to this day,
They use their shameful tongues to feud and fight;   375
When in the depths, still in the depths they curse.†
Their ribbits make each rib itself bulge out
As swearing stretches wide their gaping mouths;
Save neckless-seeming heads on backs of green,
Their body's mostly belly, white and broad.   380
Thus, through the miry lake, leapt newborn frogs.'"

[MARSYAS]†

Once this man had rehearsed the Lycians' fate,
Another called to mind Tritonia's pipes
And how the Satyr, trounced by Leto's son,
Was served. "Why tear me from myself?"† he wailed.   385
"Oh! I repent!—oh! Flutes aren't worth this much!"

He wailed on as the hide tore from his limbs
Till all was one great wound. Blood dripped all round,
His sinews were laid bare, and, stripped of skin,
His veins shuddered and shook, where you could count   390
The twitching organs clear inside his chest.
Then all the country fauns, nymphs, woodland gods,
His satyr kinfolk, and his still beloved
Olympus[5] wept for him, as did all those
Whose flocks and ox-horned herds grazed nearby slopes.   395
They soaked the fertile Earth with raining tears,
Which, soaking, she drank deep into her veins
And sent as water back into the air,
To speed by sloping banks down to the sea
As Phrygia's clearest river: 'Marsyas.'[6]   400

[PELOPS][†]

This told, the crowd returned to cares at hand,
And mourned for dead Amphion and his line.
All blamed the mother, though it's said she, too,
Was grieved by Pelops who, rending his robes,
Showed his left shoulder was of ivory.   405
At birth, its fleshy hue had matched his right,
But when his father chopped him up, they say,
The gods rejoined the bits and found them all,
Save that between the throat and upper arm.[†]
An ivory chunk replaced the missing part,   410
And, with that, Pelops was made whole again.

[TEREUS, PROCNE, AND PHILOMELA][†]

The nearby towns[†] convened to send their kings,
In sympathy, from Corinth famed for bronze,
From Calydon, then spared Diana's spite,
From Argos, Troezen—not yet Pitthean then—   415

5. Marsyas' lover
6. The name of several rivers in Anatolia

And fell Messene, full Orchomenos,
And Pelops' son's Mycenae, Sparta's realm,
Cleonae, Nelean Pylos, Patrae too,
The towns the Isthmus of two seas enfolds,
And those the Isthmus of two seas beholds.   420
Who'd think that, Athens, you alone would slack?
But duty halts in war: barbarian hordes
Had crossed the sea to menace Attic gates.
    With aiding armies, Tereus of Thrace
Defeated them and won a famous name.   425
His might in wealth and men and chance descent
From great Gradivus[7] made Pandion's[8] mind
To give him Procne's hand. But when they wed,
Did Juno, Hymen, or the Graces come?
No, Furies bore the torches, seized from pyres!   430
And Furies made the bed, while there, atop
The bridal suite, sat an ill-omened owl!
This fowl saw Tereus and Procne wed,
This fowl saw them made parents. Thrace, of course,
Gave thanks when they thanked heaven, and named the days   435
Pandion's daughter wed their famous king
And bore prince Itys as great holidays:
For "blessings" hide so much.
                                    When Titan had
Unrolled five years of autumns, Procne urged
Her husband, saying, "If my love has sway,   440
Then let me see my sister, or let her
Come here. Give father word she'll soon return,
And you'll be giving me a wondrous gift:
To see my sister!" So he launched his ships
And, faring through the sea by sail and oar,   445
Reached Cecrops' harbor and Piraeus' shores,[9]
Where his bride's father met him. Hand grasped hand,
And this auspicious sign gave way to talk.

---

7. A wartime epithet of Mars
8. King of Athens and father to Procne and Philomela
9. The port of Athens, of which Cecrops was once king

He had begun to tell of why he'd come,
Of his wife's plea and pledge of quick return,   450
When in came Philomela, richly clad,
But richer still in beauty—as we've heard
Of naiads or of dryads in the woods,
Could you but give them such array and dress!
Of course, the sight of her set Tereus   455
Ablaze, like shriveled crops brought near a fire,
Or burning leaves, or lofted stores of hay.
Her looks were cause enough, but inborn lust
Drove him as well: his tribe is quick to love,[†]
And both his vice and theirs burned hot in him.   460
   His impulse was to bribe her entourage
And loyal nurse, or tempt the girl herself
With massive gifts, though it cost him his realm,
Or rape her and defend his rape with war;
For, wild with love, he dared do anything   465
Except contain the flames inside his heart.
Now, scarce restrained, his yearning lips returned
To Procne's wish, with which he cloaked his own.
Love smoothed his speech, and when he went too far
In pleading, he claimed Procne willed it so.   470
He even cried, as though she'd told him to—
O gods, what blindness rules in mortal hearts,
That, for his monstrous evil, Tereus
Was thought devoted and won praise for sin!
Since Philomela also wished to see   475
Her sister, she embraced her father's neck,
And begged him in her interest—and against.
But Tereus was fondling her in thought,
While watching her embrace and kiss that neck:
All urged him on, all fed and fueled his lust!   480
Each time she touched her sire, her sire he wished
To be (nor would his motives have been changed!)
Her sire soon yielded to the pair. In joy,
The poor girl thanked him, taking that to be
Both sisters' gain which was both sisters' grief.   485
   Now Phoebus' toils were ending, and his steeds

Descended toward Olympus, hoof by hoof.
A royal feast, with Bacchus cupped in gold,[10]
Gave way as slumber filled their hours with peace.
But the Odrysian king,[11] though he retired,   490
Still seethed for her—her face, her walk, her hands—
And dreamed at will of all he'd yet to see,
Feeding his fires with thoughts that hindered sleep.
At dawn, Pandion turned over the girl
And shook his in-law's parting hand in tears: 495
"Dear son-in-law, since duty forces me
And both girls wish it (you, too, Tereus),
I yield her, begging you, by kinship, faith,
And heaven, to guard her with a father's love.
She's my sweet comfort in my waning years: 500
Return her soon (it will be long to me).
And come thou soon (one sister gone's enough),
My Philomela, if you care at all!"
So he implored them as he kissed his child,
And gentle tears fell as he so implored.   505
He sought and joined their hands in vows of trust,
And asked them to remember his regards
To his grandson and daughter far away.
He scarce could say 'farewell!' for all his sobs,
Foreboding so suffused his mind with fear.   510
    As soon as Philomela was aboard
The painted ship and rowing out to sea,
He cried, "I've won! My wish is at my side!"
[In triumph and scarce holding off his joy,]
The savage never turned his eyes from her;   515
But just as when Jove's bird drops from its claws
A hunted hare into its lofty nest,
The captor eyed a prey that could not flee.
    At journey's end, he left the wave-worn ship,
And dragged Pandion's child ashore with him   520
To a high shack, concealed in ancient trees,

10. That is, wine in golden goblets
11. Tereus; the Odrysians were a Thracian tribe

In which he locked her, shaking white with fear
And crying for her sister, while he showed
His true aims, raping her: a girl alone,
Who called without avail—now to her sire,   525
Her sister now, but mostly to the gods—
She quivered like a sheep struck by a wolf
And left there, yet to realize it's free,
Or like a dove with bristling blood-soaked wings,
Still fearful of more hungry piercing claws.   530
Once she'd revived, she lashed her hair [and arms
While shrieking like a mourner]. Palms outstretched,
She cried, "O savage deeds! O wicked man!
Did all my father's pleas, his faithful tears,
My sister's sorrow, my virginity,   535
And your own wedding oaths leave you unmoved?
[You've roiled all nature! Through your bigamy,
I'm made my sister's foe—and owed revenge!]
You'd better kill me, lest you skip a sin,
You traitor! I wish that you had before   540
We joined in shame: my soul would have died pure!
But if the gods are watching, if their power
Has any sway, if all's not died with me,
You'll someday pay the price! I'll put shame by
And speak your sins myself; if I've the chance,   545
I'll talk to crowds, but if kept to the woods,
I'll give the woods their fill and rouse the stones:
The air shall hear me—and the gods it holds!"
    At this, the vicious king was filled with wrath,
And fear no less, and, driven on by both,   550
He drew the sword he wore, pulled back her hair,
And forced her hands behind her back in chains.
Then Philomela offered up her throat,
For seeing the sword had raised her hopes of death,
But as she called her sire and fought to speak,   555
Tongs fixed her tongue: his cruel blade sliced it off!
Her stub of tongue throbbed, but the thing itself
Lay thrashing the dark earth and murmuring,
Till, leaping like a serpent's severed tail,

It died there, twitching toward its owner's feet.   560
And even then (I dare but hold it true),
It's said, though maimed, she often served his lust.
    Despite all this, to Procne he returned.
At sight, she asked him where her sister was,
And, faking groans, he said that she had died,   565
And backed this lie with tears. So, ripping off
Her gleaming gold-fringed garments, Procne dressed
In black, built her a sister's cenotaph,
Made offerings to her imagined ghost,
And justly mourned, though mourning the wrong fate.   570
    Through twice-six signs, the god[12] now passed a year.
And Philomela, what was she to do?
Guards blocked her flight. The shack was solid stone.
Her speechless lips had no means to inform.
But there is craft in pain, and grief breeds wit: 575
She slyly strung a loom with Thracian thread
And, weaving scarlet letters through the white,
Exposed the crime. This done, with signs she tasked
Her only slave to bring it to the queen.
The girl found Procne, clueless what she'd brought,   580
And as the tyrant's wife unrolled the cloths
And read her sister's miserable tale
In silence (it's a wonder that she could),
Pain sealed her lips. No tongue could word such wrath;
Nor could she cry, but past all right and wrong,   585
She hurled herself in dreams of her revenge.
    The Thracian women then were taking part
In their biennial nighttime Bacchic rites.
By night, bronze cymbals rang on Rhodope;
By night, the queen left home in worship dress,   590
Equipped for frenzy: grapevines round her head,
A deerskin hanging down her left-hand side,
A thyrsus on her shoulder, lightly placed.
Her mob in tow, dread Procne stormed the woods—
Her grieving frenzy, Bacchus, seeming much   595

---

12. The Sun, which cycles annually through the Zodiac

Like yours! At last, she found the secret shack,
And, howling Bacchic cries, burst through its doors,
And seized her sister, clothed her like the cult,
And, with her face obscured by ivy leaves,
Hauled off the dumbstruck girl back home with her.   600
    When Philomela reached the house of sin,
The luckless girl went white in total fear,
So Procne there stripped off her cultish clothes,
Unveiled her wretched sister's sorry face,
And held her. Still, she would not lift her eyes,   605
But, feeling she must seem her sister's foe,
With downcast face, the girl swore by the gods
That what transpired was forced against her will;
She spoke this with her hands. Then Procne raged
Unbridled, swept her sister's tears aside,   610
And said, "This is no time for tears but steel—
Or, if you have it, something stronger still!
My sister, I'm prepared for any sin:
I'll torch this palace and cast Tereus,
The author of our anguish, on its flames!   615
I'll slice his tongue and eyes out, and those parts
Which stole your virtue! Through a thousand cuts,
I'll drain his guilty soul! I'm set for some
Great feat: what, I don't know."
                              While Procne spoke,
She noticed her son Itys entering,   620
And knew what she could do. Glaring, she said,
"Ah, you're so like your father!" but stopped there,
And seethed in silence, planning tragic acts.
Yet when her son approached and greeted her,
And hugged his mother's neck with little arms,   625
And gave her kisses mixed with childish chat,
Her parent's heart was moved, her anger waned,[†]
And tears forced through her eyes. But sensing love
Had sapped her will, she caught her sister's glance,
And viewing both, said, "Why should I be moved   630
By his sweet chatter, when she has no tongue?
When he cries 'mother,' why can't she call me

Her sister? See how far you've wed below
Your birth, Pandion's daughter! For it's sin
To serve a spouse like Tereus!" At once,   635
She dragged off Itys like a suckling fawn
A Bengal tigress drags through shady woods.
Now in the furthest corners of the house,
He saw his fate, and reached to hug her neck.
As he cried, "mother, mother!" Procne stuck   640
A sword between his ribs, nor did she look
Away; and though one wound would have sufficed
To kill him, Philomela slit his throat.
While yet he breathed with life, they carved his limbs,
And soon, some pieces boiled in hollow pots,   645
Some hissed on spits, and all the room dripped gore.
    To this meal did his wife call Tereus.
Pretending it was some old rite her spouse
Alone might join, she sent the servants out.
So Tereus, aloft his family throne,   650
Sat blithely gorging on flesh of his flesh.
So blind was he, he cried, "Call Itys here!"
Then Procne could not hide her wicked joy;
Keen to make her destruction known, she cried,
"It is inside you have him!"† He looked round,   655
And asked her where, then asked and called again,
When death-crazed Philomela, tangle-haired,
Sprang forward and hurled Itys' bloody head
Into his father's face. Never did she
More wish to speak and vent her joy in words!   660
The Thracian flipped the table with a roar,
Invoked the snake-haired sisters[13] of the Styx,
And, were he able, would have split his chest,
Disgorging that vile feast of half-downed guts,
But, weeping, called himself his son's sad tomb,   665
And ran to stab the sisters. As they fled,
You'd posit the Piraean pair were poised

13. The Furies, who specialized in punishing those who murdered their own family
members

FIGURE 6. *Tereus, Procne, and Philomela* (c. 1470). Among the foremost
works of Middle English literature was John Gower's 1390 *Confessio
Amantis* (*The Lover's Confession*), a verse anthology of tales largely
borrowed from Ovid. Per typical medieval practice, the illustration in
this copy compresses multiple scenes into a single frame. Shown
mangling Philomela to the left, Tereus also attends the fateful feast at
center. Overhead, birds prefigure the coming transformation.

On pinions—and they were! One sought the woods,
One scaled the roof; but still their chests retain
The signs of slaughter in their bloodstained plumes.[†]   670
The man's own pain and swift will to avenge
Made him a bird whose crested head upholds
A running beak to match his lengthy sword:
[By name, the hoopoe, warlike in his look.]

[BOREAS AND ORITHYIA]†

These woes sent old Pandion to the shades   675
Of Tartarus before his proper time;
His crown and rule fell to Erechtheus,
A man of equal fame in laws and arms,
With four sons and four daughters, two of which
Were matched in looks: you, Procris, gladly wed   680
Aeolian Cephalus, but Boreas,
A Thracian god disgraced by Tereus,†
Was kept from Orithyia, his beloved,
Yet wooed the while, preferring prayers to force.
But when sweet words did nothing, fearsome rage,   685
Which was his normal mood, possessed the Wind:
"I'm worthy!" he cried, "Why have I put down
My weapons—fierceness, fury, force, and threats—
And turned to prayers, which do not suit my will?
Force suits me! I compel the clouds by force;   690
By force, I shake the sea, fell knotted oaks,
Compact the snows, and pelt the ground with hail!
And when I meet my brothers in the sky
(My field of war), I strive there with such strength
The middle-aether rings with our attacks   695
And flashing flames escape the hollow clouds!
And deep inside earth's hollows, my strong back
Has heaved to scare the ghosts and all the world
With quaking!† So should I have pressed my suit:
To take me as his son, Erechtheus   700
Shall no more be implored—he'll be impelled!"
When Boreas had said all this and more,
He beat his wings and sent a gusty blast
Across the lands that caused the seas to surge.
His dusty mantle skimmed both peaks and ground,   705
While, cloaked in mist, the lover's tawny wings
Wrapped terror-stricken Orithyia round;
And as he flew, the fluttering fanned his flames,
Nor did her captor check his airy course
Till they'd reached the Ciconians' city walls,   710

Where that cold tyrant wed the Attic girl,
And made her bear his twins, who looked like her
In all respects, except their father's wings.
　　And yet, they say the twins weren't winged at birth:
As boys, when ruddy down still hid their beards,   715
Both Calaïs and Zetes were unfledged.
But both soon started sprouting birdlike wings
On either side, as both turned gold of cheek.
And so, their boyhood giving way to youth,
They joined the Minyans on that first of ships,   720
And sailed strange seas to find the fleece of gold.†

Book 7

AND NOW the Minyans' vessel plowed the seas!
From Pagasae, they sped toward Phineus—
Old, blind, and starving—from whose piteous mouth
Aquilo's sons scared off the wingèd maids.†

    Famed Jason led them and, with many pains,   5
The band at last reached Phasis' muddy swirl,
Where, as they asked the king for Phrixus' fleece†
And learned the fearful terms and toils required,
Aeëtes' daughter fell to passion's spark.
She struggled long, but sense lost to desire: 10
"In vain, Medea, do you fight!" she said.
"Some god opposes you! For is this not—
Or not extremely like—that thing called love?
Why else do father's orders seem too harsh?
(They are too harsh!) Why do I fear the death   15
Of one I've scarcely seen? What's caused such fear?
Free, if you can, your virgin heart from these
Fresh flames, poor dear! I'd think straight if I could,
But new needs drive me, pulling heart and mind
In different ways; I see which one is best,   20
But take the worse. . . . Can you, a princess, burn
To wed this stranger and his alien world?

Here, too, you might find love! His life and death
Are in the hands of gods!—yet, let him live:
I'd rightly wish the same, in love or no,   25
For what has Jason done? What fiend would not
Be moved by Jason's youth, his rank, his worth?
Or, lacking these, his face? My heart sure is!
Without my help, he'll feel the cattle's breath,
Or fight foes sprung from seed he's sown himself,   30
Or feed the dragon† like a beast of prey.
If I allow this, I must call myself
A tiger's child with heart of lead and stone. . . .
But why not watch him die? Why should that sight
So damn my eyes? Should I not drive his way   35
The bulls and earth-born brutes and sleepless snake?
Oh, heaven forbid! Yet prayers don't matter now,
But deeds: shall I betray my father's rule
And save some stranger, who, safe by my aid,
Will sail without me, wed another wife,   40
And leave Medea to her punishment?
If he could do that—could prefer some girl
To me, then let the ingrate die! But no:
That face, that noble soul, that pleasing form
Mean I need fear no fraud, no thanklessness;   45
He'll pledge love *first*—I'll make the gods attest!
Why fear what's sure? Get ready—don't delay!
For Jason will forever owe his life
To you; he'll marry you, and matron throngs
Will hail you as his savior all through Greece!   50
Yet must I sail and leave my native land,
My sister, brother, sire, and gods . . .? But then,
My father's cruel, my home's a savage place,
Brother's a baby, sister's on my side,
And the best god's in me![1] I won't leave much,   55
But much awaits me: fame in having saved
The youth of Greece—a better land whose towns,
Culture, and art are known as far as here—

1. That is to say, Cupid holds her heart

And him I would not leave for all the world,
Dear Aeson's son, whose happy wife shall be   60
Called heaven's own beloved and touch the stars!
Yet what about those mountains claimed to clash
Mid-ocean, and Charybdis, curse of crews,
Who now sucks in the tides, now spews them back,
And Scylla's belt of hounds, who howl their greed   65
Through the Sicilian depths?[†] No, clasping love
In Jason's arms, I'll fare the straits, held fast
And fearless—or I'll fear for him alone. . . .
Yet, thinking 'marriage,' do you falsely name
Your faults, Medea? Rather, see what sins   70
You're hurtling toward and flee them while you can!"
This said, she gazed on Purity and Faith,
While Cupid, overcome, turned tail and fled.
    Then to the shrine of Perseid Hecate,[2]
Concealed by forest shades, she boldly went,   75
Her passions on the wane. But when she there
Saw Aeson's son, her embers flamed anew!
Her cheeks blushed as the fire reclaimed her face,
And as the smallest spark, smothered in ash,
Will feed on fanning winds and, growing strong,   80
Regain its former force, so did her love,
Which just now you'd have thought dimmed near to death,
On seeing the youth before her, blaze again!
    It chanced this day that Aeson's son was more
Than usually fair, so do excuse her love: 85
As if for the first time, she eyed his face,
Stared at his features, madly thought his looks
Not of this world, and could not turn away!
Then when the stranger spoke and took her hand,
And humbly sought her aid and promised he   90
Would wed her, she burst into tears and said:
"I see my path, nor shall my ignorance
Mislead me—just my love. I'll keep you safe;
But, saved, fulfill your pledge!" He swore it by

2. Hecate, daughter of the nymph Perse

The threefold goddess,[3] by that grove's own powers,   95
The all-seeing sire—his in-law soon to be[4]—
And by his triumphs and by all he'd risked.
Believed at once, he took her magic herbs,
Learned of their use, and happily went home.

   Once Dawn had driven out the twinkling stars,   100
Crowds gathered on the sacred field of Mars[†]
And lined its ridge. Their ivory-sceptered king
Sat with them, clad in purple robes, when—look!
Bronze-footed bulls with adamantine snouts
Came breathing flames that charred the trampled grass,   105
For, like a furnace roaring at its full
Or slaking lime within an earthen kiln
Which starts to sizzle when made wet with spray,
The pent-up fires revolved inside their chests
And rang in their burnt throats. Still, Aeson's son   110
Approached. The beasts turned towards him as he did,
With fearsome faces and horns tipped with iron,
Then pawed the dusty ground with cloven feet,
And filled the place with stifling, smoky moos.
The Minyans froze in fear, yet he pressed on   115
Unfazed by flame (so potent were the drugs!)
And, boldly scratching each beneath the chin,
He yoked and made them drag the heavy plow
Across that field no steel had ever known.

   The Colchians marveled and the Minyans swelled   120
His soul with shouts. Then, from his helm, he took
The dragon's teeth and sowed them in the seams.
Soil warmed the seeds and, steeped with poison's power,
The teeth arose in new embodied shapes.
And just as infants, in their mothers' wombs,   125
Take human form, completed piece by piece,
And don't emerge in air before they're ripe,
So, too, in pregnant soil, did they take shape,
Hatch through the ground, and—greatest shock of all—

3. Hecate, often depicted in triplicate (cf. 7.177)
4. The Sun, grandfather to Medea

Shake clanging weapons they had brought along!   130
When they beheld the sharpened spear-points aimed
And primed to strike the son of Aeson's head,
The Grecians' faces and their spirits fell.
She who'd ensured his life felt fear as well
To see one youth faced with so many foes,   135
And sat there, paling in a bloodless chill.
Then, lest the herbs she'd lent him prove too weak,
She called on spells and secret arts for aid;
But, flinging a great rock amidst his foes,
He caused them to wage war amongst themselves: 140
The earth-born brothers died by mutual wounds,
And fell in civil strife. The Greeks acclaimed
The victor, holding him in tight embrace,
As you wished to embrace him, savage maid,   144
[But for your shame. You'd have embraced him still,   146
If fear of gossip had not held you back.]   145
But you did what you could: in silent joy,
You thanked your magic and its source, the gods.
    And now, to put to sleep the wakeful snake,
Whose crest, curved fangs, and tri-forked tongue marked out   150
The watchful guardian of the golden tree.
He sprayed it with the sap of Lethean herbs,
And when he spoke three times the lulling words
Which stay the rolling sea and rushing streams,
Sleep closed those sleepless eyes. Then Aeson's proud   155
Heroic son, his golden spoil in hand,
Fared with the gift's giver, his other spoil,
Home to Iolcus' port†—victor and bride.
    The wives and agèd sires of Thessaly
Brought presents for their sons, burned incense heaps,   160
And led the gilt-horned sacrifice they'd pledged
To slaughter. Aeson, though, did not attend,
Being old and close to death. Said Aeson's son:
"Dear wife, who I confess has saved my life,
Though you've already brought me everything   165
And with your worthy deeds surpassed all hopes,
Still, if your spells can (and what can't they do?),

Please take years from my life and lengthen his."
His tears broke through. This unknown love stirred [thoughts
Of poor Aeëtes, whom she'd left behind,]   170
But hiding this, she said, "What sinful words
Just left your mouth, dear spouse? Do you think I
Can give bits of your life to anyone?
This Hecate won't bear, nor should you ask!
But I'll outdo your prayers and try to stretch   175
Your father's life through my arts, not your years—
Just let the three-formed goddess aid my cause,
And, with her presence, grace my daring deeds!"
    Three nights remained before the moon's horns met
And filled the orb, but once it shone at full   180
And gazed down at the land with solid shape,
She left home, clad in flowing robes and bare
Of head and foot, her hair about her arms,
To wander in the midnight hush alone.
The humans, birds, and beasts all soundly slept,   185
And, from the hedgerows, not a whisper came;
Still were the leaves and still the dewy air.
Only the stars shone; reaching arms to these,
She turned three times, three times submerged her hair
In water, and three times let loose a wail,   190
Then knelt on solid ground, and said, "O Night,
Who keeps all secrets; and you golden stars,
Who, with the moon, succeed the rays of day;
You, threefold Hecate, who knows our schemes,
And aids the charms and arts of sorcerers;   195
And you, O Earth, who gives them potent herbs;
You gusts and winds; you peaks and streams and lakes;
And all you gods of groves and gods of night—
Be with me! When I've wished, you streams have shocked
Your banks by flowing back! I stay the swells   200
And storm calm seas with charms; I scatter clouds
And roll them back; I call and quell the winds;
I rupture vipers' throats through spells and song,
Tear trees and living rock out of the ground,
And move the very woods; at my command,   205

Peaks quake, lands groan, and ghosts depart their graves!
I steer you, too, O Moon, though Tempsan bronze
Strives to allay your toils.[†] The chariot
My grandsire drives grows pale to hear our song,
As Dawn pales at our poisons! All for me,   210
You doused the bulls' flames, yoked their untamed necks,
And made the snake-born war upon themselves;
You lulled the wakeful beast to sleep and slipped
The golden prize, beyond its watch, to Greece!
Now I need potions to renew old age   215
And roll years backward to the flower of youth—
You'll give them! For the stars don't shine in vain,
Nor vainly comes my chariot, on wings
Of dragons!" (Here her chariot flew down.)
    Once in, she stroked the dragons' haltered necks,   220
And, pulling at their reins, was borne aloft.
She saw Thessalian Tempe down below,
And steered the serpents toward familiar lands:
The herbs of Ossa, Othrys, Pelion,
High Pindus and Olympus, higher still,   225
She raked through, ripping roots from plants that pleased,
And slicing some with scythes. Much pleased her well
Upon Apidanus' grass-laden banks—
Upon Amphrysus', too. Nor were you spared,
Enipeus; the Peneus, Sperchius,   230
And Boebe's reedy shores all gave their share.
Anthedon of Euboea's rousing grass
She plucked, though Glaucus' change[†] was not yet known,
And when nine days and nights had seen her roam
The world with her winged dragons, she returned.   235
And though they'd only touched the herbal scent,
The dragons still sloughed off their age-old skins.
    Outside her doors she stopped and did not cross,
But, sheltered by the sky alone, she shunned
Her husband's touch and built two shrines of turf,   240
The right to Hecate, the left to Youth,
Begirt with branches from the woodland wilds.
Nearby, she dug two trenches and performed

Her ritual as, with a knife, she slit
A black sheep's throat and drenched the dikes with blood.   245
On this she next poured bowls of liquid wine,
And then poured other bowls of tepid milk,
While gushing words to summon chthonic gods.
She begged the ghost-king and his stolen bride
Not yet to rob the old man's limbs of life.   250
When she'd appeased them with long, murmured prayers,
She called for weary Aeson to be brought,
And, singing him to sleep, she stretched him out,
Like someone dead, upon a bed of herbs.
His son and servants she sent far away   255
With warnings to avert their profane eyes;
They duly left Medea, bacchant-like
With streaming hair, to ring the sacral fires,
Dip broken branches in the blackened dikes,
And light them, bloodied, at the double shrine,   260
Then cleanse the ancient man three times apiece
With water, fire, and brimstone.
                                        All the while,
Her potion boils and bubbles white with foam—
A stew of roots plucked from Thessalia's vales,
And seeds and flowers and deadly saps. With these,   265
She stirs in stones brought from the distant East,
And sands the ebbing Ocean washed behind.
She adds in rime reaped under a full moon,
A screech owl's wicked wings and very flesh,
And entrails from a wolf whose shifting form   270
Could change into a man's. Nor did there lack
The scaly skin of a Cinyphian snake,
An old stag's liver, nor the beak and head—
Now added—of a crow nine ages old.
These and a thousand other nameless things   275
Comprised the witch's more than mortal plan;
She took an olive branch, long since dried out,
And, top to bottom, stirred till all was mixed.
Then, look! the dry old stick, warmed by the pot,
Turns green and soon sprouts leaves as, suddenly,   280

Fat olives bend the branch beneath their weight;
And where the hollow pot spews forth its foam,
And lets fall boiling drops upon the earth,
The ground grows green with flowers and pasture's grass.
Seeing this, Medea drew her sword and slit   285
The old man's throat, and as it bled old blood,
She poured in potion. Aeson drank this up,
Through mouth and wound at once—and his white beard
Cast off its color and returned to black!
His gauntness, paleness, weakness all dissolved,   290
His wrinkles filled with flesh, his body thrived,
And Aeson marveled, then remembered this
Had been himself, some forty years before.
      And Liber saw these miracles on high,
Learned that his nurses could regain their youth,   295
And won that favor from the Colchian.†
      To keep it up, the Phasian trickster faked
Some spousal spat and fled as suppliant
To Pelias,† whose daughters welcomed her,
Since age weighed hard on him. The Colchian soon   300
Feigned friendliness and snared them, telling tales
Of her great feats, among them how she'd turned
Back Aeson's crippling years—on this she dwelt,
So that the Pelian girls conceived a hope
That her same skill might so revive their sire,   305
For which they begged her to name any price.
She stood awhile to hold them in suspense,
And seemed to hesitate in solemn thought,
But soon she promised: "To ensure your trust
In what I do, the leader of your flock,   310
Your eldest sheep, my drugs shall make a lamb!"
At once, a woolly ram of untold years
Was brought, its hollow head hemmed in with horns.
When her Thessalian knife pierced its weak throat,
Blood barely stained the blade. The witch then threw   315
The sheep's remains into a vat of bronze
With potent drugs that shrank the body down,
Burned off its horns, and, with the horns, its years.

Then, from the vat, there came a tender bleat,
And while they listened awed, a lamb leapt forth   320
And ran off in pursuit of teats and milk.
The Pelian sisters stood amazed; and now,
The pledge fulfilled, they pressed their suit the more.
    Three times had Phoebus' steeds swum Ebro's stream,[†]
When, by the fourth night's stars, Aeëtes' child   325
Lit raging flames of treachery beneath
A liquid broth of herbs devoid of power.
And now the king and, with the king, his guards,
Were held in death-like sleep by potent chants
And magic words. The Colchian, as devised,   330
Then entered with his daughters, ringed his bed,
And said, "Why waver now, you craven curs?
Unsheathe your swords: let spill his ancient gore,
And I'll refill his veins with youthful blood!
Your father's life and age are in your hands;   335
If you love him at all and truly hope,
Then do right by your father—with your swords
Expel old age and cut out his decay!"
The girls' love set them thus against their love
To sin for fear of sinning. Still, not one   340
Would watch the strokes she struck; they looked away
And smote him sore, but blindly from the side.
Though gushing blood, he rose up on one arm
And tried to stand, half-mangled, then reached out
His ghastly arms amid the blades and said,   345
"What are you doing, daughters? Who has armed
You for my death?" Their hands and spirits sank,
And he'd have said more, but the Colchian cut
His throat and plunged his scraps in boiling broth.
    She would have paid a price, had she not flown[†]   350
Away on serpents' wings, past Pelion,
Whose shades the son of Philyra calls home,
And Othrys, and those lands made famous by
Cerambus, whom the nymphs raised up on wings,
When all the heavy earth was drowned in sea,   355
And so escaped Deucalion's Flood undrowned.

And she passed by Aeolian Pitane
And its stone statue of a giant snake,
And Ida's grove, where Liber hid the calf
His son had stolen in a stag's disguise;   360
The patch of sand where lies Corythus' sire;
The fields which feared for Maera's eerie barks;
Eurypylus, whose Coan wives grew horns
When Hercules marched out; and Phoebean Rhodes,
Where the Telchines held Ialysos,   365
Till spiteful Jove submerged their evil eyes,
Whose looks could kill, beneath his brother's waves.
    She passed Carthaea, from whose Cean walls,
Alcidamas would later gape to see
A docile dove birthed from his daughter's corpse;†   370
Lake Hyrië; and Tempe, known for swans
Through Cygnus' sudden change.† (For Phylius
Had trained the boy a lion, brought him birds,
And, asked to tame a bull, had tamed that, too,
But, angered that his love was spurned so long,   375
Refused to yield the bull, his finest gift.
Enraged, the boy cried out, "You'll wish you had!"
And vaulted off a cliff. All thought him dead,
But on new snowy wings he soared, a swan,
Though not before his mother, Hyrië,   380
Dissolved in tears into her namesake pool.)
Nearby lay Pleuron† where, on trembling wings,
Ophius' daughter Combe fled her sons.
She next spied Leto's rich Calaurean plain,
Whose king and queen it once watched turn to birds;   385
Cyllene, on the right, where Menephron
Would share his mother's bed like a wild beast;
And far Cephisus, mourning with his tears
The grandson whom Apollo made a seal,
As mourned Eumelus for his wingèd son.   390
At last, her snakes' wings reached Pirene's fount
At Corinth, where they say the dawn of time
Saw rain-soaked mushrooms spawning human forms.
    But once the Colchian poisoned the new wife,

Burned down the palace placed between two seas,   395
And soaked her wicked sword with her sons' blood,
The mother fled from Jason's arms, avenged.[†]
Astride the snakes of Titan, she was brought
To Pallas' citadel, which once saw you,
Just Phene, and you, too, old Periphas,   400
And Polypemon's grandchild all take flight.[†]
    There, Aegeus lodged her—damning in itself,
But she was no mere guest: he married her!
Then Theseus, a stranger to his sire
Who'd brought peace to the Isthmus of two seas,[†]   405
Arrived. Medea, bent on his demise,
Brewed long-held Scythian wolfsbane, which they say
Sprang from Echidna's kindred canine's[5] fangs.
There is a sightless cave of yawning gloom,
Where Tiryns' hero, up through tilting paths,   410
Dragged Cerberus in adamantine chains[†]
To struggle, strain, and screw his eyes before
The shining light of day. Gone wild with rage,
His triple heads sent barks into the air,
And sprayed the verdant meadows white with foam.   415
The drops grew, fed on fertile fruitful soil
That turned them, so it's thought, to toxic plants,
Which peasants, seeing them sprout through flinty crags,
Call "flint-wort."
              Aegeus, through his wife's deceit
Both foe and father, served this to his son,   420
Whose clueless hand had grasped it when his sire
Saw, on his ivory hilt, the family crest
And dashed the guilty goblet from his lips.
In magic mists, the witch fled for her life.[†]

[THESEUS][†]

His father, although pleased his son was safe,   425
Was stunned that such a monstrous sin had scarce

---

5. The three-headed Cerberus, child of Echidna

Been fended off. He lit the altar fires,
Filled shrines with gifts, and sent his axes through
The brawny necks of bulls with ribboned heads.
It's said no day more festive ever dawned   430
In Athens: high and low-born ate as one,
And sang these songs with wit enhanced by wine:
    "O greatest Theseus, whom Marathon
Admires for having gored the Cretan bull,†
You let Crommyonian farmers plow secure   435
From swine; through you, did Epidaurus see
Death brought to Vulcan's cudgel-wielding son,
Cephisus witness cruel Procrustes killed,
And Ceres' town Eleusis, Cercyon.
As you killed Sinis, whose great evil strength   440
Could bend trees, forcing lofty pines to earth
That he might scatter bodies far and wide,
Alcathoë's safe Lelegian gates
Stand wide, now Sciron's gone—that robber's bones
You gave no earthly grave, nor grave at sea;   445
But, tossed about at length, it's said they turned
To boulders—boulders known by Sciron's name.
    "If we should wish to count your deeds and years,
Your feats would win. We bring a nation's thanks
To you, brave one, and drain this wine for you!"   450
The palace rang with general cheers and prayers,
And nowhere in the town was sadness found.

[THE WAR WITH MINOS]†

    Not yet (since no delight is ever pure,
But some concern will interfere with joy)
Was Aegeus fully pleased to have his son: 455
War brewed with Minos, strong in men and ships
But stauncher still in his wrath to avenge,
By righteous arms, his son Androgeus' death.†
In search of allies, he first roamed the waves
In that swift fleet of ships where lay his power.   460
Astypalaea and Anaphe both

Were won—the first with vows, the other force—
And chalky Cimolus, low Myconos,
Thyme-teeming Syros, level Seriphos,
And marbled Paros, which base Arne's greed   465
Betrayed with Siphnos in exchange for gold,
And so became a bird that loves gold still:
A jackdaw with black feet and plumes of black.†
   But Gyaros, Tenos, Andros, Didyme,
Oliaros, olive-rich Peparethos—   470
All spurned the Knossian ships. So Minos sailed
For Aeacus' far realm, Oenopia.
(From Aeacus' mother, Oenopia
Received its newer name "Aegina"—hers.)†
   There, crowds rushed forth to see the famous man,   475
Whom Telamon, the younger Peleus,
And Phocus, the third-eldest son, all met,
As Aeacus himself went, slow with age,
To ask him why he'd come. His son in mind,
The ruler of a hundred cities[6] sighed,   480
And thus replied, "I seek your aid in war,
Which I am waging for my son: pray, join
This faithful fight that he may rest in peace!"
Asopus' grandson[7] said, "You seek in vain
That which we cannot do! No land's more linked   485
With Athens than are we—such is our pact!"
Dismayed, he said, "Your pact will cost you dear!"
And left, for he preferred a threat of war
To waging one and wasting his strength there.
   Atop Oenopia's walls, the Cretan fleet   490
Could still be seen when, flying at full sail,
An Attic ship put in the friendly port
With Cephalus† and news of state aboard.
The princes, though they'd not seen him in years,
Knew Cephalus at once, shook hands, and led   495
The dazzling hero to their father's house.

---

6. A Homeric epithet for Crete (cf. 9.667, 13.707)
7. Aeacus, whose mother Aegina was the daughter of the Asopus river

His former beauty still in traces seen,
And with his country's olive branch in hand,
The older man walked, flanked at left and right
By Clytus and by Butes, Pallas' sons.   500
    On greeting one another, Cephalus
Passed on Cecropid's[8] message, begging aid
And calling on their pact and ancient oaths,
Since all Greek sovereignty was now at stake.
His eloquence lent favor to their cause: 505
A hand round his bright scepter, Aeacus
Replied, "Don't beg our service, Athens—*take!*
[Nor doubt the island's force is yours, and all
My state can give.] We've troops enough to man
Both sides, and lack no strength! The time is right   510
(Thanks to the gods!) and gives me no excuse."
"May it be so," said Cephalus, "and may
Your city grow! For, landing, I rejoiced
To meet such handsome youths, so close in age;
And yet, I searched in vain for many whom   515
I met with when your town last welcomed me."
Here, Aeacus groaned. Sadly, he replied,
"A tearful start gave way to better luck.
Would I might tell the last without the first. . . .
But I'll speak plain, nor ramble while you wait: 520
Those you remember lie as bones and ash.
[They perished, as did so much of my realm!]

[THE MYRMIDONS][†]

    "A heinous plague, through hateful Juno's wrath,
Befell this realm, which bears her rival's name.
[And since it seemed a mortal malady   525
Of hidden cause, we fought the scourge with cures;
Yet death surpassed our means, which fell to ruin.]
From heaven, a heavy gloom first struck the land,
And locked its sweltering heat in swollen clouds.

---

8. Aegeus, grandson of Cecrops

Four times the lunar orb did fill its horns   530
And four times did the full orb wane again
While scorching Auster seethed with deadly heat;
And so, infection reached our springs and lakes,
As snakes in thousands ranged our untilled fields
And poured their tainting venom in our streams.   535
At first, the plague's swift slaughter kept to dogs,
And birds and sheep and cattle and wild beasts.
The luckless plowman gaped as his best bulls
Failed in their work and tumbled in the ruts.
The wool flocks bleated sickly, and their wool   540
Shed on its own and left the rest to rot.
The horse, once fierce and famous on the track,
Dishonored and forgot its old success
To groan towards helpless death inside its stall.
The boar forgot to rage, the stag to trust   545
His speed, the bear to prey on mighty herds.
All fell apart! In woods and fields and roads
Foul corpses lay, the air rank with their stench;
And—strange to say—no dogs nor hungry birds
Nor silver wolves would touch the festering scraps,   550
Whose noxious fumes drove the contagion's spread.
    "Next, pestilence fell on the peasantry
With mounting force, then gained the city walls.
It seared their organs first: as inner flames
Shone through in florid cheeks and tortured breath,   555
Their tongues swelled hard through lips scorched wide by wind
To gasp the stifling air. No cots nor clothes
Could they endure, but all unrobed they strewed
The ground, which did not keep their bodies cool—
Instead, the bodies served to warm the ground!   560
Unchecked, the vicious tragedy soon spread
To healers, now betrayed by their own art,
For those most closely tending to the sick
Most swiftly met their deaths. All, losing hope
Of life and seeing no end except the grave,   565
Indulged their whims, not caring what might help
(For nothing helped). They fastened unashamed

On springs, streams, yawning wells—and anywhere,
[Nor did they end their thirst before their lives.]
Too weak to surface, many died within   570
Those waters; others drank them all the same.
Such was the wretches' hatred of their beds,
They jumped out, or, if stopped by failing strength,
Rolled down the floor and fled their household gods,
For every home appeared a house of death,   575
[And there was naught but that small place to blame.]
Those who could stand walked half-dead through the streets,
Where you could see them weeping on the ground,
Their eyeballs rolling in the throes of death,
[Their arms stretched toward the stars and hanging sky: 580
Here—there—wherever death lurked, they expired.]
    "How did I feel then? How should I have felt
But keen to die and share my people's lot?
For everywhere I looked, they lay in heaps
Like rotting apples shaken from a branch,   585
Or acorns from an oak. You see that shrine
(Of Jupiter's) atop those towering stairs?
Whose incense did not fuel its altar fires
In vain? How many times did spouse for spouse
And sire for son say prayers, and while they spoke,   590
Breathe out their last before the heedless shrine,
With unused incense still held in their hands!
How often, while the temple priests made vows
And poured untempered wine between their horns,
Did bulls fall dead while waiting for their wounds!   595
As I myself made Jove a sacrifice
For my three sons and realm, the victim gave
An awful moo and suddenly collapsed
While yet unharmed—its blood scarce stained the knife!
And its infected entrails bore no signs   600
Or truths divine: the pest had reached its guts.
Round temple doors, I saw dead bodies thrown;
Round altars, too, to make death even worse.
Some hanged themselves, escaping fear of death
Through death, and meeting fate on their own terms.   605

Nor were the corpses given proper rites
(So many hearses would have clogged the gates),
But laid unburied on the ground, or piled
On humble pyres. By then, respect was gone:
Men fought for pyres and burned in strangers' flames.   610
With no one left to grieve, souls strayed unmourned
From boys and men and youths and agèd sires.
No space was left for tombs, nor wood for fires.
   "Astonished by such whirling storms of woe,
I cried, 'If, Jupiter, it's true you held   615
Asopus' child Aegina in your arms—
If being our sire, great sire, brings you no shame,
Then give my people back, or dig my grave!'
He flashed and thundered in acknowledgment.
'I heed these signs,' I said, 'and pray they show   620
Your favor, for I take them as a pledge.'
By chance, an oak with strangely widespread boughs,
Sacred to Jove and of Dodonaean stock,[†]
Stood near. On this, we saw a horde of ants,
Their tiny mouths amassing heaps of grain,   625
All cutting courses through the crinkled bark.
Their numbers awed me. 'Best of sires,' I said,
'Grant me as many subjects, and refill
My empty walls!' Its boughs unstirred by wind,
The great oak groaned and quaked! Fear gripped my limbs   630
And stood my hair on end, and yet I kissed
Its trunk and soil. Though trying not to hope,
I hoped the more and wishing warmed my heart.
   "When night fell and our careworn bodies slept,
That same tree seemed to stand before my eyes,   635
With all those creatures lining all its boughs,
And quake again, and shake the horde of ants
Collecting grain into the fields below,
Where they at once grew large, then larger still,
And seemed to rise and stride the earth upright,   640
And lose their blackness, leanness, and spare feet,
And take on human forms. Then sleep retired.
   "Awake, I scorned my vision and rebuked

The useless gods, when from the palace rose
The roar—it seemed to me—of human speech,   645
So long unheard. I thought it was a dream,
But Telamon burst through the doors and cried,
'O sire, this sight's beyond hope and belief:
Do come!' I came, and saw the men I'd seen
Asleep, and recognized them as the same.   650
They called me king, and I, with thanks to Jove,
Pieced out the town and fields, now emptied of
Their former farmers, to new citizens,
Whom I call 'Myrmidons'† after their birth.
Their look you've seen; their ways are as before,   655
For they're a thrifty and hardworking race,
Keen both to gain and keep what things they've gained.
Alike in mind and age, they'll fight for you,
Once Eurus, who so gladly brought you here,"
(For Eurus had) "gives way to Auster's gusts."   660

[CEPHALUS AND PROCRIS]†

  With such discourse, they passed the livelong day,
And spent its end in feasts, the night in sleep.
But when the golden sun spread forth its rays,
Still Eurus blew and stayed their homeward sails,
So Pallas' sons sought out old Cephalus;   665
And Cephalus and Pallas' sons, the king.
King Aeacus being still asleep, his son,
Young Phocus, welcomed them, for Telamon
Was with their brother, out enlisting troops.
Then Phocus led the men of Athens through   670
The keep to finer rooms where all sat down,
And, seeing Aeolus' grandson[9] held a spear
Carved from an unknown wood and tipped with gold,
Before much else was spoken, he declared,
"Though I'm a devotee of woods and hunts,   675
I'm at a loss for of what tree the shaft

9. Cephalus

You hold was cut. For sure, if it were ash,
It would be blonde; if dogwood, full of knots.
And though I cannot place its source, my eyes
Have never seen a javelin more fair."   680
One of the Attic brothers then replied,
"You will admire its use more than its shape:
It flies unchecked by chance and always hits
Its mark, then shoots back—bloodied—on its own."
Then Nereus' grandson[†] did indeed inquire   685
Whence, why, and from whom such a gift could be!   686
<There was a pause; then Cephalus, aggrieved>[†]   688a
For his lost wife, burst into tears and said,
"This spear (who could believe it?), goddess' son,   690
Now makes and long will make me weep, if fate
Long lets me live. It killed my darling wife—
And me. I wish I'd never had the gift!

    "Her name was Procris. You'll have heard about
Her sister Orithyia and her rape,   695
But seeing their shapes and sorts, you'd say that she
Was fitter prey.[†] Her sire, Erechtheus,
Joined her to me, as Love joined her to me.
Blessed I was called and was (and could be still,
But for the gods). We had been wed two months,   700
When saffron Dawn, who puts the shades to flight,
Beheld me spreading nets for antlered deer,
And from Hymettus' ever-flowering peak,
Took me by force. I beg the goddess' leave
To speak the truth: she's dazzling pink of cheek,   705
Keeps day from night, and feeds on nectar's sap—
But I loved *Procris! Procris* held my heart,
And *Procris'* name was ever on my lips!
I spoke of wedding chambers, bridal beds,
And our lost bonds of spousal intercourse,   710
Until the goddess cried, 'Enough complaints!
Keep Procris, thankless boy, but I foresee
That you'll regret it!'[†] Vexed, she sent me back.
But, heading home, I held the goddess' words
In mind, and soon I feared my wife had less   715

Than kept her vows. Her youth and looks led me
To doubt her faith; her traits led me to trust.
Still, I'd been gone, and came from one who sinned
In just that way—and we in love fear all.
In search of pain, I chose with gifts to tempt   720
Her faithful chastity. Dawn fueled my fear
And changed my shape (I felt this happening),
And so, through Pallas' Athens, I went home
Unrecognized. My house looked guilt-free, chaste,
And anxious for its lord. My thousand tricks   725
Scarce gained a viewing with Erechthida,[10]
Whose sight so stunned me that I almost dropped
My planned temptations. I could scarce hold back
The truth and all the kisses she deserved.
She was so sad (though none could look so fair   730
In sadness), longing for her stolen spouse.
Imagine, Phocus, how she then appeared:
How comely! How becoming in her grief!
Why tell how many times her virtue held,
How many times she said, 'I'm saved for one: 735
Wherever he may be, I save my joys
For him'? What man of sense would not have thought
These tests enough? But not content, I strove
To wound myself and, for one night with me,
Pledged wealth and gifts that finally gave her pause.   740
In cruel success, I cried, 'Behold! I am
No lover, but your spouse—who's found you false!'
She said no word, but silenced, crushed with shame,
She fled her wicked spouse and treacherous home,
In hatred of my wrongs and of my sex,   745
To prowl the slopes and learn Diana's ways.
     "Love's fiercer fires then reached my lonely bones:
I prayed for pardon and confessed I'd sinned
And I, too, might be overcome with gifts,
Were such gifts given me. With this avowed,   750
And once her wounded virtue was avenged,†

10. Procris, daughter of Erechtheus

She came back, and we passed the years in bliss.
And what's more, as if she were not enough,
She brought me gifts: a dog, which Cynthia[11]
Had given, saying, 'He will outrun all,'   755
And then this spear which (as you see) I hold.
    "You want the story of the other gift?[†]
Then hear this wondrous marvel! You'll be moved:
When Laius' son outfoxed all previous minds
To solve her rhymes, the cryptic riddler fell,   760
Her secrets perishing in headlong dive.
[Kind Themis, though, does not go unavenged:]
Another plague soon wracked Aonian Thebes—
A fearsome fiend who killed herdsmen and herds.
We local youths arrived with hunting-snares   765
And circled the wide fields, but that swift beast
Leapt lightly through the lines and past the tops
Of ready nets and webs. Then we unleashed
Our hounds, but as they chased the beast, she fled
With birdlike speed and sported with our band.   770
All called for me to loose my Hurricane[12]
(That was the gift-dog's name), who until now
Was held back by his striving straining neck.
He'd scarce been freed when we lost track of him:
The hot dust showed his paw-prints, but the dog   775
Escaped our eyes, for he flew swifter still
Than any spear, or ball shot from a sling,
Or arrow fired from a Gortynian bow.[13]
    "Above the fields, a nearby hilltop loomed.
From there, I gained a view of that strange race,   780
As now the beast seemed caught, and now escaped
Her wounds. She fled with cunning, never straight,
But circling back to fool his chasing jaws
And keep her foe from springing. He pressed on,
Kept pace in his pursuit, appeared to catch—   785

11. Diana, associated with Mount Cynthus
12. *Laelaps* in Greek; Actaeon had a dog of the same name (3.212)
13. Gortyna, a city on Crete, famous for its archers

But did not catch, and snapped the empty air.
I turned then to my spear, but with it poised,
My fingers on the strap, I glanced away,
And when I looked again, amid the field
I saw (a wondrous sight!) two marble forms: 790
One running, one pursuing—so you'd think.
Some god had wished, if any god was there,
That both stay undefeated in that race."†
    This said, he stopped. "What of the lance's crime?"
Asked Phocus. So, the lance's crime he told: 795
"Our blessings, Phocus, led to all our woes—
I'll tell them first. What joy, Aeacides,
To call to mind those blissful early years,
When we were happy husband, happy wife!
For we were linked by common cares and love,   800
Nor would she have preferred Jove's bed to mine,
Nor could another girl have stolen me,
Not even Venus. One love warmed our hearts.
    "The sun's first rays would scarce have touched the hills
When I'd set off to hunt about the woods,   805
A youth alone with neither horse nor slave
Nor keen-nosed hounds nor knotted nets in tow:
My spear would keep me safe. But when my hand
Had tired of slaying beasts, I'd seek the shade
And cooling zephyrs of a frigid vale.   810
These zephyrs I would seek to soothe my heat;
These zephyrs were my longed-for rest from toil.
'Come, zephyr!'† I would croon (so I recall)
'And help me—find my breast, most welcome one!
And, as you do, relieve my burning heat!'   815
Perhaps I'd add (my fate so led me on)
More fawning words: 'You are my best delight,'
I often said. 'You heal and tend to me;
You make me love the woods and lonesome ways,
And ever yearn to feel your breeze's kiss!'   820
    "But someone heard my words and misconstrued
Their double sense and, thinking 'zephyr' was

A nymphal name, believed I loved a nymph.
The rash informer rushed this fictive charge
To Procris, whispering what they had heard.   825
How gullible is love! She swooned in pain
(So I was told), and later, when revived,
She called herself a poor ill-fated wretch,
And mourned my faithlessness. Thus misinformed,
She feared a nothing with an empty name,   830
[And grieved her lot as if her foe were real.]
And yet, the wretch had doubts, hoped she was wrong,
And would not trust the charge devoid of proof,
Or else pass judgment on her husband's guilt.
     "When Dawn next banished night, I sought the woods,   835
And as I lay triumphant in the grass,
I said, 'Come, zephyr, and assuage my pains!'
It seemed, just then, a groan cut through my words,
But still I said, 'Come, dearest!' when I heard
A falling leaf, mistook it for a beast,   840
And hurled my spear. But it was Procris' voice
Which, from her wounded core, cried out, 'Ah, me!'
Thus did I recognize my faithful wife,
And seek her voice with manic headlong strides.
Half-dead, with torn and bloody clothes (poor me!)   845
I found her, drawing out the gift she gave.
I raised her frame, more dear to me than mine,
In loving arms and, tearing free her breast,
I bound the wound and tried to stanch the blood
And begged not to be guilty of her death.   850
With failing strength my dying wife forced out
These words: 'I beg you, by our wedding vows
And by the gods above and those of mine,†
By all I've done for you, and by the love
I still feel, even now it's caused my death: 855
Do not let Zephyr share our marriage-bed!'
I grasped at last that she mistook the name
And told her—but what good was it to tell?
She slumped as all the strength escaped her veins,

And while she still could look, she looked at me,   860
Then breathed her luckless last upon my lips.
Yet as she died, her face seemed more at peace. . . ."
   The tearful hero ceased his tale. Then came
King Aeacus, his sons, and their recruits,
And Cephalus received their aiding arms.   865

Book 8

[SCYLLA AND NISUS]†

THE MORNING star now bared the light of day
As night fled, Eurus fell, and rain clouds rose.
On Auster's gusts, the men from Aeacus
Returned with Cephalus before their time,
Blown haply to the harbor of their hopes.   5
    But meanwhile, Minos marred Megarian shores
And tried his martial strength on Nisus' realm,
Alcathoë,[1] whose monarch's head of hair
Contained, amid its honored white, a lock
Of splendid scarlet that preserved his throne.   10
Six times the rising moon had filled its horns,
And still the war's result hung in suspense
Between the doubtful wings of Victory.
    Atop the singing palace walls, it's said,
There rose a tower where Leto's son[2] once set   15
His golden lyre, whose sound stuck in the stone.
There, Nisus' daughter often used to climb
And cast small pebbles down the ringing rocks
In times of peace; she used it now, in war,

---

1. Megara, whose founder was Alcathous (cf. 7.443)
2. Apollo, god of music

To view the martial strife. As war dragged on,   20
She learned their leaders' names, arms, horses, clothes,
And Cretan quivers. Most of all, she learned
Their leader's face—and learned it all too well.
In her eyes, if Europa's son concealed
His head within a feather-crested casque,   25
The helm made Minos handsome; if he bore
A brazen shield, the shield became him well;
And if his aiming arms sent forth a spear,
The girl would praise his mingled strength and skill;
Or if he bent an arrow on his bow,   30
She'd swear that Phoebus stood there, shafts in hand.
But when he showed his features bared of bronze,
And, clad in purple, rode his snow-white steed,
Caparisoned and foaming at the reins,
Then Nisus' child was scarce herself—scarce sane!   35
How lucky was the lance he touched, she thought;
How lucky was the harness in his hand!
She ached to wend her maiden way between
The foemen's lines, were that allowed; she ached
To vault the tower and join the Knossian camp,   40
Or else unbar the gates, or anything
That Minos would have wished; and gazing on
The Cretan king's white tents, said, "I don't know
If this sad strife should bring me grief or joy:
I grieve that darling Minos is my foe,   45
Yet I would not have known him, save the war!
But if he took me hostage, war could end:
He'd have me with him as a pledge of peace. . . .
"If she who bore you, beauty of the world,
Was like you, she deserved the love of gods!   50
Oh, I'd be thrice as happy if I could
Fly down into the king of Knossos' camp,
Confess my burning love, and ask his price
In dowry—only not my city's walls!
My nuptial hopes shall die before they live   55
On treason—though it's often good to lose
When victors treat their victims mercifully. . . .

  "To fight for murdered sons is surely just:
His aims are valid as his weapons' aim.
I think we'll lose! if that's our city's fate,   60
Why should his martial strength unlock my walls
And not my heart? It's best he win without
Such death, delay, and loss of his own blood!
Then, Minos, I'd not fear lest you be hurt
By accident—for who's so cruel that they   65
Would dare to spear you if not by mistake?
These plans are good! I *will* give up my land
As dowry for myself, and end the war.
Yet, what good's will when sentries guard the gate,
And father holds the keys? It's him alone   70
I sadly fear, alone he halts my hopes.
Would god I had no father! Yet each man
Can be his own god: Fortune scorns the weak!
Another girl aflame with such desire
Would long since have destroyed whatever crossed   75
Her love—and gladly! Why should I do less?
I'd fare through flame and sword, though sword and flame
Aren't needed here: I need my father's hair!
That scarlet lock's worth more to me than gold,
For it will bless me with my heart's desire."   80
  Soon night, that fiercest fuel for lovers' pangs,
Arrived and, in the dark, her daring grew.
In that first hour, when day-worn spirits seal
In sleep, the silent girl (oh, dreadful deed!)
Broke in her father's room and bore away   85
His lock of life! With this ill-gotten gain,
[A sinful spoil she bore beyond the gates,]
She breached the foe (her triumph felt so sure),
Straight to the startled king, to whom she said,
"Love dealt this deed. I, Scylla,† Nisus' child,   90
Here yield to you my land and household gods!
I seek no prize but you—and know my gift,
This scarlet mark of love, is more than hair:
It is my father's head." Her guilty hand
Reached out to give, but Minos shrank from reach.   95

Appalled by her unnatural act, he cried,
"May all the gods, O horror of our times,
Expel you from our world, its lands and seas!
I'll surely not allow my world of Crete,
Jove's cradle, to feel such a monster's tread!"†   100
    And when the just lawgiver had set terms
Upon his conquered foes, he bade his fleet
Of brazen vessels launched and rowed from shore.
When Scylla saw the ships put out to sea
And knew the king would not reward her sin,   105
Her prayers gave way to wrath. Enraged, she reached
And cried through streaming hair, "Where do you flee,
Abandoning the source of your success,
You whom I set before my lord and land?
Where do you flee, cruel man, whose triumph is   110
My vice and virtue both? Are you unmoved
By all my gifts and love, when all my hopes
Depend on you? Alone, where can I turn?
My city? It lies wrecked, and if it stood,
Its gates would close to me. My father's heart?   115
I've given it to you! For what I've done,
I've won my people's hate and strangers' fear,
And walled off all the world: to live on Crete!
If you refuse that, leaving me unthanked,
Europa's not your mother—you were born   120
To Syrtis' sands, wind-whipped Charybdis, or
Armenian tigers!† Nor is Jove your sire,
Nor did he steal her in a bull disguise
(Your famed birth's false); a real bull, [too untamed
To love a heifer] sired you! Strike me now,   125
Lord Nisus! Fallen walls, enjoy my pain!
For I confess I've earned it and should die,
But let them kill me whom I have betrayed!
Why should *you* judge my crime, whom my crime crowned?
My sins toward lord and land should seem to you   130
A service! Truly, she's the wife for you
Who tricked a savage bull with wooden trysts
And bore its jumbled baby.† Do you hear?

Or are my words lost to the winds that move
Your ships, ungrateful man? [No wonder now   135
Pasiphaë preferred a bull to you
When you're more bullish still!] Alas, you bid
Them smite the sounding furrows with their oars,
While my poor land and I fade fast away,
But all for naught—you've cheated me in vain!   140
I'll force my trailing arms around your stern
And cruise across the seas!"
                        This scarcely said,
She dove and chased the craft with yearning strength;
Unsought, unloved, she grasped the Knossian keel.
Her father spied her there (for he'd become   145
A blond-winged osprey, flying overhead)
And down he swooped to peck the clinging girl.
Aghast, she lost her grip upon the stern,
But seemed to hang in air above the waves—
Hang on her wings! A wingèd bird transformed,   150
She's called a "shearer"† for the lock she sheared.

[THE MINOTAUR]†

   Once Minos had made land on Cretan soil
And offered up a hundred bulls to Jove,
He decked his house with spoils, but its disgrace
Kept growing as the monstrous two-formed child   155
Made his wife's foul adultery well-known.
So Minos chose to send the shame away
Into a sightless cage of twists and turns,
Which Daedalus, famed for his builder's skill,
Constructed, jumbling signs and leading eyes   160
Astray with multitudes of winding ways.
As clear Meander's playful Phrygian waves,†
Whose fickle flows glide back and forth and join
And see themselves—now surging toward their springs,
Now toward the sea—run through their changing course,   165
Thus Daedalus made countless puzzling paths
So even he could scarcely find the door,

Deceit so ruled the labyrinth's design!
   The twin-shaped bull-man then was locked inside,
Where Attic blood would feed the monster twice   170
Till a third nine-year tribute vanquished him.
When, with a maiden's help and spools of string,†
The door was found which none had reached before,
The son of Aegeus sailed with Minos' child
For Naxos, cruelly leaving her behind   175
Upon its shores. Left woebegone, she found
Relief in Liber's arms, which took her crown,
And hurled it in the sky that she might shine
Forever in the stars. It soared on high,
And as it soared, its gems turned bright with fire,   180
Then took their place, still looking like a Crown,
Between the Kneeler and the Strangled Snake.†

[DAEDALUS]†

Despising Crete and exile, Daedalus
Was meanwhile yearning for his distant home.
"He'll block my way by land and sea," he said,   185
"But still the sky is open—I'll go there!
Though Minos rules all, he can't rule the air."†
This said, he bent his mind toward arts unknown,
And altered nature, setting feathers so
[—First small, then larger ones—] that you would think   190
They'd grown in slanting, just as pastors' pipes
Rise one by one through their uneven reeds.
He bound the spines with string, the ends with wax,
And gave them, thus arranged, a gentle curve,
Like real bird-wings. Young Icarus stood by   195
And, unaware he handled his own doom,
First grinned and grasped at plumes the wind had stirred,
Then softened yellow wax beneath his thumb,
And slowed his father's wondrous work with play.
   When all the final touches were in place,   200
The maker poised himself between his wings,
And raised his body through the beaten air.

FIGURE 7. *Daedalus and Icarus*, Frederic Leighton (c. 1869). As President of the Royal Academy, Lord Leighton so embodied the Victorian vogue for classicism that he was nicknamed "Jupiter Olympus." While capturing Ovid's description of the concerned father aiding his overeager son, Leighton's portrayal of Icarus as a gleaming, idealized youth has been read as a racialized metaphor for enlightenment, or as revealing of the painter's homosexuality.

He taught his son next: "Icarus, be warned
To take a middle course. If you're too low,
The waves will weight your wings; too high, they'll burn.   205
Fly in between, and steer not by the Bears,
Boötes, nor Orion's sheathless sword,
But take my lead!" Then, reading him the rules
Of flight, he fixed his arms with untried wings,
And worked and warned while his old cheeks grew wet.   210
With trembling hands, the father gave his son
A kiss that would not be returned, then flew
Ahead in fear. Just like a bird who guides
A fledgling from its nest, he urged the boy
To follow him and learn the fatal skill.   215
[And flapped his wings and glanced back at his son's.]
      In wonderment, an angler's curving rod,
A shepherd's crook, and plowman's plow were clutched
To see men take the skies—they must be gods!†
With Juno's Samos³ to the left (they'd passed   220
Delos and Paros by), and honey-rich
Calymna and Lebinthos on the right,
The boy began to frolic in his flight
And boldly left his guide to roam at will
Through higher heaven, so close the searing sun   225
Made soft the perfumed wax that bound his wings—
The wax thawed through! He flapped his naked arms,
But, featherless, they could not ply the air,
And, calling out his father's name, he plunged
Into the azure sea named after him.⁴   230
His luckless sire—a sire no longer—cried,
"O Icarus! Where are you, Icarus?
Where shall I seek you? Icarus!" he cried.
Then, seeing the floating wings, he cursed his craft,
And buried the boy's body in a tomb,   235
Whose land is still named for the buried boy.⁵

3. Samos was the site of a long-established cult of Hera (Juno)
4. The Icarian Sea, a subdivision of the eastern Aegean
5. Icaria, an island in the Icarian Sea

But, seeing the man entomb his wretched son,
A chattering partridge in a muddy ditch
Looked up and clapped its wings and sang with joy.
This new-made bird—unique, not seen before—   240
Would long live to reproach you, Daedalus.
For, ignorant of fate, your sister had
Sent you a young apprentice: her own son,
A boy of twice-six years and quick to learn.
Observing once the backbone of a fish,   245
He thought of cutting teeth into a blade
Of iron and invented the first saw;
And he first made a hinge of iron legs
So one held still while one a circle drew.
The jealous Daedalus soon threw him off   250
Minerva's holy mount[6] and said he'd slipped;
But Pallas loves a genius: catching him,
She feathered him midair into a fowl.
The force of his swift genius passed into
His wings and feet, but his old name remained,[7]   255
For this bird never lifts itself on high,
Nor nests in trees, but skims along the ground
And seeks out shrubberies to lay its eggs
In fearful memory of its former fall.
    The land of Aetna welcomed Daedalus,   260
Whose weary cause King Cocalus the Kind
Took up in arms. Now, thanks to Theseus,
The tearful tribute Athens paid had stopped.
Their shrines enwreathed, warlike Minerva, Jove,
And other gods were worshiped, offered blood,   265
And shown respect with incense and with gifts.

[THE CALYDONIAN HUNT][†]

    Through all of Argos, Rumor roamed and spread
The name of Theseus. The thriving Greeks

6. The Acropolis in Athens
7. Perdix, Latin for "partridge"

Besought his aid in strife, as Calydon
Besought his aid—though Meleäger lived—   270
With proffered prayers and painful pleas. The cause:
A pig—a fiend that served Diana's wrath.
For they say Oeneus, in a fruitful year,
Had worshiped Ceres' grain, Lyaeus'[8] wine,
And Pallas, blonde Minerva, for her oil,   275
Till all the gods of field and sky received
The gifts they craved. Just Leto's daughter's shrines,
They say, were left unscented and ignored.
Gods, too, feel rage:[†] "I won't go unredressed!
Unhonored, yes," she said, "not unavenged!"   280
Thus slighted, into Oeneus' fields she sent
A vengeful boar, big as the bulls that tread
Epirus' plains and dwarfing Sicily's,[†]
With eyes ablaze in blood, a stiff-set neck,   284
[And bristles like a palisade of spears.][†]   286
Its snorts sent seething foam across its flanks;
Its tusks were tusks of Indian elephants;
Its mouth flashed flame and leaves burned in its breath.
    First trampling early corn still in the blade,   290
It then reaped farmers' tears by mowing down
Their ears of ripened hope. In vain the flails,
In vain the barns awaited promised crops!
Down heavy grapes fell with their creeping vines,
And ever-leafy olive boughs and fruits!   295
It scorned herdsmen and hounds to raid their flocks,
Nor could ferocious bulls defend their droves.
The folk took refuge in their city walls,
Till Meleäger's band of chosen youths
Came seeking fame:[†]
                        Tyndareus' twins were there,   300
Who boxed and rode; and Jason, first to sail;
That happy couple, Theseus and his
Pirithoüs; and Thestius' two sons;
Aphareus' sons, swift Idas, Lynceus too;

8. Bacchus, appropriately

Hippothoüs; and Caeneus, no maid now;   305
Spear-famed Acastus; Dryas; Actor's sons;
And fierce Leucippus; and Amyntor's child,
One Phoenix; and Echion, fastest far;
The sire of great Achilles; Telamon;
Boeotian Iolaüs; Pheres' son;   310
Panopeus; Hyleus; keen Eurytion;
Narycian Lelex; Elean Phyleus;
Fierce Hippasus; and Nestor, not yet old;
Amyclan youths sent by Hippocoön;
Ancaeus from Parrhasia; Ampycus'   315
Prophetic son; Penelope's mate's sire;
And Oecles' son, safe from his wife; and last,
The Tegean girl who graced Arcadia's groves.
Her robes were clasped, her hair was simply tied,
An ivory quiver clanged about her left,   320
A bow stood in her hand—such was her dress.
Her face you might call girlish for a boy's,
Or boyish for a girl's; but, at first sight,
The Calydonian hero⁹ longed for her
And drank love's hidden flames, despite the gods.   325
"O blessed is any man she'd deign to wed!"
He cried, but time and tact allowed no more:
The greater task of battle was at hand.
　　A crowded wood, unfelled by ages past,
Rose from the plain to loom across the fields.   330
Once there, some of the heroes set their snares,
While some unleashed their hounds, and some pursued
The path of prints, each keen to risk his life.
A valley ran there, too, carved out by streams
Of coursing rain, its swampy depths grown thick   335
With bending willows, sedges, slender sprouts,
And marshy rushes shading smaller reeds.
From here, it's said, the boar launched at its foes
With violent force, like flames from clashing clouds,
And flattened all the forest with a crack.   340

9. Meleäger

The youths cried out and held their spears aloft,
The broad points dazzling in their dauntless hands,
As on it charged among their hindering hounds
And sent them barking with a sidelong stroke.
   Echion's arm sent flying the first spear,   345
Which missed and lightly scraped a maple tree.
The next one, had it not been thrown so hard,
Would surely have hit home and struck its back,
And yet Thessalian Jason overshot.
"O Phoebus," said the son of Ampycus,   350
"As I have served and serve you, guide my spear!"
The god did what he could: the boar was hit,
Yet stood unscathed—Diana had borne off
The head midflight and left a pointless shaft!
This stoked its beastly rage to lightning heat,   355
Till flames flashed in its eyes and heaving chest.
As boulders hurtle from a catapult
When shot toward battlements or towers of troops,
So flew the baleful boar upon the youths
And struck Hippalmus down with Pelagon,†   360
Who watched the right. Their comrades dragged them off,
But still a death-stroke reached Enaesimus,
Son of Hippocoön, who, turning back
To flee in fear, was hamstrung and collapsed.
The Pylian[10] almost perished long before   365
The age of Troy, but vaulting on his spear
Into a nearby treetop, down he gazed
In safety at the villain he'd escaped.
The fiend then used an oak to hone its tusks
For death and, with its weaponry restored,   370
Slashed snout-deep into Eurytus' son's thigh.
   But now the twins, not yet two stars in heaven,
Were both seen, riding snow-white horses both,
Both shaking shining spear-points in the air.
They would have burst its bristles, had the brute 375
Not breached a pathless wood where neither spear

10. Nestor

Nor steed could pass, pursued by Telamon
Who, reckless in his zeal, tripped on a root
And fell face-down. While Peleus helped him up,
The Tegean sped an arrow on the string,   380
Shot from her bending bow. The shaft scraped past
The creature's back and fixed below its ear,
A bloody trickle reddening its hairs.
Nor did her arms' achievement please her more
Than Meleäger, who was first, it's thought,   385
To see the blood and show his group the sight:
"Your manly valor† wins you fame!" he said.
The blushing men then urged each other on
With rousing cries, and flung in disarray
An airborne spate of self-defeating spears.   390
But look! the two-bit-axed Arcadian, mad
To meet his fate, cried, "Learn how women's arms
Pale next to men's, O youths—leave this to me!
Although Latona's daughter shields its life,
Despite Diana, I will strike it down!"   395
So spoke his boastful bluster-swollen lips
As, with both hands, he raised the double axe
And stood on tiptoe, poised on point to strike.
The beast beset his boldness with its tusks,
Which tore his groin—the shortest path to death.   400
Ancaeus fell, his entrails spewing forth
In gobs of gore that soaked the soil with blood.
Ixion's son Pirithoüs came next,
A spear-point shaking in his mighty hand,
But Aegeus' son cried, "Back, my dearest one,   405
My better half!† The brave may stand aside:
Ancaeus died through recklessness of nerve!"
This said, he hurled a heavy dogwood shaft
Whose well-aimed tip of bronze would have hit home,
Had not a leafy oak tree intervened.   410
Then Aeson's son let fly a spear, which chance
Bent toward the downfall of a yapping dog,
Whose blameless bowels it drove into the ground.
    Not so for Oeneus' son! He hurled two spears:

One hit the earth, the other struck its back.   415
Then, as it raged and turned itself around,
And spewed afresh with roars and blood and foam,
Its slayer rushed to bait the creature's wrath,
And sank a splendid spear into its side.
The others showed their joy with cheerful shouts   420
And flocked to clasp the victor's hand in hand.
They gazed in wonder at the sprawling beast,
Not yet convinced that it was safe to touch,
Though each bedewed their weapons in its blood.
His foot on its fell head, he cried, "Receive   425
The prize that's mine to give, Nonacrian,[11]
And let my glory go in part to you!"
Then he awarded her its bristling hide,
Still stiff with spikes, and tusk-emblazoned head.
This pleased the giver and the gifted both,   430
But jealous murmurings rose from the rest,
Among whom waved and wailed the Thestiads,[12]
Who cried, "Girl, put those down! Don't steal our spoils!
For, be assured, your beauty won't suffice
To save you when your lavish lover leaves!"   435
Robbed of her gift and his own right to give,
Mars' son[13] snapped, gnashed his teeth, and cried, "I'll teach
You thieves of others' honors how to tell
Actions from words!" and plunged his wicked blade
Into Plexippus' unsuspecting chest.   440
Then Toxeus, doubting whether to avenge
His brother's fall or fear his fate, stood still
But soon the sword, hot from his brother's death,
Dispelled all doubt, reheating in his blood.

11. Atalanta
12. Meleäger's uncles Plexippus and Toxeus
13. Meleäger (but cf. 414)

[ALTHAEA AND MELEÄGER][†]

Althaea was at temple, giving thanks   445
To heaven for her son's triumph, when she saw
Her brothers brought in dead. She filled the town
With cries of woe and changed from gold to black,
But when she learned who'd killed them, all her tears
And sorrow fled as vengeance won her heart.   450
     There was a log the Sisters Three[14] had set
Afire when Thestia[15] was giving birth.
While thumbing through the thread of fate, they'd said,
"We give you and this wood, O newborn babe,
One span of time!" With this foretold,   455
The goddesses withdrew. At once, she'd snatched
The burning brand and doused it wet with spray.
Saved and concealed in deepest secrecy,
For years, young man, the log had saved your life!
But now the mother fetched it, called for wood,   460
And kindled flames of hate. Four times she moved
To set the brand ablaze—four times she stopped.
A mother and a sister fought in her,
The two names tugging at her single heart.
She often blanched for fear of sins she planned,   465
As often blushed with eyes of frenzied rage,
Now looking like she threatened something cruel,
And now like someone you'd have mercy on,
For when her soul's fierce fire had dried her tears,
Still more tears came. And as a wind-blown ship,   470
Tide-tossed against the wind, will feel twin pulls
And vaguely yield to both, so Thestia
By turns, caught in between half-hearted wills,
Put wrath aside and took it up again.
     At length, the sister beat the parent back,   475
And she, to soothe her blood-kin's shades with blood,
Crossed love for love. As death's fire grew, she cried,

14. The Fates
15. Althaea, daughter of Thestius

"May this pyre burn my flesh and blood to ash!"
And with the fatal log in her fell hand,
The ill-starred woman hailed the funeral shrine: 480
"O threefold goddesses of punishment,
Eumenides, gaze on my fury's rites!
My sin avenges sin: death calls for death,
Crime leads to crime, and graves bring other graves—
May heaping sorrow end this hateful house!   485
Shall happy Oeneus triumph with his son,
While Thestius has none? Both men should mourn!
But let you newborn ghosts, my brothers' souls,
Accept my service, my great sacrifice,
The wicked output of my womb—ah, me!   490
Where is this leading? Brothers, please forgive
A mother's hands for failing in their task.
He ought to die, I know—but not through me!
Yet must he live unscathed in victory
And, swollen with success, rule Calydon,   495
While you, mere dust and shade, lie cold in death?
I will not bear it! Let the villain die
And wreck his father's hopes and fatherland. . . .
But where's my mother's heart, my parent's cares,
My pangs of twice-five months?† Oh, that you'd died   500
In infancy's first fires while I stood by!
I gave you life, but now you've earned your death:
Your deed's reward is giving back the life
I gave you twice—in birth, then with the log.
Or else, seal me inside my brothers' tomb!   505
I want—I can't—what shall I do? Just now
I saw their wounds, their slaughter's sight, and yet
My spirit breaks with mother's love. Poor me!
Your triumph's tragic, brothers: triumph still!
Just let me share the solace I shall give   510
And follow you myself!" Trembling, she turned
And flung the fatal firebrand in the flames.
The very log then groaned, or seemed to groan,
Caught and consumed by the reluctant fire.
      Untold and elsewhere, Meleäger burned   515

And felt his entrails hot with hidden flames.
And though his valiance withstood the pain,
He grieved to die a coward's bloodless death,
And thought Ancaeus lucky for his wounds.
His brothers, faithful sisters, agèd sire,   520
And wife[†] he summoned with his dying groan—
Perhaps his mother, too. The fire and pain
Increased, then dulled again, then died as one,
As bit by bit his soul passed into air
And bit by bit the coals turned grey with ash.   525
    High Calydon lay low. Old mourned with young,
And lords with low-born. Calydonian wives,
Maids of Euenus,[16] wailed and tore their hair.
Prostrated in the dust, his father fouled
His ancient face and hair, and cursed his age;   530
His mother, seeing the direness of her deed,
Impaled herself with her own rueful hand.
Not if a god gave me a hundred mouths
To speak, and genius, and all Helicon,
Could I enact his sisters' woeful prayers![†]   535
With shame put by and bosoms beaten blue,
They clasped and clasped his corpse, while corpse there was,
And kissed it, kissed his bier till all was ash,
Then heaped the ashes, held them to their hearts,
And fell upon his tomb, embraced the stone,   540
And poured their tears out on his chiseled name.
Latonia,[17] finally sated by the fall
Of Portheus' house,[18] raised all the girls, except
For Gorge and Alcmene's son's new wife,[†]
On downy wings that ran along their arms,   545
Then gave them beaks and sent them, changed, on high.

16. The river at Calydon
17. Diana
18. Portheus, father of Oeneus

[ACHELOÜS]†

Now Theseus, his duty done, sought out
Tritonia's city and Erechtheus',
But rain-swelled Acheloüs blocked his way:
"Famed Cecrops' heir," he said, "enter my home,   550
And do not venture my rapacious waves!
Enormous trees and stones are swept across
The roaring swell. I've seen the banks' tall barns
Dragged under, herds and all! For in this flood,
Strength does not help the ox, nor speed the horse,   555
And many men have sunk beneath its swirl
Amid the rush of melting mountain snows.
You'd better wait until the waves resume
Their normal course and bounds." And Aegeus' son
Assented: "Acheloüs, I shall take   560
Your home and counsel!" And he took them both.
    In porous walls of soft volcanic rock,
The ground was wet with moss, the ceiling set
With conch and purple sea-snail, laid in turn.
And now Hyperion's light was two-thirds gone,   565
And Theseus lay feasting with his men:
Ixion's son here, Troezen's Lelex there,
His hero's temples growing flecked with grey,
And others deemed deserving by the stream
Of Acarnania,[19] thrilled to host such guests.   570
Barefooted nymphs soon set the banquet spread
And when the feast was gone, they laid out wine
In jeweled cups. The mighty hero then
Looked out to sea as, pointing, he inquired:
"What is that place? Pray tell the island's name,   575
Although it seems there may be more than one."
The stream replied, "It's not just one you see,
But five, though distance makes them indistinct.
You'll be less shocked by scorned Diana's deeds†
To hear they once were nymphs who sacrificed   580

19. The Acheloüs marked the boundary between Acarnania and Aetolia

Some twice-five bulls, then called the local gods
To join their sacral dance, forgetting me.
Grown to my fullest flood, I raged alike
In soul and swell, and tore the woods from woods
And fields from fields. Then, with the place they stood,   585
I flung the nymphs—who sure recalled me then!—
Into the sea. The ocean's tides and mine
Soon split the land into as many parts
As the Echinades[†] you spy to sea.

    "And look! one dear to me lies far, far off   590
Where sailors call her 'Perimele Isle.'
When, loving her, I stole her virginhood,
Hippodamas, her outraged father, threw
His daughter from a sea-cliff to her death.
But, lifting her, I cried, 'O Trident-god,   595
Who won the second world of wandering waves,
[In which we sacred streams all end our course,[†]
Come, Neptune—hear me! I bear one I've harmed.
And if Hippodamas were kind or fair,
Or fatherly, or lacking less in love,   600
He should have pitied her and pardoned me.   600a
But since her savage sire keeps her from land,]   600b
Bring aid to one a savage sire has drowned:
Please, Neptune, grant that she may have some place!
[Or let her be a place that I'll embrace!'
The sea-king's nodding set his waves ashake.
The nymph swam on in fear, but as she did,   605
I touched her trembling breasts, which shook with fright,
And while I stroked her, felt her growing hard
As surging soil engulfed her everywhere.]
And while I spoke, soil shod her swimming limbs,
And changed her body to a solid isle."   610

[BAUCIS AND PHILEMON][†]

    With this, the stream fell silent. All were awed,
Save one of untamed mind who scorned the gods
And laughed at their belief—Ixion's son:

"Lies, Acheloüs! You esteem the gods
Too much—they cannot give and take things' shapes!"[†]   615
This stunned them and they all condemned such talk,
Old Lelex most of all, who wisely said:
"The might of heaven is vast and knows no bounds,
And all the gods desire has come to pass.
In case you doubt me, in the Phrygian hills   620
A walled-off linden grows beside an oak.
(I've seen the place myself, for Pittheus[20]
Once sent me to his father Pelops' realm.)
Nearby there is a swamp, once land for homes,
But now the marshy haunt of gulls and coots.   625
There Jove, in mortal guise, went with his son,
The heir of Atlas, staff-less and unwinged.[21]
A thousand doors they knocked on, seeking rest;
A thousand doors were locked, but one flung wide—
A reed-roofed shack, where old Philemon lived   630
With pious Baucis, both alike in years.
There they had wed in youth; there shared old age,
And, knowing they were poor, there eased their lot
By thinking their condition no disgrace.
No slaves nor masters could be sought inside   635
For those two likewise ordered and obeyed.
    "When those from heaven approached this humble home
And entered, stooping, through its tiny door,
The old man laid a bench and bade them rest.
Then Baucis cushioned it with homespun cloth,   640
Raked out the cooling ashes from the hearth,
Stoked leaves between the coals of yesterday,
And coaxed a flame back with her agèd breath.
Dry twigs and broken branches from the eaves
She chopped and set beneath a copper pot,   645
Then peeled a cabbage-head her husband picked
From their well-watered plot. Meanwhile, he forked
A paltry pork-loin from the blackened beam

---

20. A king of Lelex's native Troezen and the son of the Phrygian Pelops
21. Mercury, Atlas' grandson, in disguise again

Where he'd long kept it hanging, shaved a slice,
And brought the shaven rasher to a boil.   650
   The intervening hours were passed in talk
While time flew by unfelt. Down from its nail,
They took their beechwood tub by its stiff strap,
And poured in water for their guests to bathe;
Then they laid down a mattress stuffed with sedge   655a
Across a frame with feet of willow-wood[†]   656a
And covered it with fabrics only used
For feasts, though even these were cheap and old,
As fits a willow couch. The gods reclined.
With shaky hands and hitched-up skirts, she set   660
The table; finding one leg not as long,
She used a pot to even out its length,
Then wiped green mint across its evened top,
And served Minerva's virgin mottled fruits,[22]
And bitter autumn cherries soused in wine,   665
And endives, radishes, and lumps of cheese,
And eggs turned lightly over lukewarm coals,
All in clay crocks—whose lack of silver trim
Decked both the wine-bowl and their beechwood cups
Whose insides were inlaid with yellow wax.   670
And soon, the hearth supplied their steaming feast
While wine of no great age was poured again,
Then cleared to serve the small and second course
Of nuts and figs and wrinkled dates and plums
And basketfuls of apples, sweet to smell,   675
And purple grapevines, all arranged around
A gleaming honeycomb—while, over all,
Their cheerful looks belied their poverty.
   "They meanwhile marked how, when the bowl was drained,
The wine refilled each time all on its own.   680
Then Baucis and Philemon knelt in fear
And prayed with awe and dread and upturned hands,
Beseeching pardon for the meager meal;
As hosts of godly guests, they would have slain

---

22. Olives, when not quite ripe, are speckled green and black

The single goose that watched their humble home,   685
But, fleet of flight, it wore the old ones out,
At last eluding them and fleeing, it seemed,
Unto the gods, who bid them spare its life.
'We two are gods, and justly shall we smite
This faithless land!' they said. 'But we shall spare   690
You from that punishment. Now leave your home
And walk with us up that tall mountainside.'
Both acquiesced and, leaning on their staffs,†
They struggled up the mountain step by step.
When they were but a bowshot from the top,   695
They glanced behind and saw that all around
Had sunk into a swamp, except their house;
And while they gaped and grieved their neighbors' fates,
Their home, too cramped for even two, transformed
Into a temple—pillars turned from posts,   700
The roof of straw was yellowed into gold,
The doors grew carved, and marble paved the ground.
　　"Then Saturn's son said kindly, 'Good old man,
Good worthy wife, now ask us what you wish!'
Once Baucis and Philemon talked it through,   705
He gave their shared decision to the gods:
'We ask to be your priests and temple guards,
And, having lived in harmony, to die
In the same hour, that I may never see
Her tomb, nor shall she have to bury me.'   710
Their wish came true: they lived and watched the shrine,
Till, spent with age, they chanced one day to walk
The sacred steps, remembering things past—
When Baucis saw Philemon sprouting leaves,
As Baucis did before Philemon's eyes!   715
And as a treetop thickened round each face,
Both cried as one, "Farewell, dear spouse!" before
Their mouths as one were overgrown with green.
And the Bithynians still point out that pair
Of tree-trunks side by side. I heard this from   720
Old honest men (who had no cause to lie).
Myself, I saw the branches decked with wreaths,

Placed more, and said, 'Those loved by gods are gods,
And worshippers receive their worship, too.'"

[MESTRA AND ERYSICHTHON]†

The teller and his tale had moved them all,   725
But Theseus the most, who longed to hear
More miracles. So, propped up on one arm,
The Calydonian stream said, "There are those,
Brave man, who, once transformed, retain their shape,
And those, too, who may pass through many forms—   730
You, Proteus, who swim the circling seas,
Are seen here as a lion, here a youth,
And now a raging boar, and now a snake
All fear to touch. Soon horns make you a bull,
Or else you'll seem a stone, or else a tree!   735
At times you'll be a stream and seem to flow;
At other times a flame, the waters' foe.
    "Autolycus' wife† had this gift as well.
Her father, Erysichthon, scorned the gods
And never offered incense at their shrines.   740
It's said his axe once outraged Ceres' grove,
Attacking with its blade those ancient trees,
Among which stood a large and agèd oak,
Itself a forest, hung with ribbons, wreaths,
And plaques commemorating answered prayers.   745
Beneath it, Dryads held their festal dance;
Beneath it, they would circle, hand in hand,
About the trunk full thrice-five fathoms round,
Which towered as high above the other trees,
As those trees towered above the grass below.   750
Still, Triops' son would not withhold his blade,
But bade his slaves saw through the sacred oak.
Then, seeing them shirk their task, the scoundrel seized
An axe from one and said: "Though this were not
The goddess' tree, but the goddess herself,   755
Its leafy crown would still touch earth today!'
But as he poised to make a sidelong stroke,

The oak of Deo[23] quaked and gave a groan;
As one its leaves, as one its acorns paled,
And down its running boughs the pallor spread.   760
But when his sinful hand had struck the trunk,
The shattered bark let forth a stream of blood,[†]
As at the altar, when a mighty bull
Is slaughtered, blood comes gushing from the neck.
All stood amazed, and one dared stay the axe   765
And halt the crime, but the Thessalian glared:
'Take this,' he cried, 'your virtue's own reward!'
And, from the tree, the blade swung toward the man,
Struck off his head, then sliced the oak some more,
Till deep inside the oak there came a voice: 770
'This timber's home to Ceres' favorite nymph!
Your deeds will soon be punished—I foretell,
With dying breath, this comfort to my death.'
Still on he worked his crime until, at length,
Made weak by countless blows and wrenched by ropes,   775
The tree collapsed and crushed the grove below.
    "Astonished by their—and the forest's—loss,
The dryads went to Ceres dressed in black,
And begged her to make Erysichthon pay.
The dazzling goddess nodded her assent—   780
Which caused the fields of heavy grain to quake—
Then planned a punishment most piteous,
Were pity possible for deeds like his:
A plague of Hunger. Since she could not go
(For Ceres to meet Hunger baffles fate),   785
The goddess gave a rustic mountain nymph,
An Oread, these orders: 'There's a place
In frozen Scythia's most far-flung shores,
Whose sorry soil sprouts neither fruit nor tree.
There, next to Paleness, Shivering, and Cold,   790
Lives starving Hunger.[†] Bid her hide within
That sinful scoundrel's stomach and allow
No feast nor force of mine to quell her own.

23. Ceres

Don't fear the distance—take my chariot
And drive its harnessed dragons through the sky!'   795
    "This gift gave her a ride to Scythia
Where, on a peak (the Caucasus by name),
She loosed the serpents' reins and searched and found
The rocky field where Hunger scrounged about
The scanty grasses with her nails and teeth.   800
Her hair was snarled; her lips and face were pale,
With sunken eyes and jaws gone red with scabs;
Through hardened skin, her organs could be seen.
Dry bones protruding from her crooked crotch,
Her paunch a paunch-shaped hole, you'd think her chest   805
Was dangling, scarce supported by her spine.
Emaciation swelled her joints and knees,
And made her ankles bulge in outsized bumps.
Then, from afar (not daring to approach),
The nymph obeyed her orders. Even then,   810
Though far off and though only just arrived,
She ached with hunger as she took the reins
And flew the dragons back to Thessaly.
    "Though ever her opponent, Hunger did
As Ceres bade and wafted on the wind   815
To the appointed house, then slipped inside
The sinner's room where he lay fast asleep
(For it was night) and took him in her arms.
Through throat and lungs and lips, she breathed herself
And spread starvation through his empty veins.   820
Her duty done, she fled the fertile earth,
Returning to her normal barren home.
    "Sleep's soothing wings eased Erysichthon still
As, in his dreams, he roamed in search of feasts,
And gnawed on nothing, ground tooth against tooth,   825
And gulled his gullet, full of fancied food,
With gobbled banquets born of empty air.
But now he wakes—wild cravings burn his throat
And fires of famine overtake his guts!
He calls for all sea, land, or air can bring,   830
Shouts that he's starving at the sumptuous spread,

And asks for course on course. What would suffice
Whole towns and nations now cannot feed one!
The more he crams his craw, the more he wants.
For, as the sea receives all earthly streams   835
And is not filled but drinks far rivers dry,
And as devouring flames refuse no fuel
But burn through endless wood, desiring more
When much is had, made greedier by gain,
So Erysichthon's wicked mouth receives   840
And still requests each dish. Food calls for food,
And eating only furthers him from full.
    "Soon, hunger and his stomach's endless pit
Reduced his house's wealth; but, unreduced,
Dire flames of quenchless hunger thrived inside   845
His throat and ate through all he owned except
His daughter, who deserved a better sire:
Flat broke, he sold her. But the high-born girl
Refused her master, reached to sea, and cried,
'Come steal me from my master, as you once   850
Stole my virginity!'—which Neptune had.
Nor did he scorn her prayer, but changed her form,
Which her pursuing owner had just seen,
To fit the features of a fisherman.
    "Her master looked at her: 'O you, who baits   855
His bobbing bronze and plies the rod,' he said,
'May seas be calm for you, and may the fish
Be credulous and feel no hooks but yours!
Just now an unkempt girl with ragged clothes
Stood on this shore (for sure, I saw her stand)—   860
Say where she's gone, for here her footprints end.'
Delighted that the godly gift had worked
And that he asked about herself, she said,
'Excuse me, stranger—bent upon my task,
I haven't let my eyes stray from this swell!   865
But, as the sea-god aids my art, doubt not
That for some time no man has walked this shore
Except me, nor has any woman passed.'
Befuddled by belief, her master left

To tread the sandy trail, and she changed back.   870
But, seeing that Triops' heir could shift her shape,
Her father sold her often.† Then, she'd flee,
Now as a mare, a bird—a cow—a stag!—
To fund her famished father's wrongful fare.
When evil had consumed his every store   875
And naught was left to feed the monstrous plague,
The luckless man began to bite his limbs,
And tore his flesh away to feed himself. . . .

[ACHELOÜS AND HERCULES, PART 1]†

   "Why dwell on others? I can shape-shift, too,
Although my power, young man, is limited   880
To being as now, or coiling as a snake,
Or leading herds through strength of bovine horns.
Horns!—when I could! For now, you see, my brow
Has lost one of its weapons!"† And he groaned.

Book 9

THEN NEPTUNE'S hero† asked him why he groaned
And why he hid his broken brow in reeds.
The Calydonian stream replied, "You set
A sorry task! Who speaks of fights they lost?
Still, I'll tell all, nor was it shame to fail   5
So much as glory to have fought: indeed,
It cheers me that I lost to such a man!

   "Of Deianira you'll perhaps have heard.†
She was the fairest maid and jealous hope
Of many suitors, with whom I paid court.   10
'O Portheus' son,'¹ I told her sire, 'make *me*
Your in-law!' When Alcides² said the same,
The rest gave way. He spoke of his renown,
How she'd be linked with Jove, and of his feats,
Those labors which his stepmother had set.†   15
To this, I said, 'Gods do not yield to men!'
(For he was then no god.) 'Behold in me
The lord whose waters course across your land;
I'll be no son-in-law from stranger shores,

---

1. Deianira's father Oeneus (cf. 8.543)
2. The birth name of Hercules, adopted grandson of Alcaeus

For I am of your people, of your world!   20
Let it not hurt me that queen Juno's hate
And penal labors never fell to me.
You claim, Alcmene's son, that Jove's your sire;†
Either that's false or he's a true disgrace—
A sire sought through your mother's sin. So pick: 25
Jove's not your sire, or you were born in shame!'
    "At first he answered only with a glare,
But when his rage burst through, he simply said,
'My hand outstrips my tongue: since I'll prevail
In fighting, you may take the win in words,'   30
And fiercely charged me. I, being loath to leave,
What with my boasting, shed my grassy garb,
Put up my arms, held both my fists apart
Before my chest, and so prepared to fight.
He scooped dust from the ground to cover me,   35
And tanned himself in turn with tawny sand.†
Then he was on my neck, my flashing feet,
And wounding me all over—so you'd think,
But my bulk saved me from his bootless blows,
Much as a boulder in the roaring surf   40
Will stand secure, protected by its size.
We drew apart a space, then locked again
And there stood fast, resolved against retreat.
Foot grappled foot as, bent with all my weight,
I pushed him, hand to hand and head to head.   45
So I have seen two mighty bulls collide
When fighting for the fairest mate afield,
While all the fearful herd looks on, unsure
To whom the crowning victory will fall.
Alcides tried three times without success   50
To twist his chest off mine, but on the fourth,
He broke free, slipped himself from my embrace,
And slapped me (I'm intent on speaking truth),
Then whirled and clasped me, weighing down my back.
Believe me (for such lies won't win me fame),   55
It seemed as though a mountain held me down!
My arms were streaming sweat and scarce could move

Inside his grasp, then scarce could set me free.
Nor could I catch my breath or steel my strength,
For then he rushed and wrung me round the neck   60
Until, at last, I knelt and bit the dust.
     "Outmatched in manly might, I used my arts
To change into a snake and slither out.
But when I coiled, flicked my forked tongue, and hissed,
Tirynthius[3] snickered, sneering at my arts: 65
'I vanquished vipers from my crib!'[†] he said.
'Come, Acheloüs, even if you were
The king of dragons, how could you compare,
With Lerna's Hydra[†]—you, a single snake?
It thrived on wounds! With every head I hacked,   70
Two branching serpent scions braced the neck.
It sprang and grew on death and doom—and still,
I routed it and slew it in its rout.
So what do you suppose will come of you,
A faker's snake who wields another's arms   75
While tucked inside a shifting shamming shape?'
This said, his fingers locked above my neck
And choked me as I fought his vise-like grip
And tried to tear his thumbs from off my throat:
Again I lost. The savage bull was left,   80
So in my third and bull form, I returned.
He seized my brawny shoulders from the left,
And, as I dashed ahead, dragged down my horns
Into the ground, and sank me deep in sand.
Nor was this all: he wildly grasped a horn,   85
And, grasping, tore it from my broken brow!
Then Naiads blessed it full with flowers and fruit,
And made the Horn of Plenty from my horn."
At this, there came a nymph with flowing hair,
A serving-girl dressed in Diana's style,   90
To feed them from the Horn with autumn fruits
And hallowed apples for the second course.
     Day broke. With dawn's first light upon the peaks,

---

3. Hercules, variously associated with the city of Tiryns

The youths set forth, not waiting for the stream
To strike a peaceful pace or shrink its swells,   95
While Acheloüs sank beneath the waves
And hid his rustic face and half-horned head.

[THE DEATH OF HERCULES]†

  Although this loss of splendor gave him grief,
The rest of him was sound, and he could hide
His damaged head with reeds and willow leaves.   100
But you, fierce Nessus, perished for your love
Of that same maid, an arrow in your back.
For, heading homeward with his newfound wife,
Jove's son was halted at Euenus' stream,
Whose rushing flows ran high with winter rains,   105
Replete with whirlpools and impassable.
He feared not for himself but for his bride,
But strong-limbed Nessus knew the river's shoals,
And told him, "With my help, she'll reach the bank.
You're strong, Alcides—swim!" In Nessus' care   110
The Theban left his Calydonian bride,
[Who'd paled in fear of stream and centaur both.]
Then, lion-skin† and quiver still in hand
(He'd thrown his club and bow across), he cried,
"Another stream to conquer! Why stop now?"   115
And neither paused nor sought the calmest course,
Too proud to take advantage of the tides.
Ashore and armed again, he heard her cries
And knew that Nessus had betrayed his trust.
"Where are you stealing off to," he cried out,   120
"So sure, you rapist, in your feckless feet?
Hark, two-formed Nessus—do not touch what's mine!
If you've no fear of me, your father's wheel†
Should have sufficed to stay your lawless lust.
Your horse-half is no refuge: if my feet   125
Can't chase you, my wounds will!" To prove these words,
He sent a crooked arrow through his back
So that the point protruded from his chest.

With this wrenched forth, blood gushed out on both sides,
Now mingled with the Lernaean's venomed rot.[4]   130
But Nessus thought, "I'll not die unavenged!"
And gave the stolen bride his blood-warmed shirt,
A gift, he said, whose powers could kindle love.
    Years passed and Hercules subdued the earth—
And his stepmother's hate—with wondrous deeds.   135
But while Oechalia's victor[5] honored Jove
At Cape Cenaeum, Rumor bent your ear—
Yours, Deianira—mixing false with true
And swelling trifles with her lies to say
Amphitryonides loved Iole.[†]   140
In love and fear, she held the rumor true,
And miserably mourned his latest lust,
Outpouring tears of pain. But soon she said,
"Why weep? Such tears will bring my rival joy!
If she must come, I'll make some hasty plan   145
Before I can't—before she's in my bed!
[Should I protest or brood? Stay or go back
To Calydon? Or is it best to fight?]
Recalling, Meleäger, that I am
Your sister, dare I do some deed to prove   150
The power of wounded women through her death?"
    Once she had tracked through many trains of thought,
She chose to send him Nessus' bloodstained shirt,
In hopes it might revive his fading love.
To clueless Lichas, the unwitting wretch   155
Then gave the garment that would give her grief
And sweetly bade him bear it to her spouse,
Who robed his hero's shoulders, unaware,
With Hydra's poison. By the kindling flames,
He prayed and offered incense, pouring wine   160
Before the marble shrine, whose warming flames
Let loose the bane to spread through Hercules.
At first, his usual courage curbed his cries,

4. Hercules' arrows, dipped in the Hydra's poisoned blood
5. Hercules, who conquered the city of Oechalia in a final round of heroics

But when the pain prevailed, he smashed the shrine
And filled the groves of Oeta with his groans.   165
Then, though he tried to rend the deadly robe,
Each tear tore skin and—sickening to state—
Here held despite his cuts, and there revealed
His mangled muscles and enormous bones.
His blood itself, like water quenching steel,   170
Spat hisses, boiling as the poison burned.
Unchecked, the hungry flames devoured his heart
While all his body streamed with sea-green sweat.
His marrow melting and his sinews snapped
With hidden rot, he reached to heaven and cried,   175
"Saturnia, feast on my misfortunes—feast!
Gaze, cruel one, on my doom, and gorge your heart!
Or, if my foes have pity [—that means you—],
Then end [these vicious pains] my loathsome life
Of labor! Death, a true stepmother's gift,†   180
Will be to me a blessing! Was this why†
I slew Busiris, bloodier of shrines,
Wrenched fierce Antaeaus from his mother's aid,
And faced Spain's three-formed shepherd without fear,
As I then faced you, three-formed Cerberus?   185
Why you, O hands, dehorned the mighty bull?
Why Elis knows your toil, and Stymphalus,
And the Parthenian forests? Why you won
A golden girdle by the Thermodon,
And apples guarded by the sleepless snake?   190
Why centaurs never stopped me, nor the boar
That razed Arcadia? Why, redoubling strength
With every loss, the Hydra grew in vain?
Why, when I saw the Thracian steeds were full
Of human blood, their stalls of mangled limbs,   195
Did I destroy the master, stalls, and steeds?
These shoulders laid the Nemaean monster low!
This neck sustained the sky! Jove's savage spouse
Is tired of seeing me serve her tirelessly!
But now a plague's upon me which no strength   200
Nor force of arms can fight. Fire prowls my lungs

And feeds on all my frame, yet heaven has left
Eurystheus alive!—and there are those
Who still believe in gods!"†
                    Round Oeta's peak
The man roamed dying like a bull whose flank   205
Still drags a spear-shaft, though the hunter's fled.
Then you'd have seen him groan, then growl with rage,
Then try to tear his clothes off yet again,
While felling trees and storming round the slopes,
And stretching arms up toward his father's sky.   210
Look! he sees Lichas trembling in a cave,
And, mustering madness from his rage and pain,
Cries, "Lichas, did you give this fatal gift?
Will you have caused my death?" He pales in fear
And shakes, but as he timidly explains   215
And grasps his knees,† Alcides plucks him up
And, reeling him around three times and more,
He hurls him like a slingshot out across
Euboea's waves.
                 Atop the airy breeze,
He stiffened much as icy winds, they say,   220
Turn rain to snow, then pack the snowflakes too
In fluffy lumps that harden into hail.
Thus, flung by mighty arms into the void,
He lost all blood and moisture in his fear
And turned—so goes the tale—to rocky flint.   225
Now still, in the Euboean Sea, there stands
A stone with vestiges of human shape
Where sailors fear to tread lest they be felt.
They call it 'Lichas.'†
                    Then, famed son of Jove,
You felled steep Oeta's trees to build a pyre   230
And gave your bow and quiver full of shafts,
Whose fate it was to visit Troy again,†
To Poeas' son, who lit the flames beneath.
Then, as the woodpile caught with greedy flames,
You spread your Nemean pelt across its top,   235
And lay there with your club beneath your head,

As though you were reclining at a feast,[†]
Amid full cups of wine and crowns of flowers.
Now, strong and crackling, spreading on all sides,
Flames licked his careless heedless limbs, and filled   240
The gods with fear for earth's own champion.
This pleased Saturnian Jupiter, who said
(For he could tell): "Your fear brings us delight,
And I rejoice, O gods, with all my heart
That I have sired and rule a mindful race,   245
Whose favor keeps my other offspring safe.
And, though it's for his feats you honor him,
I'm much obliged myself. Yet, free your hearts
From faithful fears and spurn Mount Oeta's flames!
You'll see them fall to him who's felled all things,   250
For Vulcan's power shall smite his mother's side,
But what descends from me is without end,
Immune to death, and subject to no flame,
And I shall bring him, done with earth, to heaven.
I trust my deed shall please. If anyone—   255
If anyone at all—should grieve or grudge
The name of 'god' to Hercules, they'll know
His prize was earned: approval will be forced!"
    The gods agreed. His queen, too, seemed to bear
The words of Jove unvexed, though vexed she'd been   260
At his conclusion when he called her out.
By then the flames of Mulciber had burned
All that they could. No semblance still survived
Of Hercules, nor of his mother's shape,
For only what traced back to Jove was saved.   265
Then, as a serpent sloughs off age with skin
To bask revived in shining newfound scales,
So, when Tirynthius shed his mortal flesh,
His finer half gained strength and seemed to grow,
Becoming fearsome in its august weight.[†]   270
Then the Almighty Father's four-horse coach
Brought him through clouds to shine among the stars—
And weigh down Atlas.

[LUCINA AND GALANTHIS]†

But Eurystheus,
The son of Sthenelus, turned his cruel hate
From sire to son.† So the long-suffering   275
Argive Alcmene poured her agèd cares,
The tales of her son's labors, known worldwide,
And her own sorrows out to Iole,
Who had been wed at Hercules' command
So high-born Hyllus' seed now swelled her womb.[6]   280
Alcmene told her, "May the gods at least
Be kind and speed your labor when you call
On Ilithyia's[7] strength in giving birth,
For, thanks to Juno, she just hindered me.

    "When labor-laden Hercules was due,   285
The sun being in its tenth of starry signs,
He stretched my womb to bear a weight so great†
You knew it must be Jove who'd sired such size;
Nor could I longer bear the labor pangs—
And even as I speak, my limbs grow cold   290
With chills, for memory is a part of pain.
I lived through seven anguished days and nights,
Till, spent with agony, I reached for heaven,
And called Lucina and the gods of Birth.
She came indeed, but she had made a deal   295
To take my life for grateful Juno's hate.
In earshot of my groans, she took a seat
Upon an outside altar, crossed her legs,
Right over left, and, with her fingers locked,
Stalled my delivery with whispered charms   300
That charmed me from further delivering.
I travailed, madly cursed ungrateful Jove,
And longed for death with words to move the stones!

    "Some Theban matrons were on hand to pray
And soothe my torment, and a serving-girl,   305

6. Iole married Hyllus, the son of Hercules and Deianira
7. Lucina, goddess of childbirth

Fair-haired Galanthis, born of common stock,
Who always did as told and earned my love
Through her attentions. Sensing Juno planned
Some hateful plot, she paced about the door,
And, seeing the goddess seated at the shrine   310
With fingers clenched, called, 'You there, come rejoice!
Alcmene, queen of Argos, has been freed.
Our mistress' prayers are heard: she's given birth!'
The great womb-goddess leapt up in dismay
With parted hands, freeing me of chains and child.   315
Galanthis laughed at having fooled the god,
Who grabbed the laugher's hair—so rumor has—
And cruelly dragged her as she tried to rise,
An act she stopped by turning arms to legs.
Yet her old diligence and skin-toned back   320
Remain, although her body has been changed.
And since her lips once lied to aid my birth,
She births with lips, yet lives here as before."†

[DRYOPE AND LOTUS]†

The memory of her servant made her groan,
But while she grieved, her daughter-in-law⁸ spoke: 325
"O mother, she whose loss of looks you mourn
Had stranger's blood. What if I told you of
My sister's wondrous fate, though tears and pain
Should stay my speech? Her mother's only child
(Our sire wed twice), she was called Dryope,   330
The loveliest of all Oechalia's maids.
Though she'd been raped by Delphi's Delian lord,†
Andraemon wed her, counting himself blessed.

"There is a lake whose tilting banks are sloped
Like ocean shores and crowned with myrtle-groves.   335
There Dryope went, blind to fate, to bring—
This ought to gall you—garlands for the nymphs,
A baby in her arms, not one year old,

---

8. Rather, her granddaughter-in-law, Iole

A darling load she nursed with lukewarm milk!
Beside the pool, a water-lotus† bloomed   340
And promised fruit in Tyrian purple flowers.
These Dryope had picked to please her son,
Just as I would have done (for I was there)
Had I not seen the flowers adrip with blood
And all the branches quivering with fright.   345
For, as slow countryfolk still tell, a nymph
Named Lotus, fleeing Priapus'† lewd assault,
Had turned into this plant that bears her name.
My sister did not know this. Starting back,
She pleaded with the nymphs and made to leave   350
But found her feet were roots which, though she fought
To free herself, held fast below the waist.
Bark slowly crept up, covering her loins,
And, watching this, she tried to tear her hair,
But plucked off leaves, for leaves had wreathed her head.   355
    "Her boy, Amphissos (named by Eurytus,
His grandsire), felt his mother's breast grow hard,
Till he could no more suck its stream of milk.
I stood by helpless, sister, as I watched
Your cruel demise! But, doing what I could,   360
I seized the boughs to stall the growing trunk
While longing, I confess, to share that bark.
Then her poor sire came with Andraemon to
Find Dryope. The Dryope they found—
I showed them—was an oak,† whose cooling wood   365
They kissed and on whose kindred roots they clung.
My sister was all tree now, save her face
Which rained tears down her former body's leaves.
And while her lips could speak, she filled the air
With grievances: 'If weeping wins your trust,   370
I swear by heaven I don't deserve this doom!
My blameless life is punished without crime,
And if I lie, let drought destroy my leaves,
Let axes hack me down, and let me burn!
But take this baby from his mother's boughs   375
And let him oft beneath my tree be nursed,

And see thou that beneath my tree he plays,
And that he greets his mother, when he speaks,
And sadly says, "My mother's in this tree!"
And let him fear all lakes, deflower no trees,   380
And think each plant a goddess in disguise.
Farewell, dear spouse and sister—father, too!
Yet, if you pity me, defend my leaves
From jagged pruning-knives and grazing flocks;
And since I cannot bend to you, reach up   385
And take my kisses while they may be felt—
Lift up my little boy! But no more words:
Soft cork is coiling round my gleaming neck
And covering my head—don't touch my eyes!†
Allow the growing bark, without your help,   390
To spread its way across my fading sight.'
And though her life and voice died out as one,
Her vanished form long warmed the new-made boughs."

[IOLAÜS AND THEMIS]†

While Iole described this miracle,
And while Alcmene (weeping, too) wiped tears   395
From Eurytus' sad child, a wondrous thing
Cut short their grief, for in the doorway stood
A teenage boy with fuzz upon his cheeks,
For Iolaüs was restored to youth.†
   This was a boon sent, at her husband's wish,   400
By Juno's daughter Hebe, who'd have sworn
Against such future gifts, but Themis said,
"There's civil war in Thebes now. . . . † Only Jove
Can smite Capaneus. . . . Brothers shall be paired
In wounds. . . . A prophet swallowed by the earth   405
Alive will witness his ancestral shades. . . .
Then parent over parent will his son
Avenge—an act both dutiful and wrong.
Next he'll be driven out of house and mind
By Furies' faces and his mother's shade   410
Until his wife demands the fatal gold,

And Phegeus soaks his sword in kinsman's blood.
Then, Acheloüs' child, Callirhoë,
Will beg Jove to mature her infant sons
[For fear the victor's death stay unavenged].   415
Jove thus reserves his step-child-in-law's gift
That he may change these beardless boys to men!"
    Once prescient Themis' far-presaging lips
Had ceased, the gods let loose a jangling growl
And asked why they might not bestow this boon!   420
Pallantis then bewailed her husband's age,†
Kind Ceres grieved Iasion's growing grey,
And Mulciber demanded back the life
Of Erichthonius. Dread moved Venus, too,
Who pled to have Anchises' years renewed.   425
Each god had favorites, and the jealous brawl
Increased till Jove unlocked his lips and said,
"Oh, as you fear me, must you squabble so?
Does any here think they can master *fate*?
For *fate* gives Iolaüs back his years!   430
To *fate* Callirhoë will owe her sons'
Maturity, not power or politics!
It should improve your mood that you and I
Are both its subjects; could I alter fate,
My Rhadamanthys' youth would always bloom,   435
My Aeacus would not stand stooped with age,
Nor would my Minos, laden down to scorn
By bitter time, not be the king he was."†

[BYBLIS AND CAUNUS]†

    Jove's words were moving: no god could complain,
Seeing Aeacus and Rhadamanthys spent   440
With years—and, with them, Minos, who, when young,
Had frightened mighty nations with his name.
Now frail, he dreaded Deïone's son,[9]
A youth proud of his strength and Phoebean sire.

9. Miletus, son of Deïone and Apollo

Though sure that this Miletus planned a coup,   445
He dared not force him from his home and land.
Yet on your own, Miletus, swift of sail,
You fled Aegean seas for Asia's shores,
And raised the walls that bear their builder's name.†
There, by her father's twisting turning banks,   450
You gained such knowledge of Meander's child,
Cyaneë of peerless form, that she
Bore Byblis unto you, and Caunus—twins.
May Byblis warn young girls about desire,†
For Byblis loved her twin, Apollo's heir,   455
[But not as sisters nor as brothers should!]
    At first, she did not comprehend love's fires
And often kissed him, thinking it no sin
To throw her arms around her brother's neck.
This front of family feeling fooled her long,   460
But slowly she lapsed into love, and dressed
With too much care to draw her brother's eye,
In jealousy of all who charmed him more.
But still her fires stayed hidden from herself:
She made no wishes, though she burned within,   465
But called him "lord" now, hating kinship's terms,
Now made him call his sister "Byblis" too,
And still she dared not let her wanton hopes
Invade her waking thoughts, till, lulled in sleep,
She dreamed desire and saw herself embrace   470
Her brother's body, blushing in her bed.
On waking, she lay still and long recalled
The slumberous sight, then spoke her troubled mind:
"Poor me! What means this silent night's mirage?
I want it gone! Why do I have these dreams?   475
I like him—even foes admit he's fair—
And, were he not my brother, I would love.
He's worthy, too—my sisterhood's a curse!
And yet, as long as I abstain awake,
May slumber often bring me back such dreams,   480
When fancied pleasure brings no spies nor stings.
By Venus and by Cupid, her winged boy,

What joy was mine! What ecstasy I felt!
Oh, how I lay there, melting in my bones!
How lovely to recall, though brief our bliss: 485
For jealous night rushed past when we began!
Oh, if I changed my name and married you,
You'd make my sire, dear Caunus, such a son!
I'd make your sire's son, Caunus, such a bride!
If heaven permitted, we would share all things—   490
Except for family: you'd be higher-born.
You'll make someone a mother, fairest one,
But since misfortune made your parents mine,
We'll be mere siblings, split by what we share. . . .
What do my visions mean to tell me, then?   495
What weight do dreams have? Have dreams any weight?
Good god!—yet gods have had their sisters' love,
For Saturn married Ops, who shared his blood;
The Ocean, Tethys; and Olympus' king
Wed Juno . . . but the gods have their own ways!   500
Should heaven's different laws rule human deeds?
I'll send forbidden passion from my heart
Or, if I fail, then let me die, I pray,
And may my brother kiss my coffined corpse. . . .
But then such things require the will of two: 505
What pleases me, he'd think a crime—and yet
Aeolus' sons shunned not their sisters' beds†—
But how do I know? Why present this case?
Where will this lead? Leave me, defiling flames,
To love my brother as a sister should!   510
Yet if he'd fallen first in love with me,
Perhaps I would indulge his mad desire;
And since I'd let him woo me, I'll woo him!
But can you speak? Can you confess? You can!
Love forces you, or if shame holds your tongue,   515
Let secret words confess your hidden fire!"
     She liked this plan. Her troubled mind was won.
Propped up on her left arm, she said, "He'll see!
Let me confess this crazy love! [—ah, me!
Where shall I end? What fires possess my mind?]"   520

And scrawled her chosen words with trembling hands,
The tablet in her left; the pen, her right.
With starts and stops, she scribbled, changed her mind,
Wrote and erased, approved, rebuked, revised,
Now put them down, now picked them up again,   525
Uncertain and upset with everything,
While shame and daring mingled in her face.
She first wrote "sister," but crossed "sister" out,
And set these words upon the clean-wiped wax:
"Good health from one whose health depends on you!   530
For shame, my shame withholds your lover's name,
And should you ask my wish, I would that I
Could plead my case unnamed and not be known
As Byblis till my hopeful prayers came true.
You might have sensed the throbbing of my heart: 535
My blush, my dwindling form, my face, my eyes,
So often tearful, and my groundless sighs,
My constant hugs and kisses would have seemed—
If you'd observed them—more than sisterly.
But still, although my heart is wounded sore,   540
Though flames burn me within, I have done all
(I swear by heaven) to stay sane to the last.
I've waged a long and luckless fight to flee
From Cupid's arrows, and I've borne with more
Than you'd think girls could bear. But, in defeat,   545
I must confess! In fear, I beg your help!
Your lover lives and dies through you alone:
The choice is yours. It is no foe that pleads,
But one who, though she's nearest to you, still
Longs to be nearer, joined by closer ties.   550
Let old men study law—what is allowed,
What's right or wrong—let them follow the rules!
But love is rash and changeful at our age:
Those ignorant of right hold all things right
And follow the example of the gods.   555
We've no strict father, no good name to save,
No fears to stop us—and should fear arise,
The sweet word 'sibling' will keep secrets safe.

I'm free to have a private word with you
As now in public we embrace and kiss.   560
What's missing? Pity me my love confessed,
For I confess it through sheer passion's force.
Don't let my tombstone say you caused my death!"
    The wax was now etched full of idle words
Down to the corner, where she promptly stamped   565
Her seal upon the sin, dripping with tears
(Though dry of tongue). Ashamed, she called a slave
But sweetly said, "Bring this, most faithful one,
To my"—a lengthy pause here—"brother's eyes!"
As she was handing them, the tablets slipped   570
And fell out of her hands—a fearsome sign!—
But still she sent him on and, in due time,
The servant passed along her secret words.
    Meandrius,[10] astounded and enraged,
Cast down the half-read tablets, scarce refrained   575
From strangling the poor servant, and cried out,
"O wicked author of forbidden lust,
Flee while you can! Were your fate less entwined
With my disgrace, you'd pay for this with death!"
In fear, he fled back, bearing the fierce words   580
Of Caunus to his mistress. Byblis paled
To hear she'd been refused, and froze with fright,
But when her mind returned, so did her love,
Although her tongue could scarcely give it voice:
"As I deserved! Oh, why was I so rash   585
To bare my wound, so quick to put in words
And rush to print what should have been concealed?
To start, I should have tested how he felt
With murky hints; in order to ensure
Fair voyaging, I should have checked the wind   590
And changed my tack, then safely sailed the sea!
But now the untried winds have filled the sheets
And borne me on the rocks, where I am wrecked
By all the Ocean, nor can I sail back.

10. Caunus, grandson of Meander

Was I not cautioned to resist my love   595
By clear-cut omens when, as they were sent,
The tablets slipped and showed my hopes must fall?
I should have switched the day, or switched my wish!—
Let's say the day. A god warned me himself
With omens clear, had I been sound of mind.   600
And yet I should have spoken, not in wax,
But there in person made my passions known;
He should have seen my tears, my looks of love!
I would have told him more than tablets hold,
And round his neck I could have forced my arms!   605
If still rebuffed, I could have seemed near death,
And fallen at his feet, and begged for life—
All things which, by themselves, may not have swayed
His stubborn heart, but might have, all in all.
Perhaps the servant should receive some blame!   610
He went ill-timed or out of turn, I'm sure,
Or did not catch him when his mind was free.
That was my downfall! He's no tiger's child!
His heart's not flint or adamant or iron,
Nor was he suckled on a lion's milk: 615
He shall be won! I'll plead my case again
And shall not rest while there is breath in me.
It would be best, if all could be undone,
Not to begin; but now that I've begun,
The next best thing's to win! Though I quit now,   620
He never would forget what deeds I've dared—
And, stopping, I'd seem fickle in desire,
Or like one tempting him into a trap,
And he'd think I'd been won not by the god
Who bends and burns my heart, but by my lust.   625
In short, I cannot now undo my sins:
I've written, wooed, and wasted our goodwill.
No matter what, I'll not seem innocent.
I've many hopes to lose, but little shame."
    This said, though she (being so unsure of mind)   630
Repented having tried, she tried again,
But every luckless tactic was repulsed.

Soon, with no end in sight, he fled her sins
To set new city walls on foreign soil.
It's then Miletus' daughter lost her mind,   635
Then, so they say, that she tore free her breast
And thrashed her frenzied arms. Now plainly mad,
She openly confessed her lawless love,
And quit her land and loathsome household gods
To follow where her brother's footprints fled.   640
A Thracian bacchant thronging thyrsus-mad
To your biennial, child of Semele,
Did Byblis, screaming through the fields, appear
To the Bubasid wives, past whom she roamed
Through Carians, Lycians, armored Leleges,   645
Round Cragus, Limyre, and Xanthus' waves,
And where the fiery-lunged Chimaera dwells[†]
With lion's head and heart and serpent's tail.
Then, where the forest cleared, tired of pursuit,
You hit the ground and lay with streaming hair,   650
Face-down, O Byblis, in the fallen leaves.
The Lelegian nymphs there often tried
To raise her soft in arms, and often spoke
Of cures for love to soothe her heedless heart,
But she lay silent, scratching at the sod,   655
And all the grass flowed wet with Byblis' tears.
From these, they say, the Naiads made a spring
That cannot dry—what more had they to give?
At once, like drops of pitch tapped from a tree,
Or like tar gushing sticky from the ground,   660
Or like once-frozen waves thawed by the sun
Dissolving in Favonius' gentle breath,[†]
Was Phoebean Byblis, fading through her tears,
Transformed into the fount that bears her name,
And gushes still beneath a holly tree.   665

[IPHIS AND IANTHE][†]

The tale of this strange marvel might have filled
Crete's hundred cities, had they not just seen

A nearer wonder: Iphis being transformed.
For once, by royal Knossos, there had lived
A low-born Phaestian, known to very few   670
As Ligdus, of no higher means than rank
But true and blameless in his mode of life.
He'd warned his wife, when she was nearly due,
"There are two things I wish: that you should have
An easy birth, and that you bear a son!   675
The other sex would cost us more than fate
Would let us bear. If, heaven forbid, you chance
To bear a girl (I speak against my will—
For Goodness' sake, forgive me), she must die!"†
When he had finished, tears were bathing both   680
The speaker's cheeks and hers to whom he spoke,
And Telethusa pleaded without cease
And vainly begged him not to halve her hopes,
But Ligdus' mind was set. And when she scarce
Could bear the heavy weight within her womb,   685
She dreamt one night the child of Inachus†
Stood there, or seemed to stand, before the bed
With all her holy train. Her brow was decked
With crescent horns, bright ears of golden grain,
And queenly pomp. Anubis howled at hand,   690
With blessed Bubastis, Apis' dappled hide,
And he who hushes with a finger raised;
With rattles came Osiris, still unfound,
And foreign serpents full of venomed sleep.†
This seemed no dream, for seeing them plain, she heard   695
The goddess say, "O Telethusa mine,
Lay down your worries, scorn your husband's words,
And rear whatever child Lucina brings!
I am a helpful god, nor shall you grieve
That you have worshiped an ungrateful power!"   700
This said, she left the room. The Cretan wife
Rejoicing, rose from bed, reached toward the stars,
And prayed that what she'd seen might come to pass.
Her pains increased and soon the weight burst forth—
A girl! To keep her secret from the sire,   705

The lying mother bade the "boy" be fed.
Trust helped this trick, which none knew save the nurse;
The sire gave thanks and named her for *his* sire—
Whose name was Iphis—to the mother's joy:
This name, being unisex,[†] was free of fraud,   710
And so the pious lie lay unexposed.
Though raised a boy, she had a face that would
Be counted beautiful on boy or girl.

   Your sire betrothed you, Iphis, at thirteen
To blonde Ianthe, of all Phaestian maids   715
The one whose fair endowments won most praise.
The daughter of Telestes, born on Crete,
She was a match in age, a match in looks,
And as a child attended the same school;
And so, one tameless love touched both their hearts   720
With wounds of equal size—unlike their hopes!
Ianthe wished the wedding day to come,
When her she thought a man would be her man;
But Iphis' love was fed on hopelessness,
Which fired her vain desire of maid for maid.   725
Just short of tears, she cried, "Is this my end?
To fall in strange, unknown, unnatural love?[†]
For, if the gods would save me, [I'll be saved,
But if the gods would slay me,] then at least
They should have sent some natural normal ill;   730
Cows never burn for cows, nor mares for mares—
Rams burn for ewes, and does chase after stags!
Thus mate the birds, and, of all animals,
There is no female females fill with lust.[†]
I wish I weren't a girl! Since Crete must bear   735
All monsters, the Sun's daughter[11] once desired
A bull—but they were male and female, too!
My love's more mad than theirs, if truth be told,
For hers had hope! For hers, a cow disguise
Sufficed to trick her bull into a tryst!   740

11. Pasiphaë, daughter of the Sun (cf. 8.131–3)

If all the wide world's cunning gathered here—
If Daedalus flew back on waxen wings,
What could he do? Could he make woman man?
Or change your sex, Ianthe, through his craft?
Be firm then, Iphis! Recollect yourself,   745
And lose these futile hopes, these foolish flames!
Accept your birth, put self-deception by,
And do what's proper: love as women should.
It's hope that brings and hope that nurtures love—
Hope which you cannot have. No guard forbids   750
Her dear embrace, nor any watchful spouse
Nor stringent sire,† nor she you seek herself,
And yet she can't be yours for all the world,
And neither gods nor men can bring you joy,
[For even now I've yet to pray in vain;   755
The gods have freely given all they can.]
Though my will is my sire's and her sire's, too,
It is not Nature's. Stronger, she alone
Assails me now when comes the longed-for hour,
My wedding, when Ianthe will be mine—   760
But won't be. In the midst of waves, I'll thirst!
Why, Juno? Hymen, why attend our rites,
Which have no groom," she said, "but both are brides?"
    No lesser passion stirred the other maid,
Who begged you, Hymen, to arrive in haste,   765
But what she sought brought Telethusa fear.
Time and again she stalled by playing sick
Or seeing bad omens, but at last she'd played
Her every trick, and when the nuptial hour,
So long deferred, was but one day away,   770
She loosed her daughter's tresses and her own,
And clutched the altar, crying through her hair,
"O Isis of the Mareotic fields,
Of Paraetonium, Pharos, and the Nile
Of seven mouths, bring help and heal our fear!   775
I've seen you, goddess, and your signs before,
[And known them all—your torches and your train,]

FIGURE 8. *Ovid's Metamorphoses*, Auguste Rodin (c. 1886). Originally fashioned for Rodin's monumental *Gates of Hell,* this sculpture was later isolated and renamed after Ovid. Although Rodin's title is pointedly broad regarding subject, the piece is commonly associated with the tale of Iphis and Ianthe, since the top figure's androgynous physique seems to evoke Iphis in transition.

Your rattles' sound—and kept your words in mind:
That she's seen daylight while I've gone unscathed
Is by your plan and gift. Take pity then   780
And aid us both!" Here, words gave way to tears.
But now—the shrine appears to move (it moves!),
Its doors shake, and the moon-like horns grow bright
To sounds of rattling.[†] Still in doubt but cheered
By these fair signs, she leaves the shrine with you   785
Behind her, Iphis, strangely long in stride;
Your cheeks look darker now, your muscles grown,
Your features sharper, and your hair cut short,
Your strength more than a girl's . . . for, though just now
A girl, you are a boy! So deck the shrines!   790
Go revel free from fear! They decked the shrines
With offerings, and there they laid a plaque
With this short verse:

NOW AS A MAN THESE GIFTS ARE PAID
WHICH IPHIS PROMISED AS A MAID

And Dawn laid bare the world as Venus met   795
With Juno and with Hymen at the fires
Where Iphis took Ianthe for his bride.

Book 10

THENCE, THROUGH the boundless air, toward Thracian shores
Soared saffron-mantled Hymen, keen to heed
The call of Orpheus, though called in vain;
For though he came, he brought no sacred words,
Nor merry looks, nor auspices of joy.   5
His torch spat smoke that wrung tears from the eyes
And would not catch, however it was held.
The end was even worse, for as the bride
Traipsed with her train of Naiads through the grass,
She took a snake-bite to the heel and died.   10
   Once through with mourning in the air above,
The Thracian bard made bold to try the shades,
And entered Taenarus' gate to the Styx.†
In weightless throngs and ghosts of buried dead,
He found Persephone with him who rules   15
That joyless realm, and to the lord of shades
He strummed and sang, "O underworldly gods
To whom we mortal creatures all return,
If I may put aside all riddling lies
And speak the truth, I've not come here to see   20
Dark Tartarus, nor chain your monstrous hound
Up by his three Medusan snake-haired necks.†

I journey for my wife, whose budding years
A trampled viper's venom stole away.
I've wished and tried to bear it, but I've lost   25
To Love, a god well-known above—though here,
I cannot say. And yet, I think he is:
If tales of ancient ravishment† are true,
Love joined you, too. So, please, by these dread lands,
By Chaos and these vast and silent realms,   30
Rewind Eurydice's untimely fate!
All things are due to you; though we abide
For long or short, we hasten to one place.
We all come here! this is our final home!
Your reign is longest over humankind.   35
When she has rightly reached a riper age,
You'll rule her, too: I seek this gift on loan.
But if the Fates deny her, I'm resolved
To stay and cheer you with our double death."

    To hear him sing, the bloodless spirits wept,   40
As Tantalus ceased chasing after waves,
Ixion's wheel stopped, liver went unpecked,
The Belides set down their empty urns,
And you sat, Sisyphus, upon your stone.†
His song, the story goes, first wet the cheeks   45
Of the Eumenides, nor could the queen
Nor king of sunken realms withstand his wish:
They called Eurydice. She was among
The recent shades and, wounded still, limped forth
To meet the Thracian hero—on one term: 50
That he not look at her till they had left
Avernus' vale, or all would be in vain.

    Through silent soundless wastes, they made ascent
On pathways steep, unclear, and thick with gloom.
They'd nearly crossed into the world above,   55
When, fearing fault and hungry for a glimpse,
The lover looked!—at once, she slipped away.
To hold or to be held, the wretch reached out,
But caught at nothing save the yielding air.
In second death, the bride made no complaint   60

(For why complain that he had loved her so?)
But gave a last "farewell" he scarcely heard,
And, with this said, fell back to whence she came.
   His wife's twin deaths astonished Orpheus,
Much like the man who, seeing the Stygian hound,   65
Its middle neck in chains, could not shed fear
Without his nature but was shod with stone;
Or Olenus, who sinned by feigning guilt
With poor Lethaea, you, whose beauty's boasts
Turned your close-coupled bodies into rocks   70
On dewy Ida.† When the ferryman
Denied his pleas to let him cross again,
He sat there on the bank for seven days,
Disheveled and devoid of Ceres' gifts,
With sorrow, tears, and anguish for his food.   75
Then, cursing the cruel gods of Hell, he fled
To wind-swept Haemus and Mount Rhodope.

[CYPARISSUS]†

   Three times did Titan swim the Piscean waves†
That bound the year, while Orpheus forsook
All women's love, either through past mischance   80
Or faithfulness. Yet, many maids still craved
The bard's embrace, and many grieved his scorn;
For it was he who taught the Thracian tribes
To love young boys† instead and pluck their flowers
Still in the early springtime of their youth.   85
   There was a hill, and on this hill a plain,
A field of perfect flatness, green with grass.
Though shade-deprived, on seeing the god-born bard
Was seated there and plucking at his strings,
The shade arrived: there came Chaonia's tree,†   90
A grove of Heliads, a leafy oak,
Soft lindens, virgin laurels, beeches too,
And brittle hazels, ash-trees fit for spears,
Unknotted pines, a holm-oak bent with nuts,
And many-colored maples, pleasing planes,   95

Stream-dwelling willows, water-lotuses,
Box evergreens, two-tinted myrtle trees,
Thin cedars, and viburnum green of seed;
Then, twisting-tendrilled ivy, you arrived
With grapevines, vine-draped elms, and ash and spruce,   100
The arbute fraught with fruit, such pliant palms
As victors prize, and bare-trunked leaf-crowned pines,†
Dear to the gods' great Mother Cybele,
Because her Attis once put manhood by
To stiffen in a pine-tree's lofty trunk.†   105
   Among this crowd, a cone-shaped cypress stood;
This tree was once a boy loved by the god
Who plies the strings of lyres and strings of bows.
For, sacred to Carthaea's native nymphs,
A mighty stag once lived whose antlers wide   110
Had furnished his own head with ample shade.
These antlers gleamed with gold, and from his neck
A jeweled collar dangled down his sides;
A silver pendant swayed about his brow
From slender straps, and, balanced at his ears   115
And round his temples, shone two brazen pearls.
Devoid of all alarm or natural fear,
He entered homes and even let his neck
Be stroked by strangers' hands; but most of all,
He pleased you, Cyparissus, fairest lad   120
Of all the Cean race. You led this stag
To pastures green, you showed him waters still,
Then wreathed his antlers round with varied flowers,
Or blithely rode him horselike back and forth,
While gently guiding him with purple reins.   125
   It was a summer's noon and, while the sun
Was boiling Cancer's wide shore-loving claws,
The stag lay weary on the grassy ground
To draw some coolness from the forest shade.
There, rash young Cyparissus sent his spear,   130
And, seeing the deer lay dead, resolved to die.
What didn't Phoebus say to comfort him,
And urge a lesser, more proportioned grief?

But, groaning, he besought above all else
For heaven to grant that he might always weep!   135
In time, his boundless tears consumed his blood
And soon his body started turning green,
His snow-white brow, but lately hung with hair,
Became a bristling crest, and, growing hard,
His narrow crown looked upward to the stars.   140
Then groaned the woeful god: "As I mourn you,
So you will mourn for others where they grieve."†
  Such was the grove assembled by the bard
And where he held his court with beasts and birds.
There, having used his thumb to test the chords,   145
Ensuring that the modes, though various,
Would harmonize in sound, he sang this song:

[GANYMEDE AND HYACINTH]†

  "Through Jove, O mother Muse (for Jove rules all),
Inspire my songs! I've told Jove's might before
And sung of Giants in a graver strain   150
And victor's bolts that fell on Phlegra's fields;†
But now I need a lighter lyre to sing
Of boys beloved of gods, and girls who felt
Forbidden flames and paid the price for lust!
  "The god-king's love for Phrygian Ganymede   155
Once prompted Jupiter to find some guise
Beside his own; but, seeing there was no bird
Deserving† save the one that bore his bolts,
He flew at once, a flapping feathered fraud,
And stole the Trojan lad, who still attends   160
Jove's nectared cups, to Juno's lasting spite.†
  "You, too, Amyclas' son,¹ would live on high,
Had your sad fate let Phoebus put you there.
Still, in a way you're deathless, for each time
That Piscean winter yields to Arian spring,   165
You rise in flowers above the verdant grass.

---

  1. Hyacinth, son of king Amyclas of Sparta

My father loved you most in all the world,
And Delphi, at its center,[†] lacked a lord
While he was out along Eurotas' streams
And unwalled Sparta.[†] Spurning lyre and bow,   170
The god forgot himself and bore your nets
And leashed your hounds and joined your toilsome climbs
To feed his flames on lasting company.
    "With Titan between dawn and banished night
And distanced equally from either side,   175
They stripped their clothes off and, both shining bright
With olive oil, began a discus game.
First Phoebus let it fly—a well-poised throw
Whose weighty force broke through the clouds above,
And much time passed before the weight returned,   180
Displaying both the thrower's strength and skill.
At once, impelled by his desire for sport,
The rash[†] young Spartan rushed to raise the disk,
But, bouncing off the ground, the weight flung back
And hit you, Hyacinth, full in the face.   185
The god turned pale—as you did in his arms—
And tried to keep you warm and staunch your wound
And stay your fading soul with poulticed herbs,
But nothing worked: the wound could not be healed.
When, in a garden-plot, plush poppy-flowers   190
And violets and lilies gold of tongue
Are snapped in two, they droop their withered heads
And cannot lift their gaze above the ground;
So sagged the dying face, his weakened neck
Slumped on one shoulder under its own load.   195
'You fall, dear Spartan, cheated of your youth,'
Said Phoebus, 'And I see your wound's my fault.
You are my grief and guilt, and by my hand
It shall be said you died. I've caused your death!
[Yet what have I done wrong? Can it be wrong   200
To play? Or else, to love: can that be wrong?]
I wish that I could give my life for you—
Or with you! But the laws of fate forbid,
So you'll live always in my thoughts and words.

[For you, my lyre—for you, my songs shall sound!   205
Then, as a flower, your marks will match my groans,
And one day, a great hero[2] will be linked
Unto this flower and known by these same leaves.]'
    "And, as Apollo's truthful lips pronounced,
Behold! the blood which stained the grassy ground   210
Was blood no more! Ashine like Tyrian dye,
There bloomed a blossom, lily-like in form,
Though this was violet where those are white.
Not pleased yet, Phoebus (being this honor's source)
Inscribed the petals with his groans: 'AI AI.'   215
And so this sad inscription decks the flower.†
    "The Spartans' pride in their son Hyacinth
Endures in their tradition every year
To hold the feast of Hyacinthia.†

[THE CERASTAE, THE PROPOETIDES, AND
PYGMALION]†

    "Yet ask ore-laden Amathus[3] if she   220
Regrets the birth of her Propoetides,
And she'll disown them and the double-horned
Cerastae, so called for their jagged brows!†
    "A shrine to Jove, the god of guests, once stood
Before her gates—had someone unaware   225
Beheld the blood, they'd have thought suckling calves
And Amathusian sheep were slaughtered there,
Not murdered guests! Appalled by these vile rites,
Kind Venus almost quit her towns and all
Of Cyprus, till she thought, 'How have my towns,   230
How have these regions sinned? What is their crime?
Much better that their faithless race were shunned
Or killed, or something in between the two—
And what could that be other than transformed?'
While choosing in what way to change their shape,   235

    2. Ajax (cf. 13.394ff)
    3. A copper-rich city on the south coast of Cyprus

She spied their horns, thought those might be preserved,
And turned their giant frames to savage bulls.†
    "As for the vile Propoetides, they dared
Claim Venus was no god! So, through her wrath,
They were the first, it's said, to sell themselves.   240
Too free of shame to blush, their blood grew hard
And turned them, scarcely changed, to solid stone.†
    "Pygmalion, though, had seen their lives of crime,
And, loathing all the faults that nature gives
The female mind, long did he live alone   245
Without a wife to share his marriage bed.
Yet all the while he used his wondrous skill
To carve an ivory figure far more fair
Than any woman born—and fell in love.
To see its face, you'd think the maid was real   250
And might have moved, if not for modesty.
Thus art concealed his art, and wonder set
Pygmalion's heart aflame for this false form.
He often touched it, seeing if it was flesh
Or ivory still, then shunned the ivory truth.   255
[He thought it met his lips. He talked, embraced,]
He felt his fingers sink into its skin,
Then feared that he'd leave bruises with his touch.
Now he spoke wooing words, now brought such gifts
As girls find pleasing: shells and polished stones   260
And little birds and thousand-colored flowers,
And lilies, ornate orbs, and fallen tears
From Heliadic trees;⁴ and clothing, too,
Rings for the fingers, pendants for the neck,
Pearls for the ears, and ribbons for the breasts.   265
Though just as fair when bared, she wore all well,
And, on a blanket of Sidonian dye,
He set her as the consort of his bed,
All swathed in down as if her neck could feel.
    "The Feast of Venus—which all Cyprus holds,   270
When snow-white heifers, led by gilded horns,

4. Amber (cf. 2.364–66)

Are slain through fumes of frankincense—had come.
His offering made, Pygmalion neared the shrine
And meekly prayed: 'If, gods, all's in your gift,
I wish to take as wife'—he dared not say   275
'My ivory maid'—'one *like* my ivory maid!'
But golden Venus, present at the feast,
Knew what he wished, and as a hopeful sign,
Flared up her flame three times into the air.
Once home, he sought his imitation girl   280
And kissed her on the bed. How warm she seemed!
He took her lips again and touched her breasts,
Then felt the ivory soften at his touch
Then sink beneath his hands, as sunlight melts
Hymettian wax which, molded by the thumb,   285
Takes many shapes, acquiring use through use.
Stunned, overjoyed, yet fearing some mistake,
The lover tried his hopes time and again:
Yes, she was flesh! His thumb could feel her pulse!
Profusely did the Paphian hero† then   290
Thank Venus as he pressed his lips at last
To living lips; and, blushing at his kiss,
The maiden met his eyes with timid eyes,
Whose first sight was her lover and the sky.†

[MYRRHA]†

"The goddess graced the wedding she had worked,   295
And when the moon had filled its horns nine times,
The bride bore Paphos, namesake of the isle,
Who then birthed Cinyras, a lucky man
Until he had a child. . . .
                    "Soon I shall sing
Of horrors! Get thee hence, girls! Hence, sires, go!   300
Or, if my songs are soothing to your souls,
Lose faith in what I tell, don't trust its truth;
Or, if you trust it, trust its punishment!
If Nature will allow such things to be,
I praise us Thracians and I praise our realm   305

For being so far from lands that bear such sin!†
Although Panchaea⁵ may grow rich in spice,
And costum, cinnamon, and frankincense,
For all the flowers it bears, it still bears myrrh,
A monstrous tree not worth so great a price!   310
Cupid himself denies you felt his darts,
And clears his torches, Myrrha, of your crime;
For with their Stygian spikes and swollen snakes
One of the Sisters Three⁶ infected you.
Sin though it is to hate one's sire, such love   315
Is greater sin than hate. As eastern youths
And nobles seek your hand from near and far,
Choose one man, Myrrha—but leave one man out!
    "Herself, she fought the love she felt and cried:
'Where shall this lead me?† What's my plan? O gods!   320
By piety and parents' sacred rights,
Check crime and stop this sin!—if sin it be,
For piety will not condemn this love
When other creatures couple as they please.†
None think the bull is base to mount his calf;   325
The stallion takes his daughter for his wife;
Goats fare through flocks they've fathered; and the birds
Conceive with those by whom they were conceived.
They're lucky to be free! But human laws
Are wicked and our jealous rules deny   330
What nature would allow. Yet there are tribes
Where mothers join with sons, and daughters sires,
To grow their bonds, they say, through doubled love.
Poor me, I was born elsewhere, stricken down
By chance of place!—but why dwell on such things?   335
Forbidden hopes, begone! He should be loved,
But as my father. Were I not the child
Of Cinyras, I'd lie with Cinyras,
But now, since he is mine, he is not mine:†
My nearness is my loss! I'd best go far—   340

5. A legendary isle of spices located near Arabia
6. The Furies

I ought to quit my home and flee my sin,
For wicked passion keeps this lover here
Where Cinyras is present to be seen
And touched and heard and kissed, if nothing else. . . .
Is something else, vile maiden, to be hoped?   345
Think of the ties, the names you would confound!
Your mother's rival! Mistress to your sire!
Your brother's mother! Sister to your son!
The snake-haired Sisters[†]—don't they stir your fear,
Whom guilty souls see brandishing fierce flames   350
Before their eyes? You've yet to sin in flesh:
Stay pure of mind and don't defile the bonds
Of nature through an act of lawless lust!
Facts bar your wish: he is a pious man,
And . . . oh, I wish this passion burned in him!'   355
    "Now Cinyras, unsure of what to do
With such a throng of suitors, name by name
Inquired of her which husband she preferred.
At first, she paused and fixed her father's face
With troubled eyes awash in tepid tears.   360
This Cinyras mistook for virgin's fear,
And dried her cheeks and kissed her sobs away.
Too happy, Myrrha, asked what man she wished,
Said, 'One like you!' But he misunderstood
And praised her, saying, 'Mayst thou ever be   365
So pious!' Hearing piety invoked,
She felt a pang of guilt and looked away.
    "Come midnight, slumber frees the flesh of cares,
But wakeful lay the child of Cinyras
In quenchless flames, her mad desire renewed,   370
Now in despair, now daring, keen, ashamed,
And clueless what to do. Much as a tree,
Struck by an axe, will stand until the end
But sway all ways, unsure of which to fall,
So did her mind, made weak with many wounds,   375
Lean here and there, drawn on toward either side,
Until it found love's sole recourse was death.
So death it was: she rose to hang herself.

Her belt bound to the beam, she said, 'Farewell,
Dear Cinyras, but know you caused my death!'   380
And slipped the noose around her pallid neck.
    "They say these murmurs reached the faithful ears
Of her kind nursemaid keeping watch outside,
Who rose, burst in, beheld the means of death,
And all at once cried out and beat her breast,   385
Clawed through her clothes, and tore the noose to shreds.
Then only had she time to weep, embrace,
And ask about the noose. The girl stood still,
Her gaze fixed on the ground in silent grief
That her too-slow attempts at death were foiled.   390
So, baring her white locks and empty breasts,
The agèd woman begged her, by her crib
And baby's milk, to trust her with her woes;
And, seeing her sob and swerve, the nosy nurse
Vowed more than confidence: 'Tell me,' she said,   395
'And let me help! My age won't slow me down.
If you are crazed, I've healing herbs and chants;
If cursed, you shall be cleansed with magic rites.
If you've enraged the gods, their rage will pass
With sacrifice. What else is there? For sure,   400
Your household thrives, your mother and your sire—'
When Myrrha heard 'your sire,' she heaved a sigh,
And still the nurse conceived of nothing foul,
But, feeling it must be some love affair,
She ceaselessly implored her to divulge   405
Whatever it might be, and brought her close,
And feebly held her weeping as she said,
'I know that you're in love, but (do not fear)
You'll have my help—your sire will never know!'
Enraged, the girl leapt up and dove head-first   410
Into the bed. 'Leave! Spare my wretched shame!
Please leave,' she said, 'or leave off asking me
About my grief: what you would know is sin!'
Aghast, her hands aquake with age and fear,
The old one pleaded at her nursling's feet,   415
Now soothing her, now making threats to tell,

Unless she heard the truth, about the noose
And suicide, yet vowing aid for love.
She raised her head and filled her nurse's breast
With rising tears and often tried to tell,   420
Yet often stopped and veiled her face in shame.
'Oh, blessed is mother in her spouse!' she said,
Then only groaned. An icy shudder gripped
The nurse's limbs and bones (for now she knew)
And all her head of hoary hair stood stiff.   425
She tried to talk away her wicked love,
Yet, knowing she spoke true, the girl stayed set
To die if barred from love. So said the nurse,
'Live, then! And have your—' she dared not say *sire*,
But, falling silent, bound her oath by heaven.   430
    "It was the time of Ceres' yearly feast,
When faithful matrons, dressed in robes of white,
Bring wreaths of wheat as first-fruit offerings
And count the love and touch of men as banned
For nine whole nights. The queen Cenchreïs, too,   435
Observed the secret rites, and since his bed
Lacked for his lawful wife, when Cinyras
Was found drunk by the all-too-helpful nurse,
Who told of one most fair who loved him true
But hid her name, he asked the maiden's age.   440
'The same as Myrrha's,' she replied. Sent home
To fetch her, she cried, 'Nursling mine, rejoice!
We've won!' But in the luckless maiden's heart,
There was no cheer—foreboding filled her heart—
Yet cheered she was, for so her mind was torn.   445
    "Now all was silent. As Boötes turned
His wagon-shaft between the Oxen's stars,
She went to work. Then fled the golden moon,
Black clouds concealed the stars, and night lacked light.
You hid your face first, Icarus, then you   450
Erigone, divine through daughter's love.†
Three times ill-omened stumbles called her back,
Three times she heard the screech-owl's mortal sign,
Yet on she walked, shame dwindling in the dark,

The nurse at one hand while the other groped   455
Her sightless way. Soon she had reached the room,
Soon cracked the doors, and soon was led inside,
But as she went she buckled at the knees,
Her blood and blush ran dry—she lost her nerve!
The nearer drew her sin, the more she shrank,   460
Deplored her pains, and longed to leave unknown.
But as she stalled, the old one took her hand,
Brought her beside the lofty bed, and said,
'Here, Cinyras, she's yours!' and doomed the pair.
    "Obscenely bedded with his flesh and blood,   465
The father fought to calm her virgin's fright,
And called her 'daughter,' owing to her age,
As she said 'sire,' the fit names for their crime.
Filled with her father's sinful seed, she left,
Their crime conceived within her horrid womb.   470
The next night twinned their sin—nor was that all!—
Till Cinyras, at length, longing to know
With whom he'd lain so often, brought a lamp
And saw his crime and child. Pain tied his tongue,
His shining sword shot from its dangling sheath,   475
And Myrrha fled, the dark of sightless night
Preserving her from death to wander through
Panchaea's fields and palm-filled Araby.
Nine moon-horns' rounds she roamed, then came to rest
In Sabaean soil, her womb about to burst.   480
At last, afraid of death yet tired of life,
Without a wish, she poured all in this prayer:
'O any power who'll bear to hear my plea!
I shall not shun the punishment I've earned.
Lest I offend the living with my life   485
And lifeless with my death, bar me from both,
And change me so I cannot live or die!'†
Some power did bear to hear her plea; or else,
Her prayers found gods,† for even as she spoke
The earth encased her legs while sidelong roots   490
Shot from her toes to brace the running trunk;
Skin changed to bark, her fingers and her arms

To branches small and large, and bone to wood,
In whose persisting pith, blood turned to sap.
And soon the tree grew round her heavy womb,   495
Enclosed her chest, and made to shield her neck;
Unable to wait further, she bent down
And sank her face into the rising wood.
    "Her former feelings vanished with her form,
But still she weeps and warms the tree with tears,   500
Which, too, are famed; for, dripping from the trunk,
Myrrh bears its mistress' name through every age.

[VENUS AND ADONIS]†

    "But in the trunk, her ill-got child still grew
And searched for where to pierce its parent's bark.
Amid the tree, the pregnant belly swelled   505
And weighed the mother down. Pangs went unvoiced,
No calls of labor called Lucina near,
But still the tree, like one delivering,
Grew bent with groans and wet with falling tears,
Till kind Lucina came; and as she touched   510
The tortured boughs and uttered childbirth's charms,
The tree cracked wide and, through the living bark,
There burst a wailing boy! In softest sod,
The Naiads wrapped him, tinged with mother's tears.
His looks could have won praise from Spite himself,   515
For he appeared as naked cupids do
In paintings, with no difference save attire—
Just give or take a quiver, here or there.
    "Time fools with furtive flight and years race past.
Born to his sister and his grandfather,   520
That son, but lately hidden in the tree
And lately born, was soon the fairest child.
Now grown to youth, now man, now fairer still,
He venged his mother's flames on Venus' heart.
For as her archer-child gave her a kiss,   525
An aimless arrow grazed his mother's breast;

The goddess pushed him back, but was deceived:
The wound was deeper than it first appeared.
　"So, taken with the beauty of this man,
She spurned Cythera's shores,† the Paphian seas,　　　530
Fish-laden Cnidos, ore-rich Amathus,
And even heaven, for she ranked heaven below
Adonis, whom she held and whom she joined—
Though wont to shade and beautify her looks—
On slopes and woods and brambly boulder-fields,　　　535
Her robes hitched up Diana's way, knee-high.
In search of safer prey, she set her hounds
On speeding rabbits, high-horned harts, and hinds,
But kept herself away from mighty boars,
From prowling wolves, bears armed with claws, and lions　　　540
Brimful with slaughtered herds. You would have feared
The same, Adonis, had you heeded her:
'With flighty beasts,' said she, 'thou shouldst be brave,
But with the daring, 'tis not safe to dare!
Do not be reckless at my risk, dear boy,　　　545
Nor smite those nature arms so well, for fear
Your valor cost me dear. Your youth and looks,
Which both move Venus so, will move no lions
[Nor bristling swine, nor feral eyes and hearts].
For boars bear lightning in their twisting tusks,　　　550
And golden lions charge with boundless wrath:
I hate their kind.'
　　　　　　"Asked why, she said, 'I'll speak
And awe you with a monstrous ancient wrong.
But I am weary with unwonted toil
And look! a handy poplar offers shade　　　555
And beds of grass: here would I lie with you.'
And, resting there upon the ground and him,
She lolled her head against the young man's chest
And spoke these words, with kisses in between:
'You will, perhaps, have heard about a maid　　　560
Who, in a race, outran the swiftest swains.
It's no mere tale (it's true!), nor could you say

Her feet deserved more praise than did her face.
As for a spouse, the god[7] had said: "No spouse
Does Atalanta[†] need—flee spousal ways!   565
Yet flee you won't: alive, you'll lose yourself."
Scared by this oracle, she dwelt unwed
Within the woods and violently repelled
Her wooing throngs: "I'll not be won," she said,
"Save in a race: come vie with me on foot!   570
The prize for swiftness is a bed and bride,
But death rewards the slow—these are the rules!"
Though she was ruthless (such is beauty's power),
Despite this rule rash wooers thronged her way.

"'Hippomenes sat out the loathsome race,   575
And, watching, said, "Who'd seek himself a spouse
At such a risk?" and cursed young love's excess;
But when he saw her face and body bared
(She looked like me—or you, were you a girl!),
He reached out awestruck, crying, "Pardon me,   580
All whom I blamed before: I did not know
You sought so great a prize!" Praise kindled love.
He wished no other youth would run so swift
And shook with jealousy. "Yet why should I
Not try my fortunes in this race?" he said.   585
"Heaven helps the brave!" But while Hippomenes
Considered this, the fleet-foot maid flew by.
She seemed no slower than a Scythian shaft,
Yet the Aonian marveled more that she,
Who was so fair, grew fairer as she raced.   590
With wings upon her heels[†] she braced the breeze,
Which fanned her tresses down her ivory back
And stirred the tinted laces at her knees.
Her body's pallor flushed a girlish pink,
Much as a drape can dye a marble hall,   595
Once pale, with purple artificial shade.
Then, as he gazed, the final post was passed!
As Atalanta donned the victor's crown,

7. Apollo, presumably; this is an oracle

The vanquished groaned and paid their promised price.
    "'And still the youth, unfazed by what befell,   600
Stood forth and looked the maiden in the face:
"Why seek an easy fame amongst the slow?
Try me!" he called. "If fortune favors me,
You shan't be shamed to lose to such a man:
Megareus of Onchestus is my sire,   605
And his grandfather's Neptune, making me
The sea's great-grandson, matched in worth and birth!
Or, should I lose, be famed for your defeat
Of great Hippomenes!" Then Schoeneus' child,
Who'd watched him sadly, doubted whether she   610
Preferred to win or lose: "What god," she cried,[†]
"For hate of handsome men, bids this one die
To wed me? I don't think I'm worth the price!
It's not his looks that touch me (though they could)—
He's just a boy: it's not him, it's his youth!   615
What of his worth, his dauntlessness in death?
What of his fourth-degree marine descent?
What of his love, which holds our match so high
That he will die if fate keeps him from me?
Flee, while you can, my wedding-bed of blood!   620
Woe to my spouse! None else would spurn your hand
And wiser girls may woo! . . . But why spare *you*,
Now with so many killed? Let him take care:
He'll die if he's so tired of life that all
My slaughtered suitors cannot warn him off. . . .   625
Then shall he die for wanting life with me?
And shall an undue death reward his love?
I'll loathe my triumph more than I can bear. . . .
That's not my fault. I wish that you'd give up,
But, since you're mad, I wish that you'll be swift!   630
How maidenly his boyish face appears—
Ah, poor Hippomenes, I'd rather you
Had never seen me: you deserved to live.
Were I more blessed and fated to be wed,
It's you alone with whom I'd share my bed."   635
This spoken in her first throes of desire,

She loved naïvely, unaware she loved.
    "'Soon, sire and city held another race.
Then Neptune's heir Hippomenes invoked
Me, vexed of voice: "May Cytherea grace   640
My trials, I pray, and aid the love she's caused!"
A kindly breeze brought me his pleasing prayers
Which touched me but gave little time to help.
There is a plain, known there as Tamasus.
It's Cyprus' richest land, and long ago,   645
The elders consecrated it to me
To fund my temples. In that field, there shines
A rustling tree, gold-leaved and gold of bough.
Come fresh from there, I chanced to carry three
Gold apples, which I taught Hippomenes   650
To use, though none could see me but himself.
To blaring trumpets, both dashed from the gates
And crossed the sandy surface with such speed
You'd think they could pass dry along the surf
Or scamper over ears of ripened grain!   655
The young man's spirits meanwhile swelled to hear
Shouts of support: "Now—now's the time! Go on!
Use all your strength, Hippomenes, don't stop!
You'll win!" It's doubtful if Megareus' son
Or Schoeneus' daughter heard this with more joy.   660
How many times she slowed instead of gained
To gaze at him, then sadly passed him by!
His breath was tired and dry, but still the end
Was far, when Neptune's heir at last threw forth
The first of the three apples from the tree.   665
Consumed with longing for the shiny fruit,[†]
She veered off-course to seize the rolling gold.
The crowd cheered as Hippomenes sped past,
But with a rush she made up for lost time,
And left the youth to trail behind again.   670
She stopped before a second flying fruit,
But caught up as they neared the final stretch.
"Now, gifting goddess, be with me!" he cried,
And hurled the shining gold, with all his strength,

Aside, whence she could not return in time.   675
The maiden seemed to wonder where to go;
I made her fetch it, adding to its mass,
That both the weight and wait might hinder her.
Then, lest my tale be longer than the race,
The girl lost and the victor took his prize.   680
   "'Adonis, did I not deserve his thanks?
His incense, too? When he forgot my thanks
And incense both, I felt my fury flash,
Stung by his slight to stave off future scorn
And make a warning lesson of them both.   685
   "'Renowned Echion[8] once, to keep a vow,
Had built the Mother of the gods[9] a shrine
Deep in a wood, where, weary of the way,
They stopped to rest; and there, untimely lust
Possessed Hippomenes—for so I willed!   690
Close by the temple stood a dim-lit den,
Much like a cave and roofed with natural rock,
Once sacred to an ancient cult and filled
With wooden figures of the olden gods.
As he befouled this shrine with blasphemy   695
The icons shunned the sight and, crowned with towers,[†]
The Mother would have plunged them in the Styx,
Had that not seemed too light! And so, less light
Their once-smooth necks grew under tawny manes;
Their fingers curved to claws, their arms to legs,   700
Their torsos spread and sprouted sweeping tails.
With wrathful features, roars in place of words,
And forests for their bed, they fright all else,
But, champing at her bit, serve Cybele.
These lions and all other beasts, my dear,   705
Who blithely bare their breasts and not their backs,
Avoid—for fear your courage wreck us both!'[†]
   "Her warning made, she soared off on her swans;
His courage, though, could not be warned, and when

8. One of the original dragon-born Thebans (cf. 3.126)
9. Cybele

It chanced his hounds tracked down a hidden hog   710
And drove it from the forest, there it met
A sidestroke from the son of Cinyras.
The wild boar's twisting tusks at once dislodged
The bloody spear and chased the panicked youth,
Fleeing for his life, then gored him through the groin,   715
And left him dying in the yellow sand.
   "Midair on cygnet wings, the chariot
Of Cytherea had not yet arrived
In Cyprus when the distant dying groans
Caused her to turn the snowy swans his way.   720
When, from on high, she saw the pool of blood
Where he lay lifeless, she rent robes and hair,
And leapt with brutal beatings of the breast
To chide the Fates: 'Still you shall not rule all!
Memorials to my grief,' she cried, 'shall last   725
Forever, reenacting every year
Your death,[†] Adonis, and my wails of woe.
Your blood will be transformed into a flower,
For, as Persephone once turned a girl
To fragrant mint,[†] shall I be grudged the right   730
Of changing Cinyras' heroic son?'
This said, she strewed sweet nectar on his blood,
Which swelled when touched, as twinkling bubbles rise
Through yellow mud; in no more than an hour,
There bloomed a blood-red flower, like that which grows   735
Red pomegranates, fruits that hide their seeds
In rigid rinds. And yet, its life is brief,
For, loose of root, it falls before that force
From which the flimsy windflower takes its name."

Book 11

SONGS SUCH as these charmed trees and beasts and stones
To seek the Thracian bard, but while they did,
Behold! a band of crazed Ciconian wives,[1]
Atop a hill, their bosoms bound in pelts,
Spied Orpheus there putting songs to strings.   5
"Look, look!" cried one, hair blowing in the breeze,
"The man who scorns us!" and she hurled her staff
To hit Apollo's songster in the face—
But it was tipped with leaves† and did no harm.
Another cast a stone but, as it flew,   10
It yielded to the chords of voice and lyre
And, as if begging pardon for its wrongs,
Fell at his feet. But they grew bolder still,
Till madness burst its bounds and Furies reigned!
All weapons would have weakened to his song,   15
Had not the clash of curving Phrygian fifes
And drums and clapping hands and bacchant howls
Drowned out his lyre. Then did their stones turn red
With blood drawn from the bard they could not hear.
First, countless birds still stricken by his song,   20

1. A group of Thracian bacchants

Then snakes and beasts—the storied audience
Of Orpheus—fell to the maenads,[2] who
Next turned their gory hands on Orpheus,
As birds of day surround a wayward owl,
Or dogs in the arena hunt a stag   25
Doomed to be slaughtered in the morning games.[†]
They rushed upon the poet, flinging forth
Their leafy thyrsi, made for other ends,
And pelting him with branches, dirt, and stones.
Then, lest their madness lack true weaponry,   30
It chanced there was an ox-team ploughing near,
While, past them, hardy farmers at their spades
Were sweating for their crops in sturdy soil.
These farmers fled before the herd's stampede
And left their tools of toil strewn round the field,   35
Great hoes and rakes and mattocks, long and large.
With these, the frenzied women tore apart
The mean-horned bulls,[†] then rushed to kill the bard,
Whose outstretched hands and words, now voiced in vain
As they had never been before, moved none: 40
The faithless women slew him. Then (by Jove!)
Out through those lips which spoke to beasts and stones,
He breathed his soul, exhaled into the air.
    For you, O Orpheus, sad birds and beasts,
For you the solid stones, for you the woods   45
Wept tears, while trees who'd thronged to hear your songs
Shed leaves like grief-shorn locks. The rivers, too,
Swelled up with tears, they say, while, robed in black,
The Naiads and the Dryads loosed their hair.
His limbs lay all about, but in your stream,   50
You, Hebrus, took his head and lyre adrift,
Which (wondrous sound!) gave forth a weeping chord,
As wept the lifeless tongue and wept the shores.
Borne out to sea, they left their native stream
And reached Methymna on the Lesbian coast.   55
There, on those foreign sands, a savage snake

2. "Raving ones," that is, bacchants

Approached the head whose tresses trickled foam,
Fangs poised to strike, but Phoebus came at last
And froze [the serpent's open jaws to stone]
And left them hardened, gaping where they were.[†]   60
    Beneath the earth, a shade reviewed the sites
He'd seen before, and in the Fields of Faith[3]
His eager arms embraced Eurydice.
Now Orpheus strolls often at her side,
And sometimes follows her, and sometimes leads,   65
But gazes safe at his Eurydice.
    Lyaeus,[4] though, refused to let such crimes
Go unavenged. To mourn his mystic bard,
He tied to tree-trunks all the Thracian wives
Who'd seen the sin, bound fast in writhing roots.   70
So far as each had traveled in pursuit,
He dug their toes into the solid ground,
And, as a bird caught in a fowler's net
Perceives its leg is cleverly entrapped
Yet with its frantic flaps constricts the snares,   75
So did these women, stuck inside the soil,
Make terrified and vain attempts to flee
As clinging roots held firm each kicking form.
Where were their toes? Where were their feet and nails?
They wondered, with their calves encased in wood,   80
And as each strove to strike her thighs in grief,
She struck on oak! For oaken were their chests,
Their shoulders oak—and if you thought their arms
Had turned to boughs, your thinking would be right.

[MIDAS][†]

Not yet contented, Bacchus left his lands   85
With better company to seek the vines
Of dear Timolus and Pactolus' sands,
Which then flowed free of gold[†] and mortal greed.

    3. Elysium
    4. Bacchus

Though other Satyrs joined this bacchant court,
Some peasants caught Silenus, old and drunk,†   90
And brought him crowned before the Phrygian lord,
King Midas, whom Eumolpus, Athens' son,
Had taught the rites† with Thracian Orpheus.
He saw it was a comrade of his cult,
And promptly gave his guest a joyous feast   95
Of twice-five days and nights. The Morning Star
Had cleared the starry sky eleven times
When, through the Lydian fields, the cheerful king
Returned Silenus to his youthful ward.
His guardian safe, the gladdened god induced   100
The king to make a great—though grievous—wish.
Predestined to pick poorly, he replied,
"Make all I touch transform to gleaming gold!"
Assenting, Liber gave the baneful boon,
But groaned that he'd not made a better choice.   105
    The Phrygian hero left in foolish glee,
And tried his power by poking everything.
[Still skeptical,] down from a [lowly] oak,
He tore a twig—the twig was made of gold!†
He heaved a stone—the stone turned gold of hue!   110
He touched the dirt—the dirt he touched was turned
To nuggets! Ceres' withered wheat he reaps
As golden grain; the apples that he picks
You'd think were sent by the Hesperides;
He watches door-beams beam beneath his hands,   115
And when he dips his fingers in the waves,
The fingered waves might well woo Danaë.⁵
His heart can hardly hold his hopes and dreams—
A world of gold!—exulting as his slaves
Set him a table, heaped with meats and loaves.   120
But then! as he takes Ceres' fruits in hand,
The gifts of Ceres harden; when he tries
The meat, with every bite the fellow takes
The meat turns into bitten yellow flakes!

5. Jupiter impregnated Danaë in a shower of gold (cf. 6.611–12)

Then he pours wine, his patron's other gift,   125
And you can see gold trickling through his teeth.
   Stunned by this curious curse, the richened wretch
Hates his old hopes and flees his wished-for wealth.
His hunger finds no food, thirst burns his throat,
And hateful gold torments him as deserved,   130
Till, hands and gilded arms upraised, he cries:
"Lenaeus, lord, pray pardon me my sins,
And spare me this foul curse which seemed so fair!"
The gods are gentle; Bacchus heard his plea,
Restored him, and recalled the granted gift: 135
"Lest you stay cased in gold unwisely wished,
Seek out that stream which near great Sardis flows,
And wend your way upstream along its banks,
Until you reach the river's source," he said.
"In that foam-flooding fountain, plunge your head,   140
And cleanse your body as you cleanse your crime."
The king obeyed; his body, as it sank,
Released its gilding power into the stream,
And to this day, where that old river runs,
The fields are hard with clods of fairest gold.   145
   Despising wealth, he took to woods and fields
And to the cult of Pan, whose haunts are caves
On mountains. But, dim-witted as before,
His foolish mind was bound for further harm.
The sloping sides of Tmolus, steep and high,   150
Look far across the sea, then tumble down
To Sardis and to humble Hypaepa,
Where Pan, while singing to the slender nymphs
And playing songs upon his waxen pipes,
Dared scorn Apollo's songs as worse than his.   155
To judge their unmatched match, old Tmolus came,
Perched on his peak, and cleared his ears of trees.[†]
With only oak to bind his sea-green hair,
And acorns hanging round his hollow brow,
He gazed upon the god of flocks and said,   160
"The judge is ready!" So, the rustic reeds
Rang out and Midas (happening to hear)

Was soothed by its crude song. When it was done,
Dread Tmolus turned his gaze and glades to face
Bright Phoebus, in Parnassian laurels crowned,   165
His Tyrian mantle trailing on the ground.
While one hand clasped an Indian ivory lyre
Inlaid with jewels, the other held a pick:
He looked the artist's part. With his trained thumb,
He strummed the strings till Tmolus, sweetly charmed,   170
Bade Pan submit his reed-pipes to the lyre.
   The sacred mountain's judgment suited all,
And none demurred or called the case unjust
But Midas. That such artless ears should sport
A human form, the Delian god redressed   175
By stretching them, stuffed full of whitish hair
And free to wave and wobble at the base.
All else stayed human save this punished part:
His ears were now those of a stubborn ass.†
[Disfigured and ashamed,] he made [to mask]   180
And hide his temples in a purple hood,
But still, the slave who cut his hair saw all.
He dared not speak about the shameful sight,
But longed to and could not keep quiet till
He'd dug a hole and hissed into the ground   185
What kind of ears he'd seen his master had.
Then, hiding what he'd whispered in the dirt,
He left in silence with the pit refilled.
But on that spot a mass of rustling reeds
Arose and, ripening with the year, betrayed   190
Their sower, echoing in Auster's breeze
The hidden hisses of his master's ears. . . .

[PELEUS AND THETIS]†

   From Tmolus, Leto's vengeful son took off,
Flew toward the Nephelean Hellespont,†
And landed in Laömedon's domain.   195
There 'twixt Sigeum and Rhoeteum stood
A shrine to the Panomphean Thunderer,†

From which he watched Laömedon at work
Upon the walls of newly founded Troy.
This toilsome task demanded great resource,   200
So he assumed a human form and joined
The trident-bearing sire of swollen seas
In raising ramparts for the Phrygian king,
Who'd promised gold in payment for his walls;
But once they stood, the king foreswore his debt   205
And crowned his perfidy with perjury.
"You shall not go unscathed!" the sea-lord cried,
And, slanting all his waves toward stingy Troy,
Transformed the land to sea, destroyed the crops,
And sank the fields in surf. Nor was that all: 210
A monster of the deep was to be fed
The king's own daughter![6] But, as she lay bound,
Alcides[7] freed her. Promised steeds for pay,
When this too was denied, he sacked the walls
Of doubly-perjured Troy, with Telamon,   215
His aide, who took Hesione as spoils,
And Peleus, whose godly wife did not
Make him less famous for her sire than did
His grandsire, for Jove's grandsons number more
Than one, but just one man has wed a god.[†]   220
    Old Proteus told Thetis, "Bear a child,
O goddess of the waves! You'll raise a youth
Whose feats shall dwarf his sire's and dim his fame!"
So, lest the world should hold a greater Jove,
Though Jupiter felt no few flames at heart,   225
He fled a match with Thetis of the deep,
And bade Aeacides,[8] his grandson, take
His place beside the virgin of the sea.
    In Thessaly, there is a scythe-shaped bay,
Whose arms, not deep enough to harbor ships,   230
Embrace a sandy bed of even sea

---

6. Hesione, future wife of Telamon and mother of Teucer
7. Hercules
8. Peleus, son of Aeacus, son of Jupiter

With solid shorelines where no footprint keeps,
No voyage falters, and no seaweed grows.
A nearby myrtle grove of mottled fruits
Surrounds a grotto (made by either art   235
Or nature†—likely art) where, Thetis, you
Would ride on bridled dolphins in the nude.
While you lay fast asleep there, Peleus
Seized hold of you and, when you spurned his pleas,
Fell back on force and flung arms round your neck!   240
If you'd not had your usual recourse
To shifting shapes, he would have had his way,
But now you were a bird (a bird he clasped),
And then a tree (a tree where Peleus perched).
But your third form, a spotted tigress, so   245
Alarmed Aeacides he loosed his grip.
He prayed then, pouring wine into the sea,
And sacral meats and fragrant frankincense,
Till the Carpathian prophet[9] rose and said:
"Aeacides, you'll win the wife you seek   250
If you, while she lies sleeping in the cave,
First bind her fast in chains before she wakes,
Then, though she take a hundred shamming shapes,
Embrace her every form till she turns back!"†
With this said, Proteus submerged his face,   255
And sank the final words beneath his waves.
    As Titan, swinging low, was holding course
Through Western waves, the noble Nereid
Slipped from the sea to seek her usual spot,
And Peleus scarce reached her when the maid   260
Began transforming; but, seeing she was bound
With arms outstretched, she groaned. "Through some god's aid,
You've won!" cried Thetis, and she showed herself.
Surrendering, she let the hero clasp
And fill her with Achilles, their great son.   265

9. Proteus

[DAEDALION AND CHIONE]†

So, blessed in son and blessed in bride, all things
Served Peleus, unless you count his crime
In killing Phocus.† Stained with brother's blood,
He fled his father's house for Trachis' land,
A realm ruled free of bloodshed, free of force,   270
By Ceÿx, offspring of the Morning Star,
Whose face, more often shining like his sire's,
Had darkened as he mourned his brother's loss.
Now, care-and-way-worn, came Aeacides
With but a few attendants to his court,   275
Concealing all the herds and flocks they'd brought
Within a glen outside the city walls.
Once he'd gained entrance as a suppliant
With olive-branch in hand, and told the court
His name and birth, but hid his cause for flight,   280
He begged asylum in the fields or town,
To which the mild Trachinian answered thus:
"Our gifts are open to the humblest folk,
Nor are we, Peleus, unkind to guests;
Consider, too, the weight your famous name   285
And grandsire, Jove, must bear:† then beg no more!
A share in all you beg for shall be yours—
Though, as you see, it is a sorry sight!"
He wept; then Peleus and all his train
Asked what aggrieved him so, and he replied: 290
"Though you perhaps had thought it always plumed,
This bird of prey, which frights all other fowls,
Was once a man (unchanged in character),
As warlike, fierce, and quick to fight as now,
And named Daedalion. Though we shared that sire   295
Who summons Dawn and leaves the heavens last,
While I craved peace and worked for peace's care
And for my wife's, my brother's love was war.
His might, which once laid low great kings and clans,
Plagues Thisbaean pigeons now in altered form.   300
    "His daughter Chione's twice-seven years,

Endowed with beauty, saw her wooed by all,
Till Phoebus chanced to pass with Maia's son
On route from Delphi and Cyllene's peak.
As one they saw her and as one they burned;   305
Apollo's dreams of love could wait till night,
But not the other's: with his slumberous staff,
He touched the girl, who fell before its touch,
And the god raped her. When night starred the sky,
Then Phoebus, in a hag's form, stole again   310
Those pre-seized pleasures! Soon, her womb grew ripe
And, to the wing-foot god, a wily child
Was born: Autolycus, whose cunning wit
Could conjure white from black and darken white—
A fitting heir unto his father's art.   315
To Phoebus also (she delivered twins),
Was born Philammon, famed for song and lyre.†
   "She'd bedded two gods and borne twins—so what?
What good were her sire's might and grandsire's sheen?
Has glory not cursed many? It cursed her!   320
For she dared rank her beauty higher than
Diana's, till the goddess, wild with rage
Replied, 'Perhaps our *deeds*† will please you more!'
And, bending then a shaft upon the string,
She shot an arrow through her guilty tongue.   325
Her tongue now stilled, of words she spoke no more,
But bled her speechless life out in my arms.
My wretched heart filled with her father's pain,
I tried to soothe my loving brother's grief.
The father listened, mourning his lost child,   330
As crags attend the breaking of the sea,
But watching her aflame, he rushed four times
To leap atop the pyre; pushed back four times,
He dashed off in a frenzy, like a steer
With bee-stings in its neck. Through pathless wastes,   335
I watched him run with superhuman speed,
So you might think his feet had taken wing,
Till, fleetly fleeing us all, intent on death,
He scaled Parnassus. There, Apollo, seeing

Daedalion hurl himself, held him aloft   340
In pity as a bird with sudden wings,
Then beaked his mouth and gave him taloned feet,
His former might, and more than wonted strength.
Now, as a hawk, he is unkind to all,
And, in his pain, brings pain to other birds."   345

[THE WOLF OF PSAMATHE]†

The Morning Star's own son was telling still
This wonder when a herdsman, Phocis-born
Onetor, rushed in, gasping, "Peleus!
O Peleus, I bring disastrous news!"
And Peleus bade him divulge the worst.   350
[As the Trachinian trembled in suspense,]
He answered: "When I'd run the weary herd
Along the shore, the Sun was at high noon
With as much left to see as he had seen.
Some cattle knelt then in the golden sand   355
And lay there gazing at the sea's expanse,
Some more were slowly straying back and forth,
And others waded in up to their necks.
But nearby, in an ancient glade, a shrine
Built not of gold or stone but densest wood   360
Exalts the Nereids and Nereus
(So said a sailor as he dried his nets)
And close by is a swamp of willow trees,
Made swampy with the spillage of the sea,
Whence, with a crash that frightened all around,   365
The reeds disgorged a monstrous beast—a wolf!
His jaws smeared thick with foam and clotted gore,
His eyes ablaze with fiery crimson flames,
He raged with fury and with hunger both,
But fury more, and took no time to sate   370
His horrid hunger on the cows he killed
But ravaged all the herd and crushed them all.
While we stood in defense, his fatal fangs
Did some of us to death. Blood stained the shore,

The water's edge, and all the moo-filled swamp.   375
But there's no time to lose or hesitate!†
While something can be saved, let us unite—
To arms, to arms!—and wield our spears as one!"
　　No harm the rube rehearsed stirred Peleus:
He knew the Nereid whose child he'd killed   380
Had done him harm to honor Phocus' death.[10]
But when the king of Oeta[11] made to go,
And bade his men take arms and raise their spears,
The racket roused his wife Alcyone,
Who burst in, tossing back her tousled hair,   385
Embraced his neck, and begged with weeping words
That he'd save two in one by sending help
But not himself. Aeacides replied,
"Put by, dear queen, these fair and faithful fears!
Though grateful, I would have none fight this fiend   390
For my sake—what the sea-nymph needs is prayer!"
　　From in a tower atop the citadel,
Whose beacons shone to beckon wandering barks,
They groaned to see their cows bestrew the shore
Where their destroyer, bloody at the lips,   395
Now prowled, his shaggy fur gone foul with gore.
There, reaching to the open sea and shore,
Did Peleus pray Psamathe to change
Her rage to aid. She spurned Aeacides
Till Thetis, begging on her lord's behalf,   400
Secured his pardon. Even so, the wolf,
Called back from slaughter, kept his thirst for blood
Until, while tearing through a heifer's neck,
He turned to stone—unchanged, save in his hue,
Whose marble color made it clear he was   405
A wolf no more, and no more to be feared.
Still, fate would not let Peleus remain,
But forced him to Magnesia, where at last
Acastus of Thessalia cleansed his sin.†

10. Phocus' mother was the Nereid Psamathe
11. Ceÿx, king of Trachis, near Mount Oeta

[CEŸX AND ALCYONE]†

His brother's death and these ensuing shocks   410
So troubled Ceÿx' heart that, to consult
Those oracles which are men's last resort,
He sought the god at Claros—Delphi's shrine
Being blocked by faithless Phorbas' Phlegyan hordes.†
But when you, dutiful Alcyone,   415
First heard his plans, your inmost bones turned cold,
Your face went boxwood-white, you streamed with tears!
Three times she tried to speak; three times she wept,
But soon her sobs gave way to loving cries:
"How have I brought you to this, dearest one?   420
Where is the care for me you used to have?
Since when can you desert Alcyone
Without concern? Since when have you enjoyed
Long trips? Since when did you prefer me gone?
Just tell me that you're traveling by land: 425
Then I shall grieve but free my cares of fear.
The ocean scares me, and the sea's grim sight;
These days I've seen planks broken on the beach,
And read the names off many empty tombs.†
Don't fool yourself that since my sire's the son   430
Of Hippotes[12] and keeps the Winds confined
That he may calm the waves for you at will,
For once the Winds are loosed upon the waves,
There is no stopping them, and helpless lie
All oceans and all lands while in the skies   435
They force the clouds to crash with crimson flames.
The more I know them (for I know them well
And often saw them in my father's house)
The more I know to fear; yet if no prayers
Can change your mind, dear spouse, but you must go,   440
Then take me, too! Together tempest-tossed,
Where I'll fear only what I face, we'll bear
Whatever comes, as through the waves we're borne!"

12. Aeolus, Keeper of the Winds

Aeolus' daughter's tears and speeches moved
Her star-sprung spouse, who flamed with love no less   445
But would not change his course across the waves,
Nor share its dangers with Alcyone.
Try as he might to soothe her anxious heart,
He could not win her blessing till he tried
This comfort, which alone convinced his wife: 450
"Though every wait is long for us, I swear
By all my father's fires that, barring fate,
I shall return before the moon fills twice."
Her hopes awakened by his pledged return,
He bade his ship be suitably equipped   455
And launched to sea at once; yet, watching this,
As though she'd seen a sign of things to come,
Alcyone was gripped by fear anew,
And, crying, clasped him with a sad "farewell"
Before at last she fainted dead away.   460
Though Ceÿx tried to halt his youthful crew,
Their twofold lines of hearty hearts rowed on
With even seaward strokes. Then, raising up
Her moistened eyes, she spied upon the deck
Her husband standing, giving her a wave,   465
Which she returned, and, as he sailed away,
Although her eyes could find his face no more,
She still gazed after the receding ship.
When that, too, slipped from sight, she watched the sails
Atop the mast and, when the sails had gone,   470
She fled distraught into her empty bed,
Where once again Alcyone broke down,
Reminded of her missing other half.
   Once out of port, a breeze bestirred the ropes,
And so the captain hung the oars aside,   475
Raised up the yard atop the wooden mast,
And spread the sails to catch the blowing breeze.
Midway or less—no more—across the sea,
The craft was cruising, far from either shore,
When night fell and the swelling waves began   480
To whiten under Eurus' rising blasts.

"Bring down the yard at once!" the helmsman cried,
"Take in the sails!" Or so he did command,
But gusting gales frustrated his commands,
For no voice carries through the crashing sea.   485
Still, on their own, some rushed to ship the oars,
Some plugged their holes, and others reefed the sails.
While here some bailed and poured sea back to sea,
And there some fastened spars, and chaos reigned,
The storm grew stronger as, on every side,   490
The Winds waged war and churned the raging waves.
In panic and, in frankness, in the dark,
The helmsman knew not what to bid or bar
So great their peril was, so past his skill.
In uproar, sailors screamed and cables creaked,   495
Wave broke on wave, and thunder rent the air.
The rising surf appeared to reach the sky
And strike the scudding cloudbanks with its spray.
And now the waves are golden with the sands
Stirred from the depths, now darker like the Styx,   500
And meanwhile flatten white with hissing foam.
So, too, is Trachis' vessel tossed and turned,
For now, heaved up as though atop a peak,
She seems to spy the depths and vales of Hell,
And now, when sunk amid the swirling swells,   505
To gaze at heaven from the abyss below.
Her wave-washed sides send forth crash after crash,
A sound as harsh as when an iron-ram
Or catapult assails a castle's walls.
[Just as ferocious lions gain in strength   510
While hurtling toward a hunter's leveled spears,
So do the wind-whipped waves increase in height
Until they tower above the towering ship.]
And soon the joints, washed of their wax, give way,
The seams crack, and the fatal flood flows in.   515
To see the clouds dissolve in sheets of rain,
You'd think all heaven was sliding down to sea
And all the swells were gliding up to heaven.
While rain soaks through the sails, the ocean tides

Are mixed with heaven's beneath a starless sky,   520
Where night's own darkness darkens in the storm
Till broken by a brilliant flash of bolts
As flames of lightning's light restart the stars.
The waves now pour inside the hollow hull,
And, as the bravest soldier in a band,   525
Though often thwarted, will, for love of praise,
At last surmount a city's circled walls
And seize the gate, a thousand men to one,
So, when nine waves had struck the ship's steep sides,
A tenth and taller torrent surged ahead,   530
Unchecked until it drowned the sagging decks
And sank within the vessel's vanquished walls.
In part, the sea still tried to breach the bark,
But part had entered. All were terrified,
Much as a town, its walls holed from without,   535
Feels terror as it holds them from within.
    Skill failed and spirits fell as every wave
Appeared a raging rush of rolling death.
Some cried, some gaped, some envied other men
Their proper tombs, and some reached up in vain   540
And called upon the heaven they could not see.
Each thought of brothers, fathers, children, homes,
And all he'd left behind, but Ceÿx' thoughts
And Ceÿx' words were of Alcyone.
For her alone he longed, though he rejoiced   545
She was at home, far off beside those shores
He would have loved to give one final glance,
Had he known where he was: for so the sea
Did swirl and froth, beneath clouds so pitch-black
They hid the sky and made night twice as dark!   550
When whirlwinds shattered both the mast and helm,
There rose a victor gloating on his spoils—
A wave that glowered above the curving waves
Then fell as hard as though it were the peaks
Of Pindus and of Athos, wrenched from land   555
And cast upon the ship, which, at a stroke,
Was sucked into the depths with most her crew,

To rise no more. But to the broken wreck
Some sailors clung, as clung the hand more used
To scepters: Ceÿx, on his flotsam float,   560
Besought his sire and sire-in-law (alas!)
To no end; but his wife, Alcyone,
Was foremost on the swimmer's mind and lips:
He prayed his corpse might drift before her gaze
And that her loving hands might bury him.   565
The waves were closing in, yet while they still
Allowed him speech, he called Alcyone.
But look, amid the surf, a black swell looms
Then breaks upon his head and sinks him down!
You'd not have recognized the Morning Star   570
Who rose so dark that dawn, for lacking leave
To stray from heaven, he cloaked his face in clouds.
    Aeolus' daughter, meanwhile, unaware
Of these misfortunes, counted down the nights
And rushed to weave the robes they both would wear   575
On his return, of which she dreamed in vain.
She offered frankincense to every god,
But worshiped most of all at Juno's shrine
And wished before her altar for the man
Who was no more, that he come safely home   580
And love no other woman but herself—
The only prayer of hers that could come true.
The goddess, when she could no more endure
Such temple-tainting pleas of mourning,† called,
"O Iris, faithful courier of my words,   585
Fly quickly to the slumberous house of Sleep
And bid him send a dream of Ceÿx' death
To tell Alcyone his truthful fate."
So Iris donned her thousand-colored cloak
And arched a rainbow through the sky to seek   590
The cloud-capped palace whither she'd been sent.
    Near the Cimmerians† runs a mountain cave,
The home and inmost lair of idle Sleep,
Where Phoebus never enters with his beams
At dawn or noon or dusk, and from the ground   595

Thick fog and twilight haze come seeping in.
No rousing rooster crows with crested head
To summon Dawn, nor is the hush disturbed
By watchdogs' barks or geese more watchful still.
[No beasts nor flocks nor breeze-stirred boughs are heard,   600
Nor are the evil tongues of selfish men.]
Mute silence reigns! but, from the grotto's depths,
The river Lethe rolls, whose babbling course
Across the rustling pebbles lulls to sleep.
Before the cave mouth, boundless poppies bloom,   605
And countless herbs, whose soporific juice
Night sprays to put the darkling world to sleep.
For fear a hinge should creak, in all the house
There are no doors, nor guardians on the step,
But at its core, a bed of ebony   610
Looms high and black through soft and dusky drapes
Where lolls the god, his limbs relaxed in sleep,
While all around him, varied in disguise,
Lie hollow dreams, as numberless as grain
Or forest leaves or sands upon the shore.   615
    On entering, she brushed these dreams aside
And set the sanctum shining with her robes.
The god scarce opened his dull listless eyes,
But, nodding off, slipped back time after time,
His chin upon his chest, till he at last   620
Shook off himself and (recognizing her)
Asked why she'd come. "O Sleep!" said she, "O Sleep,
The world's relief, the gentlest of the gods,
The peace of souls, who quells all cares and makes
Our way-worn bodies fit for further toil—   625
Command your dreams, which match the truth in form,
To change into Herculean Trachis' king†
And show Alcyone his shipwreck's shape:
This Juno bids!" Her orders thus discharged,
Swift Iris left, unable more to bear   630
The force of slumber stealing down her frame,
And fled back up the arch from which she came.
    Then, from his thousand sons, the father roused

A master of imposture: Morpheus.
No other can more cunningly portray   635
A person's walk and look and tone of voice
Down to their mode of dress and turn of phrase;
Yet he plays only people, while the one
Who apes the beasts and birds and slinking snakes
The gods call "Likeness"—"Fearmonger" on earth.   640
A third one, with a skillset all his own,
Is Phantasm, who takes on lifeless forms
To pass as clods or stones or waves or trees.
By night they show themselves to chiefs and kings,
While all the others haunt the humbler hordes.†   645
But, passing all these brothers, elder Sleep
Chose Morpheus to do as Thaumas' child
Had bidden. Then, once more, he took repose
And deep in cushions sank his drooping head.
    On noiseless wings, the other flew by night   650
And shortly entered the Thessalian town,
Where he flung off his feathers and assumed
The form and face of Ceÿx. Deathly pale
And all unrobed, he stood before the bed
Of that most wretched wife. His beard seemed wet,   655
His hair soaked through with sea. Then he bent down
And, with his face awash in tears, he said:
"Do you not know your Ceÿx, wretched wife?
Has death so changed my face? Look! Know me now
Not as your husband but your husband's shade.   660
Your prayers, Alcyone, did me no good:
I'm dead. You must deceive yourself no more.
On the Aegean Sea, our ship was seized
And wrecked by stormy Auster's giant gusts.
My lips, while vainly calling out your name,   665
Were filled with sea. Nor has some doubtful source
Brought you this news—you hear no rumored tale.
Wrecked as I am, I tell you of my fate.
Come, rise then: weep and dress in widow's weeds,
Nor send me back to Tartarus unmourned!"   670
This Morpheus said in a voice she well

Could think her husband's, crying truthlike tears,
And making gestures right for Ceÿx' hands.
  Alcyone, still sleeping, wailed and wept
And flung out arms to hold him, grasping air: 675
"Don't go! Why are you leaving? Take me, too!"
Awakened by her cries and husband's ghost,
She looked to see him where he'd just been seen,
But by the lamp her startled maids had lit
She found him nowhere. Then she slapped her cheeks   680
And bared her breast and beat the breast she'd bared;
Not loosening her hair, she tore it out,
And when her nurse asked why she grieved, explained:
"Alcyone is gone! She's gone and dead,
Killed with her Ceÿx—save your soothing words!   685
I saw him shipwrecked, knew that it was him,
And reached my hands to hold him as he fled.
Though just a ghost, it was my husband's ghost
There, clear and true! Not with his normal look,
If you would know, nor with his former glow,   690
But naked, pale, still dripping from his hair—
Oh, woe!—I saw the wretch, he stood right there!
Look! On that spot!"—she checked the spot for tracks—
"This—this my mind foretold to fear, when I
Besought you not to leave and seek the winds.   695
I wish that you, in going off to die,
Had brought me with you! I should be with you!
Then I'd have spent my whole life at your side,
Still linked in death. But now I'm dead at sea,
Afar, amid the far-off waves, afloat   700
Without myself. And yet, my mind would be
Still crueler than the waves if I lived on
And strove to bear such pain, which I won't bear,
Nor will I ever leave you, wretched man!
Now I'll be with you: if not in the urn,   705
Still, joined by epitaph, we two shall touch—
Not bone to bone, perhaps, but name to name."
Grief stopped her then as words gave way to wails,

The tortured moanings of a speechless heart.
　　At daybreak, she left home and sadly sought   710
The shoreline spot from which she'd watched him go.
And while she lingered there, and while she mused—
"Here, he weighed anchor; here, we kissed goodbye"—
And while she thought of all that there transpired,
She spied, amid the surf, a corpse-like thing   715
Though what it was she could not tell until
It floated closer, where she clearly saw
It was a corpse. Though still not guessing whose,
The omen of this unknown shipwrecked man
Moved her to tears: "Whoever you may be,   720
Alas for you and any wife of yours!"
The closer came the corpse, the more she stared,
The less and less she could contain herself,
Till on the shoals, she recognized her spouse.
"It's him!" she screamed. Her face and hair and clothes   725
She rent as one and, reaching trembling hands
To Ceÿx, cried, "My dearest spouse, is this—
Is this, poor wretch, how you come back to me?"
　　A seaside wharf stood by to break the waves
And sap the ocean's rushing strength. From this,   730
She leapt, and then—a miracle: she flew!
With newborn wings, she beat the yielding air
And skimmed the cresting waves, a wretched bird.
And while she flew, great sobs like wails of grief
Broke from her croaking mouth and slender beak.   735
But when she reached the mute and bloodless corpse,
And clasped his cherished form with newfound wings,
Her kisses only pecked his icy lips.
If Ceÿx felt this or the tossing waves
Raised up his head, those watching could not tell,   740
But feel he did; for, merciful at last,
The gods changed both to birds. Alike in doom,
So lasts their love, nor did their wings dissolve
Their vows, for still they mate and rear their young.
Each winter, seven days of peace allow   745

The halcyon to nest atop the waves
Unshaken while Aeolus guards the Winds
And keeps the sea calm for his grandsons' sake.†

[AESACUS]†

   An old man saw them soaring side by side
Along the tide and praised their lasting love.   750
Then he, or one nearby,† said: "This bird, too,
Whose legs you see there skimming on the surf"
(He pointed to a long-necked diving fowl)†
"Had royal blood, and you could trace his line†
Straight down from Ilus and Assaracus,   755
Laömedon, and Jove-snatched Ganymede,
To ancient Priam, he to whom befell
Troy's final days. Had he not strangely met
His fate before his brother Hector did,
He might have rivaled Hector in renown.   760
But, unlike Dymas' grandson,[13] Aesacus
Was born, they say, by stealth in Ida's shades
To Alexirhoë, Granicus' child.
He hated towns and, far from gleaming halls,
Dwelt in untrodden ways and secret slopes;   765
But though he rarely joined the Ilian crowds,
He was no boor with heart immune to love
But often chased Hesperia through the glades.
Beside her father Cebren's banks, he watched
The nymph dry out her tresses in the sun   770
Then flee his gaze, as frightened deer flee wolves,
Or ducks caught out of water flee a hawk.
The Trojan hero chasing after her,
He swift in love as she was swift in fear,
She ran upon a snake hid in the grass   775
Which bit her foot, envenoming her veins.
Death stopped her dead. Half-crazed, he clutched her corpse,
And cried: "No, no! How could I chase you so?

---

13. Hector, son of Hecuba, daughter of Dymas

I did not think I'd win at such a price!
We both have killed you: it's the snake that struck,   780
But I'm to blame. I am the baser one
And so I'll soothe your dying with my death!"
So saying, from a sea-cut crag he leapt
Into the surf; but Tethys pitied him,
Received him gently, plumed him as he swam,   785
And would not grant the death he so desired.
The lover fumed at so being forced to live,
His soul confined within its wretched seat,
And flew with fresh-fledged wings once more to try
And drown himself, but feathers broke his fall.   790
Enraged then, Aesacus time after time
Plunged seaward in a quenchless quest for death.
Grown lean with love, he lengthened at the legs,
Till, long of neck and long of head's extent,
His love of diving furnished him his name."   795

Book 12

NOT KNOWING his son Aesacus lived on
In bird form, Priam grieved while, at the tomb,
His brothers made a hollow holocaust.
With Hector present, none but Paris lacked,
Who'd bring a stolen bride and lasting war   5
Back home with him, pursued by allied force:
A thousand ships and all the Grecian race.†
   Revenge would have been swift, had vicious winds
Not blocked the sea and kept the fleet from sail
At fish-filled Aulis on Boeotia's shores.   10
There, gathered to pay Jove the usual rites,
His ancient altar growing bright with flame,
The Argives† saw a sea-green serpent glide
Around a plane-tree near the sacred site,
Whose branches braced a nest with twice-four birds—   15
Doomed, with their circling mother, to be seized
And swallowed by the serpent. All stood stunned,
But Thestor's son, the augur, saw the sooth,
And cried, "Rejoice, Pelasgians! We shall win,
And Troy will fall, though long will be our toil,"   20
For those nine birds he read as years of war.
And, round the tree's green boughs, just where he'd been,

There coiled a stone, stamped in the serpent's shape.†
   Fierce Nereus,¹ though, would not suffer war
To cross Aonia's seas, and some believed   25
That Neptune would spare Troy, whose walls he'd built.
But Thestor's son knew well and made it known
The virgin goddess raged for virgin's blood;
Soon king and country conquered sire and kin,†
But when Iphigenia neared the shrine,   30
With mourning maids, to spill her blameless blood,
The goddess caved, cast up a blinding cloud,
And in the midst, they say, of rites and prayers,
She swapped Mycenae's daughter for a deer.†
This seemly slaughter pleased Diana well,   35
So Phoebe and the sea both eased their rage;
And soon the thousand ships, with wind astern
And much behind, at last reached Phrygia's sands.²

[THE HOUSE OF RUMOR]†

   At the world's center,† land and sea and sky
Converge to form a threefold cosmic bound   40
From which all things, however far away,
Are seen, and open ears catch every voice.
Upon its summit, Rumor placed a house
With countless entrances, a thousand vents,
And not one door. It gapes by day and night,   45
All built of sounding bronze that echoes back,
Reverberates, and doubles all it hears.
No quiet lies within, no silent rooms,
Not even clamor: only murmurs low,
Like those one often hears from distant waves,   50
Or like the sound of thunder rumbling out
When Jupiter makes gloomy clouds collide.
Crowds fill the halls and, fickle, come and go,
As rumors in their thousands roam throughout—

---

1. An ocean god, here standing in for the whole sea
2. Troy, located near Phrygia

Part false, part true—and vague reports run wild.   55
Of these, some fill their hollow ears with talk,
And some spread tales, and so the story grows
As each new teller adds to what they've heard.
There sits Credulity; there, rash Mistake
With Undue Merriment and anxious Fears,   60
Where Treason creeps and sourceless Whispers wend.
Herself, she sees all things in heaven and earth
And in the sea, and surveys all the world.

[ACHILLES AND CYGNUS][†]

Now she spread word the Grecian ships had sailed,
And so their onslaught came as no surprise   65
But met the Trojans on their shores, where you,
Protesilaüs, were the first to fall
To Hector's dooming spear. The Danaäns
Lost much to learn of Hector's deadly strength;
The Phrygians, too, through bloodshed, learned to fear   70
Achaean hands. Sigeum[3] now grew red;
Now Neptune's Cygnus[4] killed a thousand men;
Now, in his chariot, Achilles charged,
His Pelian spearpoint[5] ripping through whole ranks,
Till, seeking Cygnus out, or Hector, he   75
Found Cygnus (Hector's death would wait ten years).[†]
Then, shouting at his steeds, whose shining necks
Strained at the yoke, he steered them toward the foe,
And brandished his bright weapons as he cried,
"Be who thou art, young man, take cheer to know   80
Achilles of Thessalia strikes thee dead!"
With this, Aeacides[6] let loose his spear,
But though the spear was sent with faultless aim,
Its hurtling iron struck to no effect,

---

3. A promontory on the Trojan coast (cf. 11.197)
4. The Trojan Cygnus, son of Neptune
5. Achilles' spear, fashioned from an ash tree on Mount Pelion
6. Achilles, son of Peleus, son of Aeacus

But bruised his breast as though its point were blunt.   85
"Son of a goddess[7]—yes, I've heard of you—
Are you surprised," he asked, "that I've no wound?"
(He was surprised.) "This golden horse-haired helm
And this small shield, which weighs upon my left,
Are not for safety but for ornament,   90
Like those of Mars. Remove them all and still
I'd go unscathed: it's something to be born
Not to a Nereid but him who rules
The Nereids, their sire, and all the sea!"
This said, his spear flung toward Aeacides   95
But hit his shield, beneath whose curving bronze
Nine leather layers burst, but not the tenth.[†]
The hero shook it free and once more hurled
A shivering shaft: once more, his foe stood safe.
Nor did a third so much as graze his skin,   100
Though Cygnus offered up his chest unarmed.
    Then, fuming like a bull inside the ring,
Whose dreadful horns assail the crimson cape
That goads him just to find his wounds unfelt,
He checked his spear: perhaps the point had gone?   105
No, there it was. "Then has my hand," he asked,
"Grown weak this once and lost its former strength?
For it was mighty when I led the sack
Of walled Lyrnessos, and when Tenedos
And Eëtion's Thebes I filled with blood,   110
And when felled foes turned the Caïcus red
And Telephus twice felt me use my spear.[†]
On this shore, too, where I've both made and seen
Great heaps of dead, I was and shall be strong!"
Then, as if doubting what he'd done, he struck   115
Menoetes of the common Lycian ranks,
Whose breast and breastplate burst beneath the shaft
And clattered dying to the solid earth.
His spear pulled from the seething wound, he cried,
"This is the winning hand and this the spear: 120

7. Achilles, son of the Nereid Thetis

May these same weapons do the same to him!"
And aimed again for Cygnus, who stood fast
And let the ashwood strike his shoulder true,
Rebounding with a thud as off a wall.
Upon the stroke, seeing Cygnus stained with blood,   125
Achilles gave a cheer, but all in vain:
There was no wound, it was Menoetes' blood.
Enraged, he leapt down headlong from his perch
To duel his dauntless foe, but once he'd watched
His shining sword hack through the shield and helm   130
Then break against his breast, he'd had enough.
With shield heaved high, three times and more he sent
His pommel pummeling down his foeman's face,
Then chased, rushed, stormed, and charged him as he fled,
And kept the man in shock till fear prevailed.   135
Then Cygnus, as the darkness drowned his eyes,
Fell back against a fieldstone in his path,
And lay there till Achilles caught him up
And flung him to the ground with mighty force.
Then, clamping down his chest with knees and shield,   140
He used the chinstrap, ripped from off his helm,
To block his airways, strangling out his soul.
But when he stripped the victim's spoils, he found
The armor empty, for the god of seas
Had changed him to the bird that bears his name.   145

[CAENIS BECOMES CAENEUS]†

   This feat—this *fight*—brought several days of truce,
As both sides sheathed their swords and took their rest.
While wakeful guards patrolled the Phrygian walls,
And wakeful guards patrolled the Argive trench,
A feast was held where Cygnus' conqueror   150
Achilles offered Pallas heifer's blood.†
And once the entrails in the altar fires
Had filled the heavens with fumes to please the gods,
What parts the rite had spared became the feast.
The lords reclined on couches, gorged themselves   155

On roasts, and soothed their thirst and cares with wine.
Nor did a lyre or voice upraised in song
Or slender boxwood flute amuse those men,
Who passed the night in talk of manly deeds!†
They told of battles—theirs, their foes'—and warmed   160
To talk in turn of dangers faced and fared.
For of what else would great Achilles tell?
What else to great Achilles would be told?
His latest triumph over Cygnus held
Their focus longest, for all were amazed   165
His body blunted blades and brooked no spear
And made the youth invincible to wounds.
    Aeacides shared the Achaeans' awe,
But Nestor said, "Your age has seen one man,
This Cygnus, scorn the sword with skin unscratched.   170
But I myself once saw a thousand blows
Leave Caeneus of Thessalia all unscathed.
Thessalian Caeneus, who called Othrys home,
Was famed for feats, but what's more wondrous still
Is he was a born a woman." All, in awe   175
At this weird wonder, begged him for the tale.
"Do tell," Achilles said, "what all would hear!
O smooth-tongued elder, wisdom of our age,
Who was this Caeneus? How'd he change his sex?
In which campaign, whose army did you meet?   180
And who subdued him, if subdued he was?"
The elder answered: "Though I'm slow with age,
And much I saw in youth escapes me now,
There's more I still recall, but naught that sticks
So firm in mind as this, mid all the deeds   185
Of war and peace. For if extreme old age
Means one has witnessed much, I have outlived
Two centuries† and live now in my third. . . .
    "Fair Caenis, child of Elatus, was famed
The finest maid in all of Thessaly,   190
Throughout whose towns (Achilles, yours being one)[8]

8. Phthia, a Thessalian town ruled by Achilles' father Peleus

Great throngs of suitors pined for her in vain.
Though Peleus might well have sought her hand
Had he not just been married or betrothed
Unto your mother, Caenis would wed none,   195
For once, beside a secret shoreside cove,
The sea-god raped her (or so rumor has).[†]
Once Neptune seized his fill of new love's joys,
He cried, 'No wish of yours will be refused:
Choose what you like!' (The rumor has this, too.)   200
'My wish,' she said, 'is mighty, like your wrongs:
Make me immune to rape. Unsex me here,
And you'll have kept your pledge.' This last she spoke
In deeper tones that might seem male in voice,
For so it was: the sea-god had fulfilled   205
His wish while also giving him the power
To bear no wound and never die by steel.
So Atrax' son,[9] pleased in his gift, set off
To roam Peneus'[10] plains in men's pursuits.

[THE CENTAUROMACHY][†]

"Ixion's son had wed Hippodame,   210
And asked the cloud-born beasts to come recline
At ordered tables in a tree-lined cave.[†]
Thessalia's lords were there, and I was there,
And all the palace rang with feasting crowds
As through the wedding hymns and smoke-filled halls   215
A train of wives led forth a bride so fair
We called Pirithoüs a lucky man
And nearly jinxed the rite! For Eurytus,
O wildest of wild centaurs, you grew hot,
Inflamed as much by wine as by the maid,   220
And doubly drunk on alcohol and lust.
Soon, tables toppled! chaos ruled the feast!
And Eurytus caught up the new bride's hair—

9. Caeneus (but cf. 189)
10. A Thessalian river, most prominently seen at 1.544a

He seized Hippodame! Each seized the girl
He would or could, as if sacking a town.   225
We leapt up at their screams, but Theseus
Cried out first: 'Eurytus! Have you gone mad?
Or don't you know to strike Pirithoüs
While I'm alive is crossing two in one?'   229
He made no answer (words could not defend   232†
Such deeds as his), but charged with frenzied fists
To beat the champion's face and noble breast.
By chance, there was an antique wine-bowl near,   235
Embossed in sharp relief, which Aegeus' son
Heaved high and higher, then hurled at his foe's face.
Blood, brains, and wine gushed from his wound and mouth
As he fell thrashing on the sodden sands.
His two-formed brothers, fuming at his death,   240
All strove as one to shout, 'To arms, to arms!'
Wine spurred their spirits and the fight began
With goblets flung and brittle cauldrons smashed,
As what had once served dinner now served war.
      "First, Amycus, Ophion's son, proved game   245
To loot the rooms inside, first tearing down
A chandelier, hung thick with twinkling lamps,
Which, like a sacral axe upraised to cleave
A bull's white neck, he hoisted high and hurled
At Lapith Celadon, leaving his face   250
A mess of bones too smashed to recognize.
His eyes leapt out, his bony face split wide,
His nose was driven down into his mouth.
Then Pelates of Pella laid him out
And used a table-leg to force his chin   255
Into his chest; while he spewed blood and teeth,
A second stroke dispatched his soul to Hell.
      "Next, grimly gazing at the smoking shrine
Before him, Gryneus cried, 'Why not use this?'
And, heaving the huge altar, flames and all,   260
Upon the Lapith line, crushed Broteas—
Orios, too. (Orios was the son
Of Mycale, well-known for drawing down

The moon's unwilling crescent with her charms.)†
'You'll not escape unscathed if I am armed!'   265
Exadius cried and, armed from off a pine
Where antlers hung as votive offerings,
He plunged the double prongs in Gryneus' eyes
And gouged them out, one sticking to the horns,
The other running down his blood-caked beard.   270
   "There, from the altar, Rhoetus snatched a brand
Of burning plumwood, swung it right, and smashed
Charaxus' temples through his tawny locks.
The fire ate through his hair like withered wheat,
While, sizzling in the wound, his blood let forth   275
An awful hiss—a hiss like red-hot iron
When clasped between a blacksmith's curving tongs
And plunged into a basin, where it seethes
And sizzles from beneath the tepid waves.
The maimed man tossed his tresses free of flame,   280
Then, heaving, tore the doorsill from the floor—
A wagon's worth of weight, too huge a mass
To reach the foe, but not his nearby friend,
Cometes, who was flattened where he stood.
Then Rhoetus could not curb his joy but cried,   285
'May all your band, I pray, be just as brave!'
And with the half-burnt brand he struck again
Three times and more until his weighty blows
Had burst the skull and splashed the brains beneath.
   "To Coryth, Dryas, and Euagrus then   290
The victor turned. With cheeks new-wreathed in fuzz,
Young Coryth fell. 'Will killing boys win praise?'
Euagrus cried, but Rhoetus stopped his speech
By ramming ruddy fire between his lips,
And, through his speaking lips, into his chest.   295
On you, fierce Dryas, too, he whirled his flames
In hot pursuit, but you escaped that fate,
For, as his string of slaughters spurred him on,
You stuck him where the shoulder meets the neck.
Then, Rhoetus groaned and tore the tempered stake,   300
Till, dripping blood, he fled. Then fled as well

Orneüs; Lycabas; and Medon, hit
In his right arm; Pisenor; Thaumas, too;
And he who once surpassed them all in speed,
One Memeros (now lagging from his wound);   305
Melaneus; Pholus; Abas, bane of boars;
The augur Asbolos, who'd counseled peace,
And Nessus, whom he told, as both fled harm,
'Don't run! You will be saved for Hercules!'†
Eurynomus, Areös, Lycidas,   310
And Imbreus, though, did not flee Dryas' hand
But took death in the face. Your face was hit,
Crenaeus, too, although you'd turned in flight,
For, glancing backward, you received a bolt
Between the eyes, where nose and forehead meet.   315
     "Amid the din, with veins suffused in sleep,
Aphidas lay, unceasing in his rest,
His languid hand still grasping at his cup,
And sprawled across an Ossaean bearskin rug.
But though unarmed, he caught the far-off eye   320
Of Phorbas, who took aim: 'You'll drink your wine
Mixed with the Styx!'† he cried, and all at once
He launched his lance and sent the ash and iron
Straight through the neck of the recumbent youth.
Death came unfelt, but his full throat spewed forth   325
Black blood upon the bed—and in the cup!
     "I saw Petraeus striving to uproot
An acorn-laden oak with both his hands,
But while the trunk was rocking to and fro,
Pirithoüs speared through Petraeus' ribs   330
And pinned his writhing chest against the tree.
Pirithoüs felled Lycus with his might;
Pirithoüs felled Chromis next, they say,
But won more fame for Dictys—Helops, too!
His lance pierced Helops, boring through his brow,   335
In at the right and out the leftward ear,
While Dictys, fleeing Ixion's charging child,
Slipped off a lofty slope and hit an ash
Which splintered into bits beneath his weight

And drove its giant splinters through his groin. 340
Then vengeful Aphareus wrenched from the slope
A stone he meant to throw, but as he threw,
His giant elbow cracked beneath the club
Of Aegeus' son, who neither stayed nor cared
To help him to his death, but leapt astride 345
Biënor, who'd borne no one else before,
And gripped his ribs and mane with knees and hand.
Then, on his face, hard brow, and cursing mouth
His club rained down its knots. Nedymnus, too,
His club dispatched; Lycotas, lance in hand; 350
The beard-enfolded breast of Hippasus;
And Ripheus who towered above the trees;
And Thereus, who'd ranged Thessalia's hills
To bring home bears, caught raging and alive.
  "Fed up with Theseus' successful streak, 355
Demoleon strove with mighty force to tear
An ancient pine-tree from the thorny brush,
But failed and snapped a piece off at his foe.
Though Theseus stood back as it shot by,
Being warned by Pallas (so he'd have us think), 360
The tree still fell to some use, slicing off
Tall Crantor's chest and shoulder from his neck.
(This was your father's squire, Achilles, whom
Amyntor, the Dolopians' conquered king,
Bequeathed Aeacides[11] in pledging peace.) 365
But Peleus, on seeing him foully cleft,
Cried, 'Crantor, dearest youth, at least accept
This offering!' and hurled with all his might
An ashen spear that stuck Demoleon's side
And pierced his ribcage, sticking in his bones. 370
He grasped and wrenched away the pointless shaft
(Which scarce withdrew), its point lodged in his lung.
But pain gave courage strength: hurt though he was,
He reared and stamped the hero with his hooves
In sounding strokes absorbed by helm and shield, 375

11. Peleus

Till, from beneath, his foe, with spear outstretched,
Speared both his chests† at once.
     "By then he'd slain
Both Hyles and Phlegraeus from afar,
And Clanis and Iphinoüs at hand;
To these he added Dorylas, who bore   380
A wolfskin and, instead of fearsome spears,
Two twisting bull's horns, rife and red with blood.
To him (for courage lends one strength) I cried,
'See how your horns retreat before my steel!'
And hurled a lance. He had no time to dodge,   385
But raised a shielding hand, and so his hand
Was pinned against his brow. A shout arose,
But Peleus (being near), as he stood fixed
In wounded agony, slashed wide his bowels.
Then, rushing forward, trailing his own guts,   390
He trod what trailed, the trodden entrails burst,
And, tripping, down he tumbled, disemboweled.
 "Nor did your beauty spare you, Cyllarus,
If we are granting beauty to your kind.†
His budding beard was gold, and golden, too,   395
The hair that hung his shoulders and his flanks.
You'd praise his lively face, neck, arms, hands, chest,
And all his human parts as works of art,
Nor did the human half outstrip the horse:
Give him the head and neck and he'd have passed   400
For Castor's mount,† so brawny was his breast,
So rideable his back! Pitch-black all round,
Except for his white tail and milky legs,
He was desired by many of his race,
But swept off by Hylonome alone,   405
The fairest half-breed maid to roam the woods.
Alone, her words and love and words of love
Won Cyllarus, as did her sense of style,
If such beings can be styled. She'd comb her hair
And braid it with a pansy or a rose   410
Or rosemary or lilies gleaming white,
And twice a day sought high Pagasae's woods

To wash her face and bathe twice in its streams,
And only clothed her leftward arm and flank[†]
In pelts of choicest beasts. Alike in love,   415
They ranged the slopes as one, strolled side by side
Through cavern depths, had reached the Lapiths' hall
Together, and together now waged war.
From hands unknown, a lance flew on the left
And pierced you, Cyllarus, where chest meets neck.   420
Though hardly hurt, his heart and all his frame
Grew colder once the weapon was withdrawn.
Hylonome caught up his dying arms,
Caressed his wound, and, pressing lips to lips,
Attempted to keep back his dying breath,   425
But, seeing him dead—with words I could not hear
Across the fray—she flung herself upon
The jutting spear, and, dying, clasped her spouse.
    "Before my eyes still rises one who bound
Six lion-skins together, laced with knots,   430
To shield both man and steed—Phaeocomes,
Who, with a log two plough-teams scarce could budge,
Brained Tectaphus, the son of Olenus.
[This crushed his skull's wide crown, and through his mouth,
Ears, eyes, and hollow nostrils oozed his brain,   435
As curdled milk runs through an oaken mesh
Or viscous fluid pressed into a sieve
Comes gushing through the strainer's thick-set holes.]
But as he made to strip the corpse of arms,
Deep in the looter's loins (go ask your sire!)   440
I sank my sword. My blade felled Cthonius, too,
Forked staff in hand, and then Teleboäs,
Who bore a spear. His spear gave me a wound—
Look here, the ancient scar can still be seen!
Then should I have been sent to capture Troy!   445
Then could my arms have stayed, if not surpassed,
Great Hector's! But there was no Hector then,
Or just a boy, and now I'm weak with age.
    "Why tell you how Pyraethus, twinned in form,
Killed Periphas, while Ampyx' headless spear   450

Fixed four-footed Echeclus in the face?
Through Pelethronian Erigdupus' chest
Went Macar's rod, and I recall a lance
That Nessus threw deep in Cymelus' crotch.
You'd not think Mopsus, son of Ampycus,[12]   455
Was just a prophet when, by Mopsus' spear,
Two-formed Hodites fell, deprived of speech,
With tongue tacked onto chin, and chin to throat.
    "Five fell to Caeneus: Bromus, Styphelus,
Antimachus, Pyracmos with his axe,   460
And Elymus. I don't recall their wounds,
But tallied them by name.† Then, having killed
Halesus of Emathia for his spoils,
Huge Latreus vaulted past; though middle-aged,
His strength was youthful, but his brows were grey.   465
With sword and shield and Macedonian pike,
He stuck out as he faced both sides, then clashed
His weapons, galloped round, and filled the air
With tauntings: "Caenis, shall I take you next?†
For you will always be a girl to me—   470
Forever Caenis! Or have you forgot
What you were born as? Has it slipped your mind
The price you paid to win your male disguise?
Be mindful of your birth and what you've borne!
Now take your wool and knitting, spin your thread,   475
And leave war to the men!' But as he jeered,
His charging flank was dashed by Caeneus' spear—
Where horse meets man. In frenzied pain, he flung
His pike at the young Phyllean's[13] naked face,
But it bounced like a hailstone off a roof,   480
Just as a pebble strikes a hollow drum.
Then, nearing his impenetrable side,
He thrust his sword: the sword found no way in.
'You'll not escape!' he cried. 'Though blunt of point,
My sword-blade's edge shall slay you!' As he slashed   485

12. A renowned seer, last seen at 8.350
13. Caeneus, a native of the Thessalian town of Phyllus

His blade aslant to curl around his loins,
The battered flesh rang out like stricken stone
And shards of sword rebounded off his skin.
When Caeneus had his fill of striking awe,
He cried, 'Come now, let's try my blade on you!'   490
And drove his deadly sword up to the hilt
Deep in his flank where, buried in his guts,
Each twist carved out a wound within the wound.
    "Now with a mighty yell, the hybrids charged.
All arms they had they hurled against one man,   495
But all fell blunted, leaving Caeneus, son
Of Elatus, unbloodied and unbowed,
To shock and awe. 'O perdurable shame!'
Cried Monychus. 'Our race succumbs to one
Who's scarce a man! Yet man he is, while we   500
With our dull deeds, are what he was! What good
Are all our monstrous limbs, our twofold strength,
Our natural mix of two most mighty beings?
We're not Ixion's kin nor any god's,
That's certain: he had such a heart he dared   505
Seek Juno, while we're won by half a man!
But let's roll boulders, trees, and mountains whole,
And crush his life out, flinging forests down—
When forests choke him, weight will deal our wounds!'
This said, he found a tree mad Auster's might   510
Had felled, and hurled it at his sturdy foe.
All followed suit and soon Mount Othrys' sides
Were bare of trees, and Pelion's void of shade.
Beneath this massive mounding, Caeneus strained,
And heaved the oaken heap with shoulders high;   515
But when he raised it past his lips and head,
He found he'd lost his breath! With failing strength,
He struggled vainly to come up for air,
Now tried to shrug the mounded forests off,
Now moved about—look there!—as you might see   520
An earthquake rippling lofty Ida's slopes.
His end remains in doubt. Some say his corpse,
Weighed down with wood, was driven into Hell;

Not Ampyx' son! For, from amid the mass,
He watched a gold-winged bird take to the skies—   525
I saw it, too, and have not seen it since.
It slowly soared in circles round the camp
On vast and whirring wings, while Mopsus tracked
Its flight with sight and soul. 'O hail!' he cried,
'To Caeneus, glory of the Lapith race,   530
A great man once, and now a bird unique!'
His telling made it true. Grief spurred our rage
To think so many foes had felled one man,
Nor did we cease to ply our grieving swords
Till half lay dead and nightfall saved the rest."   535

[HERCULES AND PERICLYMENUS][†]

   The Pylian's tale of Lapiths battling
Half-human centaurs riled Tlepolemus,[14]
Who, outraged that Alcides went unnamed
Cried, "Hercules you've left unpraised, old man!
And that's a wonder, for my father oft   540
Regaled me with the cloud-born beasts he'd tamed."
The Pylian groaned, "Why force me to recall
Old evils, pick at scars long-healed with time,
And state my hatred of your father's wrongs?
His feats (heaven knows!) defied belief to earn   545
A world of praise I wish I could deny.
And yet, we do not praise Deïphobus,
Pulydamas, nor *Hector*[15]—why praise foes?
That sire of yours once sacked Messene's walls,
Pulled Elis down and Pylos, without cause,   550
And put my household gods to flame and sword!
Say nothing of the others whom he killed:
Of twice-six sons of Neleus, fine young men,
All twice-six fell to Hercules but me.
That others could be killed must be endured,   555

14. Son of Hercules and the leader of the Greek contingent from Rhodes
15. Three Trojan heroes

But strange was Periclymenus' demise,
For he could don and doff what shape he pleased,
A power he'd gained from Neptune, Neleus' sire.
When he had vainly taken every form,
He turned into the god-king's favorite fowl,   560
Whose twisting talons bear his lightning bolts.
Then, with his wings, hooked beak, and curving claws,
He slashed the hero's face with all his might,
But the Tirynthian's[16] aim proved all-too-true,
And as his body hung aloft the clouds,   565
An arrow struck the side beneath his wing—
A slight wound, but the wounded sinews snapped,
Failed in their motion, and denied him flight.
His wings flapped feebly as he fell to earth,
Where, underneath his weight, the slender shaft,   570
Still caught among the plumes, was driven through
His breast and out the left side of his throat.
So why should I acclaim your Hercules,
O fairest leader of the Rhodian fleet?
Yet, for my brothers, to ignore his deeds   575
Is vengeance full. My love for you stays sound."
    Once Neleus' agèd son had sweetly told
His story, Bacchic gifts went round once more;
Then all withdrew to end the night in sleep.

[THE DEATH OF ACHILLES][†]

    But still the god whose trident rules the waves   580
Grieved for the son he'd turned to Phaëthon's
Dear bird,[†] and, for Achilles, long nursed hate,
Which he gave vent in less than civil rage.
The war had now dragged on some twice-five years
When he instructed unshorn Smintheus:[17]   585
"O far the favorite of my brother's sons,
With whom I built the bootless walls of Troy,

16. Hercules
17. An Anatolian epithet for Apollo

Dost thou not groan to know they soon will fall?
Dost thou not grieve the many thousands slain
To hold her gates, or even just the ghost   590
Of Hector, dragged around his Pergamum?†
Yet fierce Achilles—bloodier than war,
Our work's destroyer—lives! Were he but mine,
He'd learn what power my trident doth possess!
But since it's not my part to meet our foe,   595
Surprise him with a death by secret dart!"
Indulging both his and his uncle's wish,
The Delian, wreathed in clouds, reached Ilium's ranks
Where, mid the fray, he watched as Paris fired
Stray shots at unknown Greeks. Uncovering,   600
The god said, "Why waste darts on common blood?
To aid your people, make Aeacides
Your target and avenge your brothers' deaths!"
This said, he pointed out where Pelides
Was hewing Trojans down, there bent his bow,   605
And steered the dart home with his deadly hand.
Old Priam's only joy since Hector's death
Came when Achilles, you to whom all fell,
Fell to the coward who stole the Grecian bride;
For, had you wished to fall in girlish fight,   610
You'd fallen by the Amazon's twin-axe!†
    Now, he—Troy's fear, the guard and grace of Greece,
Aeacidcs, the tireless warlord—burned,
Torched by the self-same god who'd forged his arms.[18]
Now he is ash, and all that yet remains   615
Of great Achilles scarcely fills an urn;
But still his fame lives on and fills the world,
And in this, the true measure of the man,
Does Pelides endure and shun the void.
    His very shield, to show you whose it was,   620
Caused conflict: arms were taken for his arms!
But none—not Oilean Ajax, Atreus' sons,
One great, one small in prowess and in age,

---

18. Vulcan, god of fire, had crafted Achilles' armor

Nor Tydeus' son—dared claim the prize, except
Laërtes' son and Telamon's own child.[†]   625
To shirk the blame and burden of this choice,
Tantalides[19] convoked the Argive lords
Amid the camp, so all might judge the case.

19. Agamemnon, son of Atreus, son of Pelops, son of Tantalus

Book 13

BEFORE THE seated kings and circling crowd,
Lord Ajax of the seven-layered shield
Arose and swept a glare of boundless wrath
Past the Sigean strand and stranded fleet,
Then, pointing, cried, "By Jove and by these ships,   5
We plead our case against Ulysses' claim!
For he balked not to run from Hector's flames,
Which I withstood—from which I saved our fleet!†
It's safer far to fight with lies than fists,
But though I'm slow to talk as he's to act—   10
So strong as I'm in war, he's strong in speech—
Still, I need not remind you of my deeds,
Pelasgians, for you've seen them! Rather let
Ulysses tell of his, done out of sight,
Observed by night alone!† The prize is great,   15
I know, but such a rival robs its worth;
For Ajax won't be proud to win a prize,
However great, for which Ulysses wished.
This match already serves him his reward:
It shall be said he strove—and lost—to me!   20
   "Suppose my valor were in doubt: I still
Would bear the nobler blood of Telamon,

Who, having conquered Troy with Hercules,
Sailed a Thessalian ship to Colchian shores.[†]
His father, Aeacus, deals justice where   25
Aeolian Sisyphus strains at his stone,
And this same Aeacus is held the son
Of Jove; so Jove to Ajax is three steps!
But I'd discount descent, O Greeks, had not
My cousin, great Achilles, shared mine, too: 30
I lay a cousin's claim! Why should you, son
Of Sisyphus,[†] heir to his tricks and traps,
Taint Aeacus' pure line with strangers' names?
    "Then shall these arms be grudged me, who bore arms
Through no informer's force?[†] Shall he seem best   35
Who raised his last and tried to dodge the war
By feigning madness, till one shrewder still,
Naupliades,[1] to his own loss, exposed
The dastard's lie and dragged him into arms?
Shall he take first who first took none at all,   40
While I'm disgraced, robbed of my cousin's gifts,
Because I dared these dangers from the start?
I wish he *had* been mad, or been believed!
His voice of vice would not have joined us round
These Phrygian walls, nor would you, Poeas' son,[†]   45
Be stranded, to our shame, in Lemnos' glades,
Within whose caves, they say, you move the stones
With groans, and rightly curse Laërtes' son,
On whom, if gods exist, your curse will fall!
For now, this man who shared our vows of war—   50
Alas! one of our chiefs, heir to the shafts
Of Hercules—is wracked with ills and want,
With birds for grub and garb, in whose fowl chase,
He plies those arrows fate intends for Troy!
Still, he lives on because Ulysses left,   55
As luckless Palamedes wished he'd done,
[Who'd be alive or nobly dead,] had he,
Too mindful of his madness foully foiled,

---

1. Palamedes, son of Nauplius

Not falsely charged him traitor to the Greeks,
Then 'proved' the falsehood with pre-planted gold.   60
Such death and exile sapped our Argive strength:
So fights Ulysses, so must he be feared!
    "Though he should outtalk Nestor, I'd still think
That his deserting Nestor[†] was a crime.
For when, while hampered by his wounded horse,   65
The straggling elder sought Ulysses' aid,
His friend betrayed him! I make no false charge
As Tydeus' son well knows, who cried his name,
And called and cursed his craven comrade's flight.
But gods view mortal deeds with equal eyes,   70
And he, in need of help who'd given none,
By his own rule, should have been spurned in turn;
Yet when he called for help, I came and saw
Him trembling white, afraid to meet his death,
And, hiding him beneath my massive shield,   75
I saved his useless life[†] (small praise in that).
If still you would oppose me, let's go back:
Bring back our foes, your wound and wonted fear,
And fight with me beneath my spreading shield!
But no! he was too weak with wounds to stand,   80
Till rescued—then, he lost his wounds and ran![†]
    "Take Hector: when he led the gods in war,
Not only you, Ulysses, flinched with fear,
But brave men, too—our forces filled with fright!
That man, while yet he basked in blood and death,   85
Did I send tumbling with a far-flung stone;[†]
That man, while he was charging forth, O Greeks,
Did I confront alone, for so you prayed
And so your prayers were heard. If you should ask
How that fight went, I did not lose to him![†]   90
When Troy and Jove stormed the Achaean ships
With sword and fire, was glib Ulysses there?
Yet my breast built a bulwark for those barks
In which you hope to leave—I saved your ships,
Give me the arms! If I may be so bold,   95
Our union would bring them more fame than me:

The arms seek Ajax, not Ajax the arms.
   "Compare: the Ithacan seized Helenus,
King Priam's son, stole the Palladium,†
And then struck Rhesus and poor Dolon down—   100
All done with Diomedes, all at night!†
If that's deserved the arms, the greater share's
For Diomedes, not the Ithacan
Who prowls unarmed and traps his foes with tricks!
This helmet's golden glint would just betray   105
His ambush and reveal him where he hides.
Nor could the weak Dulichian's² head support
Achilles' casque, nor could the Pelian spear
Do aught but burden his unwarlike arms,
Nor would the shield carved with a massive map   110
Befit his meek left hand, born to despoil.
Fiend! Why seek honors that will hobble you?
If the Achaeans wrongly make it yours,
You'll give the foe more cause to steal than fear,
And flight, the one thing you do best, you coward,   115
Will just be hindered by the load you bear!
What's more, your shield, a stranger to the fray,
Is all untouched, while mine breaks from the blows
Of countless spears and calls to be replaced!
   "But why keep talking? Watch us on the move!   120
Cast forth the hero's arms amid the foe,
Then give them to the man who brings them back!"
The son of Telamon here ceased his speech
And set the crowd abuzz. Laërtes' son,
The hero, then stood forth with downcast eyes,   125
Which rose to meet the eager chiefs as he
Began to speak with pleasing eloquence:
   "Pelasgians, had my prayers—and yours—prevailed,
This contest's winning claimant would be clear:
You'd have your arms, Achilles, and we you!   130
But since unequal fate has stolen him
From you and me" (he wiped a fancied tear)

---

2. Ulysses, king of Ithaca and the neighboring isle of Dulichium

"Who better to take great Achilles' place,
Than he who first placed great Achilles here?
Let it not help this man that he should seem,   135
And be, so dull! Nor let it hurt my case,
Achaeans, that my wits have helped you so!
What eloquence I have deserves no spite;
It's served you often, though it serves me now—
Let none disown his gifts! But family, race,   140
And others' deeds—I'd scarce call such thing *ours,*
And yet, since Ajax says his grandsire's Jove,
Jove is my forebear, too, as closely linked:
My sire Laërtes' sire, Arcesius,
Was sired by Jove—no exiles in our house!†   145
Cyllenius also lent my mother's line
His royalty: on both sides I'm divine!
But neither through my mother's nobler rank,
Nor through my sire's being free of brother's blood
Seek I these arms; let worth decide this case!   150
Is Ajax worthier since Telamon
And Peleus were brothers? Discount blood,
And let to the more valiant go the spoils!
Or try the next of kin: his sire and son
Are Peleus and Pyrrhus—Ajax who?   155
Let Phthia or let Scyros take these back!†
And Teucer is Achilles' cousin, too:
Does he lay claim? As claimant, would he win?
It seems, then, we've an open duel of deeds,
And though I've done more deeds than words can tell,   160
I'll speak of them in turn.
                              "Foreseeing his death,
The Nereid mother had her son disguised
To mislead everyone—and Ajax, too—
With his deceitful dress.† But I placed arms
To lure men's eyes among the women's wares,   165
Nor had the hero shed his girlish garb,
When, clutching shield and spear, he heard me call:
'O goddess' son, Troy saves its fall for you!
Why do you wait to wreck great Pergamum?'†

Since I led this brave man to do brave deeds,   170
His works are mine—so it was I whose spear
Tamed Telephus and healed him at his plea!
I conquered Thebes! For Lesbos, credit me!
I captured Chryse, Cilla, Tenedos—
Apollo's towns—and Scyros! You must think   175
That *my* right hand pulled down Lyrnessus' walls,
For I brought him who slew—to name one man—
Fierce Hector: through me, famous Hector died!
As my arms found Achilles, I seek his,
Reclaiming from the dead my gift in life.   180
    "When one man's woe reached all of Greece and filled
Euboean Aulis with a thousand ships
In lengthy wait for winds that did not blow,
Or blew against the fleet, harsh prophecies
Bade Agamemnon slay his guiltless child   185
To cruel Diana. When her sire refused
And cursed the gods, being father more than king,
I turned his parent's heart toward common good.
Atrides,[3] grant me leave to grant it was
A tricky case to make a biased judge.   190
But still, his subjects, brother, and command
Prevailed on him to balance praise with blood
And send me to his wife—not to convince
But to connive:[†] had Telamonius gone,
Our sails would lack for breezes even now!—   195
And send me, a bold envoy unto Troy,
To Ilium's court, still full of heroes then,
Where I made Greece's case, claimed Helen back,
Indicted Paris, and dared to convince
Antenor,[4] Priam's friend—and Priam, too!   200
But Paris and his brothers and his band
Of pillagers scarce stayed their sinful hands
(As, Menelaus, you'll recall: we shared
The prelude to our perils on that day).

3. Agamemnon, son of Atreus
4. A wise elder, the Trojan counterpart to Nestor

"It would take long to tell of all I did   205
In thought and deed through this unending war.
Once we had first engaged, our foes stayed long
Within their walls and would not take the field
For nine full years! What were you doing then?
You, who can only fight—what use were you?   210
For if you want to know what deeds I did,
I ambushed foes, I trenched their ramparts round,
I soothed our allies' souls, weary of war,
And kept them calm, warned how we should be fed
And should be armed, and went where I was called.   215
    "Then Jove dispatched a dream and duped our king
To bid us leave the war we had begun!†
Let Ajax try to check so sourced a claim,
Demand Troy's downfall, and do what he does—
Make war! Why won't he stop those heading home?   220
Why not raise arms and give a rallying cry?
Would that strain one whose only words are boasts?
But he ran, too! Ashamed to see, I saw
You turn your back and raise your sorry sails.
At once, I cried, 'What are you doing, friends?   225
Have you gone mad to leave when Troy is won?
What are you bringing home from these ten years
Except disgrace?' Grown eloquent through grief,
I foiled their seaward flight and led them back
To sit in fear, convened by Atreus' son.   230
Then did the son of Telamon speak out?
He dared not! Yet Thersites dared to taunt
The kings—though not unpunished, thanks to me.†
I rose and roused my fearful fellow men,
Reviving vanished valor with my voice!   235
Thenceforth, all feats it seems this man has done
Belong to me, who dragged him back from flight.
    "Last, what Pelasgian likes your company?
Yet Tydeus' son does all his deeds with me,
Respecting me, Ulysses, as his friend!   240
Of many thousand Greeks, I was the choice
Of Diomedes! No lots made me go†

When, risking foes and dark of night, I killed
The Phrygian Dolon, who shared our fell quest—
But not before I forced him to betray   245
Each treachery the Trojans had in store.
When I'd learned all, with no more need to spy,
I could have come back home to promised praise;
But, not content, I made for Rhesus' tents
And slew him and his comrades in their camp,   250
Then, in mock Triumph,† seized his chariot
And rode it back, victorious in my prayers.
For that night's work, the foeman claimed his steeds:
Grudge me his arms, and Ajax will seem just!†
    "Why tell of how my sword slashed through the ranks   255
Of Lycia's king Sarpedon, spilling blood
From Chromius, Iphitus' son Coeranos,
Alastor and Noëmon, Prytanis,
And Halius and Alcander; how I killed
Chersidamas and Charops, Thoön too,   260
Doomed Ennomus, and lesser men—all slain
Beneath their walls. My comrades, I bear wounds
In prideful places, too! Don't trust mere words.
Behold!"—here, he unclasped his robe—"my chest
And all it's borne," he cried, "on your behalf!   265
Yet, all these years, the son of Telamon
Has spent no blood on friends but stayed unscratched.†
    "Why should he tell of how his telling strength
Fought Troy and Jove to save Pelasgia's fleet?
For sure, it did: I'll not defame his feats,   270
But don't give him sole credit when you all
Should share his praise! For it was Actor's heir,
Safe in Achilles' guise, that drove away
The Trojans, who'd have burned both ships and guard.†
He thinks that he alone dared Hector's spears,   275
Forgetting that the king, the chiefs, and I
All offered first. Though ninth, he won by lot;
And then, what was the outcome of your fight,
O brave one? Hector left without a wound!†
    "Now with what pain—poor me!—I must recall   280

The time Achilles, bulwark of the Greeks,
Was killed. Yet neither tears nor grief nor fear
Delayed me as I heaved his corpse on high.
On this back—this back, here!—Achilles' corpse
Was borne, with these same arms I now would bear.   285
I have the strength to wield your weighty gift,
And mind enough to grasp its gravity.
Come, was this why his sea-green mother wished
Her son to have such gifts of heavenly skill—
To clothe a coarse foot-soldier with no brain?   290
He has no clue what's carved upon this shield:
The Ocean and the lands and starry sky,
The Pleiads, Hyades, and sea-barred Bear,
[The varied spheres, and bright Orion's sword:†
He asks for arms he cannot understand!]   295
    "And when he scolds me that I dodged the war
And joined these labors late, does he not know
He's slandering the great Achilles, too?
If acting is a crime, we both did act!
If stalling is a fault, I got here first!   300
Kept by his mother dear and my dear wife,
We first spent time with them, the rest with you.
I'll neither fear nor fight a charge that's shared
With such a man, caught by Ulysses' wit,
When Ajax let Ulysses go uncaught.   305
No wonder his dull tongue streams with abuse
Against me, when he's shaming you as well!
Would I alone be base for a false charge
On Palamedes, when you sentenced him?
Nor could Naupliades acquit himself   310
Of such clear crimes, for you did not just hear
The evidence: you saw the bribe laid bare!
And don't blame me if Lemnos, Vulcan's isle,
Holds Poeas' son: defend the deed yourselves!
(For you approved it.) I'll admit I urged   315
That he should quit the road and wartime's toils
To soothe his pains with rest. He did—and lives!
Not only was this spoken in good faith,

Although good faith's enough, but in good luck,
For prophets warn Troy waits for him to fall!   320
But don't send me—the son of Telamon
Had better use *his* crafty eloquence
To coax him back, though raving mad with pain.
No! Ida will stand bare, the Simoïs
Stream backward, and the Greeks send aid to Troy   325
Before dull Ajax' wits replace my mind
To work your will and serve the Danaäns!
Should you despise the troops, the king, and me,
O Philoctetes, and heap on my head
Harsh streams of curses, yearning through your fits   330
To have me in your power and drink my blood,
[And have the chance at me we had at you,]
Still would I go and strive to bring you back
Or steal your shafts (should Fortune favor me),
Just as I captured the Dardanian bard,[5]   335
Just as I learned the Trojan prophecies,
Just as I stole Minerva's statue from
Her Phrygian shrine! Yet Ajax vies with *me*?
When fate decreed we could not capture Troy
Without it: where was mighty Ajax then?   340
Where were his hero's boasts? Why did you fear?
Why did Ulysses brave both dark of night
And watchmen's blades, not just to breach Troy's walls
But sack the shrine atop its highmost keep
And bear the stolen goddess through the foe?   345
For, had I not, the son of Telamon
Would hoist his shield of seven hides in vain.
Troy fell to me that night, for Pergamum
Was conquered when I made her conquerable.

    "So cease your winks and whispers, pointing out   350
My partner, Tydeus' son: he's had his praise.
Nor did your shield alone defend our ships,
You had a host of helpmates—I had one!
And if he did not know that brains beat brawn,

---

5. Helenus (cf. 98–99), whose prophetic powers are seen at 721–22

That even matchless fists don't rate this prize,   355
He'd claim it, too! As would Ajax the Less,
Andraemon's son,[6] the fierce Eurypylus,
Idomeneus and his countryman
Meriones, and Atreus' younger son.[†]
They're stout of hand, your equals in the field,   360
Yet all pay heed to me. Your fighting fists
Are useful, but your thinking lacks my sense;
Your strength is mindless, while I plan ahead;
You fight well, but I pick the time to fight,
With Atreus' son.[7] Your body's all your worth,   365
My mind's all mine; but just as captains far
Outrank their crews and generals their men,
So I surpass you! In these frames of ours,
Might matters less than mind: there, true strength lies.
    "But you, O princes, grant your guardian this   370
Reward for all my years of anxious care:
Give me the honor due for what I've done.
My work is through. I've halted hindering fate
And taken Troy, for now it's yours to take.
Now, by our hopes, by Pergamum's doomed walls,   375
And by the gods I captured from the foe,
I pray [if still some work awaits the wise,
If still some danger's waiting to be dared,
If you think something more will seal Troy's fate,]
Remember me—or give the arms to her!"   380
("Her," being Minerva's fateful effigy.)[†]
    The princes proved the power of eloquence,
Rewarding his slick tongue with hero's arms,
But he who by himself had often borne
Jove, Hector, flame, and sword could not bear rage;   385
Despair broke the unbroken man. Sword drawn,
He cried out, "Does Ulysses seek this, too?
Or is this mine? I'll use it on myself!
Its master's blood will run where Phrygians' ran,

6. The Aetolian leader Thoas
7. Agamemnon, commander-in-chief of the Greek allied forces

So none but Ajax may bring Ajax down!"   390
This said, deep in his never-wounded chest,
He set the steel and sank the fatal sword.
No strength of hand could wrench away the blade;
His *blood* expelled it, reddening the ground,
Which, from its green, brought forth a purple flower   395
That once had sprung from Sparta's wounded son.
Its lettered leaves exalt both man and boy:
The first by name, the last with cries of woe.†

[THE SORROWS OF HECUBA]†

   To Thoäs' homeland and Hypsipyle's,
Reviled for murdered men,† the victor then   400
Gave sail in quest for the Tirynthian's darts.
When, with their master, he rejoined the Greeks,
The long-drawn war at last drew to its end.   403
With Ilium burning and the flames unquenched,   408†
Jove's altar lapped old Priam's scanty blood;
The Phoebean priestess, dragged out by the hair,†   410
Reached up to heaven with unavailing arms;
And Dardan women thronged the smoldering shrines
To clasp their native icons while they could.
The conquering Grecians bore them off as spoils
And threw Astyanax from that same tower   415
His mother often scaled to show him where
His father fought to save his realm and self.†
Soon Boreas' fair breezes called the crews
To set their flapping sails. "O Troy, farewell!
We're forced to go!" the Trojan women cried,   420
Then kissed the ground and left their smoking homes.
The last to climb aboard (a wretched sight!)
Was Hecuba, torn from her children's tombs
By the Dulichian as she grasped their graves
And kissed their bones; but first she'd drained one urn, 425
So Hector's unurned ashes caked her breast,
And Hector's grave lay strewn with her white hairs:
Her meager offerings of hair and tears.

Off Phrygia's coast, where Troy had stood, lay Thrace
And Polymestor's lavish court, to which   430
Your father, Polydorus,[8] had you sent
To live in secret, far from Phrygian wars—
A prudent plan, had he not sent along
Great troves of treasure, tempting greed and vice.
When Phrygia's fortunes fell, the faithless king   435
Took up a sword and slit his young ward's throat,
Then hurled him off a cliff into the sea,
As if this act erased both corpse and crime.[†]
　　Near Thrace's shores, Atrides moored his fleet
To wait for calmer waves and fairer winds,   440
When suddenly, up through the wide-cracked ground,
There sprang Achilles' specter, large as life
And fierce of face as when he'd wrongly drawn
His sword on Agamemnon[†]—and he cried:
"Achaeans! Have you left, forgetting me,   445
And sealed my rightful thanks up in my tomb?
No! Soothe Achilles' shade through sacrifice
And grace my grave with Polyxena's death!"
To heed the ruthless shade, the crewmen seized
The mother's almost sole remaining joy,   450
And led the poor girl, braver than her sex,
Back to be sacrificed on his dread tomb.
She held her nerve, even upon the slab,
Full knowing what foul rites awaited her,
And, watching Neoptolemus draw near   455
With eyes on her and sword in hand, she cried:
"Now, take my noble blood! Don't make me wait,
But in my throat or breast come sheathe your sword"
(And here at once she bared both throat and breast)
"For Polyxena will be no man's slave!   460
[And no power shall be pleased by such a rite!]
I wish my mother did not know my fate,
For she obstructs and steals my joy in death,
Though she should grieve not my death, but her life.

8. The youngest son of Priam and Hecuba

Now leave me free to reach the Styx: step back!   465
If I seek fair, keep men's foul fingers off
My virgin corpse; whomever you would please
By spilling blood would want mine free of stain.
And if my final words have moved a soul
(For it's king Priam's daughter, not a slave   470
Who asks you) give my mother back my corpse
And let her pay the burial's mournful price
In tears, not gold. She paid gold when she could."
    At this, the crowd could no more hold its tears,
Though she held hers. When the unwilling priest,   475
Who wept as well, had pierced her proffered breast,
She crumpled to the ground on buckling knees,
But to the last she showed a fearless face,
And, even as she fell, she covered up
Her privates and preserved her modesty.   480
    The Trojan wives received her, taking count
Of all the gruesome woes of Priam's house,
And mourned you, princess, and you, lately called
The flower of Asia, dowager and queen,
But now a wretch among Ulysses' slaves,   485
Unwanted save that you gave Hector birth:
Yes, Hector's mother scarcely could be sold!
She clasped the corpse, devoid of its brave soul,
And wept into the wounds as she had wept
So often for her sons and lord and land,   490
Then kissed the lips, rebeat her beaten breast,
Swept her white tresses through the clotted gore,
And, tearing at her breast, cried this and more:
"My child, your mother's final woe (what's left?)—
My child, you fall and wound me with your wounds!   495
Yes, wounds, lest any child of mine should die
With blood unshed! I thought girls safe from swords,
But though a girl, a sword has cut you down,
And he who slew your brothers has slain you:
Achilles, doom of Troy, plague on our house!   500
When Paris' Phoebean arrows laid him low,

I thought, 'We need not fear Achilles now!'
But now, too, I must fear his buried bones.
They strike us still; entombed, he stays our foe!
My womb was fruitful for Aeacides!   505
Great Ilium's fallen and our state has reached
Its end—an awful one, but still an end.
For me alone Troy stands, and all our pain!
But lately blessed with daughters, sons, and spouse,
I'm torn in tawdry exile from their tombs   510
To give Penelope, who'll tell her friends
In Ithaca, as I sit spinning wool,
'That's Hector's mother! *That's* great Priam's wife!'
You, who alone assuaged your mother's grief
Through all her loss, now soothe a foeman's shade!   515
I birthed my foe a funeral! Am I stone?
Why don't I die? Why have I reached old age?
And why, cruel gods, if not to see more deaths,
Do you prolong my life? For who'd have thought
Of calling Priam blessed once Ilium fell?   520
Yet death has blessed him, freed from crowns and cares
And from the sight of you, our slaughtered child.
No doubt your royal dowry shall ensure
You're laid to rest in the ancestral crypt—
But such is not our fate! For rites, you'll have   525
A dash of foreign dust and mother's tears,
For I've lost all and have no cause to live
Save Polydorus, far my favorite child,
And now my only, sent when just a boy
To join the Thracian ruler of these shores—   530
But wherefore do I wait to wash your wounds
And cleanse your spattered face of gruesome gore?"
    Then, tearing her white hair, she doddered down
The shoreline, crying, "Trojan maids, an urn!"
But as she went for water from the waves,   535
The wretch saw Polydorus' washed-up corpse,
Agape with wounds from Thracian weaponry.
The Trojans screamed, but she was dumb with grief,

A grief that stopped her words and welling tears.
Still as a stone, she stared straight at the ground,   540
Then, raising her grim visage to the heavens,
Now looked at her son's wounds, now at his face,
But mostly at his wounds, till arming rage
Blazed forth within her all at once, as if
She still were queen, and set her on revenge,   545
Consumed by her vindictive fantasies.
Much as a lioness, whose suckling cub
Is snatched, will rail to track her unseen foe,
So Hecuba, her sorrow mixed with rage,
Despite her years but not despite her will,   550
Sought Polymestor, his foul murderer,
And gained an audience, pretending she
Had hid a hoard of gold to give her son.
    The Thracian king, deceived by his own greed,
Went to the hiding-place, then smoothly said,   555
"Quick, Hecuba, hand over your son's gifts!
All that you give and gave will go to him,
I swear by heaven!" She watched him falsely swear
With glaring eyes, then as her anger boiled,
She seized him, called her band of captive maids,   560
And jabbed his traitor's eyes (rage made her strong),
Gouging them out, then reaching hands again
Stained with his guilty blood, not to wrench out
His eyes (now gone) but his eye-sockets, too.
The Thracians, raging at their king's demise,   565
Began to fight the Trojan, hurling rocks,
But every stone they cast met growls and bites,
For though her jaws were set for speech, her words
Came out as barks (for which that place is named).[†]
Long mindful of her ancient woes, she howled   570
Such bursts of clamor through Sithonia's plains
That Greeks and Trojans both bemoaned her plight,
Which moved to passion all the gods of heaven—
Yes, all! for even Jove's sister and wife
Said Hecuba had not deserved her fate.   575

[MEMNON]†

Yet Dawn, although their ally, had no room
To grieve for Troy and Hecuba's demise,
But languished from the closer, private loss
Of Memnon, slain upon Achilles' spear
At Phrygia while his saffron mother watched—   580
Watched, as the rosy shades of morn went pale
And hid the sky in clouds. Then, at the pyre,
His parent could not bear to watch him burn,
So with her hair undone, just as she was,
She sank down unashamed before the feet   585
Of mighty Jove and mixed these words with tears:
"Though least of those whom golden heaven upholds
(In all the world my temples are but few),
A goddess still, I seek you, not to ask
For shrines and festal days and altar fires—   590
Though, given what this woman does for you
When each new day I guard the bounds of night,
You'd think some gifts were due. But this is not
Dawn's present care, to beg for honors earned:
I come, robbed of my Memnon, in his youth,   595
Who, bravely battling for his uncle's sake,[9]
Was slain by brave Achilles (as you willed).
Please grant the boy some honor, king of gods,
To ease his death and soothe his mother's heart!"
    A nod from Jove and Memnon's lofty pyre   600
Collapsed in flames, and plumes of sable smoke
Besmudged the sky. Much as a stream breathes forth
Dense mists that block the sun, black cinders[1] soared
Aloft and there congealed into a mass
Which took on shape, assuming from the fire   605
Both heat and life. With weightlessness for wings,
First *like* a bird, then *as* a bird indeed
It flapped, and countless sisters flapped along,

---

9. Memnon was Dawn's son with her husband Tithonus (9.421), brother of Priam

Alike in birth. Three times they passed the pyre;
Three times their cries combined to fill the air   610
Before the fourth flight saw them split in camps,
Two separate sides, each waging bitter war
With beaks and twisting talons, venting wrath
And wearying their wings and hostile hearts
Till down they plunged to their ancestral ash,   615
In tribute to the memory of their sire,
Whose hero's name has dubbed these fast-made fowls
"Memnonides." Each time the sun revolves,
They rewage war to die the family way.[†]
So, while some wept for Dymas' daughter's[10] howls,   620
Dawn's private grief took all her pious tears,
Which ever on and on bedew the world.

[THE DAUGHTERS OF ANIUS][†]

Yet Trojan hopes weren't doomed to fall with Troy,
For Cytherea's son had shouldered high
His sacred icons and more sacred sire   625
(From all he owned, the pious hero picked
His son Ascanius and that noble load),[†]
And fled Antandros[11] and the sinful shores
Of Thrace, still drenched with Polydorus' blood,
Till, helped by winds and timely tides, his fleet   630
Had reached Apollo's isle[12] with all his train,
Where Anius, priest of Phoebus, king of men,
Received them in his temple, house, and town,
Showed them the famous shrines, and led them where
Latona once gave birth between two trees.   635
There, they lit incense, drowned the scent in wine,
And, as was done, burned entrails drawn from bulls.
Then, at the palace, perched on piles of rugs,
While they shared Ceres' gifts and Bacchus' boons,

10. Hecuba
11. A town near Troy
12. Delos, birthplace of Apollo

Pious Anchises† asked: "O Phoebean priest,   640
I may be wrong, but when I saw you last,
Did you not have a son and twice-two girls?"
Then Anius shook his silver-ribboned head
And sadly said: "Great hero, you are right;
You saw me father unto five, whom now   645
(For so do mortal matters twist and turn)
You see near childless. What help is my son
Off in the land of Andros, named for him,
Where in my stead he rules? The Delian god
Gave him prophetic powers, but Liber gave   650
My girls a power beyond belief or prayer,
For everything my daughters touched transformed
To grain, to wine, or to Minerval oil.
Great was their worth, but when word reached the ears
Of Atreus' son, the ravager of Troy   655
(You'll see that your disaster has, in part,
Disturbed us, too), he had them fetched by force.
Torn from their father's arms, obliged to use
Their godly gifts to feed the Argive fleet,
Each fled where able: two Euboea claimed,   660
While two sought out their brother's Andrian isle,
But when troops came to take them, threatening war,
Fear conquered love: he gave up his own kin
For punishment. Yet do forgive his fright—
He'd no Aeneas to keep Andros safe   665
Nor Hector, who preserved you ten long years.
Awaiting chains but still at liberty,
The captives raised their arms to heaven and cried,
'Lord Bacchus, help!' And so, their patron helped,
If being destroyed by miracle is 'help.'†   670
Though in what way their bodies were destroyed
I never learned and so now cannot say,
Their awful end is known: they took on plumes
And changed into your spouse's snow-white doves."[13]
          Once they had filled the feast with talk like this, 675

13. Birds sacred to Venus, lover ("spouse") of Anchises

They left the banquet boards and slept till dawn,
Then rose and made for Phoebus' oracle,
Which bade them seek their ancient mother shores.
The king escorted them with parting gifts:
Anchises' staff, his grandson's darts and cloak,   680
And, for Aeneas' gift, a wine-bowl sent
By Therses, an Aonian guest, from Thebes.
But Therses sent what had been forged at Rhodes
By Alcon,† who engraved it with a tale:
   You could discern a town with seven gates   685
(From which one might establish where it was),[14]
Ringed round by funerals, tombs, and flaming pyres,
And mothers, whose bare breasts and streaming hair
Displayed their grief. Nymphs wept at springs run dry,
The trees stood stripped of leaves, and goatherds grazed   690
On barren rocks. Look! there the artist shows
Orion's daughters in the heart of Thebes—
One with her throat slit, not a woman's wound,
One with a spear sent bravely through her breast—
Dead for their people's sake,† borne through the town   695
In fair parade, to burn amid the square.
But, lest their line should die, the maidens' dust
Brings forth two boys, the famed "Coronae" twins,
Shown marching to entomb their mother ash.
   Such were the signs that shone in ancient bronze,   700
While gold acanthus ringed the wine-bowl's rim.
Nor did the Trojans trade him lesser gifts,
But gave the priest an incense-box, a bowl,
And, last, a coronet of gold and jewels.

[GALATEA, ACIS, AND POLYPHEMUS]†

Recalling that they sprang from Teucer's blood,   ·   705
The Teucrians made for Crete, but could not bear
Jove's thunder long and quit her hundred towns
To seek Ausonian harbors.† Tempest-tossed,

---

14. Thebes famously had seven gates

They harbored in the false-faced Strophades,†
Whence winged Aëllo frightened them to sail   710
Beyond Dulichium, Samos, Ithaca,
And Neritos, where sly Ulysses reigned;
And past Ambracia, source of godly strife—
The judge of which they saw transformed to stone—
Now known for Actium, Apollo's shrine;†   715
On to Dodona with its talking oaks,
And then Chaonia's bay, where new-fledged sons
Of the Molossian king fled faithless fires.†
    They next sought out Phaeacia's fruited plains,
But reached Buthrotum, on Epirus' coast,   720
From which the Phrygian prophet ruled New Troy.†
Thence, warned of all to come by Helenus,
That faithful son of Priam, they arrived
Where Sicily's three capes run out to sea:
Cape Lilybaeum toward the soft west winds,   725
Pachynus on the rainy south, and, last,
Pelorus by the northern sea-barred Bears.
There rowed the Teucrians on friendly tides,
And night saw them reach Zancle,[15] whose left side
Charybdis guards, while Scylla plagues the right.   730
The former sucks in ships and spews them forth,
And wild black dogs begirt the latter's waist.
And yet her face is girlish, for if bards
Are ever truthful, she was once a girl
And wooed by many, all of whom she scorned   735
To join the sea-nymphs, being the sea-nymphs' dear,
And tell them of those young men's thwarted love.
While there once, combing Galatea's hair,
She heard the nymph sigh, saying: "You, my girl,
Are wooed by quite a gentle race of men   740
To snub them as you do and feel no fear
When I, a daughter sea-green Doris bore
To Nereus, safe in my sibling crowd,
Could not escape a Cyclops' love unscathed!"

15. By Ovid's time, an already archaic name for Messina

Here, words gave way to tears, soon wiped away   745
Beneath the girl's white hands as she consoled
The goddess: "Tell me, dearest, what has caused
Your grief (for you can trust me)." Here is what
The Nereid told the child of Crataeis:[16]

    "Once, Faunus sired on a Symaethian nymph[17]   750
A son named Acis, whom his parents loved,
But I loved more, since he was mine alone.
He was a handsome youth of twice-eight years,
With tender cheeks scarce marked with hair—and yet
As I craved him, the Cyclops so craved me: 755
Unendingly! Nor could I tell you if
I loathed the Cyclops or loved Acis more,
For both were matched! How mighty is your sway,
O kindly Venus, that can force a fiend,
Whom forests fear and no man meets unharmed,   760
Who jeers at great Olympus and its gods,
To learn of love and flame with a desire
So fierce as to forget his flocks and caves!
Now, Polyphemus, you took pains to please,
Now groomed yourself and used a rake to comb   765
Or plied a scythe to shave your rigid locks,
Now practiced friendly faces in a pool.
Your love of death, your hate, your thirst for blood
All ceased, and ships could pass you safely by!

    "At this time, Telemus[18] reached Sicily.   770
On Aetna, Telemus Eurymides,
Whom no fowl fooled, warned Polyphemus thus:
'Ulysses soon shall catch your brow's one eye.'
But he laughed back, 'Fool prophet, you've been tricked—
A girl already caught it!' Spurning thus   775
The revealed truth, he clomped back down the shore,
Or wearily returned to his dark cave.
Nearby, there ran to sea a jutting crag

16. Scylla
17. That is, a daughter of the Sicilian river Symaethis
18. An augur who appeared in the *Odyssey*

Shaped like a wedge, with waves on either side.
Up this, the beastly Cyclops climbed and sat,   780
His woolly sheep there following unflocked,
And, setting at his feet a trunk of pine
Which was his staff but might well mast a ship,
He raised his pipes, bound of a hundred reeds.†
Then every wave and every mountain heard   785
His rustic strains—and in my Acis' arms
Away beneath a cliff, I heard him, too:
'O Galatea!' I recall he sang,
'Who's whiter than the privet's snowy leaves,
Who's higher than alders, lusher than the lea,   790
Outshining glass, out-frolicking young goats,
Yet smoother than the ocean's wave-worn shells,
More dear than summer shade and winter sun,
More fair than plane trees, grander still than palms—
No cygnet down or creamy cheese is soft,   795
No ice is bright, no grapes are sweet as you,
Whose charms would best all flowers, if you'd be mine!
But, next to Galatea, bulls are tame,
No sea is slick, no knotted oak is hard,
No willow-branch or chalky vine is tough,   800
These stones are pliant and these torrents calm,
Praised peacocks are not proud, flames are not fierce,
Thorns do not hurt, a suckling she-bear's mild,
Waves are not deaf, a trodden snake is kind,
And—what I wish the most were not the case—   805
A deer runs slowly, hearing hounds at bay,
For you fly faster than the winging winds.
   "'Yet if you knew me, you'd regret your flight,
Condemn delay, and try to hold me tight!
Mine are these slopes and caves of living rock,   810
Where neither summer sun nor winter frost
Is felt. Mine are the branches bent with fruit,
Mine are the vines of gold and purple grapes,
And, both being mine, I've saved them both for you;
Your hands will pick the woods' wild strawberries   815
Ripe in the shade, and cherries come the fall,

And plums, not just the juicy bluish kind,
But choice ones—too, as gold as fresh-made wax!
The arbute's berries and the chestnut's nuts
And all my trees are yours, if I am yours.   820
Mine are these sheep, and many more that range
The woods and dales, and more, penned in their caves;
I could not tell their total if you asked—
It's only paupers who must count their sheep!
But don't just take my word—see for yourself: 825
They scarce can stand for their distended dugs!
And I have little lambs, warm in their pens,
And kids, alike in age, in other pens,
And vats of snow-white milk, some set aside
For drinking, and some curdling into cheese.   830
You'll have no lazy joys nor common gifts,
But goats and rabbits, does, a deuce of doves,
Or else a nest fetched from atop a tree!
I found a pair of cubs to play with you,
So much alike you'll scarcely keep them straight.   835
Within a shaggy she-bear's peaktop lair,†
I found them and I said, "You'll be my wife's!"
Just lift your shining head above the sea
And come here, Galatea, take your gifts!
    "'Of course, I know myself. I lately looked   840
To see me in a pool—and liked my looks:
Just see how big I am! Great Jove in heaven
Does not outweigh me (since you talk so much
About some king called Jove); my locks pour down
My fearsome face and shade me like a grove!   845
Don't think, because my body bristles hair,
I'm ugly. Trees are ugly bare of leaves,
A horse is ugly shorn of its gold mane,
Plumes cover birds, and sheep look best with wool,
As men look best with beards and bristling hair!   850
True, my brow has one eye, big as a shield:
So? Aren't all things below seen by the Sun?
And yet, the Sun has but a single eye.
What's more, I'd make my sire who rules your seas

Your in-law—only pity me my prayers!   855
To you alone I kneel—I, who scorn Jove,
His heaven and thunder, fear you, Nereid;
For thunder's not so fearsome as your rage!
    "'I'd take it better if you scorned all suits,
But why reject the Cyclops and prefer   860
The love and arms of Acis over mine?
Let him be pleased and please you, too—alas!—
Dear Galatea! But give me a chance,
And he'll learn I have strength to match my size!
I'll strew his living guts about the fields   865
And (so you'll be together) through your waves!
For so I burn with ever-fiercer fire,
It seems all Aetna's power is in my chest—
And, Galatea, you don't even care!'
    "Thus having whined, he rose (I saw it all)   870
And, like a raging bull who's lost his cow,
He wandered restless through the woods and glades,
Till, taking me and Acis unawares
And blind to fate, he shouted, 'Here you are!
I'll see to it this lovemaking's your last!'   875
As loud as a mad Cyclops ought to be,
He was: Mount Aetna trembled at the sound.
I panicked, diving in the nearby sea,
But my Symaethian hero fled and cried,
'Please, Galatea, help me! Parents, help!   880
Receive me, doomed to die, into your realm!'
The Cyclops chased him, hurling forth a piece
Of splintered peak, and though its edge was all
That got to Acis, still it buried him.
Then we did all that fate would let us do,   885
And gave back Acis his ancestral powers;
At that, the mound let forth a flow of blood,
Whose redness soon began to fade and turn
The shade of streams in flood, and then quite clear,
Till, at a touch, the mound it sprung from split.   890
Then, through the cracks, there rose a slender stalk,
And, in the rock's new cavern, leaping waves

FIGURE 9. Frontispiece to *Acis et Galatée* by Jean-Baptiste Lully (1686). Superintend-
ent of Music to Louis XIV, Lully was only one of many composers to adapt the Galatea
myth. His operatic version, the last of eight Lully stage works based on Ovid, was
published with this frontispiece shortly before his death. The opera remained popular
at the French court and a 1749 revival starred the king's mistress, Madame de
Pompadour.

Roared round a wonder, for inside there stood
A youth, waist-deep, his new horns wreathed in reeds,
Who, though much larger and his face sea-green,   895
Was surely Acis—or else, Acis changed
Into the river god who bears his name."†

[SCYLLA AND GLAUCUS, PART 1]

When Galatea ceased, the Nereid band
Broke up and swam away on tranquil waves;
But Scylla (who dared brave no seas herself)   900
Went off to roam disrobed along some shore
Or cove whose sheltered eddies might refresh
Her weary limbs. But, skimming through the surf,
There came the latest dweller of the deep,
Anthedon of Euboea's son transformed!   905
He, Glaucus, froze with love of her he saw,
And anything he thought could stay her flight
He said, but still she fled, made fast by fear,
Until she'd scaled a mountain near the shore,
Whose massive seaside peak and tree-lined top   910
Curved outward, looming large across the waves.
There, safely set, she sat unsure if he
Was god or monster, gaping at his hue,
His hairy arms and back, and where his loins
Curved in a fish's tail. But, sensing this,   915
He grasped a rock and said, "No freak or fiend
Am I, dear maiden, but a god of seas!
Not Triton, Proteus, nor Palaemon, son
Of Athamas,[19] wields greater power than I.
I was a mortal once, but even then   920
Devoted to the depths, I labored there,
Now drawing up the nets that drew my fish,
Now perching on a mound with rod and line.
   "'There is a beach beside a verdant plain
Ringed here with waves and there with fields of grass   925

19. Formerly known as Melicertes (4.416–542)

Unmarred by munching heifers and their horns,
And free from grazing sheep and shaggy goats.
No busy bee has borne away its flowers,
Which never lend their heads to festive crowns,
Being strange to mowers' hands; I was the first   930
To sit there in the sod and dry my lines,
Or count, arrayed in rows, the fish I'd caught
By chance within my nets or tricked by trust
Upon my curving hooks. What happened next
Sounds like a lie (but would I lie to you?):   935
Lain on the grass, my catch began to stir
And flop about the land as if at sea!
I stopped there, stunned, as each fish fled the shore
And its new owner for their native waves.
In awe and doubt, I long stood wondering how: 940
Was this god's work? Was it the grasses' sap?
'And yet what grass,' I asked, 'could hold such power?'
Then I picked up some blades, chewed what I'd picked,
And hardly had I swallowed its strange sap
When suddenly I felt my heart aquake   945
And rapt with longing for that other world.
I could not hold back long but, crying 'Earth,
Farewell forever!' plunged beneath the waves.
The sea-gods, seeing me worthy of their state,
Asked Tethys and the Ocean to erase   950
My mortal part, and so they purged my wrongs,
First with a cleansing spell they spoke nine times,
Then bidding me to swim a hundred streams.
At once, the rivers ran from every side
To pour their swirling waters on my head.   955
This much I can recall and tell you now,
This much I know—my mind has lost the rest.
But when I woke, my form was wholly changed
From what I'd been, nor was my mind the same.
I saw then, for the first, this rust-green beard,   960
These locks of mine that sweep along the swells,
These shoulders, sea-blue arms, and twisting legs,
Tipped with a fish-like fin. Yet, why these looks?

Why please the ocean gods—why *be* a god,
If you are yet unswayed?"
                              So spoke the god,   965
Who would have spoken more, but Scylla fled.
So, raging from rejection, he sought out
The monstrous halls of Circe, Titan's child.[†]

Book 14

BOTH AETNA, heaped atop a Giant's throat,[1]
And the Cyclopes' plains, where hoes and ploughs
Are strangers and no ox-team need be paid,
Were passed on the Euboean merman's path.
He passed by Zancle, too, and Rhegium's walls,   5
And through those shipwreck straits which serve to keep
Ausonia's shores and Sicily's apart.
Then, through the Tyrrhene Sea, by strength of stroke,
He reached the grassy hills and beast-filled halls
Of Circe, daughter of the Sun. At sight,   10
They hailed each other: "Goddess," Glaucus said,
"Take pity on a god! For you alone,
Should I seem worthy, can relieve my love.
O Titaness, none knows so well as I
The power of herbs, for they transfigured me.   15
But let me tell you of my passion's cause:
Outside Messina's walls in Italy,
I spotted Scylla! I'm ashamed to tell
Of all the pledges, pleas, and prayers she scorned.
But part your sacred lips and cast a spell,   20

---

1. Typhon, still pinned under Sicily (cf. 5.346–55).

If spells have sway; or, if an herb is best,
Then use the proven strength of potent herbs.
I ask you not to cure or heal my hurt
(Don't let it end!)—just make her share my heat!"
    But Circe (for no heart's so quick to flame   25
As hers, be it through her fault or the will
Of vengeful Venus, whom her sire once slurred)†
Replied: "You'd best woo one who shares your wish,
Who's willing, and who feels your love no less!
You should be (and sure could be) sought yourself;   30
Give suitors hope and, trust me, you'll be sought!
Your beauty should assure you, seeing that I—
A goddess, daughter of the shining Sun,
Skilled in all spells, all herbs—pray to be yours!
Snub her who snubs you, welcome her who woos,   35
And so, in turn, requite us both at once!"
But Glaucus answered, "Trees will line the waves
And seaweed sprout along the mountaintops
Before my love shall change while Scylla lives."
The goddess was enraged but, with no power   40
(And, loving him, no wish) to bring him harm,
Turned all her wrath on her whom he preferred.
She ground the dreadful dregs of ill-famed herbs,
Mixed Hecataean charms into the grounds,
And, in a sea-blue robe, forsook her halls   45
Of fawning beasts to seek out Rhegium's shores,
Which face the crags of Zancle, faring firm
Atop the sea as though on solid ground,
Her feet still dry amid the seething swells.
    There was a quiet pool, bent in a bow,   50
Where Scylla loved to shelter from the heat
Of boiling sea and sky when, high above,
The sun would shine and shrink the shadows small.
This pool the goddess poisoned in advance,
Befouling it with her unnatural banes   55
And sprinkling juices squeezed from noxious roots,
While mumbling thrice-nine times through magic lips
A riddling spell of strange and secret words.

When Scylla came and waded in waist-deep,
She saw foul monsters barking round her loins   60
And did not realize at first that they
Were part of her, but shuddered, shrank, and slapped
Their hellhound snouts; but what she fled came with,
And, looking down for her thighs, legs, and feet,
She saw instead jaws fit for Cerberus!   65
And there she stood, a belt of rabid dogs
Set round her belly and her mangled loins.
    Then Glaucus wept for love, fleeing Circe's arms
Which had so cruelly worked their herbal powers,
But Scylla stayed there and, at her first chance   70
To strike at Circe, stole Ulysses' crew.†
She'd soon have wrecked the Teucrian ships as well,
Had she not first been changed to stone—a rock
Which stands there still and sailors still avoid.†

[THE SIBYL OF CUMAE]†

    With this and keen Charybdis paddled past,   75
The Trojan fleet had neared Ausonia's shores
When storm winds whisked them back to Libya.
Once there, Aeneas gained the heart and home
Of the Sidonian, who would not withstand
Her Phrygian mate's escape, but faked a rite   80
To fall atop a pyre—and on his sword,
Thus duping all as she'd been duped herself.†
    Next, fleeing† those new-built sands, he joined his friend
Acestes, worshiped at his father's tomb,
Then sailed from Eryx, though his ships were burned   85
By Juno's Iris, on past Hippotes'
Son's sulphurous isles, the Acheloïads'—
Or Sirens'—crags, unhelmed past Prochyta,
Inarime, and Australopithland,
A dung heap named for those who there reside:†   90
For the Cercopes' tricks and treasons once
So filled the father of the gods with hate
That he deformed them into mutant beasts,

Who seemed at once both like and unlike men.
He shrank their limbs down, snubbed their noses back,   95
And left their faces furrowed as with age,
Then sent them there, all wreathed in brownish fur—
Though not before he'd stopped their powers of speech
And checked their tongues, contrived for treacheries,
And left them only screeches of complaint.   100
    Proceeding leftward past Parthenope
And by the trumpeter Aeolid's tomb,[†]
He came to Cumae's marsh-infested shores,
Where, in the ancient Sibyl's cave,[†] he prayed
To cross through Hell and see his father's shade.   105
When finally she raised her downcast eyes,
She said, in frenzy from the god within,
"You wish for much, O man of mighty deeds,
Whose hand was tried by steel, whose worth by fire.
But fear not, Trojan! You will have your wish.   110
Amid Elysium's halls, the world's last realm,
I'll lead you to your sire's dear shade. With faith,
No path's impassable." This said, she showed,
Deep in Avernal Juno's grove, a bough
Of gleaming gold,[†] and bade him cut it down.   115
    Aeneas did, and in dread Orcus'[2] lands,
Beheld his forebears and the great-souled ghost
Of old Anchises, who explained death's laws,
And what fresh risks awaited him in war.[†]
Then, heading back, he passed the toilsome trek   120
In cheerful chat with his Cumaean guide;
For on their dim, dark, dreadful way, he said,[†]
"Be you a god, or one the gods hold dear,
You'll always seem divine to me! My life
Is owed to you, who showed me death's domain   125
Then led me from the dead domains I'd seen!
Once back above, I'll honor what you've done
With incense at the shrine I'll build for you."
    At this, the seer sighed. "Though I'm no god,

2. An Italian god of the underworld, here conflated with Dis

No human head deserves your sacred smoke.   130
Yet know, lest you should err, eternal life
Would have been mine, had I once let the love
Of Phoebus puncture my virginity.
While yet he yearned and hoped I'd yield to gifts,
He cried, 'Cumaean maid, choose what you will!   135
You'll have your choice.' So, pointing to a pile
Of sand heaped by, I rashly prayed to live
As many years as it had grains of sand.
I did not think to ask for years of youth.
He pledged—and would have added youth, for love—   140
But I spurned Phoebus' gifts and stayed unwed.
Now, long abandoned by my better days,
I weather the old age that creeps my way.
At seven centuries, you see me now,
And, till I match the sands, I've still to see   145
Three hundred harvest years, three hundred wines!
In time, the days will shrink my body small,
My limbs, lain waste with age, will lose their weight,
And it will seem that I was never loved
Or pleasing to a god; for Phoebus, too,   150
May say he never prized my stranger's face.
[So shall I be transformed that, seen by none,
In voice, I'll live: Fate will leave me my voice!]"†

[POLYPHEMUS]†

    Thus spoke the Sibyl, rising from the pit
Of Stygian gloom to her Euboean town.³   155
There, Troy's Aeneas made due sacrifice,
Then reached the shores not named yet for his nurse,⁴
Where Macar, poor Ulysses' Ithacan
Companion, weary of the way, had stayed,
And now spied long-lost Achaemenides,   160
Abandoned once on Aetna. Shocked to find

3. Cumae, which originated as a Euboean colony
4. Caieta, as related at 441–44

Him still alive, he asked: "What luck or god
Has saved you, Achaemenides, a Greek,
To board a foreign ship? Where do you sail?"
No longer gruffly garbed, but his own man,   165
No longer clad in garments clasped with thorns,
Said Achaemenides: "May I once more
See Polyphemus' jaws drip human gore
If I would rather be at home than here,
Or deem Aeneas less than my own sire.   170
Though I'd give all, I can't thank him enough:
To speak, to breathe, to see the sunlit sky—
How could I be ungrateful or forget?
It's through him I outlived the Cyclops' teeth,
And if I now should leave the light of life,   175
At least I'll have a grave beyond his guts!
    "What did I feel (had fear not swept away
All feeling) when I saw you set to sea?
Alone, I longed to cry, but feared the foe
Would hear me—for Ulysses almost wrecked   180
Your ship with shouting!† I saw the fiend fling
An up-torn mountainside amid the swells,
Then saw, again, his giant sinews sling
Great stones as from a catapult, and feared
The ripples or the rocks would sink the ship,   185
Forgetting that I was not then inside.
But once you'd saved yourselves from certain death,
He wandered Aetna with his sightless eye,
And, groaning, groping trees, and ramming rocks,
Reached bloodstained arms to sea and cried this curse   190
On the Achaean race: 'Oh, that some chance
Would bring Ulysses or *one of his crew*
Back here for me to vent my rage upon:
I'd gulp his guts, I'd rend his living limbs,
I'd glut my gullet on his blood and gore,   195
And feel him writhing, tangled in my teeth:
How light—how slight my loss of sight would seem!'
While on he raved, I gazed in pallid dread
At his still-gory face, his vicious hands,

His sightless socket, and his limbs and beard   200
Caked hard with human blood. [Before my eyes,
Death loomed, but was the least I had to fear.]
He'll catch me now, I thought, now in his guts
He'll sink my own! The image gripped my mind
Of how I saw him dash two comrades down   205
Three times and more against the ground, then crouch
Above them, as a shaggy lion does,
To gorge his greed upon their guts, their flesh,
Their bones' white marrow, and their half-dead limbs.
I stood there shaking as my blood ran cold   210
And watched him first chew down his gory feast,
Then spew it back, disgorging gobs with wine—
Such was the fate I feared in store for me!
For many days, I hid at every sound;
Afraid to die but longing for my death,   215
I fed myself on acorns, leaves, and grass.
Alone and helpless, hopeless, left to die,
I suffered till, at last, I spied this ship
And signed to beg for salvage, ran to shore,
And made the Trojans take a Greek aboard.   220
Now tell, dear comrade, what became of you
And all that crew with whom you set to sea."

[ULYSSES AND CIRCE]†

He⁵ said Aeolus, lord of Tuscan seas—
Aeolus, son of Hippotes—had bound
The Winds in leather as a noted gift   225
For their Dulichian captain,† whom nine days
Of sailing fair had brought in sight of land.
But at the dawning of the tenth, his men
Were overcome with plunderous jealousy
And, in pursuit of gold, unbound the Winds,   230
Which blew the ship back through the waves she'd crossed,
Returning to Aeolus' royal port.

5. Macar

"We came to Laestrygonian Lamus[†] next,
Where reigns Antiphates," he said, "from whom,
Sent with two other men, I scarce escaped   235
With one of them, while our third comrade's blood
Befouled the Laestrygonians' godless mouths.
Antiphates pursued us as we ran,
Ahead a mob whose pelting trees and stones
Sank all our men and wrecked our every ship,   240
Save that which saved Ulysses and myself.
Then, mourning our lost mates, we gained those lands
You see there, far away—and far away
Is where they should be seen from, mark my words!
O goddess' son, most righteous man of Troy   245
(For now in peacetime you're a foe no more,
Aeneas), heed me and flee Circe's shores!
We, too, on Circe's shores, being mindful of
The Cyclops and Antiphates, refused
To fare through parts unknown, and all drew lots.   250
The lots chose me; Polites, my dear friend;
Elpenor, always drunk;[†] Eurylochus;
And twice-nine more to send to Circe's walls.
    "When we arrived and stood within her halls,
A thousand wolves—or lions, wolves, and bears—   255
Rushed forth to our unjustified alarm,
For none were there but those who meant no harm.
In fact, they even wagged their gentle tails
And fawned on us and followed at our feet
Till slave-girls led us through the marble halls   260
To that grand chamber where their mistress sat
Enthroned in state, wrapped in a shining robe,
And crested by a girding veil of gold.
With her were nymphs and Nereids, whose hands
Instead of carding wool and spinning thread,   265
Were sifting into baskets heaps of plants
And fresh-plucked flowers and multicolored herbs.
Herself she managed them; knowing herself
How best to use each leaf and mix them well,
She closely checked the sorting of the herbs.   270

At sight of us, she gave our greetings back
And beamed and seemed to answer all our prayers.
At once, she ordered nectar to be mixed
With toasted barley flakes and curdled wine,
But slyly laced this honeyed brew with sap   275
And handed each of us a cursèd cup.
Just when we'd quenched our parched and thirsty lips,
The wicked witch's wand swept past our heads
And (through my shame, I'll say it) I began
To sprout with bristles! Soon I could not speak,   280
Except in grunts, while, creeping on the ground,
I felt my features stiffen in a snout,
My neck bulge brawn, and those same hands that held
A cup mere moments past now leaving tracks.
All changed and caged (such was her potions' power!)   285
We saw Eurylochus alone had not
Become a pig, for he'd refused his cup.
If he had not, I'd still be in that sty,
And never would Ulysses have been told
Of Circe's deeds, nor rescued us from ruin.   290
    "Cyllenius, who brings peace, brought him a flower
The gods call *moly*, white with roots of black,
With which, as heaven ordained, he safely came
To Circe's palace, took the traitorous cup,
And, as she stretched her wand to stroke his hair,   295
Struck it aside and drew his fearsome sword!
They soon saw eye to eye and went to bed,
But as a wedding gift he claimed his crew;
So, spraying us with secret healing sap,
She tapped our foreheads with her back-turned wand,   300
Said words to counteract the words she'd said,
And sang the more that we the more might rise,
Slough off our bristles, lose our cloven feet,
And gain again our shoulders, arms, and hands.
We wept and clasped our weeping captain's arms,   305
And hugged his neck, and said no other words
Before we'd spoken words of gratitude.

[PICUS AND CANENS][†]

"A year we lingered there, and much I saw
In that long stretch of time, and much I heard.
This, with much else, I was told privately   310
By one of those four girls who served the witch.
While Circe dallied with my liege alone,
She showed me a white statue of a youth
With a woodpecker on his marble head,
Set in a shrine and crowned with countless wreaths.   315
Being curious, I asked her who he was
And why he had a shrine and bore a bird.
'Now hear me, Macar, and you'll learn,' she said,
'What power my mistress wields: attend my words!
  "'King Picus of Ausonia, Saturn's son,[†]   320
Was mad for steeds of war. As for his looks,
You see them here: observe his handsome face,
And in these features false admire the true.
His spirit matched his shape, nor had he seen
Four of the Greeks' quadrennial Elean games[6]   325
Before the dryads born on Latium's hills
All glanced his way. Though sought by fountain nymphs,
By naiads from the Tiber, Numicius,
And Anio, from the Almo's meager stream,
From rushing Nar, the cloudy Farfa's shades,   330
And from Diana's Scythian forest pools,[7]
He spurned them all to love one nymph alone:
She whom Venilia—so it's said—once bore
To Grecian Janus on the Palatine.
When first she reached a marriageable age,   335
She wed Laurentian Picus, her preferred.
Rare though her looks were, rarer was her voice,
Whence she was known as "Canens,"[†] since her songs
Could move the stones and forests, tame wild beasts,

6. The Olympic games: Picus was under sixteen
7. Lake Aricia to the south of Rome, revisited at 15.488ff

Still rolling streams, and stay the flight of birds.   340
　"'Once, while her woman's voice was raised in song,
This Picus left their home to hunt the boars
That roamed Laurentum's plains. Astride his steed,
A pair of spears in hand, he rode beneath
A purple cloak bound with a clasp of gold.   345
In those same woods, the daughter of the Sun
Was picking fresh-grown herbs upon a hill,
For which she'd left her namesake Circaean fields.
There, hidden in the brush, she spied the youth
And stood in shock. The herbs fell from her hand,   350
She felt fire creeping through her very bones,
And, when she'd scarce recovered from the heat
To find that she could not declare desire
With all his steeds and huntsmen rushing round,
She cried, "Though borne by winds, you'd not escape,   355
If I still know myself, if still my herbs
Have power and all my charms don't fail me now!"
This said, she shaped a false and phantom boar,
Which, at her word, ran past his royal eyes
And seemed to dart into a dense-grown glade   360
Whose thickset trunks no horse could pass between.
Fooled, Picus rushed to chase his spectral prey
And, springing sprightly off his seething steed,
Ran haply through the trees in hollow hope.
Then she began to pray and speak her spells   365
And worship unknown gods with unknown charms—
The same she used to dim the moon's white face
Or hide her father's head in stormy clouds.
Then, too, her chanted charms obscured the sky
And drew mists from the ground so, wandering blind,   370
The king's men left him guardless. Time and place
Being now secured, she cried: "Oh, by your eyes
Which captured mine, and by your face so fair
It makes a goddess kneel, smile on my love,
Accept the all-seeing Sun as sire-in-law,   375
And show no scorn for Circe, Titan's child!"
But roughly he repulsed her and her pleas:

"Be who you are," he said, "I'm not for you!
I'm held by one who'll hold me long, I pray,
Nor shall I breach our bonds for stranger's love   380
While fate preserves my Canens, Janus' child!"
When all her pleas proved vain, Titania cried:
"You'll not escape, nor live with Canens more!
Now learn what might hath women scorned in love
[When Circe is," she said, "that woman scorned]!"   385
  "'Then twice to west and twice to east she turned,
Thrice tapped him with her wand, and spoke three spells.
He fled but found his flight was oddly fast,
Then noticed wings had sprouted from his frame!
Enraged at his being made a strange new bird   390
Stuck in the Latin woods, he pecked their trunks
And flecked the running boughs with angry wounds.
His purple cloak lent color to his plumes,
And, as a golden pin had clasped his clothes,
A ring of golden feathers girt his neck,   395
Till naught remained of Picus but his name.[8]
  "'Meanwhile, his men called up and down the fields,
But, finding Picus nowhere, chanced instead
On Circe (who by now had cleared the air
And let the sun and wind dispel her mists).   400
They rightly blamed her, claiming back their king,
And threatened force with readied spears, but she
Sprayed noxious poison sap and, calling forth
Night and Night's gods from Chaos and from Hell,
Prayed unto Hecate with long-drawn howls.   405
Then (wondrous sight!) the trees leapt out of place,
Groans shook the ground, and nearby trunks went pale.
As drops of blood bedewed the spattered grass,
It seemed that stones let forth a grating roar,
Dogs barked aloud, the dirt squirmed dark with snakes,   410
And slender lifeless spirits filled the air.
These horrors shocked the crowd, and, in their shock,
She touched their awestruck faces with her wand:

8. *Picus* is Latin for woodpecker

Its magic touch made monsters of them all,
And not a single youth retained his shape.   415
    "'Tartessus' banks⁹ had long seen Phoebus set
As Canens vainly watched with eyes and heart
To see her spouse come home. Now, through the woods,
Her slaves and friends bore lamps in search of him,
Nor was the nymph content to weep and wail   420
And tear her tresses (all of which she did),
But, running wild, she wandered Latium's fields.
Six nights and six new dawns discovered her
Still roaming on, deprived of food and sleep,
Past hills, past dales, wherever luck might lead.   425
The Tiber saw her last; along his banks,
She crumpled woe-and-way-worn to her knees,
And shed great tears and, in her pitch of pain,
Gushed feeble words of grief, much like the song
A dying swan will sing to mourn itself.   430
At last, with sorrow thawing through her bones,
She slowly thinned to air. Still, her renown
Lives through that spot the old Camenae called
By Canens' name,† just as the nymph deserved.'

[THE CREW OF DIOMEDES]†

    "Such things I often heard and saw that year.   435
Then tasked, though slow and slothful from disuse,
To take the seas once more, once more we sailed!
But all Titania's tales of twisting paths,
Vast voyages, and dangers yet to dare
So scared me, I admit, that I stayed here."   440
There, Macar ceased. Then, for Aeneas' nurse,
A marble urn was laid with this short verse:

    FOR ME, CAIETA, SAVED FROM ARGIVE FIRE,
    MY FAITHFUL WARD HERE BUILT A FITTING PYRE.

    Next, casting off, they left that grassy bank,   445

9. A Spanish river, here representing the far west

Steered clear of the notorious goddess' home,
And reached those shady groves where Tiber's sands
Rush golden to the sea. The hero there
Gained Faunus' son Latinus' throne and child,
But not without a fight![†] The warlike clan   450
Of Turnus, raging for his promised bride,
Led all Etruria into Latium's lands,
In long pursuit of hard-fought victory.
    Both armies swelled their ranks with foreign force.
Some joined the Trojans, some the Rutuli,   455
And though Aeneas did not vainly seek
Evander's walls, in vain sought Venulus
The city exiled Diomedes built
In Daunus of Iapygia's dowried lands.[†]
When Venulus, on Turnus' orders, asked   460
For martial aid, Aetolia's hero balked
And said he'd not commit his in-law's tribe
Nor his own self in war: he had no men.
"And lest you think I lie, though it renews
My bitter grief, I'll tell what I've endured!   465
    "Once Ilium burned and Pergamum had fed
The Grecians' fires, and Naryx' hero brought
On all of us the punishment he owed
The maiden goddess for the maid he raped,[†]
We windswept tide-tossed Danaäns endured   470
Rain, lightning, night, the wrath of sea and sky,
And, worst of all, the Cape Caphereus wreck.[†]
I'll not extend this litany of woe:
The sight of Greece would have made Priam weep!
Though warrior Minerva, loving me,   475
Saved me from drowning, I was forced from home
Again when kindly Venus, grudging still
Her former wound, took such revenge on me,[†]
Through toils at sea and wartime toils on land,
That I would often call them lucky whom   480
The storm and cruel Caphereus' cape had drowned,
And wished that I might have been one of them.
    "My crew was now fed up with wars and waves

And sought to end our roving; but our plights
Had just embittered Acmon's[10] fiery heart: 485
'What's left, men, that you could not suffer through?
What more,' he cried, 'could Cytherea now
Do (if she wished to)? While there's worse to fear,
Prayers have their place, but when the worst has come,
Fear's trodden underfoot: despair brings peace!   490
So let her hear and—as she does—hate all
Of Diomedes' men. We'll scorn her hate,
Though her great powers have greatly grown our grief.'
    "Spurred on by Acmon of Pleuronia's speech,
Which spurned her rages, Venus raged anew.   495
But few of us liked Acmon's words, and most
Rebuked him. When he tried to make reply,
His vocal tract and voice itself grew thin,
His hair turned into plumes that plumed his neck
And breast and back, and larger quills that clothed   500
His arms. His elbows bent in slender wings,
His feet absorbed his toes, and all his face
Grew rigid, ending in a pointy beak.
Rhexenor, Lycus, Idas, Nycteus,
And Abas all stared dumb—and, while they stared,   505
Changed, too! Most all the crew took flight
And flitted round the oars. If you should ask
Their shape, those sudden birds, although not swans
Were white and much like swans. That's why these fields,
My lord Iapygian Daunus' arid lands,   510
Are all the few men left me can maintain!'"†

[THE APOTHEOSIS OF AENEAS]†

So Calydonian Oeneus' grandson[11] spoke.
Then Venulus left, past Peucetia's bay
And the Messapian fields,† where he beheld
Those caverns, cloaked by trees and dripping dew,   515

---

10. A member of Diomedes' crew, not otherwise known
11. Diomedes, son of Tydeus, son of Oeneus of Calydon (cf. 8.273)

Which half-goat Pan now holds but once held nymphs,
Till an Apulian shepherd from those parts
First scared them off through sudden fear of him.
But, soon recovering, they scorned his chase,
And moved their feet again in rhythmic dance.   520
The shepherd mocked them, aped their rustic steps,
And mixed in backwoods taunts and vulgar jeers,
But then fell silent—tree-bark shut his mouth.
He is a tree now, best-known by its fruit,
And the wild olive's bitter berries show   525
The sharpness of his tongue, which passed to them.
    When envoys brought back word Aetolian aid
Had been denied, the Rutuli waged war
Without them, shedding both sides' blood—and look!
The pinewood ships are put to Turnus' torch   530
And what survived the waves now fears his flames!
Now fiery Mulciber consumes for fuel
The wax and pitch, licks up the mast and sails,
And chars the bow-shaped benches in the hull.
But, mindful that those pines from Ida fell,   535
Heaven's holy Mother[12] filled the air with sounds
Of crashing bronze and ringing boxwood flutes,
And, borne on high by her tamed lions,[13] cried:
"Vain, godless Turnus, are these fires you fling!
For I shall never let your greedy flames   540
Burn timbers of my grove!" The goddess spoke
To claps of thunder—thunder that gave way
To showers of heavy rain and leaping hail,
While sea and sky convulsed in sudden strife
As war broke out between Astraeus' sons,[14]   545
Of whom one lent the kindly Mother force
To snap the lines that held the Phrygian fleet
And plunge the ships prow-first into the waves.
At once, the planks went soft, wood turned to flesh,

12. Cybele, to whom both Ida and pine-trees were sacred (cf. 10.103–5)
13. Presumably, Hippomenes and Atalanta (see 10.686ff)
14. The Winds

The twisting shapes of sterns were changed to heads,   550
And oars transformed to toes and swimming legs.
What had been ribs stayed ribs, but, in the hull,
The deep-set keel became a working spine;
Then rigging turned to hair and spars to arms,
Their sea-green hue unchanged. Now in the waves   555
They used to fear, those ships play girlish games
As sea-nymphs. Sprung from solid mountainsides,
They roam the liquid waves, free of their past.
Yet, mindful of the risks they ran at sea,
They oft lend tide-tossed ships their helping hands—   560
Unless they carry Greeks! For they recall
Their Phrygian woes and hate Pelasgians still,
And cheered to see the Ithacan's ship wrecked
And cheered to see Alcinoüs' shipwreck
Sink through the tide, its timbers petrified.[†]   565
    Some hoped the vessels brought to life as nymphs
Would scare the Rutuli from war, but no:
Each side had gods and—what's as good as gods—
Both had resolve. No more for dowried realms,
An in-law's throne, nor you, Lavinian maid,   570
But victory and failure's shame they fought.
At long last, Venus saw her victor-son
Fell Turnus and fell Ardea[15]—a strong town,
While Turnus was alive! Once foreign flames
Had razed it and warm ashes hid its homes,   575
A bird, unknown till then, rose from the ruins
And fanned the cinders with its flapping wings.
Its gauntness, cries, and pallor all befit
The captured city whence it gained its name,[16]
So Ardea mourns itself on beating wings.   580
    Aeneas' soul had now moved all the gods—
Yes, Juno, too[†]—to stay their ancient rage;
Young Iulus'[17] state being well-secured, this left

---

15. The Rutulian capital
16. *Ardea*, a genus of herons
17. The son of Aeneas, known elsewhere as Ascanius (cf. 609)

The Cytherean hero ripe for heaven.
So Venus lobbied all the gods, embraced   585
Her father's neck, and said, "You're never harsh
With me, dear sire. Now be most kind, I pray!
Make my Aeneas, grandson of our blood,
A god—however minor, but a god.
O great one, it's enough to cross the Styx   590
But once and once see that unlovely realm!"
All heaven agreed, nor was the god-queen's face
Unmoved; no, she assented with a smile.
Then said her father, "You deserve heaven's gifts,
Both you who seek and he for whom you've sought: 595
My daughter, have your wish!" She thanked her sire
And soared in joy, aloft the wings of doves,
For the Laurentian coast. There, wreathed in reeds,
The curving mouth of the Numicius lies,
Whose silent stream she bade wash out to sea   600
Whatever of Aeneas that could die.
The horned god did as Venus ordered him,
And purged Aeneas of his mortal part
By bathing him till what was best remained.
His mother daubed him next with scent divine,   605
Touched nectar and ambrosia to his lips,
And thus made him the god whom Roman throngs
Call "Indiges"† and worship at his shrines.

[POMONA AND VERTUMNUS]†

Two-named Ascanius next held Alba's throne†
And Latium's, too; then, Silvius, whose son   610
Latinus took his forebear's name and throne.
Latinus' heir was Alba the renowned;
His, Epytus. Then Capetus, Capys—
But Capys first—and Tiberinus ruled,
Who gave the Tuscan river where he drowned   615
Its current name. His sons were Remulus
And Acrota; when elder Remulus,
Who mimicked lightning, died by lightning's stroke,†

The meeker Acrota passed on the throne
To daring Aventinus, whose court crowned   620
His namesake hill, the hill where now he lies.
   While Proca, who next ruled the Palatines,[†]
Was king, Pomona was the most adept
Of Latium's woodland nymphs at gardening,
And keenest in the care of flowering trees,   625
Whence came her name.[18] She loved no woods or streams
But only fields and branches full of fruit,
And bore in hand not spears but pruning hooks
To trim the trees' new growth, clip back their boughs,
Or slice along their bark and graft a stalk   630
To feed her foreign cuttings on their sap;
And, lest they thirst, she'd flush the fibrous twists
Of their dry quenchless roots with trickling waves.
This was her love and joy: she scorned romance!
But, fearing rapist rubes, she hid inside   635
Her orchard, barred the way, and fled all men.
What didn't the young dancing satyrs try—
And all the Pans with pine around their horns,
Silenus, ever younger than his years,
And he, the god who guards with scythe or groin[19]—   640
To vanquish her? Vertumnus loved her best,
But fared no better. Oh, how many times
With gifts of harvest grain he came disguised
In peasant rags and played the peasant's part!
He often passed enwreathed in fresh-mown grass,   645
So it might seem he'd just been tossing hay,
Or with a prod in hand, so you would swear
He'd just unyoked his team, or with a hook
For pruning vines and trimming leaves and shoots,
Or with a ladder, as if picking fruits   650
[Or sword or rod, equipped to fight or fish].
In short, his varied guises let him gain
Admittance to the joy of seeing her.

18. *Pomum*, Latin for fruit
19. Priapus

FIGURE 10. Photo by Dan Norman of *Metamorphoses* by Mary Zimmerman (1998). Zimmerman's dreamlike drama *Metamorphoses* adapts ten of Ovid's myths for the stage, Vertumnus and Pomona among them. Nominated for the Tony Award for Best Play in 2002, the work has since proven popular with schools and regional theaters. This photograph shows the Guthrie Theater's revival in 2019.

   Once, as a stooping hag with hair of grey
And painted shawls wrapped round his hair, he came,   655
Strolled through the groves, admired their fruit, and said:
"But you are better yet!" And with this praise,
He gave her several kisses no true hag
Would ever give, then hunched down in the dirt,
And viewed the boughs hung thick with fruits of fall.   660
Nearby, a handsome elm gleamed bright with grapes,
And, once he'd praised the partnered plants, he said:
"But if that tree were married to no vine,
It would be valued only for its leaves.
This grapevine, too, which wraps around the elm,   665
If not thus wed, would lie flat on the ground!
Yet, unmoved by the lesson of this tree,
You shun all mates and do not care to wed.
Oh, that you would! For you'd be courted more
Than Helen, she for whom the Lapiths fought,   670
And even bold Ulysses' prudent wife!†

Why, though you snub and spurn them, even now
You're sought by thousands: men, gods, demigods,
And all the powers that haunt the Alban hills.
But if you're wise and wish to marry well,   675
Then heed this hag, who loves you most of all—
Yes, more than you can know: make no mean match
But take Vertumnus into bed! I'll vouch
On his behalf (for I know him as well
As he does) that he wanders not the world,   680
But lives right here! And while most wooers love
Each girl in sight, he'll love you first and last
And will devote his life to you alone.
What's more, he's young, he's natural in his grace,
He can, at will, assume what shape he wants,   685
And he'll do all you ask, though you ask all.[†]
He shares your tastes as well: the fruits you grow
He's first to get, rejoicing at your gifts!
But now he wants no produce from your trees
Nor grasses from your garden, rich and sweet,   690
Nor anything but you! Pity his love
Who pleads through me in person, and beware
Of vengeful gods, Rhamnusia's[20] patient wrath,
And the Idalian's[21] hate for stony hearts!
And, so you do (for age has taught me much),   695
I'll tell a tale well-known on Cyprus' isle
And teach you to be lenient and kind:
   "When highborn Teucrian Anaxarete
First came in humble Iphis' line of sight,
The sight of her set fire within his bones.   700
He struggled long but, finding that his flames
Defied all sense, fell pleading at her door.
First trusting his poor passion to her nurse,
He begged her, by her nursling, to be kind;
Then, charming all her multitude of maids,   705
He begged them each to put in a good word,

20. Nemesis, goddess of revenge
21. Venus, worshiped at Idalium on Cyprus

And often gave them charming notes for her,
While he hung tear-drenched garlands from her gate
Or lay there limply on the stony step
And sadly cursed the bolts that barred his way.   710
But, harsher than the sea when Haedi[22] sets,
And harder than steel forged in Noric fires[23]
Or living rock still rooted in the earth,
She spurned and mocked him, mixing these cruel deeds
With haughty talk that dashed the lover's hopes.   715
Soon Iphis could bear such abuse no more,
But in her doorway cried these final words:
'You win, O Anaxarete, nor shall
I vex you more! So plan your Triumph, cheer,
Let shine your laurels, and let Paeans ring!   720
You win! I'll gladly die to your delight,
O iron maid—for then, some part of me
And what I've done will please you into praise.
But don't think my love died before I did,
For I shall lose my life's two lights as one.   725
Nor will you hear some rumor of my death,
But, doubt it not, you'll see me there myself,
That your cruel eyes may feast upon my corpse.
Yet if, O gods, you see what mortals do,
Make me remembered (I can't ask for more),   730
And tell my tale years hence, so what I lose
In span of life I gain in length of fame!'
    "Then, raising welling eyes and pallid arms
Up to the posts he'd often hung with wreaths,
He strung a noose above the door and cried,   735
'Does this wreath please you, cruel and godless girl?'
Then slipping in his head, still facing her,
He hanged his luckless self and choked to death.†
But all his thrashing sounded like a knock,
And, opening the door on what he'd done,   740
The slaves cried out and vainly carried him

22. Stars in the constellation Auriga, associated with storms
23. The Alpine region of Noricum, renowned for its iron

(His sire being dead) back to his mother's house.
Receiving him, she clasped her son's cold corpse,
And, having said what mourning parents say
And grieved the way that mourning mothers do,   745
She led his tearful funeral through the town
And bore his ghastly body to be burned.
By chance, this teary train marched past the house
Of ruthless Anaxarete, on whom
The vengeful god[24] already was at work,   750
So that the wailing moved her after all.
'A woeful funeral,' she cried, 'let's watch!'
And sought a higher view. Scarce had she seen
Where Iphis lay before her eyes went hard,
And, drained of blood, her limbs turned cold and pale.   755
She tried to leave, but found her feet stayed put;
She tried to turn, but could not! Bit by bit,
The stone within her heart spread through her limbs—
And, should you doubt the tale, her statue's still
At Salamis, where also stands the shrine   760
Of Gazing Venus.[†] Learn this lesson, pray:
Put by your scorn, my nymph, and share my love—
For then no breeze shall shake your flowering fruit,
And no spring freeze shall nip them in the bud!"
    This said, affecting age to no effect,   765
The god resumed his youth and shed his guise
Of woman's years, appearing to her then
As when the sun breaks through a bank of clouds
To shine down at its brightest, unopposed.
Though he'd have raped her, no rape was required,   770
For, seeing the god, the nymph was smitten, too.

[THE APOTHEOSES OF ROMULUS AND
HERSILIE][†]

Next, false Amulius held Ausonia's throne
By force, till Numitor, with grandson's help,

---

24. Love, presumably (the Latin *deus* here is masculine)

Won back his kingdom; and, on Pales' feast,
The City walls were built.† Thence, Tatius marched   775
The Sabine sires; Tarpeia let them in,
And lost her guilty life beneath their shields.†
The Curians[25] stole in like silent wolves,
With all their foes asleep, to force the gates
That Ilia's son[26] had barred with firmest bolts.   780
But one of these Saturnia had herself
Unlocked and now swung open and unheard
By all but Venus, who'd have locked the gate,
But gods may not undo the deeds of gods.
　Near Janus' temple sprang the frigid spring   785
Where the Ausonian Naiads made their home.
She asked their help, nor did the nymphs refuse
That goddess' just request but let their springs
Stream outward. Still, the road to Janus' shrine
Was passable, despite the welling waves,   790
So they placed yellow sulphur in the vents,
And stoked the hollow veins with smoking pitch,
And used all means to boil the very depths
Until you waves, who'd ventured once to vie
With Alpine frost, could have out-kindled fire!   795
Now, lapped with flaming foam, the gateposts fumed,
Unbarred in vain to the stout Sabine force
The wondrous spring kept back until the men
Of Mars were armed; then, Romulus advanced
And strewed the Roman soil with Sabine dead   800
And with its own, as sons and sires in-law
Commingled blood upon their faithless swords.
But they chose not to fight until the last,
And lived in peace while Tatius shared the throne.†
　When Tatius died, O Romulus, you ruled   805
Both tribes with justice. Then Mars doffed his helm,
And thus addressed the lord of gods and men:
'It's time, dear sire, since now the Roman state

25. The Sabines; Cures was a Sabine town
26. Romulus, son of Ilia

Is firmly founded and no more depends
On one man's rule, to grant my promised prize   810
And take your worthy grandson into heaven.
You told me once, in council with the gods
(For I'll remind you of the pious words
I've borne in mind): 'One shall be yours to raise
To azure heaven!' Now let your words come true!"   815
At the Almighty's nod, clouds hid the sky,
And lightning thundered terror through the world.
Aware these were the promised rapture's signs,
Gradivus,[27] bending back his spear unfazed,
Vaulted aboard his chariot of blood   820
And whipped his steeds in headlong dive to reach
The Palatine's dark peak, where Ilia's son
Was dealing justice to the Quirites.[28]
Then, snatched up as he did, his mortal flesh
Dissolved in air, much as a leaden shot   825
Fired from a sling turns molten in the skies.
In fairer form, more fit to dine with gods,
"Quirinus" now appears in kingly robes.[†]

    His wife Hersilie wept for him as lost,
Till royal Juno ordered Iris down   830
Her arching path to charge the widow thus:
"O, of the Latins and the Sabine race,
The greatest glory and most worthy wife
For such a man, and for Quirinus now,
Cease weeping and, if you would see your spouse,   835
Come with me to the Quirinal's high grove,
Which shades the temple of the King of Rome."
So Iris, gliding down her rainbow road,
Addressed Hersilie in the terms decreed.
With eyes scarce raised, she bashfully replied: 840
"O goddess (for I can't tell who you are,
Though clearly you're a god), lead on, lead on!
Show me my husband's face! Just one more glance,

27. Mars
28. A name for the Romans in their civic capacity

If fate allows it, and I'll be in heaven!"[†]
So she and Thaumas' daughter climbed the hill   845
Of Romulus, where fell a shooting star
Whose starlight set Hersilie's hair aflame.
As, with the star, she vanished into air,
Rome's founder clasped her in familiar arms,
And called her "Hora,"[†] changed in form and name,   850
To stand, a goddess, at Quirinus' side.

Book 15

THE QUESTION then arose of who could bear
Such burdens as to follow such a king,
And Rumor, being truth's herald,† set the crown
On noble Numa who, not satisfied
With knowing Sabine ways, bent his great mind   5
Toward finding out the nature of all things.†
This quest led him from Cures, his hometown,
To that which once played host to Hercules;
And when he asked who'd laid Greek city-walls
In Italy, an elder of the place   10
Who knew of ancient times gave this reply:
   "Jove's son, grown wealthy with Iberian bulls,[1]
Had left the Ocean for Lacinium's coast,
Where, as his cattle grazed the tender grass,
It's said he reached great Croton's welcome house   15
And there relieved his timeless toil with rest.
In taking leave, he said: 'Someday, your heirs
Will build a city here.' These words came true,
For once in Argos lived Alemon's son,
One Myscelus, a favorite of the gods,   20

---

1. The cattle of Geryon from Hercules' Tenth Labor (cf. 9.184)

To whom, while fast asleep, the Clubman[2] came
And cried, 'Get hence! to Aesar's rocky stream
Be off with you and leave your native land!'
With many fearsome threats should he refuse.
At that, the god was gone, and so was sleep.   25
Alemon's son then rose and pondered long,
In silent conflict over what he'd seen:
A god bade him depart, but laws had banned
Departure from the land on pain of death!

   "The bright Sun's shining face had set to sea   30
Beneath Night's face of stars, when there appeared
The selfsame god, commanding him the same,
With more and fiercer threats should he refuse.
Now terrified, he made to move at once,
But word spread through the town and he was brought   35
To trial, where his outlawry was shown
And proven without need of witnesses.
Then cried the wretch, his guilty hands raised high:
'O you whose twice-six Labors won you heaven,
Bring help, I pray, for you have wrought my crime!'   40

   "Back then, court custom called for colored rocks:
Black pebbles signaled guilt, while white absolved.
Thus was the somber sentence given then,
And every stone in that cruel urn was black.
But at the count, when out the pebbles poured,   45
They found each one had changed from dark to white—
A lighter verdict, willed by Hercules.

   "Alemon's son first thanked Amphitryon's
For his release, then sailed a friendly breeze
Through the Ionian Sea, by Sallentine   50
Neretum, Sybaris, and Thurii,
Tarentum of the Spartans, Crimisa,
And the Iapygians' land. Scarce past those shores,
The Aesar's destined delta came in view,
Close by the tomb where Croton's sacred bones   55
Lay buried. There, he built his bidden walls

2. Hercules

And named the city for the man entombed."
Such was the ancient tale of how and why
The town was founded on Italian soil.

[PYTHAGORAS]†

There lived a man from Samos in the town,†   60
Who, hating Samian despots, chose to lead
An exile's life. Though far from gods and heaven,
His thoughts drew near them, seeing in his mind's eye
What nature had denied to human sight.
Surveying all with keen and constant care,   65
He offered lessons to the dumbstruck crowds,
And taught them the beginnings of the world,
The cause of things, what god and nature are,
Where snow and lightning come from, if it's wind
Or Jupiter whose thunder claps from clouds,   70
What quakes the earth, what system moves the stars,
And what lies hidden. He was first to ban
The use of beasts for food, and first to say
Such learnèd yet unheeded things as this:
    "Cease, mortals! Spare yourselves and don't defile   75
Your frames with sinful fare! For grains exist,
And trees weighed down with fruit, and grape-filled vines!
And there are salad greens—some sweet to taste,
And some to boil with fire—nor do you lack
For milk or honey spiced with flowering thyme!   80
The lavish earth brings forth her kindly food
And offers banquets free of blood and gore.
Meat is for ravening beasts, and not for all,
Since horses, sheep, and herds survive on grass,
But those whose nature is untamed and wild: 85
Armenian tigers, raging lions, wolves,
And bears rejoice to feed on bloody feasts.
Oh, what a crime to gorge one's guts with guts,
To fatten flesh on flesh—one feed, one fed,
And live one's life upon another's death!   90
With all that best of mothers, Earth, provides,

Will nothing please you but to sink your teeth,
Cruel as a Cyclops, in their woeful wounds?
Must you destroy some other being to stop
The starving of your stomachs' wicked greed?   95
　　"In ancient times we call the 'Golden Age,'†
The fruit of trees and greenery of the ground
Were blessings, and no mouths were stained with gore.
In those days, birds soared safely through the skies,
The hare fared fearlessly about the fields,   100
And fish were never hung for trusting hooks.
Without some trick or treachery to fear,
All things were filled with peace—till some vain wretch
Or other, envying the lions' prey,
Gulped down a greedy gulletful of meat   105
And paved the path of sin. It may have been
That swords were tainted first with beasts' warm blood—
That was enough! It is no crime to kill
The things that want us dead, I do confess,
But what's been killed should not be eaten next!   110
　　"As sinning spread, it's thought that pigs went first
To slaughter, since their swollen snouts are known
To dig up seeds and ruin harvest hopes;
For grazing Bacchic grapes, goats too were led
In sacrifice. These two paid for their crimes,   115
But what did sheep do? Born to serve our race
In peaceful flocks, your udders bring us milk,
The wool you give us makes our softest clothes.
Aren't you worth more to us alive than dead?
And what did *cows* do? Guileless, simple beasts,   120
Devoid of harm and born to bear with toil!
Ingrates, indeed, unworthy of their grain
Are those who, having raised the heavy yoke,
Can slay their ploughmen, on whose work-worn necks—
Which turned the hard soil new so many times,   125
And reaped so many crops—their axes fall!
　　"Nor are such sins enough, but men must share
Their guilt with heaven, convinced the very gods
Rejoice to have their toilsome bullocks slain!

A faultless victim (cursed with fairest form)   130
Stands at the altar, decked with golden bands,
And hears the prayers, and sees, not knowing why,
The grain it grew bestrewn between its horns.
Then with its blood it stains the very knives
It's seen, perhaps, within the sacral pool.[†]   135
Next, from its living breast, they grab its guts
As if to read the mind of heaven—and *this*
(Such is man's hunger for forbidden food)
You dare devour, O mortals! End this, please:
But heed my warning words, and when you taste   140
Your cattle's corpses, be aware you chew
The farmers of your fields.
              "And since heaven moves
My tongue to speak, my tongue shall speak of heaven,
Unveil my Delphi[†] and the sky itself,
And bare their oracles of august will;   145
Of great things, long concealed and never known
To prior minds, I sing! It is a joy
To tread the stars, a joy to leave dull earth,
Reach Atlas' mighty shoulders on a cloud,
And gaze down at the people far below,   150
Who wander witless, dreading what's beyond,
And cheer them with the scroll of fate unfurled:
    "O species held in awe by icy death,
Why fear the Styx, its shades, its hollow names,
The stuff of bards and perils of false worlds?   155
For corpses, be they lost to burning pyres
Or time's decay, feel nothing, as you know.
But souls are deathless; when they leave one home,
A new one's always found to live and dwell.
Myself, I fought at Troy (for I recall)   160
As one Euphorbus, son of Panthoüs,
Whom Atreus' younger son fixed with a spear;
I lately recognized the shield I wore
At Juno's shrine in Argos, Abas' land.[†]
All changes, nothing dies. The spirit roams,   165
Now here, now there, and, to and fro, it takes

What shape it likes, transforms from beast to man,
From us to beast—but never is destroyed;
And, just as wax, which freely takes new forms
That never last or hold the selfsame shape,   170
Stays its same self, so I teach that the soul
Remains the same, though passed through sundry forms.
So, though your stomachs vanquish virtue, I,
As prophet, bid your sinful slaughter cease,
Lest blood should feed on kindred spirits' blood!   175
　　"And while I'm at it, sailing these broad seas,
There's nothing in the whole wide world that lasts.
All is in flux,† each shape's a vagrant form,
And time itself moves on in constant flow,
As rivers do; for rivers cannot stop,   180
Nor can the fleeting hour, but, wave on wave,
Each pushing forward each, each pushing back—
So time both flies and follows, always new,
As what had been is lost and what was not
Becomes and, with each moment, is renewed.   185
You've seen how passing nights stretch into day,
Whose brilliant rays succeed the black of night;
Nor is the sky one hue when all things lie
In midnight rest, when leaves the Morning Star
On his white horse, and when Pallantis³ paints   190
The planet, priming it for Phoebus' light—
His godly shield, too, rises from the depths
A morning-red, and red it plumbs the depths,
But at its height it's white, for there the air
Is purer and the fouling earth is far.   195
Nor stays Diana's nightly orb the same,
But she must ever, one day to the next,
Wax and be more, or less if on the wane.
　　"Why, don't you see the way a year runs through
Four stages, echoing our course of life?   200
Like children, spring is tender, suckling sap—
A newborn; then do fresh and fragile sprouts

3. Dawn

Rise feebly up to feed their farmers' hopes.
All is in bloom and blossoms color all
The fertile fields, though still their fronds are frail.   205
As spring gives way to hearty summertime,
The year grows into youth; no heartier age
Is there than this, no lusher fire of life.
Then autumn falls and youthful flames grow dim;
Mature and mild, between youth and old age,   210
A tempered time when temples streak with grey.
Last, agèd winter comes on shaky steps:
What hair he has is white and falling out.
    "Our bodies, too, are changing without cease,
And what we were or are we shall not be   215
Tomorrow. Once, mere human seeds and hopes,
We hid within our primal mother's womb,
But Nature set her artful hands to free
Our bodies, from their narrow home inside
Our swollen mother, into open air.   220
Thus brought to light, the infant first lies limp,
But soon crawls like a beast upon all fours,
Then—slowly, shaking, still weak at the knees—
Stands upright, braced against some near support.
Grown strong and swift, it spends its time of youth,   225
And, having likewise passed its middle years,
Slides down the sunset slope into old age,
Which saps and spoils the strength of early life.
So wept old Milo, seeing his feeble arms
Which once had bulged with brawn like Hercules'   230
Hang soft and slack;† thus wept Tyndareus' child
To see her agèd wrinkles in the glass
And wonder why she had been stolen twice.†
O jealous Age and you, devouring Time,
You waste all things and gnaw the wreck of life,   235
Consuming all in slow and steady death!
    "Nor do those so-called 'elements' endure—
(Hear me!) I'll teach the turns through which they pass:
The ceaseless cosmos holds four catalysts,
Of which two, earth and water, carry weight   240

And sink beneath their own massivity;
The other two—pure air and purer fire—
Lack gravity and, if unchecked, ascend.
Though far apart in space, each comes from each
And each to each resolves: earth rarefies   245
To water, which the breezes thin to air,
And thinnest air, by losing weight again,
Flares up as heavenly fire. Thence they return,
Unraveled in reverse, as fires condense
To thicker air, which turns to liquid waves,   250
Whose waters clot, congealing into earth.
   "No form remains itself; one yields the next
As Nature, the renewer, makes it new.
Believe me, nothing dies in all the world,
But only takes new shape! What's known as birth   255
Is just the start of not being what one was;
Death, just the end. From here to there and back,
Though things may shift, their total sum is fixed.
   "I hold that nothing keeps one look for long:
So have the Ages gone from Gold to Iron,   260
So often places have reversed their states!
I've seen the sea where once was solid ground,
And seen the ocean waves give rise to land;
Old anchors have been found on mountaintops,
And seashells lying far from any shore;   265
While waterfalls cut valleys out of plains
And floods have washed whole mountains out to sea,
Wet swamplands have dried into desert dunes
And thirsting sands turned moist as stagnant swamps.
Here Nature spouts new springs, there seals them up;   270
And rivers, churned by tremors deep in earth,
Gush forth their flows, or else recede from sight.
Thus is the Lycus swallowed by a gorge
To flow again from new springs far away;
Thus runs great Erasinus underground,   275
To reappear in Argos; Mysus, too,
Ashamed of its headwaters, so they say,
As the "Caïcus" elsewhere laps its banks;

So Amenanus swirls Sicilian sand,
Now flowing fine, now dried up at its source.   280
Once potable, Anigrus' waters now
You dare not touch (if bards may be believed),
Since there the two-formed creatures[4] bathed their wounds
Received from Hercules the Clubman's bow.
Why, don't the streams of Hypanis run sweet   285
From Scythia's slopes, then spoil with bitter salt?
Antissa, Pharos, and Phoenician Tyre,
Once ringed by waves, are islands now no more,
While Leucas, deemed a cape in ancient times,
Now stands mid-ocean. Zancle, too, it's said,   290
Was joined to Italy, till waters wore
The straits away and pushed the land to sea;[†]
And should you seek, you'll find Achaea's towns
Of Helice and Buris 'neath the waves,
Where sailors still point out their sunken walls.   295
    "Near Pitthean Troezen lies a treeless mound,
At one time an expanse of flattest field,
Now a steep mound; for (terrible to tell)
The winds, shut in their sightless cave, went wild
With wishing to breathe free in fairer skies,   300
And vainly strove, inside their seamless cell
Through which no air escaped, to swell the earth
Above them, as one uses breath to blow
Balloons up, or the skins of two-horned goats.
The swelling there remains and seems in shape   305
A lofty hill grown hard with ages past.
    "Though many tales I've heard suggest themselves,
I'll tell but few. Why, don't the waters give
And take new shapes? Horned Ammon, don't your waves,
Though cold at noon, grow warm at dawn and dusk?   310
It's said the Athamanes light their fires
With water poured beneath a crescent moon,[†]
And, as the Cicones have streams whose touch
Makes marble and turns drinkers' guts to stone,

4. Centaurs (cf. 9.191)

The Sybaris and Crathis, on our shores,   315
Dye hair to gold or amber. Stranger still
Are those whose tides are steeped with power to change
Not just the body but the mind as well.
Who has not heard of Salmacis' foul font,
And Aethiopia's lakes, whose draughts induce   320
Insanity, or deep unnatural sleep?
And he who slakes his thirst at Clitor's spring
Enjoys pure water and avoids all wine,
Whether because its waves resist wine's warmth,
Or, as folk tell, since Amythaon's son,[5]   325
His potions having cured the lunacy
Of Proetus' girls, there drained his purging drugs,
From which those waters keep their scorn for drink—
An opposite effect from Lyncus' stream,
Of which the slightest swallow sends a man   330
Careening round, as if he'd drunk straight wine.[†]
Then there's Arcadia's spot (called "Pheneus" once)
Whose wavering waves thou dare not near by night,
Being death when dark, though drinkable by day.
Thus, the assorted sorts of power displayed   335
By lakes and streams.
                    "Though once a floating isle,
Ortygia[6] now stands still. The *Argo* feared
The clashing spray of the Symplegades,
Which now hold firm, unflinching in the wind.[†]
Nor will Mount Aetna's sulfurous smithies' fires   340
Burn always; neither have they always burned.
For either earth's a living breathing being,
Which must exhale its flames at countless points
And shift its airways every time it moves
With tunnels clearing here and closing there,   345
Or else the winds, held fast in cavern depths,
Hurl rock on rock against the seeds of flame,
Whose stricken sides it is that then ignites,

5. Melampus, a legendary seer
6. Delos

And when the winds die out, the caves will cool;
Or if it's pitch that sets the fires alight,   350
Or yellow sulfur burning slight with smoke,
Then, once the fertile earth no longer feeds
The flames with fuel, their age-old strength will fade
Till famished Nature faints for want of food
And, to escape starvation, starves her fires.   355
And there's Pallene's Hyperborean men,
Whose frames are said to fledge with feathered down
On having bathed nine times in Triton's marsh;†
Of this I'm unconvinced, though Scythian maids
Are said to do the same with magic balms.   360
    "Yet, if the tested truth deserves our trust,
Have you not seen how heat and time dissolve
A rotting corpse to tiny animals?
Just bury slaughtered bulls down in a ditch
And their decaying guts (as is well-known)   365
Will bring forth bumblebees who roam the fields
In toilsome hope, just as their parents did.†
Thus warhorses birth hornets in their graves,
And if you clip a shore crab's hollow claws
And plant the rest, up from the buried part   370
Will rise a scorpion, tail poised to strike;
And in the fields (as farmers often find)
The leaves are hung with woven white cocoons,
Where larvae change to tombstone butterflies.†
In mud, the seeds that generate green frogs   375
First generate their torsos free of feet,
Next swimmers' legs, then ones to make long leaps,
With those behind outstretching those in front.
When she-bears bear a cub, it's a mere lump,
Scarce living till its mother's licking tongue   380
Has formed and framed its body like her own.
And have you not seen waxen hexagons
Where honeybees are born without their limbs,
With legs grown late and wings still later yet?
Take Juno's fowl whose tail is set with stars,   385
Jove's lightning-squire, the Cytherean's doves,

And every kind of bird—who would believe,
Had they not known, that all were born from eggs?
Some also think that when our spines decay,
The human marrow turns into a snake.   390
　　"All these arise from others, but one being
Respawns and sires itself—the phoenix bird,
As Syrians say, which eats no grain nor grass
But lives on incense drops and cardamom.
When it has passed five centuries of life,   395
It plies its claws and spotless beak to build
A nest atop an oak or waving palm,
There lining it with spikes of softest nard,
And cassia bark, crushed cinnamon, and myrrh,
Where, perched amid perfumes, it ends its days.   400
They say then, from its father's corpse reborn,
The phoenix child repeats his length of life,
And, once age lends it strength to carry loads,
Relieves the treetop of its heavy nest,
And duly flies its crib and father's grave   405
Into the town that bears Hyperion's name[7]
And sets it down before Hyperion's shrine.
　　"But if these things are wondrous, strange, and new,
The switch through which a female, mounted by
A male, in turn becomes a male herself   410
Might make us wonder at hyenas, too!
And there's that creature, fed on wind and air,
That takes on any color at a touch;
Vine-bearing Bacchus won from vanquished Ind
Its lynxes, from whose bladders all that falls   415
Turns into stone, they say, on touching air;
And coral, too, on contact with the breeze,
Grows hard, though soft as grass beneath the waves.
　　"Day will be done and Phoebus' panting steeds
Will swim the seas before I've put in words   420
All things that take new shape. We've seen times change
And nations rise in strength while others fall;

---

7. Heliopolis ("Sun City") in Egypt

Though once so powerful in men and means
It ably bore ten years of bleeding war,
Since-humbled Troy has only aging ruins   425
And ancient graves to show for its old wealth.
Yet now the rumor runs that Dardan Rome,   432[†]
Along the Tiber's Apennine-born waves,
Lays her foundations for a massive feat:
She'll change through growth to someday lead the world—   435
So prophets say and oracles foretell!
    "For I remember,[†] when Troy was to fall,
That Helenus, king Priam's son, informed
Aeneas as he mourned his doubtful state,
'O goddess' son, heed well the sooth I say   440
And, with you safe, Troy will not wholly fall,
But, spared by flame and sword, will come with you
To lands more kind to you and Troy than yours.
I see a city of your Phrygian heirs,
Unlike all that have been, are, or shall be!   445
In time, though many men will make her great,
It's Iulus' heir[†] who'll crown her queen of earth,
And when this world is done with him, the skies
Shall praise him in his final heavenly home!'
Thus was Aeneas, household gods in hand,   450
Forewarned by Helenus. This I recall,
Rejoicing that my kindred walls now rise
And Phrygians gain from their Pelasgian loss.
    "But lest my horses stray too far off track,
The sky, the earth, and all between change form!   455
Being more than flesh, we too are of this world,
And since our wingèd souls can live alike
In breasts of feral beasts and farmyard flocks,
Whose bodies might have held our parents' souls,
Our brothers, or some kith or kin of ours,   460
Let's treat them with respect and keep them safe,
Lest we should gobble down Thyestean feasts![†]
How used to wrong, how faithless and prepared
To spill men's blood is he who slaughters calves
And shuts his ears against their moving moos,   465

Or who can slit the throats of baby goats
Despite their childlike cries, or feed upon
A fowl he's fed himself! How far does this
Fall short of utmost crime? Where does it lead?
Let cattle plough and let them die from age!   470
Let sheep shield us from frigid Boreas!
Let nanny-goats give udderfuls of milk!
But lose your nets and snares and hunter's tricks;
Don't use a birdlimed branch to trap a bird,
Don't feather ropes to scare deluded deer,†   475
Don't hide a barb-tipped hook in bluffing bait.
Kill what would harm, but do no more than kill,
And feed yourselves on kinder, bloodless fare!"

[EGERIA AND HIPPOLYTUS]†

With just such teachings borne in mind, they say,
Did Numa journey home. There, he gave in   480
And gladly took the reins of Latium's tribes.
With the Camenae and his naiad wife,[8]
He shared his blessings with his warlike race
And taught them sacral rites† and peacetime's ways.
When Numa died, his life and reign complete,   485
As Latium's elders, men, and maidens mourned,
His widow fled the town and hid within
Aricia's woodland vale, where her laments
Disturbed Orestean Diana's rites.†
How many times those nymphs of woods and lakes   490
Warned her to cease and tried to comfort her!
How often Theseus' heroic son
Said as she wept, "Stop that! Your fate is not
Yours only—think of those who've shared your lot
And yours will lighten. Would I had some case   495
But mine to comfort you. . . . Still, mine will do!
    "If you've heard of Hippolytus, who died
Through stepmother's deceit and father's trust,

---

8. Egeria

I'll scarce subdue your shock that I am he.
That daughter of Pasiphaë† once tried   500
To lure me to defile my father's bed,
Then charged me with the wish she wished herself.
(Did she fear being found out, or was it spite?)
My sire condemned me, drove me from the town,
And cursed my guiltless head in banishment.   505
So I turned wheels toward Troezen, Pittheus' realm,
But as I passed the Gulf of Corinth by,
The sea rose in a massive mound of waves,
Curved like a mountain, then appeared to surge,
To roar, and, at its highest point, to split,   510
And, through the ruptured swells, there burst a bull,
Its breast and horns reared high into the air,
Brine gushing from its nose and gaping mouth.
Though terror seized my men, I stayed composed,
Thoughts fixed on exile; but my four-foot fiends   515
Stared out to sea, ears pricked and stiff with fear
Of that strange monster till, in disarray,
They dragged the chariot down the rocky cliffs!
Bent down and straining at the foam-flecked reins,
I vainly strove to pull the bridle back,   520
And might have checked the horses' frenzied strength,
Had not an axle, whence the wheel revolved,
Been struck against a stump and wrenched apart!
Thrown from the car but tangled in the reins,
My entrails trailing but my sinews caught,   525
Part of me dragged away while part remained:
Thus you'd have seen me, snapping in my bones
And gasping out my soul—but there was naught
To know me by, for all was one great wound.†
　　"Now would you, could you still compare your griefs   530
With mine, O nymph? I've seen the lightless realms,
Bathed my maimed body in the Phlegethon,⁹

---

9. One of the rivers of the underworld

FIGURE 11. Still from "Miscellaneous Myths: Hippolytus," *Overly Sarcastic Productions* (2019). Largely focusing on folklore and ancient history, the educational YouTube channel *Overly Sarcastic Productions* has cultivated a multimillion-subscriber audience with its wit, analysis, and artistic style. Many of their most viral videos deal with classical myth, often breaking down the history of a story, with Ovid's influence looming large. The video shown here has some two million views.

And still would be there, had Apollo's child[10]
Not resurrected me with tonic power.
Once healed by Paean's herbs—to Dis' dismay—   535
I sought, for safety, to slip by unseen,
Lest I stir envy with my gift of life.
So Cynthia hid me in heavy clouds
And aged my face past recognition's range.
First doubting long if I should live on Crete   540
Or Delos, she passed Crete and Delos by,
And dropped me here, then bid me drop my name,
Which smacked of horses, saying, 'Thou who wast
Hippolytus shalt now be Virbius!'[†]
Since then, a minor god dwarfed by her power,   545
I've worshiped her, here in my lady's grove."
    But stranger's loss could not console her grief,
And there, beneath the slope, Egeria's tears

10. Aesculapius, the healer god last seen as a newborn at 2.629ff

Dissolved her. Phoebe, seeing her faithful woe,
Was moved to make a cold spring of her corpse,   550
And thinned her limbs to everlasting waves.[†]

[CIPUS][†]

    This wonder touched the nymphs as well and left
The Amazonian son[11] no less amazed
Than the Tyrrhene who'd ploughed his field and found
A fateful clod—which first moved on its own,   555
Then shed its soil to take on human form
And speak with new-made lips of things to come
(Called "Tages" by the locals, he first taught
Etruscans how the future may be seen);
Or Romulus upon the Palatine,   560
Who saw the spear he'd planted there sprout leaves
And stand on new-grown roots in place of iron,
No more a weapon but a lithe young tree
Provoking awe with unexpected shade;
Or Cipus when he saw (and saw for real)   565
His horns within in a stream. Convinced they must
Be some mirage, he touched and touched his brow,
Then, feeling what he'd seen, blamed sight no more,
But, like a victor from the vanquished foe,
Raised eyes and arms on high and cried, "O gods,   570
To whom pertains this portent? Let it be
Quirinus' race and realm if it bodes well.
If ill, though, make it mine!" Then, heaping sod
Into an altar burning sweet perfumes,
He offered wine and sacrificed a sheep,   575
Then probed its quaking entrails for a sign
Till a Tyrrhene diviner took one look
And saw great things in motion, though obscure;
But when his keen eyes left the bowels and lit
On Cipus' horns, he cried, "Hail to the king!   580

---

11. Hippolytus, son of queen Hippolyta of the Amazons

For it's you, Cipus—yes, you and your horns
This land and Latium's citadels shall serve.
But don't delay! Her gates stand wide—make haste!
Thus fate decrees: once in the City's bounds,
You'll wield your kingly scepter safe and long!"   585
But he recoiled, turned from the City walls,
And grimly said, "May heaven keep all such signs
Far, far from me. Much better I should live
In exile than as Capitoline king!"†
Then, summoning stern senators and crowds,   590
He hid his horns with peaceful laurel leaves,
And, climbing up the mound his men had made,
Called on the gods with ancient prayers and cried:
"One man is here who will be king unless
You drive him from the city. Who he is   595
I'll show by sign, not name: his head is horned!
Should he reach Rome, it's augured, you'll be slaves—
And he'd have breached the open gates, had I
Not stopped him, though none's close to him as I.
O ban him from the City, Quirites!   600
Or chain him, if he's earned it, or else end
The fateful tyrant's danger through his death!"
At this, a murmuring such as is made
When raging Eurus runs through bare-trunked pines,
Or when the crash of waves is heard afar,   605
Rose from the crowd, but through their mess of noise,
One cry stood out—"Who is he?"—and they scanned
Their foreheads for the horns they'd heard foretold,
Till Cipus added, "You have him you seek!"
And fought the crowd to doff his laurel crown,   610
Revealing the twin horns that marked his brow.
All groaned with downcast gazes, loath to see
(Who'd think it true?) that justly famous head
At all dishonored. Soon a festal crown
Was brought you, Cipus; and, since you'd be kept   615
Outside the walls, the elders honored you
With all the land your team could plough around

From dawn till close of day. As for the horns,
The wonder of their beauty was engraved
In gates of bronze, for ages to remain.   620

[AESCULAPIUS]†

Reveal now, Muses,† you whose heavenly powers
Grace poets (for you know and don't forget
With passing time) how did that island, ringed
By Tiber's swirling depths, come to receive
Coronis' son among the gods of Rome!   625
    An evil plague once tainted Latium's air,
Which scourged the body, draining it of blood.
Grown tired of tombs and seeing that human toil
Was useless—useless as the doctors' arts—
Men went to Delphi, center of the world,   630
To seek heaven's help through Phoebus' oracle,
And begged a healing answer to assuage
Their sufferings and end the city's woes.
Then laurel, shrine, and godly quiver[12] all
Began to shake, as from the sanctum rang   635
The tripod's voice in these heartrending words:
"You're seeking here what should be sought back home!
Now, Roman, back at home seek help for pain,
Not through Apollo, but Apollo's child:
Good omens go with you—send for my son!"   640
    The Senate shrewdly heard the god's commands,
And, having learned where lived the Phoebean youth,
To Epidaurus sailed their envoys' ships.
Their curving keels scarce touched those shores before
They'd begged the Grecian council for the god   645
Whose presence would prevent Ausonia's race
From dying, as the oracle declared.
The elders were divided; some opposed
Withholding aid, but many spoke against
Losing their deity and source of wealth.   650

12. i.e., the quiver on the shrine's cult statue of Apollo

And while they sat there, twilight's shades drove forth
The day's last light, and darkness fell on earth.
Then, in a dream, O Roman,[13] by your bed
The healer-god arose as he appears
In temples—one hand round his rustic rod,[†]   655
The other running through his flowing beard
And uttered these heartwarming words: "Fear not!
I'll leave my statue here and come with you,
But note this snake entwined about my rod
And mark it so, when I assume its form,   660
You know me by its shape, though I shall be
Of larger size, more fit for heavenly frames."
With that, both god and voice and, with god's voice,
Sleep fled; and, on sleep's heels, came kindly day.

    Once Dawn had put the fiery stars to flight,   665
The leaders, still uncertain, met before
The splendid temple of the longed-for god
To seek some sign of where he would abide.
Scarce had they spoken when the golden god
Came forward, hissing, as a crested snake.   670
At his approach, the statues, altars, doors,
And marble floor and golden gables shook
Till there, amid the shrine, he stood chest-high,
Eyes flashing flame. All quaked with fear except
One priest, his holy hair in bands of white,   675
Who recognized the deity and said,
"Behold the god—*the god!* With mind and voice,
Let all give praise! O fair one, may this sight
Bring favor and leave all your faithful blessed!"
Then all gave praise unto the present power,   680
And, parroting the priest, were bolstered by
The pious Aeneads[14] in thought and speech.
The god pledged his assent with swaying crest
And steady hisses of his flicking tongue,
Then, sliding down the temple's shining steps,   685

13. One of the envoys
14. The Romans, descendants of Aeneas

He gave the ancient altars one last glance,
And bid his home and native shrine farewell.
Next, out across the ground bestrewn with flowers,
The giant serpent snaked and coiled through town.
Then, halting at the harbor's curving piers,   690
His gentle gaze seemed to dismiss the throng
That followed him, and all his faithful band,
Before he boarded the Ausonian ship
Whose hull dipped low beneath his godly load.

    The Aeneads, rejoicing, slew a bull   695
And cast their flower-decked vessel off from shore.
As breezes blew the ship, the god reared high
And braced his neck against the back-bent stern,
Surveying the Ionian's sea-blue waves,
Where Zephyr whisked them till, for the sixth time,   700
Pallantis rose and they reached Italy.
They passed Lacinium and its goddess' shrine,[†]
Iapygia, Scylaceum, countless crags—
Amphrisia's on the left, Celennia's right—
Romethium, Caulon, Naryx, Sicily,   705
The straits of Cape Pelorus, Hippotes'
Son's royal halls, and Tempsa's mines, then sought
Leucosia and warm Paestum's beds of rose.
Next, rounding Capri and Minerva's cape,
Vine-rich Surrentum, Herculaneum,   710
Parthenope's resorts, and Stabiae,
They sailed by the Cumaean Sibyl's shrine,
Those thermal springs, Liternum's mastic groves,
Volturnus' sandy swirl, Minturnae's marsh,
By Sinuessa, rife with snow-white doves,   715
The land where lay its namesake nurse's tomb,
Antiphates' dominion, Trachas' swamps,
And Circe's realm, for Antium's stiff strand,
To which the sailors turned their ships full-sail
(The sea being stormy), whereupon the god   720
Unfurled his coils and slithered down the shore
To his sire's temple. Once the waves had calmed,
The Epidaurian left his father's shrine,

Where he'd enjoyed his stay as kindred god,
Ploughed down the shore, scales rustling, climbed the stern,   725
And leaned his head against the ship's high deck
Till Castrum's port, Lavinium's sacred sites,
And Ostia, the Tiber's mouth, were reached.
There, all the people thronged—husbands and wives,
And, Trojan Vesta, they who tend your flame†—   730
To meet and hail the god with shouts of joy!
And as the ship sailed swiftly up the stream,
Great incense fumes and fires were smelt and heard
From rows of altars built on both its banks,
While knives grew warm with victims' sacrifice.   735
    Now, reaching Rome, the whole world's capital,
The snake stretched up the ship-mast, spinning round
And searching for a seat to suit himself.
The circling river there divides in two
And runs in equal arms around the land   740
(Known as "the Island")† lying in between;
There, Phoebus' serpent left the Latin craft,
Resumed the features of the healer god,
And brought the City's sorrows to an end.

[THE APOTHEOSIS OF JULIUS CAESAR]†

    While this god came a stranger to our shrines,   745
In his own city, Caesar is divine!
Though first in war and peace, no victory,
Domestic feat, or glory quickly won
Made him a comet† fixed among the stars:
It was his child!—for nothing Caesar did   750
Was greater than to father such a son.†
For what is having tamed the Britons' seas,
Sailed up the seven-mouthed papyral Nile
In triumph, swelled Quirinus' people with
Numidian rebels, Juba's Libyans,   755
And Pontians puffed with Mithridatic pride,
And done much else—all worthy, winning deeds—
To siring such a man, whose worldwide rule

Is your great gift, O gods, to humankind?
   Then, lest the son should spring from mortal seed,   760
The sire must be made god! When this she saw,
Aeneas' golden mother—also seeing
A plot prepared to murder her high priest†—
Went pale and cried to every god she met:
"Behold what treason's heaped upon my head,   765
What schemes are laid against the only life
That's left me from Dardanian Iulus' line![15]
Must I alone be always wracked with cares?
Struck by Tydides' Calydonian spear[16]
And in despair for Troy's ill-guarded walls,   770
I saw my son forced first to roam for years
On tossing tides and through the silent realms,
Then battle Turnus—or, if truth be told,
With Juno! But why now recall the woes
That one time wracked my house? Fresh fear forbids   775
Remembrance: watch them whet their sinful swords!
I beg you, stop them and prevent this crime—
Don't let his priestly blood douse Vesta's flames!"
   In vain did Venus fling such fretful cries
Through all of heaven; no god, though all were moved,   780
Could break the ancient Sisters'[17] laws of iron.
Instead, they gave sure signs of coming grief:
They say that, in the storm-clouds, clashing arms
And terrifying trumpet horns were heard
Foretelling evil; that the sun felt gloom   785
And cast the troubled lands in lurid light;
That brands were witnessed burning in the stars;
That clouds rained clotted gore; that rust stained black
The Morning Star's blue face, and bloodstains flecked
The chariot of the Moon. The Stygian owl   790
Warned thousands of their woe, and thousands more
Saw statues weep. They say that chants and threats

---

15. The Caesars traced their descent from Iulus (cf. 447)
16. That is, the spear of Diomedes (cf. 14.477–78)
17. The Fates

Filled sacred groves, and every sacrifice
Portended ill—the liver's severed lobe
Found in the entrails, boding great unrest.   795
And round the squares and homes and holy shrines,
They say hounds howled by night and silent shades
Roamed free, while earthquakes rocked the City streets.
    But heavenly omens could not hinder fate
Nor sheathe the traitors' swords on temple grounds—   800
For out of all the City they saw fit
To stage their murder in the *Curia!*†
Then did the Cytherean beat her breast
And strive to hide Aeneas' heir in clouds,
As she'd saved Paris once from Atreus' son—   805
Aeneas, too, from Diomedes' blades.†
Then said her sire, "Shall you alone, my child,
Shift all-unchanging Fate? Inside the house
Of those Three Sisters, you may see the mass
Of cosmic records, wrought in bronze and iron,   810
Which fear no war in heaven, nor lightning's wrath,
Nor any harm, but stand forever safe.
There, etched in timeless adamant, you'll find
Your family's fate, which I have read, recall,
And shall relate, so you know what's to come: 815
    "O Cytherea, he for whom you strive
Has done his time on earth, but he'll reach heaven,
And in his shrines be worshiped as a god
Through your hand and his son's, heir to his name,
Who'll bear the burden placed on him alone   820
And, with our aid, avenge his sire in war!†
At his command will Mutina be sieged
And sue for peace, Pharsalia feel his power,
Emathian Philippi drip blood once more,
A great name crumble in Sicilian seas,   825
And the Egyptian wife, her faith ill-wed
To Rome's commander, fall and fail to bind
Our Capitol as her Canopus'[18] slave.

18. A notoriously debauched Egyptian city

Why should I count the savage tribes that line
The Ocean's sides? Whatever land bears life   830
Shall be his realm, and every sea his slave!
With peace on earth, he'll turn to civil rights
And give his citizens the fairest laws,
Teach by example to conduct oneself,
And, looking forward to posterity,   835
Command the son born to his saintly wife
To shoulder both his duties and his name.
Nor, till he match the ancient Pylian's age,†
Shall he reach heaven and join his kindred stars.
But first go bring the slain man's soul on high,   840
That Julius the God may always gaze
Upon the Forum and my Capitol!"19
    This scarce was said when kindly Venus reached
The Senate-House unseen, caught up the soul
Released from Caesar's corpse, and whisked it off,   845
Before it could dissolve, to join the stars.
But while she did, she felt it glow and warm—
And let it go to mount beyond the moon
And stretch its flaming tail! Now as a star
He shines and, seeing his son's feats, owns that they   850
Exceed his own and cheers at being surpassed!
Though he denies his deeds outrank his sire's,
Free Fame heeds none and spites his will this once
To rank him so. Great Atreus thus gave way
To Agamemnon; Aegeus, Theseus;   855
And Peleus, Achilles. My last case
Befits them both: thus Saturn yields to Jove!
As Jove rules heaven and all the threefold world,
Augustus leads the earth as lord and sire.
O gods who spared Aeneas flame and sword!   860
O City's sire, Quirinus! Indiges!
Gradivus, conquering Quirinus' sire!
O Vesta, blessed as Caesar's household god,
And, near to Caesar's Vesta, Phoebus, thou;

19. The Capitoline Hill, site of the Temple of Jupiter Optimus Maximus

And Jupiter on high Tarpeia's rock![†]   865
And all to whom a pious bard must pray—
Let that day be not soon but past our age
When lord Augustus leaves the world he rules
To enter heaven and hear our prayers afar!

[EPILOGUE][†]

AND NOW, my work is done, which neither Jove   870
Nor flame nor sword nor gnawing time can fade.
That day, which governs only my poor frame,
May come at will to end my unfixed life,
But in my better and immortal part
I shall be borne beyond the lofty stars   875
And never will my name be washed away!
Where Roman power prevails, I shall be read;
And so, in fame and on through every age
(If bards foretell the truth at all)—I'll live.[†]

Commentary

The line numbers in this commentary refer to the numbering of the translation, which varies from that in the Latin slightly and occasionally. Subheadings are used for ease of navigation and interpretation.

BOOK 1

Prologue (1–5)

Ovid begins with a short prologue that states the theme and scope of his poem while calling on unspecified gods for help in writing it. Unlike conventional epics, which focus on the feats of gods and heroes in a contained setting, the *Metamorphoses* will range across the entirety of time and space in pursuit of the theme of transformation, which it presents as the sole obvious, if ambiguous, through-line to be found in tales of classical mythology. The prologue also establishes the narrator as an external presence in the poem, an idea Ovid will return to with his concluding epilogue in Book 15.

1   *Of new:* The opening word of an epic poem often gives some hint as to the work's theme—Homer's *Iliad* ("rage") and Virgil's *Aeneid* ("war") are prime examples. Ovid wastes no time showing his irreverent side and begins instead on a preposition, postponing the all-important *new* to second place. This also keeps the word order of the first sentence meaningfully murky; unscrambled, it would read,

"My mind moves to speak of shapes transformed into new bodies."

2–3 *O gods (for you have shaped / These matters, too):* Older editions hold the gods responsible for all transformations, but scholars now believe *these matters* instead refers to the work itself (see appendix). This would mean that the gods have transformed Ovid's poetry, a reading supported by the prologue's resonance with the opening of Ovid's earlier *Amores,* which tells how Cupid forced the poet to write in elegiac meter by stealing the ends of his lines. Also remarkable is Ovid's characterization of the relationship between the poet and his divine inspirer. Whereas early Greek poets portrayed themselves as mere vessels through whom the Muses sang, Ovid clearly claims the mental initiative for both his work (*my mind*) and its commencement (*what I've begun*), while still calling on the gods to shape it.

5   *our times:* Published in 8 CE, the *Metamorphoses'* implied temporal and geographical viewpoint is the Rome of Emperor Augustus. In addition to making the work ripe for political interpretation, the specifically yet subtly Roman focus of the writer and his intended audience underpins many of the poem's moral assertions, literary devices, and authorial intrusions.

unbroken song: Besides the verbal nicety of ending on *song* (in Latin, the same word as "poem," reflecting the oral origins of poetry), the prologue concludes with something of a paradox, as the narrator's stated aim of a single continuous work contrasts with both the sheer immensity of his undertaking and its nature as a collection of essentially disparate stories.

The First Creation (6–89)

As promised in the prologue, Ovid starts with the creation of the universe. His account combines elements from older philosophical narratives, like that found in Lucretius' *On the Nature of Things,* with mythological ones, like Hesiod's *Theogony,* but is beholden to neither. From the philosophers, he borrows the formation from chaos of a cosmic balance between opposing forces, but although he subordinates the process to a divine maker, this creator's presence is minimized and his identity kept as vague as possible. The episode's supposed climax, the origin of humanity, is similarly murky, setting up the poem's uneasy tension between the world and the mortals who inhabit it.

7   *nature bore one face:* Ovid subscribes to the classical theory that sees physics as a series of reactions among four elements of decreasing weight: earth, water, air, and fire. In this primordial state of Chaos, however, the undifferentiated elements present a unified appearance, or *face*. Though unelaborated, this personifying metaphor foreshadows the poem's world of nymphs and spirits, one where sentient power may be found lurking inside every rock or tree.

11–14   *No Titan . . . embraced her banks:* To contrast with his present and underline the lack of individuated entities, Ovid starts several lines running with a negative word, even as he refers to the sun (Titan), moon (Phoebe), and sea (Amphitrite) by the names of gods who have yet to possess them. The name "Titan" will be used throughout the poem to refer to the god of the sun, though often while conflating him with Phoebus Apollo, who was not a Titan at all (see note to 2.23).

21   *A god and better nature:* Whether "better nature" is the god or a separate entity is kept ambiguous. Although fulfilling a similar function, this god should not be conflated with Judeo-Christian notions of a God or Maker. As becomes clear in line 33, the creator's identity will remain meaningfully unknown, ceding center stage to creation itself. The gods usually signified by the word do not appear until line 74.

46ff   *And, as two regions on both left and right . . . :* In this ancient model, earth and heaven are both divided into five climatic zones, comprising two polar regions of inhospitable cold, an equatorial region of inhospitable heat (the tropics), and two temperate zones in between. Ovid borrows this picture from Virgil's *Georgics* (1.231–

58), but the concept itself was often traced back to the philosopher-mathematician Pythagoras, whose speech in Book 15 will rehash much of this creation narrative.

62–67   *Arabian lands of dawn . . . Auster's hand:* A geography with Arabia and Persia to the east and the Black Sea region of Scythia to the north is one that takes the Greco-Roman world for its center.

68–69   *aether . . . earthly trace:* A fifth element of which the heavens are made, theorized by Plato and Aristotle. Unlike the baser four, aether was incorruptible and incapable of change.

77ff   *But still there lacked . . . :* While the appearance of gods occupies half a line, that of humans is a major event, heralded by the assertion that humanity is holier and fitter to rule than divinity—a blasphemy not contradicted by the conduct of the poem's gods. On this topic, however, Ovid is especially slippery. His bald announcement *"the human race was born"* (79) might be profound in its simplicity or just anticlimactic, and he not only refuses to favor either of the two origin stories told here, he provides several others throughout the poem (1.157ff, 1.401ff, and the especially strange 7.392–93). The fundamental question of where people come from goes neither unaddressed nor unanswered, yet remains wholly unresolved.

The Ages of Man (90–150)

First appearing in Hesiod's seventh century BCE *Works and Days,* the Ages of Man is a mythic framework narrating the devolution of humans from a state of innocent paradise through successively degraded generations of Gold, Silver, Bronze, and Iron. Still playing fast and loose with convention, Ovid adopts this model but undermines it with details culled from Lucretius, who instead presented early humans as primitives on an ascending path to civilization. Civilization, however, has its discontents, and many read the brutal anarchy of Ovid's Iron Age as an echo of Rome's recent civil wars.

104–6   *bitter strawberries . . . tree:* In a subversive gesture, Ovid undercuts the picture of bounteous felicity he has just painted to describe a nasty barebones diet borrowed from Lucretius, implying that—by modern standards— the Golden Age may not have been so great after all. (A similar point is made with regard to housing in lines 121–22.) Since Virgil had heralded the reign of Augustus as a return of the Golden Age, this move may be read as politically subversive. At the least, it warns readers against identifying too closely with the mythic past. *Jove's wide-spreading tree* is the oak, so called after the grove of prophetic oaks at the Oracle of Jupiter at Dodona (in Latin, Jove and Jupiter are forms of the same name). This is the poem's first mention of the king of the gods, and the unappetizing acorn makes for a particularly unimpressive introduction.

113–14   *Once Saturn was dispatched . . . Jove made king:* The Golden Age was also known as the reign of Saturn, a Roman god of agriculture who had become identified with the much crueler Greek Titan Cronus, best known for eating his children. In a war between generations, the gods overthrew their Titan parents and imprisoned Cronus/Saturn in the underworld, whereupon Jupiter assumed rule of the universe.

150   *the maid Astraea:* Astraea was the divine personification of justice. After finally quitting the earth, she joined her fellow gods in heaven as the constellation Virgo ("the maiden").

The Gigantomachy (151–62)

A favorite theme in older art, the war with the Giants (or "Gigantomachy") was by Ovid's time considered too coarse for sophisticated modern tastes. Ovid himself once joked that trying to write an epic on the subject had cost him a girlfriend (*Amores* 2.1.11ff). This may explain the brevity of his rendition, but it lends additional interest to his positing the Giants as another possible source of the human race.

152 *They say:* Ovid often uses such phrases, known as "Alexandrian footnotes," either to question the credibility of a story or, as in this case, to distance himself from its narration. The feeling here must be especially keen since he uses the phrase again at 158.

157 *Mother Earth:* A comparable idiom exists in Latin ("*Tellus Mater*"), but in contrast to the modern view of a benevolent nature goddess, the Greco-Roman Earth was a mother of monsters (see 434–38). The term Giants (or *Gigantes*) means "earth-born" in Greek.

Lycaön (163–239)

The story of the cannibal king Lycaön of Arcadia marks not only the poem's first tale of human metamorphosis but also its first instance of an internal secondary narrator, with most of the story told by Jupiter himself. As a result, it immediately raises questions of narrative viewpoint and reliability. Lycaön's extreme cruelty is an Ovidian innovation not found in earlier versions, but with only a wrathful god to attest to it, what are we to believe?

167ff *He called a council:* The council of the gods is a familiar set piece of epic poetry but is usually convened to render help to a suffering hero. Ovid's council will instead vote to destroy humanity. Consequently, the poet's cheekily flattering depiction of heaven's government as comprising patricians, plebeians, and a Palatine palace mirroring the social structure of Rome masks a deeply subversive implication.

174 *household gods:* Penates, the guardian gods of Roman households, were often employed as a poetic metonym for homes. Ovid amusingly stretches the image to absurdity, portraying the gods as cherishing household gods of their own.

188–89 *this I swear, / Upon the . . . Stygian groves:* As seen several times in the poem, an oath sworn by the river Styx was unbreakable. Jupiter will swear another one at 1.737.

202   *with Caesar's blood:* The allusion is disputed. Ovid may
refer either to the assassination of Julius Caesar in 44
BCE, or to any number of attempts that had been made
on the life of Augustus Caesar, directly addressed at 205.
The ambiguity is perhaps intentional.

237   *some signs of old remain:* Since the name Lycaön takes
after the Greek word for wolf (*lykos*), the transformation
carries a sense of continuity bordering on the inevitable:
Lycaön becomes the wolf he always was inside. Many
metamorphoses to come will allow for similar inferences,
but the moralizing aspect of this one should be read in
light of its inherently biased source. The second half of
Book 1, with Ovid back in the narrator's seat, will detail
transformations that result from divine rapes perpetrated
by Jupiter and others. In those cases, the reader will find
no such justification.

The Deluge (240–312)

This deluge follows the familiar format: a wrathful god drowns
humanity for its sins, with one or two devout exceptions—comparisons to the Biblical Noah and the Mesopotamian Utnapishtim are
inevitable. Ovid's version, however, is notably lacking in pathos, and
focuses mainly on humorous "opposite day" descriptions of land
underwater. This is the viewpoint of the immortals, who here join
forces to eradicate all landed life.

241   *the Furies:* Better known in their later moralizing role
punishing murderers of family members, for most of this
poem the Furies are simply demons of wholesale discord.

256–58   *a day was prophesied:* Long before Robert Frost, Stoic
philosophers already espoused the belief that the universe
was periodically consumed by fire. Co-opting their
prophecy, Ovid words it so as to prefigure the world's
near-destruction at the hands of Phaëthon in Book 2.

262–64   *Aeolus . . . Aquilo . . . Notus:* Aeolus was the Homeric
Keeper of the Winds, whom we met during the creation.
Evidenced as early as line 11, Ovid was an avid practitioner

of antonomasia, the poetic use of epithets, monikers, and aliases to refer to characters and locations, instead of their normal names. In addition to displaying the author's erudition, antonomasia can be used to sow suspense (see note to 1.673–77) or intentional confusion, particularly when depicting the chaos of battle. Accordingly, the North and South Winds, introduced as "Boreas" and "Auster" at 1.65–67, are here called Aquilo and Notus.

277   *This is no time . . . to give a speech:* Neptune violates convention by dispensing with the expected pre-battle pep talk, indicating a cruelty comparable to his brother's. Note that this scene takes the form of a second council of gods.

Deucalion and Pyrrha (313–415)

For all the rivers' thoroughness, one human couple is left alive: Deucalion, son of Prometheus, and his cousin-wife Pyrrha, daughter of Epimetheus. In this passage, Ovid works hard to deprive Jupiter of any sympathetic qualities. The pair's undeniable piety vitiates Jove's claims that humanity is uniformly depraved, and the role of oracular restorer, played by Jupiter in previous versions of the myth, is reassigned to Themis.

317   *Parnassus:* This story takes place on the slopes of Mount Parnassus, in and around Delphi, site of the Greek world's most famous oracle. In addition to the Delphic temple itself, Deucalion and Pyrrha will visit the Corycian cave and the Castalian Spring, whose waters were mythically connected to the Cephisus river. All these sites were typically associated with Apollo, though at the early date described in the story he had yet to assume their patronage.

378–79   *Tell us, Themis, how . . . restored:* If Deucalion and Pyrrha appeared dimwitted before, their ignorance of where children come from would seem to confirm appearances.

400ff   *who'd believe but on the ancients' word:* Playing on Romans' trademark reverence for tradition, Ovid is of course being sarcastic. This will be the fourth human creation story proffered in the poem, with lines 1.414–15 mirroring 1.162 in the previous one.

The Second Creation: Python (416–52)

After briefly sketching the rebirth of animal life as a series of spontaneous creations without need of a divine agent, Ovid just as briefly shades in the picture with a cosmological digression that echoes the primordial Chaos described at the book's outset. Mythology returns soon enough, however, as philosophy mercifully gives way to an enormous snake. The reptile's death at the hands of Apollo will finally transition the poem out of its narratives of creation.

422ff   *when the seven-channeled Nile*: To illustrate the process, Ovid gives the example of the Nile (which splits in seven at its delta), whose regular, predictable, and benevolent floods struck the ancients as miraculous and lifegiving.

442   *archer-god*: This is Phoebus Apollo, god of archery, music, and prophecy (among other things). Delaying the name-drop until the right moment—or indefinitely—is among Ovid's favorite tricks, so the god is not identified until 1.451. Also typical is the lack of introduction. As the poem abandons all but the broadest sense of chronology, tales will transition across wide expanses of time, with characters rapidly appearing and disappearing from the story. The birth of Apollo will not be narrated until Book 6, where it is told twice (6.186–91, 332–36).

447   *Pythian games*: Like the Olympics, the Pythian games were one of the four great Panhellenic ("all-Greek") tournaments, though it featured competitions in art and music as well as athletics, befitting its association with Apollo. Ovid unexpectedly glosses over this myth's connection to Delphi, where the games were held outside the temple of Apollo's famous oracle. The Python's death was typically portrayed as the founding incident for both the games and the oracle, whose high priestess was known as the "Pythia," but we have already seen the oracle in action under the auspices of Themis.

Apollo and Daphne (453–567)

Apollo's attempted rape of the nymph Daphne is the first of the poem's dozens of scenes of sexual assault, some nineteen of which are treated at length. Whole books have been written on interpretive approaches to rape in Ovid, yet the subject is still too often met either with relativist dismissal or with simple handwringing that fails to earnestly engage with a topic so central to the epic and so disturbing to read. The Daphne episode in particular has historically attracted far more attention for its aesthetic qualities—in part owing, no doubt, to Bernini's famous statue (fig. 1)—than for the violent assault they depict.

Each rape story naturally brings an individual set of circumstances, character dynamics, and narrative stylings that deserve separate treatment. In many cases, Ovid's general inclination to sympathize with the oppressed and disparage divine or royal oppressors leads him to create near parables on the effects of power abused, sometimes with startling psychological intensity as in the rapes of Callisto in Book 2 and Caenis in Book 12. Just as often, however, these sincere explorations of power collide with a male-dominated viewpoint that is at least as willing to take artistic pleasure in the portrayed subjugation of a usually female and always beautiful victim. Paradoxical sympathy with both the agony of the oppressed and the mindset of the oppressor are present throughout the poem, and translators have often failed to grapple with them.

As it happens, Ovid does take rape seriously, but only when it conforms to his narrow definition of the crime. Coercion is of little concern and, though he never faults the victim, he takes the frustration of Apollo's desires in this scene as license for levity, presenting Daphne's flight as an emotionally fraught kind of roadrunner cartoon. During the chase, Daphne's body is literally bared, and while it is true that, as some critics have argued, the ensuing voyeuristic description cleverly and uncomfortably puts the reader in the position of the divine assailant, this implicit criticism of the audience only somewhat counteracts the truth that accessing the passage's aesthetic appeal calls for a male gaze blithely directed at a woman under attack.

Still, the *Metamorphoses* remains an "unbroken song," and the story of Daphne does not exist in isolation but instead moves straight into that of Io, where the narrator will sympathize far less equivocally with the sufferer. Ovid structures that tale's opening so as to parallel Daphne's story directly, with the key difference that, since Jove succeeds in his attempt, he handles the material with much more gravity, painting the aggressor in a significantly harsher light. In a sense, Daphne's preceding plight is there to tee off Io's—a narrative fact that makes Daphne's fate no less awful but is truer to the broader project of Ovid's poetic inquiry into the abuses of power.

458   *our frame:* Characters in Latin literature often use a poetic "we" when speaking only about themselves—a rhetorical device usually smoothed over by translators. This time, however, Ovid makes a point of Apollo's arrogance by having him refer to himself exclusively in the plural, while Cupid responds in the singular.

477   *Like unwed Phoebe:* As an outdoorsy huntress who spurned the company of men, the goddess Diana (Phoebe) represented an alternative kind of femininity to the homebody wives of Greco-Roman convention. Daphne stands first in the poem's long line of virgins striving to emulate Diana's lifestyle, many of whom will unfortunately lack her divine power to repel unwanted advances.

559   *Laurel:* The name Daphne means "laurel" in Greek. The wording of Apollo's speech is reminiscent of religious hymns; in contrast to his earlier conduct during the chase, the god treats the literally objectified woman with relative reverence.

560–63 *You'll be there . . . oak that hangs between:* Victorious Roman generals wore laurel crowns in a ritual parade called the Triumph, which ended with an ascent of the Capitoline Hill in Rome. This symbolism also led the Senate to decree that laurel trees should flank the oak-garlanded doors of the house of Augustus, which abutted a temple to Apollo. Ovid's tendency to inject Roman associations into myths with Greek settings may be regarded as an ancient form of modernization, with a similar blend of cheek and cross-cultural connection to that found today in the works of Neil Gaiman and Rick Riordan. Cf. 13.251, 14.719.

567   *seemed to nod:* One translation unfortunately adds the
       phrase "in full consent," but the point of interest lies in the
       seeming. Daphne might be acquiescing now that Apollo's
       intentions are loftier, but line 552 implies that she retains
       no consciousness at all. Besides keeping Apollo at least
       somewhat on the hook (not that he minds), this note of
       ambiguity adds another dimension to the poem's rapidly
       complicating concept of metamorphosis; in the next
       scene, the other river gods will be unsure whether to
       congratulate Daphne's father or console him for his loss.

Io, Part 1 (568–667)

This long, layered story retells a very old myth most prominently featured in the Greek play *Prometheus Bound,* once attributed to Aeschylus. Io's story first seems to be an abbreviated rehashing of Daphne's: a
self-aggrandizing deity propositions the daughter of a river god, then
pursues her in an abrupt comedic chase. As soon as Jove succeeds in
raping her, however, Ovid's tone and focus changes, settling in for an
extended narrative that, despite its happy ending, elaborates the theme
of divine injustice by skewering Jupiter's worthless guilt and Juno's
misdirected wrath. Two stories within stories complement the action.

568ff   *In Thessaly, there is a wooded vale . . . :* The Vale of Tempe
         was literarily synonymous with natural beauty. It is
         therefore a natural subject for the work's first extended
         depiction of a *locus amoenus* (pleasant place), a poetic
         trope often heralded by the telltale phrase *there is.* Ovid's
         locus amoenus leads into a brief example of another epic
         staple, the list or catalog (in this case, of rivers).

634–36   *She wished to reach out supplicating arms . . . moos:*
          Supplication was a ritualized plea for mercy involving spe-
          cific gestures, like the clasping of knees, that Io is unable
          to perform. (Actaeon will have the same problem at
          3.240–41.) These lines also reveal that Io has undergone a
          different kind of metamorphosis from Daphne, one in
          which her mind is left intact but unable to express itself.

650   *Poor me:* Even as it reveals the father's painful selfishness,
       this phrase conceals a bilingual pun. The letters Io

scratches in the dust are presumably those of her name, *io*, which happens also to be a standard Greek expression of woe, much as *me miserum* ("poor me") is in Latin. In crying out, Inachus simultaneously translates the message and reacts to it.

Argus: Pan and Syrinx (668–721)

Continuing the theme and variation, if Io is a sequel reacting to Daphne, then Syrinx is a burlesque of it, narrated by Mercury to Io's guard Argus in a rushed progression through the same narrative beats. In fact, the story has now become so tired that it quickly puts the listener to sleep, whereupon Mercury gruesomely kills him. In a sense, this has a moralizing quality: death awaits those who close their eyes to rape. But Mercury is still acting on the orders of Jupiter, and the god-king's transgressions have just racked up another (relatively) innocent victim.

673–77 *Jove's son . . . pipes:* Besides the humor of having Mercury put on his favorite outfit and immediately take it off, these lines contain two other features of note. First, at no point in this episode is Mercury referred to by name, and the haze of epithets and patronymics in the narration mirror the disguise he has assumed in the narrative. Second, the pipes he plays are panpipes ("syrinx"), a stock attribute of herdsmen in classical pastoral literature, and the subject of the coming story within the story within the story.

710 *This will stay my bond with you!:* Pan echoes Apollo at 558 ("At least you'll be my tree!"), but where Apollo elevates the laurel, tying it to the future glory of Rome, Pan makes the vulgar promise that Syrinx will live on forever in his mouth. The point is driven home in Book 11, when Pan plays his pipes in a musical contest with Apollo, who arrives wearing laurels (153ff). Spoiler: Apollo wins.

Io, Part 2 (722–46)

731 *her face—up toward the stars:* In Ovid's creation story (1.85–86), the upward gaze was portrayed as a distinguishing feature of humans; on the inside, Io is still Io.

736 *She'll cause you no more pain:* As if Io were to blame. Slimy as
     ever, Jupiter should really swear off all further activities, but
     restricts his oath to Io alone.

Phaëthon, Part 1 (747–79)

In another smart transition, Io's story ends on the opening of Phaëthon's, one of the longest in the poem. Never one to bother with formal convention, Ovid gives only a foretaste of this myth before concluding Book 1 on a (gentle) cliffhanger, but the lighthearted feel of the
passage, which sees demigods bickering like boys in the schoolyard,
rounds out his opening chapter with a refreshing shift in tone.

747   *worshiped by a linened throng:* By Ovid's time, Io's
         association with Egypt had led her to become identified
         with the Egyptian goddess Isis, whose cult of linen-robed
         priests was increasingly popular in Rome. Io will
         reappear as Isis in Book 9 (686ff). Her son Epaphus was
         identified with Apis, the sacred bull of Egypt.

773–74   *his household gods . . . near our land:* The geography is
         absurd. Besides the historical regions of (A)ethiopia and
         (A)egypt that bordered each other in northern Africa,
         there was also a mythological Aethiopia that reached east
         toward India and the land of the sunrise. For narrative
         expediency, Ovid has conflated the two, allowing
         Phaëthon to at once live at home with king Merops of
         Aethiopia, see Epaphus in neighboring Aegypt, and walk
         to the realm of the rising sun. In order to conjure a sense
         of mythic geography while also diminishing the sugges-
         tion that the two countries share a border, this translation
         opts for the regions' archaic English spellings, rather than
         the modern "Ethiopia" and "India."

BOOK 2

Phaëthon, Part 2 (1–328)

The rest of Phaëthon's adventure, and its aftermath, will occupy the
first half of Book 2, offering a comparably calamitous narrative of fire
to balance Book 1's narrative of the Flood. This is an etiological myth,

meaning it purports to explain the origin of some aspect of the world, in this case climatic zones (though Ovid gave another explanation at 1.49ff). The story of Phaëthon was popular in antiquity and had been treated by tragedians, but Ovid's telling is the best-known version of the tale and appears to be largely his own.

1–18   *For Mulciber himself had there engraved:* In another epic trope, this grand visual opens the book with an extended *ekphrasis,* or still-life description. Ovid nods particularly to the Shield of Achilles passage from Homer's *Iliad,* the grandfather of all classical *ekphrases.* Like Achilles' shield, the doors of the Sun's palace were forged by Vulcan (Mulciber) to depict the world in microcosm—a fitting image for a story where that world will soon be imperiled.

9–10   *Melodious Triton, changing Proteus, / Aegaeon with two monstrous whales in hand:* With his hundred hands, Aegaeon (better known as Briareus) would have been unusually equipped for this task. Triton's association with a musical horn has already been seen (1.335), while the prophetic sea god Proteus was, appropriately, protean (8.731ff).

23   *Phoebus:* The identity of Ovid's Sun is unsettled, reflecting the syncretism of the god Phoebus Apollo with the sun deity Sol (Helios in Greek), son of the Titan Hyperion (see note to 1.11–14). Throughout, he is called both "Phoebus" and "Titan," with no obvious method to the monikers.

53ff   *But be dissuaded:* A major component of Roman education was the writing of *suasoriae,* persuasive soliloquies from the viewpoint of mythical or historical figures whose highly artificial style tended to lean on emotional appeals. Ovid's rhetorical training shines through in many of his characters' speeches, with the Sun's outburst here being especially obvious.

70   *the constant motion of the heavens:* The geocentric model of the universe envisioned the heavens and heavenly

bodies as a series of concentric spheres, each circling the globe while spinning around the geographic poles of the Earth.

117   *the moon-horn's tips*: The Romans conceived of the crescent moon as a horn.

172–73 *the Oxen . . . forbidden seas*: As will be explained at 527–30, because Ursa Major never set, it was considered the sole constellation in the heavens forbidden to bathe in the sea. Perhaps because the etiology of Ursa Major ("the Great Bear") will be related later in the book, Ovid here uses another Roman term for the constellation, *Triones* ("Oxen"). He was less careful at 132.

219–24 *Chaste Helicon . . . Haemus . . . Sacred Cithaeron*: Mount Helicon is home to the virginal Muses. Mount Haemus is elsewhere associated with Orpheus, son of Oeagrus (10.77), but that tale has yet to occur or be told. Mount Cithaeron's proximity to the temple of Apollo at Delphi renders it sacred.

236   *turned the Aethiopian peoples black*: The Greek word *Aithiops* approximately means "burned-face," though the Alexandrian footnote in the previous line (see note to 1.152) suggests that Ovid is distancing himself from this origin story.

245   *Xanthus, doomed to burn again*: As related at *Iliad* 21.328ff, during the Trojan War, the god Vulcan set fire to the Xanthus (or Scamander) in retaliation for attacking Achilles.

255   *hid its unfound head*: A clever etiology for the unknown source of the Nile, a great mystery in the ancient world not fully unraveled until 1862.

259   *Tiber, pledged to someday rule them all*: Having run through all of the Romans' known world, the catalog of rivers reaches its climax with Rome itself, the city that will govern most of them and through which the Tiber flows.

261   *Light entered Hell and scared its queen and king*: An unprecedented circumstance, but one foreshadowed by

the Sun earlier: "And may the waves by which gods' oaths
are sworn, / *Though unknown to our eyes,* bear witness
here!" (45–46).

302–3   *withdrew her face / Inside herself:* When portraying
personifications of nature or allegorical concepts, Ovid
delights in depicting such characters with dual identities
both part of and individuated from the entity they
represent. Thus, the Earth hides her face within the
Earth, Mount Tmolus perches atop his own peak
(11.156–57), and the god Sleep is very, very sleepy
(11.612ff). The effect is amusing, but further mystifies the
concept of consciousness within nature, so central to the
world of the poem.

307   *to cloud the spreading lands:* Jupiter is a storm god, but we
have seen him performs this act for nefarious purposes
as well (1.600).

The Heliads and Cygnus (329–401)

So far, transformations from the human to the inhuman have taken
the form of punishment (Lycaön), merciful escape (Daphne, Syrinx),
memorial tribute (Argus), and even temporary expedient (Io). Phaëthon's mourners introduce another kind of change that will become
prevalent in the poem: metamorphosis as the utmost expression of
emotion.

366   *the wives of Rome:* An abrupt jolt into the future and one
of the poem's occasional contemporary references. As he
did with Daphne, Ovid ends the tale of the Heliads with a
turn toward Rome, but the missing triumphal mood
gives the move a messier meaning. Is it a criticism of
modern decadence that tragic tears should be so tempting? Or simply a comment on the oblivion wrought by
time?

368–69   *One Cygnus ... still closer, Phaëthon, in heart:* This is the
first of the poem's three men named Cygnus who will be
turned into a swan (*cygnus*). The circumlocution implies
that Cygnus was Phaëthon's lover as well as his kinsman,
an association Virgil confirms.

Callisto (402–530)

Supervising the world's recovery, Jupiter quickly gets sidetracked when he spots another unlucky maiden, a huntress of Diana named Callisto. The rape of Callisto, however, takes a very different tone from those that preceded it. Ironic jokes are replaced by tragic realism, physical descriptions of Callisto evoke sympathy rather than eroticism, and there is no question as to the baseness of the gods' actions. Unlike with Io, Jove opts for deceit from the start before switching to unconscionable indifference, whereupon Diana and Juno engage in unfeeling displays of what would today be called victim-blaming. Furthermore, where Io's sufferings depended on her forced silence, Callisto's status as a sworn virgin turns hers into a disturbing story of trauma and its aftermath: she has trouble sleeping, avoids reminders of the incident, and undergoes shifts in personality, becoming paranoid, absent-minded, and plagued by unwarranted guilt—a psychological profile unchanged by her cruel but circumstantially negligible transformation. Rarely does Ovid write a human so thoroughly innocent in their own suffering or show the gods so horribly at fault.

410   *A girl:* Callisto is never named in the story, emphasizing the ostracism and loss of identity that results from her suffering. (The myth was too well-known in Ovid's time for this to have caused confusion.) This choice carries special symbolism because the name *Kallisto* is Greek for "fairest," yet it is her name-brand beauty that will make Callisto a target and which her miserable metamorphosis will subsequently erase.

411   *to weave in wifely wool:* In the Roman imagination, weaving wool was the archetypal activity of a good wife, who stays at home spinning instead of painting the town. The contrast is no indictment of Callisto, however, for in the most famous instance of the trope, the spinning of the legendarily dutiful Lucretia did nothing to dissuade her rapist. Leucothoë will make the same discovery in 4.220ff.

495   *wolves, though her father then was one:* As the next line will reveal, Callisto's father is Lycaön. Readers wondering how either father or daughter managed to survive the flood will find many further inconsistencies to deal with.

507 *made them stars:* This kind of metamorphosis, called catasterism, happens only rarely in the poem, likely because Ovid was saving them for another work, the *Fasti,* where this myth is retold. Callisto and Arcas have become Ursa Major (the "Great Bear") and Boötes, or *Arctophylax* (the "Bear-Watcher"). Readers realizing that these stars already appeared under different names will enjoy line 528.

527 *nursling:* Ocean and Tethys briefly stood as Juno's foster parents.

528 *ban the Oxen from your sea-green swirl:* Paradoxically, Juno calls Callisto's stars by their alternate name, the Oxen. Ursa Major was considered the one constellation that never sets. (See note to 172–73).

The Raven and the Crow (531–632)

A comically forced transition leads into a set of interlocking bird etiologies, with a preview of the coming story of Aglauros shuffled in. As with previous tales, the fatal rashness and sexual misconduct of the gods is on full display, but Ovid's constant shifting between narratives undercuts any real chance for pathos to develop, instead directing attention toward his Russian-doll storytelling, the true star of the show. Chaucer enthusiasts will recognize the plot of "The Manciple's Tale."

538 *Whose watchful wails would save the Capitol:* According to legend, during the Gallic invasions of 390 BCE, the honking of geese warned soldiers on the Capitoline Hill of a nighttime attack, saving the city. Romans consequently considered geese proverbially vigilant, as opposed to proverbially irritating.

553–55 *Erichthonius, whom no mother bore . . . Cecrops sired :* Ovid elides the sordid details. While attempting to rape Minerva (Pallas), Vulcan spilled his semen on the Earth, impregnating the soil. The resulting "chthonic" (earthborn) child was Eri*chthon*ius, a future Athenian king. Together with the chest of *Attic* reeds and the appearance of the *two-formed* king Cecrops, depicted as a man above the waist and a serpent below, the reference signals that the poem has arrived at Athens.

561   *Inside, she saw an infant—and a snake:* Though an
         alarming detail in the absence of context, the snake was a
         standard attribute of Erichthonius; the statue of Athena
         that once occupied the Parthenon depicted him as a
         snake rearing behind her shield. The Crow's ability to
         report this sight reveals that she, too, broke Minerva's
         order against peeking.

570   *it's well known:* Likely a joke; King Coroneus of Phocis is
         not otherwise attested.

630   *brought the child to two-formed Chiron's cave:* Apollo's son
         is Aesculapius, the god of medicine, who will reappear
         so-named in Book 15. The centaur (half-man, half-horse)
         Chiron was a skilled archer, healer, and musician
         entrusted with the training of many heroes, including
         Achilles, Hercules, and Jason.

Ocyrhoë (633–75)

In an odd sequel to the birth of Aesculapius, Chiron's prophetic
daughter Ocyrhoë begins spouting forbidden knowledge, ceasing
only when divine punishment stops her tongue. Ovid makes clear,
however, that Ocyrhoë's speech was not her fault but forced by Apollo,
god of prophecy, who supplies the next transition.

644–48   *twice will you mold your fate anew:* Predictably,
              Aesculapius' ability to raise the dead engendered
              vociferous complaint in the underworld. Jupiter
              consequently smote his grandson, only to later
              resurrect him as a god.

651–54   *Will wish you could die:* When Hercules inadvertently
              wounded him with a poison arrow, the subsequent
              unending pain caused Chiron to wish for death. The
              threefold goddesses who grant his wish are the Fates,
              who weave, measure, and cut the threads of life. (That
              Chiron would reappear later in the mythos as tutor to
              Achilles is just one of those things.)

675   *The monstrous marvel was renamed:* Ocyrhoë was
         henceforth known as Hippe ("mare"), in most versions
         a different daughter of Chiron's.

Battus (676–708)

This short tale of entrapment begins with a double fake-out. First hinting at the story of Apollo's love for the boy king Admetus, whom the god served as cowherd for a year (his compunction over Coronis was evidently short-lived), Ovid then teases the myth of Apollo's stolen cattle. He finally settles on the much more obscure tale of Battus, landing our attention on Mercury (still disguised and still unnamed) in preparation for the next story.

707 *Still called by the informer's name:* The point of this etiology is lost to time. Ovid's statement that the stone is known as "chatterbox" makes little sense. The myth's only other extant version, that of Nicander, says the stone is always either hot or cold, which makes even less.

The Envy of Aglauros (709–832)

Tying up the loose end of Erichthonius' birth, Ovid returns to the daughters of Cecrops for a long parable on greed and envy—the former sin exemplified by Aglauros, the latter inflicted on her by Minerva. Both sins are prompted by Mercury's courtship of Aglauros' sister Herse, whose feelings on the subject are never voiced. By this point, however, we know they are of little account: no matter what, the god will have his way.

712–14 *It chanced to be the feast . . . Pallas' hilltop shrine:* As part of the Great Panathenaia festival, a procession of girls carried baskets of offerings up to the Parthenon, the temple to Pallas that sits atop the Acropolis to this day. Since the oppression of women in Athens was extreme even by ancient standards, such festivals were common literary settings for love-at-first-sight, furnishing rare occasions on which Athenian girls might be seen outside their homes.

727–29 *burned like lead . . . never had before:* In a tradition today carried on by Rafael Nadal, the people of Mallorca and the other Balearic Islands were renowned as powerful and accurate shots, a skill they employed as slingers in the Roman army. The science here is, of course, nonsense.

738   *Pandrosos, yours*: The vocative is the only form of
Pandrosos' name that fits Ovid's meter, partially explaining this abrupt address. However, Ovid has already
shown a propensity for short-lived second-person
interruptions (1.728), and his odd emphasis on the least
important of the three sisters is rather droll.

741   *Mercury*: Having at last shed his various disguises,
Mercury is finally named.

760ff   *house / Of Envy*: Envy is the first of the poem's four great
allegorical personifications, the others being Hunger in
Book 8, Sleep in Book 11, and Rumor in Book 12. Each
passage describes the entities' dwellings as well as the
inhabitants, all four of whom both inflict and suffer the
conditions they represent (see note to 302–3).

Europa (833–75)

Ovid ends the second book with a lighthearted rendition of another
famous rape, that of Europa. Because the story cuts off before the
obvious outcome, the tone mostly matches Europa's unsuspecting
cheerfulness, closing on a weirdly pretty abduction scene familiar
from countless works of art. What eroticism there is concentrates not
on Europa, but in the playful description of Jove in bull form, largely
cribbed from the Greek poet Moschus, whose long narrative poem on
Europa is the chief source here. The caustic editorializing that "majesty and love do not mix well," however, is entirely Ovid's.

839   *The land that spies your mother from the left*: Since Phoenicia
lay to the east, from Jupiter's celestial vantage point, it views
the stars of the Pleiades (including Mercury's mother Maia)
from the left. Ovid poetically conflates the two great Phoenician cities Sidon and Tyre.

BOOK 3
Cadmus and the Dragon's Teeth (1–130)

Since Phaëthon's story straddled the last book division, readers might
expect Book 3 to open with a lengthy conclusion to the tale of Jove and
Europa. Instead, Ovid abruptly abandons them on Crete (where their

son Minos will be found ruling in Book 7), shifting attention to Europa's brother Cadmus, founder of Thebes and another child of King Agenor of Tyre. Thus begins a long cycle of Theban myths chronicling the sorrows of the city's ruling family. With few exceptions, the gods are squarely to blame.

13–14   *Boeotia's name . . . Castalia's cave:* Boeotia is the region of Greece surrounding Thebes. The name is reminiscent of the word for cow: *bos.* The cave is that of the Castalian Spring at Delphi.

28   *Amidst an ancient wood no axe had harmed:* The scene of Callisto's rape was described in similar terms (2.418). By now, the reader may have realized that Ovid's idyllic locales tend to serve as the backdrop to extreme violence. This pattern is counted among the work's most analyzed subversions, transforming the literary topos of the *locus amoenus* ("place of pleasure"; see note to 1.568ff) into a *locus terribilis* ("place of fear").

32   *dragon-snake of Mars:* As may be evident already, Latin does not honor English category distinctions between dragons, snakes, and serpents. The relation of the dragon to Mars is not explicit; in some versions, it is the god's son.

46   *Phoenicians:* Tyre was a Phoenician settlement.

91–92   *Backed up against / An oak:* Throughout this passage, the serpent varies so absurdly in scale as to constitute a kind of joke. It must have shrunk considerably to be pinned against a single oak, given that it earlier "glowered down on all the woods" (43–44) and "split the hindering forest with its breast" (80).

111–14 Another of Ovid's appeals to his contemporary audience (cf. 1.560–63, 2.366). In contrast to modern practice, curtains in the Roman theater began folded at the front of the stage and were raised from the bottom up, rather than lowered from the top down.

117   *civil wars:* A touchy subject considering the civil wars that gripped Rome just twenty years before Ovid's writing. The line also presages the fratricidal strife of the

Theban War, one of the great sagas of Greek myth, but one that Ovid handles only in passing (9.403ff).

126   *Echion*: The name means "viper." Echion would go on to marry Cadmus's daughter Agave and become the father of Pentheus.

Actaeon (131–252)

The sufferings of the house of Cadmus begin with his grandson Actaeon, whose fate recalls the cruelty Diana exhibited toward Callisto. Some versions of the myth had the goddess defending herself against a would-be rapist, but Ovid's Actaeon is wholly innocent, and the unjust vengeance Diana exacts on him contrasts sharply with the powerlessness of mortal women in the face of divine advances. His subsequent death mixes sympathetic echoes of Callisto and Io with a Dantesque *contrapasso* verging into wit, as the unrecognized hunter is himself hunted to death.

132–37   *Besides . . . lacks his funeral rites*: Unfortunately for Cadmus, Ovid's poem will never see him pass, and his family will furnish many of the book's remaining characters. With his wife Harmonia, daughter of Mars and Venus, Cadmus had four daughters: Autonoë, Ino, Agave, and Semele. Autonoë is the mother of Actaeon, Semele's tale is next, and Agave's son Pentheus will rule Thebes by the end of the book. (Ino escapes unscathed, at least until Book 4.) Roman audiences may have detected an echo of Emperor Augustus' own difficulties in securing an heir.

156   *close-garbed Diana*: Being a huntress, Diana gathered her robes closely about her to enable movement.

198   *heroic son turned tail*: The dissonance is surely intended. Ovid usually mentions his characters' heroism just as they are fleeing, dying ignominiously, or dissolving into tears. Other examples are a weepy Chiron (2.676), the useless Pygmalion (10.290), a mangled Adonis (10.731), the pigheaded Midas (11.106), and a nymph-raping Peleus (11.264). This will prove especially true of Perseus, who is by turns cowardly and lazy.

206ff   *his bloodhounds:* In one of his most comical subversions
of epic convention, Ovid here pauses the action for a
catalog listing—of all things—Actaeon's hounds, each of
whom is endowed with a stately Greek name that would
have been understood by Ovid's sophisticated audience.
(For the untranslated originals, see the appendix's note
on 206–25; the only unaltered entry is Ladon, presumably, if oddly, named for the Ladon river in the
Peloponnese.)

232–35   *and got there first:* In spite of the narrator's ironic claim
that it would waste time to name more than the first
thirty-three dogs, it turns out that the three hounds of
greatest consequence were not even mentioned.

Semele (253–315)

Readers who marked Juno's ire toward Io and Callisto may have been
surprised to find her absent from the myth of Europa, but that was
merely the calm before the storm. For the next book and a half, Juno
will pursue a program of vengeance against Europa's extended family,
whetted by Jupiter's latest (consensual) affair with Semele. The resulting child, Bacchus, will join the pantheon as a dynamic new god, but
one who will soon prove as violent as the others.

271   *So self-assured is beauty:* Juno repeats the narrator's comment on Mercury from 2.731. The same trait that comes off
as a bit cocky in a god, however, will be a death sentence for
a mortal woman.

282   *Gods' names are often used to gain chaste beds:* An ironic
statement in a poem where it is the gods who are constantly
engaging in such impersonation.

289   *I'll have naught be denied:* Another echo. Phoebus used these
exact words in making the same foolhardy promise to
Phaëthon (2.97).

304   *the hundred-handed Typhon:* Typhon was the father of all
monsters and the greatest enemy of the gods. Their struggle
to defeat him is narrated, in haphazard installments, at
5.321–31 and 5.346–58.

Tiresias (316–38)

Blind old Tiresias, the most famous prophet in Greek mythology, will provide foreboding prefaces for two of the book's upcoming stories. To quickly introduce him, Ovid first tells the myth of his repeated sex change, a tale that again exhibits Juno's wrath while furthering the motif of holy visions beheld by profane eyes (Cadmus and the dead serpent, Actaeon and the nude Diana, Semele and Jupiter's true form).

335   *damned her judge's eyes to endless night:* Ovid leaves the matter unresolved, but the nature of the punishment would hint that Tiresias has seen the truth.

Echo and Narcissus (339–510)

Taking a break from the beleaguered Theban royals, the poet treats us to the off-topic but tour-de-force myth of Narcissus, paired—in a brilliant Ovidian innovation—with the story of the nymph Echo. In another permutation of the fatal vision theme, the boy Narcissus, too self-obsessed to love anyone else, is finally cursed to love himself. Yet his passion is more intriguing than the simple narcissism to which he lends his name, for the self that Narcissus falls in love with is his own reflection, a perceived entity separate from himself and one he ultimately dies because he cannot have: he is the only thing he can't possess. For her part, the personified Echo loves selflessly, but her incapacity for independent expression forces her to become a reflection of him as well. Brought together by their love of Narcissus, both are undone by their deficiencies in love, the nymph unable to initiate action, the boy doubly unable to do anything else. Yet what love is truly expressible, what lover fully accessible? Ovid's wordplay, parallelism, and thematic exploration are seen here at their sparkling best.

348   *If he never knows himself:* Tiresias utters a witty inversion of one of antiquity's most famous aphorisms, "Know thyself" (*gnōthi sauton*, or in Latin, *temet nosce*), purportedly inscribed on the portico of Apollo's temple at Delphi. Narcissus will fulfill this prophecy at 463.

362   *This Juno wrought:* Like the divine rape perpetrated at 343, the anger of Juno is by now so commonplace as to become incidental backstory.

386–88 *"I want you"* . . . / *"Come? Here!"*: The original pun is more
        explicit, playing on the double meaning of *huc coeamus*
        ("let us meet here"), in which the word *coeamus* can also
        mean "let us have sex."

466   *Gain has made me lose:* This exclamation (in Latin,
        inopem me copia fecit) and the several that follow it are
        prime examples of Ovid's tendency to inject passionate
        situations with a clashing cleverness that pointedly
        undercuts the narrative moment, whether to emphasize
        the absurdity of the situation, distract from its sordid-
        ness, or sustain its artistic appeal. As Dryden com-
        plained in the preface to his *Fables, Ancient and
        Modern* of 1700:

> Would any man who is ready to die for love describe his
> passion like Narcissus? Would he think of *inopem me
> copia fecit*, and a dozen more of such expressions, pour'd
> on the neck of one another, and signifying all the same
> thing? If this were wit, was this a time to be witty, when
> the poor wretch was in the agony of death? . . . On these
> occasions, the poet should endeavor to raise pity; but
> instead of this, Ovid is tickling you to laugh.

        That Ovid might have had aims in mind other than verisi-
        militude was not dreamt of in Dryden's philosophy.

510   *A yellow flower with petals ringed in white*: The narcissus, or
        daffodil.

Pentheus and Acoetes (511–733)

Meanwhile, back at Thebes, Bacchus has aged into full divinity, a fact
the current king, Pentheus, refuses to recognize. His death at the
hands of the god's followers is most familiar from the sensational version found in the *Bacchae* of Euripides, whose story beats Ovid naturally goes out of his way to avoid. Though Bacchus himself is fairly
absent from Ovid's telling, those who oppose his worship are characterized as fools or criminals, a far cry from the innocents persecuted
by Diana and Juno. The story accordingly pits the forces of impiety
and oppressive authority against those of a terrifying but devout and
transgressively matriarchal cult. The myth's conclusion consequently

eschews the harrowing pathos of Euripides' play, opting for a climactic display of violence too extravagant to be taken seriously.

542   *thyrsi*: A fennel stalk entwined with leaves of ivy, the thyrsus was a ritual staff associated with the cult of Bacchus, whose frenetic female devotees were called bacchants. Pentheus' accusation is ironic since the poem's bacchants often do use their thyrsi as weapons, as he himself will discover at 712.

544   *Take up the serpent's spirit*: Ovid gives an in-universe example of the various meanings a myth can contain as Pentheus vaunts his descent not from Cadmus but from his other grandfather, the dragon of Mars encountered at the book's outset, whose brutality he deems heroic. His cousin Bacchus, by contrast, shares only the Cadmeian lineage.

559   *Acrisius*: Acrisius was the king of Argos. His opposition to Bacchus is briefly seen at 4.604 as a transition to the adventures of his grandson Perseus.

576   *Tyrrhene-born*: But at 583, the disciple will identify himself as Lydian. Roman poets used the appellation "Tyrrhene" to refer not only to the Etruscans of Italy (near the namesake Tyrrhenian Sea) but also to the Lydians of Asia Minor from whom they supposedly descended. Etruscan Tyrrhenes will appear in Book 15.

658–59 *for there's no god / So close as he*: This common metaphor of divine presence masks a sly joke if, as many scholars have suggested, Acoetes is Bacchus in disguise. In Euripides' play, it is Bacchus himself whom Pentheus interrogates.

710   *he watched the rites with profane eyes*: A final nod to the motif of profane eyes beholding forbidden sights, which previously led to the deaths of Actaeon and Semele. The reminder is especially apt since these secret rites are performed by Semele's surviving sisters, including Actaeon's mother, soon to reenact her son's gruesome death.

721–22 *she tore / Off his right arm*: In the height of frenzy, bacchant worshipers were said to tear sacrificial animals apart with their bare hands, an act known as *sparagmos*. We will witness another sparagmatic episode in Book 11.

BOOK 4

The Daughters of Minyas, Part 1 (1–54)

The death of Pentheus may have taught the Thebans a lesson, but the daughters of Minyas, king of nearby Orchomenos, remain staunch in their heresy. Their decision to stay home during a Bacchic festival and pass the time in storytelling lends Ovid his next framing device, which will carry the poem through three other tales and the first half of this book. If Acoetes truly was Bacchus in disguise, then the daughters of Minyas are the poem's first human narrators, a condition reflected in the anthropocentric stories they choose to tell.

1 *But:* An oddly dependent opening for a book in an epic. Though Ovid does not split a story across two books here as he did with Phaëthon and Europa, he continues to eschew the trappings of formal structure.

11ff *Bromius . . . :* The following lines take the structure of a hexameter hymn, beginning with an invocation of the god by his various names: Bromius ("thunderous") refers to the tumult of Bacchanalian celebrations; Lyaeus ("the relaxer") refers to the effect of wine; Twice-Born, Lone Two-Mothered Son, and Child of Fire refer to his miraculous double-birth recounted in Book 3 (first in his mother Semele's combustive death and later from Jupiter's thigh); Thyoneus refers to his descent from Thyone, another name for Semele; and Nysan refers to his rearing by the nymphs of Nysa (3.314–15). Lenaeus derives from the Greek word *lenos* ("wine-press"); Nyctelius ("by night") from his nocturnal worship; and Iacchus, Elelean Sire, and Euhan from his cult's ritual cries, *iacche, eleleu,* and *euoe.* The list ends with a standard formula covering any possible omissions (cf. 15.866), and is followed by a brief recitation of the deity's deeds, including references to the axe-wielding king Lycurgus of Thrace, another vanquished heretic along the lines of Pentheus, and the "drunk old" satyr Silenus, the god's steadfast companion, who will appear in Book 11. By the hymn's concluding plea for divine favor, the narrator's voice has given way to that of the Thebans at prayer.

33   *Minerval tasks*: Minerva was the goddess of weaving (see
note to 2.411). Like Lucretia and the soon to be met Leucothoë, the daughters of Minyas will not be saved by this
supposedly devotional act.

44ff *Dercetis of Babylon . . .* : The prospective narrator's hesitation
allows Ovid to stage a quick parade of mini-metamorphoses.
Little more is known of the myth of the naiad beyond what
Ovid describes (49–51), but the sister's thoughts are evidently on Babylon, since she begins with the Eastern fertility
goddess Dercetis (or Atargatis), whose shame at bearing a
mortal man's child turned her into a fish, then shifts to her
daughter, queen Semiramis, who famously walled the city in
brick (a novelty for Europeans accustomed to stone fortifica-
tions). Such deliberations begin painting the backdrop for
the upcoming myth set in Babylon, wherein references to
Semiramis and her husband king Ninus (founder of Nin-
eveh) furnish the tale's local color.

Pyramus and Thisbe (55–166)

The sisters' substitute activity for attending a religious festival begins
with a tale fittingly low on divinity, the poem's first narrative of two
humans in love. Familiar to readers of Shakespeare through its similarity to *Romeo and Juliet* and its burlesqued enactment in *A Midsummer Night's Dream*, Ovid's original tale of Pyramus and Thisbe provides the first of the epic's many examples of human lovers whose
devotion and sincerity far outstrips any godly romance.

121–24 *his blood gushed high / Much as a faulty pipe whose lead has
burst:* For this gruesome and anachronistic analogy, which
pulls the reader out of Babylon and into the poisonous
plumbing of first-century Rome, one can do no better than
appeal to previous commentators. To quote E. J. Kenney,
"this is not the only place in the poem where blood jets
from a wound with implausible force" (Melville 396:
122n). But William S. Anderson disagrees: "I have been
assured that it would be possible for such a jet to reach a
height of six or seven feet briefly, high enough, then, to
strike the mulberries." I defer judgment to the reader.

The Loves of the Sun (167–270)

The second sister, Leuconoë, responds with a tragedy of her own, a love triangle between the Sun, the girl he loves (Leucothoë), and the girl who loves him (Clytië). Yet the story's emphasis lands solidly on its human characters, both of whose narrative arcs are reminiscent of previous tales. Like Callisto, Leucothoë is raped by a god in a trusted disguise; like Aglauros, Clytië is destroyed by her consuming jealousy over his advances. In typical fashion, Ovid starts with a famous tale only to segue into a much more obscure one. Leuconoë therefore begins with the love affair of Mars and Venus.

192   *Hyperion's son*: The Sun's return reopens his identity crisis (see note to 2.23).

204–6   *Clymene . . . Clytië, who still lusts after you*: We have already met Clymene, mother of Phaëthon. The Sun's other lovers include the island of Rhodes, where a famously wondrous colossus of the Sun once stood, and the unnamed mother of the witch Circe, who will be seen living on the mythical isle of Aeaea in Book 14. Of Clytië's passion for the god we will hear more shortly.

233   *raped without a word*: As discussed in my Translator's Note, many translators and critics consider Leucothoë's acquiescence consensual on the basis of the phrase *posita . . . querela* ("with complaint dropped"). But the act is described as a "suffering of force" (*uim passa*), and the girl's protestation at 239 ("He forced himself upon me!") ought better to be believed. See also the notes on 2.229–32 in the appendix.

254   *frankincense*: Since frankincense was typically burned as an offering to the gods, Leucothoë will, in a sense, still reach heaven. This development was foreshadowed by her mother's hailing from "the lands of spice" (210).

270   *Turns with the Sun*: Clytië has turned into heliotrope ("sun-turning"); flowers that follow the path of the sun are still called "heliotropic." Heliotrope's purported motion was also captured in the flower's Middle English name "turnsole."

Hermaphroditus and Salmacis (271–388)

The third sister's tale offers an etiology for Salmacis, a spring near Halicarnassus whose waters purportedly rendered men effeminate. Her story centers on the rape of the boy Hermaphroditus by the spring's namesake nymph, whose body is subsequently fused with his in a shocking divine act, countering the benevolent prayer-granting that honored Pyramus and Thisbe. This is also the only rape in the poem to contain a graphic description of physical assault, a fact probably owing to the role reversals it involves. Like Daphne and Leucothoë before him, the boy is described as attractive in his fear, while Salmacis (already the most atypical of nymphs) shows all the intensity, duplicity, and violence of a male deity. Unlike one of their crimes, however, Salmacis' assault results in a permanent and ongoing confusion of sexes—in the world of the poem, a female aggressor is far more transgressive.

> 276ff *I need not tell:* Like the first sister, Alcithoë runs through a few transformational appetizers before settling on her main course. A stock character from pastoral poetry, the shepherd Daphnis was turned to stone by a nymph he had spurned to marry a princess. Jove's childhood friend Celmis turned into metal when he later questioned the god's divinity. The Curetes were a Cretan tribe who also attended the infant Jupiter, though their pluvial birth is not otherwise attested. The tale of Sithon's sex changes is unknown.

> 333 *When cymbals idly crash to aid the moon:* Ovid seems to scorn the popular belief that human noise could strengthen the moon against magic or eclipse (cf. 7.207–8).

> 388 *queering:* The manuscripts divide as to whether the fountain's power, and thus Hermaphroditus' intersex condition, is one of inflicted ambiguity (*incerto*) or unholy defilement (*incesto*). The former is adopted here on the logic that, since the narrator's sympathies in this tale lie overwhelmingly with Hermaphroditus, it would be odd to label him so callously at its conclusion. (For a fuller explanation, see the appendix.)

The Daughters of Minyas, Part 2 (389–415)

415   *named for how they bat their wings by night:* The Latin word
for bat, *verspertilio,* is derived from *vesper* ("evening"). My
English pun, however, is an etymological quirk.

Athamas and Ino (416–562)

With local opposition to Bacchus thoroughly suppressed, it will fall to
the still-wrathful Juno to exact vengeance on Ino, the one daughter of
Cadmus and Harmonia not yet afflicted. Other than being related to
Europa, Ino's specific offense is having cared for the infant Bacchus,
son of Juno's rival Semele. That her downfall should be sealed by her
piety toward her nephew after so many have died for lacking it shows
the utter futility of working to appease the gods. Ovid's choice to char-
acterize Ino as blissfully innocent, rather than the cruel stepmother
seen in other versions (see note to 7.6–7), makes her fate all the more
tragic.

426   *Can Juno only weep in unearned pain:* The question,
already ironic given the unearned pain she will shortly
cause, is further vitiated by the narrator's earlier assertion
that gods cannot cry (2.621–22). The queen of heaven is
a drama queen.

438   *Dis:* Dis was the standard name for the Roman god of the
underworld, despite a modern literary convention
insisting on the name Pluto, actually a Latinization of the
Greek *Plouton,* another name for Hades. Although Dante
and Milton both opted for Dis, the name Pluto was
codified in English literature with Arthur Golding's
influential 1567 translation of the *Metamorphoses.* Most
other translators have followed his lead.

446   A portion of text has probably been lost following 445.
The transmitted line 446 appears only in the margins of a
handful of manuscripts and is widely considered
spurious. However, line 445 is ungrammatical alone,
leading editors to posit a lacuna, which 446 was likely
invented to fill. Indeed, the imprisoned residents of

Tartarus soon to be described do not really belong on a list of wandering ghosts.

456ff   *the "Seat of the Accursed"*: Describing the infamous inmates of the "Seat" was a trope of underworld journeys. For attempting to rape the goddess Latona, the Giant Tityos had his liver pecked out daily by vultures, only for it to regrow every night. Tantalus, whose attempt to feed his son Pelops to the gods is briefly narrated in Book 6, was sentenced to starve in proximity to fresh water and fruit trees, both of which eluded his grasp. In punishment for cheating Death, the Corinthian trickster king Sisyphus was damned to roll a stone for all time. King Ixion of the Lapiths was strapped to an ever-rolling wheel of fire for his attempted rape of Juno. Finally, the fifty granddaughters of king Belus of Egypt were doomed to draw water in broken jugs for the crime of murdering their husbands, the fifty sons of their uncle Aegyptus.

486   *Aeolus' house:* This Aeolus is not the Keeper of the Winds, but the namesake king of Aeolia, and father to Athamas.

537–38   *if depths of foam . . . my name among the Greeks:* The Greek name for Venus, Aphrodite, is reminiscent of the word *aphrós,* "sea-foam." Ovid here exploits the conflicting versions of the birth of Venus: if she was indeed born from sea-foam following the castration of Uranus (*à la* Botticelli), then she could not have been the daughter of Jupiter and Dione, meaning Neptune was not her uncle (cf. 532).

Cadmus and Harmonia (563–603)

At last, the poem bids farewell to Thebes. With his daughters and grandchildren thoroughly ruined, it is finally time for Cadmus to meet his fate and turn into a snake (3.97–98). Realizing that he, too, has trespassed on the sacred, Cadmus and his wife undergo transformations that release them from the human world, but not from life. Though Ovid will now call our attention elsewhere, the curse on the royal house of Thebes will continue unfolding in the background, glimpsed occasionally in oblique accounts of the reign of Oedipus (7.759ff), and the war between his sons (9.403ff).

568   *reached Illyria's borders:* The elderly pair have "wandered
         long" indeed. From Thebes to Illyria (modern Albania) is a
         mountainous journey of some four hundred miles.

Perseus, Atlas, and Andromeda (604–764)

In Ovid's irreverent telling, Perseus, canonically the most flawless of
heroes, cuts a decidedly flimsy figure. By the time he appears in the
poem, courtesy of his grandfather Acrisius, he has already completed
his most famous quest—killing the snake-haired Medusa—and is
busy using Mercury's winged sandals as a toy. For the next four-hun-
dred-plus lines he will exhibit little heroism, instead using Medusa's
severed head (which turns those who view it into stone) as a super-
power to get him out of all scrapes, incidentally creating coral,
Saharan snakes, and the Atlas mountains of Morocco. Terse summa-
ries of how he came by the head, along with the rest of his personal
backstory, will be shoehorned in along the way.

607   *Acrisius:* A distant cousin of Cadmus, king Acrisius of
         Argos has already been noted for his opposition to
         Bacchus (3.559–60). His refusal to recognize the pater-
         nity of another child of Jove, his grandson Perseus, is
         enough of a transition for Ovid.

611–12 *begat by raining gold / On Danaë:* When a prophecy
         stated that his future grandson would kill him, Acrisius
         locked up his daughter Danaë to prevent her conceiving
         one. Ever resourceful, Jupiter contrived to impregnate
         her by raining down on her cell in a shower of gold,
         whereupon mother and child were cast out to sea. In the
         words of Stephen Fry, "We do not know whether or not
         Danaë enjoyed the experience. There are those, it is said,
         for whom the prospect of a golden shower is rather . . .
         well . . . quite" (22).

645   *A son of Jove shall take its plundered fame:* A bit of
         dramatic irony; the prophecy actually refers to Hercules,
         who will plunder the golden apples of the Hesperides in
         the course of his Labors (9.190).

670–71 *her mother's tongue . . . Ammon's cruel command:* Cassi-
         ope, wife of king Cepheus of Aethiopia, had blasphe-

mously claimed to rival the Nereids in beauty. As punishment, Neptune forced the Egyptian god Ammon (commonly identified with Jupiter) to order her daughter Andromeda sacrificed to a sea monster. Ovid's editorializing adjectives (*innocent, cruel*) identify the situation as yet another divine miscarriage of justice.

675   *A statue:* The prototype of all beautiful damsels in distress, Andromeda's complete lack of agency makes her a perfect match for her cardboard hero. All her dialogue is delivered in second-hand narration, and her initial statuesque appearance stays uncompromised for nine whole lines, to be interrupted only by the act of weeping. This specific analogy has caused modern confusion, since Ovid makes clear in his *Ars Amatoria* that he imagined Andromeda as Black—she is, after all, an Aethiopian princess (see figure 4). But ancient statuary was polychrome and could be painted any color.

710   *Balearic slings:* Presumably, too close for comfort (cf. 2.727–29).

Perseus and Medusa (765–803)

Having watched him petrify Atlas and rescue Andromeda, we are finally treated to the story of how Perseus slew Medusa, which is told as quickly and unimpressively as possible. Once she is dead, however, Ovid produces an original twist that reorients sympathy toward the slain monster, revealing that Medusa had once been a beautiful woman, undone by the typical divine double-punch of rape and wrongful wrath. In Ovid's mythos, even the most fearsome horror might be the result of an Io or Callisto story gone an extra step too far.

767   In the original Renaissance numbering, lines 767a and 768 provide only a garbled version of 766–7 and are so certainly spurious that few editors bother to print them. As commentator W. S. Anderson explains, they

> do not appear in any major early manuscripts, but have been added in the margin of some by later hands. We assume that some scribe, who did not realize that Perseus was *Lyncides,* tried to fix the text by creating a short con-

versation, question and answer, between *Abantiades* and *Lyncides,* with the absurd result that Perseus is talking to himself!

770   *what craft:* Knowing the story, Ovid's readers would have recognized that all credit for strategy was due elsewhere. The gods Mercury and Minerva not only told Perseus how to kill Medusa, they loaned him the winged sandals, sword, and mirrored shield to get the job done.

773   *frigid Atlas:* Ovid is playing with chronology again. As part of his quest to slay Medusa, Perseus visited a cave in the Atlas mountains. Yet as we have just seen, the mountains only formed through his later use of Medusa's already severed head.

774–75   *Phorcys' daughters—twins / Who shared one eye:* Ovid condenses a familiar story. The primordial sea god Phorcys had two sets of daughters: the Gray Ones, ancient hags who shared a single eye and single tooth between them, and the Gorgons, snake-haired monsters whose glance could turn viewers to stone. Perseus stole the Gray Ones' eye and ransomed it back in exchange for information on their sisters' whereabouts, allowing him to discover Medusa's lair.

786   *his swift brother:* The winged horse Pegasus's brother was a man, Chrysaor, of whom little more is known.

803   *she wears these self-made snakes:* Minerva was often depicted wearing the *Gorgoneion,* an amulet featuring a Gorgon's head, sometimes in the center of her aegis. This final, fearsome image draws attention to the goddess, who will shortly appear and remain on the scene well into Book 6.

BOOK 5

Perseus and Phineus (1–235)

Throughout the wedding, Cepheus and Cassiope have neglected to mention that their daughter is already betrothed to her uncle Phineus. When the jilted fiancé appears at the head of an army, Perseus naturally does nothing and has to be attacked before launching a defense. This results in the first of the epic's two great battle scenes, but the ridiculous odds (by the end, one versus a thousand), coupled with an exaggerated gore factor reminiscent of a Tarantino film, make Ovid's clash a burlesque of the epic set-pieces found in Virgil and Homer. As plot concerns recede behind a haze of one-off names and gruesome injuries, just who's fighting for whom feels increasingly irrelevant—which, ultimately, it is: in the end, Perseus falls back on his trusty *caput ex machina*, throwing in some unheroic taunts to boot.

25   *It . . . it . . .* : Cepheus employs neuter forms in this sentence, making it clear that the king refers to the "prize" of the previous line, completely objectifying his daughter (cf. note to 4.675).

47ff   *There was an Indian boy:* Much of this battle scene takes after Virgil's *Aeneid*, where Aeneas and Turnus wage war for the hand of Lavinia while her father Latinus runs around ineffectually. The male lovers Athis and Lycabas further this parallel by mirroring Virgil's heroic couple Nisus and Euryalus, whose noble deaths in Book 9 of the *Aeneid* make for one of that epic's most graphic and poignant episodes. Ovid's exoticized pair meets an even fouler (if less tragic) demise, forming the first in a series of vignettes that lend variation to the violence.

111ff *You too, Lampetides:* Poets in the *Metamorphoses* are few and far between. Perhaps out of respect for a fellow practitioner, Ovid lavishes a direct address on this one, but still delivers him to a cleverly lurid end. He will do the same for the bard Orpheus in Book 11.

148   *infamous for parricide:* As usual when Ovid makes such lofty claims, the father-murdering Agyrtes is not otherwise known (cf. 2.570).

155   *Bellona:* Bellona is the Roman goddess of war. In a poem with so many decidedly incarnate divine actors, this reference is more likely metaphorical.

Proetus and Polydectes (236–49)

With Phineus gone, "Abas' heir" (that is, Perseus) returns home for a bonus round of two more petrifications, before bowing out of the poem permanently. He first arrives in Argos, where Acrisius has been usurped by his brother Proetus. Using predictable means, Perseus reinstates his grandfather, who has shown himself in no way deserving of such vengeance (3.559–60, 4.607–12), then makes for the small island of Seriphos, where he and his mother lived following their exile (see note to 4.611–12). The local tyrant, Polydectes, had sent Perseus on the suicide mission to kill Medusa in the first place; Ovid not only assumes his audience's familiarity with the story of Perseus, he neglects to mention its beginning until the end.

248 *Don't look:* A confusing statement. As he did with Phineus at 5.180, Perseus presumably directs this command at everyone in the room except Polydectes.

Pyreneus and the Muses (250–93)

With better things to do than watch Perseus live happily ever after, Minerva flies off for a visit with the Muses, patron goddesses of the arts and sciences, at their home on Mount Helicon. There, she will linger for the remainder of the book, listening to the goddesses' transformation-filled news. Their first tale relates their recent escape from the deranged king Pyreneus, the first in a string of mortals who radically overestimate their own power to contend with the gods.

254–57 *sprang from his hoof:* Medusa's equine son Pegasus, mentioned in passing at 4.786, has caused a magical spring to well on "maiden" Helicon, so called after the virgin Muses who live there. Appropriately named the Hippocrene ("Horse's Fountain"), its waters were purported to cause poetic inspiration.

The Pierides, Part 1 (294–340)

As Book 6 in particular will make abundantly clear, comparing yourself to the gods is a bad idea and competing with them is even worse. But making your entry in such a contest purposefully blasphemous is an especially poor strategy, as the nine daughters of Pierus discovered when they challenged the Muses to a battle of songs. The remainder of Book 5 details the contents and outcome of that sprawling battle, beginning with the Pierides' revisionist song of the gods' war against the Giants, a choice of subject matter unlikely to win points religiously or artistically: see note on the Gigantomachy at 1.151–62. As with the tale of Lycaön, however, if the Pierides come off as talentless and rude, we do well to remember that it is a hostile Muse narrating.

318   *With lots undrawn:* Like a coin-toss, the drawing of lots would normally determine the order of competition. The Pierides rudely insisted on going first.

326ff   *she said:* This clumsy story, in addition to being a poor testament to the supposed talents of Pierus' daughters, purports to explain the hybrid animal forms of the Egyptian gods. We have already seen the horned god Ammon identified with Jupiter. Diana was similarly syncretized with the cat god Bastet, Mercury with the ibis-headed Thoth, and so on.

The Rape of Proserpine (341–571)

For their turn, the Muse Calliope unfolds a long, rambling song of interlocking stories, loosely coalescing around the figure of Ceres, goddess of agriculture. Though various digressions will relate the creation of the gecko, the Sirens, and two springs on the island of Sicily, the song begins with a harsh ending to the story of Typhon, putting the Pierides firmly in their place. It then takes up its principal story, an etiological myth of the seasons—or, less pleasantly, the rape of Ceres' daughter Proserpine at the hands of her uncle Dis, though the narrative focus rests less on the princess than on the anguish of those who care for her. Notably for a song sung by, for, and about women, a major subplot sees the nymph Cyane try to intervene with a theory of consent-based romance; her failure to halt the crime will cause her to literally dissolve in tears.

349–53   *Ausonia's capes:* The three capes of Sicily (whose most prominent landmark is the volcanic Mount Etna) are Lilybaeum, Pachynus, and Pelorus, the last of which reaches toward Italy (Ausonia).

359ff   *The darkling lord*: Like his brother Jupiter at 2.402ff, Dis starts out as a conscientious king, careful to ensure his realm has survived recent catastrophe. Also like his brother, he will be distracted by an opportunity for sexual aggression.

368   *Allotted but the last of three domains*: Legend held that, after defeating the Titans, the three sons of Saturn drew lots for kingdoms. Jupiter won the sky and Neptune the sea, leaving Dis the underworld. Mother Earth alluded to this myth at 2.291–92.

386–87   *singing swans . . . Caÿster's coursing waves*: The Caÿster in Anatolia is still a major habitat for swans (2.252–53). Pergusa Lake, however, is now better known for its racetrack.

405ff   *Palici's sulphurous pools*: A brief exhibition of Sicilian geography. The Palici were local chthonic gods whose cult centered on a group of small volcanic lakes. The two-harbored city of Syracuse was founded in 734 BCE as a colony of Corinth, a Greek city then ruled by the Bacchiadae clan and located on an isthmus.

412   *the best-known nymph in Sicily*: Surprise, surprise, the myth of the nymph Cyane is unknown prior to Ovid. Both the springs of Ciane and Arethusa, however, flow at Syracuse to this day.

460–61   *Its naming fits / Its shaming, for the gecko's flecked with specks*: The Latin is, unsurprisingly, more convincing: the skin of the gecko (*stellio*) is star-spangled (*stellatus*) with spots.

468   *a clear, familiar sign*: Though not a direct object of assault, Cyane's loss of voice requires her to seek alternate modes of expression in a manner reminiscent of Io (1.649) and, later, Philomela (6.574–79), identifying her with other rape victims.

487   *Then Alpheus' nymph rose from her Elean waves*: This is Arethusa, whose connection to Alpheus and Elis will be explained further on (5.575–637). In older versions of

the myth, it was the all-seeing Sun who informed Ceres of her daughter's whereabouts. Ovid's promotion of assault survivor Arethusa to that role provides a neat parallel to the tale of Proserpine, while also preserving the gynocentrism of the Muse's song.

540   *Not the least famous of Avernal nymphs:* Orphne was, of course, not famous at all. Her partner, the Acheron, is a river of the underworld, to which the Romans believed Lake Avernus was an entrance.

555   *O Sirens skilled in song:* The Sirens were bird-woman monsters, most famous for their appearance in the *Odyssey,* where their seductive voices lure sailors to their deaths. Depicted here as daughters of the river Acheloüs, they receive a surprising degree of sympathy (including direct address) from the Muse, who has shown little such regard for the dubiously just transformations of Ascalaphus and the nameless gecko-boy. All three stories prefigure the Pierides' fate at the hands of the Muses.

Arethusa (572–641)

As promised, Arethusa gets to tell her tale. Seldom in the poem does a character narrate their own metamorphosis and only here and in the Crow's short backstory from Book 2 is that narrative one of rape. Accordingly, her flight from the river Alpheus runs like a horror replay of Apollo and Daphne, even recycling the same hare-and-hound metaphor (1.534–40; 5.628–29). But this nymph will not need to lose her identity to escape; in fact, her metamorphosis is notably lacking in change, since Arethusa retains not only her consciousness but some version of her form. The main alteration is the welcome distance that has sprung up between her, now located in Sicily, and her Peloponnesian assailant, now seas away. Arethusa is a rare female character that manages to foil her rapist, and it is small wonder that both Ceres and Calliope decide to spend some extra time with her.

577   *those Achaean nymphs:* That is to say, she was originally Greek rather than Sicilian. With Arethusa taking over the

narration, Ovid now has Urania telling Minerva what Calliope told the Pierides Arethusa told Ceres.

607–9 *Past Psophis . . . nor was I outsped:* According to Arethusa's catalog of landmarks, she made it over 150 miles before beginning to tire.

Lyncus and Triptolemus (642–61)

Calliope ends on a short anticlimactic coda recalling the agrarian hymn with which she began. Having heard Arethusa's tale, Ceres finally gets around to undoing the havoc she wrought at 474–86 and dispatches her Athenian minion Triptolemus to spread agriculture to the world. The story was well-known in Ovid's time, which may explain his neglecting to really tell it. Usually a venerable culture hero, here Triptolemus does little more than nearly die and hurry home.

656 *will bring ripe food and fruit:* Calliope concludes her hymn to Ceres with language that mirrors its opening (5.343), though the reader is about to discover that this signal act will not be shown.

661 *The Mopsian youth return her sainted team:* With its obscure synonym for "Athenian" and abrupt ending, this final line is nearly as uninspired as that used by the Pierides at 331. With the book's much more convincing conclusion following shortly after, the contest's real winner is clearly Ovid.

The Pierides, Part 2 (662–78)

677–78 *Now, too . . . boundless will to speak:* Much as Ceres unleashed the lynx inside Lyncus and Jupiter justified the 'aptness' of changing Lycaön into a wolf (1.236–9), Urania contends that the transformed Pierides merely continue their idle prattling, chatty as ever. But the narrator has already informed us that they are mourning their dismal fate (298); as he returns to the mainframe of the poem, Ovid reminds us not to put our trust in gods.

BOOK 6

Arachne and Minerva (1–145)

Although the Muses and Pierides have been left behind, the theme of ill-advised contests continues. Inspired by their example, Minerva decides to confront a rival of her own, a girl named Arachne who dares to match her skill at weaving. In the resulting competition, both girl and goddess prove adept at thematic consistency: Minerva's tapestry portrays the punishment of other presumptuous mortals, while Arachne's unfolds a litany of divine injustices (all rapes). Unlike Urania's song-driven account, however, this story is as much about the contestants as the contest, with the narrator's return delivering a fresh slew of humanizing details.

23   *You'd know that Pallas must have trained the girl:* Arachne's denial is easier to swallow if one takes this line metaphorically, that is, as an assertion that all talent is a gift from the gods. This reading makes Minerva's revenge even more arbitrary, however.

70–72   *the ancient fight / To name that land:* In the heart of Athens ("Cecrops' city") sits a stone outcropping called the Areopagus ("Hill of Mars"), where court proceedings were traditionally conducted. There, Minerva (Athena) and Neptune once vied to be the city's patron and namesake, with Neptune's gift of a salt spring easily bested by Minerva's olive tree. Minerva has woven a testament to her own glory and munificence; the rest of her tapestry will be more menacing.

72   *Jove, august:* The first of only three instances of the adjective *augustus* in the poem, this description links the name of the Emperor with that of the king of the gods. The next occurrence will be less flattering (9.270).

85ff   *four contests in the corners four:* These are all somewhat obscure. Since they *called each other by the names of gods*, it seems the mortals Haemus and Rhodope "contested" the nature of divinity and were punished accordingly. The Pygmies were a mythical race of dwarves said to war with cranes after their queen Oenoë became one, but neither she nor Antigone, daughter of king Laömedon of Troy (not the child of Oedipus found in Sophocles), were otherwise known to have engaged in a contest. The story of Cinyras' staircase full of daughters is completely unknown.

103ff   *The Lydian likewise wove:* There is no clear structure to Arachne's weaving, but Ovid's catalog of its contents comprises an astonishing number of stories, all involving gods who underwent temporary transformations in order to assault women. Opening with the familiar tale of Europa (and recycling the narrator's phrase "bull disguise" from 3.1) lends Arachne's list credibility. Jove's other victims are the Titan Asteria, in an otherwise unknown story; the Spartan queen Leda, who bore him Helen of Troy; the Theban king Nycteus' daughter Antiope, mother of Amphion; Alcmene, wife of Amphitryon of Tiryns, in whose guise Jove fathered Hercules; Danaë, mother of Perseus; Asopus' daughter Aegina, mother of Aeacus (the flame disguise is Ovid's invention and rather alarming); Mnemo(sy)ne, mother of the Muses; and Proserpine, his own daughter with Ceres (Deo).

115ff   *Neptune:* The sea god also has a track record of sexual deceptions, beginning with Canace, daughter of king Aeolus. Ovid's Neptune unprecedentedly impersonates the river Enipeus to sire the giant Aload twins on Iphimedia, while his ram-shaped relations with Theophane, daughter of Bisaltes, resulted in the ram of the Golden Fleece. He further coupled with Demeter in the form of a horse, and with Medusa in an unspecified winged form not elsewhere attested, but which might account for the pinions of Pegasus. His rape of Deucalion's daughter Melantho in a dolphin's guise spawned Delphi's founder Delphus.

123ff   *Next:* These stories are very murky. Apollo's peasant service to king Admetus is not usually characterized as assault (2.678–83), and the hawk and lion myths are unknown. Isse was the daughter of *Aeolus' girl* Canace, raped by Neptune. Bacchus' seduction of Erigone *aux raisins* is not otherwise known (though the painting by Charles André van Loo is delightfully batty). Saturn's equine siring of Chiron would explain the centaur's form.

140   *Of Hecate's:* A very odd detail. Hecate was a goddess of witchcraft, but how Minerva came by her potion and why she would need it is unclear; to effect a transformation, a god's emotional impulse has hitherto proven sufficient.

Niobe (146–312)

By now, the citizens of Thebes are well-schooled in the risks of religious inobservance, but their queen Niobe has yet to learn the lesson. Whereas Arachne and the Pierides foolishly challenged the gods in contests, Niobe believes she has already won: the goddess Latona, mother of Apollo and Diana, has only two children, while Niobe boasts fourteen. Narrated in a complex array of tones ranging from fanciful melodrama to aching pity, Niobe's consequent and violent humbling begins a short series of revenge stories about Latona and her children.

149   *While living close on Phrygian Sipylus:* To effect his transition, Ovid explains that Arachne had been childhood friends with Niobe, daughter of the Phrygian king Tantalus of Sipylus. As Ovid's audience would have known, Niobe moved to Boeotia on marrying the musician-king Amphion of Thebes.

173ff   *My sire was Tantalus:* In this list of traits, feats, and relations, readers may recognize the structure of a formal hymn (cf. 1.515ff, 4.17ff): Niobe is quite literally singing her own praises. Her points of pride, however, are notably dubious; lauding her father Tantalus as the only man to dine in heaven is especially questionable, given how he abused the privilege (see note to 4.457ff).

176–79 *And Jove . . . the walls my husband's lyre / Once built:* Jupiter was the father of both Niobe's father Tantalus and her husband Amphion, whose mother Antiope, daughter of Nycteus, appears on Arachne's tapestry (110). Amphion was a magical musician in the mold of Orpheus whose playing charmed the Theban walls into building themselves.

191   *floating Delos:* A fuller version of the story is given at
        332–36. In typical fashion, Juno tormented her husband's
        latest lover by forbidding her to give birth on any
        landmass. However, since the isle of Delos drifted across
        the seas unmoored, it did not qualify as "land" and
        welcomed her. In reward, the island was finally fixed to
        the ocean floor and was held sacred to Latona's children
        (the Delian gods) ever after, as shown at 13.631–35.

312   *As, even now, her tears bedew the stone:* Water still trickles
        from the Weeping Rock of Sipylus (now Mount Spil in
        modern Turkey), which passingly resembles a human
        head.

Latona and the Lycians (313–81)

Niobe's demise reminds her frightened subjects of other stories of
Delian vengeance, which they swap with one another as if over a
campfire. For a relieving change, Latona's rage in this story is entirely
sympathetic, and the Lycian peasants she punishes seem thoroughly
deserving of their fate. Having the Thebans tell it, however, is no mere
framing device; by fearfully narrating Latona's miseries immediately
after Niobe's, they show that even the most weak, isolated, and
oppressed of deities can still destroy mortal lives.

339 *the Chimaera's land:* The Chimaera was a fire-breathing
     Lycian monster whose lion's body sported extra goat and
     snake heads (cf. 9.647–48). It does not appear in this tale.

376 *in the depths, still in the depths:* The Latin repetition hides an
     amphibian onomatopoeia, mimicking the sound of a
     croaking frog: *sub aqua, sub aqua.* I attempt something
     similar in the following line.

Marsyas (382–400)

The story of yet another ill-fated contest both responds to the tale of
the Lycians and echoes that of Arachne. This myth was familiar
enough to allow Ovid's omission of context: the satyr Marsyas, having
discovered a set of pipes discarded by Minerva, challenged Apollo to a
musical competition. Marsyas played well, but since his instrument

prevented him from matching the god's feat of playing his lyre upside-down, he lost and Apollo had him flayed. Like Titian's painting, Ovid's portrayal concentrates on the punishment rather than the contest, saving those details for Apollo's other musical match-up in Book 11.

> 385–86   *Why tear me from myself:* A famous line and, along with the following, one of the most oft-cited examples of Ovid's oddly timed wit (see note to 3.465).

Pelops (401–11)

Another brief sketch returns the narrative to its present, where Niobe is mourned by her brother Pelops—the son Tantalus once tried to feed to the gods (the crime's punishment is described at 4.458–59). A broader vision of Niobe's funeral provides the transition to the next tale.

> 409   *Save that between the throat and upper arm:* Ovid is being dainty. The traditional explanation was that Ceres, distracted with grief over Proserpine's disappearance, had eaten it.

Tereus, Procne, and Philomela (412–674)

Leaving Thebes and the gods (mostly) behind, Ovid hits upon the appalling story of king Tereus of Thrace and the two daughters of king Pandion of Athens, Procne and Philomela. In previous tales, we have often encountered unscrupulous rapists who abuse their power, jealous wives who misdirect their rage, and tormented victims struggling to speak. This time, however, all three characters will be humans, each as capable of suffering great pain as inflicting it, with sickening results that make this myth perhaps the poem's most disturbing to read. The utter sordidness of Tereus' intentions and the gruesomeness of their fulfillment all but force the reader into a degree of sympathy with the abominable vengeance that follows, but both the action and reaction channel their traumas and transgressions into such sheer violence that the final transformation brings not so much climax as relief. Those familiar with Shakespeare will recognize the inspiration for *Titus Andronicus* in Philomela's sufferings and the horrific form of her revenge.

412ff   *The nearby towns:* Ovid recycles the "all-but-one" transition
he used between the tales of Daphne and Io (1.568–85), but
his catalog of cities jumbles chronology. Corinth was not
famed for bronze until the Hellenistic period, *Diana's spite*
toward Calydon looks forward to the great boar hunt of
Book 8 (271–72), and although it is true that, since we have
just seen Pelops alive, his son Pittheus cannot yet have ruled
Troezen, the same should apply to his other son Atreus and
the city of Mycenae. The rule of king Neleus of Pylos is
more plausibly contemporaneous. Lines 419–20 merely
refer to the lands either side of the Isthmus of Corinth.

459   *his tribe is quick to love:* Greek prejudice held that the
inhabitants of Thrace, a borderland on the northern fringes
of Greece and thus semi-barbarian, were given to violence
and lust. Ovid, however, states that Tereus' debauchery is
individual as well as inbred.

627ff   *Her parent's heart was moved, her anger waned:* This short
scene, in which Procne first voices then overcomes her
indecision, prefigures several of the later poem's grand
monologues, particularly that of Althaea, who will also
convince herself to kill her son to avenge a sibling (8.445–
514). The stories of Medea (Book 7), Scylla and Althaea
(both Book 8), Byblis and Iphis (both Book 9), and Myrrha
(Book 10) will all show similarly hesitant women talking
themselves in and out of transgressions of varying intensity.
Though in most cases the established mythic plots make
their ultimate decisions inevitable, it is telling that the
Ovidian characters inside whose minds we spend the most
time are, without exception, women.

655   *It is inside you have him:* With the words "it is," this
translation acknowledges a morbid pun in the Latin: when
Tereus calls for Itys, Procne homophonously directs him to
look inside (*intus*). Tereus' blithe eating of his own child is
a reminder that he is human; in the preceding story of
Pelops, the gods recognized boy meat right away.

670   *their bloodstained plumes:* The sisters were transformed into
a swallow and a nightingale, both presumably speckled.

There was some debate among previous authors as to which sibling became which, so Ovid tactfully neglects to specify.

Boreas and Orithyia (675–721)

The dark tale of king Tereus gives way to the much lighter one of the north wind Boreas. Disgraced by the conduct of his fellow Thracian, Boreas sails over the spectacularly low bar set by his countryman even as he forcibly abducts an Athenian maiden of his own, Pandion's granddaughter Orithyia. But this is a story of neither eroticism nor deceit, and the focus gently lands first on the Wind's pomposity, then on the cliffhanger ending that draws both book and story to a close.

680–82 *you, Procris . . . Tereus:* The story of Procris and Cephalus will be told at 8.694ff. Identifying the sisters' suitors geographically reinforces the anti-Thracian prejudice stated at 459. Compared to the boorish Boreas, the ethnically Greek (and human) Cephalus will seem fairly noble.

696–99 *flashing flames . . . With quaking:* Ancient "scientific" explanations pointed to wind as the cause of lightning and earthquakes. Pythagoras is seen teaching on the subject at 15.69–71.

720–21 *the Minyans on that first of ships . . . the fleece of gold:* Book 6 ends with an abrupt teaser for the *Argo*'s voyage in quest of the Golden Fleece, one of the great subjects of ancient epic, though readers hoping for a conventional retelling will be sorely surprised. The *Argo* was purportedly the first ship ever built (but cf. 511), and its crew, the Argonauts, were largely descended from king Minyas, whose daughters appeared in Book 4, giving rise to their other name, the "Minyans."

BOOK 7

Medea (1–424)

As hinted at the end of Book 6, Ovid now tells his version of the quest for the Golden Fleece, a magical MacGuffin owned by king Aeëtes of the far-off land of Colchis (modern Georgia). The adventures of young

Jason of Iolcus and his all-hero cast of sidekicks had received its definitive treatment in Apollonius of Rhodes' third century BCE epic the
Argonautica. But where Apollonius spun a tale of masculine camara-
derie, focusing on feats of daring and the exploits of such accompany-
ing heroes as Hercules, Orpheus, and Peleus (none of whom figure in
this version), Ovid's interest centers firmly on another character:
Medea, daughter of Aeëtes, lover of Jason, granddaughter of the Sun,
and invincible sorceress.

Medea seems to have been Ovid's favorite character. Prior to the
Metamorphoses, where she occupies the first half of this book, the poet
had given her voice twice before, first in his *Heroides* and later in a
tragic drama, now lost (her soliloquy at 11–71 would be at home in a
play). Yet her best-known act, the murder of her children as famously
dramatized by Euripides, is here dispensed with in four obligatory lines
(394–97), ceding space to three major tales of her transformative witchcraft: her assistance in winning the Golden Fleece (5–158), her rejuve-
nation of Jason's father Aeson (159–293), and her murder of Aeson's
wicked brother Pelias (297–349). Her subsequent flight opens up a geographical catalog of mini-metamorphoses (350–401), ending in her
attempted poisoning of Theseus (402–24), which leads into the rest of
the book. In these renditions, the heroism of the Argonauts, the treachery of her father, and even the infidelity of Jason are of little account.

In her deeds, Medea is metamorphosis in microcosm. As her
incantations show (191–219), her powers are ill-defined, wide-ranging,
driven by both great malignity and great good, and about as likely to
help as to hurt. As a character, she occupies a similarly complex place
in the Greek mythos: a mighty, terrifying, barbarian female driven by
a sympathetic love to commit norm-shattering transgressions that go
unpunished by man or god. In a poem filled with betrayed women
and powerless mortals, Medea cuts a towering figure, forging her own
way amid heroes and kings with her ruthlessness, kindness, and
magic.

2–4   *From Pagasae . . . wingèd maids:* Aside from these three
        lines, which smooth the transition from Boreas (Aquilo),
        the venturesome trials and tribulations that take up the
        first half of the *Argonautica* are pared down to the "many
        pains" of line 5. Setting out from the Thessalian port of

Pagasa, along their way the Argonauts encounter Phineus, not the ex-fiancé of Andromeda but a blind Thracian prophet beset by the Harpies (winged tormentors with female faces), who kept the old man from eating. Equipped with wings of their own, Calaïs and Zetes drive them off.

6–7 *Phasis' muddy swirl . . . Phrixus' fleece:* When his stepmother Ino plotted to have him killed, prince Phrixus of Thebes was rescued by a flying golden ram who bore him to Colchis, a Black Sea city on the Phasis river. (Midflight, his sister Helle fell off and drowned in the namesake Hellespont.) At Colchis, Phrixus sacrificed the ram and bequeathed its fleece to king Aeëtes.

29–31 *the cattle's breath . . . feed the dragon:* As will be seen, to prove himself worthy of the Fleece, Jason will have to yoke a team of bronze-footed, fire-breathing bulls forged by Vulcan, defeat a band of warriors sprung from dragon's teeth, and defeat the dragon guarding the treasure.

62–66 *those mountains claimed to clash . . . Sicilian depths:* Three classic perils faced by mythic seafarers. The Symplegades ("Clashing Rocks") smashed ships that sailed between them, while Charybdis was a massive whirlpool that, together with the sea monster Scylla, choked the Strait of Messina. Scylla's origin story is told at 14.50–67.

101 *the sacred field of Mars:* Not the Campus Martius at Rome; many cities had a field dedicated to military exercise.

158 *Home to Iolcus' port:* Ovid continues to dance around his literary predecessor, polishing off in a single line a journey that occupies the final quarter of the *Argonautica*. He omits the crew's betrayal and chase by Aeëtes, along with Medea's murder of her brother.

207–8 *I steer you, too, O Moon . . . allay your toils:* Medea caps off her litany of magical tropes (borrowed by Shakespeare for Prospero's use in Act 5 of the *Tempest*) with an allusion to the "Thessalian Trick" of drawing down the moon (cf. 12.263–64). The clashing of bronze cymbals was believed to give the moon strength in such instances (cf. 4.333), and Tempsa was the site of a large copper mine.

232–33   *Glaucus' change:* As described at 13.934ff, the fisherman Glaucus was transformed after eating herbs grown at Anthedon, a Boeotian town in fact located opposite Euboea.

294–96   *And Liber . . . / . . . the Colchian:* An odd coda to the episode, this otherwise obscure tale of Bacchus and his nurses was the subject of a lost play by Aeschylus. These cannot be the immortal nymphs of Nysa invoked at 3.314.

299   *Pelias:* As he did with Perseus and Polydectes (5.242–49), Ovid circles back to the hero's origin story without ever explaining it. After Pelias usurped the throne of Iolcus from his brother Aeson, he sent his nephew Jason to retrieve the Golden Fleece on the assumption that the quest would get the young man killed.

324   *Ebro's stream:* Dividing the Iberian peninsula, the Ebro river marked the western end of the known world.

350ff   *had she not flown:* Medea's murder of Pelias necessitated the couple's flight for sanctuary at Corinth, where Jason will soon throw her over for another woman. Naturally, Ovid has her take a ridiculous route, allowing for allusions to an additional twenty or so myths. Philyra's son is the centaur Chiron, who lived near Iolcus on Mount Pelion in Thessaly, in northern Greece. The lands made famous by Cerambus are of uncertain location; in the known version, he escaped drowning only by becoming a beetle. The stone statue of a giant snake at Pitane, way off by Lesbos, is more fully glimpsed at 11.54–60. Corythus' sire is Paris, the disgraced prince of Troy (see 12.4ff), who was ignominiously buried in a pit of sand. The stories of the calf that Bacchus' son had stolen in a stag's disguise, of Maera's eerie barks, and of how the Coan wives grew horns are all obscure. Furthest of all from Corinth is Ialysos, a major city of Rhodes, held by the Telchines in their capacity as the island's mythic aboriginals, whose wicked sorcery (and, in this telling, evil eyes) earned them divine punishment.

370   *A docile dove birthed from his daughter's corpse*: When Alcidamas of Carthaea (on the isle of Cea) went back on his oath to force his daughter Ctesylla into marriage, the gods punished him by having her die in childbirth, supposedly making it up to her by transforming her corpse into a dove.

372   *Cygnus' sudden change*: A different Cygnus from Book 2 (see note to 2.368–69).

382ff   *Nearby lay Pleuron*: This further lightning round of metamorphoses is extremely obscure. Of Combe, the Calaurean royal family, Menephron, and the grandson of Cephisus, nothing is known. A devotee of Apollo, Eumelus killed his son Botres for his impiety toward the god, who in turn took pity and resurrected the boy as a bird. The delightful tale of creation *ex fungo*, sketched out at 392–93, is also unknown but seemingly contradicts the already supernumerary narratives of human origins given in Book 1 (see note to 1.77ff).

394–97 *poisoned the new wife . . . fled from Jason's arms, avenged*: In four lines, Ovid summarizes the entire action of Euripides' tragedy. Upon returning to Corinth, Medea discovered that Jason had taken a new wife, whom she promptly dispatched with a poisoned robe. She continued her retaliation by killing her own children, burning the palace, remounting her chariot, and fleeing to romantic refuge at the court of king Aegeus of Athens, who had promised her sanctuary.

400–1   *Just Phene . . . all take flight*: A final couple of transformations relocate the scene to Athens. When the people of Attica began giving their king Periphas the honors due to Jove, the god changed him and his wife Phene into an eagle and a vulture. In a separate tale, Polypemon's granddaughter Alcyone was hurled from a cliff for her inchastity, whereupon she became a 'halcyon,' or kingfisher. (Ovid will present the tale of a different Alcyone in Book 11.) That Medea has had to borrow the flying dragons of her grandfather the Sun to get to Athens indicates the gods remain on her side. The image is borrowed from the end of Euripides' play.

404–5   *Theseus, a stranger to his sire . . . Isthmus of two seas:* Shortly to be introduced at greater length, Theseus was an illegitimate son of Aegeus who presented himself to his father only after reaching adulthood. His journey to Athens via the Isthmus of Corinth saw him dispatch a number of monsters, as detailed at 433ff.

411   *Dragged Cerberus in adamantine chains:* For the last of his Twelve Labors (covered in Book 9), the Tirynthian hero Hercules kidnapped Cerberus from the underworld. The poisonous quality of the hellhound's saliva has been seen at 4.501.

424   *the witch fled for her life:* There is no myth detailing Medea's death and, for all her crimes, she never appears to lose the favor of heaven. In a sign of true character agency, the worst fate Medea ever suffers is that she chooses for herself.

Theseus (425–52)

Having left Perseus behind in Book 5, Ovid now introduces Theseus, the second of Greek mythology's three great heroes (Hercules will appear in Book 9, mostly in order to die). Expectations are again subverted, however, as the poet gives short shrift to the character's two most familiar narrative arcs. His famous labors on the journey to Athens, hinted at in 405, are told only in the form of a rapid-fire hymn (433–50), and we are treated to just the barest beginning of the tale of the labyrinth before Ovid transitions away, leaving the story of Theseus and the Minotaur to be resumed—sort of—at 8.151.

433ff   *O greatest Theseus . . .:* In a previous effort to get him killed, Medea had tasked Theseus with subduing *the Cretan bull,* father of the Minotaur, then busy ravaging the city of Marathon. He had similarly slain the *Crommyonian Sow,* a monstrous pig destroying the town Crommyon. On his way to Athens, Theseus also killed *Vulcan's cudgel-wielding son* Periphetes (a persistent menace to wayfarers), the *cruel Procrustes* (who strapped his victims to a bed and racked or hacked them until they fit its dimensions), King Cercyon of Eleusis (who wrestled travelers to death), the brigand Sinis (who tied his victims to the tops of two bent trees which he then released, tearing them apart), and the robber Sciron (who enticed his victims to the edge of a cliff from which he kicked them, and from which Theseus in turn hurled him). The eponymous Scironic Rocks of 447 refer to a sea-cliff on Mount Gerania still known as *Kaki Scala* ("dangerous climb").

The War with Minos (453–522)

As it happens, the powerful king Minos of Crete (the child Europa bore to Jupiter) holds Aegeus at fault for the death of his son Androgeus, though precisely why Ovid does not say. His vast war of vengeance against Athens will give rise to several stories before it is quietly dropped at 8.263, but readers expecting the normal narrative of a quick Athenian defeat resulting in the blood tribute that fed the Minotaur will first have to wait through extended scenes of diplomatic intrigue, with both Minos and Aegeus seeking military aid from the island kingdom of Aegina.

458   *Androgeus' death*: Multiple versions of the story exist; all hold the Athenians at fault.

465–68 *plumes of black*: The tale of Arne's treason against Paros and Siphnos is not found elsewhere but prefigures the treachery of Scylla in Book 8. Like crows, other birds, and the present author, jackdaws exhibit an attraction to shiny things.

473–74 *Aeacus' mother ... "Aegina"—hers*: King Aeacus is the son of Jupiter and Aegina, daughter of Asopus. His conception is mentioned at 6.113, and his three sons (Telamon, Peleus, and Phocus) recur throughout the latter half of the poem. This strange couplet will turn out to provide important information for the coming tale (see 523–24).

493   *Cephalus:* Last seen marrying Procris at 6.681, the
       Athenian diplomat arrives with Clytus and Butes, the two
       narratively inconsequential sons of Aegeus' brother
       Pallas.

The Myrmidons (523–660)

Aeacus explains the strange absence of his former subjects with an account of the horrific plague that annihilated his people. Plague narratives—known to modern readers through zombie movies, Camus, Defoe, and the prologue to Boccaccio's *Decameron*—were already familiar in Ovid's time from the works of Lucretius and Virgil, who modeled theirs after the great plague of Athens described by the historian Thucydides. Ovid's rendition is predictably hyperbolic, though his capacity for gruesome wit does not entirely rob the scene of pathos. Though the focus remains on human matters, the gods (who have been notably absent from this book) here return in major narrative roles, with Juno's jealous wrath causing the plague and Jupiter mercifully "resolving" it.

623   *Sacred to Jove and of Dodonaean stock:* That is, sprung from
       the seed of an oak in the sacred grove of Jove's sanctuary at
       distant Dodona (cf. note to 1.104–6).

654   *Myrmidons:* In Greek, "Ant-People." Aeacus' grandson
       Achilles would lead them in the Trojan War, where they
       distinguished themselves by their unswerving, antlike
       loyalty.

Cephalus and Procris (661–865)

Of the poem's few passingly happy couples, Cephalus and Procris are the most tragic and the most thoroughly treated. Endowing a typically melodramatic myth with tenderness and even believability, Ovid glosses over its more salacious plot points to fashion a two-part parable on the dangers of jealousy, where each partner's suspicion of the other wins lasting pain for both (though Cephalus' doubts are far less reasonable). The grieving widower is upfront about the guilt he feels, but repressed shame and trauma continually belie his narration; his attempt to distract his audience and stop halfway results in the amusing digression of the Teumessian Fox.

685   *Nereus' grandson:* Phocus was the son of Psamathe, a
       Nereid (cf. 690: *goddess' son*). This will prove important
       in Book 11, when Psamathe decides to avenge his
       murder.

688a   *There was a pause:* The manuscripts transmit line 687 in
       no less than three different versions, all transparently
       corrupt. Taken together with the transmitted 688, each
       seems to indicate that Cephalus' silence is connected
       with his shame at the price of obtaining the spear (see
       note to 751, below). Since these readings are redundant
       with 751 and of dubious authenticity, editor R. J. Tarrant
       inserted a line of his own composition—*ipse diu reticet
       Cephalus tactusque dolore*—to serve as a placeholder
       transition between 686 and 689, conjecturing its content
       from Ovid's style while cobbling together phrases
       gleaned from the corrupt transmission.

694–97 *You'll have heard about . . . fitter prey:* We have indeed
       heard of Orithyia's rape (6.677ff). This clever metatextual
       statement contains a disturbing equation of rape and
       marriage not unheard of in Greek culture (as well as
       being a troubling remark to make about one's wife).

712–13 *but I foresee / That you'll regret it:* Unlike every other
       mortal object of divine lust in the poem, Cephalus was
       apparently free to refuse. Note that Dawn, who com-
       plains about her powerlessness in her only other major
       appearance (13.587–90), merely foretells his downfall,
       rather than causing it. She will, however, be there to
       watch it happen (835).

751   *once her wounded virtue was avenged:* As the preceding
       lines hint (and Cephalus here obliquely concedes), his
       own comparable infidelity was not entirely hypothetical.
       In alternate versions of the myth, Procris made her point
       by disguising herself as a boy and using the gifted spear
       to bribe Cephalus into a homosexual affair, proving that
       his virtue was no more incorruptible than hers. Ovid's
       elision of this episode preserves the two-part structure of
       his retelling while casting a knowing wink at readers who

know the story. Even so, gender and sexuality still bubble on the margins of his rendition; rather than directly addressing Cephalus' homosexual liaison, the poet has Procris renounce all men and join the aggressively homosocial huntresses of Diana.

757ff   *You want the story . . . ?*: As Cephalus distracts from his own humiliation, a comically clumsy transition allows the poet to insert an additional tale. The digression briefly returns us to the still-suffering city of Thebes, where Laius' son Oedipus has won the kingship by ridding the populace of the monstrous Sphinx, a cryptic riddler who killed all passersby that failed to answer the question of what walks on four legs in the morning, two at noon, and three in the evening. Oedipus correctly responded "man," understanding that humans crawl early in life, later walk upright, and adopt the use of a cane in their dotage. In defeat, the Sphinx hurled herself from a cliff, but the appearance immediately afterward of another *fearsome fiend*, an enormous vulpine generally known as the Teumessian Fox or the Cadmean Vixen, shows that the curse of Cadmus is still in effect: see the earlier note to the story of Cadmus and Harmonia (4.563–603). The allusion to the malice of Themis in line 762 is nonsensical and likely spurious.

793   *That both stay undefeated in that race:* The god (in other versions, Jupiter) addresses himself to the old paradox about an unstoppable force meeting an immovable object: rather positing an answer, he eliminates the question.

813ff   *zephyr:* The word *aura* ("breeze") is used four times in four lines, and thrice thereafter in the remainder of the book. Ovid's repetition is emphatic (the first four instances occur in line initial or terminal positions), and a translation issue arises in that the word must both accurately refer to a meteorological phenomenon and plausibly be mistaken for a person's name, as happens at 822 and 856. This would appear to preclude such obvious translations as "wind." I have adopted "zephyr," albeit with slight misgivings given its typically masculine character, especially with regard to this story. Nonetheless, its plausibility as both a weather pattern and a name makes it the clear choice. For other translators' choices, see the appendix.

853   *the gods above and those of mine:* Since Procris is close to death, "her" gods are presumably those of the underworld below.

BOOK 8

Scylla and Nisus (1–151)

Readers have likely forgotten all about Crete's war with Athens, but we soon catch up with Minos laying siege to the town of Megara, where Nisus reigns by virtue of his magical lock of hair. The problem turns out to be Nisus' daughter Scylla (not the sea monster commonly paired with Charybdis), whose love for Minos contends with her duty toward her homeland and father in an echo of Medea's predicament. Also like her Colchian predecessor, Scylla expresses her mind in long, conflicted speeches of deliberation. Her decision is predictably heinous, but her treasonous love benefits by comparison with the poem's other examples of the "traitress-within-the-walls" trope (Arne, 7.465–66; Tarpeia, 14.775–77), who are motivated solely by greed.

90   *I, Scylla:* Scylla's name goes unstated until she announces it herself (see note to 1.442).

99–100   *I'll surely not allow . . . monster's tread:* Ironic, considering Crete was proverbially rife with monsters (9.735–36), including one Minos will soon take great pains to house (152ff). The infant Jupiter was hidden on Crete to escape his father Saturn (see note to 1.113–14).

120–22   *you were born / To Syrtis' sands . . . Armenian tigers:* To avoid confusing the reader, Scylla mentions Charybdis but not the other Scylla. The Syrtes are dangerous sandy gulfs off the Libyan coast. Medea made a similar tiger comparison at 7.32–33.

131–33 *she's the wife for you . . . jumbled baby:* A cleverly disguised piece of exposition. As will shortly come to bear, when Minos' wife Pasiphaë fell in love with the Cretan bull (a sacred bovine sent by Neptune), she had the inventor Daedalus build her a wooden cow-suit so she could seduce the beast. Their union produced a man-bull hybrid called the Minotaur.

151 *shearer:* The species has not been convincingly identified.

The Minotaur (152–82)

Bowing to obligation, Ovid ties up a few loose ends even as he severs some new ones. Unable to abide the Minotaur's presence, Minos orders Daedalus to build an enormous labyrinth for its cage. Meanwhile, the war against Athens has been quietly won, forcing the vanquished city to feed the monster with its citizens, a menu of whom are offered by way of tribute every nine years. Theseus momentarily resurfaces to save the day and resume the story arc left off at 7.458, but soon abandons it along with the princess who aided him. This desertion sets up the poem's second catasterism before attention turns to the passage's most metamorphic character, the inventor Daedalus.

162–65 *Meander's playful Phrygian waves:* The name of the winding Meander River of Anatolia (modern Büyük Menderes) gave rise to the verb. The poem's other two mentions of the stream make similar references: 2.246, 9.450–51.

171–72 *a third nine-year tribute . . . with a maiden's help and spools of string:* Theseus volunteered himself for the third tribute. Minos' daughter Ariadne fell in love with the prince and gave him a ball of string with which to navigate his way back through the labyrinth.

181–82 *Crown / Between the Kneeler and the Strangled Snake:* The constellation Corona Borealis (the Northern Crown) sits adjacent to Engonasin ("the Kneeler," now known as Hercules) and Ophiuchus, which depicts a man grasping a snake.

Daedalus (183–266)

It happens that the brilliant Daedalus is an exiled Athenian, held at Crete against his will. Ovid gives his famed escape attempt with his son Icarus an affecting narration, with special emphasis on the boy's childlike qualities and the inventor's fatherly feeling. Only after tragedy transpires do we learn the reason for Daedalus' exile, and the sympathetic image of the grieving old man is vitiated by his criminal past. A further transition sees the city of Athens finally restored to peace.

185–87   *by land and sea . . . / Though Minos rules all, he can't rule the air*: Daedalus echoes the scope of Minos' power as portrayed by the king himself at 98: "our world, its lands and seas!" Like Scylla, he will thwart the tyrant's thrall by taking to the air.

217–19   *an angler's curving rod . . . they must be gods*: The clear inspiration for Bruegel the Elder's painting of Icarus, the country-folk's impression foreshadows the fliers' tragic downfall: time and again, we have seen what happens when mortals come too close to divinity. That Ovid called Daedalus a "maker" (*opifex*) at 201 only worsens the matter.

The Calydonian Hunt (267–444)

Once again, the return of Theseus signals a quick transition to another story. Having robbed his readers of one show of heroic solidarity in his version of the Argonauts, Ovid compensates with the gory, all-hero hunt of the Calydonian boar, a monster set by Diana on the people of Calydon to punish their insufficiently devout king Oeneus. The "heroes," led by Oeneus' son Meleäger, distinguish themselves mostly in their inability to wound the beast (this is Ovid, after all), yet the chief narrative distraction lies not in the incompetence of the hunters but in the romantic feelings Meleäger develops for the sole female member of the band, the inscrutable, androgynous, and unnamed Atalanta. When their male comrades detect bias in his treatment of this capable and transgressive woman, the scene is set for Meleäger's downfall in the following tale.

279   *Gods, too, feel rage*: Bold of Ovid to assume we had forgotten, given the utter bloodbath of the poem's first six books. But with the age of heroes dawning, this story

will, for the first time, see an organized band of mortals successfully oppose a god without divine aid.

283   *Epirus' plains . . . Sicily's:* An anachronistic reference to the enormous cattle bred by king Pyrrhus of Epirus (c. 319–272 BCE), whose war with the nascent Romans briefly saw him take charge of Sicily.

285–86   Lines 285 and 286, as transmitted, are mutually exclusive, and I have chosen to translate 286. See the appendix for further detail.

300ff   *Came seeking fame:* Ovid here composes his most conventional catalog yet (cf. note to 3.206ff), listing the heroes who will take part in the coming action. Several are worthy of comment. Tyndareus' twin sons are Castor and Pollux, a horseman and boxer respectively, later catasterized as the Gemini (see 372). Jason arrives fresh from the Argo, while Theseus brings the obnoxious Pirithoüs, his constant companion (see note to 405–6), who reappears numerous times in the poem. Thestius' two sons (the "Thestiads"), are Meleäger's maternal uncles Plexippus and Toxeus, who will prove vital to the story. Caeneus is no maid now, but the tale of how he once was will be told at 12.189ff. Echion is an Argonaut, not the dragon-born Theban of 3.126. The sire of great Achilles is Peleus, here joined by his brother Telamon, both of whom we met at the court of their father Aeacus. The elderly Lelex narrates a tale later in this book. Nestor will more famously fight in the next generation's Trojan War, where he will be noted for his age (cf. 12.169ff), and he, Caeneus, Peleus, and Ampycus' prophetic son Mopsus all reappear at the wedding of Pirithoüs in Book 12. Penelope's mate's sire is Laertes, father of Ulysses (husband of Penelope). Oecles' son Amphiaraus joined the Theban War at the malign urging of his wife Eriphyle, as will be (somewhat) explained at 9.405ff. Finally, the unnamed Tegean girl is Atalanta, described here with striking resemblance to the hunters' enemy Diana.

360   *Hippalmus . . . Pelagon*: Two hunters absent from the earlier catalog (cf. note to 3.232–35).

387   *manly valor*: Though the *uir* (man) in *uirtus* (strength, bravery, or the cognate "virtue") need not always be emphasized in translation, Atalanta's ability to hold her own in an all-male band proves crucial to the story (cf. 392, 433–35).

405–6   *my dearest one, / My better half*: Theseus and Pirithoüs shared perhaps Greek mythology's most famously homoerotic friendship, though (unlike that of Achilles and Patroclus) theirs was not usually portrayed as sexual. Ovid has been proposed as possibly the earliest author to make their romantic subtext explicit; Theseus will defend his friend in similarly affectionate terms at 12.227–29.

Althaea and Meleäger (445–546)

When Meleäger's mother Althaea objects to her son murdering her brothers, her vengeful deliberating vents itself in Ovid's next great speech of inner conflict. Like Scylla, Althaea can take fate literally in her own hands, since Meleäger too leads a charmed life, in this case tied not to a scarlet lock but to a log of firewood. Ovid's heartfelt portrait of her dilemma stands in sharp contrast to the glib tone of the earlier hunt, though the bonus metamorphosis of Meleäger's sisters makes for a melodramatic coda reminiscent of the Heliads in Book 2.

500   *pangs of twice-five months*: Since the Romans counted inclusively, the human gestation period of nine-plus months was rounded up to ten.

521   *wife*: In some versions, her name is Cleopatra. Ovid contrived not to mention her existence while her husband was falling in love with Atalanta.

533–35   *Not if a god . . . woeful prayers*: Classical poets often used displays of false modesty to sow suspense at climactic moments, insisting they have not the talent to capture what their next lines will capture quite well. Ovid lightly plays on this trope by employing it at a rather uninspired juncture; we have seen this kind of mourning before.

544   *Gorge and Alcmene's son's new wife:* The desire to set up
the next book's tales of Hercules (Alcmene's son) leads
Ovid to engage in a rare bout of fastidious consistency.
We will see Hercules win Deianira's hand at 9.8ff, while
her sister Gorge is spared to become the grandmother of
Diomedes, a major figure in Books 13 and 14. The
remaining sisters turn into guineafowl (*meleagrides*).

Acheloüs (547–610)

Heading home from Calydon, Theseus apparently goes the wrong
way, for he comes upon the flooding Acheloüs—the longest river in
Greece and a suitably pompous god. Welcomed to shelter in the river's
lavish home (the subject of a fine painting by Rubens), the heroes and
their host spend the rest of the book feasting, trading stories, and
ruminating on the power of the gods. The self-assured stream gets the
discussion off to a startlingly frank start with two short tales of his
own divine might: the first in which he kills five naiads, the second in
which he rapes a girl.

579   *You'll be less shocked by scorned Diana's deeds:* Acheloüs,
to his (partial) credit, is quite upfront about his own
misdeeds, and here compares them to Diana's summoning of the Calydonian boar to punish Oeneus' lack of
devotion (273–78). His treatment of the nymphs shares
both Diana's motivation and cruelty.

587–89   *The ocean's tides . . . the Echinades:* Ovid takes note of the
real-life transformative power of running water, which he
will address more directly at 15.287ff. In the fifth century
BCE, Herodotus wrote that alluvial deposits from the
Acheloüs had already connected half of the Echinades
archipelago to the mainland (2.10). By contrast, Ovid
ascribes the same mixed state of affairs to the opposite
process, erosion.

597ff   The text here is very patchy, with multiple transmission
issues; some lines may be spurious, but for reasons of
readability I have opted to translate them all. For details,
see the appendix.

Baucis and Philemon (611–724)

The next tale is narrated by the old and wise Lelex, who casts it as a proof of heavenly power. In a turn of events recalling the biblical story of Lot, Lelex tells of how Jupiter and Mercury once wandered Phrygia in disguise, finding no one willing to shelter them but a humble peasant couple. The fate of that pious pair comes as close to heartwarming as the poem gets, and the description of their paupers' generosity shows that Ovid's skills are just as suited to the mundane as to the epic.

612–15   *one of untamed mind . . . they cannot give and take things' shapes:* A preposterous statement at this juncture in the poem, but one that punches a complex hole in the suspension of disbelief—readers may well both agree in reality and disagree in universe. Calling Pirithoüs by his blasphemous father's name is surely a pointed gesture (see note to 4.457ff).

655–56a   As at 597ff, the manuscripts produce two sets of lines in this passage, with one version skipping from 651 to 655–6, and the other following 654 with the couplet known as 655a and 656a (lines 655–56 and 655a–56a contain similar information and are mutually exclusive). I follow most modern editors in preferring the latter version.

693   In yet another example of variant texts, some manuscripts contain an expanded, two-line version of 693. I follow most editors in opting for the briefer version.

Mestra and Erysichthon (725–878)

In case the previous story of divine reward taught Pirithoüs too gentle a lesson, Acheloüs rejoins with a tale of divine retribution. He purports to tell of shapeshifters, like the sea god Proteus and the mortal Mestra, but soon gets carried away narrating the sinfulness of Mestra's father Erysichthon, who is everything Baucis and Philemon were not, even chopping down a sacred tree reminiscent of the couple's final form. Unlike their portrayal in Ovid's source, Callimachus' *Hymn to Demeter,* Mestra's metamorphic dealings with the twin evils of rape and slavery are here used to lighten the mood, so unreasoning is Erysichthon's cruelty, so extreme his punishment (though, as usual, we do well to remember it is a god who is talking—and one proving a point at that).

738   *Autolycus' wife:* The roundabout reference to Mestra sets up a double subversion in expectation, since the girl's shapeshifting is really an excuse to tell the story of Erysichthon. Mestra herself is never named in the story and does not even appear until 847. Her husband Autolycus will not appear at all, though his birth is described at 11.311–15.

762   *The shattered bark let forth a stream of blood:* The original bleeding tree was Polydorus in *Aeneid* 3 (see note to 13.437), but Ovid's female versions lent the motif much of its renewed currency in the Renaissance, when it recurred in the works of Dante, Spenser, Tasso, and Dryden (among others). Ovid appears to have been fond of the image, using it twice elsewhere in the poem (2.358–60, 9.340–45).

791ff   *starving Hunger:* The home and personification of Hunger is the second of the poem's four great allegorical descriptions (see note to 2.760ff).

871–72   *But, seeing that Triops' heir . . . sold her often:* Ovid makes Mestra (Triops' granddaughter) something of an object lesson in abuse as she manages to parlay Neptune's assault into a measure of personal power, only to have that power exploited by her father. Slavery was a widespread institution in the ancient Mediterranean, though conditions, prevalence, and legal status varied greatly between societies. Impoverished Romans were allowed to "rent" their children into bondage, though a legal fiction differentiated the practice from enslavement.

Acheloüs and Hercules, Part 1 (879–84)

Ovid uses the last six lines of the book to tease the start of the next one.

884   *one of its weapons:* River gods were typically depicted with horns. The story of how Acheloüs lost one of his will occupy the opening of Book 9.

BOOK 9

Acheloüs and Hercules, Part 2 (1–97)

Though its first words refer to Theseus, the first half of Book 9 is all about Hercules, the third great hero of Greek mythology, and the only one Ovid allows a measure of convincing heroism. Instead of the normal tales of his miraculous birth and Twelve Labors, however, the poem will concern itself mostly with the hero's death, for which this story, detailing Hercules' defeat of Acheloüs for the hand of Deianira, forms a kind of prologue.

1   *Neptune's hero:* Theseus was the son of Neptune as well as Aegeus, both of whom slept with Theseus' mother Aethra on the same night. Such dual paternity was a common feature in the backstories of heroes, who could thereby inherit both semi-divine power and earthly thrones. We have seen a less prominent example with Meleäger, son of both Oeneus (8.414) and Mars (8.437).

8   *Of Deianira you'll perhaps have heard:* Ovid recycles his metatextual joke on Orithyia (see note to 7.694–97). Freshly arrived from the court of Deianira's brother Meleäger, Theseus most likely has heard of her (she was spared at 8.544). For those who know Greek, her name ("husband-destroyer") rather gives the game away.

15   *Those labors which his stepmother had set:* Being an illegitimate child of Jupiter, Hercules was predictably no favorite of Juno's. After she contrived to have him kill his wife and children in a bout of insanity, Hercules did penance by serving king Eurystheus of Tiryns, who assigned him a series of impossible *labors* on Juno's advice. The Labors themselves will be summarized at 181ff.

23   *Jove's your sire:* Jupiter impregnated Hercules' mother Alcmene in the guise of her husband Amphitryon.

36   *And tanned himself in turn with tawny sand:* A standard practice; wrestlers threw dust on one another to counteract their slippery body oil.

66 *I vanquished vipers from my crib:* In another bout of family feeling, Juno sent two monstrous serpents to kill the newborn Hercules, who instead strangled them. The image of the infant hero grasping a snake remained popular in Roman art.

69 *Lerna's Hydra:* For the second of his labors, Hercules slew the many-headed Lernaean Hydra, a serpentine monster that spawned two new heads with each decapitation. As will become important, he also dipped his arrows in its poisonous blood.

The Death of Hercules (98–273)

Rather than follow Theseus home, Ovid transitions to continue the long, convoluted narrative of Hercules' death, with details largely drawn from Sophocles' play *Trachiniae*. In its various episodes, from the killing of the centaur Nessus (98–133) to Deianira's unwitting betrayal (134–73), Hercules' dying recitation of his Labors (174–204), the murder of his slave Lichas (204–29), and the hero's ultimate immolation and catasterism (229–73), the story's tone swings wildly from the grandiose to the satirical, befitting a character who could be both admirable and pigheadedly wrathful—and who by Ovid's time had become associated with the Emperor: the apotheosis sequence neatly prefigures the deification of the Caesars in Book 15.

113 *lion-skin:* Among Hercules' most famous attributes was the pelt of the Nemaean Lion, slain as his First Labor, which he often wore draped about his shoulders. His club is another mainstay.

123 *your father's wheel:* Like Pirithoüs, the centaurs were descended from Ixion, whose wheel-based punishment for another attempted rape was glimpsed at 4.461.

140 *Iole:* Hercules was the stepson of Amphitryon, and Iole was the daughter of king Eurytus of Oechalia. In other versions (including Ovid's *Heroides*), the rumor is correct, but Ovid seems intent on heightening the sense of tragedy.

180   *Death, a true stepmother's gift:* Like writers of later fairy
tales, the Romans considered stepmothers proverbially
wicked (cf. 1.147–48). Taken with the similarly archetypical
wrath of Juno, this makes Hercules' assumption of her guilt
understandable, though misplaced.

181ff   *Was this why:* Here, Hercules launches into a retrospective
catalog of his own feats. He begins with his killings of
Busiris, an Egyptian king who sacrificed strangers, and
Antaeus, a Giant who was invincible so long as he remained
in contact with his mother Earth, but whom Hercules slew
while hoisting him off the ground. He then obliquely
alludes to all Twelve Labors, most of which involved
monstrous beasts:

1. Slaying the Nemaean Lion (197)
2. Slaying the Lernaean Hydra (192–93)
3. Capturing the Ceryneian Hind near Mount Parthenius
   (188)
4. Capturing the Erymanthian Boar ravaging Arcadia
   (191–92)
5. Cleaning the massively filthy Augean Stables at Elis (187)
6. Slaying the man-eating Stymphalian Birds (187)
7. Capturing the Cretan Bull (186), later killed by
   Theseus (see note to 7.433ff)
8. Slaying the man-eating Mares of Diomedes, after
   feeding them Diomedes (194–96)
9. Stealing the girdle of the Amazon queen Hippolyta at
   the river Thermodon (188–89)
10. Capturing the cattle of Geryon, a three-bodied
    herdsman, whom he slew (184)
11. Fetching the Golden Apples of the Hesperides (190; cf.
    4.645)
12. Fetching Cerberus (185), as narrated at 7.409ff

    As a side quest while pursuing the Erymanthian Boar,
Hercules blundered into a battle with centaurs (191),
mortally wounding Chiron (2.649–54). In capturing the
Golden Apples from Atlas' garden, he briefly took over
the task of holding the sky (198).

203–4   *and there are those / Who still believe in gods:* For a character who has personally dealt with numerous deities, this is a scathing if somewhat nonsensical pronouncement. Hercules' apotheosis will shortly vindicate his own situation, but his condemnation of divine injustice rings true for much of the poem. Unlike Christian problems of theodicy ("why would a good god let evil exist?"), however, this criticism carries no logical conundrum—no one ever accused these gods of benevolence.

216   *grasps his knees:* That is, in the typical gesture of supplication (see note to 1.634–36).

229   *They call it Lichas:* Mount Lichada stands on the northwestern tip of Euboea.

232   *to visit Troy again:* This prophecy, recurring at 13.320, portends how Philoctetes (Poeas' son) will use the arrows to kill Paris in the Trojan War. Hercules and his arrows have already paid a "visit" to Troy when he sacked the city and saved its princess, though this is not related until 11.211ff.

237   *As though you were reclining at a feast:* Hercules' equanimity in the face of death, though somewhat compromised by his last seventy lines of vigorous agonizing, is emblematic of the ideals of Roman Stoic philosophers, who took Hercules as their patron saint. This specific image also carries a political association, since Horace had foretold of the Emperor Augustus banqueting with Hercules in heaven (*Odes* 3.3.9–12).

270   *its august weight:* The poem's second use of the word *augustus* as an adjective (cf. 6.72, 15.145) occurs at the moment Hercules becomes a god, appearing to further this episode's allusive flattery of the Emperor. Yet the sharp anticlimax of line 273 reveals the "august weight" to be quite literal and burdensome enough to hurt Atlas, so Ovid may be sneaking in an imperial fat joke: he has already established that the gods are heavy (4.449–50).

Lucina and Galanthis (273–323)

In a typically Ovidian inversion, Hercules' death gives way to Hercules' birth, which quickly cedes the spotlight to an etiological myth about the reproductive system of weasels. The reader is by now thoroughly acquainted with the unfairness of divine wrath, but not since the plague of Aegina in Book 7 have we seen a god's vengeance as poorly motivated as the attempts of Lucina (goddess of childbirth) to prevent Hercules' mother from delivering her son. The culprit is naturally Juno, but as with the Calydonian Hunt, human resource is here shown to be capable of thwarting the will of heaven, even if (like Meleäger) the clever Galanthis will suffer for her triumph.

273–75   *But Eurystheus . . . from sire to son:* After the death of
Hercules, Eurystheus began harassing his late enemy's
sons, eventually pursuing them to Athens, where they
killed him in battle.

287–89   *a weight so great . . . labor pangs:* The language surrounding
Hercules' birth mirrors that of his death, where his enormous weight (270) and the precedence of his divine
paternity (265) are similarly stressed. Furthermore,
Alcmene is dealing with a *labor* of her own. The reference in
286 is to the tenth month of pregnancy; see note to 8.500.

323   *She births with lips, yet lives here as before:* Belief that the
weasel gives birth through the mouth was old enough for
Aristotle to refute it in his *On the Generation of Animals.*
The ancient Greeks kept weasels domestically, valuing
them for their skill as mouse-catchers.

Dryope and Lotus (324–93)

Iole tops Alcmene's story with her own tale of tragic transformation, telling how her half-sister Dryope turned into a plant after innocently wounding another bleeding tree (see note to 8.762), itself a former nymph who—like Daphne and Syrinx—had transformed to escape a god's sexual assault. The cruel revenge inflicted on Dryope, who describes the process in wrenching real-time narration, would seem to indicate that, although the nymph's body and mind have disappeared into the greenery, some part of her pain has survived the metamorphosis to live malignantly on.

332 *Delphi's Delian lord:* Apollo raped Dryope in the form of a snake, resulting in the child Amphissos.

340 *water-lotus:* Precisely what plant the semi-magical "lotus-tree" of Greek mythology refers to is a matter of longstanding debate. It is certainly not a water lily.

347 *Priapus:* Priapus was a Roman horticultural god best known for his vast and permanent erection, though by Ovid's time he was closer to a literary joke than an object of genuine worship. In function, Priapus was a bawdy kind of ancient garden gnome, warding thieves off from vegetable plots with the threat of rape.

365 *oak:* The manuscripts say *loton* ("lotus") and all modern translations with which I am familiar have rendered it accordingly. However, as scholar E. J. Kenney wrote in his notes, "the story lacks point unless the word *loton* has ousted the name of some other tree" (Melville 428: 365n). Indeed, there is no more reason for the word *loton* to here refer to Dryope instead of the aforementioned lotus-tree than there is for Iole to be pointing to anyone but her sister. Nor is there any indication elsewhere in the poem that Dryope became a lotus, or any other specific kind of tree (in another version she turns into a poplar). The line remains heavily disputed, with some editors conjecturing such words as *robur* and *quercum*—both meaning oak. Since the name Dryope is reminiscent of the Greek word for oak, I take that tree for the most appealing contender and have translated accordingly.

389 *don't touch my eyes:* As in the present day, traditional Roman practice involved closing the eyes of the deceased. In this case, the encroaching tree-bark will render the act superfluous.

Iolaüs and Themis (394–438)

The conversation between Iole and Alcmene ends while leading into a convoluted transitional passage rife with vague mythological allusions. Pursuing broad themes of fate and mortality, in under forty lines Ovid delivers an extremely elliptical summary of the entire Theban War, while checking in on a whole string of the gods' favorite mortals. Last to be mentioned is the now elderly king Minos, who will bring us to the following tale.

399   *Iolaüs was restored to youth:* Iolaüs was Hercules' nephew, lover, and general sidekick, best known for helping him defeat the Lernaean Hydra, though we briefly met him at the Calydonian Hunt (8.310). He has been rejuvenated in order to aid the sons of Hercules in their fight against Eurystheus (cf. 273–5). As will be seen, this miracle has been sent by the deified Hercules' new wife Hebe, goddess of youth, whom Juno bore without a father.

403ff   *There's civil war in Thebes now . . . :* Ovid compresses one of the great epic narratives of Greek mythology into fifteen lines. After the abdication of Oedipus, a civil war for the kingship of Thebes broke out between his sons Eteocles and Polynices, the latter of whom attacked the city with a band of allies known as the Seven Against Thebes. In the ensuing war, Jupiter smote the physically enormous Capaneus with a lightning bolt (403–4), while Eteocles and Polynices killed each other in single combat (404–5). The prophet swallowed by the earth alive was Amphiaraus (mentioned at 8.317), one of the Seven, who indeed died by falling directly into the underworld (405–6, but see the appendix). Despite foreseeing his own death, Amphiaraus was pressured into the war by his treacherous wife Eriphyle, who had been bribed with a gold necklace. Their son Alcmaeon then killed her, avenging parent over parent (407–8), in an act Ovid describes with the same terms he used for Agenor's treatment of Cadmus (3.5). In punishment for matricide, the Furies drove Alcmaeon insane (409–10), but he eventually recovered and married Alphesiboea, daughter of the Arcadian king Phegeus, and gave her his mother's necklace. When a relapse of madness drove him off again, he married Callirhoë, daughter of the river Acheloüs, who also asked him for the necklace (*the fatal gold*, 411). He then returned to Phegeus' court to seek it, whereupon his former father-in-law murdered him (412). His new widow next begged Jupiter to prematurely mature her infant sons into adolescence (414), that they might avenge their father all the sooner (415). It is because Jupiter will answer Callirhoë's prayer, Themis explains, that Hebe (Jove's step-daughter and daughter-in-law) must not forswear all future gifts of youth (416–17).

421–25 *Pallantis then bewailed ... Anchises' years renewed:* Ovid refers to four humans beloved of gods. Dawn (daughter of the Titan Pallas) bewails the fate of her husband Tithonus, who was granted immortality but not eternal youth. Iasion was a mortal lover of Ceres, as Anchises was of Venus (we will meet him and their son Aeneas in Book 13). The origins of Erichthonius, son of Vulcan (Mulciber), figured at 2.552ff.

435–38 *My Rhadamanthys ... not be the king he was:* Jupiter also has mortal sons. We have seen Aeacus ruling Aegina and Minos ruling Crete (where his brother Rhadamanthys likewise reigned), but here and in the next tale we learn that a generation has passed and all three are now old men. After their deaths, the three brothers would serve in the underworld as judges of souls.

Byblis and Caunus (439–665)

A brief digression into Cretan politics swiftly leads the narration into the longest tale in this book and the first in a series of myths concerning unnatural love—in this case, the incestuous passion of Byblis for her brother Caunus. Once again, a rhetorically sparkling monologue brings us inside the head of a conflicted heroine as she convinces herself to commit a shocking sin. This time, however, Ovid outdoes himself with two additional passages: a love letter to Caunus in which Byblis recasts her soliloquy in persuasive terms, and a further monologue in response to her inevitable rejection, which sees Byblis' despair unthinkably-yet-convincingly turn to reawakened hope. After two hundred superbly crafted lines of character distress and reader discomfort, the metamorphosis at the story's conclusion comes as a well-earned relief.

449   *the walls that bear their builder's name:* Miletus was a
       major city on the Anatolian coast, built at the mouth of
       the Meander. Other versions of the myth have Miletus
       fleeing Crete to escape not Minos' political malice but his
       sexual advances, preferring those of Minos' brother
       Sarpedon. Ovid likely changed the circumstance to avoid
       distracting from the more crucial sexual impropriety of
       Byblis.

454   *May Byblis warn young girls about desire:* A rare bit of
       outright moralizing for Ovid, and a difficult one to take
       seriously since the ensuing tale makes little effort to drive
       home its purported point. The theme of lustful maidens
       will be much more expressly handled in Book 10—but
       there the narrator will be the misogynist Orpheus.

507   *Aeolus' sons shunned not their sisters' beds:* In fact, the six
       sons and six daughters of Aeolus intermarried, brother to
       sister. This line—especially when taken with 508—is
       something of an intertextual joke; Ovid's *Heroides* had
       included a love letter from one of the sisters, Canace, to
       her brother Macar.

646–47 *Cragus . . . Chimaera dwells:* Mount Cragus and the rivers
       Limyre and Xanthus are all in Lycia, land of the Chi-
       maera (cf. 6.339). This puts Byblis well past the Carian
       city of Caunus—she has missed her brother entirely.

662   *Favonius' gentle breath:* The return of the west wind
       Favonius (or Zephyrus) was associated with the start of
       spring.

Iphis and Ianthe (666–797)

The barest of transitions returns us to Crete for the final tale in Book
9, the love of Iphis for Ianthe. In a cheerful change of pace, their story
will end happily, but not before Ovid launches into yet another soliloquy for a distressed heroine. Unlike Byblis, however, Iphis knows what
she wants right from the beginning, and rather than gradually goad-
ing herself into drastic action, she ends her speech in the same place of
helpless indecision where she began. But hers is a different problem
entirely, originating not from a heinous inner conflict of morals but

from the social strictures imposed on her by a gently-yet-murderously misogynist father and a society whose sexual naïveté renders all lesbian desire incomprehensible. We have seen the poem's previous women (Medea, most obviously) overcome comparable constraints only through violent transgression. Iphis will instead achieve her aims by forsaking her womanhood—a solution that, in the narrative, yields perhaps the most unreservedly happy ending in the poem, but which would have been impossible outside of it. Even as Iphis undergoes her metamorphosis, the misogyny and social norms that she so innocently violated remain inescapably in place.

679   *she must die:* Romans were known to abandon (or "expose") infants deemed undesirable or unviable, a practice even more prevalent in ancient Greece. Part of the point of exposure, however, was to sidestep straight-up murder in the hope that the forsaken baby might be found (as occurs in the stories of Oedipus, Romulus, and Moses). Yet for all his supposed misgivings, Ligdus eliminates all chance of mercy: he orders the child to be killed.

686   *the child of Inachus:* This is the Egyptian goddess Isis, identified with Inachus' daughter Io at 1.747. In the other known version of the myth, Telethusa's patroness is Leto (Latona), but Ovid's alteration allows him to preserve his nastier characterization of Latona from Book 6, while attributing Iphis' eventual salvation to a goddess who was once herself a long-suffering and unwanted daughter (cf. 1.650ff). In the context of Ovid's portrayals of divine power, it is notable that this uncomplicatedly kind and helpful goddess should also be the rare deity in the poem to exist solidly outside the Greco-Roman pantheon.

690–94   *Anubis . . . foreign serpents full of venomed sleep:* Isis' entourage is a line-up of Egyptian deities. Anubis, god of death, howls because he has the head of a dog. Bubastis was a protective cat goddess. Apis was a sacred bull identified with Io's son Epaphus (cf. 1.748–49). The boy god Horus was depicted with a finger to his lips in an Egyptian attribute of childhood the Greeks misinterpreted to create

the Hellenistic deity Harpocrates, god of silence (692).
Osiris, husband of Isis, was dismembered by his brother
Set, and annual festivals reenacted Isis' search to reassem-
ble him. The rattling refers to the noise of the *sistrum*, a
percussion instrument used in Egyptian worship and
mentioned again at 778 and 784.

710   *unisex:* A male Iphis even appears in Book 14.

727   *strange, unknown, unnatural love:* This display of
ignorance should not be taken at face value. Although
instances of female homosexuality were rare in myth, its
practitioners were sufficiently well-known to have a
Latin term (*tribas*) and appear in the works of other
writers, such as Phaedrus and Martial. Indeed, the
innocent tenor of Iphis' soliloquy would seem to connote
a silly wholesomeness on the part of both love and lover,
particularly in contrast to the tale of Byblis (see note to
731–34), still fresh in the minds of Roman readers—
who, in any case, would likely have known their Sappho.

731–34   *Cows never burn for cows . . . no female females fill with
lust:* We have just seen a similar set of case studies lead
Byblis astray (497–500), so this argument is literarily as
well as scientifically uncompelling. Book 10 will provide
an even closer parallel when Myrrha uses animal
behavior not to rule out her incestuous desire but to
justify it (10.324–28). The comparisons make clear that,
despite Iphis' self-abnegating befuddlement, her wishes
are sympathetic rather than monstrous.

750–52   *No guard forbids . . . nor stringent sire:* These are the
standard obstacles to lovers typified in the genre of love
elegy—the form in which Ovid made his name (cf.
Byblis at 556–57). Ironically, considering Iphis' profes-
sions of ignorance, many of these tropes have their
earliest roots in Sappho.

783–84   *moon-like horns . . . sounds of rattling:* To the sound of
sistra (see note to 690ff) the goddess' statue has begun to
glow. Isis was often depicted with cow horns and
appeared sporting them at 689.

BOOK 10

Orpheus and Eurydice (1–77)

The myth of Orpheus, the Thracian singer who almost resurrected his wife, was as commonplace in Ovid's time as in ours. True to form, the poet throws his retelling off balance, emphasizing piquant details over its most poignant moments. Eurydice's death, the terms of her release, and her final farewell (so affecting in Virgil's *Georgics*) are all minimized, and where Virgil wisely avoided trying to capture the magical charm of Orpheus' song, Ovid leaps at the chance to contrive another anticlimax, assigning the widower a speech more rhetorical and polished than emotional or persuasive. This is Ovid's sly way of going through the necessary motions to bring Orpheus into the poem; as the rest of the book will show, he has other plans for the famous bard in mind.

13   *Taenarus' gate to the Styx:* Like Lake Avernus (5.540, 10.52), the cave at Cape Taenarum on the Peloponnese was traditionally considered a gateway to the underworld.

21–22   *chain your monstrous hound . . . his three Medusan . . . necks:* An allusion to Hercules, who shackled the three necks of Cerberus during his Twelfth Labor (7.409ff), as will be mentioned at 65–66. Why Cerberus should be Medusan is uncertain (see note in appendix).

28   *tales of ancient ravishment:* The rape of Proserpine, narrated at 5.385–571 by Calliope, the Muse of epic poetry and Orpheus' own mother. Given the Machiavellian character of Cupid's involvement in that tale, Orpheus' remark is more accurate than romantic.

41–44   *Tantalus ceased . . . Sisyphus, upon your stone:* These same five inmates of hell were seen on Juno's visit to the underworld in Book 4 (see note to 4.457ff).

65–71   *the man who . . . on dewy Ida:* These two tales are otherwise unknown. Evidently, some poor fellow glimpsed Cerberus during Hercules' Twelfth Labor and was literally petrified with fright. For her part, Lethaea dared rival the gods in beauty and suffered the expected fate, in which her faithful husband Olenus apparently joined her.

Cyparissus (78–147)

Despite his performative grief, life goes on for Orpheus, who now adopts a quintessentially Greek way of life combining misogyny with pederasty ("Greek love"), the institutionalized formation of romantic relations between an older man and a teenage boy. These twin priorities will be reflected in Orpheus' subsequent song, but Ovid beats the bard to the chase by inserting a quick pederastic narrative of his own, that of Apollo and Cyparissus, whose plot prefigures Orpheus' tale of Apollo and Hyacinth. To make matters sillier, their story will occur in the middle of another of the poem's ridiculous catalogues, in this case a list of walking trees.

Any academic engagement with pederasty is inevitably complicated by the practice's deplorability in light of modern moral standards and developmental psychology. Even relative to the slavery and rigidly sexist gender roles that litter ancient texts, the concept's utter foreignness to the present day has made it one of the most uncomfortable aspects of antiquity to discuss. Unfortunately, this discomfiture has combined with centuries of homophobic scholarship to spawn a tendency to identify the custom with either homosexuality—a term of sexual identity as out of place in the context of classical culture as the institution of pederasty is in ours—or pedophilia, a recognizedly transgressive act of child abuse. By contrast, in an antique world without current conceptions of childhood or sexual maturity as divorced from pubescence, pederasty was a widespread social practice that— far from the covert, coercive crimes of present-day pedophiles— enjoyed the sanction of parental and state authorities as a kind of nurture, difficult as it is now to imagine. Ancient sources (and presumably ancient societies) differed as to the age of the youths and the degree of sexuality involved, but it appears that such relationships generally required parental approval, respected an age of consent, were preceded by courtship, did not preclude outside heterosexual activities, could last well into adulthood, commonly constituted a form of mentorship, and were thus closely tied to other societal structures, especially the military. While it would be naïve to suppose that such an institution was not prone to misconduct or was somehow protected against predation (Orpheus' first example, Ganymede, will suffer an unequivocal rape), for the purposes of poetry it is a cultural misread-

ing to view the junior members in fictional representations of pederasty as the categorical victims of physical and psychological abuse.
Within the ethical framework of the Greek culture that spawned it,
pederasty was constructed as a consensual form of partnership—that
is, as a *relationship*. In a society where brides were commonly as young
as twelve, its closest parallel may well have been marriage.

Likewise, although pederasty was the most accepted form of same-
sex coupling in the ancient world, the descriptor "homosexual" is best
used only insofar as it is of interest to modern audiences, who may be
understandably eager for historical gay content. Broadly speaking,
Greek and Roman cultures conceived of sexuality in terms not of
identity or orientation but of activity, and presumed the possibility of
attraction toward either sex, at least in men. Readers may consequently be surprised at seeing same-sex pairs portrayed in ways anti-
thetical to modern stereotypes surrounding homosexuality. In Greece,
and militaristic Sparta especially, homoeroticism was linked not to
effeminacy but to masculinity—after all, what could be manlier than
multiple men? Accordingly, the stories of Cyparissus (and subsequently Hyacinth) will see the role of the older lover filled by the
archetypically athletic god Apollo, who by this point in the poem has
proven himself fully capable of both attraction to females and the
most bloodthirsty excesses of male behavior. It is revealing of commentators' prejudices that the comparable youth of the heterosexually
coupled Adonis never seems to scandalize, despite Ovid drawing clear
parallels between him and Hyacinth.

By the same token, a great deal has been written about Ovid's
alleged aversion to same-sex stories, a supposed stance translators
have been all too happy to augment. This avoidance is purportedly
proven by two lines in the poet's *Ars Amatoria* (2.683–84), which in
reality just express his personal preference for women. Admittedly,
male same-sex couples have so far appeared only on the sidelines—
Cygnus and Phaëthon (2.367–69), Athis and Lycabas (5.47–73), Marsyas and Olympus (6.393–94), Phylius and another Cygnus (7.372–79),
and a few other scattered references—but the incidental nature of
these appearances would seem to belie rather than confirm aversion,
since Ovid could just as easily have omitted them. It would be more
accurate to say that same-sex attraction is simply a part of the world of
the poem, to be downplayed (see notes to 2.676–708 and 7.751) or

played up (8.403–6) as suits the needs of the literary moment. With same-sex attraction taking center stage in this next set of myths, it would seem that its moment has arrived.

78   *Piscean waves:* As the twelfth sign of the Zodiac, Pisces marks the end of the year. Ovid uses similar astral references to denote the start of summer (Cancer) at 127 and the spring (Aries) at 165.

83–84   *taught the Thracian tribes / To love young boys:* The geographic specificity is odd. Thracians were proverbially lustful (cf. note to 6.459), so this adoption of a practice already disseminated elsewhere may even be seen as a civilizing move. More practically, this detail motivates the rage of the specifically *Thracian* women who attack Orpheus in Book 11.

90ff   *There came Chaonia's tree . . . :* As is about to become extremely clear, the music of Orpheus had the power to compel animals, rocks, and trees. *Chaonia's tree* is a variety of oak. Heliads are poplars (descended from Phaëthon's sisters, cf. 2.345ff). Laurels are virginal since Daphne, the original laurel, saved herself from Apollo's assault (1.453ff).

102   *bare-trunked leaf-crowned pines:* Italian stone pines have no boughs below their crowns. (Pliny the Younger used their shape to describe a mushroom cloud over Vesuvius.)

103–5   *the gods' great Mother Cybele . . . lofty trunk:* In a moment of desperation during the Second Punic War, the Senate took advice from the Sibylline books (see note to 14.153) and imported the foreign cult of the goddess Cybele. Known in Rome as the "Great Mother of the Gods," her priests were initiated through a self-castration ritual imitating her mythic consort Attis, whose enactment of the rite received definitive literary treatment in Catullus 63. In transforming into a tree, Attis has therefore *put manhood by* in more ways than one. Cybele will reappear in the penultimate story of this book.

142   *So you will mourn for others where they grieve:* The
Romans associated cypress trees with funerals and
mourning, often planting them around graves.

Ganymede and Hyacinth (148–219)

The song of Orpheus will occupy the remainder of this book. Just as
Calliope called on Ceres at the outset of her song in Book 5, Orpheus
uses a standard formula to call on his mother Calliope, promising to
begin his song with Jove, vanquisher of Giants. This grand invocation
(148–51) is immediately undercut, however, when the bard announces
lighter themes befitting his newfound pederasty and misogyny: namely,
boys beloved of gods and *girls who felt forbidden flames* of lust. Naturally, Orpheus will stray far off topic, but he starts by making good on
his pledge; after a perfunctory nod toward Jupiter with the story of the
Trojan prince Ganymede, we are treated to the sweet and surprisingly
gentle tragedy of Apollo and the Spartan cult hero Hyacinth.

151   *victor's bolts that fell on Phlegra's fields:* Ovid subtly
identifies himself with Orpheus, since he too has sung of
the gods and Giants at war (cf. 1.151–62). Their battle
was traditionally located on the Phlegraean fields around
Mount Vesuvius, whose volcanic activity was attributed
to the residual effects of Jupiter's bolts.

157–58 *no bird / Deserving:* A ludicrous assertion; the idea that
Jupiter was at all picky about the dignity of his disguises is
thoroughly contradicted by previous stories (cf. 6.103–14).

161   *nectared cups, to Juno's lasting spite:* Once on Olympus,
Jupiter granted Ganymede the extraordinary gift of
immortality, making the boy his personal "cupbearer"
and inciting Juno's lasting rage against the Trojans.
Wishing to move on to Hyacinth, Ovid refrains from
editorializing on a myth whose meaning was unsettled
even in antiquity, owing to the contradiction between
Jupiter's use of force and the story's happy (?) ending, a
tension that allowed Roman writers to cast Jupiter and
Ganymede as the pederastic ideal even while depicting
the prince's abduction as a traumatic kidnapping.
European artists of the Renaissance and after worsened

matters by exaggerating Ganymede's youth; in Rembrandt's painting, the prince is a bawling toddler.

168   *Delphi, at its center:* The ancient Greeks regarded Delphi as the center of the world. The ritual stone navel (or *omphalos*) that marked the spot is still displayed at the site.

170   *unwalled Sparta:* Such was the Spartans' confidence in their martial prowess that they proudly left their city unfortified. Spartan culture poses a particular challenge to modern stereotypes of emotionless masculinity, since the state's militarism coexisted with the adoration of Hyacinth and the worship of Aphrodite as a war goddess.

183   *rash:* The same word was used at 130 to describe Cyparissus, whose story plays like an inversion of Hyacinth's. Both are lovers of Apollo undone by an accidental killing and transformed into a plant.

215–16   *Inscribed the petals ... decks the flower:* "AI AI" was a Greek phrase of lamentation. The ancients apparently imagined such markings on the inside of hyacinth petals, though the flower described is clearly not the modern hyacinth, but something closer to an iris or a larkspur. Hyacinth's vegetable mode of immortality is even less convincing than usual, since only his blood undergoes the transformation.

217–19   *The Spartans' pride in their son Hyacinth ... feast of Hyacinthia:* Soldiery lay at the heart of Sparta's society (see note to 170), and the Spartan army (its entire male citizenry between ages seven and sixty) standardized pederasty as a form of apprenticeship. The midsummer Hyacinthia festival celebrating a native hero so closely identified with the institution was unsurprisingly one of the city's most important holidays, and Spartan armies at war were reportedly known to negotiate temporary truces specifically in order to attend.

The Cerastae, the Propoetides, and Pygmalion (220–94)

While Sparta reveres Hyacinth, Cyprus reviles two groups of its mythic natives, neither of whom are found in other sources. Orpheus is already veering off track, since the Cerastae are neither beloved boys nor lustful women but a tribe of murderers. As prostitutes, the Propoetides come closer, but they quickly transition into the famous story of Pygmalion, the sculptor who fell in love with his own creation—a plot point added by Ovid. The three tales are unified not so much by theme as by their setting on Cyprus, an island sacred to Venus, who effects all three transformations. There is, however, a persistent undercurrent of misogyny, crystallized in the character of Pygmalion, whose perfect artificial female is not even named ("Galatea" is an Enlightenment appellation). In the twentieth century, George Bernard Shaw would give her the name Eliza and the good sense to rebel against her creator, but here the narrator is still Orpheus, and much as readers of Book 5 should remember that it is the Muses who are speaking and painting their enemies in so poor a light, we should bear in mind just whose dim view of women is shining through.

221–23   *Propoetides . . . so called for their jagged brows: Propo-*
etides means simply "the daughters of Propoetus," but the
significance of the name is unknown. *Cerastae* is Greek
for "horn-bearing," though why the tribespeople have
horns in the first place is not exactly clear.

237   *savage bulls:* A fitting punishment; they are themselves
now suitable for sacrifice.

242   *scarcely changed, to solid stone:* They were already
hardened to shame. Herodotus wrote of Cyprus as a
center of cult prostitution.

290   *Paphian hero:* An absurd epithet; not only is Pygmalion
decidedly devoid of heroism, but his child Paphos,
founder of the eponymous city, has not even been born
(see note on 3.198).

294   *first sight was . . . the sky:* Once again, gazing upward
signals humanity (cf. 1.85–86, 731).

Myrrha (295–502)

Orpheus finally lands on his second theme with the tale of Pygmalion's great-granddaughter Myrrha. Contrasting Myrrha's incestuous passion with that of Byblis in Book 9, Ovid cleverly takes things up a notch by making Myrrha's story both more sympathetic and more repulsive: unlike Byblis, Myrrha genuinely tries to stifle her desires, but unlike Byblis, Myrrha will fulfill them. Ovid's version likely owes a debt to *Zmyrna*, Helvius Cinna's lost epic on the tale, but the remaining fragments are too scant to tell.

305–6   *I praise us Thracians . . . such sin:* Something of a joke, since the Thracians were proverbially depraved (cf. 6.549).

320ff   *Where shall this lead me?:* The reader knows by now what kind of speech to expect from a conflicted heroine. Myrrha's particular obsession is with the Roman virtue of piety (321, 323), which in Latin denotes dutiful respect, especially toward one's family. Cinyras is presented as a paragon of piety (354), of which incest would be the ultimate transgression.

324–28   *other creatures couple as they please . . . :* Iphis followed similar logic to the opposite conclusion (see note to 9.731–34). Ovid draws on his Roman rhetorical education, which required students to practice arguing for both sides of an issue (see note to 2.53ff).

339   *But now, since he is mine, he is not mine:* This paradox most obviously echoes the plight of Narcissus (cf. 3.466), who cannot gain his object of desire because, in another sense, he already possesses it. Byblis (9.493–4) and Iphis (9.760–1) framed their predicaments in similar terms.

349   *The snake-haired Sisters:* These are the Furies, who punished crimes against family, but who—unbeknownst to Myrrha—are the cause of her unnatural lust (cf. 314; see note to 1.241).

446–51   *As Boötes . . . Erigone, divine through daughter's love:* Sidereal periphrases convey both setting and foreboding. Boötes turning his wagon-shaft indicates that it is midnight, while an apposite set of celestial bodies flee the scene of the crime. The golden moon is associated with Diana and therefore with chastity, while Icarus (not the son of Daedalus) and Erigone symbolize a maximally pious father-daughter relationship. When Erigone hanged herself in grief over her father's murder, the pair were catasterized for her devotion as the constellations Virgo and, confusingly, Boötes.

487 *change me so I cannot live or die:* According to Venus, the only other option (232–34).

489 *Her prayers found gods:* These anonymous gods apparently have a soft spot for female molesters; the same odd phrase occurred at 4.373 in response to the prayers of Salmacis.

Venus and Adonis (503–739)

Despite the inbreeding, Myrrha's son emerges from the tree an epitome of beauty—the original Adonis. Venus catches a glimpse of him and we are hurtled back to the first theme, boys beloved of gods, with strong parallels to the story of Apollo and Hyacinth. But Orpheus seems intent on finishing his song with a mix of his two subjects, and the goddess' desire to shield Adonis from harm prompts her to narrate her own admonitory tale, which (if you squint a little) touches on forbidden female love. Such an unkind categorization, however, redounds only to Orpheus' discredit; not only is Atalanta's love not immoral, but it is her beloved Hippomenes who brings down on them the familiar wrath of the gods.

530ff *She spurned Cythera's shores:* In describing Venus' lovesick change into a dedicated huntress, Orpheus uses much the same language as he did when capturing Apollo's love for Hyacinth (168–73).

565 *Atalanta:* It is debated whether this is the same aloof, athletic Atalanta who took part in the Calydonian Hunt in Book 8, but Pseudo-Apollodorus identifies them as one individual and they could certainly be less similar.

591 *With wings upon her heels:* The Latin word is not "wings" but the ambiguous *talaria*, a substantive adjective relating to ankles, in most cases referring to winged sandals, which she is clearly not wearing. This translation

follows a separate school of commentary (see appendix) that reads her *talaria* as a metaphor for speed.

611ff   *"What god," she cried:* Though there will be more great speeches from such women as Alcyone in Book 11 and Hecuba in Book 13, Atalanta's monologue is the last in Ovid's series of soliloquies for conflicted heroines that began with Medea in Book 7. Her deliberations mirror that first speech in particular, dwelling on Hippomenes' youth much as Medea did on Jason's, and likewise wondering if she has the heart to let the man die. New here, however, is a note of humor; line 617 crosses over into absurdity.

666   *Consumed with longing for the shiny fruit:* Other poets emphasized Atalanta's supposed greed or frivolity, but some degree of symbolism is clearly at play: in chasing after Venus' golden apples, Atalanta instinctively pursues the fruits of love.

696   *crowned with towers:* As was customary for patron deities of cities, Cybele was often depicted wearing a turreted headdress or "mural crown."

705–7   *These lions . . . wreck us both:* Venus ends the story with a flimsy attempt to tie it back to her original warning, for though she has explained her personal antipathy toward beasts (or lions at least), she fails to accurately represent the danger they pose. And in any case, Cybele's lions are tamed.

725–27   *Memorials to my grief . . . reenacting every year / Your death:* In addition to their similar deaths and metamorphoses, Adonis parallels Hyacinth in that he was commemorated in an annual festival, the Adonia (cf. 217–19).

729–30   *as Persephone once . . . fragrant mint:* In the myth mentioned, Proserpine turned the nymph Minthe to mint after she attempted to seduce Dis. Venus' jealous tone further alludes to a much older myth in which Venus and Proserpine competed for Adonis' affections. Since Adonis is dead, Proserpine has in a sense won him for the underworld.

BOOK 11

The Death of Orpheus (1–84)

Having allowed their enemy to sing unmolested for six hundred lines, the women of Thrace, last seen "grieving his scorn" at 10.82, at last make their displeasure felt. As luck would have it, the women are bacchants and proceed to do unto Orpheus as they did unto Pentheus in Book 3, before Apollo and Bacchus arrive to avenge the death of their respective son and priest. Throughout, Ovid employs his signature gruesome wit to revel in the gory details, relishing the demise of this poet no less than he did at 5.111–18 when killing Lampetides—though the happy ending, in which Orpheus and Eurydice reunite after death, is also Ovid's original contribution.

9   *But it was tipped with leaves:* This detail indicates that the bacchant has, appropriately, thrown a thyrsus (see note to 3.542).

26   *the morning games:* In the usual schedule of Roman entertainment, afternoon gladiatorial games were preceded by wild animal hunts. This is Ovid's most directly anachronistic reference in some time but fits with the poem's broader pattern of locating its audience in contemporary Rome (see note to 1.560–63).

37–38 *tore apart / The mean-horned bulls: Sparagmos!* (See note to 3.721–22.)

60   *gaping where they were:* Medea glimpsed this statue during her flight at 7.357–58. Despite his having been with us for eight hundred lines, this is the only real metamorphosis with which Orpheus is involved.

Midas (85–192)

Bacchus transitions us into the myth of Midas, a foolish king whose back-to-back stories give ample room to display his ampler stupidity. The famous tales of his golden touch and donkey's ears are mentioned in earlier sources but have come down to us in their familiar forms thanks to Ovid. Notably, Midas is believed to have been a real person who ruled a Phrygian kingdom of vast wealth in the eighth century BCE; as promised in its prologue, the poem has begun to flirt with the fringes of history.

88   *Which then flowed free of gold:* Ovid presents the myth of
         the Midas touch as an etiology for the lucrative gold
         deposits found in the river Pactolus.

90   *Silenus, old and drunk:* A comic figure, the drunk old
         satyr Silenus was Bacchus' foster father and constant
         companion. He appeared briefly at 4.26.

93   *taught the rites:* The Athenian Eumolpus was famed as
         the legendary founder of the Eleusinian mysteries, a cult
         of Persephone and Demeter (Ceres). Ovid presents him,
         Orpheus, and Midas as fellow initiates of the mysteries of
         Bacchus.

109   *the twig was made of gold:* This passage is rife with
         mythological allusions (114, 117). Roman readers
         would have recognized an oak tree (*ilex*) with a branch
         of gold as an unmistakable reference to the Golden
         Bough episode in Book 6 of Virgil's *Aeneid*. Ovid will
         give short shrift to the Golden Bough when he reaches
         that tale himself (14.113–14), and prefigures that choice
         here by demoting the bough (*ramus*) to a mere twig
         (*uirga*).

156–57   *Tmolus . . . cleared his ears of trees:* On this clever personi-
         fication, furthered at 164, see note to 2.302–3.

179   *his ears were now those of a stubborn ass:* Apollo's choice
         of animal is explained by the existence of several Greek
         proverbs describing an unappreciative or intransigent
         person as "an ass with an *aulos*," "an ass trying to play the
         cithara," or (most pertinently here), "an ass listening to a
         lyre." As a rule, lyric verse was held in higher esteem than
         pastoral, making Apollo's victory incontestable.

Peleus and Thetis (193–265)

This short passage carries a heavy expositional load in preparation for
the next book's handling of the Trojan War. Ovid's desire to save Troy
(and the foundation of Rome it entails) for last is reflected in that the
stories told here should really have appeared much earlier: the narrator
was already referring back to Hercules' sack of Troy at 9.232, and Peleus
ought to have married Thetis by the time the *Argo* sailed in Book 6. But

delaying them until now means that the birth of Achilles, the divine origin of the walls of Troy, and the city itself will all be fresher in the reader's mind when the war seizes the spotlight. These tales also serve as a reminder. In every telling, Thetis is less than thrilled at being forced to marry a mortal, but her acquiescence is rarely so brutally won. In a book where gods have thus far restricted themselves to avenging a murder and making an example of a fool, the divinely ordained rape of Thetis reaffirms how nasty and self-serving the gods can be.

194   *the Nephelean Hellespont:* Now usually called the Darda-
          nelles, the Hellespont is a strait separating Europe and
          Asia. It is named for Helle, daughter of Nephele, who
          drowned in it when she fell off the ram of the Golden
          Fleece (see note to 7.6–7).

196–97   *Sigeum and Rhoeteum ... Panomphean Thunderer:* The
          Thunderer is Jupiter, invoked here in his capacity as
          "author of all oracles" (*panomphaios*). Mentioned
          frequently in the coming books, Sigeum and Rhoeteum
          were coastal promontories near Troy, here seen under the
          rule of Priam's father Laömedon.

214–20   *When this too ... just one man has wed a god:* Ovid's
          transition is unusually convoluted. When Hercules,
          Peleus, and Telamon sacked Troy together, Telamon
          took the king's own daughter Hesione for his wife. His
          brother Peleus, however, was already married to Thetis—
          a rare match between male mortal and female immortal.
          It is therefore more remarkable that Thetis' father was
          Nereus (making her a Nereid goddess) than it is that
          Peleus' grandfather was Jupiter, whose descendants are
          legion.

235–36   *made by either art / Or nature:* A picturesque spot once
          again serves as the setting for a violent transgression, this
          time specifically echoing the description of the cave
          Gargaphië (3.155–60), where Actaeon stumbled upon
          Diana. Unlike Actaeon, Peleus will act with criminal
          intent; unlike Actaeon, he will suffer no consequences.

254   *till she turns back:* In Book 4 of the *Odyssey* and of Virgil's
          Georgics, this tactic is used against Proteus himself. In the

most charitable reading, his double-dealing counseling of both Peleus and Thetis is an effort to avoid further wrestling matches.

Daedalion and Chione (266–345)

Proceeding with Peleus, we learn that he is not only a rapist but a murderer as well, and has fled to the court of King Ceÿx of Trachis to escape punishment for his crime. Though he departs at 408, we will stay with Ceÿx for the next three tales and four hundred lines. In the first tale, Ceÿx narrates his grief at the loss of his brother Daedalion, who himself fell to grief at the loss of his daughter Chione. Largely original to Ovid, this story reads like a Frankensteining together of *Metamorphoses* tropes, as a typical start (beautiful girl raped by the powers that be) turns on a dime into a Niobe-like parable of a mortal fool enough to challenge the gods. The myth finishes with a focus-shift to the mourning father and the first of the book's three bird metamorphoses. The other two will be handled more carefully.

268   *killing Phocus*: Phocus was the son of the Nereid Psamathe and king Aeacus of Aegina, at whose court we met him in Book 7. His half-brothers Peleus and Telamon murdered him for variously reported reasons, though the usual motive is jealousy.

285–86   *the weight . . . and grandsire, Jove, must bear*: An amusing contradiction of 217–20.

313–17   *Autolycus . . . Philammon*: Autolycus' comparably cunning wife Mestra appeared in Book 8 (cf. 8.738). In some versions of the tale, Philammon takes Orpheus' place as the musician aboard the *Argo*.

323   *Perhaps our deeds*: That is, as opposed to her looks.

The Wolf of Psamathe (346–409)

As Ceÿx is finishing his story, a herdsman of Peleus bursts in to deliver a breathless yet oddly rambling report about an offstage catastrophe—readers of Greek drama will recognize a parody of the typical messenger speech (see note to 15.506–29). The master's cattle, carefully hidden at 276–77, are being savaged by an enormous wolf, which Peleus recognizes as Psamathe's revenge for the murder of her son. As he sets about addressing the situation (getting his wife to help), we are introduced to the character of Ceÿx' anxious queen Alcyone, whose fears for her husband's safety are only temporarily without cause.

376   *there's no time to lose or hesitate:* A patent absurdity given the length of this speech, which did not come to the point until 366. The elevated diction of Onetor's monologue is pointedly unrealistic; the narrator calls him a *rube* at 379.

409   *Acastus of Thessalia cleansed his sin:* Killers could not participate in worship until they had been purified by innocent hands. Acastus had joined Peleus on the Calydonian Hunt (8.306). Peleus later killed him, too.

Ceÿx and Alcyone (410–748)

Greatly perturbed by all he has endured, Ceÿx sails off to consult Apollo's oracle at Claros, ceding the stage to the fretful Alcyone. There follows one of the poem's most artful, extensive, and self-contained stories, whose four dynamic sections have been likened to the movements of a symphony. Alcyone's grave misgivings at Ceÿx' departure bring us to 473, when a violent storm overtakes her husband's ship and we are treated to ninety-nine lines of Ovid's finest hyperbolic description. The third part of the story also contains the third of the poem's four great allegorical personifications (see note to 2.760ff), as Juno's messenger Iris petitions the House of Sleep to send Alcyone a vision of what has transpired (573–673). In the final section (674–748), Alcyone wakes and mourns her way to a transcendent transformation, when she rejoins her husband to poise the poem in a rare moment of perfect peace.

413–14   *at Claros . . . Phorbas' Phlegyan hordes:* Apollo's oracle at Claros was second only to that at Delphi. The bandits of prince Phorbas of the Phlegyes serve no other narrative purpose than to rule Delphi (and an overland journey) out.

429   *many empty tombs:* Readers familiar with Sophocles' *Antigone* will recall the importance of proper burial in

Greek religion. The idea of one's corpse being lost at sea thus carried a special horror (cf. 539–40).

584   *temple-tainting pleas of mourning:* Without a proper funeral, the deceased's home and family were considered unclean. Despite her ignorance, Alcyone's persistent praying is therefore sinful.

592   *the Cimmerians:* The Cimmerians were a proto-historic Scythian people, long vanished by Ovid's time. In the *Odyssey*, they inhabit a cave near the underworld, much like that described here. Reports of them worshipping the mountain-dwelling Crom or moth goddess Lo are later elaborations.

627   *Herculean Trachis' king:* As narrated in Book 8, Hercules spent his later years in Trachis, dying on nearby Mount Oeta. The term "Herculean Trachis' king" is an anachronism, however, since the Spartans only renamed the settlement Heraclea in Trachis in 426 BCE. Ghostly apparitions are common in epic, though it is usually the deceased that appears (cf. Achilles at 13.442), rather than a divine imitation. But Ovid is always interested in narrative authority (cf. 666–67); here, Alcyone is being tricked into a justified true belief.

640–45 *The gods call "Likeness" . . . humbler hordes:* Ovid's dreams, like his gods (1.171–73), conform to class distinctions. The names "Likeness" and "Fearmonger" are translated from the Greek "Icelos" and "Phobetor," with "Phantasos" rendered as the related "Phantasm." Morpheus ("Shaper," 633) has been kept on the grounds of familiarity, though the modern identification of Morpheus with the god of sleep (rather than dreams) is a medieval innovation.

745–48 *Each winter, seven days of peace . . . grandsons' sake:* Thus the English expression "halcyon days." The mythical halcyon is the kingfisher, believed in ancient times to nest atop the waves. Another, less sympathetic Alcyone (Polypemon's grandchild) underwent the same change at 7.401.

Aesacus (749–95)

Daedalion, Alcyone, and Ceÿx all became birds through the pity of the gods. In the book's last tale, the same will hold true for Aesacus, but although his metamorphosis is certainly the sorriest and most sordid of the bunch, it packs a relatively light punch after the saga of the Trachinian royal family. The story's main purpose is transitional. Aesacus is a son of king Priam of Troy; in little more than a page, a Greek army will besiege his father's gates.

751   *or one nearby:* Once again, Ovid defies epic convention by making his omniscient narrator's sourcing playfully sloppy. This may be a nod to the tale's originality; Aesacus was usually characterized as a clear-eyed prophet, a detail Ovid omits.

753   *diving fowl:* The Latin *mergus* ("diver") seems to refer to a broad category of birds rather than a specific species (see appendix).

754ff *you could trace his line:* This genealogy recalls previous tales while looking ahead to the Trojan War. Troy's eponymous founder Tros had three sons: Assaracus, Ganymede (10.155ff), and Ilus (after whom Troy was also called "Ilium"). Ilus' son was Laömedon (197ff), whose son Priam was king when the city fell—an event that seems, curiously, to have happened already (757–58). Priam's fifty sons included both Aesacus and the greatest of the Trojan heroes, Hector.

BOOK 12

The Greeks at Aulis (1–38)

The next three books contain Ovid's telling of the Trojan War and its aftermath, a mythic cycle that had already received definitive treatment by Homer, Virgil, and the Greek dramatists. As we might expect, given Book 7's Argonaut-free handling of the *Argonautica,* Ovid shows no interest in retreading familiar territory, instead skirting the highlights of his predecessors' works to pursue digressions and side plots of his own. Accordingly, Book 12, in which Ovid tackles the subject matter of Homer's *Iliad,* is the shortest in the poem. In this first section, the entire inciting incident for the war (the abduction of Helen) is condensed into three lines, while the great tragedy of Iphigenia takes only fifteen.

4–7   *none but Paris ... Grecian race:* These lines are decipherable only to those who already know the story. Paris was the sole Trojan prince absent from the funeral because he was busy abducting the incomparably beautiful Queen Helen of Sparta from her husband Menelaus. Unfortunately for Paris, the former suitors for Helen's hand (every king in Greece) had sworn a collective oath to protect her in just such an event. Their forces therefore amassed at Aulis under the banner of Menelaus' brother Agamemnon, who led them in a retaliatory siege of Troy. Whether or not Helen ("the face that launched a thousand ships") conspired in her own capture varies from telling to telling. In Ovid's lopsided version, however, she barely appears at all.

13   *Argives:* Classical writers developed several poetic monikers for the Trojan War's combatants. Otherwise an adjective specific to the city of Argos, "Argive" henceforth refers to the Greeks writ large, as do the terms "Danaans," "Achaeans," and "Pelasgians." Similarly, the Trojans are called "Phrygians" or "Dardanians" as often as not, while Troy is also called "Ilium" or "Pergamum."

22   *stamped in the serpent's shape:* The rare metamorphosis to be found in Homer, this transformation closely follows the telling at *Iliad* 2.299–330.

28–29   *The virgin goddess raged ... sire and kin:* This highly mannered couplet again compresses a well-known story. The augur Calchas, Thestor's son (18), correctly divined that the poor weather hindering the fleet was caused by the wrath of Diana, who demanded the sacrifice of Agamemnon's virgin daughter Iphigenia to appease her. Ulysses, as he himself relates at 13.181ff, convinced Agamemnon to acquiesce, thereby putting "king and country" duties over those of "sire and kin." True to form, Ovid declines to lend Diana's actions the slightest motiva-

tion; typically, it is Agamemnon's killing of her sacred
deer.

34   *swapped Mycenae's daughter for a deer:* Agamemnon was
the king of Mycenae. This *deus ex machina* happy ending
is found in the oldest version of the myth. Euripides and
other later writers tended to leave it out.

The House of Rumor (39–63)

The poem's fourth great allegorical personification is also its least inte-
grated: after her long ekphrastic introduction, Rumor lingers for just a
single line (64). But by invoking the spirit of hearsay at the outset of
his narrative of the Trojan War and the founding of Rome, Ovid makes
a nod toward skepticism at the very moment his poem crosses into the
supposedly historical. Modeling his House of Rumor on a similar
description in *Aeneid* 4, Ovid outdoes his predecessor by adding
throngs of clients and parasites, subversively characterizing his own
House of Rumor as the palace of a Roman aristocrat.

39   *At the world's center:* This phrase typically refers to Delphi
(cf. 10.168); Apollo's oracular voice has been swapped out
for its shadowy imitation—gossip.

Achilles and Cygnus (64–145)

Robbed by Rumor of the element of surprise, the Greek attack goes
poorly, with the Trojan heroes Hector and Cygnus proving a particular nuisance. Achilles reacts by going after Cygnus, whose handy
invincibility only briefly forestalls the metamorphosis already suffered
by two others of his name (see note to 2.368–69). The blend of violence
and silliness, along with the portrayal of Achilles as more halfwit than
hero, recall Perseus' battle from the start of Book 5. Though not original to Ovid, the story of Cygnus does not appear in Homer.

76   *Hector's death would wait ten years:* The siege of Troy
lasted a decade, and Homer describes only a few weeks of
its final year. Ovid will pass through all ten at line 584.

97   *Nine leather layers burst, but not the tenth:* A preposterous detail, especially since the famously huge shield of
Ajax had only seven layers (cf. 13.2).

108–12   *For it was mighty . . . felt me use my spear:* Just as Hercules
rattled off his feats while dying at 9.181ff, Achilles' crisis
of confidence occasions a recitation of his prewar
exploits. On his way to Troy, Achilles sacked the city of
Lyrnessos, the isle of Tenedos, and the Anatolian city of
Thebes (not the Boeotian kingdom of Cadmus), killing
its king, Eëtion. While repulsing an attack from the
Greeks, who had mistaken his city for Troy, king Telephus of Mysia (through which the Caïcus river flows)
was wounded by Achilles' spear. Advised by oracle that
he could only be healed by his attacker, Telephus sought
out Achilles, who mended the wound with rust scraped
from his spear.

Caenis Becomes Caeneus (146–209)

For Nestor, the proverbially ancient wise man of the Greeks, the invincibility of Cygnus recalls the tale of Caenis, who gained the same
impenetrability only after suffering an act of forced penetration.
Raped by the god Neptune, she asked to be rendered unrapable—a
state synonymous in the universe of the poem with being a man. Neptune's additional boon of making Caenis (now Caeneus) invincible to
literal swords as well as the kind found in Shakespearean puns draws
an equation of sexual with martial violence that will be elaborated in
the following tale, when Caeneus himself assumes the role of the
invulnerable masculine fighter but is jeered as a woman all the same.
Nestor's narration is digressive and incredulous, but when Caenis
addresses her rapist, the tone becomes direct and trenchantly cold.

151   *Achilles offered Pallas heifer's blood:* There was no special
reason to thank Minerva. Not appeasing Neptune after his
son's death will prove to be Achilles' undoing (580–83).

159   *manly deeds:* A striking choice of words, given the gender
play in the coming tale. The Latin term is *uirtus,* which Ovid
used to similar effect in detailing the deeds of Atalanta (see
note to 8.387).

188   *Two centuries:* Homer described Nestor as living through his
third generation, but the Latin *saeculum* could mean both
generation and century. Ovid's exaggerated reading makes

Nestor over two hundred years old, a translingual pun
contradicted by the poem itself, since Nestor appeared as a
young man only a generation earlier (8.313).

197   *so rumor has:* Together with its echo at 200, this parenthetical casts doubt on the story's central miracle. While Ovid is
always happy to muddy the waters of narrative authority
with a note of incredulity, in this case skepticism of Caenis'
transformation doubles as a skepticism of women's ability to
escape the sexual aggression of men: cf. note to 9.666–797.
Also notable is the recurring presence of *rumor.*

The Centauromachy (210–535)

Troy aside, perhaps Greek mythology's most famous battle scene was
the Centauromachy, a brawl that pitted the centaurs against the Lapiths,
a human tribe ruled by Theseus' old friend Pirithoüs. In the *Iliad,* Nestor gives Achilles a short rendition of this fight that mentions Caeneus
only once (1.262–72); but pursuing his usual program of frolicking in
Homer's margins, Ovid expands that brief passage into a tangential
escapade so long that one might call Ovid's Trojan War a Trojan horse
for his Centauromachy. Not even its closest parallel, the Book 5 battle
between Perseus and Phineus, ascends to such heights of absurd gore
and melodrama, compounded here by the thematic tensions caused by
the presence of the half-beast centaurs on the one hand (who are the
real savages?) and the transgender Caeneus on the other (who is a real
man?) Although distinctions between combatants will again fade into a
blurry onslaught of names and injuries, this time a series of transphobic
attacks from the centaurs will snap the division back into focus just as
the battle reaches its climax. By the time Nestor is done explaining how
he met Caeneus, the reader has surely forgotten that Achilles ever asked.

210–12   *Ixion's son ... the cloud-born beasts ... tree-lined cave:*
Last seen in Book 8, Ixion's son is king Pirithoüs of the
Lapiths. In addition to winning him the eternal damna-
tion described at 4.461, Ixion's attempted assault of Juno
led the would-be rapist to impregnate a cloud mirage of
the goddess, producing the *cloud-born* race of centaurs.
Pirithoüs is thus the centaurs' half-brother, which
explains their presence at his wedding.

232   Lines 230–31 are missing from some major manuscripts and are widely considered spurious, since they completely undermine the drama of the episode. Finding them too anticlimactic to inflict upon the reader, I have taken the extra step of omitting them from my text, but proffer this translation here:

> [The great-souled hero, lest he vaunt in vain,
> Broke through the mob and saved the stolen girl.]

262–64   *Orios was the son / of Mycale . . . with her charms:* A humorously abortive attempt to humanize the fallen Lapith. Seneca and Nemesianus describe Mycale as a Thessalian witch capable of drawing down the moon, an ability Medea also professes (cf. 7.207–8).

309   *You will be saved for Hercules:* Asbolos prophesies correctly, for we watched Hercules kill Nessus at 9.101ff. Despite his absconding, Nessus reappears at 454, a circumstance Dryden "fixed" in his translation: "Nessus, now return'd from flight . . ."

321–22   *You'll drink your wine / Mixed with the Styx:* Several of the "close-ups" in this battle sequence mirror those in the fight with Perseus from Book 5, where Paetalus made a similar crack while killing Lampetides (5.115).

377   *Both his chests:* That is, first Demoleon's human chest, then the equine barrel behind.

393ff   *Cyllarus . . . your kind:* A thirty-five line interlude breaks up the carnage to bring us the centaur couple Cyllarus and Hylonome. Even more so than Athis and Lycabas at 5.47–73, their devoted and tragic love story lends the enemy force a note of complicating sympathy. Though Nestor is persistent in his characterization of the pair as belonging to a lesser race (394, 409), they certainly cannot seem savage compared to what Peleus has just done to Dorylas!

401   *Castor's mount:* We have read that Castor was a keen equestrian (8.300–1). His horse was indeed canonically named *Kyllaros*.

414   *clothed her leftward arm and flank*: Like an Amazon, she keeps her right side free to fight.

461–62   *I don't recall their wounds / But tallied them by name:* At this late juncture in the story, an absurd statement. Ovid enjoys making a pretense of sparing the reader information only after first overloading them with it (cf. 3.225).

469ff   *Caenis, shall I take you next . . .* : In a rather satisfying bit of action and reaction, Caeneus responds to Latreus' transphobic dead-naming (469–71) and victim-blaming (472–74) by tearing the centaur a literal new one. The "manhood" of both the ex-woman and the half-man would appear to be in question, but Caeneus settles the matter by wounding his opponent at the very point of contention ("Where horse meets man," 478), whereas Latreus' metaphorical attempt at rape ends with his sword discovering that Caeneus' genitals are inviolable (485–88). The sexist terms of Latreus' verbal assault recall the male hunters' reaction to Atalanta at the Calydonian Hunt (8.388–93); Monychus takes up the theme anew at 499–506.

Hercules and Periclymenus (536–79)

Much as the catalog of Actaeon's dogs in Book 3 left out the three that mattered most (see note to 3.232–35), it turns out Nestor has neglected to mention the greatest hero present at the Centauromachy—Hercules. Nor is this the result of an old man's forgetfulness, for Nestor admits to deliberately editing him out due to an (admittedly sympathetic) personal grudge. In addition to elaborating on the theme of rumor and unreliability, the resulting tale further postpones the resumption of Ovid's Trojan War narrative.

The Death of Achilles (580–628)

When we finally get back to the war, it is only to fast forward through it and find Achilles in his final moments. Though the poet's grandiloquent eulogy for the hero (612–19) makes a show of epic emotion, he has done nothing to give the character's demise real meaning: Achilles' victory over Hector comes up only in passing (591), Patroclus—the dead lover typically so central to Achilles' story—has yet to be mentioned, and the closest thing to a feat we have seen him achieve is his befuddled triumph over Cygnus, which in this version leads to his death. Even when Ovid pretends to extol his heroes, he keeps them unworthy of the name.

581–82 *Phaëthon's dear bird:* A reference to the first of the three Cygnus stories, narrated at 2.367ff. Only in Ovid is Achilles' death motivated by Neptune, typically the hero's ally. In drawing a direct line from the fate of Cygnus to that of Achilles, Ovid sketches an arc for the hero of the *Iliad* that is almost sarcastic in its brazen circumvention of Homer. Why would Neptune's *less than civil rage* (583) wait *twice-five years* (584) to bear fruit?

591 *Hector, dragged around his Pergamum:* Pergamum is another poetic term for Troy. After slaying Hector (who had killed his beloved Patroclus), Achilles dishonored his enemy's body by dragging it behind his chariot for twelve full days, though Apollo took care to keep the corpse undamaged. Hector's death, the climactic moment of the *Iliad*, is here little more than a sidenote.

610–11 *For had you wished ... Amazon's twin-axe:* An obscure allusion to another episode of the war, after the events of the *Iliad*, when Achilles slew Penthesilea, the fierce queen of the Amazons and an ally of Troy. Since Paris was constantly mocked for his effeminacy, the narrator implies that the Amazon would have been a worthier "woman" to kill Achilles.

622–25 *Oilean Ajax ... Telamon's own child:* Now that he is safely past Homeric territory, Ovid finally introduces the slate of Greek heroes that typically populate Trojan War narratives, albeit only as potential squabblers over the inheritance of a dead man's armor. These include Ajax "the Lesser," son of Oileus; the sons of Atreus, Agamemnon and the inferior Menelaus; the son of Tydeus, Diomedes, and his crafty comrade, Ulysses (Odysseus), son of Laertes; and Ajax "the Greater," son of Telamon and thus Achilles' cousin.

BOOK 13

The Judgment of Arms (1–398)

The epic's shortest book gives way to its longest, of which the first four hundred lines comprise the speeches of Ajax and Ulysses contesting the inheritance of Achilles' armor. This "Judgment of Arms" was a standard (if post-Homeric) set piece of Trojan War poetry, but Ovid mostly uses it as a vehicle to rehash the most famous episodes of the *Iliad*—only a few of which came up earlier. Issues of narrator reliability remain central, however, as the pair repeatedly contradict each other in a biased rhetorical battle of brawn (Ajax) against brains (Ulysses). Readers who know Ulysses primarily through Homer's Odysseus may be surprised at his slimy, duplicitous characterization here, drawn from a large corpus of ancient accounts by other poets and playwrights. For the Roman audience, however, both heroes' arguments would have been familiar, and focus would have fallen not on the points made in their speeches, but on the fresh flourishes and recombinations the oratorically trained Ovid creates with them.

7–8   *For he balked not . . . I saved our fleet*: As related at *Iliad* 15.674–746, when Hector and the Trojans took advantage of Achilles' absence to breach the Greek camp, force a retreat, and set their fleet aflame, it was Ajax who rallied the allies to repulse the attack. Homer says nothing of Odysseus fleeing the scene, however. Ajax returns to this subject at 91–95.

15   *Observed by night alone*: A reference to the "Doloneia," a nighttime quest undertaken by Odysseus in *Iliad* 10. Ajax elaborates at 98ff. (See note to 100–1.)

22–24   *Telamon . . . Colchian shores*: We met Ajax' father Telamon at the court of his father Aeacus, then watched him aid Hercules in an earlier sack of Troy (11.211–16). He also took part in the Argonauts' voyage to Colchis (though one would never know it from Ovid's account).

31–32   *son / Of Sisyphus*: Seemingly an odd embellishment of Aeacus' job as judge in the underworld, the mention of Sisyphus at 26 turns out to have been teeing up this zinger. Suspicions that Ulysses had been fathered by the similarly sly Sisyphus, rather than Laërtes, were a common trope.

35   *no informer's force:* In a tale not found in Homer, Ulysses had attempted to avoid service in the Trojan War by feigning madness and sowing his fields with salt. When Palamedes (the informer) placed Ulysses' son Telemachus in front of the plow, Ulysses stopped plowing rather than kill his child, showing his sanity and foiling his own ruse. As Ajax relates at 56–60, Ulysses later retaliated by planting gold in Palamedes' tent, then using it as evidence that he was taking enemy bribes, a crime for which Palamedes was executed.

45   *Poeas' son:* This is Philoctetes, who attended Hercules at his death and inherited the hero's bow and arrows (9.229–33). On the voyage to Troy, he was bitten by a snake and the festering wound gave off a stench so unbearable that Ulysses convinced their other comrades to abandon Philoctetes on the isle of Lemnos, where he subsisted in miserable conditions until being retrieved later in the war (399–403). Since prophecy held that Troy could not be defeated without the arrows of Hercules (320), the marooning of Philoctetes was a major tactical blunder.

64ff   *deserting Nestor . . .:* As related at *Iliad* 8.66–129, Odysseus fled the field at Hector's attack, despite the vociferous insistence of Diomedes (son of Tydeus) that he save Nestor, whom Diomedes ultimately rescued himself. Homer's Nestor makes no direct appeal (66), however.

76   *I saved his useless life:* Ajax' retelling is particularly uncharitable. As related at *Iliad* 11.411–88, Odysseus fought bravely against a Trojan attack before succumbing to wounds and calling to Ajax and Menelaus for rescue.

80–81   *he was too weak with wounds . . . he lost his wounds and ran:* Following Homer, an outright lie. Not only was Odysseus gravely wounded, but he managed to kill his assailant before calling for help (*Iliad* 11.435–48).

86   *send tumbling with a far-flung stone:* Ajax exaggerates his prowess. As related at *Iliad* 14.409–32, Ajax threw a stone and struck Hector from behind, stunning him briefly, but to no lasting effect.

90   *I did not lose to him:* As related at *Iliad* 7.37–312, in Achilles' absence, Hector challenged the remaining Greeks to send a champion against him in single combat. His ensuing bout with Ajax ended in an amicable draw, but Ulysses' rebuttal to this point is particularly withering (275–79).

98–99   *the Ithacan seized Helenus . . . stole the Palladium:* In a story not found in Homer, Odysseus (the king of Ithaca) captured the Trojan prince Helenus and forced him to divulge the secret of the Palladium, a wooden icon of Pallas that protected Troy. Odysseus and Diomedes then entered the city in disguise and stole it.

100–1   *then struck Rhesus and poor Dolon down . . . all at night:* In the "Doloneia" episode of *Iliad* 10, Diomedes and Odysseus set out on a nocturnal reconnaissance mission, during which they apprehended the enemy spy Dolon, who was engaged on the same errand for the Trojans. As related at 242–52, having extracted intelligence from Dolon, Ulysses killed him, then fell upon the camp of the Trojan ally Rhesus.

145   *no exiles in our house:* This is an attack on Ajax' father Telamon, who fled his homeland after murdering his half-brother Phocus (though Ovid's version at 11.226–29 has Peleus acting alone). With this genealogy, Ulysses implicitly rebuts Ajax' accusation that he is the son of Sisyphus (31–32), but conveniently omits his grandfather Autolycus, another notoriously wily forebear (cf. 11.313–15).

155–56 *Peleus and Pyrrhus . . . let Phthia or let Sycros take these back:* Achilles' father Peleus is home at Phthia. Achilles' son Pyrrhus (or Neoptolemus) is still on Scyros with his mother, but will shortly join the war (13.455).

161–64 *Foreseeing his death . . . deceitful dress:* Less obscurely, Thetis disguised Achilles as a girl and sent him to Scyros,

where he fathered Neoptolemus. As alluded to at 134 and
explained at 164–69, Ulysses unmasked Achilles by
offering him a variety of gifts, the most masculine of
which he proved unable to resist.

169   *Why do you wait to wreck great Pergamum?:* Like stealing
the Palladium and using Hercules' arrows, the presence
of Achilles was a prophesied prerequisite for Troy's fall.

193–94   *send me to his wife . . . to connive:* For the story of
Iphigenia, see note to 12.24–38. When Agamemnon sent
Ulysses to retrieve Iphigenia from her mother
Clytemnestra, Ulysses accomplished his task by claiming
the girl was being fetched to marry Achilles.

216–17   *Then Jove dispatched a dream . . . the war we had begun:*
This is a simplified rendition of *Iliad* 2.1–141. After a
deceitful dream from Jupiter convinced Agamemnon to
lead an attack on Troy, he first tested his men's resolve
with a proposal to return home and was disappointed to
find the offer widely accepted. While Ulysses was
instrumental in staying their flight, Ajax does not figure
in Homer's telling.

232–33   *Yet Thersites dared . . . thanks to me:* A famous minor
character in the *Iliad*, Thersites was noted for his
ugliness and vulgar, obnoxious behavior. In response
to his insubordinate opposition to Agamemnon,
he was upbraided and beaten by Odysseus
(*Iliad* 2.244–69).

242   *No lots made me go:* As opposed to Ajax, who was chosen
to fight Hector by lot (cf. 87–90, 275–79).

251   *in mock Triumph:* One of the poem's most egregious
modernizing touches; the Triumph was a distinctly
Roman ceremony (see note to 1.560–63).

253–54   *the foeman claimed his steeds . . . Ajax will seem just:* The
logic here is tortuous. Hector had promised Dolon the
steeds of Achilles as a reward for his quest, the success of
which Ulysses foiled. Since Ajax suggested that Ulysses
and Diomedes split Achilles' arms in reward for a similar

mission (102), the possibility that Ulysses might instead be awarded nothing at all makes the judges appear ungrateful by comparison.

266–67   *the son of Telamon . . . stayed unscratched:* Whether this is due to Ajax' adept fighting, his enormous shield, or his physical invulnerability (as some versions have it), only through Ulysses' sophistry does this fact redound to his opponent's discredit.

272–74   *Actor's heir . . . both ships and guard:* Despite the heroism of Ajax (91–94), Hector's attack was only repulsed when the appearance of Patroclus (son of Menoetius, son of Actor) disguised in Achilles' armor scared the Trojans off. Patroclus had first joined Achilles in retiring from the field to vent rage against Agamemnon (see note to 443–44), but later gained Achilles' permission to return in his armor and save the fleet. The guard is Ajax.

279   *Hector left without a wound:* In the *Iliad*, Ajax' spear hits Hector in the neck (7.262).

291–94   *what's carved upon this shield . . . Orion's sword:* Ovid gives a brief selection of the many sidereal and geographical scenes detailed in Homer's Shield of Achilles, forged by Vulcan at the request of Thetis (*Iliad* 18.478–608). See note to 2.6–18.

356–59   *He'd claim it, too . . . Atreus' younger son:* Together with Ajax and Ulysses, these are the seven other men who drew lots to duel with Hector (*Iliad* 7.161–69), further minimizing Ajax' accomplishment.

381   *Minerva's fateful effigy:* Ulysses concludes his address by gesturing to the Palladium, a physical reminder of his useful service. Ajax opened his speech with a similar move, gesturing toward the fleet (4–8).

395–98   *a purple flower . . . cries of woe:* As foretold at 10.206–8, Ajax shares a memorial with *Sparta's wounded son* Hyacinth in his namesake flower. The letters AI AI (10.215) both represent Greek lamentation ("alas") and resemble Ajax' name (in Greek, AIAS).

The Sorrows of Hecuba (399–575)

Rolling rapidly through the fall of Troy, Ovid alights on the sorrows of Priam's widow Hecuba, perhaps the most unequivocally piteous figure in the poem. Already devastated by the death of Hector, losing her last two children turns her into an epitome of grief and a paragon of paradox, as the childless mother lets forth a meditative lament in which Ovid's mannered wit for once emphasizes rather than undercuts the character's misery. Unlike Philomena, who followed her appalling sufferings with appalling retribution, Hecuba retains the reader's full sympathy while taking revenge against the king who killed her son. In the end, however, the queen reduced to slavery is reduced further still, so that even the gods, so recently divided in the war to destroy her city, are united in belief that "Hecuba had not deserved her fate" (575). Largely drawn from Euripides' play *Hecuba*, Ovid's account seemingly pours all the tragic emotion drained from his version of the Trojan War into the story of Hecuba and her daughter Polyxena, both of whom evince a stoic power and self-possession unmatched by the villainous men in the story, but which still cannot save them from their fates.

399–400   *Thoas' homeland . . . reviled for murdered men:* Ulysses is sailing to Lemnos to retrieve Philoctetes and the arrows of Hercules. In one story, when the women of Lemnos murdered all the men on their island, their queen Hypsipyle proved the sole exception in saving her father Thoas.

408   Lines 404–7 are almost certainly an interpolation, summarizing the coming action in a manner emphatically redundant with 408–9 while spoiling the whole story to follow. Since they pose too great a detriment to the reading experience to stand in the printed text, I instead proffer a translation here:

> [Troy fell with Priam; Priam's luckless wife,
> Once she had lost all else, lost human form   405
> To fright the foreign air with strange new barks
> Along the narrows of the Hellespont.]

410   *The Phoebean priestess, dragged out by the hair:* This is Cassandra, a Trojan princess and prophetess of Phoe-

bus. Her assailant is Ajax the Lesser, who will rape her in the Temple of Minerva, bringing the wrath of that goddess down on the entire Greek fleet (14.466–72).

415–17   *threw Astyanax . . . his realm and self:* Little more than an infant, Astyanax was the son of Hector and Andromache, who predicted this fate at *Iliad* 24.734–35. The famous tower scene where Astyanax watches his father fight occurs at *Iliad* 6.390–496. Depending on the version, Astyanax is killed by either Neoptolemus or Ulysses.

438   *erased both corpse and crime:* In *Aeneid* 3.22–56, Aeneas is harvesting myrtle and cornel shoots for altar decorations when the plants begin bleeding and cry out with the voice of Polydorus, who narrates his own fate. Ovid's decision to omit this otherwise apt metamorphosis reflects his continuing desire to steer clear of the trodden epic path. The poem may also have reached its limit on screaming, bleeding trees (see note to 8.762).

442–44   *large as life . . . His sword on Agamemnon:* An allusion to the opening episode of the *Iliad*, in which Agamemnon's seizure of Achilles' concubine Briseis so enraged Achilles that he began to draw his sword (1.188–94). Achilles and Patroclus subsequently withdrew from the war until Hector's assault on the fleet.

569   *for which that place is named:* Cynossema ("Dog's Tomb") is a promontory on the Thracian coast—Hecuba has become a dog.

Memnon (576–622)

Coming after the vast arcs of Hecuba, the Trojan War, and the Centauromachy, the tale of Memnon, son of Dawn, reads like a tender vignette, briefly pausing the narrative to zoom in on one in the legion of faceless dead who fell on the fields of Troy. That Memnon was a major hero, the king of Aethiopia, and himself the titular subject of an epic (the *Aethiopis,* now lost) are not recoverable from Ovid's telling. Like the previous story, Memnon's death is about a mother's grief; yet despite her divinity, Dawn seems powerless in comparison to Hecuba.

Instead of channeling sorrow into action, she will make a monument of her pain.

601–3   *sable smoke . . . black cinders:* Though it is hazy whether the Aethiopia of Homer's contemporaries was closer to Africa or India (see note to 1.773–74), in Roman times Memnon was portrayed as a Black African, which may account for the emphasis on these color words.

618–19   *Memnonides . . . die the family way:* The birds' annual battles mirror the gladiatorial games that took place during the Parentalia, a Roman festival honoring dead ancestors. While no match has gained consensus, the Memnonides are traditionally identified as ruffs, dark-plumed sandpipers known for their aggressive fighting.

The Daughters of Anius (623–704)

It is finally time to leave Greece. For the rest of this book and most of the next, the poem will follow the journeys of Venus' son Aeneas, ancestor of the Romans, as he sails the Mediterranean to manifest his Italian destiny. Ovid, however, will show no more interest in rehashing Virgil's *Aeneid* than he did with Homer's *Iliad,* and not until his death will Aeneas manage to hold the narrator's attention. In this first section of his voyage, the poet takes a pry bar to *Aeneid* 3, breaking up Aeneas' visit to king Anius of Delos with a long feast scene containing two tales of metamorphoses, neither of them mentioned in the original. As with Homer, the few Virgilian details required for continuity are so compressed as to be nearly indecipherable.

624–27   *For Cytherea's son had shouldered . . . that noble load:* Though both epics preserve the famous image of Aeneas escaping with his father Anchises on his shoulders, Virgil's hero must be talked into leaving by repeated divine visitations, and the loss of his wife Creusa comes as a particularly tragic blow. Ovid's Aeneas, by contrast, seems unhurried in his flight and quite deliberate about leaving her behind.

640   *Pious Anchises:* Ovid is at it again. Virgil famously referred to his hero as *"pius Aeneas,"* an epithet Ovid adopted at 626 in an echo of Dawn's tears from 621. But

since we are still waiting for Aeneas to be named (see note to 1.442), the phrase "pious Anchises" would have teasingly thwarted Roman expectations.

670   *If being destroyed by miracle is 'help':* Anius provides an unusually pointed reminder that the central act of the epic, metamorphosis, is a deeply ambiguous one. By this stage in the poem, we have seen metamorphoses routinely performed as punishment, salvation, memorial, tragic downfall, or reward. As for which applies to the Delian princesses, Anius and Bacchus apparently disagree.

681–84   *Aeneas' gift . . . Therses . . . Rhodes / By Alcon:* Otherwise content to belie and belittle, Ovid here takes the extra step of directly contradicting Virgil, in whose account the craftsman was named Alcimedon. The geographical descriptor ascribed to the artist is hotly disputed (see appendix), unlike the identity of Therses, which is simply unknown.

695   *Dead for their people's sake:* An oracle had decreed that Thebes' latest plague would end only with the self-sacrifice of two virgins, a duty for which Orion's daughters gamely volunteered.

Galatea, Acis, and Polyphemus (705–897)

Another transitional passage takes Aeneas on a circuitous voyage that, like Medea's flight in Book 7, allows the narrator a parade of mini-metamorphoses. The voyage and the parade both end in Sicily, where Ovid teases the origin story of the sea monster Scylla, only to digress immediately into the story of Galatea. Despite its austere introduction, Galatea's tale of her love triangle with Acis and Polyphemus is among the poem's most lighthearted. A monster in the *Odyssey,* the Cyclops Polyphemus will resume his cruel ways at 14.167–213, but for now the presence of this proto-*kaiju* is used to comedic, rather than horrific, effect. Ovid's song for the lovesick ogre explores the heights of rhetorical absurdity, and even the minor details of his pipes and staff are exaggerated into farce. Capped off with a (mostly) happy ending, this rustic parody sees Ovid at his whimsical finest—a tone picked up in John Gay and G. F. Handel's pastoral opera *Acis and Galatea,* which remains the story's best-known adaptation.

705–8   *Recalling ... Ausonian harbors:* Acting on the oracle that *bade them seek their ancient mother shores* (678), the Trojans (or, in this case, Teucrians) make for Crete, the homeland of their ancestor king Teucer—not the cousin of Achilles. Driven off by the climate (*Jove's thunder*), Aeneas has a dream advising him toward Italy (Ausonia), the birthplace of Dardanus, another Trojan forebear.

709   *false-faced Strophades:* The welcoming appearance of the Strophadic isles was deceptive because they harbored monstrous harpies, including Aëllo.

713–15   *Ambracia, source of godly strife ... Actium, Apollo's shrine:* An arcane double reference conceals one of Ovid's most politically subversive moves. Each claiming the patronage of Ambracia, Apollo, Diana, and Hercules appointed the shepherd Cragaleus as arbiter; when he decided in favor of Hercules, the disappointed Apollo turned him to stone. More important, however, was a promontory on the Ambraciot Gulf known as Actium, which was much less famous in Ovid's time for its shrine to Apollo than as the location of the Emperor's decisive victory over Mark Antony in the last civil war (31 BCE). This dispassionate mention of the site is especially unimpressive beside that of Virgil, who has Aeneas spend an entire winter there (*Aeneid* 3.278–89).

717–18   *new-fledged sons ... faithless fires:* When bandits torched the palace of Munichus, the Molossians' pious king, Jupiter aided his family's escape by turning them into birds.

719–21   *Phaeacia's ... Buthrotum ... New Troy:* Ovid cheekily skims over the traditional sites. Odysseus found himself on Phaeacia for the bulk of the *Odyssey,* and the visit to Buthrotum occupied much of *Aeneid* 3. The *Phrygian prophet* is the Trojans' fellow refugee Helenus (98, 335), whose prophetic powers recur at 15.438ff.

784   *a hundred reeds:* Seven was standard.

834–36 *I found a pair of cubs . . . she-bear's peaktop lair:* This
entire speech is a burlesqued patchwork of details drawn
from the pastoral poetry of Theocritus and Virgil. To use
these lines as an example, in Virgil's *Eclogue* 2, the
shepherd Corydon promises the boy he loves no fearsome bear cubs from the slopes, but "two frightened
fawns" he found "deep in a dell" (40–42).

897   *the river god who bears his name:* The Acis (modern
"Jaci") is a Sicilian river rising at the foot of Mount Etna.

Scylla and Glaucus, Part 1 (898–968)

Returning to shore, Scylla finds that she, too, is wooed by a monster—
for so she considers the sea god Glaucus who pursues her. Perhaps
because he was once a human, Glaucus is less aggressive in courtship
than most of the poem's gods and tries using his life story to impress
her. His failure to do so, and the more drastic measures he then adopts,
will carry us into Book 14.

968   *The monstrous halls of Circe, Titan's child:* In a bit of a
cliffhanger, Ovid ends the book by introducing Circe,
daughter of the Sun, a renowned mythical witch and
major character from the *Odyssey* who will figure
prominently in Book 14. As shall be seen, her palace is
"monstrous" on account of the many beasts into which
she has transformed her victims.

BOOK 14

Scylla and Glaucus, Part 2 (1–74)

Resolved on winning Scylla's love through the power of magic, Glaucus
seeks the help of Circe, in Homer a fearsome witch on the order of her
niece Medea, but in Ovid's telling a rather ridiculous figure, constantly
undone by her boundless lust, which now fixes on Glaucus. Their ensuing love triangle recalls that of Galatea, Acis, and Polyphemus, but here
it is the undesiring Scylla who will end up as the monster.

27   *Venus, whom her sire once slurred:* The Sun discovered and
reported the affair between Venus and Mars, as narrated at
4.169ff. Circe is one of the most variable characters in the

mythos, appearing in an enormous number of tales and consequently linked with an enormous number of lovers. Ovid exploits the comedic potential involved, providing the above explanation; by contrast, Madeline Miller has won success in recent years for the literary feat of giving Circe relatable motivations, transforming her story into a first-person meditation on immortality.

70–71   *But Scylla stayed . . . stole Ulysses' crew:* This attack is related at *Odyssey* 12.73–100, but Ovid is the first to ground it in malice toward Circe. The witch's love for Ulysses is detailed at 297ff.

72–74   *She'd soon have wrecked . . . sailors still avoid:* The Rock of Scilla continues to mark the mainland side of the Strait of Messina. To spare the Trojan (Teucrian) fleet, Scylla must have been petrified overnight; she was still active at 13.729–32.

The Sibyl of Cumae (75–153)

Having left Aeneas to kick his heels at Zancle since 13.729, Ovid now resumes his five-minute parody of the *Aeneid* with another series of cartographical metamorphoses, draining the first six books of Virgil's epic of both content and intent. The prophetic Sibyl of Cumae talks primarily about the past, the search for the Golden Bough occupies a line and a half, and even the great journey to the underworld from *Aeneid* 6 passes uneventfully. Where Virgil's Aeneas is constantly driven by the force of fate, Ovid's hero seems to wander almost at random. Far from fulfilling a divinely ordained destiny, here it is a stroke of luck that Rome will be founded at all.

78–82   *Once there . . . duped herself:* A radical reduction of the first four books of the *Aeneid,* this is Ovid's only nod toward that epic's grand romance between Aeneas and queen Dido of Carthage, whom he does not even name. When Aeneas abandoned her to fulfill his destiny, Dido ordered a pyre built on the pretext of burning all reminders of him, then vaulted atop the flames and killed herself with his sword.

83–88   *Next, fleeing . . .:* These lines brutally summarize *Aeneid*
         5. After leaving the *new-built sands* of Carthage (83),
         Aeneas and his band arrive at the Sicilian court of
         Acestes, where they hold funeral games for Anchises
         (84). While the men are playing, Juno dispatches Iris to
         beguile the way-weary Trojan women into setting fire to
         the fleet (85–86), though a rainstorm sent by Jupiter
         quickly douses the flames. They next sail past the
         volcanic Aeolian Isles (named for Aeolus, son of Hip-
         potes) and the islands of the Sirens, daughters of
         Acheloüs (5.552–63). Thence, the fleet proceeds
         unhelmed (88), a tiny reference to the death of Aeneas'
         helmsman Palinurus, which Virgil treated at length.

89–90   *Australopithland . . . named for those who there reside:*
         Home to the monkeylike race of Cercopes, this island's
         Latin name is *Pithecusae*, after the Greek *pithekos*
         ("ape")—a word best known in English from the early
         hominid genus *Australopithecus* ("southern ape"), which
         gives rise to this rendering. Other translators have used
         "monkey island" and similar monikers. The modern
         name is Ischia. This is the only metamorphosis in the
         catalog on which Ovid dwells; unsurprisingly, Virgil does
         not mention it.

102   *the trumpeter Aeolid's tomb:* Misenus, son of another
         Aeolus, was trumpeter to Aeneas' fleet. Ovid is making a
         chronological joke. Whereas in *Aeneid* 6, the Sibyl of
         Cumae counsels Aeneas that he must bury the drowned
         Misenus before entering the underworld, Ovid here shows
         Misenus fully buried even before Aeneas reaches Cumae.

104   *the ancient Sibyl's cave:* The most famous of antiquity's
         "Sibyls," each a site-specific prophetess, the long-lived
         Sibyl of Cumae was a recurring character in the legends
         of early Rome, in some sense a Latin counterpart to
         Tiresias. Virgil describes her cave in grandiose terms, but
         Ovid has already cannibalized the details for his House
         of Rumor (12.39ff).

114–15   *she showed ... a bough / of gleaming gold:* A Virgilian
invention, the much-studied Golden Bough was a
prerequisite for entering the infernal regions (*Aeneid*
6.136–211), the idea being that the bough would be
presented as a gift to Proserpine, queen ("Juno") of the
underworld (Avernus). Virgil portrayed an arduous
search for the bough among all the grove's trees, but here
the Sibyl simply points it out.

118–19   *who explained ... in war:* Notably absent is the main
thrust of Virgil's underworld visit, in which Aeneas
receives a vision of the grandeur that is to be Rome.
Perversely, Ovid concentrates more on the ascent from
the underworld than the descent into it.

122   *he said:* What follows is Aeneas' only dialogue in the poem.

153   *Fate will leave me my voice:* The Sibyl predicts for herself
a fate to match Echo's, and Petronius later recorded her
shriveled form hanging in a cage and longing for death, a
passage now best known as the epigraph to Eliot's *The
Waste Land*. For Roman readers, however, the Sibyl's
prediction may have held an additional meaning, since
to her were attributed a series of secret prophecies
known as the Sibylline books, purportedly purchased
from her by Rome's last king, and which the Senate and
Emperors consulted in times of dire crisis. In this sense,
Fate would leave the Sibyl her voice well into the
imperial period.

Polyphemus (154–222)

Much as Ovid toys with the *Iliad* in Book 12, the voyagers in Virgil's
Aeneid dance cheekily around the *Odyssey,* landing on Polyphemus'
shores shortly after Ulysses departs and sailing right past Circe's. Naturally, Ovid responds by importing great swaths of the elided material, which he does in the form of a three hundred–line conversation
between two members of Aeneas' entourage, both Greek stragglers
from the crew of Ulysses, neither found in Homer. Virgil's invention of
Achaemenides was a clever spin on the Homeric tradition, but Ovid's

cooption of the character, along with the creation of a new one, Macar, reads more like a sarcastic contribution to it, especially since they receive far more attention than any of the story's usual protagonists. The first part of this dialogue, in which Achaemenides retells the *Odyssey* 9 tale of Polyphemus, contains no transformations. The only metamorphosis is what Ovid does to Homer and Virgil.

180–81   *Ulysses almost wrecked / Your ship with shouting:* As related at *Odyssey* 9.473–542, having blinded him and escaped to sea with his men, Odysseus began taunting Polyphemus, nearly allowing the Cyclops to sink their ship by hurling boulders at the sound of his voice.

Ulysses and Circe (223–307)

In regurgitating Book 10 of the *Odyssey*, Macar provides an even fuller account of Ulysses' adventures, for although Ovid's Aeneas accords with Virgil in never visiting Circe's isle, Ovid's narrative violates him in spirit by arriving there at 242 and staying for two hundred lines. Given his theme, Ovid is unsurprisingly more taken than his predecessors were with the practicalities of Circe's witchcraft, but the sorceress' weakness for men remains a weakness.

224–26   *Aeolus . . . Dulichian captain:* As related at *Odyssey* 10.1–79, Aeolus bound the Winds in a leather bag as a gift to Odysseus (*their Dulichian captain*), allowing him to sail unmolested by storms. The crew presumed the satchel held treasure their king was unwilling to share.

233   *Laestrygonian Lamus next:* As related at *Odyssey* 10.56–132, after Aeolus spurned Odysseus' request to have his gift again, the expedition next made land in Lamus, the realm of the giant man-eating Laestrygonians.

252   *Elpenor, always drunk:* An allusion to the *Odyssey*, where an intoxicated Elpenor falls off Circe's roof and dies (10.552–60), later appearing to Odysseus in the underworld (11.51–80). Some historical commentators managed to moralize the whole visit to Circe's isle into a parable on the effects of drunkenness.

Picus and Canens (308–434)

At *Odyssey* 10.467–68, Homer says Odysseus and his crew stayed on Circe's isle for a year. As he did with Aeneas' visit to Delos (see note to 13.623–704), Ovid exploits a gap in the tradition to insert a metamorphosis. The love triangle of Picus, Canens, and the ever-lustful Circe recalls the story of Scylla, but also signals a lasting shift from Greece to Italy: Canens hails from the Palatine Hill in Rome (334). Ovid uses this detail to replace the fateful scene in *Aeneid* 8 when Aeneas visits the site of the future city; in the *Metamorphoses*, a secondary character in a story within a story within a story gets there first.

320   *Picus of Ausonia, Saturn's son:* Like the coming list of rivers (326–31), the Ausonian location emphasizes the story's Italian setting. Picus' paternity also reflects Saturn's place in the pre-Greek tradition as a benevolent local ruler (see note to 1.113–14), though, according to the poem itself, he has been imprisoned in the underworld for eons.

338   *Canens:* "Singing." The subsequent lines depict her as a kind of female Orpheus, whose "good" songs contrast with the wicked incantations of Circe.

433–34 *that spot the old Camenae called / By Canens' name:* No such location is known. The Camenae were Italian water-goddesses identified with the Greek Muses (cf. 15.482).

The Crew of Diomedes (435–511)

Breaching the second half of the *Aeneid,* Aeneas and his crew set forth from Caieta and finally reach the region of Rome. There, they promptly go to war with the local Rutuli, who seek help from the Greek hero Diomedes, also resettled in the area. The tale of how he lost his men, a four-line story in Virgil (*Aeneid* 11.271–74), is expanded to delay the action another few dozen lines.

448ff   *The hero there ... but not without a fight ...:* This *fight* occupies all of *Aeneid* 7–12. On arriving in Latium, the "hero" Aeneas impressed the local king Latinus into making him his heir and son-in-law. But Latinus' daughter Lavinia was already betrothed to king Turnus of the Rutuli, who immediately led an Etruscan army against the Trojans.

456–59 *And though Aeneas ... Iapygia's dowried lands:* Much of *Aeneid* 8 follows Aeneas on a quest to win military aid from Evander, who rules Pallantium on the future site of Rome. Turnus simultaneously dispatches Venulus to seek help from Aetolia's "hero" Diomedes, the Aetolian son of Tydeus from Book 13, who has now traveled to Italy and married the daughter of the local king Daunus, receiving Iapygian real estate as dowry.

467–69 *Naryx' hero ... the maid he raped:* As mentioned at 13.410, during the sack of Troy, the "hero" Ajax the Lesser (a native of Naryx) raped the Trojan princess Cassandra in the temple of the maiden goddess Minerva, incurring the divine wrath that would follow many of the Greek warriors home.

472 *the Cape Caphareus wreck:* In revenge for the death of his son Palamedes (13.55–60), Nauplius lit false beacons at Cape Caphereus on the isle of Euboea, leading the Greek fleet to shipwreck on its voyage back.

476–78 *I was forced from home ... such revenge on me:* As related at *Iliad* 5.311–54, Diomedes wounded Aphrodite (Venus) on the field of Troy. In revenge, she caused Diomedes' wife to betray and force him into exile, hounding him through subsequent wanderings much as she aided her son Aeneas on his.

511 *Are all the few men left me can maintain:* In Virgil's telling, Diomedes' crewmen still turn to birds, but the real reason for his refusal to fight is the invincibility of Aeneas, whose might on the Trojan battlefield he equates to that of Hector (*Aeneid* 11.281–93; Homer would have been surprised). Ovid, of course, glosses over so aggrandizing a detail.

The Apotheosis of Aeneas (512–608)

The last section of Ovid's Aeneas narrative is as digressive and scattershot as the previous ones, but finally delivers Aeneas to his fate.

Notwithstanding the incidental metamorphoses of an Apulian shepherd, a fleet of ships, and an Italian town, the narrator at last gets around to polishing off the Rutulians and making a god of Aeneas, who becomes the first in the poem's series of deified Romans. But Ovid is as happy to minimize the god as the man. Unlike Hercules in Books 9 and 15, neither Aeneas nor the Romans who supposedly follow him to heaven will return to the narrative to confirm their divinity by appearance or action.

513–14   *Peucetia's bay / And the Messapian fields:* Both regions are in the heel of Italy; Venulus is going the wrong way.

563–65   *the Ithacan's ship wrecked . . . its timbers petrified:* The fate of Aeneas' ships is drawn from Virgil (*Aeneid* 9.69–122), where the rare metamorphosis reads as a novelty rather than a standard feature. In these lines, Ovid draws a comparison to two of Odysseus' ships in Homer, one scuttled by Zeus (*Odyssey* 12.403ff), the other, a gift from king Alcinous of Phaeacia, turned to stone by Poseidon in Ithaca's harbor, signaling that Odysseus' wanderings were at an end (*Odyssey* 13.159–64).

582   *Yes, Juno, too:* An all-important force in the *Aeneid*, Juno's hatred of the Trojans is nearly absent from Ovid's erratic retelling (cf. 85–86), but is mentioned here to parallel the apotheosis of Hercules (9.259–61). Juno's opposition to Romulus will be similarly glancing (781–84).

608   *Indiges:* In reality, Aeneas was likely assimilated to an indigenous cult. The visual similarity of *Indiges* to "indigeneity" may well be grounded, but even in ancient times the precise meaning and origin of the epithet was disputed.

Pomona and Vertumnus (609–771)

In pressing ahead with the legends of early Rome, Ovid remains discursive as ever, interrupting the by-then standard list of pre-Roman kings (609–621) to narrate the tale of Pomona and Vertumnus, two Roman gods of horticulture. The desperate love of the shapeshifting Vertumnus for the indifferent Pomona plays out many of the tropes of Roman love elegy, made even clearer in the largely original fable of the lowborn youth Iphis and the highborn maiden Anaxarete (698–764), which Vertumnus narrates as a warning to his desired. Pomona yields only when her suitor reveals himself, but this potentially heartwarming lesson on the beauty of one's true form is vitiated with a comment from the narrator—but for the success of his final ploy, Vertumnus would have simply raped her.

609   *Alba's throne:* By Ovid's time, Rome's origin myth had become convoluted. To fill the gap between Aeneas' flight from Troy (canonically, 1184 BCE) and the founding of Rome by his descendant Romulus (canonically, 753 BCE), Hellenistic historians invented the Alban king list, a roster of intermediate heirs to Aeneas who supposedly ruled the proto-Roman polity of Alba Longa. These nebulous monarchs were used to explain local topographical names, including the river Tiber (614–16) and the Aventine Hill (620–21).

618   *Who mimicked lightning, died by lightning's stroke:* According to Dionysius of Halicarnassus (*Ant. Rom.* 1.71.2–3), when Remulus feigned divinity by simulating lightning—he does not mention how—the gods smote him accordingly.

622   *the Palatines:* An odd way of referring to these proto-Romans, since the Palatine Hill had yet to acquire importance. Even when telling Roman legends, Ovid makes anachronistic nods toward modern Rome (see note to 1.560–63).

670–71   *Helen . . . bold Ulysses' prudent wife:* The abductions of Helen and the Lapith queen Hippodame caused the Trojan War and the Centauromachy, respectively (12.5–7, 210ff). In the *Odyssey*, Ulysses' wife Penelope is seen fending off a large cohort of aggressive suitors, who assume her long-absent husband must be dead (see appendix).

686   *And he'll do all you ask, though you ask all:* Depending on how the Latin is punctuated, Vertumnus may instead be making the kinkier promise to assume any form Pomona desires. The translators are about evenly divided.

738   *choked to death:* The elegiac motif of the locked-out lover
       was sufficiently common as to merit a name, *parak-*
       lausithyron (cf. Narcissus at 3.449). However, as is natural
       for the primarily first-person genre of elegy, actually
       following through on the threat of suicide is rare. By
       contrast, the immortal Vertumnus, who could not do so
       if he wanted to, has no problem making Iphis go the
       extra mile of sincerity, yet conforms to standard proce-
       dure by completely neglecting Anaxarete's point of view.
       With no recourse to the beloved's thoughts and reasons,
       the classical elegist's characterization of her (or some-
       times him) as inexplicably and inexcusably cruel is
       almost always allowed to go unchallenged. While this is
       to be expected in the motif's native element of first-
       person narration, for the storytelling Vertumnus, it is an
       artificial oversight constructed to aid his selfish cause.

761   *Gazing Venus:* This strange detail would appear to make
       the myth an etiology. Scholars have accordingly theo-
       rized the existence of some Cypriot ritual, attested in
       Eastern art, involving the placement of cult statues in
       windows.

The Apotheoses of Romulus and Hersilie (772–851)

Resuming the Alban king list, Ovid finally reaches the foundation of
Rome in one of the poem's greatest anticlimaxes. Romulus, the city's
founder, is allotted barely fifty lines, and the epic set-pieces of his life
and reign—his suckling by a wolf, his murder of his brother Remus,
the rape of the Sabine women, and the betrayal of Tarpeia—are all
omitted or brutally compressed. If the apotheosis of Aeneas felt dispassionate in tone, it colors in comparison to that of Romulus. Yet
draining Rome's heroes of their heroism is clearly a deliberate choice,
for the brief-yet-affecting apotheosis of queen Hersilie that follows
makes it plain that the poet has not lost his touch: unlike her husband,
she at least gets to talk.

772–75 *false Amulius . . . on Pales' feast, / The City walls were built:*
        Years after the Alban throne was usurped by his brother
        Amulius, Numitor reclaimed his rightful kingship

with the aid of his grandson Romulus (whose brother
Remus the poem completely elides). Striking out on their
own, the twins then built Rome ("The City"), an act Ovid
puts in the passive voice without even naming a founder.
"Pales' feast" is the Palilia, a shepherds' festival celebrated
annually on April 21—apparently, Ovid's Rome was built
in a day.

775–77   *Tatius . . . beneath their shields:* After the Romans' mass
abduction of their daughters, an army of Sabines led by
Titus Tatius marched on Rome. There, in an utterly
ludicrous legend, the traitress Tarpeia opened the city
gates to them after being promised "what the Sabines
wore on their arms." She had been referring to their
golden bracelets, but once inside, the Sabines crushed her
to death with their shields. In her memory, traitors to the
Roman state were executed by being hurled from the
Tarpeian Rock (cf. 15.865).

803–4   *they chose not to fight . . . shared the throne:* In the
traditional telling, the kingdoms merged at the interces-
sion of the Sabine women (now Roman wives), who
begged their fathers and captor-husbands not to kill each
other. Ovid seems intent, however, on keeping the joint
kingdom's foundation myth as agentless as the City's
itself.

827–28   *more fit to dine with gods, / "Quirinus" now appears in
kingly robes:* The gods were often depicted at a celestial
banquet (see note to 9.237). Augustan writers were oddly
explicit about identifying Romulus with the indigenous
war god Quirinus, indicating that the link had propagand-
ist applications and was probably quite new. If so, Ovid
may be poking a hole at 836 when Iris refers to the
Quirinal Hill, which cannot possibly have been renamed
for Romulus already (but see note to 622).

844   *I'll be in heaven:* A joke, since she will be.

850   *Hora:* The name's meaning is unclear but may have to do
with speaking; it is pronounced differently from *hōra*
("time, hour, season").

BOOK 15

Hercules and Croton (1–59)

The second king of Rome was a Sabine, Numa Pompilius, whose traditional role as the founder of Rome's foremost political and religious institutions Ovid rewrites into an un-Roman passion for Greek philosophy. Since the southern coasts of Italy were then dominated by Greek colonies, Numa seeks instruction at the Calabrian city of Croton, where he hears the town's origin story. Notably, this tale depends on the intervention of the deified Hercules, who displays a divine power not dreamt of in Book 14's cosmogony (see note to 14.512–608).

3 *Rumor, being truth's herald:* She is depicted less favorably in Book 12 (see note to 12.39–63), where her invocation strikes a note of skepticism. Since this whole episode is grounded in ahistorical rumor (see note to 60), Ovid may be winking at us.

6 *the nature of all things:* This phrase, *rerum natura,* recalls the title of Lucretius' great philosophical epic *De rerum natura* (*On the Nature of Things*), whose atheistic vision of the universe heavily informs Pythagoras' speech in the next story.

Pythagoras (60–478)

Another man soon begins to speak, revealing the real reason we are in Croton. For the next four hundred lines, the philosopher and mathematician Pythagoras (who goes unnamed in the text) will harangue the reader in a (more Epicurean than Pythagorean) extended address ostensibly extolling vegetarianism, but really teaching a lesson on the nature of all things, fulfilling Numa's wish from line 6. Presenting his view of a cosmos in a constant state of flux, Pythagoras' diatribe on nature and the transmigration of souls constitutes Ovid's most sustained meditation on transformation, attempting to account for the continuing possibility of change in a poem whose world appears increasingly settled, tree by tree and bird by bird. With its vivid details, abrupt shifts, and throaty rhetoric, the resulting speech is a spectacular read, but its quasi-scientific godlessness lies at odds with the whole epic's worth of metamorphoses that precede and succeed it, most of which are effected by divine beings. To what degree Pythagoras is special—a mouthpiece for the author's truer beliefs, commenting on the rest of the poem—or just another of Ovid's contradictory characters is a subject of perennial debate.

60   *There lived a man from Samos in the town:* Pythagoras founded his school at Croton around 530 BCE, so the legend that he might have taught Numa (traditionally reigning by 715 BCE) was thoroughly debunked by Ovid's time, with Cicero deeming the story "not only totally false, but ignorant and nonsensical as well" (*Rep.* 2.28). The historian Livy ridiculed the notion that Numa could even have made it to Croton (1.18.2–3):

> The source of [Numa's] learning is falsely said, in want of some other figure, to have been Pythagoras of Samos, known to have held assemblies of young disciples near Metapontum, Heraclea, and Croton on the furthest shores of Italy during the reign of Servius Tullius, over a hundred years later! But even if [Pythagoras] had lived at that time, how would his fame have reached from those lands to the Sabines? And in what common language could he have roused anyone to learn from him? And under whose protection could a lone man have traveled through so many nations, differing in speech and custom?

Pythagoras' persistent appearance here is therefore one of Ovid's most flagrant violations of chronology. Perhaps this is why he is never named.

96   *Golden Age:* In a pleasing callback to the beginning of the poem, Pythagoras paints a picture of society's origins extremely reminiscent of the narrator's at 1.90ff. However, where Ovid's Golden Age seems to end at the hands of Jupiter, the anthropocentric worldview of Pythagoras will dump the blame squarely at the feet of (carnivorous) man.

135   *seen, perhaps, within the sacral pool:* Sacrifices were conducted with the victim's head placed over a water vessel. From this and a similar passage in Callimachus (fr. 75.10–1), it seems the notion that animals might have glimpsed the blade descending carried a special horror.

144   *Unveil my Delphi:* A strange metaphor for personal insight, derived from the identification of *Pyth*agoras

with *Pyth*ian Apollo (see note to 1.147). Ovid's Pythagoras treads a careful line that allows for the existence of the gods, but ascribes no natural influence to them.

160–64   *I fought at Troy . . . Argos, Abas' land:* In contrast to the Epicurean view that the soul dies with the body, belief in the reincarnation of souls is authentic to Pythagoras, underpinning his vegetarianism (173–75). Homer relates Menelaus' killing of Euphorbus at *Iliad* 17.43ff, and his shield reportedly adorned the Heraeum at Argos, where Abas more famously dedicated the shield of his grandfather Danaus.

178   *All is in flux:* This aphorism is an ancient philosophical tenet originally attributed to Heraclitus (he of not stepping in the same river twice).

229–31   *old Milo . . . soft and slack:* Milo of Croton was a Pythagorean disciple and famed athlete, six times victorious at the Olympic games. This anecdote of his later decrepitude (which makes no chronological sense for Pythagoras to know) is found in Cicero's *On Old Age* 27.

231–33   *thus wept Tyndareus' child . . . stolen twice:* This is, yet again, the apocalyptically beautiful Helen, whom Theseus once kidnapped long before her abduction by Paris.

287–92   *Antissa . . . Zancle, too . . . pushed the land to sea:* Pythagoras' topographical digression is too long to merit explaining every detail, so this section may serve as an instructive example. Of the places named, only the Lesbian village of Antissa could have undergone such a natural change in antiquity. Both Pharos (site of the Lighthouse of Alexandria) and Tyre were connected to the mainland by causeways on the orders of Alexander the Great, two hundred years after the time of Pythagoras. In contrast, Leucadia was cut off by a canal in the seventh century BCE, while Sicily separated from Italy in the refilling of the Mediterranean basin 5.33 million years ago—an event geologists have accordingly named the "Zanclean flood."

309–12   *Horned Ammon . . . Athamanes light their fires / With water:* Most of these details are incompletely understood.

The Athamanes (supposed descendants of Athamas) were a tribe in Epirus, near Dodona. According to Pliny the Elder, Jove's Fountain at Dodona ran cold, but torches extinguished in its waves would rekindle if brought near it again (*Nat.* 2.228).

331 *straight wine:* The strength (and savor) of Roman wine was such that it was typically watered down to be rendered palatable and potable. The consumption of undiluted "straight wine," then, was considered an act of dissolution.

338–39 *Symplegades . . . unflinching in the wind:* These are the "Clashing Rocks" of the Bosporus (see note on 7.62–66). After the Argonauts managed to row past them at ramming speed, the Symplegades ceased moving forever; they have remained stationary enough for Istanbul to be built on top of them.

356–58 *Pallene's Hyperborean men . . . Triton's marsh:* An extremely obscure reference. Pallene, a town in Chalcidice, is not otherwise associated with the Hyperboreans, a mythical race of polar giants, and neither is elsewhere linked with Lake Tritonis, which is in Libya.

364–67 *bury slaughtered bulls . . . as their parents did:* Widely believed in ancient times, this form of spontaneous generation is known as *bugonia*, and was precisely detailed by no less an authority than Virgil (*Georgics* 4.81ff). The absurd origins in the following lines (wasps from horses, scorpions from crabs, bear cubs licked into shape) are similarly well-attested, making it all the more jarring for the modern reader to find the accurate metamorphoses of butterflies and frogs entered on the same ridiculous list. Truth, Ovid seems to hint, is often stranger than fiction.

374 *tombstone butterflies:* In a bit of suitably metamorphic symbolism, butterflies were often carved on graves to represent the continuity of the soul.

432 The preceding five lines (426–30 in the Latin) are widely deleted as spurious, being more at home in the mind of a

medieval copyist than an ancient philosopher. Not only were the cities of Sparta, Thebes, and Athens still flourishing in the time of Pythagoras, but even in Ovid's time the city of Athens was much more than a mere name. The logic of the text is also much improved if Pythagoras continues directly from Troy to Rome. For the record, my translation would be:

> [So Sparta prospered, great Mycenae thrived,
> And Cecrops' and Amphion's citadels;
> Now Sparta's wasteland and Mycenae's wrecked.
> What's Thebes of Oedipus now but a name?   430
> What's left Pandion's Athens but a name?]

437   *I remember:* That is, from his previous life (160–62).

447   *Iulus' heir:* The Julian clan (*gens Iulia*) claimed descent from Iulus, whose "heir" could thus refer to either Julius Caesar or, more likely, Augustus. Helenus' prophecy of Rome's future dominance is somewhat belied by Pythagoras' assertion that all empires must fall (421ff).

462   *Thyestean feasts:* That is, acts of cannibalism. In a myth that had become recently popular at Rome through a dramatization by Lucius Varius Rufus (now lost), king Thyestes of Mycenae unwittingly ate his own sons, served to him by his brother Atreus in revenge for Thyestes having stolen his throne and seduced his wife. While many faiths subscribe to vegetarianism on the basis of similar belief in reincarnation, the regularity with which characters in this poem have indeed transformed into animals lends Pythagoras' precept particular force.

475   *feather ropes to scare deluded deer:* Hunting practice called for the use of garish feathers to frighten deer into nets.

Egeria and Hippolytus (479–551)

Pressing on, the narrator now relates the deaths of king Numa and his wife Egeria, which primarily serve as a vehicle for the story of Hippolytus—yet another apotheosis. With Pythagorean concepts of change and flow still fresh in the reader's mind, however, the poem's abrupt return to its usual business of immortality and permanent transformation calls both concepts implicitly into question.

484 *taught them sacral rites:* Presumably, the kind of animal sacrifice Pythagoras taught him to deplore (see "unheeded" at 74).

489 *Orestean Diana's rites:* According to Euripides' *Iphigenia in Tauris,* when Diana rescued Iphigenia from sacrifice (cf. 12.34), the girl landed among the Taurian people of Scythia. She would later escape with her brother Orestes, carrying with them a cult image of Diana to the town of Aricia, near Rome, where it was worshiped in the shrine of Diana Nemorensis ("of the woods").

500ff *daughter of Pasiphaë:* This is Phaedra, wife of Theseus and stepmother of Hippolytus. As famously recounted in dramas by Euripides, Seneca, and Racine, her incestuous love for her stepson turned to murderous spite at his rejection, whereupon she told her husband that Hippolytus had made advances on her. Theseus then called on his father Neptune to smite Hippolytus, as narrated in the following lines. As he did with Medea in Book 7, Ovid here avoids his Euripidean model, emphasizing incidental details of transformative magic over the traditional tale of tragic desire.

506–29 *. . . To know me by, for all was one great wound:* Because theatrical convention kept violence offstage, Greek tragedies' most tragic moments were narrated by breathless heralds in a trope known as the messenger speech. By instead allowing Hippolytus to relate his own death, Ovid effectively recasts a standard messenger speech in the first person, subverting both the dramatic trope and his literary model.

542–44 *my name, which smacked of horses . . . Virbius:* Hippolytus is Greek for "undone by horses," an inauspicious reminder of his death. (As J. Jonah Jameson might say, what are the odds?) Under his new name, Virbius (Latin for "twice a man"), he served as a minor god sharing Diana's shrine at Aricia.

551   *everlasting waves:* A stark contrast to Pythagoras' pronouncements on springs (and nature generally) at 270. The next tale will end similarly (*for ages to remain,* 620).

Cipus (552–620)

Three mythological similes carry us from the pre-Roman period (here represented by Tages, the founding prophet of Etruscan religion) through Romulus to the semihistorical early days of the Roman Republic. The story of the legendary magistrate Cipus, who thwarted his own fate to save Rome from returning to tyranny, puts a metamorphic twist on common Roman tales of incorruptible ancestors who gave up personal power in favor of public wellbeing. Since the Caesars had recently become Rome's first post-republican monarchs—yet had refused many of the trappings of kingship—Ovid's telling may be read as either politically flattering or subversive.

588–89   *Much better . . . than as Capitoline king:* As in the early United States and the French First Republic, the overthrow of Rome's last king (traditionally dated to 509 BCE) ushered in a period where fear of would-be monarchs constituted a perennial political bogeyman.

Aesculapius (621–744)

The son of Apollo and Coronis, Aesculapius was born—but never named—near the beginning of the poem (2.542–47, 598–634); he now returns to bring it to a close. The healer-god's journey from his traditional cult center of Epidaurus to Rome comes as the final entry in a series of westward migration myths symbolizing the shift in cultural and political power from Greece to Italy through the travels of Aeneas, Helenus, Diomedes, Myscelus, Pythagoras, and Hippolytus. As Ovid promised in the prologue, we are now drawing quite near to his times; Livy dated the advent of Aesculapius to 292 BCE.

621   *Reveal now, Muses:* Invoking the omniscient Muses for help getting through a particularly lofty or difficult passage was

a common move for epic poets, famously used by Homer while describing the Greek army in his catalog of ships (*Iliad* 2.484–92). Ovid, however, does it only here, just as the transition from legend to history ought rather to allay any such need for divine knowledge.

655 *his rustic rod:* Still used as a symbol of medicine, the Rod of Aesculapius consists of a staff entwined with a single serpent (now often conflated with the doubly-entwined caduceus of Mercury).

702ff *Lacinium and its goddess' shrine:* The poem's final list of place names neatly charts the god's course around the boot of Italy. Among the sites meriting a word of explanation are the Temple of Juno Lacinia near Croton, whose single remaining column names the modern Cape Colonna; the *royal halls* of *Hippotes' son* Aeolus (706–7), meaning the Aeolian Islands off Sicily; *Parthenope's resorts* (711), still frequented as Naples; and "those" *thermal springs* (713), referring to Baiae, then a ubiquitous Roman spa town. The *namesake nurse's tomb* (716) we saw give rise to Caieta at 14.157, 441–44. Finally, *Antiphates' dominion* at 717 is the realm of the Laestrygonians from 14.233ff, purportedly located in southeast Sicily.

730 *Trojan Vesta, they who tend your flame:* One of the corner-stones of Roman religion was the order of the Vestal Virgins, priestesses of the hearth goddess Vesta who were entrusted with the tending of an eternal flame (cf. 778). Vesta is Trojan in the sense that she metaphorically moved with Aeneas when he made Italy his home.

741 *the Island:* The Temple of Aesculapius was built on the only island in Rome, Tiber Island, which is still associated with healing as the location of Fatebenefratelli Hospital since 1585.

The Apotheosis of Julius Caesar (745–869)

The poem's final tale extends into recent history, taking for its subject the assassination of Rome's dictator-for-life Julius Caesar in 44 BCE, the year before Ovid's birth. Caesar's subsequent deification by the Senate was at the time unheard of (in Rome anyway), and Ovid enters into its narration with a pretend enthusiasm that draws attention to the political motives underpinning the decree. Looming large is Caesar's *adopted* son, the Emperor Augustus, whose own precedent-confirming deification Ovid correctly foresees in his concluding prayer (860–69). Having fulfilled his pledge to draw the universe from creation to current times, Ovid puts forth an impressive but bleak view of his present as an age of artifice, when the most power-hungry mortals improbably strive to erase the distinction between themselves and the gods—in this poem, unsavory figures to begin with and perilous ones to impersonate.

749   *Made him a comet:* Romans interpreted "Caesar's Comet," a weeklong cometary outburst observed in July of 44 BCE, as proof of the apotheosis of Julius Caesar, who had died two months earlier. There is a pun here, since the name *Caesar* means "hairy" and the Latin for comet (*stellam comantem*) means "hairy star." Julius Caesar was famously bald.

750–51   *nothing Caesar did . . . father such a son:* Augustus was not sired by Julius Caesar, but was a great-nephew adopted posthumously in the dictator's will. Even so, after Caesar's deification, Augustus styled himself the "son of a god." Ovid's mock zeal emphasizes the legal fiction, whose political calculations he brazenly states at 760–61, only afterward imputing his logic to Venus (762). Ovid's brief rundown of Caesar's conquests supposedly pales beside this "siring" of his adopted son (758), but is actually quite impressive. Prior to his kingdom' s annexation, King Mithridates the Great of Pontus had opposed Rome in his eponymous Mithridatic Wars (756).

763   *high priest:* Among other offices, Julius Caesar was *pontifex maximus*, the high priest of the Roman state religion. The title "Supreme Pontiff" is still held by the Pope.

802   *the Curia:* Adding blasphemy to murder, the assassination of Caesar took place in the Curia Pompeia, a sacred building then being used as a Senate House.

804–6   *to hide Aeneas' heir . . . from Diomedes' blades:* As related at *Iliad* 3.380–2 and 5.311ff, Venus made a habit of thus rescuing her favorites from danger on the battlefield.

821ff   *avenge his sire in war:* Jupiter now forecasts the civil wars that followed Caesar's assassination and which saw Augustus (then known as Octavian) defeat all opposition to become sole ruler of Rome. Octavian would avenge his sire in 42 BCE by defeating Caesar's assassins at the Battle of Philippi, a site close enough to Pharsalia (the location of Caesar's decisive victory in the previous civil war) for the two to be poetically conflated (823–24). He was also present for the death of the Republican government at Mutina (822–23), though in both cases victory was due to the generalship of his sometime comrade Mark Antony, "Rome's commander" whose later ill-wed alliance with his Egyptian wife, Queen Cleopatra VII, fell to Octavian at Actium (826–28; see note to 13.713–15). The "great name" that crumbled in Sicilian seas was his last common enemy with Antony, Sextus Pompeius Magnus, whom they defeated in 36 BCE; *magnus* means "great."

838   *the ancient Pylian's age:* That is, the three generations of the proverbially ancient Nestor (but see appendix). Augustus was nearly seventy when the *Metamorphoses* was published. He would die at seventy-five in 14 BCE, three years before Ovid.

863–65 *O Vesta . . . Tarpeia's rock:* Temples to Apollo and Vesta abutted the imperial palace on the Palatine Hill. The Capitoline Hill sported both the Temple to Jupiter (842) and the Tarpeian Rock, from which traitors were executed (see note to 14.775–77).

Epilogue (870–79)

Ovid's formal coda contains one final apotheosis: his own. Calling the poem his *better and immortal part* (874; cf. 9.268–72), Ovid foretells a future for his work and self as lofty as the deified rulers of Rome and as lasting as the adamantine records of fate. The claim that the poet or poet's beloved would live forever through their art is found everywhere from Theognis to Shakespeare to Whitman, but Ovid's profession of immortality takes the thematically perfect extra step of collapsing his identity into the work itself—the *Metamorphoses*' final metamorphosis.

879   *I'll live:* In sharp contrast to the main body of the poem, which ends on the deified Augustus' absence (*afar*, 869), Ovid claims for himself an eternal life on earth.

Appendix

Text and Translation Notes

All engagement with classical works depends on corrupted texts. In the fourteen centuries between the death of Ovid and the opening of Gutenberg's print shop, the only way to create new copies of books was for scribes to copy them by hand. And scribes—being not only humans but often bored, bigoted, and untutored humans at that—make mistakes. As a result, modern editors must compare the readings of existing medieval manuscripts and reconstruct what the original most likely said. The fruits of such "textual criticism" are rarely definitive and sometimes impossible. In the case of the *Metamorphoses,* an unusually late set of manuscripts makes the process especially difficult; the earliest pieces of the poem are found in fragments dating from the ninth century CE, and nothing close to complete appears until the eleventh.

The source text for this translation is the Oxford Classical Text edited by Richard J. Tarrant and published in 2004. Founded on an unprecedentedly exhaustive review of the poem's surviving manuscripts, Tarrant's work has been widely heralded as a major contribution to Ovidian scholarship, though at the time of writing no other English translator has made use of it. In the vast majority of cases, I have deferred to Tarrant's judgment on textual matters, endeavoring to explain my few deviations from his edition in this appendix. Besides incorporating numerous superior readings, Tarrant's edition is notable for the large number of lines he brackets as likely interpolations. Translators have tended to smooth over such textual problems, keeping as many lines as reasonable in the laudable interests of conservation and readability, though this creates an illusion that the text is much more certain than it ever is. I have taken the unusual step of including Tarrant's brackets in the printed translation and conforming to the line numbering of his Latin edition, alerting the reader to the presence of vexed passages and potentially spurious verses.

Listed below are the readings translated at some of the more infamous points of contention, most of which accord with Tarrant. Readings adopted against Tarrant are in **bold**. Readings adopted where Tarrant's text is obelized, indicating that he deemed no reading acceptable, are *italicized*.

1.2	illa for illas
1.92	**legebantur** for ligabantur
1.190	**temptata** for temptanda
1.345	**sola** for iuga or loca
3.242	**rabidum** for rapidum
3.641	opheltes for ac(o)ete
4.260	nimborum patiens for nympharum impatiens
4.388	**incerto** for incesto
4.417	**numen** for nomen
6.184	**causam** for laudem
6.201	infectis propere ite sacris for various
6.582	germanaeque for fortunaeque
7.246	**uini** for mellis
7.612	natorumque for matrumque
7.865	consortibus for cum fortibus
8.117	obstruximus orbem for exponimur orbe
8.237	limoso . . . elice for ramosa . . . ilice
8.724	sunt . . . coluntur for sint . . . colantur
9.74	*peremi* for †reduxit (or perussi or reclusi)
9.365	*robur* for †loton†
10.115	parilesque ex aere for parilique aetate or parilique decore
10.380	causam te for causamque
11.71	in quantum for uia quam tum
	quaeque secuta for quisque secutus
11.361	templi for ponti
11.523	ignes for imbres

12.24	Nereus for Boreas
12.356	dumo for trunco or terra
13.602	flumina **densas** for flumina natas and others
13.619	moriturae more for periturae uoce
13.694	telo for tela
14.334	Ionio . . . Iano for ancipiti . . . Iano
14.493	*ut magno stet magna* for et †magno stat magna†
14.639	Silenusque for Siluanusque
14.671	*prudens audacis* for †timidi aut audacis† and others
14.817	**orbem** for urbem
15.104	*leonum* for †deorum†
15.271	*aut imis commota* for †antiquis tam multa†
15.364	*in scrobe deiecto* for †i quoque delectos†
15.838	senior Pylios for senior similes or senior meritis

Listed below are the lines translated at points where multiple sets of verses exist:

1.544a, 1.546–47 over 1.544–45

4.766–67 over 1.767a–68

7.186 over 7.186a

7.688a over 7.767–68

8.286 over 8.285

8.597–610 over 8.601–2 and 8.609–10

8.655a–56a over 8.655–56

8.693 over 8.693a–b

BOOK 1

1–2   *Of new embodied shapes transformed, my mind / Is moved to speak! (In noua fert animus mutatas dicere formas / corpora):* For a poem about continuous renewal, my translation follows Ovid's carefully curated opening phrase, beginning on a preposition and followed immediately by the programmatic statement "new." Most translators instead foreground the grammatical subject, starting with "My mind" (*animus*), while others ranging from Dryden to Melville apparently misread the sentence such that it is no longer the shapes (*formas*) but the bodies (*corpora*) undergoing change. Golding got it right back in 1567: "Of shapes transformed to bodies straunge. . . ."

2–3   *for you have shaped / These matters, too . . . what I've begun (coeptis nam uos mutastis et illa / . . . meis):* The pronoun *illas,* transmitted by the majority of manuscripts, indicates that the gods have been responsible for the shapes transformed. Hence Miller's translation: "O gods, for you yourselves have wrought the changes." Concurring with recent scholarship, Tarrant prints the alternate reading *illa,* which instead refers to the poet's undertakings (*coeptis*). My translation opts for a middle ground, albeit favoring the latter reading.

93   *Were read on plaques of bronze (aere legebantur):* Tarrant is somewhat unusual in printing the transmitted *aere ligabantur* ("were fastened to bronze"), of which I fail to see the sense. My translation concurs with Anderson, Possanza, and Barchiesi in following Heinsius's elsewhere-attested conjecture *legebantur.*

104–5   *plucked bitter strawberries / On mountainsides, hard cherries, thorny fruits (arbuteos fetus montanaque fraga legebant / cornaque et in duris haerentia mora rubetis):* The Latin could be more literally translated as: "They picked unripe arbute berries and mountain strawberries / And cornel cherries and sticky mulberries from sharp brambles. . . ." In order to more accurately convey the import of Ovid's lines to an audience less aware of the fruits (and nasty flavors) in question, my translation strays more than usual from the original's precise meaning. For more on this passage, see Soucy 2022.

111–12   *nectar rolled . . . honeyed gold (nectaris ibant / flauaque . . . mella):* A. G. Lee points out in his commentary that Ovid reinforces the sense of serene prosperity at the end of the Golden Age with a series of end-stopped hexameters, culminating in a modified Golden Line. English syntax does not allow for this effect, so my translation employs a heroic couplet in pursuit of a similar one.

128   *An age of baser mettle (uenae peioris . . . aeuum):* The Latin more literally means "an age of a worse vein," playing on both the moral character and the metallic value of the period. My version adopts from Lee's suggested translation, nor am I the first translator who failed to resist some version of his pun.

190   *All else has now been tried (cuncta prius temptata):* Tarrant follows the majority of manuscripts which transmit *temptanda* for *temptata,* indicating that Jupiter swears to try other cures first, rather than saying he has done so already. Most other editors, however, reason that the partially attested *temptata* is a better fit for the tone and timing of Jupiter's speech, and I concur.

325–26   *And, from thousands of men, just one alive, / And just one woman out of thousands more (et superesse uirum de tot modo milibus unum / et superesse uidet de tot modo milibus unam):* While my translation of these two verses shows the repetition of sense contained in the Ovidian original, English syntax and metrical constraints prevent so complete a repetition of sound from being reproduced.

345   *waves gave way to ground (crescunt sola decrescentibus undis):* Tarrant prints Slater's *iuga* ("ridges") in place of the nonsensical transmitted *loca.* My translation instead follows Housman's emendation, *sola* being a more proper contrast for *undis.*

361–62   *If the sea now held you, too, / It would hold me, for I would follow you (si te quoque pontus haberet, / te sequerer, coniunx, et me quoque pontus haberet):* Ovid represents the couple's hypothetically identical situations with two lines containing nearly identical endings. My translation partially captures the effect through rhyme.

544a–47   *seeing Peneus' waves . . . all too pleasing shape (spectans Peneidas undas . . . figuram):* Conflicting manuscripts have Daphne appeal to Mother Earth (the transmitted 1.544–45), her father Peneus (1.544a, 546–47), or versions of both, with similar language employed in each instance. Deeming it unlikely that both readings should stand, and unconvinced by Anderson's argument that river gods are insufficiently divine to effect transformations, I have followed Tarrant (who brackets 1.544–45) in giving precedence to Peneus. My rendering, therefore, translates the Latin 1.544a, 546–47 and omits 1.544–45, thus according with the text employed by the majority of modern translations.

615   *From thin air! (e terra genitam):* The Latin phrase, literally "sprang from the ground," is an expression for inexplicable origin. I have substituted a comparable English idiom.

664   *eye-bespangled Argus (stellatus . . . Argus):* Ovid's description more literally means "star-studded Argus" and relies on the conventional Latin identification of eyes with lights or stars. Since English speakers are more used to star-spangled objects (or at least one particular banner), my translation adopts the adjective "bespangled" in a nod to the original's sidereal imagery.

771   *You gaze upon the Sun who are his son (hoc te, quem spectas, hoc te . . . / Sole satum):* The emphatic repetition of "you" is difficult to capture. I pray to be forgiven for this pun.

775   *If your mind's so moved (si modo fert animus):* As Ovid brings Book 1 to a close, he recycles the diction of his opening line (*in noua fert animus,* "of new . . . my mind is moved"). The diction of this translation has been adjusted to match.

BOOK 2

92   *Fatherly fear affirms my fatherhood (et patrio pater esse metu probor):* Ovid is fond of undercutting a scene's emotional content with verbal style, especially allitera-

tion. The effect in this verse is only exacerbated by the *petis* and doubled *pignora* of the previous line. I have therefore made my rendering as alliterative as possible.

107 *Gold was its axle, gold its pole, and gold (aureus axis erat, temo aureus, aurea):* Ovid illustrates the excessive splendor of the Sun's chariot by employing the adjective *aureus* ("golden") three times in a single line. Although his doing so drew censure from Seneca, who thought such opulent descriptions conducive to greed (*Ep.* 115.12–13), I find the effect humorous and worth replicating.

115 *The Morning Star (Lucifer):* Ovid calls the Morning Star, a recurring figure in the poem, by his Latin name Lucifer ("bringer of light"). Since that moniker has since been tainted by Christian writers who associated it with Satan, my translation uses the name of the celestial body.

179–80 *Poor Phaëthon, from paradise's peak, / Peered down upon the distant, distant lands (ut uero summo despexit ab aethere terras / infelix Phaethon penitus penitusque patentes, / palluit):* After describing Phaëthon gazing down from the very top of heaven (*uero summon despexit ab aethere*), Ovid composes a brilliantly alliterative line in which the word *penitus* is given twice for emphasis: "far, far below." Unable to reproduce these effects combined, I have settled for capturing them separately, moving the alliteration to the act of Phaëthon gazing down, with only minor alliteration present for the repeated adjective: "down upon the distant, distant lands."

239–59 *Boeotia . . . Tiber (Boeotia . . . Thybrin):* Ovid's list of rivers poses a difficulty in translation on account of its geographical diversity, with the catalog's entries ranging from the near and familiar (to the Roman mind, anyway) to the extremely remote and esoteric. Although any modifications render true consistency of approach impossible, I have largely conformed to my normal practice in avoiding unwonted obscurity in place names, while also trying to capture Ovid's sense of range. Consequently, large waterways whose names have present-day currency are allowed modern nomenclature (the Don, *Tanais*; the Danube, *Hister*; the Po, *Padus*), while most regional markers are smoothed into more recognizable forms (Thracian for "Mygdonian"; Lydian for "Maeonian"; etc.). In other cases, however, I felt that updating place names would only further foreignize the reference, producing the opposite of the intended effect. The modern names for such streams as the Caïcus ("Bakırçay") and the Caÿster ("Küçük Menderes"), therefore, do not appear in my translation.

284   *My lids and lips are all, all caked in ash (inque oculis tantum, tantum super ora fauillae):* My translation attempts to capture the careful composition of this line, which counterpoises the alliterative *oculis* ("eyes") and *ora* ("mouth") alongside the emphatic repetition *tantum, tantum.*

327–28   *HERE PHAËTHON, WHO DROVE HIS FATHER'S STEEDS, / LIES DEAD: HE CRASHED. STILL, DARING WERE HIS DEEDS (HIC SITVS EST PHAETHON CURRVS AVRIGA PATERNI / QVEM SI NON TENVIT MAGNIS TAMEN EXCIDIT AVSIS):* The Latin most strictly means, "Here lies Phaëthon, driver of his father's chariot, / Though he did not keep control of it, he still failed with great daring." My translation is fairly faithful to the original, though it is difficult to tell how bathetic the second line is intended to be. My earlier drafts leaned rather too far in the opposite direction:

> HE DROVE HIS FATHER'S CAR AND WAS SO BRAVE
> HE LOST CONTROL AND WRECKED IT: HERE'S HIS GRAVE.

Most translations have trended toward the extremely solemn, but I hope mine preserves a hint of the absurdity in suggesting that Phaëthon's daring is praiseworthy or defensible.

381   *To dwell in floods, the opposite of flames (quae colat elegit contraria flumina flammis):* With a pair of similar-sound-

ing words—*flumina* and *flammis*—Ovid emphasizes the opposition of fire and water, an effect I preserve with "floods" and "flames."

409   *while he went and came (dum redit itque):* The word order in the Latin is deliberately counterintuitive, the normal idiom being *itque reditque* ("he went and went again," or, more freely, "he came and went"). The English idiom is therefore reversed as well.

424   *how, oh, how worthwhile! (sunt, o sunt iurgia tanti!):* A closer translation would read: "O, the quarrels are so worth it, they are!" My rendering sacrifices specificity for a more idiomatic version of the repetition, while preserving the interjection "*o*" which, in Anderson's opinion, "reveals the god's comically lyrical eagerness for this sexual adventure."

433   *and showed himself through crime (nec se sine crimine prodit):* Literally, "nor did he reveal himself without a crime" (that is, the act of rape). However, Ovid recycles this same verb-noun pair at 2.447 (*crimen . . . prodere*) and a similar one at 2.462 (*patuit . . . crimen*), with the *crimen* now referring to the evidence of the transgression. My translation therefore adopts "show/share" and "crime" as the words best able to bear this tripartite burden, using them at all three points.

472   *pregnant, except publishing my pain (fecunda fores fieretque iniuria partu / nota):* While Anderson holds that the alliteration in this line captures Juno's "sputtering" anger, I find it more of an amusing distraction that belies the import of deity's words. Whatever its effect, my translation reproduces the device.

518   *Who would hold back from wounding Juno now? (†est uero quisquam† Iunonem laedere nolit):* The text in the first portion of this line is extremely uncertain, but the rough sense of the whole is still easily translatable; Juno poses a rhetorical question asking what indefinite person, given this latest slight, would hesitate to slight her in turn.

532–33 *painted peacocks . . . peacocks painted (pauonibus . . . pictis / . . . pictis . . . pauonibus):* The Latin also repeats the phrase with reversed word order.

580–81 *arms reached out: / The arms began (tendebam bracchia caelo: / bracchia coeperunt):* When a similar fate befell Callisto at 2.477–78, Ovid used these same words in the same metrical location. My translation reproduces this mirroring.

608–9 *O Phoebus, I'd have paid a proper price / Were I not pregnant (potui poenas tibi, Phoebe, dedisse, / sed peperisse prius):* Once again, my translation recreates excessive alliteration rendering an emotional moment slightly ridiculous.

626 *poured thankless incense on her breast (ingratos in pectora fudit odores):* In the Latin, it is unclear whether the adjective *ingratos* ("thankless") should be paired with *pectora* ("breast"), as Bömer believed, or with *odores* ("incense"), as argued by Anderson. Keeping in mind Ovid's general eagerness to rob divine action of potential sympathy, I have sided with Anderson and translated accordingly. Barchiesi is silent.

627 *and performed unrighteous rites (iniustaque iusta peregit):* Apollo gives Coronis the proper rituals (*iusta*), but since he is responsible for their occurrence, his performing them is still impious (*iniusta*). An etymological quirk of homophony between the Latinate "rite" and the Germanic "right" allows the pun to preserved in English.

760 *rotten (tabo):* The word used here, *tabus*, really means "putrefied slime," and refers to the substance discoloring the house and turning it black. However, Ovid makes this word a kind of verbal leitmotif for Envy and uses derived forms of it three more times before she exits the narrative. My translation employs versions of the similarly variable word "rot" to render all of them:

2.780, *intabescit* ("she wastes away"): "she rots within"
2.784, *infice tabe tua* ("infect with your decay"): "Infect . . . with your rot"

2.807–8, *tabe / liquitur* (she melted from decay): "rot / Dissolving her"

763–64 *firelight's glow / Gleams never round and gloom ever abounds (igne uacet semper, caligine semper abundet):* More literally translated, this verse means "always devoid of fire, always abounding with fog." The line is exquisitely constructed, counterpoising two consonant nouns (*igne / caligine*), two assonant verbs (*abundet / uacet*), and a repeated adverb (*semper / semper*). My rendering attempts a similar effect.

776 *teeth grown green with mold (liuent rubigine dentes):* Ancient color words are notoriously murky. Anderson glosses this phrase as "Her teeth are black with mold," though the hues typically associated with the words *liuent* and *rubigine* are blue and red, respectively. However, the verb *liuere* carries the figurative double meaning "to be envious"—Ovid is making a pun. Since in English parlance envy is associated with *green,* my translation changes the color to preserve the wordplay.

818 *"We'll stand," said swift Cyllenius, "by those terms!"* *(stemus, ait, pacto, uelox Cyllenius, isto):* The effect of this line's word order is impossible to replicate in English. Mercury speaks only three words, *stemus . . . pacto . . . isto,* each of which stands alone, broken up by *ait* ("said") and *uelox Cyllenius* ("swift Cyllenius"). English syntax comfortably allows only one such interruption.

BOOK 3

10 *shall meet thee . . . (fac condas . . . uocato):* Befitting an oracular pronouncement, the imperative-subjunctive phrase *fac condas* ("do you build") and the future imperative *uocato* ("thou shalt call") employ solemnly archaic grammatical constructions. This is one of several places where I have used archaic English pronouns in translating archaic speech. I will do so again at 3.284.

60   *gave the mass a massive throw (magnum magno conamine misit):* A close rendering of the original doublet.

120   *His slayer, too, did not outlive the slain (hunc quoque qui leto dederat non longius illo / uiuit):* A nearer rendering might read, "The former also did not live longer than the latter whom he delivered unto death," but the point of interest is the careful balancing of *hunc* ("this man") and *illo* ("that man") on opposite ends of the line. My translation therefore condenses and adapts to preserve this feature.

139–41 *your grandson . . . / you, his dogs . . . / should you ask (nepos . . . tibi . . . / uosque, canes . . . / quaeras):* In translating this passage, I have followed Tarrant's punctuation with the amusing result that, in three successive lines, the pronoun "you" refers to three different entities (Cadmus, Actaeon's dogs, and the reader).

206–25 *his bloodhounds:* In the ancient art that is chocking hexameters full of proper nouns, the catalog of Actaeon's hunting dogs makes for one of Ovid's most dazzling feats. Though my first draft left the names untranslated on the grounds that most of them are Greek instead of Latin, I found not only that doing so created a metrical nightmare but also that relegating the meaning of the names to a footnote deprived the passage of much of its comedic charm. Moreover, Ovid's Roman audience would have been fairly well-versed in Greek, and while there may be no clear English counterpart to the foreign-yet-intelligible quality of Greek names in Latin (one friend did suggest I give the names in French), the utter opacity of Hellenic nomenclature in vernacular English is hardly a suitable substitute. In consequence, I duly translated the list from the following originals:

> *Melampus* (Blackpaw), *Ichnobates* (Tracer), *Pamphagos* (Bottomless), *Dorceus* (Sharpeye), *Oribasos* (Mountaineer), *Nebrophonus* (Deerslayer), *Theron* (Hunter), *Laelaps* (Hurricane), *Pterelas* (Flyingfoot), *Aegre* (Chaser), *Hylaeus* (Woody), *Nape* (Vale), *Poemenis* (Shepherdess),

Harpyia (Harpy), *Ladon* (Ladon), *Dromas* (Runner),
Canache (Barker), *Sticte* (Spot), *Tigris* (Tiger), *Alce*
(Plucky), *Leucon* (Snowy), *Asbolos* (Ash), *Lacon* (Spar-
tan), *Aëllo* (Whirling-Wind), *Thoös* (Lightfoot), *Lycisce*
(She-Wolf), *Cyprius* (Cypriot), *Harpalos* (Snapper), *Mela-
neus* (Sable), *Lachne* (Shaggy), *Labros* (Rager), *Argiodus*
(Wildtooth), *Hylactor* (Yelper)

Of these, only "Ladon," the name of a river, is left as is.
Commentators also note an ambiguity as to whether
Lycisce's brother is named "Cyprius" or is Cypriot by
birth. This is grammatically true, but it strikes me as
strange that in a catalog of thirty-three dogs this one
alone should go nameless; I therefore present the former
option. Additionally, lines 232–33 furnish the names of
three more hounds: *Melanchaetes* (Blackfur), *Therodamas*
(Beastbreaker), and *Oresitrophos* (Cragside). As far as
I know, Johnston, Mandelbaum, and (to my surprise)
Gregory are the only modern verse translators who do
not translate the dogs' names into English.

243   *The raging pack (rabidum . . . agmen):* Here I have read
against Tarrant's printed *rapidum* ("swift") in favor of the
alternate *rabidum,* which Tarrant notes is *fort. recte*
("perhaps correct"). Since the dogs, whose speed is
otherwise attested, have already caught up with their
quarry, noting the frenzy of their actions strikes me as
the superior option.

271–72   *set that straight, / I will (fallat eam faxo):* A closer
translation of this phrase would read "I will make [her
faith in her own beauty] deceive her." My looser rendering more nearly captures the pithy and alliterative sound
of the original, while also recognizing the nonstandard
nature of the unusual form *faxo.*

285   *The form and face, the size and state (quantusque et qualis
. . . / tantus talisque):* There are no English equivalents for
the related and similar-sounding Latin pairs *quantus/
tantus* (how large/as large) and *qualis/talis* (of what kind/
of such a kind), which together concern quantity and

quality, as etymologically implied. As a substitute, my translation uses alliterative pairs of English words, achieving the same sense, though with lessened rhetorical effect.

307   *Known to the gods as "Firearm Number Two" (tela secunda uocant superi):* Unlike Anderson, who holds that Ovid has lent these secondary thunderbolts "official status and nomenclature," I concur with Barchiesi and Rosati in taking the expression as a joke on the epic motif of gods calling entities by other names. My translation is only marginally sillier than the moniker's Latin form.

386–88   *I want you to come here . . . I want you, too! / Come? Here! (huc coeamus . . . coeamus):* My translation fails to achieve the brazen brilliance of Echo's original response, but is a genuine echo and does manage to recast Narcissus' originally innocent words with a new amorous, if not quite sexual, intent. Most translations have struck me as either too literal ("Let us meet!") or painfully colloquial, though Martin's pairing of "Here let us come together" with "*Come! Together!*" is not without inspiration.

403   *so in the beds of men (sic coetus ante uiriles):* The Latin word *coetus,* more familiar in its alternate spelling *coitus,* refers to union in general and can mean "group" in addition to its better-known sense. (Hence, Melville's "many a man" and Martin's "host of male admirers.") However, Anderson notes that the sexual nature of the word is inescapable and wrongly ignored; he proposes the rendering "sexual relations with men," a cue my translation follows in effecting a kind of compromise.

568–71   *observed . . . obstructed . . . obstacles (obstabat . . . obstructa . . . obice):* In a sustained parenthetical on the effects of blockage, Ovid uses three words with the prefix *ob* in the space of four lines. Since the syllable retains something of its sense in English, my translation does the same, albeit with somewhat altered positions and meanings.

641–42   *Opheltes said . . . / Turn left! they cried (inquit Opheltes / persequitur retinens laeuam pete):* This passage is textually fraught. I have followed Tarrant's printing of 641, which identifies Opheltes as the speaker, over an alternate reading addressing Acoetes as part of the direct speech. For 642, however, I have followed the transmitted text, in which the remainder of the crew speaks for themselves, believing it constitutes a likelier transition to the following verse.

670   *The men leapt up (exsiluere uiri):* At this point, several translators portray the crewmen leaping overboard. However, the verb *exsilire* merely indicates an upward burst, and the succeeding lines make clear that at least the sailors depicted have stayed aboard the ship.

BOOK 4

37   *liar's rites (commentaque sacra):* Ovid has Pentheus speak the same phrase when describing the rites of Bacchus at 3.558, where my translation uses the similar construction "his rites are lies."

54   *begins to weave (orsa):* A conventional word in epic to mark the start of a speech, the verb *orsa* ("began") originated as a textile term, a sense Ovid exploits here by having Minyas' daughter begin speaking and spinning simultaneously. Since English has a comparable idiom regarding woven tales, my translation prints both senses.

116   *Beneath the tree, as planned (pactae . . . arboris umbram):* In this line, Ovid's diction echoes that of the planning sequence in 4.88–91. My translation has recycled words accordingly.

169–70   *The Sun, whose starlight lights all, also loves. / Now we'll recount the lovers of the Sun (hunc quoque, siderea qui temperat omnia luce, / cepit amor Solem; Solis referemus amores):* In the second of these lines, Ovid employs his favorite trick of juxtaposing two different forms of the same word (*Solem Solis,* "the Sun, of the Sun"), also managing to do something similar with the two forms of *amor* ("love") which embrace the solar pair. My translation sacrifices this precise effect in order to capture the sense of the two lines as a whole, but pulls a similar trick with the syllables "light" and "all." Separately, I have attempted to preserve Ovid's emphasis on the Sun with an opposite device, bookending.

174   *Not just their lie, but on whose bed they lay (furta tori furtique locum):* The coincidental similarity in English between the noun for deception, lie/lied, and the verb for reclining, lie/lay, allows for a pun nodding toward the original's repetition, which delineates both the how and where of the *furta* ("deception").

175   *The blacksmith dropped his work with drooping heart (et mens et quod opus fabrilis dextra tenebat / excidit):* The sentence in Latin relies on a clever zeugma. The verb *excidit* ("to fall out") here governs both *mens* ("mind") and *opus* ("work"), the pun being that the sad news caused Vulcan's spirits to metaphorically sink while the object he was forging literally sank out of his hand. My attempts at something similar in English yielded comically forced results, so I have instead opted for a pun by way of homophony.

191–92   *So he who'd bared her love was met in turn / With barren love (inque uices illum, tectos qui laesit amores, / laedit amore pari):* A nearer translation might read, "And in turn, he who wounded her hidden loves is wounded by love as well." My translation exchanges the original verb for a different word pair (bared/barren) to create a pun of similar effect, while still capturing the sense of the whole.

229–32   *Afraid ... fright / ... fear ... / scared (pauet ... metuque / ... timor ... / territa):* In the space of four lines, Ovid employs four unrelated words for fear, fearing, or fearfulness, an effect my translation endeavors to replicate. The verbal display underlines Leucothoë's utter dread at the prospect of the Sun's sexual assault.

260   *Through ... cloudy skies, she sat (nimborum patiens):* With some misgivings, I have translated Tarrant's text for this phrase, which literally means "putting up with rain-clouds." Other editors print *nympharum impatiens* ("not putting up with nymphs"), presumably referring to

Clytië's sympathetic sisters. This gives Melville his "shunning the nymphs" and Martin his "unable to endure the other nymphs." I find the nymphs' abrupt appearance at this juncture incongruous, and while the mention of clouds in a passage that presents its subject staring fixedly at the sun does give me pause, the god's occlusion would make a nice pathetic fallacy of his abandonment.

294   *unknown . . . unknown (ignotis . . . ignota):* Based on a single Homeric precedent, poets of classical epic were fond of using the same word twice in one line with different metrical stresses. English words tend to resist such attempts, but the ambiguously stressed "unknown" makes for a happy exception.

372–76   *Disjoin this boy from me nor me from him . . . / The two were joined in form and face . . . / . . . when someone grafts a branch in bark, / The joint is seen to seal (et istum / . . . a me nec me diducat ab isto. / . . . corpora iunguntur faciesque inducitur . . . / . . . si quis conducat cortice ramos / . . . iungi . . . cernit):* Ovid's description of Hermaphroditus and Salmacis mixing together makes use of some complex wordplay. To begin with, Salmacis prays to the gods that neither she nor Hermaphroditus shall ever leave the other, an action described in the verb *diducat* (literally, "lead apart"). When her prayer is granted, their faces are described as melding in the related but antonymous verb *inducitur,* while their bodies are likewise "joined" (*iunguntur*). Both these verbs are played upon in the subsequent horticultural simile, where a branch is grafted (*conducat*) onto a tree and the two are seen growing together (*iungi*).

Unable to find space in my translation to play on both verbs, I have opted to use one throughout: "join." Consequently, Salmacis prays for the gods not to "disjoin" her from the boy, to whom she is later "joined." Though I translate the verb *conducat* as "graft" for purposes of clarity, the English word for the point of graftage is, helpfully, "joint."

374   *as one (una):* Ovid draws special attention to the numerical result of the union through forceful enjambment,
setting *una* ("one") to end the sentence by itself at the
beginning of the next line. Doing likewise in English
verse with a monosyllabic word is perhaps too jarring; I
have therefore set it at the end of the line with just a dash
for sequestration.

377   *merged their forms in passionate embrace (complexu
coierunt membra tenaci):* My translation is not so different
from the literal meaning: "their limbs came together in a
fierce embrace." However, as seen in some earlier puns
(3.387, 3.403), the verb *coierunt* and those derived from it
carry a sexual connotation. I have tried to capture something of that here by rendering their embrace "passionate."

380–82   *man / ... semi-male ... / ... emasculate (uir ... / semimarem ... / ... uirili):* Like English, Latin has different
words for "man" (*uir*), "male" (*marem*), and "masculine"
(*uirilis*). In three consecutive lines depicting Hermaphroditus unmanned, Ovid uses forms of each. My translation
does likewise, albeit with the somewhat odd adjectival
form of "emasculate."

388   *steeped the fountain with its queering power (incerto
fontem medicamine tinxit):* A perhaps controversial
translation for a controversial line. Manuscripts are
divided here, with a typically reliable family presenting
incesto (sexually perverse) in place of *incerto* (ambiguous). In this case, I am reading against Tarrant and most
modern editors, who print *incesto,* and defer to Possanza
2005; I have interposed quotes from my translation
where appropriate:

> the transformation of Hermaphroditus is not a violation
> of religious taboo and it does not involve sexual inter-
> course that is forbidden by law or custom. Defenders of
> *incesto* cite *infamis ... Salmacis* (4.285–286) and Pythago-
> ras's phrase *obscenae Salmacis undae* (15.319), but neither
> *infamis* nor *obscenae* is weighty enough in its opprobrium
> to justify the epithet. ... *Incerto,* on the other hand, which

is defined by *neutrumque et utrumque* ["neither and both"] (379), follows naturally after *semimarem* ["semi-male"] (381), *semiuir* ["unmanned"] (386), and *biformis* ["two-shaped"] (387). Moreover, if *incesto medicamine* is read, we are confronted with the scandalous situation in which Hermaphroditus's divine parents are themselves involved in committing what is *incestum* in response to their son's prayer.

Since the narrator's sympathies in this story hew firmly to the side of Hermaphroditus, I am also disinclined to believe Ovid would have labeled him so cruelly at its conclusion. Moreover, it is extremely easy to imagine such a slip issuing from the prudish mind of a scribe in a medieval monastery, a point made by both Anderson and Possanza.

Deciding to read *incerto,* then, raises the question of how to translate it. Anderson found the adjective appropriate because it "applies to the sexual ambiguity of the hermaphrodite, the subject of this story." Casting about for a verb that would capture the fountain's power to blur the binary of sexual identity, I settled upon "queering," which, being an old word with a new meaning, I hoped would not ring too false on the ear.

417   *Divine (numen):* Another contested reading, the question being whether all of Thebes came to know Bacchus as a god (*numen*) or came to know his name (*nomen*). Tarrant prints *nomen,* but notes in his apparatus that *numen* is *fort. recte.* Considering that *nomen* appears only two lines earlier in an unrelated context, I deem it an improbably unartful repetition and translate against it (though a form of *numen* does occur at 421).

456   *the "Seat of the Accursed" (sedes Scelerata):* In naming this site of everlasting torments, some translators have opted to preserve the original's alliteration; thus, Melville's "Dungeon of the Damned," itself borrowed from a seventeenth-century translation by George Sandys.

Doing so, however, misses a pun: the *sedes* ("seat") in question is also a literal one, from which the Furies have just risen.

471   *And Athamas dragged madly into sin (in facinus traherent Athamanta furores)*: Translators have tended to take *furores* to mean the Furies, making Juno explicitly wish for the goddesses themselves to do the dragging: "the Fury-sisters should drive Athamas to madness" (Miller); "Athamas dragged down / to crime and horror by those Sisters three" (Melville). This is possible (*OLD* 1c), but also slightly redundant, since Juno is imploring the Furies to act anyway. Tarrant prints the word in lower-case and Anderson connects it to Ino's *furoribus* of 4.431, a much more compelling parallel, and one in which the term clearly refers to insanity.

476   *this unending tale (longis . . . ambagibus)*: Pentheus used the same words in the same metrical positions to make a similar dismissal at 3.692. My translation follows suit.

573   *And sowed the soil with serpent seeds—its teeth? (uipereos sparsi per humum, noua semina, dentes?)*: In word choice, word order, and narrative content, this recalls 3.105: *spargit humi iussos, mortalia semina, dentes* ("And sowed the ordered mortal seeds: the teeth"). This echo brings the tale of Cadmus to a tidy end that I have tried to preserve.

766–67   *the life and lineage of the place / . . . the mien and manner of its race (cultusque genusque locorum / . . . moresque animumque uirorum)*: These two phrases might be more literally translated as "the culture and the race of the region" and "the customs and the spirit of its men." My rendering follows this fairly closely, but preserves the structural similarity of the Latin, as well as its rhyme.

BOOK 5

53   *his hair, which dripped with myrrh (madidos murra . . . capillos)*: This phrase closely follows 3.555, where

Pentheus described Bacchus as having *madidus murra crinis* ("hair dripping with myrrh"), the implication being that scented hair is exotic or effeminate. In any case, my translation adheres to the repetition.

234–35 *his meek supplicating face, / Defeated hands (os timidum ... supplex / summissaeque manus):* In the final lines dealing with Phineus, Ovid resonantly recycles much of the diction earlier used to illustrate the character's abjection. Phineus' timidity returns from the *timidissime* of 224 ("O meek one," in my translation), and his suppliant look and concessive gestures closely mimic the word choice and metrical position of his initial capitulation in lines 214–15, *supplex / confessasque manus,* which I translated as "supplication and defeat." Accordingly, I have striven to string together a series of comparable repetitions.

393 *She stuffed her clothes (sinumque / implet):* It is unclear precisely what Proserpine is filling. The noun *sinus* may refer to any number of cavities or hollow spaces (including pockets, cleavage, laps, bodies of water, and folds of garments), some of which are easier to fill with flowers than others. I take it to mean the folds of her clothing, the better for the blossoms to fall out when her robe is torn six lines later. Though Innes, Kline, Lombardo, Mandelbaum, Raeburn, and Simpson do likewise, Golding, Johnston, Melville, Sandys, and Arthur Mainwaring instead opt for "lap," while More, Martin, and Miller each choose "bosom." Watts has "breast." For his part, Gregory (who persistently calls Dis "Death") is keen to elaborate on Proserpine's "hollow of small breasts." Humphries is silent.

416 *You need rapport, not rape! (roganda, / non rapienda fuit):* As Anderson rather lightly puts it, "The contrasted verbs, emphasized by alliteration, are so different in connotation that Cyane's linking of them raises a smile at her silliness." My translation aims to preserve this striking effect.

568 *her look and outlook (facies et mentis et oris):* Though it captures something of the original's sense, the light

wordplay of my version compensates for the loss of the
Latin's somewhat untranslatable zeugma: the "look" or
"state" (*facies*) pertains to both her mind and face (*et
mentis et oris*).

578–79 *the keenest one of all to traipse / The glades; the keenest one
of all with traps (nec me studiosus altera saltus / legit nec
posuit studiosus altera casses):* A fairly faithful translation
of yet another Ovidian mirrored couplet.

580–81 *fame . . . fair / . . . fearless, fairness (formae . . . fama . . . / . . .
fortis . . . formosae):* The profound alliteration in these
lines serves to contrast the differences between being
fortis ("bold") and *formosae* ("beautiful"). The effect has
been preserved.

BOOK 6

103 *the bull disguise (imagine tauri):* For his brief reprise of
the Europa story, narrated in Books 2–3, Ovid recycles
this phrase in the same metrical position that it occupied
in 3.1. My translation does likewise. The phrase appears
again at 8.123.

118–20 *how, as a steed, / The crops' kind corn-haired mother knew
your force; / The winged steed's snake-haired mother knew
your wings (et te flaua comas frugum mitissima mater /
sensit equum, sensit uolucrem crinita colubris / mater equi
uolucris):* In these three lines, Ovid constructs a series of
paralleled repetitions that my translation carefully
reconstructs. Besides the repeated verb (*sensit*), the lines
deal with two steeds (*equum, -i*), two winged creatures
(*uolucrem, -is*), and two mothers (*mater*), each with
distinctive hair (*comas; crinita*).

184 *First ask what's caused our pride (quaerite nunc, habeat
quam nostra superbia causam):* I translate *causam* ("cause")
in place of Tarrant's printed *laudem* ("praise"), noting that
Tarrant considers the alternate reading "*fort. recte.*" While
praise proved a vital theme in the preceding tale of
Arachne, I concur with Anderson that "Niobe does not

invite the Thebans to award *praise* to her pride, but rather
to determine the strength of her *case.*"

201–2   *rites undone . . . / . . . undone rites (infectis . . . sacris . . . / . . .*
sacra infecta): Line 201 is notably vexed. I have followed
Tarrant's text in translating Korn's conjecture, whereby
Ovid springs for his old trick of using different grammatical forms of the same phrase in quick succession.

399   *speed (rapidus):* Tarrant prints this line with the transmitted *rapidum* obelized. Despite being the overwhelming
reading of the manuscripts, the neuter form of the adjective
can only go with *aequor,* and the absurdity of the sea being
called swift led Housman to conjecture the masculine
rapidus, applying to the *amnis* of the following line.
Unconvinced by this, Anderson in turn proposed an
adverb: *rapide.* However, although I agree with the
reasoning of Antonio Ramírez de Verger, who, in an
argument published after Tarrant's recension, explained
away Anderson's grammatical qualms in favor of Housman's emendation, the implied difference in translation
between *rapidus* and *rapide*—that is, between "a swift
stream flowing" on the one hand and "a stream swiftly
flowing" on the other—is not very great. Therefore, I have
pursued a kind of middle course, using the word "speed"
as a verb describing the action of the river flowing to
the sea.

438   *For "blessings" hide so much (usque adeo latet utilitas!):*
Finding more straightforward translations, such as
Miller's "even so is our true advantage hidden," nearly
incomprehensible, I have presented a rendering that I
believe better captures the tone of the original adage.
Lombardo's lengthened "We never know / Where our
true advantage lies" is closer to the original.

615   *The author of our anguish (artificem):* A clarifying
addition. The noun *artifex* most simply means "artist" or
"creator," but in some cases carried a derogatory connotation. Elsewhere in Ovid and Virgil, the word is paired
with such terms as *scelus* ("crime") or *caedis* ("slaughter"),

and translators have consequently taken a similar meaning in this line as implied. Golding had "the worker of our shame," while Miller printed "the author of our wrongs," and Martin "the mastermind of all our woes." Melville's translation gives "scheming fiend."

667–68   *You'd posit the Piraean pair were poised / On pinions—and they were! (corpora Cecropidum pennis pendere putares; / pendebant pennis!):* This sentence might be literally translated, "You'd think the bodies of the Cecropid [Athenian] girls were suspended on wings—they were suspended on wings!" I have unfortunately had to dispense with the strict repetition of *pendere pennis* to make way for the pounding alliteration, but both this effect and the meaning have been preserved. For *Cecropid,* a form of antonomasia referring to the legendary Athenian king Cecrops, I have substituted the alliteratively apt "Piraean," which refers to the port of Athens.

701   *Shall no more be implored—he'll be impelled (non orandus erat mihi sed faciendus):* In this line, Ovid draws a contrast between Boreas' attitude toward Erechtheus and the approach taken by Tereus toward Pandion in the previous tale, at once recycling *orandus* from the previous scene and inviting comparison by pairing it with another verb of the same grammatical construction. In capturing this, I have therefore borrowed "implore" from 504–5 and juxtaposed it with the similar-sounding "impel."

721   *the fleece of gold (uellera . . . nitido radiantia uillo):* Though the Latin phrase more strictly means "gleaming fleece of shining tufts," Humphries and Mandelbaum are the sole verse translators who do not explicitly mention the "Golden Fleece." However, Ovid clearly intended to refer to the famous object via circumlocution, a choice befitting his version of the tale in which the Fleece itself is downplayed as much as possible. Wishing to preserve a sense of the implicit without causing the reader any genuine confusion, I have opted for "fleece of gold."

BOOK 7

124   *new embodied shapes (noua corpora):* An echo of the
opening lines of the *Metamorphoses,* where the
phrase *noua . . . corpora* is prominently featured.
I have consequently recycled the language used in the
opening line of my translation.

141   *The earth-born brothers died by mutual wounds (terrige-*
nae pereunt per mutua uulnera fratres): A clear echo of
the story opening Book 3, in which Cadmus watches a
similar fight to the death among soldiers sprung from
dragon's teeth. Those men are also called *terrigenis*
fratribus, "earth-born brothers" (3.117) and likewise die
per mutua uulnera, "by mutual wounds" (3.123). My
translation once again recycles the relevant diction.

186a   *([sopitae similis, nullo cum murmure serpens]):* Though
Anderson argues to the contrary and even defends a
more redundant reading with *serpens* ("serpent")
switched for the same *saepes* ("hedgerows") of 186, I
follow Tarrant in deeming it unlikely that both this line
and the transmitted 186 can stand. While *serpens* is more
credible than a second round of hedges, it also violates
the course of imagery transitioning from the animate
beings of 185 to the inanimate ones of 187. I have
therefore opted to entirely excise the alternate line from
my translation. Literally translated, it would read, "As if
sleeping, from the serpents not a whisper came."

246–47   *On this she next poured bowls of liquid wine, / And then*
poured other bowls of tepid milk (tum super inuergens
liquidi carchesia uini / alteraque inuergens tepidi carchesia
lactis): The final word of 246 is disputed. Tarrant prints
mellis ("honey"), the predominant reading, but other
manuscripts supply wine (*uini* or *bachi*) or another
serving of milk (*lactis*). Anderson deems it "quite
inconceivable that Medea would have tried to pour
unmixed honey, because it would not pour," and while
this line of argument does not entirely convince me, I
have allowed myself to be persuaded on grounds of

metric convenience, reasoning that the close mirroring of diction in the two lines is of greater poetic importance.

297   *To keep it up (Neue doli cessent):* This phrase literally means "and lest the trickery cease," but I believe my wording is closer to the jocular brevity of the original clause, which several translators expand to fill a whole line. Raeburn's "Black treachery next" takes the idea in another direction, signaling that Medea's next tricks will be more malicious.

339–40   *The girls' love thus set them against their love / To sin for fear of sinning (his ut quaeque pia est hortatibus impia prima est / et, ne sit scelerata, facit scelus):* In under two lines, Ovid uses some fifteen words to express the daughters' complex state of mind. Miller's rendering ("Spurred on by these words, as each was filial she became first in the unfilial act, and that she might not be wicked did the wicked deed") is more faithful than mine, but I felt it important to preserve the repetition of *pia / impia* and *scelerata / scelus,* on which the wit of the sentence depends. Though I was forced to condense, I also believe my translation may be somewhat more intelligible.

418–19   *Which peasants, seeing them sprout through flinty crags, / Call "flint-wort" (quae quia nascunture dura uiuacia caute, / agrestes aconita uocant):* Relying on the Roman reader's knowledge of Greek, this miniature digression makes for one of Ovid's most opaque etymologies and a particularly thorny problem for translators. The plant in question, known in English as wolfsbane, was the Greek *akoniton,* derived from the word *akóne* ("whetstone"), itself vaguely related to the Latin word *cautes* ("crags"), which Ovid uses in the previous line. The matter of capturing in English what is only esoterically present in the Latin is a difficult one. Johnston, Lombardo, Miller, More, Simpson, and Nahum Tate are faithful to the text and consequently confusing. Kline, Mandelbaum, Martin, Raeburn, and Watts offer clarifying translations, ranging from the fanciful (Martin: "the rustics call them, since they grow on rocks, the aconites, or 'flowers lacking soil'") to the more accurate, if incomplete (Mandelbaum: "a plant the peasants call aconitum [in Greek the word for whetstone is *akóne*]"). Meanwhile, Innes renders the word "rock-flowers," Humphries "the flower of stoniness," and Gregory omits the etymological implication entirely. My timid solution is similar to Melville's and is taken from the sixteenth-century translation of Arthur Golding, who drew the connection by describing the *caute* of 418 as "Flints" and subsequently supplied the name "Flintwoort." Though it has the advantage of appearing in the *OED* and the *Dictionary of the Scots Language,* the word "flint-wort" is likely as obscure to English speakers as *akoniton.* Nevertheless, I have employed it here, believing its effect superior to the confusion, caginess, and clumsiness inherent in more faithful, faithless, and clarifying translations, respectively.

709–10   *I spoke of wedding chambers, bridal beds, / And our lost bonds of spousal intercourse (sacra tori coitusque nouos thalamosque recente / primaque deserti referebam foedera lecti):* In keeping with typical Roman symbolism, Ovid supplies Cephalus with three similar topics of discussion relating to his marriage, all of which involve words having to do with beds (*tori, thalamos, lecti*). While most translators have stressed the metonymy, Ovid's further inclusion of the word *coitus* makes clear that the emphasis on fleshly delights is intentional. In Anderson's interpretation, this is Ovid's "delicate way" of "saying that Cephalus refused to sleep with the goddess because of his loving loyalty to Procris." My translation attempts to encapsulate both sides of the symbolic coin by creating three phrases, each pairing a nuptial word with a more sexually suggestive one.

810ff   *zephyr (aura):* See the note in the commentary for my choice (according with Innes and Melville) of "zephyr" for this word, techically meaning "breeze." For their

parts, Lombardo and Miller confusingly use "breeze" in
narration and "Aura" in dialogue, as does Gregory, who
downplays the mistaken identity entirely. Kline and
Mandelbaum do similarly, as did Nahum Tate, but their
italicization of *aura* is surprisingly effective. Martin opts
for a clarifying translation ("I named that cool breeze
'Aura'"), as do Humphries, Johnston, More, and Watts;
Golding and Sandys proffered "Aire," and Raeburn
countenances absurdity: "please never allow your Breeze
to take my place as your wife." Simpson does likewise.

865   *aiding arms (consortibus . . . armis):* The transmitted text
is *cum fortibus armis* ("with strong arms"), and this
reading underpins most modern translations. However, I
follow Tarrant in accepting Housman's conjecture
consortibus, which carries more circumstantial meaning
and would have been paleographically indistinguishable
in the scribal days of the long s.

BOOK 8

118   *walled off all the world (obstruximus orbem):* One of many
vexed passages in this book. I have followed the textual
authorities of Tarrant and Hollis, but most modern
translators side with Anderson in reading the alternate
passive construction *exponimur orb(a)e* ("I have been
banished from the world"). Raeburn's "I banished myself
from the rest of the world" and Martin's wordier "I have
made myself an exile everywhere, throughout the world"
may be regarded as compromises between readings.

123   *bull disguise (imagine tauri):* This is the third time Ovid
has used this phrase in this metrical position to refer to
this story. My translation does the same, having rendered
3.1 and 6.103 likewise.

238   *a muddy ditch (limoso . . . elice):* The manuscripts read
ramosa . . . ilice ("a branchy oak"), but a medieval
grammarian quoted the line as translated. I have
followed Tarrant, Kenney, and Anderson on the logic

that locating the bird in a tree would seem to negate this
narrative, which purports to explain why partridges
avoid heights, pear-trees seasonally excepted. Possanza's
objection does not even address this point, and Hollis'
defense of the transmitted text ("Ovid merely says that
the bird does not nest in the topmost branches") leaves
me, frankly, unamused.

285–86   At several points in Book 8, the manuscripts briefly
divide into what appear to be alternate versions of the
same passage, leading some scholars to believe that Ovid
at some point revised the poem for a second edition (the
"double recension" theory, now largely abandoned; see
above note to 1.544a–57 for another good example).
Lines 285 and 286 constitute a minor instance of this
phenomenon, being redundant with one another and
both possibly spurious, but while 285 is more egregious,
it also has better manuscript authority. Anderson
defends 285, Hollis defends 286, and Tarrant brackets
both. Reasoning that including both would have a
detrimental effect on reading, and since 286 strikes me as
both more likely and more likable, I have allowed it to
stand in brackets and relegated 285 to this appendix. The
full passage would read as follows:

> With eyes ablaze in blood, a stiff-set neck,   *284*
> Its bristles bristling stiff as though with spears,   *285*
> And bristles like a palisade of spears.   *286*

414   *Not so for Oeneus' son (At manus Oenidae uariat):* The
meaning of this phrase is ambiguous. Literally translated, it
might read, "But the hand of Oeneus' son differed,"
indicating that Meleäger's next performance was at variance
either with that preceding it or within itself. My translation
sides with the former option. Melville's rendering, "Now it
was miss and hit for Meleager," exemplifies the latter.

434   *For, be assured, your beauty won't suffice (nec te fiducia
formae decipiat):* Ovid echoes the verbiage of his earlier
statement *tanta est fiducia formae* ("so self-assured is

beauty") about Mercury at 2.731 and Semele at 3.271. My
translation does likewise.

597ff   Something has gone very wrong in transmission, and the
full scope of the issue is not captured in my translation.
The most reliable manuscripts skip directly from 596 to
601, and again from 602 to 609, all of which reads well.
But another set of manuscripts includes a series of
alternate lines that are not transparently unworthy of
Ovid but clash with the rest of the passage. Simply, lines
597–600b would appear to be mutually exclusive with
601–2 (the repetition of *feritate paterna*, "savage sire," in
600b and 601 is especially ungainly), while 603–8 is
mutually exclusive with 609–10 (line 610, beginning *dum
loquor*, "while I spoke," demands to be placed closer to
602 where the act of speaking occurs). Much is at
interpretive stake in the issue, since 598 contains an
avowal of guilt, whereas the river's conduct at 606–7
would conversely stand out as one of the poem's most
graphic descriptions of physical violation. Not believing
that either version is clearly superior to the other, I have
printed Tarrant's brackets and translated the full sixteen
lines, warts and all, albeit smoothing over some textual
tensions in the interest of readability.

668   *whose lack of silver trim (caelatus eodem / ... argento):* A
clarifying translation. Literally rendered, the Latin states
that the cups and wine-bowl were embossed with the
same silver finish as the earthenware previously mentioned—the joke being that such embellishment adorns
none of them.

693a–b   In yet another example of variant texts, some manuscripts contain an expanded, two-line version of 693. I
follow most editors in opting for the briefer version and
have excluded the extra lines from my translation as
being redundant with 693.

698   *their neighbors' fates (fata suorum):* My translation reads
the reflexive pronoun *suorum* ("of theirs") as an idiom
referring to the couple's neighbors. In doing so, I accord

with nearly all previous translations, but Melville read the word differently and wrote "their lost possessions."

723–24 *Those loved by gods are gods, / And worshippers receive their worship, too (cura deum di sunt, et qui coluere coluntur):* My translation follows Tarrant, who is unusual among modern editors in printing this sentence with two indicative verbs; the Anderson and Miller-Goold texts have subjunctives for both (*sint* and *colantur*). The effect of their alternate reading is to change Lelex's words from simple statements to wishes or commands. This may be seen in Goold's translation: "Let those beloved of the gods be gods; let those who have worshiped be worshiped."

748 *thrice-five fathoms (ulnas / quinque ter):* Only Humphries tries to avoid the mathematics involved here. The traditional translation of *ulna* is "ell," an archaic English form of cubit whose length could reach up to forty-five inches, but was often much less. Lombardo, Martin, Miller, and More adopt the word, as did Edward Vernon, while Mandelbaum prefers "arm's-breadths," Watts and Kline "arm's-lengths," and Gregory "yards." Sandys, Innes, and Simpson are content with "cubits." As for the commentators, Anderson makes no attempt at sums, but Hollis "reckoned" the ell at eighteen inches for a total of just over twenty-two feet, the number taken by Raeburn. Johnston gives forty and Melville fifty, a count seemingly supported by a recent anthropological history of the cubit, which puts the *ulna* at four feet (Stone 4). Wishing to avoid such dreary controversies while both preserving Ovid's numerical oddity (*quinque ter,* "thrice five") and giving a reasonable impression of the tree's size, I have rejected the diminutive ell in favor of the more familiar fathom, though this exaggerates the girth in question. Generally pegged at six feet in length, the fathom also once meant "cubit" (*OED* 3a), and its verb form, meaning "to encircle with extended arms" (*OED* 1a), describes precisely what the nymphs are doing. Only after arriving at this solution was I amused to discover myself in the

company of Golding's 1567 translation: "Full fifteene fadome."

860   *Stood on this shore (for sure, I saw her stand) (litore in hoc steterat nam stantem in litore uidi):* In attempting to preserve something of Ovid's effect in using *litore* ("shore") twice in one line, along with two forms of the verb *stare* (to stand), I have resorted to the homophones "shore" and "sure."

BOOK 9

66–71   *vipers . . . dragons . . . Hydra . . . snake . . . serpent (angues . . . dracones . . . serpens . . . echidnae . . . colubris):* In a display of sophisticated diction, Ovid employs five different synonyms for "serpent" over the course of seven lines, before finally repeating one at 75. My translation attempts the same.

73   *I routed it and slew it in its rout (domui domitamque peremi):* My rendering is somewhat effective in mimicking the play of the first two words in this phrase, but the third is more troublesome. Tarrant prints the transmitted *reduxi* between obelisks, with Anderson concurring that, whatever Hercules may have done with the newly vanquished Hydra, he certainly did not bring it back. Other conjectures would elaborate further aspects of the myth, showing Hercules burning (*perussi*) the carcass or splitting it open (*reclusi*) to dip his arrows in its blood. Finding no reading particularly preferable, I have timidly translated the variant *peremi* ("I slew"), which yields a more narratively conservative rendering.

405–6   *a prophet swallowed by the earth / Alive will witness his ancestral shades (subudctaque suos manes tellure uidebit / uiuus adhuc uates):* In the familiar episode of the Seven Against Thebes here narrated, the prophet-king Amphiaraüs was swallowed alive by the earth, whereupon he found himself in the underworld. Ovid's brief rendition covers the typical ground but adds the compelling detail that, once there, the still-living prophet (*uiuus adhuc uates*) will behold (*uidebit*) an entity most literally rendered as "his own spirits" (*suos manes*). What exactly this phrase means is the subject of disagreement.

The simplest explanation is that Amphiaraüs arrives in the underworld and is greeted there by the sight of his own ghost. How the king's soul should already be present among the dead while the man himself is still alive, however, remains unclear. Many translators facing this issue have bent the grammar of the timeline so that Amphiaraüs glimpses his ghost *at the moment* of passing into the underworld. Versions of this are given by Gregory, Johnston, Melville, Miller, and Raeburn, but Innes' is perhaps the most expansive: "and the prophet Amphiaraus, while still alive, will see his own ghost, as the ground yawns open to receive him." While this interpretation minimizes the temporal overlap between the living and the dead Amphiaraüs, it does not really address the absurd bilocation at issue.

Further confusion arises from a brief gloss in Anderson's commentary: "Amphiaraus (*vates*), swallowed up alive in the earth, will descend to the underworld to see the spirits which he once controlled (*suos manes* 406)." Mandelbaum and Martin closely follow Anderson's prosaic phrasing, perhaps because its meaning is so unclear. Does Anderson think that he controlled these spirits in his capacity as *uates*, and, if so, why would his knowledge anomalously stem from them instead of the usual god of prophecy? The king was a seer, not a necromancer.

My translation comes as the result of a conversation with Melissa Haynes, who proposed the rendering "will see the shades of his own ancestors past," since the simple reflexive adjective *suus* can specifically refer to family members (*OLD* 6b). This interpretation is especially strong considering how, as Robert Kaster put it to me in another discussion of the phrase, "the idea of seeing the shades of one's ancestors in reaching the underworld has the robust endorsement of epic," with famous parallels in the *Odyssey* and the *Aeneid.*

408   *an act both dutiful and wrong (facto pius et sceleratus eodem):* Ovid used exactly the same description at 3.4 when waxing moral on Agenor's banishment of Cadmus. My translation preserves the match.

432   *not power or politics (non ambitione nec armis):* An *ambitio* was a Roman act of political door-knocking, as attested in Raeburn's rendering: "not a matter for canvassing votes or for fighting." Melville's "not to canvassing / Or conflict" also preserves the pleasing alliteration of the original, as does my clarifying translation, which opts for broader categories.

728–29   *For, if the gods would save me, [I'll be saved, / But if the gods would slay me] (si di me [parcere uellent, / parcere debuerant; si non, et] perdere uellent):* Tarrant brackets the end of the 728 and most of 729 as spurious, and the resulting splice is certainly seamless. The supposed interpolation, however, shows markedly Ovidian cleverness, pairing balanced conditional clauses with a near rhyme. My translation preserves these traits.

797   *Iphis took Ianthe for his bride (potiturque sua puer Iphis Ianthe):* English grammar prevents the replication of Ovid's charming end to the book, wherein the names of the lovers, united at last, comprise its last two words.

BOOK 10

12   *to try the shades (temptaret . . . umbras):* As Anderson writes, "The exact sense of *temptaret* is unclear; does Orpheus merely seek an audience?" With Melville rendering the verb "make trial" and Raeburn offering "appeal to," I settled on a literal translation similarly ambiguous to the original.

22   *Medusan (Medusaei):* It is unclear why Cerberus is described as "of Medusa." While Johnston, Kline, Mandel-

baum, Martin, Miller, and Raeburn all innovate mythology (and contradict Ovid: 7.408) to make Cerberus her son, Melville and Congreve excise the reference, and Gregory dispenses with the dog entirely (my "hound" in the previous line is a clarifying addition) to posit the existence of "Medusa's children, / Three-throated beasts with wild snakes in their hair," a translation concurring with Humphries and More, but which would seem to nullify the effect of Orpheus' words by removing the comparison to Hercules as a previous visitor to the underworld. Simpson accepts Anderson's accounting for the reference on the grounds that Cerberus shares Medusa's power to petrify at a glance, while Nathaniel Bailey's edition makes a similar argument based on Cerberus' serpentine hair. I find this final point the most persuasive but have joined Lombardo in translating "Medusan" and leaving the issue unresolved. Innes and Watts are similarly cagey.

115–16   *and, balanced at his ears / and round his temples, shone two brazen pearls (parilesque ex aere nitebant / auribus e geminis circum caua tempora bacae):* I have adhered to Tarrant's text, in which the words *parilesque ex aere* ("equal and made of bronze") begin a new clause describing the pearl earrings in the following line. In so doing, I am joined by few modern translators, with the exceptions of Humphries, Johnston, Simpson, and Kline. Others mostly translate the text printed—with great misgivings—by Anderson, reading the manuscripts' *parili aetate* ("of equal age") in conjunction with the previous clause describing the *bulla . . . argentea* ("silver pendant"). They interpret the awkward phrase to mean that the deer has worn the pendant his entire life. Gregory, Innes, Lombardo, Mandelbaum, Melville, Miller, More, and Watts subscribe to this reading, while Martin appears to skip the phrase. Only Raeburn seems interested in a different conjecture, Madvig's *parilique decore,* which he translates "no less fetchingly." The last word should perhaps belong to Golding, whose "perles of all one growth" would seem to indicate that the original *aetate* might as well be applied to the pearls anyway.

200–1   *Yet what have I done wrong? Can it be wrong / To play? Or else, to love: can that be wrong? (quae mea culpa tamen? Nisi si lusisse uocari / culpa potest, nisi culpa potest et amasse uocare):* My translation neatly captures the repetitive diction and parallel endings of these two lines but cannot approach the sheer phonetic nonsense (*nisi si lusisse*) of the original.

266   *fair when bared, she (nuda . . . formosa):* After introducing the statue, Ovid carefully distracts by introducing a long series of objects before returning to the work of art, now grammatically feminine. I have attempted to follow the same pronoun trajectory.

293   *met his eyes with timid eyes (timidumque ad lumina lumen / attollens):* Ovid's fondness for punning on *lumen*, which can mean both "light" and "eye," here becomes a problem. Since both Pygmalion and the sky are ready to greet her upward gaze, I have opted for "eyes" in order to preserve something of the original's repetition, accentuated by the twin pairs of "lips" a few lines earlier. Melville evinced the same choice, if not the same motivation, with his "shyly raised / Her eyes to his," but Lombardo's "lifting her shy eyes up to the light" represents a far more popular school of translation.

380   *but know you caused my death! (causam te intellige mortis):* My translation follows Tarrant's text. The more common reading, underpinning most translations, is far more tepid: *causamque intellige mortis* ("and know the cause of my death").

591   *With wings upon her heels she braced the breeze (aura refert ablata citis talaria plantis):* The word *talaria* in this line has been the subject of much consternation, a fuller discussion of which may be found in Anderson's 1966 article "Talaria and Ovid *Met.* 10.591." Briefly summarized, *talaria* is a substantive adjective relating to ankles and in most cases refers to the winged sandals worn by

Mercury and Perseus. Early commentators interpreted the word as indication that Atalanta was clothed in ankle-length robes, a suggestion whose awkwardness is apparent in Innes' correspondent translation: "the wind blew back her long robes, as she held them up out of the way of her swift feet." A secondary school of thought assigns Atalanta a set of laces or ankle-ribbons, so that More writes of "streamers on her flying ankles," which strikes me as particularly ill-advised foot-racing apparel.

As Anderson notes, both these interpretations are profoundly flawed. Either would involve a unique definition of *talaria*, and, as concerns the first, Ovid explicitly states at 578 that Atalanta has disrobed in accordance with standard athletic practice. Moreover, while the long *tunica talaris* bears the advantage of being a garment that actually existed, that is more than can be definitively said of anklet sandal laces. Anderson's solution, which I fear will only suffer in summary, involves applying the standard mythic meaning of *talaria* ("wings at the ankles") in a metaphorical sense connoting speed. This interpretation more neatly conforms to Ovid's use of the word in the poem and is strengthened by the flying imagery already employed to describe Atalanta at 587.

Of the existing options, I find Anderson's far the most palatable, though this is not a universal belief (the translations of Melville and Raeburn both stick to their ribbons despite postdating Anderson's article; Johnston opts for "ankle straps"). There remains, however, the matter of rendering it. Curiously, such recent translations as adhere to Anderson's interpretation (Lombardo: "Her sandals' feathers swoosh in the breeze") seem intent on retaining the specific image of winged *sandals*, which Anderson specifically argues against and confusingly literalizes the metaphor: Atalanta is not really wearing winged sandals. On the other hand, I find that a more straightforward version (Martin: "the breezes blew back the wings attached to her ankles") too ambiguous in force. As a result, I have adapted the English expression "wing-footed" in hopes of approximating the original.

739 *windflower takes its name (idem, qui praestant nomina, uenti):* A convenient translation. Ovid is not so explicit as to name the flower itself, speaking only of "the wind from which they take their name," and counting on his audience to connect the anemone with the Greek wind word *anemos*. Happily, anemones are commonly called "windflowers" in English, allowing the connection to be preserved (and, in my version, made explicit).

BOOK 11

71 *So far as each had traveled in pursuit (in quantum est quaeque secuta):* Centuries of editors have flagged this phrase as obscure and possibly corrupt. As Murphy explains, the unemended text can mean only two things: that each bacchant is "rooted to the ground by her toes *at the point which* she reached in her pursuit," or that "Bacchus drew down the Bacchantes' toes *as far as* (the same distance as) each had pursued Orpheus, i.e. the length of the roots was proportionate to the length of the pursuit." Tarrant quizzically proffers the first explanation in his apparatus, and though Murphy admits that "at the point which" makes for an unusually strained rendering of *in quantum,* he dismisses the more grammatically feasible second option as "bizarre and pointless." Griffin concurs, but his adoption of Bentley's gender-bending conjecture *in quantum est quisque secutus* (excluded from Tarrant's apparatus) produces an image of Bacchus "stretching out the maenads' toes like pieces of elastic or rubber" that I find far more objectionable.

At the risk of Murphy's bizarrerie and pointlessness, I have consequently opted for the second explanation, deriving amusement, despite him and Griffin, from this Dantesque notion of proportional punishment. In so doing, I find myself in the company of Golding, Innes, and Sandys, while Melville and Raeburn are clear adherents to the first. Most other translations are unclear in their interpretations or fail to provide one. Notably, Lombardo, Martin, Simpson, and Kline all appear to adopt a conjecture of Housman's, replacing *in quantum* with *uia quam tum* so that it is the path on which the bacchants tread that tugs upon their toes.

123–24 *The meat, with every bite the fellow takes / The meat turns into bitten yellow flakes!* (*siue dapes auido conuellere dente parabat, / lammina fulua dapes admoto dente premebat*): I have made use of rhyme in rendering the wordplay of this couplet, which, in addition to repeating the noun *dapes* ("meat" or "meal"), closely mirrors its lines' final two feet: *dente parabat* and *dente premebat*.

146–47 *he took to woods and fields, / And to the cult of Pan* (*siluas et rura colebat / Panaque*): An attempt at recreating the original syllepsis, wherein the verb *colebat* first means "frequented" and then "worshiped."

295 *Though we shared that sire* (*illo genitore creatus*): This is Tarrant's printed text, which literally reads "a son of that sire." However, there is no point in Ceÿx mentioning his brother's parentage except as a mark of unity that will contrast with the disparities described in subsequent lines: though Ceÿx and Daedalion shared a father, they differed in character, with one as peaceable as the other was warlike.

Accordingly, multiple conjectures have adjusted the text so as to make Ceÿx refer to both brothers at once, either directly (*nostro genitore*, "our father") or obliquely (the more popular *creatis*, a plural). Whether or not emendations are necessary to carry such force, I feel that the arc of contrast in these lines is enough to justify my clarifying translation. Griffin's interpretive defense of the original reading—"It is in keeping with Ceÿx' modest manner that in talking to Peleus about Daedalion he should draw attention to his brother's ancestry without mentioning himself"—is needlessly complicating.

362 *So said a sailor as he dried his nets* (*hos nauita templi / edidit esse deos, dum retia litore siccat*): In full, the Latin

might be translated, "While drying his nets upon the shore, a sailor explained that these were the temple's gods." (My rendering is somewhat condensed; the temple appears in previous lines.) Tarrant is unusual in this reading, however, and most all other editors and translators follow the manuscripts in printing *ponti* ("of the sea") in place of *templi,* with the preposterous result that the sailor identifies Nereus and the Nereids as divinities of the sea—an obvious and unmotivated statement whose absurdity is only compounded when Onetor takes the incredible trouble of relating it to his master Peleus, who is married to a Nereid and presumably already knows. Finding it far better that this aside should instead provide the reader with an explanation of how Onetor came to know the temple's function, I have broken with tradition and followed Tarrant's lead.

523   *As flames of lightning's light restart the stars (fulmina fulmineis ardescunt ignibus ignes):* My translation of this obscure line conforms to the explanation of Hugo Magnus, requiring the first set of flames (*ignibus*) to refer to lightning and the second (*ignes*) to the stars. In mimicking the original's sonorous repetition, I have deployed the homophonous verb "restart" to pair with "stars."

753   *diving fowl (mergum):* Since line 795 will show the bird being named for its tendency to dive, this is an odd but nearly standard translation. Historical translators were bolder, with Golding, Sandys, and Dryden identifying the fowl as a cormorant; but as W. G. Arnott explained (258):

> *mergus* is clearly a blanket term, covering a number of species that have certain attributes in common.... The etymology of the word, which the Romans themselves knew, makes it highly probable that *mergus* was originally applied to some or all diving birds.... [C]onsequently, any attempt to discover a basic 'accepted translation' of *mergus,* applicable to all the passages where the word occurs, irrespective of author and context, is doomed to failure.

In this regard, the most accurate English rendering yet has probably been Brookes More's "divedapper." Simpson thinks it is a gull.

777   *Death stopped her dead (cum uita suppressa fuga est):* I offer this as a substitute for the original zeugma, which Melville more faithfully renders as "Her flight, her life cut short!"

BOOK 12

24   *Fierce Nereus (Nereus uiolentus):* With misgivings, I have adhered to Tarrant in printing the transmitted *Nereus,* who would here serve as a metonym for the sea in general. However, as Housman contended, calling the sea "Nereus in one breath and Neptunus in the next" is hardly elegant (171). Housman's substitute conjecture *Boreas* makes good sense, since most versions of the myth have Artemis interfering with the winds rather than the waves, but it is the wrath of the sea (*maris ira*) that subsides at 36.

262–64   *(Orios was the son / . . . with her charms) (Orio / . . . cornua lunae):* This aside is sufficiently odd that I felt it necessary to put it in a parenthetical, violating my normal practice of punctuating thus only following Tarrant.

357   *from the thorny brush (solidoque . . . dumo):* This is Tarrant's reading of an old intractable phrase. As Hill pithily writes, "*dumo;* what does it mean?" The *OLD* defines the word as a "thorn or briar bush," but gives this as its sole instance in the singular—a particular concern since the plural *solidis . . . dumis* is metrically feasible. An alternate reading (*trunco*), printed in the Miller-Goold text, appears to be the source of Raeburn's translation ("with trunk intact"), and most translations have something similar. But as Robert Kaster pointed out to me in conversation, *trunco* nullifies what should really be an ablative of separation, and Tarrant excludes it even from his apparatus. Martin appears to follow a minor variant, *terra,* with his "from the ground." My translation repre-

sents my best attempt at making sense of Tarrant's text but is forwarded with little confidence. Kaster suggested to me that *dumo* be obelized.

389–92   *slashed wide his bowels. / Then, rushing forward, trailing his own guts, / He trod what trailed, the trodden entrails burst, / And, tripping, down he tumbled, disemboweled. (mediam ferit ense sub aluum. / prosiluit terraque ferox sua uiscera traxit / tractaque calcauit calcataque rupit et illis / crura quoque impediit et inani concidit aluo)*: These lines present an extreme example of Ovidian wordplay. Besides his favorite pairing of a verb with its own past participle in quick succession (a trick occurring twice in this passage: *traxit, tracta*; *calcauit, calcata*), consonance abounds, and both the first and last lines end with a form of the noun *aluum* ("bowel"). Albeit with some variation in specifics, my translation has been able to reproduce much of these effects, with the result that Dorylas, beginning with his *bowel*s slashed wide, finds his en*trail*s *trailed* and *trodden* till he falls down disem*bowel*ed.

416–18   *as one . . . side by side / Together, and together (una / . . . simul . . . / . . . pariter, pariter)*: Regarding these lines, Hill writes, "in context, *una, simul* and *pariter* are synonymous . . . but the English 'together' has no suitable synonym." I have taken this as a challenge.

434–38   Sporting a number of metrical anomalies, these five lines are so firmly regarded as spurious that Tarrant, who refers to them as "*uersus illepidos*" ("graceless verses"), takes the extraordinary step of sequestering them in his apparatus rather than printing them in brackets. The grotesque imagery has proven more popular with translators, however; to my knowledge, only Raeburn omits them.

BOOK 13

602–3   *Much as a stream breathes forth / Dense mists (ueluti cum flumina natas / exhalant nebulas)*: The text of this line is extremely contested and my translation is something of a compromise. The disagreement centers on the word *natas*, which superfluously describes the mists as "born" from the river. Several editors have posited other readings, including Postgate's *lentas* ("sluggish"), Shackleton Bailey's *opacas* ("dark"), Burman's *latas* ("broad"), and Ramírez de Verger's *densas* ("thick"). My translation ("dense") is a nod to several of these, though I must admit the attractions of Housman's conjecture (*ueluti cum flumine Nais / exhalat nebulas*, "just as when a Naiad blows mists from her river"), printed in the Miller-Goold text. Housman's reasoning makes for an amusing and intriguing display of paleographic fireworks, but his introduction of a singular, unspecified nymph and river perhaps raises more questions than it answers.

619   *They rewage war to die the family way (parentali moriturae more rebellant):* This is Tarrant's printing of another heavily contested line with no obviously superior reading. Besides *parentali moriturae more* ("doomed to die in the manner of their parents"), there is also manuscript support for reading the synonymous *periturae* for *moriturae* and *uoce* ("voice," "call") for *more*. Hopkinson accepts the latter of these alternatives, leading him to translate the phrase, "they renew their warfare, destined to die with a cry such as was made by their parents," and though Tarrant's reading makes better sense, the similarity between *more* and *moriturae* smacks of corruption (as does that between *periturae* and *parentali*). Some manuscripts preserve the preposterously redundant *periturae morte* ("destined to die from death"), but Heinsius' consequent conjecture *periturae Marte* ("destined to die in battle") is clever and may well be right.

622   *on and on bedew the world (et toto rorat in orbe):* Dawn's Latin name is *Aurora,* a phonetic cluster Ovid hides in the story's last words, "*toto rorat in orbe*" ("bedews all the world"). I have attempted something similar with the phrase "*on and on*."

683–84 *forged at Rhodes / By Alcon (fabricauerat Alcon / Lindius):*
Ovid's calling the sculptor by name already occasions
comment, but his adjective describing the artist has
occasioned despair. Some manuscripts read *lidius* or
hyleus and make Alcon a native of Lydia or the crafts-
men's city of Hyle, though that should really be *Lydius*
and *Hylaeus*. I follow Tarrant in reading *Lindius*, attested
in a late antique commentary, which would locate Alcon
in Lindus on Rhodes, the isle where Pliny mentions a
sculptor of that name (*Nat.* 34.141). Unconvinced by this,
Hopkinson and Hardie both obelize the transmitted
nileus, which is meaningless.

694   *spear (telo):* Lines 693–94 are tortuously obscure and were
deleted by Bentley (whom Raeburn follows). Though
many of the textual matters involved are too arcane to be
worth explaining here, a number of other translators
(Humphries, Innes, Melville, Miller, and More) show the
second daughter stabbing herself with a weaving-shuttle,
as in a version of the story recorded by Antoninus
Liberalis. Such translations are founded on an alternate
text reading, *tela,* but as Hopkinson notes, "*tela* means
'loom', not 'shuttle', for which the Latin is *radius*." I
therefore follow Tarrant who prints the weapon word *telo.*

698   *Coronae twins (geminos . . . / . . . coronas):* The significance of the name is not clear in any surviving version,
and manuscripts even differ as to the gender of the word.
Ovid does seem to draw a verbal parallel to the crown in
line 704, which I translate as *coronet* accordingly.

788ff   The nineteen lines that begin Polyphemus' song contain
some twenty-six comparative statements, with two often
appearing in the same line. In the Latin, all twenty-six are
accomplished through comparative adjectives for a
striking rhetorical effect. However, this is one sphere in
which English is far less consistent than Latin, since some
English adjectives take an "-er" suffix in the comparative
while others require an auxiliary "more." I have therefore
abandoned any attempt at consistency across this speech,

instead opting for a varied array of sentence structures
that I hope will be comparably impressive.

BOOK 14

278   *wicked witch (dea dira):* The phrase more literally means
"dreadful goddess," but the staccato alliteration struck
me as an effect worth the alteration to preserve.

297   *They soon saw eye to eye (inde fides dextraeque datae):*
Lombardo's translation ("They came to an understanding") gives an elegant rendition of the original's pithy and
idiomatic wit, while Melville's ("Then trust was pledged
and hands were clasped") is closer to the text. My
rendering attempts to combine the wryness of Lombardo's version with something of the transactional "hands
were clasped" sense of the original.

334   *To Grecian Janus (Ionio . . . Iano):* Many translators prefer
the variant *ancipiti Iano* ("to two-headed Janus"), despite
the clear phonetic wordplay (sadly obscured in English)
of this reading, which also enjoys superior manuscript
support.

493   *Though her great powers have greatly grown our grief (ut
magno stet magna potentia nobis):* This is a corrupt and
contentious line, which Tarrant prints obelized: *et
†magno stat magna† potentia nobis.* Most translators
seem drawn either to Heinsius' conjecture *et paruo stat
magna* (Raeburn: "Her power may be great, but it counts
for little with *us!*") or Ellis' *haud magno stat magna*
(Lombardo: "Great powers are anything but great to us").
Either produces a result called "blatantly untrue" by
Myers, whose unenthusiastic endorsement of Charles
Simmons' 1899 conjecture *ut magno stet magna potentia
nobis* ("even granting that her great power costs us
dearly," in Myers' translation) guides my rendering.
Simmons' emendation is very close to the original and
makes good sense; I am at a loss as to why it is not more
popular.

494–95   *Spurred on by Acmon of Pleuronia's speech / Which*
         spurned her rages, Venus raged anew (talibus iratam
         Venerem Pleuronius Acmon / instimulat uerbis stim-
         ulisque resuscitat iram): These lines are more literally
         rendered by Innes: "By such provocative words, Acmon
         of Pleuron goaded Venus to fresh rage, and roused her
         wrath again." My freer version, however, attempts to
         capture the contrived repetition (*iratam, iram; instimulat,*
         stimulis) of the original.

639   *Silenus, ever younger than his years (Silenusque suis*
         semper iuuenalior annis): Miller-Gould prints *Silu-*
         anusque, Silvanus being a Roman forest god not out of
         place in this list. Silenus, however, makes a more usual
         companion for Pan and satyrs, and Ovid's *Fasti* 1.413–14
         addresses him in tellingly similar terms, speaking of the
         quenchless lust (*inexstinctae . . . libidinis*) which keeps
         him from aging (*quae te non sinit esse senem*).

649–50   *trimming leaves and shoots / . . . as if picking fruits*
         (frondator . . . uitisque putator / . . . lecturum poma
         putares): The second phrase might be more literally
         translated "so you would think he was about to gather
         apples." The clear point of interest, however, is in the two
         line-terminal words, which play on the double meaning
         of the verb *putare,* both "to think" and "to prune." Since
         anything similar is hardly to be found in English, I
         proffer a simple rhyme.

657   *But you are better yet! (†tantoque potentior†):* What
         exactly Vertumnus says to Pomona here may be hope-
         lessly garbled. Most simply, the phrase means "much
         more powerful," which Myers expands into "How much
         more capable are you." Various editors have conjectured
         any number of positively connoted comparative adjec-
         tives (*beatior, decentior, placentior, peritior,* etc.) praising
         Pomona's state, beauty, allure, skill, and so on. Ultimately,
         the only seeming certainty is that Pomona is *better* than
         the fruit on display, so I have made that the basis of my
         translation.

671   *And even bold Ulysses' prudent wife! (nec coniunx*
         prudens audacis Vlixi): Tarrant prints *nec coniunx*
         †*timidi aut audacis*† *Vlixi.* The obelized phrase is a clear
         contradiction ("timid or daring") and the most popular
         conjectures (*nimium tardantis*, Riese; *tarde remeantis*,
         Postgate) make plausible allusions to Ulysses' protracted
         journey home (cf. Lombardo: "the wife of late-returning
         Ulysses"). However, seeing as such emendations come at
         the expense of the fitting epithet *audax* for Ulysses, I
         have pursued Possanza's conjecture that the corrupted
         phrase instead contained a descriptor for Penelope, who
         is anyway the supposed focus of the comparison.
         Possanza's *prudens* is apt, if paleographically far-fetched,
         and I have tentatively adopted it as at least superior to
         the next-best option involving *audax*, Heinsius' *timidis*
         audacis (whence Melville's "brave when foes' hearts
         failed"), which strikes me as irrelevant to the
         sentence.

817   *world (orbem):* Tarrant prints *urbem* ("city"), meaning
         Rome. With one letter's difference, either is quite
         possible. I prefer the broader setting for its global view of
         Jupiter's power and Romulus' importance, though the
         specifying potential of *urbem* is not lost on me.

                              BOOK 15

47   *a lighter verdict (candidaque . . . sententia):* A partially
         preserved pun. The adjective *candida* can signify both
         paleness of hue and general favorability, much as the
         English "light" can apply as well to a thing as to the
         metaphorical weight of a judicial sentence.

104   *the lions' prey (uictibus . . . leonum):* Tarrant prints the
         obelized word *deorum* ("of the gods"), but the gods do
         not eat meat. The reading *leonum,* printed by Hardie, is
         relevant to the context and seemingly in line with
         Seneca's later quotation of the Pythagorean philosopher
         Sotion, *alimenta tibi leonum et uulturum eripio* ("I take

from you only the food of lions and vultures," *Ep.*
108.21). Another conjecture, *ferarum* ("of the beasts"),
would produce much the same result.

199   *Why, don't (Quid? non):* As Mark Twain advises in *A
Connecticut Yankee in King Arthur's Court,* in order to
differentiate a character through dialogue,

> you ought to give him a brogue, or at least a characteristic
> expletive; by this means one would recognize him as soon
> as he spoke, without his ever being named. It is a common
> literary device with the great authors. You should make
> him say, 'In this country, be jabers, came never knight
> since it was christened, but he found strange adventures,
> be jabers.' You see how much better that sounds.

The "be jabers" of Ovid's unnamed Pythagoras is clearly
the vocal tic *quid? non,* which recurs at 285 and 308. I
preserve this effect in my translation.

271   *churned by tremors deep in earth (aut imis commota
tremoribus orbis):* Though the result is not particularly
satisfying, I follow most translators in adopting Merkel's
conjecture in place of the widely obelized transmitted
reading †*antiquis tam multa*† *tremoribus orbis.* After all,
what does an ancient tremor matter now?

364   *down in a ditch (in scrobe deiecto):* Some translators stick
to the transmitted text, obelized by Tarrant (†*i quoque
delectos*†), describing the slaughtered bulls as "choice."
This makes sense but is ungrammatical in the sentence. I
have adopted Madvig's conjecture, which Tarrant deems
haud male ("not bad").

577   *a Tyrrhene diviner (Tyrrhenae gentis haruspex):* Some
translators render this phrase with a definitive article,
indicating that the Etruscan diviner is Tages himself,
rather than one who profited from his instruction.
Hardie tacitly opposes this reading. Since Tages is
generally depicted aging with extreme rapidity, even
dying at the end of the episode in the field, I have avoided
such an interpretation.

637–38   *You're seeking here what should be sought back home! /*
         Now, Roman, back at home seek (quod petis hinc propiore
         loco, Romane, petisses, / et pete nunc propiore loco): In
         addition to the clever repetition of verbs displayed in
         these lines, there is the obscure phrase *propiore loco*
         ("from / at / for a nearer place"). Commentators are
         divided as to whether this should refer to Epidaurus or
         Rome. While Epidaurus will be the destination of the
         questing Romans, it is barely nearer their home than
         Delphi (though, as Hardie notes, Epidaurus is on the way
         to Rome should one travel via the Peloponnese), whereas
         Rome is the destination of the god being sought. Favor-
         ing Rome, Hermann Fränkel freely renders these lines as
         "You might have found such relief in Rome itself, O
         Roman. It is high time for you to have in Rome itself the
         healer god. . . ." (224: 95n). My translation favors this
         latter option.

728   *And Ostia, the Tiber's mouth (Tiberinaque ad ostia):* The
         Latin merely means "the mouth of the Tiber," but the
         word used is *ostia,* which Roman readers would have
         recognized as the name of the port city there located.
         Since Ostia remains a well-known location in modern
         Italy, I have settled on a rendering that both translates
         and reproduces the word.

838   *Nor, till he match the ancient Pylian's age (nec, nisi cum*
         senior Pylios aequauerit annos): This reading is Heinsius'
         emendation, printed by Tarrant. The manuscripts
         transmit the dull *senior similes,* from which Housman
         cleverly conjectured *senior meritis,* printed and translated
         in Miller-Goold as "when his years have equalled his
         benefactions." This reading fits well with the passage as a
         whole, but Ovid makes similar allusions to Nestor's age
         with regard to the Emperor Augustus at *Trist.* 5.5.61–62
         and *Pont.* 2.8.41–42, a fact that seems, in my mind, to
         settle the matter.

ACKNOWLEDGMENTS

This book exists thanks to many patient people who took a chance and gave me one.

Excerpts from Book 1 previously appeared under the title "The Two Creations" in the Winter 2021 issue of *Arion: A Journal of Humanities and the Classics*. I am grateful that this work reached its first audience through its extremely considerate editors, Nicholas Poburko, Herbert Golder, and Brandon Jones.

There is neither world enough nor time to express my thanks to Tamsen Wolff, who taught me everything, who is the kind of person superlatives (*optima maxima*) were made to describe, and who lent me superlative encouragement when it counted most. Also to Christian Wolff, who gave the translation its first thumbs up and so sent me on my much merrier way.

I am similarly grateful to Eric A. Schmidt at the University of California Press for picking this project and for his spectacular care steering it out of the subjunctive and into reality. Also to LeKeisha Hughes for her attention and tolerance in the face of all my many problems, and my glorious copyeditor Catherine R. Osborne for sandblasting the volume into shape.

At Princeton's English department, I am delighted to thank Sophie Gee and especially Jeff Dolven for their key support, as well as R. N. Sandberg for being so very difficult to impress. At Princeton Classics, Robert A. Kaster and Andrew Feldherr for their thoughtful answers to my impertinent questions, and Johannes Haubold for introducing me to Ovid. Also Daniela Mairhofer for making me a Latinist, Yelena Baraz for keeping me one, Denis Feeney for taking a benign interest, and Melissa Haynes for being effortlessly great, but making efforts on my behalf all the same. At Princeton Music, I am indebted to the friendship and encouragement of Wendy Heller and Chris Parton. At

Molecular Biology, to Matt Montondo, Veronica Diaforli, Eric F. Wieschaus, and Owen Dunkley.

To my early teachers of myth and verse: Julie Light, Jon Fagerson, Jean Prokott, Bill Vieth, and Kathryn Kottke. To my supportive friends: Brennen Ohlemann, Charlie Leonard, John Hoffmeyer, Taylor Kang, Calvin Van Zytveld, Allison Young, Sam Weisberg, Maureen O'Malley, Caleb and Lucy Zarns, Lahiru Samarasinghe, Eliana Cohen-Orth, Karin Kraml, M Berry, Thomas Zhang, and especially Daniel Krane and his flowing red pen. To Maddi. To David and Vicki, and Xin and Greg. And to Red and Blue at *OSP*, for their wonderful work and my wonder at their working with me.

Finally, to the poor people who had to live with me for any part of the turbulent, plague-ridden time I was writing. Martin F. Semmelhack and Christina Kraml, at whose dining table this whole thing began. My parents, Peter and Ai Soucy, who sweetly didn't ask too many questions. My dear Ryan J. Skarphol, who took naps long enough for me to translate Book 8. And my grandmother, Sara Soucy, at whose dining table this whole thing ended, and who was first to read it.

But most of all to Timothy Ruszala, the ex-bassoonist and software engineer whose cranky, stubborn, withering, voluminous, infuriatingly thorough, and hilariously illustrated comments shaped this book in more ways than I care to remember—though he remembers, often reminds me, and is happy to tell you about it if you ask him. Tim demanded I acknowledge him with a poem, so I will:

> There once was a grumpy young Redditor,
> who cried, 'Fix the line as I said it, or
> your crimes against meter
> will surely defeat yer
> one chance of impressing an editor!'

If not for his stinting support and untimely contributions, this book would have been completed much sooner and been staggeringly worse in every way. But then, so indeed would my life.

SELECTED BIBLIOGRAPHY

TEXT AND COMMENTARIES

Anderson, W. S. 1972. *Ovid's Metamorphoses Books 6–10*. Norman: University of Oklahoma Press.

———. 1996. *Ovid's Metamorphoses Books 1–5*. Norman: University of Oklahoma Press.

Barchiesi, A. 2005. *Ovidio Metamorfosi*, vol. I. Milan: Arnoldo Mondadori Editore.

———, and A. Rosati. 2007. *Ovidio Metamorfosi*, vol. II. Milan: Arnoldo Mondadori Editore.

Bömer, F. 1969. *P. Ouidius Naso Metamorphosen: Kommentar*, vol. I. Heidelberg: C. Winter.

Griffin, A. H. F. 1997. "A Commentary on Ovid *Metamorphoses* Book XI." *Hermathena* 162/163: 1–290.

Hardie, P. R. 2015. *Ovidio Metamorfosi*, vol. VI. Milan: Arnoldo Mondadori Editore.

Hill, D. E. 1999. *Ovid Metamorphoses IX–XII*. Warminster: Aris & Phillips.

Hollis, A. S. 1970. *Ovid Metamorphoses Book VIII*. Oxford: Clarendon Press.

Hopkinson, N. 2000. *Ovid Metamorphoses Book XIII*. Cambridge: University Press.

Kenney, E. J. 2011. *Ovidio Metamorfosi*, vol. IV. Milan: Arnoldo Mondadori Editore.

Lee, A. G. 1953. *Metamorphoses, Book I*. Cambridge: Cambridge University Press.

Murphy, G. M. H. 1972. *Ovid Metamorphoses XI*. Oxford: Oxford University Press.

Myers, K. S. 2009. *Ovid Metamorphoses Book XIV*. Cambridge: Cambridge University Press.

Tarrant, R. J. 2004 *P. Ouidii Nasonis Metamorphoses*. Oxford: Oxford University Press.

ENGLISH TRANSLATIONS

Dryden, Congreve, Tate, Mainwaring, Vernon, et al. 1727. *Ovid's Metamorphoses, in Fifteen Books*. Dublin.

Golding, Arthur. 1567. *The. Xv. Booke of P. Ouidius Naso, entytuled Metamorphosis*. London.

Gregory, Horace. 1958. *Ovid: The Metamorphoses*. New York: Viking.

Humphries, Rolfe. 1955. *Ovid: Metamorphoses*. Bloomington: Indiana University Press.

Innes, Mary M. 1955. *Ovid: Metamorphoses*. London: Penguin.

Johnston, Ian. 2012. *Ovid: Metamorphoses*. http://johnstoniatexts.x1ohost.com/ovid/ovidtofc.html.

Kline, Anthony S. 2000. *Ovid: The Metamorphoses*. https://ovid.lib.virginia.edu/trans/Ovhome.htm.

Lombardo, Stanley. 2010. *Ovid: Metamorphoses*. Indianapolis: Hackett.

Mandelbaum, Allen. 1993. *The Metamorphoses of Ovid*. Boston: Harcourt Brace.

Martin, Charles. 2004. *Ovid: Metamorphoses*. New York: W. W. Norton.

Melville, A. D. 1986. *Ovid: Metamorphoses*. Notes by E. J. Kenney. Oxford: University Press.

Miller, F. J. 1916. *The Metamorphoses*. Cambridge, MA: Harvard University Press.

———. 1977. *Ovid: Metamorphoses*. Loeb Classical Library. Revised by G. P. Goold. Cambridge, MA: Harvard University Press.

More, Brookes. 1922. *Ovid's Metamorphoses*. Boston: The Cornhill Publishing Company.

Raeburn, David. 2004. *Ovid: Metamorphoses*. London: Penguin.

Sandys, George. 1632. *Ovid's Metamorphosis Englished*. Oxford.

Simpson, Michael. 2001. *The Metamorphoses of Ovid*. Amherst: University of Massachusetts Press.

Slavitt, David R. 1994. *The Metamorphoses of Ovid*. Baltimore: Johns Hopkins University Press.

Watts, A. E. 1954. *The Metamorphoses of Ovid*. Berkeley: University of California Press.

SECONDARY SOURCES

Ahl, F. 1985. *Metaformations: Soundplay and Wordplay in Ovid and Other Classical Poets.* Ithaca: Cornell University Press.

Anderson, W. S. 1966. "*Talaria* and Ovid *Met.* 10.591." *Transactions and Proceedings of the American Philological Association* 97: 1–13.

Arnott, W. 1964. "Notes on *Gauia* and *Mergus* in Latin Authors." *The Classical Quarterly* 14: 249–62.

Bailey, N. 1815. *Ovid's Metamorphoses in Fifteen Books; with the Notes of John Minellius, and Others, in English. With a Prose Version of the Author.* Dublin.

Barolsky, P. 2014. *Ovid and the Metamorphoses of Modern Art from Botticelli to Picasso.* New Haven: Yale University Press.

Feeney, D. 1991. *The Gods in Epic.* Oxford: Clarendon Press.

Feldherr, A. 2010. *Playing Gods.* Princeton: Princeton University Press.

Fränkel, H. 1945. *Ovid: A Poet Between Two Worlds.* Berkeley: University of California Press.

Fry, S. 2018. *Heroes: The Greek Myths Reimagined.* London: Michael Joseph.

Hamilton, E. 1942. *Mythology.* Boston: Little, Brown and Company.

Hardie, P. 2006. Review of *Ovid and the Moderns* by T. Ziolkowski. *Translation and Literature* 15, no. 2: 261–65.

Hill, D. E. 1973. "The Thessalian Trick." *Rheinisches Museum für Philologie* 116: 221–38.

Housman, A. E. 1890. "Emendations in Ovid's *Metamorphoses.*" In *The Classical Papers of A. E. Housman,* vol. I, edited by J. Diggle and F. R. D. Goodyear, 162–72. Cambridge: Cambridge University Press.

Ingleheart, J. 2018. *Masculine Plural: Queer Classics, Sex, and Education.* Oxford: University Press.

McCarter, S. 2018. "Rape, Lost in Translation." *Electric Literature,* May 1, 2018. https://electricliterature.com/rape-lost-in-translation.

McGrath, E. 1992. "The Black Andromeda." *Journal of the Warburg and Courtauld Institutes* 55: 1–18.

Miller, J. F. 1994. "The Memories of Ovid's Pythagoras." *Mnemosyne* 47: 473–87.

Penrose, W. D. 2014. "A World Away from Ours: Homoeroticism in the Classics Classroom." In *From Abortion to Pederasty,* edited by N. S. Rabinowitz and F. McHardy, 227–47. Columbus: Ohio State University Press.

Possanza, M. 2002. "Penelope in Ovid's *Metamorphoses* 14.671." *The American Journal of Philology* 123: 89–94.

———. 2005. Review of *P. Ouidi Nasonis Metamorphoses.* Oxford Classical Texts. *Bryn Mawr Classical Review,* June 27, 2005.

Ramírez de Verger, A. 2006. "Notas Críticas a las *Metamorfosis* de Ovidio (I 386, VI 399, VII 77, IX 653, XIII 602, XV 364)." *Revista de Lingüística y Filología Clásica* 74: 29–39.

Richlin, A. 1992. "Reading Ovid's Rapes." In *Pornography and Representation in Greece and Rome*, edited by A. Richlin, 158–79. Oxford: Oxford University Press.

Segal, C. 1969. *Landscape in Ovid's Metamorphoses.* Wiesbaden: F. Steiner Verlag.

———. 1998. "Ovid's Metamorphic Bodies: Art, Gender, and Violence in the *Metamorphoses.*" *Arion* 5, no. 3: 9–41.

Soucy, C. L. 2022. "Scrounging in a Land of Milk and Honey: Ovid's Golden Age." *Arion* 29, no. 3: 31–51.

Stone, M. H. 2014. "The Cubit: A History and Measurement Commentary." *Journal of Anthropology* (2014): 1–11.

Tarrant, R. J. 1995. "The Silence of Cephalus: Text and Narrative Technique in Ovid, *Metamorphoses* 7.685ff," *Transactions of the American Philological Association (1974–2014)* 125: 99–111.

Wordsworth, D. 2019. "Where Did 'Aconite' Spring From?" *The Spectator*, December 14. https://www.spectator.co.uk/article/where-did-aconite-spring-from.

Wieden Boyd, B., ed. 2002. *Brill's Companion to Ovid.* Leiden: Brill.

Ziolkowski, T. 2004. *Ovid and the Moderns.* Ithaca, NY: Cornell University Press.

Zuckerberg, D. 2018. *Not All Dead White Men.* Cambridge, MA: Harvard University Press.

GLOSSARY OF NAMES AND PLACES

This glossary of proper names includes all characters and locations of any importance in the poem, along with the patronymics, epithets, and other forms of antonomasia Ovid uses to refer to them. In polysyllabic names, accents mark the stressed syllable. A diaeresis (or *umlaut*) signals that adjacent vowels which might form a diphthong are pronounced separately.

Ábas (1)	king of Argos and father of Acrisius: 4.607, 673; 5.236; 15.164
Ábas (2)	a casualty in the fight between Perseus and Phineus (1): 5.126
Ábas (3)	a centaur: 12.306
Ábas (4)	a member of Diomedes' crew: 14.505
Abas' heir	see **Perseus**
Acástus	king of Thessaly and participant in the Calydonian Hunt: 8.306; 11.409
Achaéa	(adj. Achaean) a Peloponnesian region of Greece: 5.577; 15.293
	representing all allied **Greece** in the Trojan War: 12.71, 168; 13.91, 113, 137, 445; 14.191
Achaeménides	a member of Ulysses' crew: 14.160, 163, 167
Achelóïads	see **Sirens**
Achelóüs	the longest river in Greece, dividing Acarnania and Aetolia, where Calydon lies

591

	as the river's god, father to the Sirens and Callirhoë: 5.552; 8.549, 560, 614; 9.67, 96, 413 as the **Calydonian stream:** 8.728; 9.3
Achílles	the foremost Greek warrior of the Trojan War; son of Peleus and Thetis; grandson of Aeacus; slayer of Cygnus (3) and Hector: 8.309; 11.265; 12.73, 81, 126, 138, 151, 162, 163, 177, 191, 363, 582, 592, 608, 616; 13.30, 108, 130, 133, 134, 157, 179, 273, 281, 284, 298, 442, 447, 500, 502, 579, 597; 15.856 as **Aeacides:** 12.82, 95, 168, 602, 613; 13.505 as **Pelides:** 12.604, 619
Ácis	lover of Galatea; son of Faunus and grandson of the Symaethus; later god of the Sicilian river Acis (modern Jaci): 13.751, 757, 786, 861, 873, 884, 886, 896 as the **Symaethian hero:** 13.750
Ácmon	a member of Diomedes' crew: 14.485, 494, 496
Acoétes	a Lydian sailor and follower of Bacchus: 3.582, 696
Acrísius	king of Argos; son of Abas (1), father of Danaë, and grandfather of Perseus: 3.559; 4.607, 612; 5.69, 239
Actaéon	a Theban hunter; grandson of Cadmus and son of Autonoë: 3.230, 243, 244, 720, 721 as **Autonoë's son:** 3.198
Áctor (1)	father of Erytus: 5.79
Áctor (2)	father of Menoetes and grandfather of Patroclus: 8.306; 13.272
Adónis	lover of Venus, son of Myrrha and Cinyras (2): 10.533, 542, 681, 727 as **Cinyras' son:** 10.712, 731
Aeácides	patronymic of **Phocus**, son of Aeacus: 7.667 patronymic of **Peleus**, son of Aeacus: 9.388, 11.227, 246, 250, 274, 399; 12.365 patronymic of **Achilles**, grandson of Aeacus: 12.82, 95, 168, 602, 613; 13.505
Aéacus	king of Aegina (1); son of Aegina (2) and Jupiter; father of Telamon, Peleus, and Phocus; grandfather of Achilles; later a judge in the underworld: 7.472,

473, 478, 494, 506, 517, 667, 797, 864; 8.3; 9.436, 440;
13.25, 27, 33
    as **Asopus' grandson:** 7.484

Aeëtes   king of Colchis and father of Medea: 7.9, 170, 325

Aegéan Sea   the sea separating Greece from Asia Minor: 9.448;
11.663

Aégeus   king of Athens; grandson of Cecrops and father of
Theseus: 7.402, 419, 455; 8.174, 405, 559; 12.236, 344;
15.855
    as **Cecropid:** 7.502

Aegína (1)   (formerly known as **Oenopia**) an island near
Athens ruled by Aeacus: 7.474
    as **Oenopia:** 7.472, 473, 490

Aegína (2)   namesake of the island; daughter of Asopus and
mother of Aeacus: 7.616
    as **Asopus' child:** 6.113; 7.616

Aenéas   a Trojan hero; son of Anchises and Venus; ancestor
of the Romans; later deified as **Indiges:** 13.665, 681;
14.78, 116, 156, 170, 247, 441, 456, 581, 588, 601, 603;
15.439, 450, 762, 804, 806, 860
    as **Cytherea's son** or the **Cytherean hero:**
    13.624; 14.584
    as **Indiges:** 14.608

Aeneas' heir   see **Julius Caesar**

Aeólia   (adj. Aeolian) an archaic term for **Thessaly:** 7.357;
13.26

Aeólus (1)   the Keeper of the Winds; son of Hippotes; father
of Alcyone: 1.262; 9.507; 11.444, 573, 747; 14.223,
224, 232
    as **Hippotes' son:** 4.663; 11.431; 14.86; 15.706

Aeólus (2)   namesake king of Aeolia; father of Athamas,
Sisyphus, and Canace; grandfather of Cephalus:
4.486, 512; 6.115; 7.672

Aeolus' daughter   see **Alcyone**

Aeolus' girl   Canace, daughter of Aeolus (2); raped by Neptune:
6.115

Aeolus' son   see **Athamas**

Aeolus' sons	the Winds (**Auster, Boreas, Eurus,** and **Zephyrus**): 9.507
Aésacus	Trojan prince; son of Priam and Alexirhoë: 11.761, 791; 12.1
Aesculápius	god of healing; son of Coronis and Apollo as **Apollo's child:** 15.533, 639 as **Coronis' son:** 15.625 as the **Phoebean youth:** 15.642
Aéson	king of Iolcus and father of Jason: 7.60, 77, 84, 110, 132, 155, 162, 163, 252, 287, 292, 303; 8.411
Aethiópia	(adj. Aethiopian) a geographical term referring to either a country in Africa or a mythical land bordering India: 1.778; 2.236; 4.669; 15.320
Aétna	a volcanic mountain in Sicily, associated with Typhon: 2.221; 4.664; 5.352, 442; 8.260; 13.771, 868, 877; 14.1, 161, 188; 15.340
Aetólia	(adj. Aetolian) a region of central Greece home to Diomedes: 14.461, 527
Agamémnon	king of Mycenae and commander of the Greek forces at Troy; son of Atreus, brother of Menelaus, and father of Iphigenia: 13.185, 444; 15.855 as **Atreus' son:** 12.622; 13.230, 365, 655; 15.805 as **Atrides:** 13.189, 439 as **Tantalides:** 12.627
Agáve	a bacchant; sister of Autonoë and Ino, and mother of Pentheus: 3.725
Agénor	Phoenician king of Tyre; father of Cadmus and Europa: 2.858; 3.8, 51, 81, 90, 97, 257, 303; 4.563, 772
Agenor's heir	see **Perseus**
Aglaúros	daughter of Cecrops; sister of Herse and Pandrosos: 2.559, 739, 748, 785 as **Cecrops' child:** 2.797
Ájax (1)	("Ajax the Greater" or "Telamonian Ajax"): a Greek hero in the Trojan War known for his enormous shield; son of Telamon and cousin of Achilles: 13.2, 17, 28, 97, 142, 151, 155, 163, 218, 254, 305, 326, 338, 340, 390 as **Telamonius:** 13.194

	as **Telamon's child** or **son:** 12.625; 13.123, 231, 266, 321, 346
Ájax (2)	("Ajax the Lesser" or "Oilean Ajax"): a native of Naryx (1) and Greek hero in the Trojan War; son of Oileus and rapist of Cassandra: 12.622; 13.356 as **Naryx' hero:** 14.467 as **Oilean Ajax:** 12.622
Álba	(adj. Alban) a proto-Roman kingdom founded by Aeneas: 14.609, 612, 674
Alcáthoë	see **Megara**
Alcídes	see **Hercules**
Alcíthoë	daughter of Minyas and denier of Bacchus: 4.1, 274
Alcméne	queen of Argos; wife of Amphitryon and mother of Hercules: 8.544; 9.23, 276, 281, 312, 395 as the **Tirynthian wife:** 6.112
Alcýone	wife of Ceÿx and daughter of Aeolus (1): 11.384, 415, 422, 447, 458, 472, 544, 562, 567, 588, 628, 661, 674, 684 as **Aeolus' daughter:** 11.444, 573
Alémon	father of Myscelus: 15.19, 26, 48
Almighty	("*Omnipotens*"): an epithet of **Jupiter:** 1.154; 2.304, 402, 505; 3.336; 9.271; 14.816
Alphéüs	the longest river in the Peloponnese (and its god): 2.250; 5.487, 600
Althaéa	mother of Meleäger, wife of Oeneus, daughter of Thestius, and sister of Plexippus and Toxeus: 8.445 as **Thestia:** 8.452, 472
Ámathus	(adj. Amathúsian) an ore-rich city on Cyprus sacred to Venus: 10.220, 227, 531
Amazonian son	see **Hippolytus**
Ámmon (1)	the horned Egyptian god Amun, syncretized with Jupiter: 4.671; 5.18, 327; 15.309
Ámmon (2)	a boxer, twin of Broteas (1); follower of Perseus killed by Phineus (1): 5.107
Amphíon	lyre-playing king of Thebes (1); husband of Niobe: 6.222, 271, 402
Amphítryon	Theban general; husband of Alcmene and stepfather of Hercules: 6.111; 15.48

Apídanus	a river in Thessaly: 1.579; 7.228
Apóllo	god of music, poetry, healing, oracles, and archery; born on Delos to Jupiter and Latona, brother of Diana, father of Aesculapius and Orpheus; lover of Daphne, Coronis, Cyparissus, and Hyacinth; associated with ravens, Delphi, and Claros; also known as **Phoebus**, especially when conflated with the **Sun:** 1.474; 3.421; 7.389; 9.455; 10.209; 11.8, 155, 306, 339; 13.175, 631, 715; 15.533, 639

as **Aid-Bearer:** 1.523
as the **Delian:** 1.455; 5.329; 6.250; 9.332; 11.175;
    12.598; 13.649
as the **Delphian** or **Delphic one:** 2.544, 677; 9.332
as **Leto's son:** 6.384; 8.15; 11.193
as **Paean:** 1.566; 15.535
as **Phoebus** (adj. Phoebean): 1.451, 453, 490, 553,
    752; 2.23, 36, 110, 399, 545, 608, 628; 3.9, 10, 18,
    130, 151; 4.349; 5.389; 6.123, 215, 486; 7.324, 364;
    8.31, 350; 9.444, 663; 10.132, 163, 178, 197, 214;
    11.58, 165, 303, 310, 316, 594; 13.410, 501, 632, 640,
    677; 14.133, 141, 150, 416; 15.191, 419, 631, 642,
    742, 864
as **Smintheus:** 12.585

Apollo's heir	see **Caunus**
Apúlia	see **Iapygia**
Áquilo	see **Boreas**
Aquilo's sons	see **Calaïs** and **Zetes**
Arabia	(or **Áraby**; adj. Arabian): 1.62; 5.163; 10.478
Aráchne	a Lydian weaver and the daughter of Idmon: 6.6, 133, 150
	as the **Lydian:** 6.103
Arcádia	(adj. Arcadian) a region of the central Peloponnese; homeland of Ancaeus: 1.219, 689; 2.244, 405; 8.318, 391; 9.192; 15.332
Árcas	son of Callisto and Jupiter: 2.469, 496, 500
Árdea	a Rutulian city: 14.573, 580
Arethúsa	a spring in Sicily, formerly a Pisan nymph: 5.409, 497, 573, 599, 625, 642

Árgos

(adj. Argive) a city in the Peloponnese: 2.239; 3.560; 4.608; 6.415; 8.267; 9.276, 312; 15.19, 164, 276
Argive, representing all allied Greece in the Trojan War: 12.13, 12.149, 627; 13.61, 659; 14.443

Árgus

a hundred-eyed monster loyal to Juno; son of Arestor: 1.624, 625, 664, 670, 680, 720; 2.533

Arícia

a town in Latium (modern Ariccia): 15.488

Armenia

(adj. Armenian) a Caucasian country associated in the Roman imagination with tigers: 8.122; 15.86

Ascánius

see **Iulus**

Asia

Asia Minor, a large peninsula corresponding roughly with modern Turkey: 5.649; 9.448; 13.484

Asópus

father of Aegina (2) and grandfather of Aeacus: 6.113; 7.484, 616

Assýria

(adj. Assyrian) an empire of the ancient Near East: 5.60
as **Syria** (adj. Syrian): 5.145; 15.393

Astraéa

virgin goddess of justice; the final god to forsake the Earth: 1.150

Astýanax

infant son of Hector: 13.415

Atalánta

Tegean huntress from Nonacris; beloved of Meleäger; daughter of Schoeneus and wife of Hippomenes: 10.565, 598
as the **Nonacrian**: 8.426
as the **Tegean**: 8.318, 380

Áthamas

king of Boeotia; wife of Ino, uncle to Pentheus, son of Aeolus (2), father of Learchus and Melicertes: 3.564; 4.420, 467, 471, 489, 497; 13.919
as **Aeolus' son**: 4.512

Áthens

(adj. Attic) a city in Attica sacred to Minerva: 2.554, 721; 5.652, 661; 6.421, 423; 7.431, 486, 592, 507, 670, 681, 723; 8.170, 263; 11.92

Áthis

an Indian youth and follower of Phineus (1) killed by Perseus; son of Limnaeë and beloved of Lycabas (2): 5.48, 62, 72

Áthos

a mountain in Macedonia: 2.216; 11.555

Átlas	a Titan who holds up the sky; father of Maia, grandfather of Mercury, son of Iapetus; identified with the Atlas mountains of northwest Africa: 1.682; 2.296, 685, 704, 742, 834; 4.368, 628, 632, 644, 646, 653, 657, 773; 6.175; 8.627; 9.273; 15.149
	as **Iapetus' son**: 4.632
Atlas' heir	patronymic of **Mercury**: 2.704, 834; 8.627
	patronymic of **Hermaphroditus**: 4.368
Átreus	king of Mycenae, son of Pelops, father of Agamemnon and Menelaus: 12.622; 13.230, 359, 365, 655; 15.162, 805, 854
Atreus' son	see **Agamemnon**
Atreus' younger son	see **Menelaus**
Atrídes	see **Agamemnon**
Áttic	see **Athens**
Augústus Caesar	(63 BCE–14 CE) reigning Emperor of Rome at the time of Ovid's writing; adopted son of Julius Caesar and victor at Actium: 1.205, 562; 15.859, 868
	as **Caesar**: 1.202; 15.863, 864
Aúlis	a port town in Boeotia opposite Euboea: 12.10; 13.182
Ausónia	(adj. Ausonian) an ancient name for southern Italy; by extension, a poetic name for **Italy**: 5.349; 13.708; 14.7, 76, 320, 772, 786; 15.646, 693
Aúster	the South Wind; also known by his Roman name **Notus**: 1.67; 2.853; 5.285; 7.532, 660; 8.3; 11.191, 664; 12.510
	as **Notus**: 1.264
Australópithland	("*Pithecusae*," modern Ischia) a monkey-infested island in the gulf of Naples: 14.89
Autólycus	wily shapeshifting son of Chione and Mercury, husband of Mestra, grandfather of Ulysses: 8.738; 11.313
Autónoë	a bacchant; mother of Actaeon, sister of Ino and Agave: 3.198, 720
Avérnus	(adj. Avernal) a lake in southern Italy opening into the underworld: 5.540; 10.52

Bábylon   (adj. Babylónian) a Mesopotamian city on the Euphrates river: 2.248; 4.44, 99

Bácchus   (adj. Bacchic) god of wine and wildness; son of Jupiter and Semele: 3.317, 421, 518, 573, 629, 630, 691; 4.3, 11, 273, 416, 523, 765; 6.488, 588, 595, 597; 11.85, 134; 12.578; 13.639, 669; 15.114, 414

    as **Lenaeus:** 4.14; 11.132

    as **Liber:** 3.520, 528, 636; 4.17; 6.125; 7.294, 359; 8.177; 11.104; 13.650

    as **Lyaeus:** 4.12; 8.274; 11.67

    as **Semele's child:** 3.520; 9.642

Báctria   (adj. Bactrian) a region of Central Asia north of the Hindu Kush range: 5.135

Bálearic Islands   islands east of Spain known for their slingers: 2.727; 4.710

Báttus   an elderly Pylian herdsman: 2.688

Baúcis   elderly peasant; wife of Philemon: 8.631, 640, 681, 705, 714, 715

Bélides   fifty Libyan princesses damned to haul water eternally in bottomless jugs for the murder of their husbands; granddaughters of Belus: 4.463; 10.43

Bellóna   goddess of war: 5.155

Bithýnia   (adj. Bithynian) a Black Sea country in Asia Minor: 8.719

Boeótia   (adj. Boeotian) a region of central Greece including Thebes (1): 2.239; 3.13, 146; 5.313; 8.310; 12.10

Boötes   a northern constellation depicting a ploughman: 2.177; 8.207; 10.446

Bóreas   the North Wind, associated with Thrace; rapist of Orithyia; also known by his Roman name **Aquilo:** 1.65; 6.681, 702; 13.418; 15.471

    as **Aquilo:** 1.263, 328; 5.286; 7.4

    as the **North Wind:** 2.132

Bróteas (1)   a boxer, twin of Ammon (2); a follower of Perseus killed by Phineus (1): 5.107

Bróteas (2)   a Lapith: 12.261

Bubássus   (adj. Bubasid) a town in Caria in Asia Minor: 9.644

Búris	a city in Achaea destroyed along with Helice by a tsunami in 373 BCE: 15.294
Bútes	an Athenian envoy sent with Cephalus to Aegina (1); son of Pallas (2): 7.500 as **Pallas' son:** 7.500, 665, 666
Býblis	daughter of Miletus and Cyaneë; twin sister of Caunus: 9.453, 454, 455, 467, 534, 581, 643, 651, 656, 663 as **Miletus' daughter:** 9.635
Caiéta	a port town in southern Italy (modern Gaeta), named for the wet-nurse of Aeneas buried there: 14.443
Cádmus:	(adj. Cadmeian) founder of Thebes (1); son of Agenor, sister of Europa, husband of Harmonia, father of Semele, and grandfather of Actaeon and Pentheus: 3.3, 14, 24, 115, 131, 138, 174, 287; 4.470, 546, 572, 591, 592; 6.177, 217 as **Agenor's son:** 3.8, 51, 81, 90, 97; 4.563
Caéneus	Thessalian hero of dubious parentage; born as the girl **Caénis**, raped by Neptune: 8.305; 12.172, 173, 179, 189, 195, 459, 469, 471, 477, 489, 496, 514, 530 as **Atrax' son:** 12.208 as the **Phyllean:** 12.479
Caésar	cognomen referring to **Augustus Caesar:** 1.202; 15.863, 864 cognomen referring to **Julius Caesar:** 15.746, 750, 845
Caïcus	a river in the west of Asia Minor (modern Bakırçay): 2.243; 12.111; 15.278
Cálaïs	a member of Jason's crew; winged son of Boreas and Orithyia: 6.716 as **Aquilo's son:** 7.4
Callíope	the **Muse** of epic poetry; mother of Orpheus: 5.339
Callírhoë	daughter of Acheloüs; avenging widow of Alcmaeon: 9.413, 431
Callísto	Parrhasian huntress of Diana raped by Jupiter; mother of Arcas as **Parrhasis:** 2.460
Cálydon	(adj. Calydónian) city in Aetolia menaced by a monstrous boar; built on the Euenus and near the

Acheloüs; home of Oeneus, Meleäger, and Deianira; associated with Diomedes: 6.414; 8.269, 324, 495, 526, 527, 728; 9.3, 111, 148; 14.513, 769

Calydonian stream   see **Acheloüs**

Caménae   Roman goddesses identified as the Italian Muses: 14.433; 15.482

Cánens   ("Singing") daughter of Janus, wife of Picus: 14.338, 381, 383, 417, 434

    as **Janus' child:** 14.381

Capáneus   Greek hero of immense strength; one of the Seven Against Thebes (1): 9.404

Cápitol   (adj. Capítoline) one of Rome's seven hills; site of the Temple of Jupiter and endpoint of Triumphal parades: 1.561; 2.538; 15.589, 828, 842

Cária   (adj. Carian) a region bordering Lycia in Asia Minor: 4.297; 9.645

Cárpathos   (adj. Carpáthian) an island in the Sporades, home to Proteus: 11.249

Carthaéa   (adj. Carthaean) a city on the isle of Ceos: 7.368; 10.109

Cárthage   Phoenician city in north Africa; home to Corythus (1): 5.125

Cassíope   wife of Cepheus and mother of Andromeda: 4.736

Cástor   son of Leda and Tyndareus and twin of Pollux; a noted horseman and participant in the Calydonian Hunt: 12.401

Cástrum   the port town of Ardea in ancient Latium: 15.727

Caúcasus   a mountain range in Scythia: 2.225; 8.797

Caúlon   a city in southern Italy: 15.705

Caúnus   son of Miletus and Cyaneë; twin brother of Byblis; grandson of Meander: 9.453, 488, 489, 581

    as **Apollo's heir:** 9.455
    as **Meandrius:** 9.574

Caÿster   a river in the west of Asia Minor frequented by swans (modern Küçük Menderes): 2.253; 5.387

Cébren   a river (and its god) near Troy; father of Hesperia: 11.769

Cecrópid	patronymic of **Aegeus**, grandson of Cecrops: 7.502
Cécrops	snake-bodied first king of Athens; father of Herse, Pandrosos, and Aglauros: 2.555, 784, 797, 806; 6.71, 446; 8.550
Cecrops' heir	see **Theseus**
Céladon (1)	a native of Mendes killed in the fight between Perseus and Phineus (1): 5.144
Céladon (2)	a Lapith: 12.250
Celénnia	an unidentified location in southern Italy: 15.704
Cenaéum	a cape on the isle of Euboea; site of a shrine to Jupiter: 9.137
céntaurs	a race of man-horse hybrids, all but Chiron being descended from Ixion and the cloud nymph Nephele; they include Nessus: 2.636; 9.112, 191; 12.219, 537
Céos	(adj. Cean) an island in the Cyclades home to Cyparissus: 7.368; 10.121
Céphalus	an Athenian prince and envoy; beloved of Dawn, husband of Procris, and grandson of Aeolus (2); owner of Hurricane (2): 6.681; 7.493, 495, 501, 512, 665, 666, 687, 865; 8.4 as **Aeolus' grandson**: 7.672
Céphene	an Aethiopian people ruled by Cepheus: 5.2, 97
Cépheus	king of Aethiopia; husband of Cassiope, father of Andromeda, brother of Phineus (1): 4.669, 736, 764, 769; 5.13, 42, 43
Cephísus	a river in Boeotia; father of Narcissus: 1.369; 3.20, 343, 351; 7.388, 438
Cérberus	the three-headed snake-haired guard-dog of the underworld; son of Echidna: 4.450, 501; 7.411; 9.185; 14.65
Céres	goddess of agriculture and harvests; mother of Proserpine and lover of Iasion: 1.123; 5.109, 341, 343, 376, 415, 533, 572, 655, 659; 7.439; 8.274, 741, 771, 778, 785, 815; 9.422; 10.74, 431; 11.112, 121, 122; 13.639 as **Deo**: 6.114; 8.758

Céÿx	king of Trachis; son of the Morning Star, brother of Daedalion, and husband of Alcyone: 11.271, 411, 461, 543, 544, 560, 587, 653, 658, 673, 685, 727, 739 as the **Morning Star's son:** 11.346
Chaönia	(adj. Chaonian) northwestern region of Epirus, home to Molpeus and near the Molossians; known for a distinctive variety of oak tree: 5.162; 10.90; 13.717
Cháos (1)	the primordial formlessness from which the universe was made: 1.8; 2.299
Cháos (2)	a part of the underworld: 10.30; 14.404
Cháriclo	a nymph; wife of Chiron and mother of Ocyrhoë: 2.636
Charýbdis	a monstrous whirlpool between Italy and Sicily, opposite Scylla (1): 7.63; 8.121; 13.730; 14.75
Chersídamas	a Trojan killed by Ulysses: 13.260
Chimaéra	a fire-breathing lion-goat-snake hybrid monster native to Lycia: 6.339; 9.647
Chíone	daughter of Daedalion; raped by Mercury and Apollo: 11.301
Chíos	(adj. Chian) a large island in the north Aegean Sea: 3.598
Chíron	an immortal centaur; son of Saturn and Philyra, husband of Chariclo, and father of Ocyrhoë; foster-father of Aesculapius: 2.630; 6.127 as **Philyra's son:** 2.676; 7.352
Chrómis (1)	a follower of Phineus (1) in the fight against Perseus: 5.103
Chrómis (2)	a centaur killed by Pirithoüs: 12.333
Chrómius	a Trojan killed by Ulysses: 13.257
Chrýse	a town near Troy sacred to Apollo and sacked by Achilles: 13.174
Cícones	(or **Cicónians**) a Thracian tribe whose women killed Orpheus: 6.710; 11.3; 15.313
Cilícia	(adj. Cilician) a region of southern Asia Minor home to the Taurus range: 2.217

Cílla	a town near Troy sacred to Apollo and sacked by Achilles: 13.174
Cimmérians	an ancient proto-historic tribe inhabiting Scythia: 11.592
Cimólus	a chalk-rich island in the Cyclades: 7.463
Cínyps	(adj. Cinýphian; modern Wadi Ka'am) a small river in modern Libya: 5.123; 7.272
Cínyras (1)	a man whose daughters turned to marble: 6.98
Cínyras (2)	king of Cyprus, son of Paphos, father of Myrrha and Adonis: 10.298, 338, 343, 356, 361, 369, 380, 437, 464, 472, 712, 731
Cípus	a legendary Roman general: 15.565, 580, 581, 609, 615
Circaéan fields	a promontory in Latium (modern Cape Circeo) home to Circe: 14.348
Círce	an amorous sorceress; daughter of the Sun (Titan) and lover of Ulysses: 4.205; 13.968; 14.10, 25, 68, 71, 247, 248, 253, 290, 294, 312, 376, 399; 15.718
	as the **Sun's daughter:** 14.346
	as **Titaness:** 14.14
	as **Titania:** 14.382, 438
Cithaéron	a mountain in Boeotia sacred to Apollo: 2.224; 3.702
City, the	see **Rome**
Clánis (1)	brother of Clytius; casualty of the fight between Phineus (1) and Perseus: 5.140, 143
Clánis (2)	a centaur: 12.379
Cláros	a city an Ionia, home to an Oracle of Apollo: 1.516; 11.413
Cleónae	a city in the Argolid: 6.418
Clítor	a town in Arcadia: 15.322
Clubman	see **Hercules**
Clýmene	mother of Phaëthon, lover of the Sun, and wife of Merops: 1.757, 766; 2.19, 37, 43, 333; 4.204
Clýmenus	a follower of Phineus (1) in the fight against Perseus: 5.98
Clýtië	a sea-nymph in love with the Sun: 4.206, 234, 256

Clýtius	brother of Clanis (1); a casualty of the fight between Phineus (1) and Perseus: 5.140, 143
Clýtus (1)	a follower of Phineus (1) killed by Perseus: 5.88
Clýtus (2)	an Athenian envoy sent with Cephalus to Aegina (1); son of Pallas (2): 7.500 as **Pallas' son:** 7.500, 665, 666
Cnídos	a city on the Carian coast: 10.531
Cócalus	a Sicilian king who offered refuge to Daedalus: 8.261
Coéranos	a Trojan killed by Ulysses; son of Iphitus: 13.257
Coéus	a Titan and the father of Latona: 6.185, 366
Cólchis	(adj. Colchian) a Black Sea kingdom home to Medea: 7.120, 296, 300, 330, 348, 394; 13.24
Cólophon	a city on the Lydian coast home to Idmon: 6.8
Cómbe	a native of Pleuron transformed into a bird; daughter of Ophius: 7.383
Cométes	a Lapith: 12.284
Córinth	a city on the Isthmus of Corinth: 2.240; 5.407; 6.413; 7.392; 15.507
Corónae	twin Theban boys sprung from the ashes of Orion's daughters: 13.698
Coróneus	a king of Phocis; father of Crow: 2.569
Corónis	a princess of Larissa, lover of Apollo, and mother of Aesculapius: 2.543, 599; 15.625
Corýcian	a cave on Mount Parnassus: 1.320
Córythus (1)	a Carthaginian participant in the fight between Phineus (1) and Perseus: 5.124
Córythus (2)	Trojan son of Paris: 7.361
Córyth (3)	a Lapith youth: 12.290, 292
Cos	(adj. Coan) an island in the Sporades: 7.363
Crágus	a mountain in Lycia: 9.646
Crántor	squire to Peleus: 12.362, 367
Crátaeis	mother of Scylla (1): 13.749
Cráthis	a river in southern Italy near Croton (modern Crati): 15.315

Crenaéus	a centaur: 12.313
Crete	(adj. Cretan) a large Mediterranean island; home to Minos and the Minotaur, birthplace of Zeus: 3.2, 208, 223; 7.434, 490; 8.22, 43, 99, 118, 152, 183; 9.667, 701, 717, 735; 13.706; 15.540, 541
Crímisa	a town in southern Italy: 15.52
Crócale	a Theban attendant of Diana: 3.169
Crócus	a young man transformed into a flower: 4.283
Crómmyon	(adj. Crommyónian) a small town near Corinth: 7.435
Cróton	a hospitable settler; namesake of the town in southern Italy: 15.15, 55
Crow	daughter of Coroneus transformed into a crow; attendant of Minerva: 2.547
Cthónius	a centaur killed by Nestor: 12.441
Cúmae	(adj. Cumaéan) a city on the Italian coast home to the Sibyl, originally a colony of Euboea: 14.103, 121, 135; 15.712 as a **Euboean town:** 14.155

Cúpid	winged archer god of love; son of Venus: 1.454; 4.321; 5.367; 7.73; 9.482, 544; 10.311
	    as **Love:** 4.759; 5.374; 7.13; 10.26, 29
	    as **Venus' son:** 1.464

Cúres	(adj. Curian) a Sabine town in Italy home to Numa (modern Fara in Sabina): 14.778; 15.7
Curétes	a Cretan tribe devoted to Jupiter: 4.282
Curia	the Senate House in Rome; site of Julius Caesar's assassination: 15.802
Cýane	a spring (and its nymph) at Syracuse: 5.409, 411, 426, 465
Cyáneë	daughter of Meander; mother of Byblis and Caunus: 9.452
Cýbele	a cult mother goddess known as the **Mother** of the Gods: 10.103, 704 as the (**Gods' Great**) **Mother:** 10.103, 687, 697; 14.536, 546

Cýclades	an island archipelago in the Aegean Sea: 2.264
Cýclops	(pl. Cyclópes) a race of one-eyed giants on Sicily who forge Jupiter's thunderbolts: 1.259; 3.305; 14.2; 15.93
	spec. **Polyphemus:** 13.744, 755, 757, 780, 860, 876, 882; 14.174, 249
Cýgnus (1)	king of Liguria; son of Sthenelus (1), lover of Phaëthon: 2.368
Cýgnus (2)	son of Hyrië and lover of Phylius: 7.372
Cýgnus (3)	a Trojan hero; son of Neptune: 12.72, 75, 76, 101, 122, 125, 136, 150, 164, 170
Cýllarus	a centaur beloved of Hylonome: 12.393, 408, 420
Cylléne	a mountain in Arcadia; birthplace of Mercury: 1.217; 5.609; 7.386; 11.304
Cyllénius	see **Mercury**
Cymélus	a Lapith: 12.454
Cýnthia	see **Diana**
Cýnthus	a mountain in Delos identified with Diana (Cynthia): 2.222; 6.204
Cyparíssus	a Cean youth beloved of Apollo: 10.120, 130
Cýprus	(adj. Cypriot) a large island off the coast of Asia Minor sacred to Venus: 10.230, 270, 645, 719; 14.696 as **Paphos** (adj. Paphian): 10.530
Cythéra	an island south of the Peloponnese and the birthplace of Venus (Cytherea): 10.530
Cytheréa(n)	see **Venus**
Cytherea's son	see **Aeneas**
Cytherean hero	see **Aeneas**
Cýthnus	an island in the Cyclades: 5.252
Cytórus	(adj. Cytoran) a mountain in Asia Minor famous for its boxwood: 4.311, 6.132
Daedálion	son of the Morning Star, brother of Ceÿx, and father of Chione: 11.295, 340
Daédalus	Athenian architect and inventor at the court of Crete; father of Icarus (1): 8.159, 166, 183, 241, 250, 260; 9.742

Damasíchthon	a son of Niobe: 6.254
Dánaän	a poetic name for the allied Greeks at Troy: 12.68; 13.327; 14.470
Dánaë	mother of Perseus and daughter of Acrisius raped by Jupiter in a shower of gold: 4.612; 5.1; 6.112; 11.117
Dánube	the longest river in Europe: 2.250
Dáphne	a nymph beloved of Apollo; daughter of the Peneus: 1.453, 490 as **Peneus' daughter:** 1.504
Dáphnis	a shepherd on Mount Ida: 4.276
Dárdan or Dardánian	a poetic name for the Trojans: 13.335, 412; 15.432, 767
Dardanian bard	see **Helenus**
Daúlis	a town in ancient Phocis: 5.276
Daúnus	king of the Iapygians or Apulians; father-in-law to Diomedes: 14.459, 510
Dawn	saffron-robed goddess of dawn; mother of Memnon, wife of Tithonus, and daughter of the Titan Pallas: 2.112, 144; 3.150; 4.630; 5.440; 6.48; 7.100, 210, 701, 721, 835; 9.795; 11.296, 598; 13.576, 594, 621; 15.665 as **Pallantis:** 9.421; 15.190, 701
Déianira	a Calydonian princess; daughter of Oeneus, sister of Meleäger, wife of Hercules, and beloved of Acheloüs: 9.8, 138 as **Alcmene's son's new wife:** 8.544
Deïone	mother of Miletus: 9.443
Deïphobus	a Trojan hero: 12.547
Délian	an epithet of **Apollo:** 1.455; 5.329; 6.250; 9.332; 11.175; 12.598; 13.649 an epithet of **Diana:** 5.638
Délos	(formerly **Ortygia**) a once "floating" isle in the Cyclades ruled by Anius; birthplace of Apollo and Diana: 3.597; 6.191, 334; 8.221; 15.541 as **Ortygia:** 1.694; 15.337
Délphi	a city in Phocis home to an Oracle of Apollo; believed to be the center of the universe: 1.515; 10.168; 11.304, 413; 15.144, 630

Delphian or **Delphic one**	see **Apollo**
Demóleon	a centaur: 12.356, 369
Déo	see **Ceres**
Deo's child	see **Proserpine**
Dércetis	a Syrian fertility goddess (Atargatis); mother of Semiramis: 4.44
Deucálion	flood survivor; son of Prometheus and husband of Pyrrha: 1.319, 350; 7.356
	as **Prometheus' son:** 1.390
Día	see **Naxos**
Diána	virgin goddess of the hunt and the moon, noted for her loose style of dress; born near Mount Cynthus on Delos to Jupiter and Latona; sister of Apollo and granddaughter of the Titan Coeus; also known as **Phoebe:** 1.487, 695; 2.425, 451; 3.156, 180, 185, 252; 4.304; 5.376, 619; 6.414; 7.746; 8.272, 353, 395, 579; 9.90; 10.536; 11.322; 12.35; 13.186; 14.331; 15.196, 489
	as **Cynthia:** 2.464; 7.754; 15.538
	as the **Delian:** 5.638
	as **Dictynna:** 2.441
	as **Latonia:** 1.696; 8.542
	as **Leto's daughter:** 8.277
	as the **Moon:** 2.208; 7.207; 15.790
	as the **Ortygian:** 1.694
	as **Phoebe:** 1.12, 477; 2.415, 723; 5.329; 6.216; 12.36; 15.549
	as **Titania:** 3.173
	as **Trivia:** 2.416
Dictýnna	see **Diana**
Díctys (1)	a member of Acoetes' crew: 3.615
Díctys (2)	a centaur: 12.334, 337
Dídyme	a tiny island near Syros: 7.469
Díndyma	a mountain in Phrygia: 2.223
Diomédes	an Aetolian native and Greek hero at Troy and companion of Ulysses; later a settler in Iapygia; son of Tydeus, grandson of Oeneus, and son-in-law of Daunus: 13.101, 103, 242; 14.458, 492; 15.806

	as **Aetolia's hero:** 14.461
	as **Oeneus' grandson:** 14.512
	as **Tydeus' son:** 12.624; 13.68, 239, 351
	as **Tydides:** 15.769
Dírce	a spring in Boeotia near Thebes (1): 2.239
Dis	god of the underworld; husband of Proserpine, son of Saturn, brother of Jupiter: 4.438, 511; 5.384, 395, 569; 15.535
	as **Orcus:** 14.116
	as **Saturn's son:** 5.420
Dodóna	(adj. Dodonaean) a city in Epirus home to an Oracle of Jupiter noted for its oaks: 7.623; 13.716
Dólon	a Trojan spy captured by Ulysses and Diomedes: 13.100, 244
Dolópia	(adj. Dolopian) a region between Epirus and Thessaly ruled by Amyntor: 12.364
Don	a Black Sea river in modern Russia: 2.242
Dóris	a sea-goddess; wife of Nereus and mother of the Nereids: 2.11, 269; 13.742
Dórylas (1)	a rich Nasamonian follower of Perseus gruesomely killed in the fight with Phineus (1): 5.129, 130
Dórylas (2)	a centaur gruesomely killed by Peleus: 12.380
Drýads	wood nymphs: 3.507; 6.453; 8.746, 778; 11.49; 14.326
Drýas	a Lapith and participant in the Calydonian Hunt: 8.306; 12.290, 296, 311
Drýope	Oechalian maiden; daughter of Eurytus (2), sister of Iole, husband of Andraemon (1), mother of Amphissos: 9.330, 336, 342, 364
Dulíchian	see **Ulysses**
Dulichium	an island near Ithaca ruled by Ulysses: 13.711
Dýmas	king of Phrygia; father of Hecuba and grandson of Hector: 11.761; 13.620
Earth	the personified goddess of the earth; mother of Giants, Python, Typhon, and the Titans: 1.13, 102, 157, 394, 434; 2.272, 301; 5.321, 315, 325; 6.396; 7.196; 15.91

Ébro	a Spanish river in the extreme west: 7.324
Echéclus	a centaur: 12.451
Echémmon	an Arabian follower of Phineus (1) in the fight with Perseus: 5.163, 169
Echídna	snake-woman hybrid monster; mother of Cerberus: 4.501; 7.408
Echínades	an island archipelago off the coast of Acarnania: 8.589
Echíon (1)	Theban settler and hero sprung from dragon's teeth sown by Cadmus; father of Pentheus: 3.126, 513, 526, 701; 10.686
Echíon (2)	participant in the Calydonian Hunt: 8.308, 345
Echo	a nymph in love with Narcissus: 3.357, 359, 380, 386, 493, 501, 507
Eëtion	king of Cilician Thebes (2): 12.110
Egéria	a nymph and wife of Numa: 15.548
Egypt	a country in Africa on the river Nile: 5.323
Egyptian wife	Cleopatra VII (69–30 BCE); queen of Egypt and wife of Roman commander Mark Antony defeated by Augustus at the Battle of Actium in 31 BCE: 15.826
Élatus	father of Caeneus / Caenis: 12.189, 497
Eleúsis	a town in Attica; site of the Eleusinian mysteries honoring Ceres: 7.439
Élis	(adj. Elean) a region in the western Peloponnese containing the river Alpheus; site of the Olympics: 2.680; 5.487, 494, 576, 607; 8.312; 9.187; 12.550; 14.325
Elpénor	a tippling member of Ulysses' crew: 14.252
Élymus	a centaur killed by Caeneus: 12.461
Elýsium	the land of the blessed in the underworld: 14.111 as the **Fields of Faith**: 11.62
Emáthia	(adj. Emathian) a plain in Macedonia home to the daughters of Pierus: 5.313, 669; 12.463; 15.824
Emáthion	a casualty in the fight between Perseus and Phineus (1): 5.100
Enaésimus	a participant in the Calydonian Hunt and son of Hippocoön: 8.362

Enípeus	a river in Thessaly: 1.580; 6.116; 7.230
Énnomus	a Trojan killed by Ulysses: 13.261
Eoüs	a flying horse of the Sun: 2.153
Épaphus	son of Io and Jupiter, grandson of Inachus, and playmate of Phaëthon: 1.748, 757 as the **heir to Inachus**: 1.753
Epidaúrus	(adj. Epidaurian) a city in the Argolid home to Aesculapius: 3.279; 7.436; 15.643, 723
Epimétheus	brother of Prometheus and father of Pyrrha: 1.391
Epírus	a region in northern Greece known for its large bulls: 8.283; 13.720
Epópeus	member of Acoetes' crew: 3.618
Épytus	an Alban king: 14.613
Erasínus	a river in Achaea (modern Vouraikos): 15.275
Eréchtheus	king of Athens; son of Pandion and father of Procris and Orithyia: 6.677, 700; 7.697; 8.548
Eréchthida	see **Procris**
Erichthónius	earth-sprung son of Vulcan: 2.553; 9.424 as the **Lemnian child**: 2.756
Erídanus	a western river, possibly the Italian **Po**; site of Phaëthon's fall: 2.324, 371
Erigdúpus	a Pelethronian centaur: 12.452
Erígone	daughter of Icarus (2) raped by Bacchus; later made a star for her filial piety: 6.126; 10.451
Erycína	see **Venus**
Erymánthus	a river and mountain in Achaea: 2.244, 499; 5.608
Erysíchthon	king of Thessaly; son of Triops and father of Mestra: 8.739, 779, 823, 840 as **Triops' son**: 8.751
Érytus	a follower of Phineus (1) killed by Perseus; son of Actor (1): 5.79
Éryx (1)	a city and mountain in Sicily sacred to Venus: 2.221; 14.85
Éryx (2)	a follower of Phineus (1) in the fight against Perseus: 5.195

Etrúria	(adj. Etruscan or Tuscan) a region of central Italy populated by Rutulians and Tyrrhenes (2): 3.624; 14.223, 452, 615
Euágrus	a Lapith: 12.290, 293
Euboéa	(adj. Euboean) a large island east of mainland Greece opposite Anthedon and Aulis: 7.232; 9.219, 226; 13.182, 660, 905; 14.4, 155
Euboean town	see **Cumae**
Euénus	a river near Calydon in Aetolia: 8.528; 9.104
Euíppe	Paeonian wife of Pierus: 5.303
Eumélus	father who killed his son for impiety to Apollo: 7.390
Euménides	see the **Furies**
Eumólpus	an Athenian priest of Apollo: 11.92
Euphórbus	Trojan son of Panthous, supposedly reincarnated as Pythagoras: 15.161
Euphrátes	a river bounding Mesopotamia: 2.248
Európa	Tyrian princess raped by Jupiter; daughter of Agenor, sister of Cadmus, and mother of Minos; namesake of Europe: 6.104; 8.24, 120
	as **Agenor's child:** 2.858
Europe	5.649
Eurótas	a river near Sparta: 2.247; 10.169
Eúrus	the East Wind: 1.62; 2.160; 7.659, 660, 664; 8.2; 11.481; 15.604
Eurýdice	wife of Orpheus: 10.31, 48; 11.63, 66
Eurýlochus	a member of Ulysses' crew: 14.252, 286
Eurýmides	patronymic of Telemus, son of Eurymus: 13.771
Eurýnome	mother of Leucothoë: 4.209, 218
Eurýnomus	a centaur: 12.310
Eurýpylus (1)	king of Cos: 7.363
Eurýpylus (2)	a Greek hero at Troy: 13.357
Eurýstheus	king of Tiryns; son of Sthenelus (2); enemy and master of Hercules: 9.203, 273
Eurýtion	a participant in the Calydonian Hunt: 8.311

Eúrytus (1)	father of Hippasus (1): 8.371
Eúrytus (2)	father of Dryope and Iole, grandfather of Amphis-sos: 9.356, 396
Eúrytus (3)	a particularly lustful centaur: 12.218, 223, 227
Eurytus' son	see **Hippasus (1)**
Evánder	Roman culture hero; king of Pallantium in Italy and ally of Aeneas: 14.457
Exádius	a centaur: 12.266
Fárfa	a river in Latium: 14.330
fauns	see **satyrs**
Faúnus	a Roman forest god identified with **Pan**; father of Acis and Latinus (1): 6.329; 13.750; 14.449
Favónius	see **Zephyrus**
Fields of Faith	see **Elysium**
flint-wort	aconite or wolfsbane, a toxic flowering plant: 7.419
Forum	a public plaza for civic activity in the center of Rome: 15.842
Furies	three winged goddesses of vengeance, including Tisiphone; daughters of Night; euphemistically known as the **Eumenides** ("kindly ones"): 1.241, 725; 4.490; 6.430, 431; 9.410; 11.14
	as the **Eumenides**: 8.482; 10.46
	as the **Sisters Three**: 10.314
Galánthis	attendant of Alcmene: 9.306, 316
Galatéa	a Nereid; lover of Acis and beloved of Polyphemus: 13.738, 788, 798, 839, 863, 869, 880, 898
Gallia	(adj. Gallic) a region in modern France with prized hunting dogs: 1.534
Gánges	a river in India (and its god); father of Limnaeë: 2.250; 4.21; 5.48
Gánymede	a Trojan prince; son of Laömedon and beloved of Jupiter: 10.155; 11.756
Gargáphië	a valley and prized bathing spot of Diana: 3.156
Giants	monsters born from the Earth: 1.152, 156, 183; 5.320; 10.150
	spec. **Typhon**: 5.346; 14.1

Glaúcus	a fisherman from Anthedon transformed into a merman; lover of Scylla (1): 7.233; 13.906; 14.11, 37, 68
Górge	daughter of Oeneus and sister of Meleäger; mother of Tydeus: 8.544
Górgons	snake-haired daughters of Phorcys whose gaze turned the viewer to stone: 4.779 spec. **Medusa:** 4.618, 699, 801; 5.180, 196, 202, 209
Gortýna	(adj. Gortynian) a town in ancient Crete, an island noted for its archers: 7.778
Graces	three benevolent sister goddesses associated with weddings: 6.429
Gradívus	see **Mars**
Granícus	a river beginning at Mount Ida (modern Biga); mother of Alexirhoë: 11.763
Grecian bride	see **Helen**
Greece	(adj. Greek or Grecian): 1.602; 3.512; 4.17, 538, 606; 5.306; 7.50, 57, 133, 142, 214; 8.268; 12.7, 64, 600, 609, 612; 13.29, 59, 87, 181, 198, 241, 281, 325, 402, 414, 572; 14.325, 334, 467, 474, 561; 15.645
Grýneus	a centaur: 12.259, 268
Gyáros	an island in the Cyclades: 5.252; 7.469
Haédi	stars whose setting was associated with stormy weather: 14.711
Haémus	a mountain range in Thrace associated with Orpheus; formerly a Thracian king and husband of Rhodope: 2.219; 6.87; 10.77
Halcyóneus	a Bactrian follower of Phineus (1) in the fight against Perseus: 5.135
Halésus	an Emathian Lapith: 12.463
Hálius	a Trojan killed by Ulysses: 13.259
Hárpies	bird-woman monsters, including **Aëllo** as **wingèd maids:** 7.4
Hébe	goddess of youth; daughter of Juno and wife of Hercules: 9.401 as **Jove's step-child-in-law:** 9.416
Hébrus	a river in Thrace: 2.257; 11.51

Hécate	(adj. Hecataéan) goddess of magic often shown in triplicate; daughter of Perses: 6.140; 7.74, 174, 194, 241; 14.44, 405
Héctor	the foremost Trojan warrior and prince; son of Priam and Hecuba, grandson of Dymas, and father of Astyanax: 11.759, 760; 12.4, 68, 69, 75, 76, 447, 548, 591, 607; 13.7, 82, 178, 275, 279, 385, 426, 427, 486, 487, 513, 666 as **Dymas' grandson:** 11.761
Hécuba	queen of Troy; daughter of Dymas, wife of Priam, and mother of Hector, Polyxena, and Polydorus: 13.423, 549, 556, 575, 577 as **Dymas' daughter:** 13.620
Hélen	proverbially beautiful wife of Menelaus whose abduction by Paris incited the Trojan War; daughter of Leda and Tyndareus: 13.198; 14.670 as the **Grecian bride:** 12.609 as **Tyndareus' child:** 15.231
Hélenus	Trojan prince and prophet; son of Priam: 13.98, 722; 15.438, 451 as the **Dardanian bard:** 13.335 as the **Phrygian prophet:** 13.721
Héliad(e)s	(adj. Heliádic) daughters of the Sun and sisters of Phaëthon later transformed into poplars: 2.340; 10.91, 263
Hélice	a city in Achaea destroyed along with Buris by a tsunami in 373 BCE: 15.294
Hélicon	a mountain in Boeotia home to the Muses: 2.219; 5.254, 664; 8.534
Hélix	a follower of Phineus (1) killed by Perseus: 5.86
Héllespont	a narrow strait in Asia Minor (the modern Dardanelles) named for Helle, daughter of Nephele: 11.194
Hélops	a centaur killed by Pirithoüs: 12.334, 335
Hénna	a city in central Sicily, near Lake Pergus: 5.385
Herculáneum	a town near Naples: 15.710

Hércules   (adj. Hercúlean) club-wielding preeminent
mythical hero who performed twelve Labors for
Eurystheus of Tiryns; born **Alcides** to Jupiter and
Alcmene; stepson of Amphitryon; husband of
Deianira and Hebe; father of Hyllus and Tlepolemus: 7.364; 9.134, 162, 257, 264, 279, 285; 11.627;
12.309, 539, 554, 573; 13.23, 52; 15.8, 47, 230, 284
    as **Alcides**: 9.12, 50, 110, 216; 11.213; 12.538
    as **Alcmene's son**: 8.544; 9.23
    as **Amphitryonides** or **Amphitryon's son**: 9.140;
    15.48
    as the **Clubman**: 15.21, 284
    as **Jove's son**: 9.104; 15.12
    as **Oechalia's victor**: 9.136
    as **Tiryns' hero**: 7.410
    as the **Tirynthian**: 6.112; 12.564; 13.401
    as **Tirynthius**: 9.65, 268

Hermaphrodítus   son of Mercury and Venus raped by Salmacis: 4.383
    as **Atlas' heir**: 4.368

Hérse   daughter of Cecrops beloved of Mercury; sister of
Aglauros and Pandrosos: 2.558, 725, 739, 747, 809

Hersílie   wife of Romulus deified as **Hora**: 14.829, 839, 847
    as **Hora**: 14.850

Hesíone   daughter of Laömedon rescued by Hercules; wife of
Telamon: 11.216

Hespéria   a nymph; daughter of Cebren and beloved of
Aesacus: 11.768

Hespérides   three nymphs in Atlas' garden of golden apples:
11.114

Hippálmus   a participant in the Calydonian Hunt: 8.360

Híppasus (1)   a participant in the Calydonian Hunt and son of
Eurytus (1): 8.313
    as **Eurytus' son**: 8.371

Híppasus (2)   a centaur: 12.351

Hippocoön   king of Sparta and father of Enaesimus:
8.314, 363

Hippódamas   father of Perimele: 8.593, 599

Hippódame   wife of Pirithoüs: 12.210, 224

Hippólytus	son of Theseus and the Amazon Hippolyta deified as **Virbius:** 15.497, 544
	as the **Amazonian son:** 15.553
	as **Theseus' son:** 15.492
	as **Virbius:** 15.544
Hippómenes	Aonian-born son of Megareus, great-grandson of Neptune, and husband of Atalanta: 10.575, 586, 609, 632, 639, 650, 658, 668, 690
	as the **Aonian:** 10.589
	as **Megareus' son:** 10.659
	as **Neptune's heir:** 10.664
Híppotes	father of Aeolus (1): 4.663; 11.431; 14.86, 224; 15.706
Hippóthoüs	a participant in the Calydonian Hunt: 8.305
Hodítes (1)	a noble at the court of Cepheus: 5.97
Hodítes (2)	a centaur killed by Mopsus: 12.457
Hóra	see **Hersilie**
household gods	domestic deities representing an individual's home: 1.174, 231, 773; 3.539; 5.155, 496; 7.574; 8.91; 9.639; 12.551; 15.450, 863
Hurricane (1)	(*"Laelaps"*) a hound of Actaeon's: 3.212
Hurricane (2)	(*"Laelaps"*) a magical hunting dog owned by Cephalus: 7.771
Hýacinth	a Spartan youth beloved of Apollo; son of Amyclas: 10.185, 217
	as **Amyclas' son:** 10.162
Hýad(e)s	seven stars in the constellation Taurus: 3.595; 13.293
Hýale	an attendant of Diana: 3.171
Hýdra	a many-headed serpent from Lake Lerna killed by Hercules; it had poisonous blood and sprouted two heads with each decapitation: 9.69, 159, 193
	as the **Lernaean:** 9.130
Hýles	a centaur: 12.378
Hýleus	a participant in the Calydonian Hunt: 8.311
Hýllus	son of Heracles and Deianira, husband of Iole: 9.280
Hylónome	a female centaur beloved of Cyllarus: 12.405, 423

Hýmen	torch-wielding god of marriage: 1.480; 4.759; 6.429; 9.762, 765, 796; 10.2
Hyméttus	(adj. Hymettian) a mountain in Attica known for its honey: 7.703; 10.285
Hypaépa	a small Lydian town at the foot of Mt. Tmolus, home to Arachne: 6.13; 11.152
Hýpanis	a river in modern Ukraine (modern Southern Bug): 15.285
Hyperbóreans	a race of polar giants, possibly residing at Pallene: 15.356
Hypérion	Titan of the sun and father of the Sun; associated with Heliopolis in Egypt: 4.192, 241; 8.565; 15.406, 407
Hýpseus	a follower of Phineus (1) killed by Perseus: 5.98
Hypsípyle	queen of Lemnos and daughter of Thoas: 13.399
Hýrië	mother of Cygnus (2), later an Aetolian lake: 7.371, 380
Iálysos	a town on the isle of Rhodes: 7.365
Iánthe	Cretan girl beloved of Iphis (1): 9.715, 722, 744, 760, 797
Iápetus	a Titan; father of Prometheus and Atlas: 1.83; 4.632
Iapetus' son	referring to **Prometheus**: 1.83
	referring to **Atlas**: 4.632
Iapýgia	(adj. Iapygian) a region of southern Italy ruled by Daunus and Diomedes: 14.459, 510; 15.53, 703
	as **Apulia** (adj. Apulian): 14.517
Iásion	a mortal lover of Ceres: 9.422
Iberia	location of the cattle of Geryon stolen by Hercules: 15.12
Ícarus (1)	son of Daedalus: 8.195, 203, 232, 233
Ícarus (2)	father of Erigone; later made a star for filial love: 10.450
Ída	(adj. Idan) a forested mountain near Troy home to Daphnis and Hermaphroditus; sacred to Cybele: 2.218; 4.277, 289, 293; 7.359; 10.71; 11.762; 12.521; 13.324; 14.535

Idálian	see **Venus**
Ídas (1)	a casualty in the fight between Perseus and Phineus (1): 5.90
Ídas (2)	a participant in the Calydonian Hunt; son of Aphareus (1): 8.304 as **Aphareus' son:** 8.304
Ídas (3)	member of Diomedes' crew: 14.504
Ídmon	a dyer from Colophon; father of Arachne: 6.8
Idómeneus	king of Crete; a Greek hero at Troy: 13.358
Ília	mother of Romulus: 14.780, 822
Ilióneus	son of Niobe: 6.261
Ilithýia	see **Lucina**
Ílium (adj. Ilian)	see **Troy**
Illýria	a region of the western Balkans: 4.568
Ílus	the founder of Troy: 11.755
Ímbreus	a centaur: 12.311
Ináchides	a patronymic for **Perseus**, a tenth-generation descendant of Inachus: 4.718
Ínachus	a river in the Argolid (and its god); father of Io and grandfather of Epaphus: 1.583, 611, 641, 644, 753; 4.718; 9.686
Inárime	a coastal island of central Italy: 14.89
India	(or **Ind**; adj. Indian): 1.778; 4.21, 605; 5.47; 8.288; 11.167; 15.414
Índiges	see **Aeneas**
Íno	wife of Athamas, daughter of Cadmus, sister of Semele, mother of Learchus and Melicertes, aunt of Bacchus and Pentheus; later deified as **Leucothea:** 3.313, 722; 4.430, 497, 528 as **Leucothea:** 4.542
Ío	daughter of Inachus raped by Jupiter and transformed into a cow; mother of Epaphus; later identified with **Isis:** 1.585, 627, 628 as **Inachus' child:** 1.611; 9.686 as **Isis:** 9.773 as **Phoronis** or **Phoronides:** 1.669; 2.524

Ioláüs	a Boeotian hero and participant in the Calydonian Hunt; nephew and lover of Hercules: 8.310; 9.399, 430
Iólcus	a town in Thessaly home to Jason: 7.158
Íole	wife of Hyllus, daughter of Eurytus (2), and sister of Dryope: 9.140, 278, 394 as **Eurytus' child:** 9.396
Iónian Sea	a body of water separating Greece and Italy: 4.535; 15.50, 699
Iphigenía	daughter of Agamemnon sacrificed at Aulis: 12.30 as **Mycenae's daughter:** 12.34
Iphínoüs	a centaur: 12.379
Íphis (1)	child of Ligdus and Telethusa, beloved of Ianthe: 9.668, 709, 714, 724, 745, 786, 794, 797
Íphis (2)	a Cypriot youth in love with Anaxarete: 14.699, 716, 754
Íphitus	a Trojan hero; father of Coeranos: 13.257
Íris	goddess of the rainbow; messenger of Juno and daughter of Thaumas (1): 1.270; 4.480; 11.585, 589, 630; 14.86, 830, 838 as **Thaumas' child** or **daughter:** 4.480; 11.647; 14.845
Ísis	Egyptian goddess with a major cult in Rome, here syncretized with **Io:** 9.773
Island	an island in the Tiber at Rome; site of a temple to Aesculapius: 15.741
Isménus (1)	a river near Thebes (1): 2.243
Isménus (2)	a son of Niobe: 6.224
Ísse	daughter of Macar (1) raped by Apollo: 6.125
Isthmus	a strip of land dividing the Peloponnese from mainland Greece; site of Corinth: 6.419, 420; 7.405
Italy	(adj. Italian): 14.17; 15.10, 291, 701; 15.59
Íthaca	(adj. Ithacan) an island in the Ionian Sea home to Ulysses: 13.512, 711
Ítys	son of Tereus and Procne: 6.437, 620, 636, 652, 658

Iúlus	(also known as **Ascanius**) king of Alba and son of Aeneas; purported ancestor of Julius Caesar: 14.583; 15.447, 767 as **Ascanius**: 13.627; 14.609
Iulus' heir	an epithet referring to either **Augustus** or **Julius Caesar**: 15.447
Ixíon	king of the Lapiths; father of Pirithoüs and the centaurs; damned to spin forever on a wheel of fire for his attempted rape of Juno: 4.461, 465; 8.403, 567, 613; 10.42; 12.210, 337, 504
Jánus	two-faced god of beginnings with an ancient temple in the Roman Forum; associated with Greece; father of Canens: 14.334, 381, 785, 789
Jáson	hero of the quest for the Golden Fleece and participant in the Calydonian Hunt; born at Iolcus in Thessaly; son of Aeson and husband of Medea: 7.5, 26, 27, 48, 67, 397; 8.301, 349 as **Aeson's son**: 7.60, 77, 84, 110, 132, 155–6, 163; 8.411
Jove	see **Jupiter**
Jove's step-child-in-law	see **Hebe**
Jove's daughter	see **Minerva**
Jove's son	patronymic of **Mercury**: 1.673; 2.697, 726 patronymic of **Hercules**: 9.104; 15.12
Júba	king of Numidia defeated by allies of Julius Caesar in 46 BCE: 15.755
Július Caesar	(100–44 BCE) Roman general and dictator assassinated by a conspiracy of Roman Senators; adoptive father of Augustus and purported descendant of Aeneas through Iulus; later deified as **Julius the God**: as **Aeneas' heir**: 15.804 as **Caesar**: 15.746, 750, 845 as **Julius the God**: 15.841
Juno	queen of the gods, goddess of marriage, sister and wife of Jupiter, daughter of the Titan Saturn, and mother of Vulcan; associated with peacocks; known for jealousy and enmity toward Thebes (1), Troy,

and Rome: 1.270, 602, 678; 2.469, 508, 518, 525; 3.264, 286, 287, 320, 362; 4.173, 422, 426, 448, 473, 479, 523, 548; 6.91, 94, 206, 337, 429; 7.523; 8.220; 9.21, 284, 296, 308, 401, 500, 762, 796; 10.161; 11.578, 629; 12.506; 14.86, 114, 582, 830; 15.164, 385, 774

    as **Saturnia:** 1.612, 616, 722; 2.435, 532; 3.294, 333, 365; 4.464; 5.330; 9.176; 14.781

Júpiter or **Jove**   omnipotent king of the gods, ruler of the sky, god of thunderbolts, brother and husband of Juno, son of Saturn and Ops, brother to Neptune and Dis, and father of Apollo, Bacchus, Diana, Hercules, Mercury, Minerva, Minos, Perseus, and others; rapist of many; associated with the eagle and the oak: 1.106, 114, 116, 166, 205, 244, 274, 324, 517, 589, 590, 615, 623, 673, 733, 748; 2.62, 378, 397, 422, 429, 437, 444, 473, 480, 488, 678, 697, 726, 744; 3.6, 26, 256, 260, 266, 270, 273, 280, 281, 283, 288, 318, 333, 363; 4.3, 281, 610, 640, 645, 650, 697, 698, 714, 755, 799; 5.11, 297, 326, 370, 512, 514, 523, 528, 565; 6.51, 72, 74, 94, 110, 176, 516; 7.366, 587, 596, 615, 623, 651, 801; 8.100, 122, 153, 264, 626; 9.14, 23, 26, 104, 136, 198, 229, 242, 260, 265, 288, 302, 403, 414, 416, 427, 439; 10.148, 149, 156, 161, 224; 11.41, 219, 224, 225, 286, 756; 12.11, 52; 13.5, 28, 91, 142, 143, 145, 216, 269, 385, 409, 574, 586, 600, 707, 842, 844, 856; 15.12, 70, 386, 857, 858, 865, 870

    as the **Almighty:** 1.154; 2.304, 402, 505; 3.336; 9.271; 14.816

    as **Diana's father:** 1.487

    as **Panomphean Thunderer:** 11.197

    as **Saturn's son:** 1.163; 8.703

    as the **Thunderer:** 1.170; 2.466; 11.197

Knóssos   (adj. Knossian) capital and palace on Crete: 7.471; 8.40, 52, 144; 9.669

Lacínium   a promontory in southern Italy near Croton; site of a temple to Juno: 15.13, 702

Ládon   a river in the Peloponnese: 1.702; 3.216

Laërtes   son of Arcesius and father of Ulysses: 12.625; 13.48, 124, 144

    as **Penelope's mate's sire:** 8.316

Laestrygónians	a race of man-eating giants from the city of Lamus: 14.233, 237
Láius	a Theban king and father of Oedipus: 7.759
Lampétia	one of the **Heliades**: 2.348
Lampétides	a bard killed in the fight between Phineus (1) and Perseus: 5.111
Lámus	the land of the Laestrygonians: 14.233
Laömedon	king of Troy; father of Antigone and Priam: 6.95, 11.195, 198, 756
Lápiths	a Thessalian tribe famed for a battle with the centaurs: 12.250, 261, 417, 530, 536; 14.670
Laríssa	a city in Thessaly home to Coronis: 2.543
Látins	the proto-Roman people of Latium: 14.832 as the **Palatines**: 14.622
Latínus (1)	eponymous king of the Latins; son of Faunus and father of Lavinia: 14.449
Latínus (2)	an Alban king; son of Silvius: 14.611, 612
Látium	(adj. Latin) a region of central Italy surrounding Rome: 14.326, 391, 422, 452, 610, 624; 15.481, 486, 582, 626, 742
Latóna	mother of Apollo and Diana; daughter of the Titan Coeus; also known by her Greek name **Leto**: 6.160, 162, 171, 186, 199, 214, 280, 335; 8.394; 13.635 as **Coeus' child**: 6.366 as **Leto**: 6.274, 384; 7.384; 8.15, 277; 11.193 as **Titania**: 6.346
Latónia	see **Diana**
Látreus	a centaur: 12.464
Lauréntum	(adj. Laurentian) a city in Latium: 14.336, 343, 598
Lavínia(n maid)	daughter of Latinus (1) and wife of Aeneas: 14.570
Lavínium	a city in Latium founded by Aeneas and named for Lavinia: 15.727
Leärchus	son of Athamas and Ino; brother of Melicertes: 4.516
Lebínthos	a small island in the Sporades: 8.222

Léda	wife of Tyndareus raped by Jupiter in the form of a swan; mother of Castor, Pollux, and Helen: 6.109
Léleges	(adj. Lelegian) a pre-Greek tribe inhabiting Megara: 7.443; 9.645, 652
Lélex	an elder participant in the Calydonian Hunt, associated with Naryx (1) and Troezen: 8.312, 567, 617
Lemnian child	see **Erichthonius**
Lemnian	see **Vulcan**
Lémnos	(adj. Lemnian) an island in the Aegean sacred to Vulcan; site of Philoctetes' abandonment: 2.756; 4.185; 13.46, 313
Lenaéus	see **Bacchus**
Lérna	(adj. Lernaean) a lake region of the Peloponnese, near the Inachus river; home to the Hydra: 1.599; 2.240; 9.69, 130
Lésbos	(adj. Lesbian) an island in the north Aegean sacked by Achilles: 2.591; 11.55; 13.173
Lethaéa	vain wife of Olenus (2): 10.69
Léthe	(adj. Lethean) an underworld river associated with sleep: 7.152; 11.603
Léto	see **Latona**
Leto's daughter	see **Diana**
Leto's son	see **Apollo**
Leúcas	an island on the Acarnanian coast: 15.289
Leucíppus	a participant in the Calydonian Hunt: 8.307
Leucónoë	a daughter of Minyas and denier of Bacchus: 4.167
Leucósia	a coastal island of southern Italy (modern Licosa): 15.708
Leucóthea	see **Ino**
Leucóthoë	a Persian princess raped by the Sun; daughter of Eurynome and Orchamus: 4.196, 208, 220
Líber	see **Bacchus**
Libya	(adj. Libyan) a name for the continent of Africa: 2.237; 4.617; 5.75, 327; 14.77; 15.755

Líbys	a member of Acoetes' crew: 3.617, 676
Líchas	a servant in the household of Hercules: 9.155, 211, 213, 229
Lígdus	a Phaestian commoner; husband of Telethusa and father of Iphis (1): 9.671, 684
Ligúria	a region of northern Italy ruled by Cygnus (1): 2.370
Lilybaéum	the westernmost of Sicily's three capes (modern Marsala): 5.351; 13.725
Limnaéë	daughter of the Ganges and mother of Athis: 5.49
Límyre	a town in Lycia: 9.646
Liriópe	a nymph raped by the Cephisus; mother of Narcissus: 3.342
Litérnum	a town in southern Italy noted for its mastic trees: 15.713
Lótus	a nymph pursued by Priapus: 9.347
Lucína	goddess of childbirth loyal to Juno: 5.304; 9.294, 698; 10.507, 510 as **Ilithyia**: 9.283
Lyaéus	see **Bacchus**
Lýcabas (1)	a particularly heinous member of Acoetes' crew: 3.623, 673
Lýcabas (2)	Assyrian lover of Athis killed by Perseus in the fight against Phineus (1): 5.60
Lýcabas (3)	a centaur: 12.302
Lycaéus	a mountain in Arcadia: 1.217, 698
Lycáön	heretic king of Arcadia; father of Callisto and grandfather of Arcas: 1.164, 198, 221; 2.496, 526
Lycétus	a Thessalian follower of Phineus (1) killed by Perseus: 5.87
Lyceum	the school of Aristotle in Athens: 2.711
Lýcia	(adj. Lycian) a region of southwestern Asia Minor, home to Menoetes, Sarpedon, and the Chimaera: 4.296; 6.317, 339, 382; 9.645; 12.116; 13.256
Lýcidas	a centaur: 12.310

Lycórmas (1)   a river in Aetolia: 2.245

Lycórmas (2)   a follower of Perseus in the fight against Phineus (1): 5.119

Lycótas   a centaur: 12.350

Lycúrgus   a Thracian king inimical to Bacchus: 4.23

Lýcus (1)   a centaur: 12.332

Lýcus (2)   a member of Diomedes' crew: 14.504

Lýcus (3)   a partially underground river in Phrygia: 15.273

Lýdia   (adj. Lydian) a kingdom in western Asia Minor home to Acoetes and Arachne: 2.253; 3.583; 4.423; 6.5, 11, 103, 146; 11.98
    its citizens, as **Tyrrhene:** 3.576, 696; 4.24

Lýnceus (1)   great-great-grandfather of Perseus: 4.769; 5.99, 185

Lýnceus (2)   a participant in the Calydonian Hunt and son of Aphareus (1): 8.304
    as **Aphareus' son:** 8.304

Lynceus' heir   see **Perseus**

Lýncus (1)   a Scythian king: 5.650

Lýncus (2)   a region of western Macedonia: 15.329

Lyrcéa   a town near the Inachus river: 1.599

Lyrnéssos   a town near Troy sacked by Achilles: 12.109

Mácar (1)   father of Isse: 6.125

Mácar (2)   a Lapith: 12.453

Mácar (3)   a member of Ulysses' crew: 14.158, 318, 441

Macedónia   (adj. Macedonian) a para-Greek kingdom to the north of Greece: 12.466

Maénalus   a mountain in Arcadia sacred to Pan and Diana: 1.216; 2.415, 442; 5.607

Maéra   a woman in Asia Minor transformed into a dog: 7.362

Magnésia   a region of Thessaly: 11.408

Máia   mother of Mercury; daughter of Atlas and Pleione, hence one of the Pleiades: 2.685; 11.303
    as **Atlas' child:** 2.742

Mánto	Theban prophetess; daughter of Tiresias: 6.157
Márathon	a town near Athens: 7.433
Mareótis	(adj. Mareotic) a lake in northern Egypt (modern Mariout): 9.773
Mars	god of War; lover of Venus; father of Harmonia, Meleäger, and Romulus; ancestor of the Romans: 3.32, 132, 531; 4.172; 7.101; 8.437; 12.91; 14.799, 806 as **Gradivus** ("the Strider"): 6.427; 14.819; 15.862
Mársyas	a pipe-playing Satyr and lover of Olympus (2); later a river in Phrygia: 6.400 as the **Satyr:** 6.384
Meánder	a meandering river in southwestern Asia Minor (modern Büyük Menderes); father of Cyaneë and grandfather of Caunus: 2.246; 8.162; 9.451
Meándrius	see **Caunus**
Medéa	Colchian sorceress; daughter of Aeëtes; wife of Jason and then of Aegeus: 7.11, 41, 70, 257, 285, 406 as **Aeëtes' child** or **daughter:** 7.9, 325 as the **Colchian:** 7.296, 300, 330, 348, 394 as the **Phasian trickster:** 7.297
Médon (1)	a member of Acoetes' crew: 3.671
Médon (2)	a centaur: 12.302
Medúsa	(adj. Medusan) a Gorgon killed by Perseus; daughter of Phorcys; mother of Chrysaor and Pegasus: 4.656, 743, 781; 5.70, 217, 247, 249, 257, 312; 10.22 as the **Gorgon:** 4.618, 699, 801; 5.180, 196, 202, 209 as **Phorcys' daughter:** 4.743; 5.230
Mégareus	king of Onchestus and father of Hippomenes: 10.605, 659
Mégara	(adj. Megárian) a town on the Isthmus of Corinth: 8.6 as **Alcathoë:** 7.443; 8.8
Meláneus (1)	a follower of Perseus killed in the fight with Phineus (1): 5.128
Meláneus (2)	a centaur: 12.306

Melántho	a daughter of Deucalion raped by Neptune in the form of a dolphin: 6.121
Melánthus	a member of Acoetes' crew: 3.617
Meleäger	son of Oeneus (or Mars) and Althaea; leader of the Calydonian Hunt; lover of Atalanta: 8.270, 299, 385, 515; 9.149
	as the **Calydonian hero:** 8.324
	as **Mars' son:** 8.437
	as **Oeneus' son:** 8.414;
Melicértes	son of Athamas and Ino; later deified as the sea-god **Palaemon:** 4.522
	as **Palaemon:** 4.542; 13.918
Mémeros	a centaur: 12.305
Mémnon	son of Dawn killed by Achilles; nephew of Priam: 13.579, 595, 600, 618
Méndes	a city of ancient Egypt (modern Tell El-Ruba); home to Celadon (1): 5.144
Meneláüs	king of Sparta and Greek hero at Troy; brother of Agamemnon and son of Atreus; first husband of Helen: 13.203
	as **Atreus' younger son:** 12.622; 13.359; 15.162
Menéphron	an incestuous man in the region of Mount Cyllene: 7.386
Menoétes	a Lycian foot soldier: 12.116, 127
Mércury	the messenger god; born on Mount Cyllene to the Pleiad Maia and Jupiter; grandson of Atlas and Pleione; father of Hermaphroditus; associated with his winged sandals and sleep-inducing caduceus wand: 2.741; 4.288, 754
	as **Atlas' grandson** or **heir:** 1.682; 2.704, 834; 8.627
	as the **bearer of Caduceus:** 2.709
	as **Cyllenius:** 1.713; 2.720, 818; 5.176, 330; 13.146; 14.291
	as **Jove's son:** 1.673; 2.697, 726
	as **Maia's son:** 2.685; 11.303
	as **Pleiad's child:** 1.670
Meríones	a Greek hero at the Trojan War; nephew of Idomeneus: 13.359

Mérops	king of Aethiopia; husband of Clymene and stepfather of Phaëthon: 1.764; 2.185
Messápia	(adj. Messapian) a region in southern Italy: 14.514
Messéne	a city in Messenia sacked by Hercules: 6.416; 12.549
Messénia	a region of the southwestern Peloponnese including Messene: 2.680
Messína	a Sicilian city on the tip of Cape Pelorus facing the Italian mainland, formerly known as **Zancle:** 14.17 as **Zancle:** 13.729; 14.5, 47; 15.290
Méstra	shapeshifting daughter of Erysichthon and wife of Autolycus as **Autolycus' wife:** 8.738
Methýmna	a town on the coast of Lesbos: 11.55
Mction	father of Phorbas (1): 5.74
Mídas	Phrygian king, follower of Bacchus, and musical philistine: 11.92, 162, 174
Milétus	namesake of the Carian city on the Meander; son of Deïone, father of Byblis and Caunus: 9.445, 447, 635 as **Deïone's son:** 9.443
Mílo	Olympian wrestler born at Croton in the 6th century BCE: 15.229
Mímas	a mountain on the coast of Asia Minor: 2.222

Minérva	(adj. Minerval) blonde virgin goddess of wisdom, weaving, and war; daughter of Jupiter, half-sister of Perseus, and patroness of Athens; associated with olives, owls, weaving, the aegis, and Lake Tritonis; also known as **Pallas:** 2.563, 588, 710, 749, 787; 4.33, 756, 798; 8.251, 264, 275, 664; 13.337, 381, 653; 14.475; 15.709
	    as **Jove's daughter:** 5.297; 6.51
	    as **Pallas:** 2.552, 567, 714, 834; 3.101; 4.38; 5.45, 263, 335, 375; 6.23, 26, 36, 44, 70, 129, 135, 335; 7.399, 723; 8.252, 275; 12.151, 360
	    as **Tritonia:** 2.782, 794; 3.127; 5.250, 269, 645; 6.1, 383; 8.548

Minerva's cape	a promontory near Sorrento (modern Punta Campanella): 15.709

Mínos — warlike king of Crete and enemy of Athens; son of Jupiter and Europa; husband of Pasiphaë; father of Androgeos and Ariadne: 7.456, 471; 8.6, 26, 42, 45, 64, 95, 152, 157, 174, 187; 9.437, 441
as **Europa's son:** 8.24

Mintúrnae — a marshy city in Latium: 15.714

Mínyans — the crew of Jason and the *Argo* in the quest for the Golden Fleece, many of whom claimed descent from Minyas: 6.720; 7.1, 115, 120

Mínyas — king of Orchomenos; father of Leuconoë and Alcithoë; ancestor of Jason and other Argonauts: 4.32, 389, 425

Mínyas' girls — the daughters of Minyas, including **Leuconoë** and **Alcithoë**; heretics rejecting the divinity of Bacchus: 4.32, 389, 425

Mithridátes — (120–63 BCE; adj. Mithridatic) Mithridates VI Eupator, king of Pontus and enemy of Rome defeated in the hard-fought Mithridatic Wars: 15.756

Mnemó(sy)ne — goddess of memory and mother of the Muses: 5.267, 280; 6.113

Molóssians — a Greek people of Epirus: 1.227; 13.718

Mólpeus — a Chaonian follower of Phineus (1) in the fight against Perseus: 5.162, 168

Mónychus — a centaur: 12.499

Moon — the celestial body; sister of the Sun; identified with **Diana**: 2.208; 7.207; 15.790
as **Phoebe:** 1.12, 2.723

Mópsian — see **Triptolemus**

Mópsus — a Lapith prophet; son of Ampycus (3) and participant in the Calydonian Hunt: 12.455, 456, 528
as **Ampycus'** or **Ampyx' son:** 8.315–6, 350; 12.524

Morning Star — celestial body (and its god) heralding the dawn; father of Ceÿx and Daedalion: 2.115, 722; 4.629, 664; 8.1; 11.96, 271, 346, 570; 15.189, 789

Mórpheus — god of human manifestations in patrician dreams; son of Sleep: 11.634, 647, 671

Múlciber — see **Vulcan**

Munýchia	a steep hill at the port of Athens: 2.711
Muses	nine specialized virgin goddesses of literature, science, and the arts; daughters of Jupiter and Mnemone, including **Urania** and **Calliope**; associated with Mount Helicon in the Thespiae region of Aonia: 5.294, 337; 10.148; 15.621 as **Aonians**: 5.333; 6.2
Mútina	a city in northern Italy (modern Modena) besieged in the civil war following Julius Caesar's assassination: 15.822
Mýcale (1)	a mountain on the west coast of Asia Minor: 2.223
Mýcale (2)	a Thessalian witch; mother of Orios: 12.263
Mycénae	a city of the northern Peloponnese ruled by Agamemnon: 6.417; 12.34
Mycénae's daughter	see **Iphigenia**
Mýconos	an island in the Cyclades: 7.463
Mýrmidons	("ant-people") the people of Aegina (1): 7.654
Mýrrha	daughter of Cinyras (2) and mother of Adonis: 10.312, 318, 363, 402, 441, 476
Mýscelus	a native of Argos and founder of Croton; son of Alemon: 15.20 as **Alemon's son**: 15.19, 26, 48
Mýsia	(adj. Mysian) a region in Asia Minor where the Caïcus flows: 2.243
Mýsus	a purported name for the headwaters of the Caïcus: 15.276
Náiads	water-nymphs, including Syrinx and Salmacis: 1.641, 701; 2.325; 3.506, 4.49, 289, 302, 356; 6.329, 453; 8.580; 9.87, 657; 10.9, 514; 11.49; 14.328, 786
Nar	a river north of Latium: 14.330
Narcíssus	vain son of Liriope and Cephisus; beloved of Echo and himself: 3.346, 370 as **Cephisus' son**: 3.351
Náryx (1)	(adj. Narýcian) a town in Locris home to Lelex and Ajax (2): 8.312; 14.467
Náryx (2)	a Narycian colony on the southern tip of mainland Italy: 15.705

Nasamónes	a Berber tribe of the Libyan Desert, of whom Dorylas (1) was a member: 5.130
Nauplíades	see **Palamedes**
Náxos	(formerly **Dia**) the largest island in the Cyclades; sacred to Bacchus: 3.636, 640, 649; 8.175 as **Dia:** 3.690
Nedýmnus	a centaur: 12.349
Néleus	(adj. Nelean) king of Pylos; son of Neptune and father of Nestor: 2.689; 6.418; 12.553, 558, 577
Némea	(adj. Nemean) a town in Argolis home to a lion killed by Hercules: 9.197, 235
Neoptólemus	son of Achilles born on Scyros; elsewhere known as **Pyrrhus:** 13.455 as **Pyrrhus:** 13.155
Néphele	an attendant of Diana; not the mother of Helle: 3.171
Nephélean	see **Hellespont**
Néptune	god of the sea and earthquakes; brother of Jupiter, husband of Amphitrite, father of Theseus, Neleus, and Cygnus (3), and great-grandfather of Hippomenes; associated with the trident: 1.283, 330; 2.270; 4.533, 539; 6.115; 8.598, 602, 851; 10.606, 639, 664; 12.26, 72, 198, 558
Neptune's heir	see **Hippomenes**
Neptune's hero	see **Theseus**
Néreïds	fifty sea nymph daughters of Nereus and Doris, including Amphitrite, Psamathe, Thetis, and Galatea: 5.17; 11.258, 361, 380; 12.93, 94; 13.162, 749, 857, 898; 14.264
Nerétum	a town on the Ionian coast of Salento in southern Italy (modern Nardò): 15.51
Néreus	a primordial sea god; father of the Nereids and grandfather of Phocus: 1.187; 2.268; 7.685; 11.361; 12.24; 13.743
Néritos	an island near Ithaca ruled by Ulysses: 13.712
Néssus	a centaur killed by Hercules: 9.101, 108, 110, 119, 122, 131, 153; 12.308, 454

Néstor   proverbially wise, old, and loquacious king of Pylos
and Greek hero at Troy; son of Neleus and brother
of Periclymenus: 8.313; 12.169; 13.63, 64
   as **Neleus' son:** 12.577
   as the **Pylian:** 8.365; 12.536, 542; 15.838

New Troy   Buthrotum, a city in Epirus founded by Helenus
after the Trojan War: 13.721

Nile   a river in Egypt (and its god) whose mouth splits
into seven channels and whose source was long
unknown; purported father of Nileus: 1.422, 728;
2.254; 5.187, 324; 9.774; 15.753

Níleus   a follower of Phineus (1) in the fight against
Perseus; alleged son of the Nile: 5.187

Nínus   legendary Assyrian king and husband of Semiramis: 4.88

Nióbe   Phrygian-born queen of Thebes (1); wife of
Amphion, daughter of Tantalus (1), sister of Pelops,
and mother to fourteen children: 6.148, 156, 165,
273, 287
   as **Tantalus' child:** 6.210

Nísus   king of Megara and father of Scylla (2): 8.7, 17, 35,
90, 126

Noëmon   a Trojan killed by Ulysses: 13.258

Nónacris   (adj. Nonácrian) a mountain in Arcadia: 1.690;
2.409; 8.426

Nonácrian   see **Atalanta**

Nóricum   (adj. Noric) a Celtic kingdom of modern Austria
famous for its steel: 14.712

North Wind   see **Boreas**

Nótus   see **Auster**

Núma   second king of Rome and husband of Egeria; native
of Cures: 15.4, 480, 485

Numícius   a river in Latium: 14.328, 599

Numídia   (adj. Numidian) a kingdom of north Africa
conquered by Julius Caesar: 15.755

Númitor   an Alban king; brother of Amulius and grandfather
of Romulus: 14.773

Nýcteus (1) — father of Antiope, raped by Jupiter in the form of a satyr: 6.110

Nýcteus (2) — a member of Diomedes' crew: 14.504

Nyctímene — princess of Lesbos transformed into an owl for incest: 2.589, 592

Nýsa — (adj. Nysan) mythical mountain where Bacchus was reared: 3.314; 4.13

Ocean — the great river circling the world (and its god); husband of Tethys: 2.510; 7.267; 9.499, 594; 13.292, 950; 15.13, 830

Ocýrhoë — prophetic daughter of Chiron and Chariclo: 2.638

Odrýsians — a people of Thrace ruled by Tereus: 6.490

Oeágrian — see **Orpheus**

Oechália — a city of uncertain location sacked by Hercules: 9.136, 331

Oécles' son — Amphiaraus; a prophet and participant in the Calydonian Hunt; later betrayed by his wife and swallowed alive by the earth during the Theban War: 8.317

Oéneus — king of Calydon; husband of Althaea, son of Portheus, grandfather of Diomedes, and father of Meleäger and Deianira: 8.273, 281, 414, 486; 14.512
  as **Portheus' son**: 9.11

Oenópia — see **Aegina (1)**

Oéta — a mountain near Trachis in central Greece; site of the death of Hercules: 2.217; 9.165, 204, 230, 249; 11.382

Oetaéa — a region of Thessaly surrounding Mount Oeta: 1.313

Oilean Ajax — see **Ajax (2)**

Ólenus (1) — father of Aege, later transformed into Capella, the Goat-star: 3.594

Ólenus (2) — husband of Lethaea: 10.68

Ólenus (3) — father of Tectaphus, a Lapith: 12.433

Olíaros — an island in the Cyclades allied with Minos: 7.470

Olýmpus (1) — (adj. Olympian) a mountain in northern Thessaly home to Jupiter and the gods: 1.154, 213; 2.60, 226;

6.487; 7.225; 9.499; 13.761

Olýmpus (2)	lover of Marsyas: 6.394
Onchéstus	a town in Boeotia home to Megareus: 10.605
Onétor	herdsman to Peleus; native of Phocis: 11.348
Ophéltes	a member of Acoetes' crew: 3.605, 641
Ophíon	father of Amycus: 12.245
Óphius	father of Combe: 7.383
Ops	wife and sister of Saturn: 9.498
Órchamus	king of Persia and father of Leucothoë: 4.212
Orchómenos	a town in Arcadia (not the Boeotian kingdom of Minyas): 5.608; 6.416
Órcus	see **Dis**
Óreads	mountain nymphs: 8.787
Oréstes	(adj. Orestean) a Greek hero; founder of temple of Diana at Aricia: 15.489
Oríon	hunter; later a belted constellation; father of the Coronae: 13.692
Oríos	a Lapith; son of Mycale (2): 12.262
Orithýia	daughter of Erechtheus, sister of Procris, wife of Boreas, and mother of Calaïs and Zetes: 6.683, 707; 7.695
Ornéüs	a centaur: 12.302
Oróntes	a river in Asia Minor: 2.249
Órpheus	Thracian singer, bard, pederast, and priest of Bacchus; husband of Eurydice; son of Apollo (or Oeagrus) and Calliope; associated with Mount Haemus: 10.3, 64, 79; 11.5, 22, 23, 44, 64, 93 as **Oeágrian:** 2.220 as the **Thracian bard:** 10.12; 11.2
Órphne	an underworld nymph; mother of Ascalaphus: 5.539
Ortýgia (1)	an island in Syracuse named for Diana (the Ortygian): 5.499, 640
Ortýgia (2)	(adj. Ortygian) an old name for **Delos**, associated with Diana: 1.694; 15.337

Osíris
incompletely resurrected Egyptian god; husband of Isis: 9.693

Óssa
(adj. Ossaean) a mountain in Thessaly near Pelion, Olympus (1), and the Vale of Tempe: 1.155; 2.225; 7.224; 12.319

Óstia
the port of Rome, located at the mouth of the Tiber: 15.728

Óthrys
a mountain in Thessaly near Pelion: 2.222; 7.224, 353; 12.173, 512

Pachýnus
the southernmost of Sicily's three capes (modern Capo Passero): 5.350; 13.726

Pactólus
a river in Asia Minor rising from the base of Tmolus known for its gold deposits: 6.16; 11.87

Paéan (1)
an epithet of **Apollo** as the god of healing: 1.566; 15.535

Paéan (2)
a ritual song of triumph, originally addressed to Apollo: 14.720

Paeónia
(adj. Paeonian) a region of Macedonia: 5.314; 5.303

Paéstum
a coastal city of southern Italy: 15.708

Paétalus
a follower of Phineus (1) in the fight against Perseus: 5.115

Págasae
a Thessalian port from which the Argo was launched: 7.2; 12.412

Palaémon
see **Melicertes**

Palamédes
Greek hero at Troy who exposed Ulysses' feigned madness; son of Nauplius: 13.56, 309
    as **Naupliades:** 13.38, 310

Pálatine
one of Rome's seven hills; site of temples to Vesta and Apollo, and the Palace of Augustus: 1.176; 14.334, 822; 15.560

Pálatines
a name for the proto-Roman **Latins**, derived from the hill: 14.622

Páles
Roman god of shepherds whose festival marked the founding of Rome (April 21st): 14.774

Palestínians
a people of ancient Syria: 4.45

Palíci
two Sicilian gods of agriculture associated with sulphuric lakes: 5.405

Palládium	a sacred effigy of Minerva (Pallas) protecting Troy: 13.99
Pallántis	see **Dawn**
Pállas (1)	a name for **Minerva**: 2.552, 567, 714, 834; 3.101; 4.38; 5.45, 263, 335, 375; 6.23, 26, 36, 44, 70, 129, 135, 335; 7.399, 723; 8.252, 275; 12.151, 360
Pállas (2)	Athenian royal; son of Pandion, father of Clytus (2) and Butes: 7.500, 665, 666
Palléne	a town in Macedonian Chalcidice, vaguely linked with the Hyperboreans: 15.356
Pan	satyr god of nature and the wild; lover of Syrinx and inventor of panpipes; father of Acis and Latinus (1): 1.699, 705; 11.147, 153, 171; 14.516, 638 as **Faunus**: 6.329; 13.750; 14.449
Panchaéa	a mythical island paradise east of Arabia famed for spices: 10.307, 478
Pandíon	king of Athens; son of Erichthonius; father of Procne, Philomela, and Erechtheus: 6.427, 436, 494, 520, 634, 675
Pandion's child	see **Philomela**
Pandion's daughter	see **Procne**
Pándrosos	daughter of Cecrops; sister of Herse and Aglauros: 2.558, 738
Panómphean	an epithet of **Jupiter** as the author of all oracles: 11.197
Pánope	a Boeotian town near Delphi: 3.19
Pánopeus	a participant in the Calydonian Hunt: 8.311
Pánthoüs	a Trojan elder; father of Euphorbus: 15.161
Paphian hero	see **Pygmalion**
Páphos (1)	(adj. Paphian) daughter of Pygmalion and namesake of Paphos (2): 10.290, 297
Páphos (2)	(adj. Paphian) another name for **Cyprus**: 10.530
Paraetónium	a port city on the Egyptian coast (modern Marsa Matruh): 9.774
Páris	a Trojan prince; son of Priam and Hecuba, brother of Aesacus and Hector; abductor of Helen; father of

Corythus (2) and favorite of Venus: 12.4, 599; 13.199, 201, 501; 15.805
　　as **Corythus' sire:** 7.361

Parnássus
(adj. Parnassian) a double-peaked mountain near Delphi sacred to Apollo and the Muses: 1.317, 468; 2.221; 4.643; 5.278; 11.165, 339

Páros
(adj. Parian) an island in the Cyclades famous for its marble: 3.419; 7.465; 8.221

Parrhásia
a region of Arcadia home to Callisto: 2.460; 8.315

Parthénius
(adj. Parthenian) a mountain in Arcadia: 9.188

Parthénope
a city on the southern coast of Italy (modern Naples): 14.101; 15.711

Pasíphaë
wife of Minos, daughter of the Sun, and mother of Phaedra; mother of the Minotaur by the Cretan Bull: 8.136; 15.500
　　as the **Sun's daughter:** 9.736

Pasiphaë's daughter
Phaedra, wife of Theseus in love with Hippolytus: 15.500

Pátara
a city in Lycia; site of an oracle of Apollo: 1.516

Pátrae
a city in the Peloponnese: 6.418

Patróclus
a Greek hero at Troy; lover of Achilles and grandson of Actor (2)
　　as **Actor's heir:** 13.272

Pégasus
a winged horse born from Medusa; brother of Chrysaor and creator of the Hippocrene spring on Helicon: 4.786; 5.262

Pélagon
a participant in the Calydonian Hunt: 8.360

Pelásgia
(adj. Pelasgian) a term representing all allied **Greece** in the Trojan War: 12.19; 13.13, 128, 238, 269; 14.562; 15.453

Pélates (1)
a Cinyphian casualty in the fight between Phineus (1) and Perseus: 5.123

Pélates (2)
a Lapith from Pella: 12.254

Pélethron
(adj. Pelethronian) a valley in Thessaly home to Erigdupus: 12.452

Péleus
king of Phthia; father of Achilles and husband of Thetis; son of Aeacus, brother of Telamon, and

half-brother of Phocus; a participant in the
Calydonian Hunt and the fight with the centaurs:
7.476; 8.379; 11.217, 238, 244, 260, 267, 284, 289, 348,
349, 350, 379, 398, 407; 12.193, 366, 388; 13.152, 155;
15.856

> as **Achilles' sire:** 8.309
> as **Aeacides:** 9.388; 11.227, 246, 250, 274, 399;
> 12.365

Pelian girls or **sisters**	the daughters of Pelias: 7.304, 322
Pélias	king of Iolcus, brother of Aeson, and enemy of Jason: 7.299
Pélides	patronymic of **Achilles**, son of Peleus: 12.604, 619
Pélion	(adj. Pelian) a mountain in Thessaly near Ossa and Olympus (1) home to Chiron; its ash trees furnished Achilles' spear: 1.155; 7.224, 351; 12.74, 513; 13.108
Pélla	(adj. Pellan) the capital of Macedonia; home of Pierus and Pelates (2): 5.302
Pélops	son of Tantalus (1) and brother of Niope; father of Pittheus of Troezen and Atreus of Mycenae: 6.404, 411, 417; 8.623
Pelórus	the northernmost of Sicily's three capes (modern Faro Point near Messina): 5.350; 13.727; 15.706
Penélope	steadfast wife of Ulysses; daughter-in-law of Laertes: 8.316; 13.511
Penéüs	(adj. Peneian) a Thessalian river (and its god); father of Daphne: 1.473, 504, 544, 569; 2.242; 7.230; 12.209
Péntheus	heretical king of Thebes (1); son of Agave and Echion (1); grandson of Cadmus: 3.513, 532, 561, 577, 693, 707, 712; 4.22, 429
	> as **Cadmus' grandson:** 3.174 > as **Echion's son:** 3.513, 526, 701
Peparéthos	an island in the Sporades noted for its olives (modern Skopelos): 7.470
Pérgamum	see **Troy**
Pérgus	a lake in Sicily near Henna: 5.386
Periclýmenus	son of Neleus and brother of Nestor killed by Hercules: 12.556

Periméle	daughter Hippodamas beloved of Acheloüs: 8.591
Périphas (1)	king of Attica and husband of Phene: 7.400
Périphas (2)	a Lapith: 12.450
Perséphone	see **Proserpine**
Pérseus	son of Jupiter and Danaë; husband of Andromeda; half-brother of Minerva; slayer of Medusa: 4.611, 639, 697, 699, 730; 5.16, 31, 33, 34, 56, 80, 128, 137, 167, 175, 177, 190, 201, 218, 224, 248
	as **Abas' heir:** 4.673; 5.236
	as **Acrisius' grandson:** 5.69
	as **Agenor's heir:** 4.772
	as **Danae's son:** 5.1
	as **Inachides:** 4.718
	as **Lynceus' heir:** 4.769; 5.99, 185
Persia	(adj. Persian) a country in Asia Minor ruled by Orchamus: 1.63; 4.212
Petraéus	a centaur: 12.327, 330
Peucétia	a region of Apulia in southern Italy: 14.513
Phaeácia	a mythical island ruled by Alcinous: 13.719
Phaédimus	a son of Niobe: 6.239
Phaeócomes	a centaur: 12.431
Phaéstos	(adj. Phaestian) a town on Crete home to Iphis (1) and Ianthe: 9.670, 715
Pháëthon	son of the Sun and Clymene; stepson of Merops and beloved of Cygnus (1): 1.750, 756, 776; 2.34, 54, 99, 111, 179, 228, 319, 327, 342, 369, 382; 4.246; 12.581
	as **Clymene's son:** 2.19
Phaëthúsa	one of the **Heliades:** 2.347
Pháros	an island on the Egyptian coast: 9.774; 15.287
Pharsália	a town in Thessaly; site of Julius Caesar's victory over Pompey in 48 BCE; later conflated with Philippi: 15.823
Phásis	(adj. Phasian) a river in modern Georgia near Colchis, home of Medea (modern Rioni): 2.249; 7.6, 297

Phégeus	a king of Arcadia; murderer of Alcmaeon: 9.412
Phéne	Attic queen and wife of Periphas (1): 7.400
Phéneus	a town in Arcadia: 15.332
Phéres	father of Admetus, a participant in the Calydonian Hunt: 8.310
Phíale	an attendant of Diana: 3.172
Philámmon	son of Apollo and Chione: 11.317
Philémon	husband of Baucis: 8.630, 681, 705, 714, 715
Philippi	a Macedonian city; site of the defeat of Julius Caesar's assassins in 42 BCE; later conflated with Pharsalia: 15.824
Philoctétes	son of Poeas; heir to Hercules' arrows; left on Lemnos in the Trojan War: 13.329 as **Poeas' son:** 9.233; 13.45, 314
Philoméla	daughter of Pandion and sister of Procne raped by Tereus: 6.451, 475, 503, 511, 553, 572, 601, 643, 657 as **Pandion's child:** 6.520
Philyra	mother of Chiron: 2.676; 7.352
Phíneans	the followers of Phineus (1) in the fight against Perseus: 5.157
Phíneus (1)	brother of Cepheus previously betrothed to Andromeda; rival of Perseus: 5.8, 36, 89, 92, 93, 110, 156, 210, 231
Phíneus (2)	a Thracian prophet rescued from Harpies by the Argonauts: 7.2
Phlégethon	a river of the underworld: 5.544; 15.532
Phlégon	a flying horse of the Sun: 2.154
Phlégra	a volcanic region near Vesuvius, site of the thunderous battle between the gods and the Giants: 10.151
Phlegraéus	a centaur: 12.378
Phlégyas (1)	a follower of Phineus (1) in the fight against Perseus: 5.87
Phlégyas (2)	(adj. Phlegyan) a town in Boeotia ruled by Phorbas (2): 11.414

Phocaéa	(adj. Phocaean) a city on the western coast of Asia Minor: 6.9
Phócis	(adj. Phocian) a region of central Greece home to Coroneus and Onetor: 1.314; 2.570; 5.276; 11.347

Phócus	son of Aeacus and the Nereid Psamathe; half-brother of Peleus and Telamon: 7.477, 668, 670, 732, 795, 796; 11.268, 381
	    as **Aeacides:** 7.797
	    as **Nereus' grandson:** 7.685

Phoébe	an epithet of **Diana**, sister of Apollo (Phoebus), especially when serving as goddess of the **Moon:** 1.12, 477; 2.415, 723; 5.329; 6.216; 12.36; 15.549
Phoebean youth	see **Aesculapius**
Phoebean priestess	Cassandra, a Trojan prophetess and priestess of Apollo; sister of Helenus and daughter of Priam and Hecuba; raped by Ajax (2): 13.410
Phoébus	(adj. Phoebean) an epithet of **Apollo**, brother of Diana (Phoebe), especially when conflated with the **Sun:** 1.451, 453, 490, 553, 752; 2.23, 36, 110, 399, 545, 608, 628; 3.9, 10, 18, 130, 151; 4.349; 5.389; 6.123, 215, 486; 7.324, 364; 8.31, 350; 9.444, 663; 10.132, 163, 178, 197, 214; 11.58, 165, 303, 310, 316, 594; 13.410, 501, 632, 640, 677; 14.133, 141, 150, 416; 15.191, 419, 631, 642, 742, 864
Phoenícia	(adj. Phoenician) a country on the Syrian coast whose cities included Tyre and Sidon: 3.46; 15.287
Phoénix	son of Amyntor and participant in the Calydonian Hunt: 8.308
phoénix	a mythical bird with the power to respawn at death: 15.392, 402
Phólus	a centaur: 12.306
Phórbas (1)	son of Metion from Aswan; casualty of the fight between Phineus (1) and Perseus: 5.74, 78
Phórbas (2)	king of Phlegyas (2) who sacked the oracle at Delphi: 11.414
Phórbas (3)	a Lapith: 12.321

Phórcys	father of Medusa and the Gray Ones: 4.743, 774; 5.230
Phorcys' daughter	see **Medusa**
Phorcys' daughters	the Gray Ones, twins with one eye to share who kept secret the location of their Gorgon sisters: 4.774
Phoróni(de)s	see **Io**
Phríxus	son of Athamas and brother of Helle; original owner of the Golden Fleece: 7.7
Phrýgia	(adj. Phrygian) a country in central Asia Minor ruled by Midas: 6.45, 147, 149, 166, 177; 8.162, 620; 11.16, 91, 106; 13.429 representing **Troy:** 10.155; 11.203; 12.38, 70, 148; 13.45, 244, 338, 389, 432, 435, 580, 721; 14.80, 547, 562; 15.444, 453, 612
Phrygian prophet	see **Helenus**
Phthía	a city in Thessaly ruled by Peleus and home to Achilles: 13.156
Phýleus	a participant in the Calydonian Hunt native to Elis: 8.312
Phýlius	lover of Cygnus (2): 7.372
Phýllus	(adj. Phyllean) a city in Thessaly home to Caeneus: 12.479
Pícus	king of Latium; son of Saturn and husband of Canens; beloved of Circe: 14.320, 336, 342, 362, 396, 398
Piérus	father of nine daughters who challenged the Muses: 5.302
Píndus	a mountain in Thessaly: 1.570; 2.225; 7.225; 11.555
Piraéus	(adj. Piraean) the port of Athens: 6.446, 667
Piréne	a spring at Corinth: 2.240; 7.391
Piríthoüs	an uncouth Lapith; son of Ixion, husband of Hippodame, and constant companion of Theseus: 8.303, 403; 12.217, 228, 330, 332, 333 as **Ixion's son** or **child:** 8.403, 567, 613; 12.210, 337

Písa	(adj. Pisan) a village in the western Peloponnese home to Arethusa: 5.409, 494
Písces	(adj. Piscean) a sign of the Zodiac associated with winter: 10.78, 165
Pisénor	a centaur: 12.303
Pítane	a town in Aeolia, near Lesbos: 7.357
Píttheus	(adj. Pitthean) king of Troezen and son of Pelops: 6.415; 8.622; 15.296, 506
Pleíad(e)s	a constellation comprising the seven daughters of Atlas and Pleione, including Maia, mother of Mercury: 1.670; 6.174; 13.293
Pleíone	mother of the Pleiades, including Maia, mother of Mercury: 2.742
Pleúron	a town in Aetolia: 7.382
Pleurónia	the region surrounding Pleuron; home to Acmon: 14.494
Plexíppus	son of Thestius; brother of Althaea and Toxeus; uncle of Meleäger: 8.440
Po	a long river in northern Italy; possibly the same as the **Eridanus**: 2.258
Poéas	father of Philoctetes: 9.233; 13.45, 314
Polítes	a member of Ulysses' crew and friend of Macar (3): 14.251
Polydaémon	a Babylonian follower of Phineus (1) in the fight against Perseus: 5.85
Polydéctes	king of Seriphos and enemy of Perseus: 5.242
Polydórus	a Trojan prince; youngest son of Priam and Hecuba; ward of Polymestor: 13.431, 528, 536, 629
Polyméstor	king of Thrace and guardian of Polydorus: 13.430, 551
Polypémon	grandfather of Alcyone (not Ceÿx' wife) who became a kingfisher: 7.401
Polyphémus	man-eating, goat-herding Cyclops; lover of Galatea and enemy of Ulysses: 13.764, 772; 14.168
	as the **Cyclops**: 13.744, 755, 757, 780, 860, 876, 882; 14.174, 249

Polyxéna	a Trojan princess; youngest daughter of Priam and Hecuba: 13.448, 460
Pomóna	a Roman fruit goddess beloved of Vertumnus: 14.623
Póntus	(adj. Pontian) a Black Sea kingdom ruled by Mithridates: 15.756
Pórtheus	father of Oeneus, king of Calydon: 8.543; 9.11
Príam	king of Troy; son of Laömedon and husband of Hecuba; father of Aesacus, Hector, Paris, Helenus, Polydorus, and Polyxena; uncle of Memnon: 11.757; 12.2, 607; 13.99, 200, 409, 470, 482, 513, 520, 723; 14.474; 15.438
Priápus	obscenely endowed god of gardens; wooer of Lotus and Pomona: 9.347
Próca	an Alban king: 14.622
Próchyta	an island off the coast of Naples (modern Procida): 14.88
Prócne	daughter of Pandion, sister of Philomela, wife of Tereus, mother of Itys, and bacchant: 6.428, 433, 439, 468, 470, 563, 567, 580, 594, 603, 609, 619, 640, 653 as **Pandion's daughter:** 6.436, 634
Prócris	daughter of Erechtheus, wife of Cephalus, and sister of Orithyia: 6.680; 7.694, 707, 708, 712, 825, 841 as **Erechthida:** 7.726
Procrústes	infamous brigand killed by Theseus: 7.438
Proétus	usurper king of Argos and brother of Acrisius; his daughters were cured of madness by Melampus, son of Amythaon: 5.238; 15.327
Prométheus	son of Iapetus, brother of Epimetheus, father of Deucalion; possible creator of the human race: 1.390 as **Iapetus' son:** 1.83
Propoétides	a band of heretic women from Amathus: 10.221, 238
Próreus	a member of Acoetes' crew: 3.635
Próserpine	plant and springtime goddess; queen of the underworld; daughter of Ceres and Jupiter;

	abductee and wife of Dis; also known by her Greek name **Persephone**: 5.391, 505, 530, 554
	as **Avernal Juno**: 14.114
	as **Ceres' girl**: 5.376
	as **Deo's child**: 6.114
	as **Persephone**: 5.470; 10.15, 729
Protesiláüs	a Greek hero at Troy; first casualty of the Trojan War: 12.67
Próteus	a prophetic, shape shifting sea-god: 2.9; 8.731; 11.221, 255; 13.918
	as the **Carpathian prophet**: 11.249
Prothoënor	a follower of Perseus in the fight against Phineus (1): 5.99
Prýtanis	a Trojan killed by Ulysses: 13.258
Psámathe	a Nereid; mother of Phocus and sister of Thetis: 11.398
Psécas	an attendant of Diana: 3.171
Psóphis	a city in Arcadia near Elis: 5.607
Pulýdamas	a Trojan hero: 12.548
Pygmálion	a misogynist Cypriot sculptor, father of Paphos (1): 10.243, 253, 273
	as the **Paphian hero**: 10.290
Pýgmies	a mythical tribe of dwarves said to wage war on cranes: 6.90
Pýlos	a city in the southern Peloponnese ruled by Neleus and sacked by Hercules; home to Nestor (the Pylian): 2.684; 6.418; 12.550
Pyrácmos	a centaur killed by Caeneus: 12.460
Pyraéthus	a centaur: 12.449
Pýramus	a Babylonian youth beloved of Thisbe: 4.55, 71, 105, 142, 143
Pyréneus	king of Thrace and harasser of the Muses: 5.274, 287
Pyróïs	a flying horse of the Sun: 2.153
Pýrrha	daughter of Epimetheus, granddaughter of the Titan Iapetus, and wife of Deucalion: 1.350, 384
	as **Epimetheus' daughter**: 1.391

as **Titania:** 1.396

Pýrrhus   see **Neoptolemus**

Pýthon   (adj. Pythian) a serpentine monster killed by
Apollo: 1.439, 447, 460

Quírinal   one of Rome's seven hills, named for Quirinus:
14.836

Quirínus   see **Romulus**

Quírites   a name given to the Roman citizens in their civic
function: 14.823; 15.600

Raven   a talking bird attendant on Apollo: 2.534, 596, 631

Rémulus   an Alban king; son of Tiberinus and brother of
Acrota: 14.616, 617

Rhadamánthys   king of Crete and son of Jupiter: 9.435, 440

Rhamnúsia   Nemesis, goddess of revenge; her primary sanctuary was located at Rhamnus in Attica: 3.406;
14.693

Rhánis   an attendant of Diana: 3.171

Rhégium   a town on the Italian coast facing Sicily (modern
Reggio di Calabria): 14.5, 46

Rhésus   king of Thrace and Trojan ally killed by Ulysses:
13.100, 249

Rhexénor   a member of Diomedes' crew: 14.504

Rhine   a river in modern Germany; to Romans, the
boundary of the known world: 2.258

Rhodes   (adj. Rhodian) an island near Asia Minor associated with the Sun; home to the Telchines, Tlepolemus, and Alcon: 4.204; 7.364; 12.574; 13.683

Rhódope   a mountain range in Thrace associated with
Orpheus; formerly a Thracian queen and wife of
Haemus: 2.222; 6.87, 589; 10.77

Rhoetéüm   with Sigeum, one of two promontories near Troy:
11.196

Rhoétus   a centaur: 5.38; 12.271, 285, 293, 300

Rhône   a river in modern France and Switzerland: 2.258

Rípheus   a centaur: 12.352

Rome (adj. Roman): 1.202, 561; 2.366; 14.607, 800, 808, 837, 849; 15.432, 597, 625, 638, 653, 736, 827, 877
  as **the City**: 14.775; 15.584, 586, 600, 744, 798, 801, 861
  its citizens, as the **Quirites**: 14.823; 15.600

Rométhium an unidentified location in southern Italy: 15.705

Rómulus founder king of Rome; son of Mars and Ilia; grandson of Numitor and husband of Hersilie; later deified as **Quirinus**: 14.799, 805, 846; 15.560
  as **Ilia's son**: 14.780, 822
  as **Quirinus**: 14.828, 834, 851; 15.572, 754, 861, 862

Rútuli an ancient tribe of Latium led by Turnus: 14.455, 528, 567

Sába (adj. Sabaean) the biblical Sheba, a kingdom in South Arabia: 10.480

Sabine an ancient tribe of Latium led by Titus Tatius; they later joined with the Latins and became Romanized: 14.776, 797, 800, 832; 15.5

Sálamis a city on Cyprus; site of a temple to Venus Prospiciens: 14.760

Sállentine a people of southern Italy: 15.50

Sálmacis a spring in Caria purported to make men effeminate; its nymph: 4.285, 305, 337, 347; 15.319

Sámos (1) (adj. Samian) an island off the coast of Asia Minor sacred to Juno; home to Pythagoras: 8.220; 15.60, 61

Sámos (2) an island in the Ionian Sea near Ithaca: 13.711

Sárdis the capital of Lydia: 11.137, 152

Sarpédon king of Lycia; a Trojan ally killed by Patroclus: 13.256

Sáturn (adj. Saturnian) a Titan; Roman god of agriculture who ruled in the Golden Age; wife of Ops and father of Jupiter, Juno, Dis, Chiron, and Picus: 1.113, 163; 3.272; 4.448; 5.420; 6.126; 8.703; 9.242, 498; 14.320; 15.857

Satúrnia see **Juno**

sátyrs	goat-men creatures of the wild, including Marsyas; also known by their Roman name **fauns**: 1.692, 193; 4.26; 6.110, 384, 393; 11.89; 14.637 as **fauns**: 1.193; 6.392
Schoéneus	father of Atalanta: 10.609, 660
Scíron	an infamous brigand near Megara, killed by Theseus: 7.444, 447
Scylacéum	a town on the southern coast of Italy (modern Squillace): 15.703
Scýlla (1)	a sea-monster with a belt of snapping dogs located near Sicily, often paired with Charybdis; daughter of Crataeis and beloved of Glaucus: 7.65; 13.730, 900, 966; 14.18, 39, 51, 59, 70 as **Crataeis' child**: 13.749
Scýlla (2)	daughter of Nisus in love with Minos: 8.90, 104 as **Nisus' child or daughter**: 8.17, 35, 90
Scýros	an island near Euboea, home to Neoptolemus and conquered by Achilles: 13.156, 175
Scýthia	(adj. Scythian) a vague northerly region near the Caucasus ruled by Lyncus (1): 1.66; 2.224; 5.86, 650; 7.407; 8.788, 796; 10.588; 14.331; 15.286, 359
Sémele	daughter of Cadmus; mother of Bacchus by Jupiter: 3.260, 275, 279, 293, 520; 5.328; 9.642 as **Cadmus' child**: 3.287
Semíramis	legendary queen of Babylon; daughter of Dercetis and wife of Nisus: 4.58; 5.85
Sériphos	an island in the Cyclades home to Perseus and ruled by Polydectes: 5.242, 251; 7.464
Síbyl	an immortal prophetess at Cumae; beloved of Apollo: 14.104, 154; 15.712
Sícily	(adj. Sicílian) a large three-cornered island off the coast of mainland Italy; home to the Cyclopes and Mount Aetna: 5.361, 412, 464, 476, 495; 7.66; 8.283; 13.724, 770; 14.7; 15.279, 705, 825
Sícyon	(adj. Sicyónian) a region of the northern Peloponnese: 3.216

Sídon	(adj. Sidónian) a Phoenician city associated with purple dyes; home to Cadmus and Dido; sometimes interchangeable with **Tyre**: 2.840; 4.572; 10.267; 14.79
Sidónian	Dido, queen of Carthage and lover of Aeneas: 14.79
Sigéüm	(adj. Sigean) with Rhoeteum, one of two capes near Troy: 11.196; 12.71; 13.4
Silénus	drunken companion and foster-father of Bacchus: 11.90, 99; 14.639
Sílvius	an Alban king; son of Ascanius and father of Latinus (2): 14.610
Símoïs	a river near Troy: 13.324
Sínis	a brigand with a penchant for dismemberment killed by Theseus: 7.440
Sinuéssa	a town in Latium: 15.715
Síphnos	an island in the Cyclades: 7.466
Sípylus (1)	a mountain in Lydia home to Niobe (modern Mount Spil): 6.149
Sípylus (2)	a son of Niobe: 6.231
Sírens	companions of Proserpine and daughters of Acheloüs; later bird-women who preyed upon sailors: 5.555; 14.88
	as **Acheloüs' daughters:** 5.552
	as the **Acheloïads:** 14.87
Sisters Three	referring to the **Fates:** 8.451
	referring to the **Furies:** 10.314
Sísyphus	wily son of Aeolus (2) condemned to roll a stone forever as punishment for cheating death; alleged father of Ulysses: 4.459, 465; 10.44; 13.26, 32
Síthon	an otherwise unknown individual who underwent a sex change: 4.280
Sithónia	a peninsula in Thrace: 13.571
Smílax	a nymph transformed into a flower: 4.283
Smíntheus	a Trojan epithet for **Apollo:** 12.585
Spárta	(adj. Spartan) a city in the southern Peloponnese home to Hyacinth and Helen: 2.247; 3.208, 219, 223; 6.417; 10.170, 183, 196, 217; 13.396; 15.52

Spercheüs	a river in Thessaly: 1.579; 2.251; 7.230
Stábiae	a resort town near Naples: 15.711
Sthénelus (1)	father of Cygnus (1): 2.367
Sthénelus (2)	father of Eurystheus: 9.274
Stróphades	two small islands on the east coast of Greece, home to Aëllo: 13.709
Strymón	a river in Thrace (modern Struma): 2.257
Stýmphalus	(adj. Stymphálian) a region in Arcadia once infested with man-eating birds killed by Hercules: 5.585; 9.187
Stýphelus	a centaur killed by Caeneus: 12.459
Styx	(adj. Stygian) a river in the underworld by which the gods swore binding oaths; by extension, the underworld and death in general: 1.139, 189, 737; 2.101; 3.273, 291, 505, 695; 4.434, 437; 5.504; 6.662; 10.13, 65, 313, 697; 11.500; 12.322; 13.465; 14.155, 590; 15.154, 790
Sun	the celestial body and brother of the Moon, variously identified with the Titan **Hyperion** and his son Sol (**Titan**); later conflated with **Apollo** (**Phoebus**); father of Phaëthon, Pasiphaë, Circe, and the Heliades; grandfather of Medea, lover of Clymene, Rhodes, Clytië, and Leucothoë: 1.338, 750, 771; 2.1, 31, 154, 161, 395; 4.169, 170, 214, 235, 238, 270, 634; 9.736; 11.353; 13.852, 853; 14.10, 33, 346, 375; 15.30
	as **Hyperion**: 8.565
	as **Hyperion's son**: 4.192, 241
	as **Phoebus** (adj. Phoebean): 1.752; 2.23, 36, 110, 399; 3.151; 4.349; 5.389; 6.486; 7.324, 364; 11.594; 14.416; 15.191, 419
	as **Titan**: 1.11; 2.118; 6.438; 7.398; 10.78, 174; 11.257; 13.968; 14.376
Sun's daughter	referring to **Pasiphaë**: 9.736
	referring to **Circe**: 14.346
Surréntum	a town near Naples (modern Sorrento): 15.710
Sýbaris	a town and river (modern Coscile) on the southern coast of Italy: 15.51, 315

Symaéthus	(adj. Symaethian) a river in Sicily and its god; grandfather of Acis: 13.750, 879
Symplégades	magical shipwrecking cliffs at the Bosphorus: 15.338
Sýria	see **Assyria**
Sýrinx	an Arcadian nymph beloved of Pan: 1.691, 705
Sýros	an island in the Cyclades not typically associated with thyme: 7.464
Sýrtis	sandy gulfs on the Libyan coast proverbially dangerous to ships: 8.121
Taénarus	a cape at the southernmost point of the Peloponnese (modern Cape Matapan), where a cavern provided an entrance to the underworld: 10.13
Táges	an Etruscan prophet: 15.558
Tágus	a river in Iberia famed for its gold-bearing sands: 2.252
Támasus	a plain in Cyprus sacred to Venus: 10.644
Tantálides	patronymic of **Agamemnon**, great-grandson of Tantalus (1): 12.627
Tántalus (1)	son of Jupiter; father of Pelops and Niobe; punished with eternal starvation in the underworld for feeding his son to the gods: 4.458; 6.173, 210; 10.41
Tántalus (2)	son of Niobe named for his grandfather: 6.239
Taréntum	a city on the southern coast of Italy (modern Taranto), founded by Spartan colonists: 15.52
Tarpeía	a Roman traitor to the Sabines: 14.776; 15.865
Tártarus	a region of the underworld: 6.676; 10.21; 11.670
Tartéssus	an Iberian settlement at the western extent of the known world: 14.416
Tátius	king of the Sabines; later co-king of Rome: 14.775, 804, 805
Taúrus	a mountain range in Cilicia: 2.217
Taÿgete	one of the **Pleiades**: 3.595
Téctaphus	a Lapith; son of Olenus (3): 12.433
Tégea	(adj. Tegean) a town in Arcadia home to Atalanta: 8.318, 380

Télamon	son of Aeacus, father of Ajax (1), brother of Peleus, half-brother of Phocus, and husband of Hesione; participant in the Calydonian Hunt: 7.476, 647, 668; 8.309, 377; 11.215; 12.625; 13.22, 123, 151, 231, 266, 321, 346
Telamónius	see **Ajax (1)**
Telchínes	an ancient tribe of sorcerers on Rhodes: 7.365
Teléboäs	a centaur killed by Nestor: 12.442
Télemus	a prophet; son of Eurymus: 13.770, 771
Télephus	king of Mysia, wounded and healed by Achilles: 12.112; 13.172
Telethúsa	wife of Lygdus and mother of Iphis (1): 9.682, 696, 766
Témpe	a proverbially beautiful vale in Thessaly: 1.569; 7.222, 371
Témpsa	(adj. Tempsan) a town in southern Italy noted for its mines: 7.207; 15.707
Ténedos	an isle near Troy sacred to Apollo and sacked by Achilles: 1.516; 12.109; 13.174
Ténos	an island in the Cyclades: 7.469
Téreus	king of Thrace, husband of Procne, and father of Itys: 6.424, 433, 455, 473, 478, 497, 614, 635, 647, 650, 682 as the **Odrysian king**: 6.490
Téthys	primordial sea-goddess, wife of the Ocean, and attendant of the Sun; mother of Clymene and grandmother of Phaëthon: 2.68, 156, 509; 9.499; 11.784; 13.950
Teúcer (1)	(adj. Teucrian) a Greek hero at Troy; cousin of Achilles and founder of Salamis: 13.157; 14.698
Teúcer (2)	(adj. Teucrian) Cretan ancestor of the Trojans: 13.705, 706, 728; 14.72
Thaúmas (1)	father of Iris: 4.480; 11.647; 14.845
Thaúmas (2)	a centaur: 12.303
Thebes (1)	(adj. Theban) a seven-gated city in Boeotia founded by Cadmus: 3.131, 169, 549, 553, 561, 732; 4.31, 416,

543, 561; 5.253; 6.159, 163; 7.763; 9.111, 304, 403; 13.682, 692

Thebes (2)   a city near Troy ruled by Eëtion and sacked by Achilles: 12.110; 13.173

Thémis   sometime goddess of oracles: 1.321, 378; 4.643; 7.762; 9.402, 418

Théreus   a Thessalian centaur: 12.353

Thérmodon   a river in Pontus home to the Amazons (modern Terme): 2.249; 9.189

Thérses   a Theban guest at the court of Anius: 13.682, 683

Thersítes   an obnoxious Greek soldier at Troy: 13.232

Théscelus   a follower of Phineus (1) in the fight against Perseus: 5.182

Théseus   king of Athens; son of Aegeus or Neptune; participant in the Calydonian Hunt; lover of Ariadne, constant companion of Pirithoüs, and father of Hippolytus: 7.404, 433; 8.262, 268, 302, 547, 566, 726; 12.226, 355, 359; 15.492, 855

    as **Aegeus' son:** 8.174, 405, 559; 12.236, 344
    as **Cecrops' heir:** 8.550
    as **Neptune's hero:** 9.1

Théspiae   (adj. Thespian) a Boeotian town at the foot of Mount Helicon: 5.310

Théssaly   (or **Thessália**, adj. Thessalian; formerly known as **Aeolia**) a region of northern Greece home to Olympus (1) and other mountains, the centaurs, the Lapiths, the Muses, Coronis, Jason, Ceÿx, Achilles, and Caeneus: 1.568; 2.81, 542, 599; 5.87, 306; 7.159, 222, 264, 314; 8.349, 766, 813; 11.229, 409, 651; 12.81, 172, 173, 190, 213, 353; 13.24

Théstiads   patronymic of **Plexippus** and **Toxeus**, sons of Thestius: 8.432

Théstius   father of Althaea, Plexippus, and Toxeus: 8.303, 452, 472, 487

Théstor   father of Calchas, a Greek prophet at Troy: 12.18, 27

Thétis   a Nereid; wife of Peleus and mother of Achilles: 11.221, 226, 236, 263, 400

Thísbaea	(adj. Thisbaean) a town in Boeotia famously rife with pigeons: 11.300
Thísbe	a Babylonian girl beloved of Pyramus: 4.55, 72, 93, 99, 116, 143, 145
Thoáctes	a casualty in the fight between Phineus (1) and Perseus: 5.147
Thóäs	king of Lemnos and father of Hypsipyle: 13.399
Thóön	a Trojan killed by Ulysses: 13.260
Thrace	(adj. Thracian) a region northeast of Greece home to the Haemus and Rhodope mountains; home to Pyreneus, Tereus, Boreas, Orpheus, and Polymestor: 2.247, 257; 5.277; 6.88, 424, 434, 576, 587, 661, 682; 9.194, 641; 10.1, 12, 50, 83, 305; 11.2, 69, 93; 13.429, 439, 530, 537, 554, 565, 629
Thracian bard	see **Orpheus**
Thunderer	("*Tonans*") an epithet of **Jupiter:** 1.170; 2.466; 11.197
Thúrii	a city on the southern coast of Italy: 15.51
Thyéstes	(adj. Thyestean) brother of Atreus who inadvertently ate his own sons: 15.462
thýrsus	(pl. thyrsi) an ivy-wound staff topped with a pinecone wielded by followers of Bacchus: 3.542, 712; 4.7; 6.593; 9.641; 11.28
Tíber	the river flowing through Rome: 2.259; 14.328, 426, 447; 15.433, 624, 728
Tiberínus	an Alban king; namesake of the river: 14.614
Til	a river in Thrace (modern Manavgat): 2.247
Timólus	see **Tmolus**
Tirésias	a blind Theban prophet and father of Manto: 3.323; 6.157
Tíryns	(adj. Tirýnthian) a city in the Peloponnese associated with Hercules: 6.112; 7.410; 12.564; 13.401
Tiryns' hero or **Tirynthius**	see **Hercules**
Tirynthian wife	see **Alcmene**
Tisíphone	one of the **Furies:** 4.474, 481
Títan	see the **Sun**

Títaness	see **Circe**
Titánia	referring to **Pyrrha,** granddaughter of the Titan Iapetus: 1.396 referring to **Diana,** granddaughter of the Titan Coeus: 3.173 referring to **Latona,** daughter of the Titan Coeus: 6.346 referring to **Circe,** daughter of the Sun (Titan): 14.382, 438
Títyos	a Giant punished in the underworld by having his regenerating liver eternally pecked out by vultures: 4.457
Tlepólemus	leader of the Rhodians at Troy; son of Hercules: 12.537
T(i)mólus	a mountain in Lydia and its god: 2.217; 6.15; 11.87, 150, 156, 164, 170, 193
Tóxeus	son of Thestius; brother of Althaea and Plexippus; uncle of Meleäger: 8.441
Tráchas	a coastal town in Latium (modern Terracina): 15.717
Tráchis	(adj. Trachínian) a region in Thessaly ruled by Ceÿx; location of Hercules' death: 11.269, 282, 351, 502, 627
Tríops	father of Erysichthon and grandfather of Mestra: 8.751, 871
Triops' heir	Mestra, shapeshifting granddaughter of Triops: 8.871
Triptólemus	inventor of agriculture and acolyte of Ceres: 5.645, 653 　　as the **Mopsian:** 5.661
Tríton	a sea-god known for his conch-shell horn: 1.331, 335; 2.9; 13.918; 15.358
Tritónia	see **Minerva**
Triton's marsh	Lake Tritonis in Africa; site of Minerva's birth: 15.358
Triumph	(adj. Triumphal) a Roman ceremony celebrating military victory and culminating in a garlanded general's parade up the Capitol: 1.560; 13.251; 14.719

Trívia	see **Diana**
Troézen	a small town in the Peloponnese ruled by Pittheus and home to Lelex: 6.415; 8.567; 15.296, 506
Troy	(adj. Trojan; also known as **Ilium** and **Pergamum**) a city in Asia Minor with walls built by Neptune and Apollo; site of the Trojan War; ruled by Laömedon, later by Priam: 6.96; 8.366; 9.232; 10.160; 11.199, 208, 215, 758, 773; 12.20, 26, 66, 445, 587, 605, 612; 13.23, 54, 91, 168, 196, 219, 226, 246, 269, 274, 320, 325, 336, 339, 343, 348, 374, 379, 419, 420, 429, 481, 500, 508, 534, 538, 566, 572, 577, 623, 655, 702, 721; 14.76, 110, 156, 220, 245, 455; 15.160, 425, 437, 441, 443, 730, 770
	its citizens, as **Dardan(ian)**: 13.335, 412; 15.432, 767
	as **Ilium**: 11.766; 12.598; 13.197, 408, 506, 520; 14.466
	as **Pergamum**: 12.591; 13.169, 348, 375; 14.466
	as **Phrygia**: 10.155; 11.203; 12.38, 70, 148; 13.45, 244, 338, 389, 432, 435, 580, 721; 14.80, 547, 562; 15.444, 453, 612
Túrnus	king of the Rutulians, sometime betrothed of Lavinia, and enemy of Aeneas: 14.451, 460, 530, 539, 573, 574; 15.773
Tuscan	see **Etruria**
Týdeus	father of Diomedes: 12.624; 13.68, 239, 351
Tydídes	patronymic of **Diomedes**, son of Tydeus: 15.769
Tyndáreus	father of Castor, Pollux, and Helen: 8.300; 15.231
Tyndareus' child	see **Helen**
Tyndareus' twins	**Castor** and Pollux, participants in the Calydonian Hunt: 8.300
Týphon	a hundred-handed Giant monster defeated in war by the gods and buried beneath Mount Aetna in Sicily; son of the Earth: 3.304; 5.321, 325, 348, 353
	as the **Giant**: 5.346; 14.1
Tyre	(adj. Tyrian) a Phoenician city ruled by Agenor, home to Cadmus and Europa, and noted for its purple dye; sometimes interchangeable with **Sidon**:

2.845; 3.35, 129, 258, 538; 5.51; 6.61, 221; 9.341; 10.211; 11.166; 15.287

Týrrhenes or Tyrrhénes (1) a term for **Lydians**: 3.576, 696; 4.24

Týrrhenes or Tyrrhénes (2) a people of Etruria: 14.8; 15.554, 577

Tyrrhene Sea the body of water separating mainland Italy from Sardinia and Corsica: 14.8

Ulýsses wily king of Ithaca and Dulichium; a Greek hero at Troy, whence he wandered long in returning; husband of Penelope, son of Laërtes, and companion of Diomedes; beloved of Circe: 13.6, 14, 18, 55, 62, 66, 83, 92, 240, 304, 305, 342, 387, 485, 712, 773; 14.71, 158, 180, 192, 241, 289, 671
  as the **Dulichian**: 13.107, 424; 14.226
  as the **Ithacan**: 13.98, 103; 14.563
  as **Laërtes' son**: 12.625; 13.48, 124

Uránia the **Muse** of astronomy: 5.260

Venília wife of Janus and mother of Canens: 14.333

Vénulus Rutulian ambassador: 14.457, 460, 513

Vénus goddess of love and beauty; daughter of Jupiter, wife of Vulcan, and mother of Cupid, Hermaphroditus, and Aeneas; lover of Mars, Adonis, and Anchises; associated with doves, Eryx (1), Cyprus, and her homeland of Cythera: 1.464; 3.132; 4.172, 531; 5.331, 379; 7.803; 9.424, 482, 795; 10.229, 239, 270, 277, 291, 524, 548; 13.759; 14.27, 477, 495, 572, 585, 602, 761, 783; 15.779, 843
  as **Cytherea** or the **Cytherean**: 4.190, 288; 10.640, 718; 13.624; 14.487, 584; 15.386, 803, 816
  as **Erycina**: 5.363
  as the **Idalian**: 14.694

Vertúmnus Roman god of gardens and lover of Pomona: 14.641, 678

Vésta goddess of the hearth; a cult tended her flame in Rome: 15.730, 778, 863, 864

Vírbius see **Hippolytus**

Voltúrnus a river in central Italy: 15.714

Vúlcan	god of fire and the forge associated with Lemnos; husband of Venus; son of Jupiter and Juno; father of Erichthonius: 2.106; 7.437; 9.251; 13.313
	as **Juno's son:** 4.173
	as the **Lemnian:** 4.185
	as **Mulciber:** 2.6; 9.262, 423; 14.532
Vulcan's son	Periphetes, a club-wielding bandit near Epidaurus killed by Theseus: 7.437
Xánthus (1)	a river near Troy: 2.245
Xánthus (2)	a river in Lycia (modern Eşen Çayı): 9.646
Záncle	see **Messina**
Zéphyr(us)	the West Wind; also known by his Roman name **Favonius:** 1.65, 108; 15.700
	as **Favonius:** 9.662
Zétes	a member of Jason's crew; winged son of Boreas and Orithyia: 6.716
	as **Aquilo's son:** 7.4

ABOUT THE TRANSLATOR

PHOTO: TIM RUSZALA

C. LUKE SOUCY is a translator, poet, and vocal Minnesota native. Born gay and biracial, he began writing in ninth grade out of the foolhardy belief he could impress a boy with a string of acrostic sonnets. More recent efforts ranging from light verse to classical scholarship have appeared in *Arion*, *Light*, and on *Poets.org*. Soucy is a 2019 graduate of Princeton University, where he concentrated in English and received the E. E. Cummings Society Prize of the Academy of American Poets. In addition to literary translation, he has worked in the regional theater, in a chromatography lab, and as a university bureaucrat. He now resides in Princeton, New Jersey.